The War Was Better

Also by Miodrag Bulatović
HERO ON A DONKEY

THE WAR WAS BETTER

by MIODRAG BULATOVIĆ

Translated from the Serbo-Croatian by
B. S. BRUSAR
ADAPTED BY MICHAEL WOLFERT

McGRAW-HILL BOOK COMPANY
New York St. Louis San Francisco
Dusseldorf London Mexico
Sydney Toronto

Library of Congress Catalog Card Number: 79-38518

First Edition

07-008846-2

The War Was Better

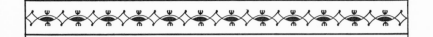

First Part

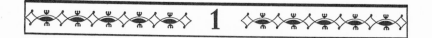

MAJOR ANTONIO PEDUTO, commanding officer of the routed Venezia Division, stumbled out of the smoldering blackberry bushes talking to the turtle he held cupped in his hands. "Anna-Maria Cattolica, I love you," he said, and burst into tears.

"You're my only true love, you little Balkan whore, you," the Major went on, sobbing hysterically and not bothering to wipe his eyes. He hardly heard the rifle shots and machine-gun bursts echoing around him; the tears were streaming down his cheeks. "You're the only woman who can make me forget this miserable heart of mine that has been broken and mended and pierced through again a thousand times!" A grenade exploded near him, blowing off his hat, but he paid it no attention. He stood rocking back and forth on his heels, blinded by smoke, blackberry juice, and tears.

"I love your sad old stomach," he whispered to the turtle. "I love your Byzantine eyebrows. I love your eyes—deep, dark eyes that see everything and hide everything. I love your little legs which are so wide apart and always have something dripping in between. Above all, I love your black, evil, hunched-over, whore's heart. It's beating so calmly in your little shell."

This brought on fresh tears. Choking with sobs, his hands scratched and bleeding from the blackberry thorns, yet taking care not to let Anna-Maria drop, Antonio Peduto set off down the dusty road.

"Darling," he began again, lifting the turtle from his bosom and gazing at her tenderly like a mother at her infant child.

"Darling," he repeated drunkenly, tottering. "You're growing!"

Antonio Peduto took a brandy bottle from his pocket, uncorked it, and poured down another large mouthful.

"You were nothing but an orphan the day I found you," he murmured. "A tiny, miserable wretch... You even cried. You peeked out from your little shell and cried. There was no one to help you, nobody to wipe the ashes off your little feet. You were so helpless, abandoned by everyone, the most woebegone little creature... and I made you my eternal beloved... fiancée! If somebody had told me what a slut you'd become, I'd have gouged out his eyes."

[3]

He pressed her again to his chest and felt her warm moistness and sighed.

"I can't tell you exactly where it happened. It was in the Balkans somewhere, in the morning. What I remember is the blood. Blood was everywhere. When the sun rose, the sky and the earth were all red.

"It was dry. The Balkan earth was thirsty. It swallowed whatever fell on it. It was dry and quiet and dewless that morning, the morning I met you, when we embraced for the first time, when the right moment came and I knew happiness at last.

"They were torturing a soldier—the Greeks or the Serbs. I saw his uniform—it was Italian—thrown on the embers and the ashes. I was lying near them. He must have been young, beardless. I could see his chest was narrow and his neck was thin, like a boy's. They weren't satisfied with cutting his ears off and throwing them in the bushes near my legs. They clipped off his nose too. They hadn't touched his eyes. I thought they must be saving the eyes for the end. I heard them talking in some strange, peasant language:

" '*Taliano, Taliano, Taliano* . . .' I heard the horror in their voices, the commiseration and dark love. '*Taliano, Taliano.*' Tears seemed to well up in their eyes.

"The *Taliano*, my little soldier, naked and bloody, was wringing his arms as they castrated him. They—the Greeks or the Serbs —they did it the way they geld an ox or a stallion: some of them were holding him while the others hammered his balls with hammers, and then with stones. When his testicles softened up, and they were sure the crushed flesh would never heal again, they started burning the soles of his feet and whispering very tenderly. Then they tore his toenails out, asked him something, and all of them cried.

"The boy had been lying on his back, and they turned him over to peel the skin off and then sprinkled the raw wounds with salt, ashes, and dirt. His arms strained helplessly. His groin and all the skin around it was twitching silently. His mutilated head dropped on his chest; the peasants kept lifting it, trying to fix it on his neck. They looked again and again at the smashed cock between his legs, shaking their heads back and forth, so that the tears would not cling to their eyelashes.

" '*Taliano, Taliano,*' they were saying again, adding in their dark, South Balkan language: 'Why . . . why . . . *perché* . . . ?'

"Then they stopped torturing him. All five of them were tired out; their eyes were overflowing. They were pulling on his tongue to keep him from passing out, pointing first at their own eyes and

then at his. Then it dawned on me what they were saying to him:
" '*Taliano*, little lost boy, we're leaving your tongue alone, so it
can tell the rest of your army what your unharmed eyes have
seen. . . .'

"They left my little soldier, the *Taliano*, lying in the thick Balkan forest with his knees spread apart. I don't know whether anybody ever found him."

Antonio Peduto could hardly keep on his feet anymore. It
seemed to him the ugly, bloody head of the soldier was drinking
from his bottle. He cursed the Balkan gods and, making a fist, inad-
vertently squeezed Anna-Maria. He looked into the turtle's eyes.

"Now you're not so small and innocent as you were on the
night we lay near our soldier," he said. "Our first night in the ferns
and the moonlight, *Taliano* was saying good-by to his lost Venezia
Division, and his crushed cock. He even called it by its real name.
He squealed quietly and uttered the names of many women. He
moaned and punched at the ashes and coals until your little legs
trembled with fear. That day and that moonlit night I fell in love
with you. I swore we would never part. Hush now, quiet down.
We were betrothed in the blood of the little soldier *Taliano*. Even
now we're walking on blood. Blood is our way.

"Don't go now. What would I do alone? Don't try to wriggle
out of my arms. You're what makes me a man. You're my memory,
my star, my darkness, my laughter, my tears. Whenever I feel really
lost, I look at you, and all the bayonets and knives ever forged by
men begin to cross before my eyes. Cattolica, you're my sin."

Anna-Maria calmed down in Antonio's arms. He adjusted his
knapsack on his back and began to walk again. Grenades were
bursting on all sides. He paused and poured brandy down his throat,
choking with dust and words. Then he put the bottle back in his
pocket. In spite of the explosions and the bullets whistling past his
head, he remained on his feet. He had lost all fear long before.

"Darling," he said to her. "You've had enough blood, words,
and smoke for today. It's time for you to go back to your own familiar place, where it's much cozier than out here."

Antonio slipped the knapsack off his back and opened it. He
placed the turtle tenderly on the pages of his unfinished manuscript,
The Time of Shame. "Now you can shit on it all over again," he
said, smiling wryly. "There you are," he added, "my evil and my
happiness in one shell, my sin and my salvation. You sleep now, my
darling, or stay up and listen while they chase us out of burning
Montenegro."

Totally drunk and straddling the slope to keep upright, he

wished that one of the thousands of bullets whistling by would hit him and pierce his heart. He laughed uproariously and looked down at the trucks crawling and toiling along the tortuous dusty road that stretched out across the landscape. In retreat, the Italians were singing and cursing the Montenegrin dust.

"I'm ashamed of you, soldiers!" Peduto shouted hoarsely. "You're running away and singing! And when you advance—you weep! Bah!"

Antonio jerked his red beard with rage.

The Italians who could find no room in the trucks were running for their lives along the road. Antonio could see them emerging sometimes from clouds of dust and then vanishing again. Disarmed, often half-naked, in extreme disorder and panic, they were like swarms of locusts escaping from a fire. Those unable to hold their own in the stampede behind the trucks fell at the others' feet and were trampled over. They could be seen still lying in the road when the dust had cleared, apparently dead.

Antonio watched the peasants rush after the army. Armed with rifles and grenades and often with machine guns, they seemed to crop up from the soil, simply, like an outgrowth from the rocks. There they waited for the dusty grasshoppers and shot.

Mowed down by their bullets, cut at with axes and pitchforks, the soldiers were falling. Those who managed to escape the multitude of bullets, the scythes and hammers, were pursued and preyed upon by fire.

For the forest was burning in earnest now. Peduto could see a flaming crescent spread through the old pines and low junipers. Fire whipped through the treetops and scorched and blackened whatever it touched with almost invisible tongues of flame. Dried out by drought, moistened only by tears and blood, the soil itself was burning. It smoked, and the air above it palpitated with a life of its own. Even in the rocks, cocoons and lurking hornets' nests of fire were sealed in alive; when stepped on, they turned into flowers of flame scorching the frightened Italian skin.

"What a send-off!" Antonio Peduto said aloud and felt the turtle move in his knapsack.

Then he saw that even the trees were chasing his soldiers. Sawed through by machine-gun volleys, shattered and split by grenades that seemed to fall out of the red-hot sky, the trunks were leaning and plunging to the earth.

"This could be God's punishment," he thought aloud, watching a huge pine trunk fall and crush a heap of wounded men he had imagined would be spared. "But it isn't. It isn't God who is punishing us. It's the land!" He was choking on smoke and soot, coughing out his words. "We godlessly raped and humiliated and insulted this land. It's the punishment of the land!"

The grenades were coming so fast they caught up with each other in mid-air and burst open the earth at closer and closer intervals. The living and the dead tumbled headlong into the warm pits and embraced there.

"The punishment of Montenegro, Malić's homeland," the red-bearded Major said to himself, and remembered Gruban Malić and his donkey.

Everything he could see from the glade was burning. He felt like closing his eyes. He asked himself for the hundredth time since he had come out of the blackberry bushes with his bottle and his turtle:

"Is it possible that the visible and the invisible, the living and the dead, even the earth itself, is being thrown against my army?"

He shivered.

"If so, and it certainly seems so," he reasoned, "may the punishment fully atone us. Let none of us try to stop the fire. Why did we come here in the first place? It was the greatest fraud our nation has perpetrated since God planted us on our peninsula, and we must pay for it."

Antonio Peduto remembered the soldier *Taliano* and the peasants crushing his balls and peeling the skin from his back. A cold sweat drenched him.

"You won't be setting fire to our houses anymore or chasing our girls, *soldato*," he thought the mustached peasants had said, the tearful ones, with round caps on their skulls, "and you'll never again ... never again ..."

From Antonio's eyes, full of smoke, tears gushed again.

"My sorrowful mother," he wailed, "help me get out of this burning valley. Do not pray, my only one, that my head be spared. I don't deserve it. I myself, especially at the beginning, killed many of them. My hands are dirty and bloody, and not only with soil and blackberries. But pray that I may trudge up the highest Montenegrin mountain and behold alive, clearly and fully, this common evil, this pornography of death.

"Don't expect me to, Mother, my dear old mother, with your freckles. ... I can't do it anymore, I can't look into your eyes. I'm a soldier, a killer. That's my trade. And I didn't learn it from you."

He waded through smoke and ferns which burned green. He thought it was a dream. Sweating, exhausted, falling and picking himself up from swamps and heaps of ashes, he did not know whether it was his former or future life he was dreaming. It lasted so long that he could not imagine it would ever end. He walked and walked, craving the pain that suffused his body. The only thing he could tell himself or Anna-Maria was they were climbing, they had been going uphill for a long time and finally the moment would come when he would throw himself down and not know whether his mouth was full of dirt or smoldering Montenegrin ashes.

Fire, driven on by the wind, was catching up with him. The tails of his jacket and the edges of his socks were already singed. He was crawling on all fours, coughing and thinking aloud:

"If this continues, my beard and my memory will go up in smoke."

His knapsack was hot. He was afraid the fire was already kindling his manuscript and nestling in the shell of the turtle. The other things did not worry him: "Medals, maps, pornographic war souvenirs—it is only right that they should be lost from time to time, to be rediscovered and possessed by others."

His knapsack felt like a heap of tar melting and pouring down his back.

"My soul is in my nose, and my heart is in my throat, like a mouse's," Antonio Peduto said, watching the rocks rolling down from the top of the mountain he had been climbing, at first in a trickle and then in a flood; it was a real landslide. "They'll bury me and I won't have time to burn up," he said, pleased at the thought of such a death.

He decided not to budge, and watched the heap of rocks mounting around him. Smiling blissfully, he took hold of some roots and ferns and waited. His eyes were full of tears and light.

But the slide changed direction. A tumult of rocks and earth suddenly swept away everything he had been looking at. Even the uproar vanished into the precipice that yawned beside him. Antonio rose and looked down the big black mouth of the pit, thicketed by blackberries and vines. Underneath, the earth was rumbling. In the depths, further down than he could see, he thought fire and water must be heaving and clashing, white heavy rocks with cold darkness.

"Major! Man!"

A voice was calling from above, from the earth, from the only thing that existed for him at that moment.

"Major . . . if you're alive, look up . . . do you hear me?"

THE WAR WAS BETTER

The human voice echoed eerily in the pit. He trembled violently.

"I understand you. ... I hear you," he answered. "I don't know where you are. ... I'm alive. ... That's why I can't call back." This was a whisper. "I'm still alive, but happily not for long."

He pressed himself against the soil and heard his heart, full of ashes and smoke, beating as against a drum. Pitifully shrunk, tangled in vines and roots, he felt as though he had been sleeping a long time, very long.

"Major!" The voice was full of terror. "Rocks! ... Look out! ... This time they'll crush you!" The voice was vanishing into the tumult of the landslide. "Grip! Hold fast! ..."

The voice was gone. Only smoke remained, and rocks and roots.

Antonio looked up, to see where the sun was. He caught sight of the end of a rope and stared at it for a moment in disbelief, as if stricken dumb. Through the din of sliding rocks and earth moving heavily toward the dark opening, the voice came again:

"Man, grab it! ... Or the landslide will sweep you away! ... Hallo! Hallo!"

An underground echo drowned out the man's voice again.

Still without fear, more like a machine than a man, Antonio took hold of the knot of the rope, gripped it fast and let himself go, dangling against the side of the precipice. He looked up. On the edge of a stublike crag, he could see a man bending and pulling.

"A soldier," Antonio thought in the smoke, smiling grimly. "A soldier, a man." For an instant he stared at the black silhouette against the sky. "A soldier. Instead of pushing his Major into the abyss, he saves his head. Any major would have let his soldier ride the landslide. Then he'd shit down in his war notes: "In an encounter with the far more powerful enemy forces, only one of our soldiers was killed.' He'd probably conclude with the wisdom that war is the most terrible, stupid, senseless thing ever witnessed on the face of this earth. Then the shit-eating writer-observer would hold his stomach and laugh until, as in novels, tears would well up in his eyes! He's a strange man, this maniac soldier who's pulling up the rope."

"We've overcome the danger. ... You're alive!"

"It's almost not import," he said to himself as he watched flaming rocks, earth, and coals stream down under his dangling feet. "If you, soldier, think it's so important, so be it!"

Antonio's strength ebbed; slowly he began to slip down the rope again. At any moment he would drop. Yet it was all the same to him. The stench of the earth dripped over his face like polluted honey. His head swam. The black, hairy, vaginal mouth of the pit loomed in front of his eyes. It seemed to him that the time had come to return to where he had come from.

The sky itself seemed to be plunging into the abyss; rocks, uniformed bodies, pierced helmets, bootfuls of dead soldiers' feet and ankles, rifles and machine guns, boxes of medicines, bandages and contraceptives, flags with golden fringes and brass medals; all these mingled before Antonio's eyes; all these streamed somewhere, lost, irrecoverable, like tears from the eyes of a man who is tired to death, who is ready to escape his torture chamber, to go to that place from which there is no return.

"Now!" the soldier yelled. "Now . . . put your feet in the loop!"

The soldier's scream frightened Antonio. His muscles tensed. With the top of his boot he found the loop under the knot and stopped slipping. "Look now," he said to himself. "For the second time, this unknown soldier has saved your life. Now you must hold out because of him. You must scramble up. Because of men like this, one must postpone one's death."

Antonio got his second wind. Clutching the rope vigorously, he looked down at the avalanche sweeping away the living and the dead below him. He said something to the soldier, but his voice vanished in the hot dust. He began to cough and cry with exhaustion.

"We've won!" the soldier said when he pulled Antonio up to the edge of the crag. "How happy I was to be near you!"

For a full minute the Major lay on his side, without realizing that the soldier was taking the knapsack off his back. Then, slowly, he opened his eyes and looked up at the soldier's boyish face. He wanted to tell him something beautiful and bitter but could not close his mouth. The soldier understood and smiled. Then they stared at each other for a long time and did not speak.

A new landslide of earth and smoldering coals rushed past them. Antonio propped himself on one elbow and peered down into the pit. It was even more horrible from above, plunging steeply and then yawning open like a vast, hairy mouth. He thought of asking the soldier what the warm opening reminded him of, but succeeded only in cursing and spitting and holding out a trembling hand to him.

"They've invented the blackest revenge," the soldier said. "Hundreds of our men have gone since I came here. Some went down there alive. I saved only about thirty."

THE WAR WAS BETTER

"Where are they now?"

"Where we are, Major."

"You say they're revenging themselves on us?" Antonio said, looking at the rope in the soldier's hands: it was bloody. "Is it an ingenious revenge?"

"I think such a revenge has never yet been imagined, Major. They've hunted us with fire for weeks now. They have no mercy." His voice was calm and self-possessed. "They're filling the pit of hell with our bodies."

He looked at the rope and his hands.

"Sometimes I think at least half of our Venezia Division has died down there. Not to speak of the Murge Division: it was they who began to withdraw first."

"Are your eyes open, soldier?" Antonio whispered, suddenly overcome with fatigue, falling half asleep and stretching himself on the soil.

"They are. I never shut them."

"Then tell me what you see."

"The earth and the sky are burning."

"You expressed it beautifully: the earth and the sky ... both the earth and the sky ... What's your name?"

Giuseppe."

"Very well," Antonio said. "And is anything else burning besides the earth and the sky, Peppe?"

"It seems ... even water, Major," the soldier said as he looked out over the distance, letting the rope drop beside him. "Water. Rivers. Ponds."

"You say they're hunting and chasing us with fire," Antonio said quietly, happy not to be talking just to himself. "With whose fire, Peppe? Tell me."

The soldier owed him an answer. He fumbled for the rope, thinking he should take it up again and throw the knotted loop into the abyss; human voices could be heard there, echoing.

"Who cast the fire here, Peppe?"

"I don't understand you, Major. Anybody ... everybody ... fire is everywhere. It seems this is the time of fire and calamity."

"But who put the fire here first, who planted it like wheat?" Seen from below, the soldier looked huge, almost like a tree. "Who set the land afire, Peppe? The forest, the rivers? Who made the rocks flame? You see they are full of heat."

"We did, Major," the soldier answered shamefully, "while running away. It was we Italians. Who else could it have been?"

[11]

"We, of course, Peppe," Antonio said bitterly. "We came with fire. Therefore, they are pursuing us with it. Therefore we will perish from it. From our own fire."

"It isn't fair," the soldier mused aloud. "Instead of killing us like men, or at least like dogs, they're roasting us like . . . rats."

"We are rats, Peppe."

The soldier stared at the rope and the hairy opening of the abyss. Then he drew his head in between his shoulders.

"What will happen to us, Major?" he muttered.

"You wonder what will happen to the rats?" Antonio rested on his elbow, his head thrown back. "You know what happens to rats."

The sudden explosion of a grenade buried them with dirt and the smell of sulphur.

"Peppe, lend me your hands," Antonio said, when he had opened his eyes again. "I'd like to stand up." He did not wipe his face; it was as soot-stained and dirty as the soldier's. "Lend me your hands."

"I can't," the soldier said as he knelt to look at the Major, who still lay on his back. "They're bloody."

"Mine are too, Peppe."

"Yours are bloody only up to the elbows, Sir. And mine up to my shoulders."

"I'm bloody and dirty everywhere, Peppe. Everywhere! Look more closely."

"You're only raw," Peppe said. "The rocks bruised you; fire scorched your skin. It was that damn landslide!"

"I'm bloodier, Peppe."

"I'm bloodier and dirtier, Major."

"No, Peppe. I'm bloodier—I'm an officer!"

"I'm sorry I must refute you, Sir, but the truth is on my side." The soldier almost burst into tears. "You haven't seen my back, the skin is all peeled, and my legs are raw up to the, excuse me, Sir, up to my testicles." He lowered his scorched head and showed his teeth. "I'm dripping everywhere. That's why I'm resting here, hoping that all my wounds will close and dry."

"Why are you throwing the rope down then? Why are you straining yourself so much?"

"I found the rope here," Peppe said quietly. "Somebody was already doing what I tried to do. I'm sure he saved more than I."

"That isn't important, Peppe. What counts is that our wounds don't get infected."

[12]

"And that we forget them one day," Peppe added. "Yes, the wounds. To forget them utterly. To tell no one about them, about what we saw and did."

"But if we can't manage it, soldier? If we won't be able to?"

"I come from a village near Naples," Peppe said. "We forget everything, and we've had something to remember." Peppe watched the Major lying on the warm, burrowed earth; he was slowly opening his eyes again. "We are known throughout the world for that."

"And what about me, Peppe, who wasn't born in your village near Naples?" Antonio's voice sounded sad; his eyes were full of smoke. "What about me, my little one, with my wounds and so many memories?"

The soldier did not answer.

"The only thing I can do is curse my freckled mother for not giving birth to me in your village, Peppe."

Both of them paused.

"What's your last name? Do you have one? Or is being a Neapolitan enough for you?"

"My last name is indecent, Major," the soldier answered. "It's so ugly I can't say it."

"What did the fishermen call you?"

"Well...fishermen!" the soldier smiled. "For a while they called me Bonaccia. They were drafted into the army." Peppe paused. "Since none returned ... nobody called me that anymore." He paused again, looking at the rope. "My fishermen."

"Now, at last, will you give me your hands, Giuseppe Bonaccia? You see, I'm waiting for you to lift me up. Come on, Bonaccia. Make this one extra effort."

The soldier obeyed. Antonio spat out dirt and sulphur and peered into the soldier's big joyless eyes. Peppe was sitting beside him, drying his wounds in the sun. Antonio liked his tiny, frightened, still unhardened face with the mustache budding under his nose. Peppe reminded him of many of the soldiers with whom he had been living for years now, roaming through vast areas of Italy, Africa, and the Balkans.

"Thank you," Antonio Peduto said. "You're a real find." He paused. "And I hope all the fishermen haven't died."

The soldier sighed.

"One fisherman at least will return. Perhaps then the whole village will call you the same name as that one surviving fisherman."

"I'm a miserable find," the soldier said, he too spitting dirt and sulphur out of his mouth. "There are unhappy people in this world, Major, but I am misfortune itself!" With evident pain, he gesticulated with his raw, extended fingers. "Misfortune!"

"Why?"

"Because I remember too much, Major. I remember even what others have forgotten." His eyes were glassy, his lips cracked. "As you see, I suffer."

"You're wonderful, Peppe," Antonio said, perking up. "And to remember what others have forgotten is magnificent. I'm happy to have met you. You're a genuine poet, soldier!"

"I'm illiterate," Giuseppe Bonaccia said and looked at his bloody hands. "With hours of trouble and sweat I can just about read a page that is written in large printed letters."

"I envy you, Peppe."

"Other soldiers write my letters to girls," he continued. "And I overflow with love. Most of them I haven't met at all, or seen. I'm not even sure whether the addresses are right."

"So you've thought them up?"

"The others thought some of them up," Peppe said, blushing with embarrassment. "I got several addresses from Augusto Napolitano, from Salvatore Paolone, and even from Pietro Portulu." The soldier lowered his voice. "They're gone now, you know it better than I; it would be unkind to blame them now. If the addresses are false, what then? Anyhow, there are few true and honest things on earth," Peppe said, growing inspired. "Augusto and I came from the same village. Several times I thought of killing myself after he was killed. We were so close." His voice was warming up. "I'm a stinking scoundrel, and still living, and I know Augusto couldn't live without me, or sing . . . as he couldn't breathe with both lungs without his Bolognese girl. That's what he used to say before he started singing—or barking at the stars. My brother, my Augusto, used to howl and snarl a full hour like a dog or a wolf; he would call the stars one by one, by their real names, or make up filthy names. . . ."

"Please stop there, at the stars," Antonio said quietly. "Although I do not remember as much as you, I know a few things myself." Antonio's eyes were hazy with smoke; his hair was full of dirt and ashes. "Let's not talk about Augusto and the others now. Italians are famous for singing to the stars, and then spitting at them and crying like babies because they can't get them down from heaven and dirty them." A weird light flickered in his eyes. "Let's discuss your whores instead," he said. "I could talk about whores forever, you know, night and day."

[14]

"They aren't whores, Major. I don't even know them. They'd be whores if they started answering my letters, though."

The soldier stopped, and his eyes assumed their former, glassy shine.

"But they're silent," he said. "They don't write. I'd be ready to sacrifice my life for any one of them."

"How many lives do you have, Peppe?"

"I don't know," the soldier said, puzzled. "About fifty, Major. Or one hundred. As many as girls."

"And how old are you?"

"Nineteen and a half, minus five months and thirteen days," the soldier said excitedly. "I generally end my years in the fall, when harvesting and weddings begin."

"Hmm. On the subject of grape gathering and girls, Peppe, hmm ... have you or haven't you yet ... I think, in the folk and Neapolitan way, have you been putting your little bunny rabbit between girls' legs and up into their little shell? Hm? Tell me, Peppe, don't be ashamed."

"I have, yes ... but only in songs and letters."

"No wonder they don't answer your letters, Peppe!" Antonio Peduto was talking like a country teacher, extending his forefinger: "Girls don't like the bunny only in letters. Keep that in mind." They looked into each other's eyes, like plain-spoken men. "Because you're a warrior and an Italian, in addition to being a Neapolitan, you should know how things stand. And things stand ..."

"I know best how they stand, Major: mine is always a little up." His voice was boyishly pure. "And I don't hide it in letters—or in songs either." It was an angel's face in a fresco. "Today, for instance, just as if I weren't raw and, actually, scorched ... I feel, as you say, my bunny: he's breathing and wiggling his ears...."

"And should we write, Peppe, to your ..." Antonio was roaring with laughter. "To your ... I'm so sorry I'm not allowed to say, whores! Ha! Ha! Ha! Peppino, we'll write them in verses!" A cough was strangling him. "My pen is strong, I am strong with the pen, believe me."

"There's no use writing to girls with bloody hands, Major," the soldier protested. "When we go down. Or if we remain alive." His voice was confident. "And we must remain alive, if we want to run, with our bunnies in our hands, to run after ... whores!"

"Bravo, Peppe!" Antonio shouted, almost weeping with happiness. "Bravo, my wonderful Peppe! My Neapolitan!" Thunder began to be heard. The soil was smoking and the air smelt of sulphur and burnt grass. "Peppe, here's what I say: if we can't write to girls with bloody hands, can't we at least sing to them?"

"It's a question whether wounds heal faster due to singing, Major," the soldier said quite seriously. "I've seen that tears have a negative effect. I don't know about songs. Maybe a song isn't bad, especially if there are two or more singers."

"Yes, Peppe. One should never sing alone. Here, I'm humming a chord. You join in if you remember the song and the melody."

"There's not one single song my fellow soldiers ever sang that I wouldn't remember," Peppe said. "I know our own songs and the songs of the rest of the armies too, not to mention the dirty ones that Augusto used to sing. That's what I told you before, why I'm so sad and sick of everything; it's because I remember too much."

"When two or three sing, they usually embrace," Antonio suggested. "I don't want to touch your wounds, Peppe, but I embrace you in my thoughts. Here, I've closed my eyes in order not to look at the fire and the rocks. I've embraced you like an older and more sensible brother. I've hugged you to my heart and am about to utter a few pure words. Do you hear me, Peppe?"

"I've embraced you too, and don't want to break away. If you weren't a major, I'd call you my brother. I've shut my eyes in order not to see that we're separated and that the unfortunate soldier, Augusto Napolitano, isn't between us."

They were sitting one beside the other. If someone had looked at them from the side, he would have thought they were blind.

"Well, we sing in two parts," Antonio said and began to try out his throat. "Do you know the song of the whore, the helmet, and the flag, Peppe?" Curling his lips, he began to hum. "I see you know it. Good. How about that *porcheria* about the general before the battle?" As the Major listed each song, the soldier nodded his head. "You Neapolitan devil, do you really know all the songs that have ever been composed?"

They sang the song about the whore, the helmet, and the flag.

"Lower your voice, Major. Still softer. The song must be so tender and soft that Augusto's heart can hear it," Giuseppe Bonaccia said without moving. "It must be almost a whisper. Although Augusto isn't here, his heart is alive. Perhaps he's somewhere here, between us, buried under the earth. Or perhaps in that raging fire." His voice did not tremble; his fingers were spread apart, like a beggar's ready to catch a stone from afar. "Do you hear? ... Oh, listen to that thunder!"

"I don't know if I understand you, Peppe," Antonio Peduto

THE WAR WAS BETTER

whispered. "Continue, please." He too was not moving. "I think I'm dreaming. I beg you, please go on." He paused, listening to something. "You say that Augusto's heart is alive?" His red beard turned to the sun. "Oh God, have mercy on my soldier and say where Augusto's heart is hidden!"

"Wherever it is, Augusto's heart is good," Giuseppe Bonaccia whispered. "It vomits blood and fire only when people anger it."

They both paused, listening to the pealing sky.

"Let's stay faithful to it, Major, let's not forget it." The soldier's voice was hollow and soft. "Let's sing just his songs for a while."

It seemed to Antonio that he had never been so composed. He felt blood rushing up to his burnt skin. He saw Giuseppe's raw hands in front of him and wanted to blow on them and kiss them and put them under his shirt. Although the smoke grew thicker and thicker, he was sure he would not cough or weep. The soldier sat beside him motionless and enraptured, like a sage by the wayside.

A song broke out by itself. At first it was not made of words, but of letters and smoke. It was like breathing that turned into a whisper.

The two men's lips hardly moved as they uttered Augusto's tenderest words:

Se te la rompo, non te la pago . . .

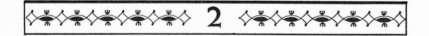

2

"Take another shot, Peppe," Antonio Peduto urged the soldier as he pressed the bottle into his hands. "Knock it down if you can, bottoms-up, leave only one swallow, which . . . I'd like to share with her," he added, stammering and looking at the turtle. "So, drink, my soldier! *Rakia*, this divine plum brandy, this slivovitz of theirs, I'm sure is good for wounds. For all wounds!"

Giuseppe Bonaccia trembled after he had swallowed as if he had drunk poison. Black and ashy, with his dark hair glued to his temples, he looked affectionately at the Major for a long time. It was clear that he had many nice words to say, but his tongue too seemed to have been scorched by fire. So he only stared at the Major, ready to strike the ground with his forehead and pray.

"Men have never invented another poison like this," Antonio

said as he looked at what remained in the bottle. "And the people who made this miracle, this *rakia*, must have suffered much."

"I agree fully that it's a miracle," the soldier said. "I never tasted anything like it and never want to again! You're right, too, when you say it's a poison, Major. Poison like that can make your heart stop."

"That wouldn't be so terrible, Peppe," Antonio said. "The heart and memory often pause. It often happens to us, the real soldiers, and to the whores. Your heart and your memory stop for a moment, and you cringe in shame."

"If I was sure I could cloud up my memories with brandy, I'd never stop guzzling it," the soldier said. "Even if my heart stopped forever."

"I like you, Peppe," Antonio said, clasping the turtle to his breast.

"I like you too very much and respect you tremendously, boundlessly," the soldier said. "Because you wouldn't even guess how long I've known you." They stared at each other. "One day perhaps . . . or in Italy, I'll tell you everything."

Antonio Peduto racked his brains. He knotted his forehead and cursed his sluggish memory. He blamed even the brandy, but most of all Abyssinia and Greece.

"It's quite understandable that you don't remember me, Major. For more than two years I've been the most despicable, the most insignificant, the most ridiculous soldier of the Venezia Division."

Peppe's voice quavered.

"I'm remembered that way in the Murge Division too, but I was only there a few months. Before that, however . . ."

"Take the turtle away from my breast, Peppe," Antonio said, holding onto the bottle. "So. See how good and gentle a boy you are. A true soldier and lover, worthy of the Venezia Division, which they've massacred now."

Antonio looked at him compassionately.

"So you were also in the Murge, which I commanded too, ha! and was famous for evil deeds and immorality."

Antonio's eyes were full of ashes and light. The soldier held the turtle in his hands as a moment before he had held the bottle, without the faintest idea what he should do.

"Turn her on her back, Peppe," Antonio said enthusiastically. "On her back!"

Peppe obeyed. Then both of them examined her tender, hairy little stomach. The skin around her groin trembled; ants were trying to crawl in and hide under her coffee-colored shell. She was craning her neck with her eyes tightly closed, as if ashamed to be overturned.

"She's scared, the poor thing," the soldier whispered. "She's trembling."

"My love," Antonio Peduto said to the turtle as he carefully began to pour brandy, drop by drop, into her throat. "We must fuddle you first, so as to dim your memory. Here, love, so." It seemed to the soldier that the turtle knew a great deal about brandy and drank it thirstily.

"Anna-Maria," Antonio said. "You've got the last drop. And you'll pay for it dearly, you Balkan, Byzantine whore!"

Peppe was embarrassed. He looked at Antonio's nervously moving lips and then at the turtle's little belly, overgrown with tender little hair. "And what now?" he asked. He could see Antonio's fist raised to smash the turtle's shell and her little craning neck. "I'm afraid her heart will break," he said.

"The heart doesn't break from brandy, Peppe. The heart breaks from sorrow ... or from shame." Antonio's voice cracked; he was enthusiastic yet strangely frightened. "Now we're going to rape her, soldier. Don't you see how she's thrown up her little legs already and is just waiting for it?"

"Do it without me, Major. I come from an honest peasant family."

"Come on, my bunny," Antonio insisted, inviting the soldier on. "What are you waiting for if you come from an honest peasant family, and even from around the bastard dog city, magnificent Naples!" His eyes widened. "Look! I'll move her little paws apart and put a stone on each of them." As he spoke, so he did; it had always been thus with him. "Here, see. This is the way you have to treat them."

"Major ..."

"Come here, Peppe." Antonio's voice was trembling with a strange, awe-struck sadness; there were tears in his eyes. "Fall on your knees and say you've never seen a more beautiful worn-out belly. Say that you've never seen a female thrown on her back and her shell before, that you'll go off your head if she doesn't consent." Antonio babbled on; his forehead and neck were sweating. "Do you hear me, Peppino?" A smoky avalanche was descending rapidly toward the gorge; the soldier did not know which way to turn. "Look, I'm going to embrace her long, black neck; I'm going to stroke her mussed-up hair." The landslide had tumbled into the chasm; only the noise remained, and the ashes that were falling down on them. "Look, ashes. I'm near her now, quite near. Damn! I've forgotten something. I just had it on the tip of my tongue, a minute ago, when I had her in my arms." His eyes were mad and quiet. "Was I going to insult her, or repeat that I couldn't live without her? Perhaps I was about to tell her that I love her and that even the sun does not shine when she is near me ... that I love her darkly, hopelessly, sickly, adoringly, as one loves one's own betrayer!" Antonio's shoulders were shaking; his words were hard to follow. "Peppe, don't pick on her little stomach too long. I don't want the little Byzantine brat to die in such pain right before my eyes."

"I'm drunk as an owl, Major," the soldier whispered, with his forehead glued to the turtle's belly. "I don't know what I'm doing anymore. I can't tear myself away from her." He also was trembling. "For God's sake, tell me what to do now! She's frightened; her body is small; her little paws have been scorched by fire like my palms," he moaned. "Tell me something or I'll turn into stone, as I am now, bent over on my knees."

"Now I am erect and in my full strength," Antonio began to babble as he lay on his back weeping, with his arms and legs spread out. "I cannot stop myself, yes, I'm taking my revenge, I'm revenging myself, this is my revenge—to look at her, on her back under you, Bonaccia." He was speaking quite softly, almost whispering. "Whatever evil she has done wouldn't be so serious if we hadn't been given birth by the same mother," he whispered sadly, his mouth again full of ashes. "I'm standing on the locks of her long hair. It doesn't matter to me that she's pleading with me to stop. I won't let her hair go. I won't let the soldier relax, I won't, I can't. I'm threatening them with the moon which is in my arms. Peppe ... watch out!"

Antonio saw before his mind's eye the half-naked body of a young woman and a frightened soldier whose raw and bleeding body was plunging headlong between her knees. The woman seemed to have grown into the soil and the burning grass and even into the soldier's flesh. She was waiting for the man with his peeled back and sore feet to put his hard and blooming knife into the wound between her legs. He heard her panting and moaning smothered by the soldier's strength, and he did not move; he did not turn. The sweetest pain he had ever experienced electrified his bones. He saw Peppe's maddened face and his black hands stroking the turtle's paws.

THE WAR WAS BETTER

"Horror, Major."

"Your real life has only begun, Peppe," Antonio murmured from the earth. "Now you'll sing less and write fewer letters."

"I never imagined it would begin this way," Peppe said. He burst into tears and rose to his knees.

"Now you've become a man, Peppe."

"Well, so quickly?" He was kneeling, stooping, peering at the turtle on her back. "Couldn't it have been different?"

"We're burning, Peppe. Don't you see? We're burning!"

"So much the less need for me to become a man," the soldier replied, and with his sleeve he smeared soot and dust on his face. "Why all this . . . today? . . ."

"Now you're just like me, if not worse, Peppe."

Antonio lay on his back and listened to the soldier's sobs. Cannons were booming nearby; grenade shrapnel was buzzing over their heads.

"Now you're a true soldier of the Venezia Division. If anybody denies it, just tell him what you've done today. If he doesn't believe you after that—cut his throat!"

"If only I could be once again what I was before I knelt and leaned my forehead on her miserable stomach!" The soldier broke down and cried again, throwing himself at Antonio's feet. "Let me become what I was . . . if you're my commandant . . . if you're the former friend of Pietro Portulu, Paolone, Augusto Napolitano, and all the other poor devils who will stay in this bloody country forever!"

"What's done is done," Antonio gloated. "You're a man now, like other men, and there's no use in your dying like an angel," Antonio said quietly. "You tortured her stomach for a long time, but I forgive you. Why? Because I know that the landslide will sweep you away in a minute or two. Anyway it will sweep me away. And then, Peppe, those dirty, filthy, lascivious songs of yours . . ."

"It's true, I was holding my head on her stomach without listening to the ticking of her heart," the soldier said impetuously. "And I want to answer for my songs! I want to die, disappear! But how?" He looked around. The fire was approaching them from pine to pine, from stone to stone. "How? . . Tell me!"

"Someone else will take care of that, my little one," Antonio interrupted. "Don't you feel . . . ?"

"I feel even more, Major!" Peppe hurried on. "That I'm contaminated, that after this day there will be no place for me among the living, nor among the dead!" He stared about him with his eyes widening. "When the flame comes, please don't defend me from it! Forget me! Forget me right away!"

Antonio noticed that the turtle was walking up his arm. She walked as on a bridge, careful not to slip and dodging falling ashes. A feeling of guilt and a fear so strong it was like terror preyed on him again. She arrived at his shirt and stopped there. She scratched with her little paw and uncovered his chest; then she nestled in on a clean part of his skin and quieted down. Extending her neck and peering out, she seemed to be waiting for something to happen.

Suddenly Antonio no longer saw the defeated, sprawling body of the woman who had so often invaded his imagination, nor did his eyes linger on her round, mole-flooded knees. He knew at last that he was on the earth, that his head hung down, that his eyes were staring at a sky full of heat and smoke, and that his eternal and beloved burden was resting on his breast. He heard the soldier curse and speak of God, his mother, and his adolescent sisters. He had an urge to stroke his hair, to tell him there was no use crying like a wild fire.

"Neither among the living, nor among the dead," the soldier was repeating softly and shivering. "Neither among the living . . ."

"Among the living, my Peppe," Antonio muttered, rising slowly. "Only among the living," he added as he urged the turtle to climb back down his arm. "It must be dreary among the dead, since they're for peace at any price, to say nothing of good health and morals."

He laughed at the dead and their sense of hygiene, justice, and equal rights.

"Come, Peppe, calm down and wipe my tears. Leave the dead alone, so they can distribute their medals and spoils among themselves." He was laughing as if he were not insulting the dead, but the living. "Wipe my tears, soldier."

"With what?"

"With your hands," Antonio said as, in his thoughts, he took leave of the dead.

"But . . . my hands are raw and sinful."

"Peppe, I want your hands to wipe my tears," Antonio lifted his voice. "Your hands are cleaner than my tears. Do you understand?"

Peppe wiped his tears and repeated that he had never seen a more beautiful beard. He stressed that there had been red ones in his family too, but that everyone had feared them. Antonio's eyes grew light and mad again.

"Bonaccia," he shouted and embraced him. "Look down there,

but not through tears." The turtle was between them, on both their breasts; she was quiet, for their hearts were beating on both sides of her shell. "Not through tears, Peppe."

"How can we stop them, Major?" the soldier said, grimacing in an effort to become serious. "Whenever I laugh or cry, it's usually hard for me to stop." He pressed his jaws and ground his teeth. "When I cry, it's somehow harder." By raising his voice he was able to calm down somewhat. "Tears don't flow from my eyes only," he explained. "They seem to come from inside of me, from down below, from my guts and my flesh."

"Look carefully," Antonio said. "If my eyes aren't deceiving me, I see some of our men."

"Those are the ones who have escaped the landslide and the chasm, Major," Peppe said. "The ones we were looking at while we sang." The soldier was winking. "It isn't easy to catch an Italian!"

"And you, do you see anything, Anna-Maria?" Antonio asked the turtle. "Or are your eyes overflowing with lust like mine, so that we see everything backwards?" The turtle stretched her neck but did not see, Antonio thought, as much as Peppe. "Listen, darling," he continued, caressing her shell. "There are fifty fleeing soldiers, and twice as many women." He was happy he could talk to her about it. "They're all whores, *Ortodosse*, your sisters. Greek, Macedonian, Montenegrin, and Albanian whores. They're in uniform, and so tough the peasants shoot more at them than at the soldiers. Look: one of them has the rank of a captain; look at all the rare medals they have! Now you continue, Peppino."

"They're bracing up the soldiers, imploring them not to weep. They really look brave, those damned Balkan women! When one of our men falls, they run up with bandages and medicine. They don't abandon anyone, even the most badly wounded. The soldiers are dying so fast now that the ratio of women to men is two and a half to one. They're shooting too, and shrieking 'Long live Italy, nation of lovers, heroes and singers!'; they're fantastically gallant and musical. But the Montenegrins are faster. They're catching up with them and . . . what they're doing . . . I can't tell you, I'm ashamed."

The turtle seemed to be frowning.

"Our *Ortodosse* are perishing, our whores are croaking," Antonio muttered. "The peasants are faster; they're waiting behind every bush." His face pressed against her shell. "They're grabbing your sisters, Anna-Maria; they've got no time to roll them down on the still unliberated ground. Some of them are grabbing them by the throats and cutting their hair off, while others, the younger ones, are tearing their pants down their thighs and torpedoing them right there, standing up. You can see the women's army shirts cave in; you can see their backs sweat and give off the smell of powder. Their drilled behinds are blazing white. The peasants are coming one after the other, pitching into it with their dirty, whipped-up tails. Still the invincible *Ortodosse* are holding out, sticking out their behinds and yelling to their soldiers to run away faster. They don't complain the way city whores usually do. They're shouting at their Italian lovers and singers; they're ordering them to wait for them; they say they'll join them soon and cross the Adriatic Sea with them. The *Ortodosse* are a real living wall. Thanks to them, maybe forty of the luckless devils will get away."

"Oh, what a shame!" Peppe groaned, about to hide his face in his hands.

"Oh, what a picture!" The idea seemed to leap from Antonio's throat. "What a defeat!" he roared. "Peppe, don't you see the defeat is total?! One thousand per cent and magnificent!" He gasped. "Cattolica, rejoice, the defeat is complete and pure: the victors are on the whores! The heroes and liberators are ridiculed and disdained!"

3

The path, most traveled probably by vampires and wild goats, led Antonio and Peppe along the slope. Below them the waters were roaring, full of ashy foam and human wailing. When they looked up, they saw pines and black roots gripping boulders like human hands. The treetops were burning. It seemed as though the invisible mouth of the sky were sucking in the flames. They crawled along on all fours, fearful that the stones they caught hold of would slip and pull them down.

"Take it easy, Major," Peppe warned him. "Easy. Easy. Don't let the rope go. Don't forget there's a loop under the knot."

"Don't mention that loop to me again," Antonio groaned, hardly able to keep his knapsack on his back. "How could I forget it?" The soldier, crawling along on his hands and knees like a spider, only grumbled in reply. "Where are you leading me, Peppe?"

"We must be going the right way," Peppe answered as he tied the end of the rope to a thick root. "I hear voices. Hold on!"

THE WAR WAS BETTER

Antonio threw his head back and saw a black eagle in the fire of the sky, blacker from the smoke, huge, with wings that seemed to burn; in his talons, he was holding a hare or a small lamb. He was about to point him out to Peppe and tell him to look, there was so much fire that the eagle had nothing to land on and shake the ashes from his wings. But a rock slipped under his foot and tumbled down the cliff, and Antonio forgot the eagle and his desperate shrieking, fell down trembling and clung to the earth and thorns. "Don't look up into the smoke, Major," Peppe said, looking back and then continuing to pull him along.

Finally they came to a clearing in the sunlight which seemed to be waiting for them. Sweaty and exhausted, they threw themselves down on their knees. The moment they knelt there seemed to them to vanish out of time, to last an eternity in which the cool wind touched and lapped against them like waves. A plateau opened out before them, full of flames and flowers. Human voices approached, but they did not have the energy to move. They knelt in the sunlight and waited.

"I'll drink water," Peppe muttered.

"Brandy for me," Antonio said, sensing the turtle move in the knapsack on his back.

"Lord, how many flowers!" the soldier exclaimed excitedly, looking at the meadow which ended in a thin piny wood and a pool; it was a vast mountain glen with steep edges and reeds at the approaches. "I've never seen so many colors except in flower stores!"

"I'm drunk and want more brandy," Antonio murmured. "I can feel my brains boiling in my skull. Only brandy can stop that, or make me forget it. I don't want other drinks! How are you doing, Peppe?"

"Pardon me, Major, I want to piss and I would piss if it weren't for the flowers and the fire," the boy said. "I've been holding my water since we sang those songs."

"The Greeks and the Turks pissed on their wounds when they wanted to heal them quickly," Antonio said, and stretched out slowly on the grass. "Lord, turn over a bottle and pour down a drop or two of whatever wets and burns the tongue, the throat, the bowels ... Don't be so stingy, take pity on me. ... Even when You were creating this mad and corrupted world, You weren't as thirsty and lost as I am!"

Antonio lay on his side, his red beard full of mountain flowers and blades of grass, his mouth gaping wide, as if he were some monstrous fish thrown out upon the land. "You mentioned a few minutes ago that there were some streams," he said. "Can you see a pond?"

"I can see even from here that the water is stagnant, dirty, dense."

"But still, Peppe."

"It is a hole full of frogs and tadpoles."

"And do you know, Peppino, that frogs are the most erotic beings . . . on the earth?"

"I thought the English were," the soldier argued. "Anyway the English are the richest."

"Some other time about the English, Peppe," Antonio said, laughing. "We're discussing eroticism now. Well, when a he-frog mounts a she-frog, he squeezes her armpits so fiercely he breaks the skin. She, of course, wouldn't feel a thing even if he broke her ribs; the female is a whore, an unquenchable sponge." He spat; the wind blew against his head. "The he-frog is a libertine; neither time nor place matter to him when he's in heat. How many times I used to watch them fucking in the middle of a road, or on the steps of a church! You ought to know, Peppe, that with the possible exception of Italians, the he-frog is the most reckless male on the face of this earth!" His cracked lips broke into a smile; he spat no more. "At any rate, we Italians eat frogs; the Montenegrins and the Greeks will never forgive us for that." His eyes were closed. "Don't forget, Peppino: a he-frog and an Italian are real ladies' men, but there are no greater shit-ass cowards than lovers." His mouth touched the ground and he began to chew on the dirt. "Are we already on the highest mountain of this unforgettable Montenegro?"

"Conserve your energy, Major, don't talk so much," Peppe warned him. "There'll be water. Right now I'm looking for a brook or a stream."

His eyes wandered over the plateau which was full of abandoned farms, cottages, and animal pens.

"I didn't know there was such a similarity between he-frogs and the English," he thought out loud. "I've heard about them, the English. And now I know they're as slimy as worms. It's quite possible the war is dragging on because of them."

Peppe turned back and noticed that Antonio's body, slumped in the grass, was shaking with a tearless sobbing. He rose above him and screened him from the sun. Antonio brought his hands up to his face and licked them.

"If it's true that urine dries and heals wounds . . . don't frown,

THE WAR WAS BETTER

Peppe . . . if that really holds true . . . make no bones about it, go ahead, piss on me! Make sure you don't make the flowers and the fire dirty. As for me, I don't matter; I've always been a pig anyway, and you'll see for yourself the Greeks and the Turks are right to put it on their wounds."

From the earth, Peppe's head looked like a stone—it was no longer that youthful, still unshaven face; it was serious and sharpened, like a bird's, looking for a spring. "The eagle is there no more," Antonio thought and was lost again. "The wind, the light, maybe that last avalanche took him away," he went on as in a dream. "But no wind can sweep away the sun . . . and Peppe's head . . . This soldier, Peppe, who doesn't even know where to piss, and this mad Montenegrin sun are eternal."

Bonaccia protected him from the wind that was bending the flowers and the grass and the flames. Condemned to an unquenchable thirst, Antonio's lips moved in pain:

"Peppe, you don't want to wet my wounds, don't forget I was born in a fog like this. In fog and blood, tearing the entrails of my poor mother for the tenth time." He was shaking and his teeth were chattering. "Since then fog and blood have been my star and my religion."

Then, for a moment, he was quiet, with his arms stretched out in the grass, with his feet wrapped in old army shirts. He seemed to be sleeping, although his eyes could be seen, half open, under the eyelashes which were long and reddish like his hair.

"What's your religion, Peppe?"

The boy jumped—as if a bullet had hit him. He pressed his heart with his hand; that must be his religion, Antonio thought. The soldier said nothing, and his eyes continued to look for water. He kept his hand on his bosom.

"You've answered me wonderfully," Antonio mused. He remembered similar conversations with Pietro and Augusto. "All these soldiers are alike, all magnificent," he began to mumble; Peppe could not catch his words. "They are children, maddened, egged on against each other. And when someone tells me that some division, some army of this or that country, was irresistible when it stormed the enemy, I remember frogs; I think of our passionate games; I remember when we were armed with arrows and bows of willow twigs, with hen feathers around our heads; when we were fearless in our dreams, when we stormed the fortresses of our toughest foes like Indian braves."

Peppe wanted the Major to continue the story of the English

and the frogs, and he listened attentively, hoping he would come to that subject.

"With these miserable compulsive children, who play at warfare and history, I have spent my most beautiful days, and then my blackest ones."

Antonio closed his eyes. He wanted to be left alone for a moment. He wanted to dream, with his raw fingers in Peppe's tousled hair.

His dim dream was short. Greeks, Turks, and Albanians, rubbing piss into their numerous wounds, filed before his mind's eye. Antonio asked them whether it was true that urine was so wholesome. They did not understand him. Then he showed them his wounds and burns, and in a mixture of Balkan languages requested them to treat him. But they wetted only their own wounds, and Antonio could do nothing but watch them with envy and scorn. Then his dream narrowed down and warmed up. The hunched soldier, Peppe, wept from between the knees of a stripped woman thrown on her back; without wiping his tears, he was staring awe-struck at her crescent, which was bordered by a turtle's little hairs and paws, ferns and fragrant mountain flowers. Then only a vague reality remained from the dream: Antonio knew he was lying on the ground, helpless, and that his weakness was sweet and comfortable, but he did not understand that his hands were not in Peppe's hair, but in the sharp, short grass. His dream thawed in the sun like ice mixed with dirt; he could see the panting, fearful soldier pulling him along the ground and trying to hide him behind a stone. The Greeks and the Turks were departing forever, with their swollen skin and reddish piss; the woman without a face or voice, given over to Peppe's mercy, was vanishing; the intoxicating smell of the wound between her thighs was thinning into the air.

"They'll kill us, Major!"

"It's high time, Peppe," Antonio replied, looking up from the turtle's embrace; "who is it? The Greeks or the Turks? Or the miserable Albanians?"

"Look!" A machine-gun volley cut Peppe's voice. "Look at the pond! Look carefully!" Peppe hid behind the stone and began to chatter.

A small grenade fell near them and exploded, blowing dirt in their eyes.

"That one was one of ours," Peppe said. "I know the sound and the smell."

"I'm remembering another smell, Peppe," Antonio said, rising beside the stone and looking out over the plateau covered with flowers and corpses. "Peppe, who are those men at the pond, waiting for our army and the *Ortodosse?*" He did not wait for an answer. A strange joy irradiated his face. "How many whores there are, Bonaccia! At least two or three hundred! They're the ones who're flinging our little grenades, the red ones, to cover our soldiers' retreat!" He stared out avidly, without fear of the bullets that whistled in the air across the valley and around their stone. "Giuseppe, maybe I'm still dreaming."

"You aren't dreaming, but you can't get rid of whores," Peppe commented from the grass.

"So long as there are whores, life will also exist, my little one," Antonio succeeded in observing through a salvo. "And when they're gone, neither war, nor life, nor anything human will remain."

"Speaking of whores, just look at the other side of the pond," Peppe suggested, laughing at his own bitter joke. "Those whores will gouge out our eyes."

"Boches!"

Antonio Peduto wheezed and pressed the turtle to his shirt. "Boches! There'll be no salvation for us now, Bonaccia!"

"Nor for them," the soldier said.

A sickly laugh which he could not resist was on the point of bursting out of Antonio.

"Germans, Germans," he kept repeating, cock-a-doodle-doing like a rooster. "Whores, whores," he neighed, gasping for breath. "The whores of the whole world are the same; first they attack the eyes, and then the heart!"

The soldier wanted to ask him to squat down, to hide behind the stone, but he did not dare to.

"The Boches are worse than the Abyssinians, Major!" Giuseppe Bonaccia shouted from behind the stone. "I've never seen them, but they say they're cannibals; they say that now they'd rather kill us, the Italians, than the others.... They say they're real Negroes!"

With great difficulty, Antonio climbed the boulder, shielding his eyes from the wind with his free hand. The large pond blazed in the sun. The bodies of the dead and wounded were falling from almost every side and breaking into the water as through the broad surface of a looking glass. On the other shore, German helmets, well fortified and concealed behind rocks, were waiting. Machine guns sputtered above the reeds and rushes. Bombs of all calibers were bursting and throwing up wild blooms of earth and rock. Wounded Italian soldiers tottered toward the swamp, which was full of algae, roots, and frogs. The *Ortodosse* were also falling, their bodies gliding toward the water as if in slow motion, with their legs apart.

Standing on the stone like some ancient marshal, Major Peduto watched a new group of soldiers running down into the valley, half-naked and barefoot. They wept and wailed as they went, saying over and over again that they were surrendering, they were surrendering once and for all.

"Peppe, now only the Germans are shooting!" Antonio yelled. "They keep silent, wait, and kill!"

"I told you, Major, they're worse than the Africans," Bonaccia replied. "They like our white Italian flesh!" He raged and spat. "Damned ravens from the North, why don't you let us escape quietly like men?" He was curling himself into a ball, wishing fervently that he could sink into the earth. "Cowards, greedy pigs! ... Why don't you show your faces instead of squatting behind screens like whores?!"

He had never been so courageous; his voice seemed to emerge from the soil itself: "Squat, Major! Take cover! Squat!"

He was weeping: "Since you don't want to get down, tell me your last desire!"

"That we two never part, Peppino!" Antonio grunted from the stone. "Never, never, never!"

He balanced himself on the boulder as on a crossbeam, swaying from side to side. "Since we have to go, let's go together!"

"But I don't want to go, Major!" Giuseppe Bonaccia burst into tears. "Just then, when I had to do ... it ... with Anna-Maria, I wanted to vanish into the flames. But it's different now. I want to piss, even if I have to do it on the flowers and the fire! Please allow me to; don't look at me!" With a trembling hand, he unbuttoned the remnants of his trousers, and then urinated in the direction of the pond and the German gun barrels. "Excuse me, for God's sake," he chattered. "I've also shit. It doesn't take much. As soon as I hear a shot behind me, I fill up my pants."

"I adore you and embrace you, my illegitimate son!" Antonio cried, beaming amorously as he looked out at the soldiers who were tottering through the flowery valley. "Peppino, my first and dearest son!"

"Don't despise me because my stomach broke down. And watch out. You'll get killed up there! You're completely exposed!"

"I've been dead for a long time, Bonaccia!" Antonio riposted, looking at the pond into which helmets, broken skulls, and frightened military game were splashing. "I'm already dead, my little one; it's all the same to me how many bullets pass through!"

Antonio Peduto would have remained on the stone for hours watching the other side of the pool if the Montenegrins had not come, looming up suddenly from behind the pine forest and crying out sometimes in Serbian and sometimes in Italian:

"Soldiers! Hey, soldiers! Italians! *Soldati! ... Poveri!* Run to us!" A male voice was echoing in the valley: "Poor devils, don't you see the Germans are waiting for you, killing you from ambush like lambs? Listen to us! Run to us! We won't do anything to you! ... We've chased you so far. ... This is the end now!" More and more peasants were appearing everywhere. "You've already paid too much, *poveri soldati!* It's over now!"

Peasants dodged out from behind the young pines and waved to the soldiers and the uniformed women. The *Ortodosse* fell down, rolled over, and started shooting at the peasants, together with the German machine-gun nests.

"Soldiers!" Antonio Peduto shouted from the stone as from a cross. "Soldiers, don't you hear that the people are calling you?!" His voice suddenly became full and deep. "Men, real men are calling you now! Toward *them*, my poor devils! Stop! Turn around! The Montenegrins aren't shooting at you anymore! These are real men!"

But the soldiers did not hear Antonio. It was as if they were drunk and mad with fear. They rushed past his rock, catching up with each other and falling on their faces. Some of them were writhing and jerking on the ground, lifting themselves on the tips of their fingers, trying to stop up their wounds with their bare hands. Blood hissed as it jetted out of their cut throats and their rattling bodies; far and wide the mountain flowers were soiled with blood. With his shoulders sagging, Antonio turned his eyes from the pond and the helmets and searched for the Montenegrins, who were still inviting his soldiers to come and promising them water and bread.

"Major!" the balled-up soldier screamed. "The Boches are firing from all their machine guns... only at the stone! Come down to me! Or they'll split you in half with lead!"

"They'll split us both, Bonaccia!" Antonio Peduto howled. "I know them well, these Africans of the North! Good-by, my son, Peppino!"

Then he turned toward the forest and the hands that were waving to his army: "Men! Montenegrins! Poor unfortunates whose country is burning up, don't let the Boches kill me! Shoot, my good

THE WAR WAS BETTER

ones! I want your fire to shatter my heart and cut up my guts!
Only quick, on the double! Don't let me be in agony too long!"

Hands waved from the forest, but no shots came. Pressed against
the ground, Peppe was trying to tell Antonio that the Negroes from
the North were firing now from at least one thousand machine guns
and several cannons, and that both of them, if they did not find
cover, would soon not even be among the dead.

"I want you to kill me!" Antonio screamed toward the forest.
"I'm personally guilty of all the shit and misery brought here by the
Venezia and Murge divisions! Shoot! Better you than the Ger-
mans!"

"Soldier, come here!" a voice called from the wood. "The
Boches will cut you up!" they shouted into the smoke. "Do you
hear?! We know who and what you are! None of that matters anymore! Come to us!"

Antonio could hardly stand on the rock. The soles of his feet
were burning. His knees trembled. Bent and crooked, coughing,
choked by wind and light, all he could do was speak:

"You good waving hands, I'm asking you for the first and last
time to spill my drunken, rotten brains on this plateau! Do it before
the Boches do, for God's sake, by your honor and your Montenegrin mustaches. Shoot! My name is Antonio Peduto, and I've done
much evil! It is I who was responsible for our common shame and
pornography!"

The peasants were shouting something, but he did not listen.

"For my first and illegitimate son, the soldier Giuseppe Bonaccia,
save his life! Save him from the Germans today, direct him toward
the Adriatic Sea, and tell him never to come back!"

"Don't bother about it, Major!" Peppe wailed. "I wouldn't remain in this country even if they made me a general!" He curled
into a ball again. "Oh, misery! There goes my stomach again! Even
if they don't cut off my head, I'll have to hold onto my pants for
the rest of my life, planting shit behind me wherever I go. . . ."

Antonio could see a horse galloping down the plain, overloaded
with ammunition and tied-on boxes and bags. Its legs and reins were
bloody. Neighing in panic, it rushed toward the forest and the
pond, trampling over the Montenegrin earth and the dead who were
lying on it, together with those who were just taking leave of their
lives. Both the Germans and the Montenegrins were firing at it, and
it could do nothing but buck and rear and rush on, unable to get rid
of its damned burden. Antonio feared a bullet would hit one of the
boxes of ammunition or explosives. Through his tears, the pony ap-

peared even bloodier and madder, and its deathly whinnying came as far as the smoke. Since everyone was firing, Antonio no longer knew whose horse it was; for a moment he thought it was going to spread its legs and sail out of the valley and the flowers.

His head swam. He felt he was going to fall down without being able even to tell his name to whoever came up to him first. And he would have dropped down then if the horse had not flung down his pack at last and galloped past them. Its back was peeled and bloody, its mouth full of foam. It whinnied and neighed and began galloping in circles.

"Men!" he shouted, addressing all the smoking gun barrels at once. "Men!" Only Peppe, clinging to the earth, heard him. "If you're still men, save the horse's life at least... if you don't save each other's!" The horse was floating through Antonio's tears, full of flowers. "Let it go! It's bloody and scared out of its wits! Let it dry its wounds in the forest!" To Antonio, the horse no longer seemed to be touching the earth. "Now it's swimming," he thought. "They can't hit my Montenegrin pony," he whispered. "And he's just swimming and swimming, and he doesn't know how to stop, or doesn't want to."

Antonio began to weep as he whispered to the turtle, which he did not realize was no longer in his arms:

"*Ortodossa*, darling, the mouth of our pony is full of the leaves of the smoke, juicy grass and water; now he's no longer thirsty. Look, *Ortodossa*, and do not forget Montenegro and its pony; rye and mountain flowers are growing in his back!"

Antonio seemed to be falling for a long time, slowly. He still saw a shoreless, petrified sea and smoke billowing everywhere. He muttered on and on without realizing he had hit the rock with the back of his head:

"Montenegro, country cast from the moon, God must have been mocking us when he carved you out of the globe!"

His dark red beard was still. The pony swam in the endlessness of his eye sockets and tears; it flourished its flaming tail like a dragon, and shook ashes, lead, and coals from its long mane. Antonio saw nothing but flame and heard nothing. It had been a long time since his beard had been so golden, so completely drenched with sun.

"*Ortodossa*, where are you?"

THE WAR WAS BETTER

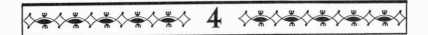 4

All that remained from the dream was light and the bitterness in Antonio's mouth. He felt that the invisible hands would wake him up if they continued to shake him so. He was bent over his rock and could open his eyes now because the backs of the three men screened off not only the setting sun, but also half the sky. He looked at them a long time before he told himself they were Germans. He looked at them and listened to Peppe's weeping while the Germans raved at them both.

"Wake up!" a sweaty and sooty soldier was saying. "Wake up, Colonel!" he snarled in bad Italian. "Quick!"

"I haven't even slept," Antonio answered in good German.

"Look, the General is a polyglot," another soldier remarked; his sleeves and eyebrows were also charred. "Then up, Marshal!"

"I'm only a Major," Antonio said as he saw the third soldier, with torn pants legs, grab hold of Peppe's shoulders. "Only a Major," he said again, admitting to himself that he had imagined them differently when they were firing from the other side of the pond.

"Perhaps, in the meantime, you've been promoted to a higher rank," the first soldier said when he took him down from the rock.

"Why don't you kill me?" Antonio asked all three.

The Germans looked at each other, at a loss what to answer. All three were out of breath and scared, and their faces looked badly burnt. Antonio riveted his eyes on the first soldier, the one who had mentioned a promotion; in spite of his exhaustion, his face, even under the helmet, seemed to smile.

"Why didn't you lift your sights a few inches a minute ago?" Antonio asked. "I was a superb target!" He looked into the soldier's beautiful wolf's eyes.

"We have orders to bring you back alive," the soldier answered as he glanced back at the pond. "*Herr Oberst* takes a lively interest in you in particular." His feet were wrapped in old rags like Antonio's and Peppe's. "*Herr Oberst . . .*"

"I'd have killed you if it was up to me," the second German snarled as he put him in shackles. "You were an exquisite target," he added, binding Peppe's right arm with the same shackles. "It didn't bother us that you were waving and shouting something in two languages. But everything was translated for Colonel Schlotterer, which is why he ordered us to aim lower."

"I'm not interested in you or your Colonel!" Antonio replied dryly, sensing suddenly that he would fall down. "Let's shorten our conversation, soldiers. Kill me!" He was staring right into their eyes. "My regards to your Colonel, and tell him I requested that a bullet be fired into the middle of my heart."

The second German, the one who had shackled him, seized his revolver mechanically, and Antonio's eyes brightened with joy.

"If possible, save the life of the war orphan beside me. He's guilty of nothing in this world, except that he has filled his pants up."

The soldiers did not know how to stop him; he was talking on, coughing, and choking with words:

"His name is Peppino Bonaccia; since he comes from the surroundings of Naples, from a village where they don't remember evil things very long, he will soon forget that today, in front of German heroes and knights, he has made such a nauseating stink . . ."

"Do you have any additional wishes?" the first soldier asked him brusquely.

Antonio stared at each of them separately. He was reeling. If it had not been for Peppe, who was sobbing convulsively, without tears, and the first soldier, who was frowning, Antonio would have struck the ground with the back of his head again. "One should never ask the Germans for things," he mused. "One has to shout at them, or at least order them."

"Put my knapsack, *bitte*, where it belongs," he said and stooped. "So." He felt the load on his back. "And the turtle on my breast, please."

The first soldier obeyed and bent down; he observed Anna-Maria for a long time with tenderness and admiration and Antonio felt jealousy surge up in him.

"I'm ready," he informed the soldier. "Which means, I can't budge."

"What are you talking about, and in what language, Major?" Peppe sputtered. "Again something about whores?" He was weeping. "If there had been no whores, perhaps all this would never have happened."

Everyone looked at him while he driveled on:

"Try to get away with it. As for myself, nobody needs me anyhow. I'm going to be court-martialed. I've got to answer for a great number of letters I've sent throughout Italy, Greece, and Montenegro."

"*Marsch!*" the first German barked out.

"Calm down, Peppino," Antonio soothed him. "Let's be dignified at least. They won't do anything to you."

It had been a long time since Bonaccia had believed in anyone's word.

"They won't kill you. The Germans save ammunition."

"Then they'll strike me with their fists, Major.... My poor mother," he spluttered out in dialect, "you've no idea that the Negroes of the North are going to execute me!"

"The conversation between the Colonel and his adjutant has ended," the first German warned; somehow he spoke even Neapolitan. "Get moving!"

He pushed Antonio and began to walk:

"To the devil!" he snapped at Peppe, who had sagged to his knees. "God in heaven, what a stench!"

"Poor devil, he's shitting again," Antonio remarked and almost burst his sides holding in his laughter. "He's been doing it nonstop ever since the war began." He looked at all three with wide eyes. "And for that reason he should be released, into the forest, freely to ... shit!"

Then all five hobbled on. First the first German fell, then Antonio: then the soldier with the scorched pants, then Peppe. They helped each other up and pushed on, each, in his own heart, cursing the fate that had brought him to this Montenegrin plateau.

Antonio did not know which of the five of them was the more miserable. He wanted to say that to the others, but he knew long and unnecessary explanations would ensue and would get on his nerves, as they always did when the Germans were involved. This was the reason why he did not reply to the first soldier, who had asked him something. The German repeated the question and requested a reply by his eyes; they slipped and banged each other's heads. Then they stared at each other fiercely for a moment and burst out laughing. Afterwards, without words, they compared wounds and burns. Instead of telling him he was sorry he could not embrace him, Antonio once again implored him to release Peppe.

"Then I would be your adjutant," the soldier replied and returned the turtle to Antonio's bosom.

"I won't look when you kill him."

"Perhaps we'll only shoot him," the soldier remarked. "Or simply throw him into the pond. In any case, I don't decide anything."

"You only obey. Isn't it so? You're a German."

"Yes, I'm from the north. My name's Eckart Cordes. And yours?"

"Ecky," Antonio enunciated with his eyes full of tears. "Cordes or Cordialis, have a heart and kill me before we come to the pond and your Colonel." Antonio was looking at his beautiful almond eyes. "Cordialis, I'd like to remain here. Look around you: there's no more beautiful spot in the world for a man's final departure and eternal rest."

"I'm not allowed to, Major," Cordes replied spontaneously. "Pardon me. I'm only a German, and from the north, to boot. This country is truly damned, you're right. God, Montenegro is made of nothing but stone, flowers, and fire!" Cordes seemed to wail. "I cannot, *Taliano;* I am not allowed to kill you until they order me to. Oh, what a country!"

"This country was flung down from the moon, Cordialis!" Antonio stumbled through his words while all three German soldiers pulled him along by his legs. "This is the most unbelievable and most beautiful country, Ecky," he muttered. Tears were pouring into his beard. "Pull the trigger, Cordes. I see you've got a rifle and a revolver. Come on, soldier! Come on, Cordes!" They pulled him on and on, with his head bouncing against the ground. "Cordes, man from the north, if you want to save your bullet, trample on my throat!"

With one hand fettered to Antonio's hand, Peppe fell over, was pulled along for a moment, and then regained his balance and crept after him. Then he fell again and the process was repeated. He would have liked to be carrying his Major, and tried to support his red head with his free hand. He succeeded only in weeping, in striking the ground with his forehead. Looking steadfastly into Antonio's large eyes, he was afraid he had gone mad again.

"Cordes, soldier from the north," Antonio murmured as though enraptured. "The earth under my back is so soft, so good, so warm; I want it to receive me immediately. Don't lead me to your superiors. Don't humiliate me."

Cordes seemed to be sorry for Antonio. The Major's face looked maniacal again; his beard was full of grass and flowers.

"Cordes, look up there: it's only the eighth day after our celebrated defeat; we're only in the middle of September and the valley is still blooming and burning; but look, there is snow glittering up there."

Cordes hurried on, sweating; he could hear rifle shots coming closer, approaching from north and south; perhaps they would be surrounded.

"The first snow," Antonio continued, "the same snow which Augusto Napolitano wanted to touch before he died. Cordes, did you know a guitarist with tin teeth and a permanently crooked throat? Do you remember his songs? Did you know he never saw the snow?"

"I knew another soldier, Major," Cordes answered. "He did not sing much, and he did not want to leave his bones in Montenegro."

"Perhaps his name was Pietro Portulu, known as Sardo?" He paused for the reply which did not come. "Well, what was the name of the soldier who did not want to die?"

"His name was Cordes," the German answered gruffly. "Eckart Cordes, Major."

"I've never heard the name," Antonio sighed and closed his eyes. "Cordes? God, how strange! ... Cordes ... Probably from the suburbs of Rome with a name like that. How come he didn't want to die if he was a Roman?"

"He wanted to live at least as long as the others, and to love his Frauke tenderly, as well as a few other girls," Cordes explained. "To love them much, Major, very, very much."

The two other Germans wondered why Cordes was speaking with an Italian who was not only a prisoner, but in addition stammered and did not allow them to put him on their shoulders and carry him away. They cursed, and moaned and said that Cordes was not the only German who had several girls. In constant fright, they tramped on, watching the rocky mountains and the fire that rushed toward them from every side like water from opened dikes.

Antonio was no longer talking about Augusto Napolitano, nor inviting his Bolognese girl to his own lap. He seemed to be sleeping, and since they were dragging him along the ground, his shirt and jacket rolled up almost to his throat, and Peppe could see his burns and the old wounds on his torso.

They were nearing a big tree and its shadow. Cordes and the other two soldiers had just woken up Antonio with great difficulty and set him on his knees; they were making an effort not to let him drop down again on his back. All three of them were crawling by this time, and tried to put their rag-wrapped feet, unbuttoned jackets, and belts in some semblance of order. Cordes could not understand why Antonio's face seemed to be illuminated by a strange joy, and he was afraid he might try to run away if he, Cordes, in addition to everything else, should begin to laugh. He was carrying Antonio's knapsack and turtle and had no strength left to prevent him from breaking away.

Finally they knelt like acolytes before the officers who were sitting at a table made of stone blocks and pine boards. For a moment they stared at each other without a word or gesture. There were many maps, binoculars, and pots in front of the officers. The bulkiest of them, Colonel Schlotterer, his shirt unbuttoned like the others, stroked his closely cropped hair; then he adjusted his spectacles and, gazing at Antonio, asked Cordes:

"Where's the fifth?"

Eckart Cordes turned and, seeing no Peppe, almost fainted. He did not know what to reply, and looked at Antonio with an emotion almost of sympathy. Antonio noticed for the first time that the shackles did not hold Peppe's hand anymore; he was about to cry out in rapture, but remained quiet, with his eyes pinned on the Colonel and his pots.

Cordes was turning around and around. The other two Germans were staring straight ahead; they expected a bullet in the back of their necks.

"Where's the fifth?" Colonel Schlotterer's voice was severe. "Where have you lost him? Speak!" He looked at them almost with disgust. "Where? Where's your . . . fifth?!"

"If he's escaped . . . this is unbelievable," Cordes muttered. "He was bound; we were pulling him." He shot a glance at the shackles. "How could he disappear?"

"I'm asking myself the same question," Colonel Schlotterer said curtly. "I watched you with the binoculars, even while you were coming back." Anger began to boil up in him. "I saw him clearly," he said not only to Cordes and the other three, but also to the officers beside him. "I even remember his face: a small bird's head; and the expression on his face . . . pooh!"

"He was here a few seconds ago," Cordes said, trying to excuse himself. "I was holding his shoulders. He stank horribly."

"It still stinks where he was standing," the second soldier put in, continuing to look straight ahead. "He must be around here somewhere."

"But where?" the Colonel snarled again. "Where?!" He glued

his eyes to the officers, as if to stir them into an answer; they were surprised, almost frightened. "Unbelievable bad taste; he's run away from us all!"

"And who knows who he was and what he knew," the Captain near the Colonel sighed.

"And what kind of secrets he has carried away with him," the Lieutenant pondered. "It's incredible—as if he had sunk into the earth!"

"Perhaps the Major knows something about it," Cordes suggested, pointing at Antonio. "It seems his name was Mario Taliano Soldato. But all of them have names like that, when they don't lie about it. Special caution is needed when dealing with people with several names—usually they are communists or fellow travelers, which is even worse. I had the impression that he was an old friend of the Major's."

All turned to Antonio. He eyed the tall ashen Colonel calmly. Schlotterer's feet were wrapped in burnt rags, and he seemed hardly able to stand on his feet. He had a dirty bandage around one knee, and his throat and elbows were scratched and bruised. Leaning over the pots, the Colonel stared back at Antonio suspiciously.

"Well, Major?" he began as he adjusted his spectacles. "Before we handle your case, tell us where this strange omnipotent Mario Taliano Soldato could be."

The Colonel filled a glass and drank; as if responding to a command, the other officers did the same.

"I understand that you spoke German with the soldiers who brought you here, but with me you may speak Italian; I understand it perfectly."

He smiled broadly, uncovering his big beautiful teeth. "*Dunque* that *soldato*, that strange character?"

Antonio watched the water that was dripping from the table for a long time without speaking. His throat was dry, his mouth full of ashes and dirt. With his hands resting on the still unburnt grass and stones, he cowered before the Colonel like a whipped dog. His head swam. It seemed to him that there were numberless pots on the Colonel's map and that water was pouring down even from the sky. He knelt so long without speaking that he forgot the Colonel and his question. And just when it seemed that they would all be left without an answer, a messtin of water arrived and was given to him.

"You surely know who and where the so-called Peppe is?" the Colonel said, after Antonio had drunk the water. "If I'm not mistaken, that was his name?" He leaned forward to examine the Major's eyes, into which light and life were returning. "Give him some bread too," he told one of the soldiers who was sitting in the shade and eating. "A lot of bread and a good piece of meat." Colonel Schlotterer wiped sweat and ashes from his forehead. "So," he said to the soldiers. "And now the bottle."

The Colonel moaned suddenly, rose, and sat down on a stone near Antonio. He did not want to have to look at the pond and what was swimming in it. One of the officers tried to unfasten the shackles on his right wrist, but Antonio shook his head. Then the Colonel asked him what he knew about the man who had vanished in such a weird fashion.

"He's Italian," Antonio said and stared straight ahead.

"And then?"

"He told me his name was Giuseppe—Peppe—Bonaccia, that he came from the vicinity of Naples, from a village where people forget evil. I met him in the morning and believed everything he said. He saved my life several times."

"Is that all, Major?" the Colonel asked, sniffing at his glass.

"Almost," Antonio said, feeling blood and water wash over his temples. "He said he loved life tremendously, that he wrote to perhaps a hundred girls, of whom he didn't know more than ninety-nine. He asked me for forgiveness."

"What?" Schlotterer perked up his ears.

"He asked me to forgive him for being a coward with an uncontrollable stomach, trailing shit behind him wherever he went," Antonio said. Looking up, he saw the Colonel's lips puckered in disgust.

"Did you forgive him?"

"I pleaded with him to stay with me, so we could be together to the bitter end," Antonio said, staring ahead vacantly.

"To which and whose end?"

"To the end," Antonio said tersely. "To the end of us all."

"Don't exaggerate, Major," Colonel Schlotterer rebuked him. "Germans don't like death." He adjusted his spectacles. "That is, they don't like to die."

Antonio gazed over the Colonel's shoulders for a long time. Although dirty, the pond was glazed over like a dead eye; only the surface was visible. Algae and rotten water lilies emerged sometimes, and then bodies in Italian uniforms and peasant clothes. The water was polluted; it gave off a stench of gunpowder and festering wounds, weapons floating on it like toys and long female hairs intertwined with frog spawn.

THE WAR WAS BETTER

"Don't be sad," Carl Schlotterer said. He poured again from his bottle into the messtin, trying to cheer him up. "Germans love life, Major," he remarked significantly as he looked out at the other officers, who were filling their messtins or helmets. "Germans like *rakia*," he continued, happy that Antonio had begun to sip from the messtin. "This magnificent Balkan poison, *Taliano*, is not unknown to you either. So here, have some more! Drink freely!"

The Colonel asked him something else, and then stressed again how mad the Germans were about Montenegrin plum brandy. Antonio was silent; his thoughts wandered. The officers gathered around Colonel Schlotterer without knowing why tears were glittering in the Major's eyes.

Antonio was ashamed that the Germans had seen him licking his hands after he had spilled brandy on them. He had licked the shackles too.

The Colonel poured more. Antonio wept silently.

"It's very strange that you don't know anything more about the soldier who escaped," the Captain behind Schlotterer's back said. "He's the only one who got away with it in the last seven days." Nervously, he poured more brandy for himself. "We've got to have him, dead or alive," he said, imitating the Colonel. "Perhaps *he* is the man—we were thinking that a moment ago—the high military personality we are looking for." Antonio's dirty face angered the Captain. "Tell us, then! Anything!"

"He told me several times that he was a coward and could not resist anyone, just as he couldn't control his bowels," Antonio began, feeling the brandy sting his throat and warm his entrails. "He kept repeating, when we were coming down, that he was so ashamed he was going to sink into the earth or vanish," he added with an aching joy in his voice. "And so, as you can see, the great General Giuseppe-Peppe Bonaccia, the commandant of all our forces in the Balkans, has disappeared in a manner worthy of attention and admiration."

"General?" the Captain's mouth opened wide with astonishment. "Now I see, yes, I was right when I said he was no private!" He gloated triumphantly. "First, the manner in which he hid behind the rock. Then, the way in which he wept, falling on his knees. An ordinary soldier, especially an Italian, would never . . ."

"Thank you, Captain," Colonel Schlotterer said with undisguised disdain. "The Major's explanation seems to me to be more interesting." He looked into Antonio's dimmed eyes. "Continue. You've made a good beginning."

"I regret as deeply as you do, Colonel, that General Bonaccia, the commander of all our land forces, is not here," Antonio said, his beard full of brandy and tears. "Since you have no heart and no imagination, you can't even guess how many addresses, military secrets, plans, and medals Peppino carried away with him."

Eckart Cordes was looking at the officers significantly. Only the Colonel did not feel insulted.

"Peppino," Antonio murmured. "The inexorable Peppino. He was so kind to my wife, up there in the mountains."

"To your wife?" Colonel Schlotterer's big eyes bulged. "Where's your wife? Perhaps...she has disappeared...with him?"

"With my wife," Antonio caught up with the rhythm of the sentence. "With my wife, and when we were expecting the landslide and the wind to sweep us away into the black, gaping pit." His words flowed by themselves, like brandy from the Colonel's bottle. "I was standing on her long hair, on her arms; I tried to peer into her whorish heart. And he, our first soldier and the commander of our navy and air force, knelt and stroked the damned flower between her legs. Then he leaned his forehead on her belly and loins; he was trembling; he pushed his nose right up into the sacred blossom where the smells of flesh and earth meet and surge."

Colonel Schlotterer was excited. He wanted to stop the Major with a new messtin of brandy. But Peduto saw no one and nothing beyond the freckled knees of the woman on her back. And without moving, paying no attention even to the Colonel, he followed his own mad words on and on:

"With my wife. And then I knew defeat. Listening to them, seeing them heaped up in my mind's eye, I felt defeated; I felt as I feel now, with you getting me drunk and keeping me on my knees, alive. And she, my only wife, my treason...is right in front of you....She'd like some brandy too."

The Colonel passed the bottle to him. They watched him drinking and saw his Adam's apple bobbling in his throat. They thought he would pause and say something else. Finally his swollen hands let the bottle drop.

"And that is why," he began again, "I request you to humiliate me too. This is what you must do. Spread the little legs of my *Ortodossa* and if you don't wish to do something else, or are too tired and can't do it, at least spit into her wound. If she resists, tear up her entrails—then we'll see what stuff the whorish female heart is made of!"

THE WAR WAS BETTER

Antonio exploded with a madman's laughter. He hugged the turtle to his bosom in a burst of rapture. He would have fallen down but for the soldier, Eckart Cordes, and the two others who supported him.

The Colonel thought Antonio's mind had collapsed and he, also drunk, kept repeating: "What's your name, Major? Name! ... Do you hear me?"

All of them started shouting at once. The other officers leaned over him, already tired out and dissatisfied. While the Colonel argued with him, they took some pieces of paper out of his pockets and tried to read them. The Captain pulled an old book out of his knapsack. The name of Pietro Aretino appeared on the cover. The Captain asked who he was, and Antonio had an urge to spit on him.

Proud of his sharpness, the Captain inquired whether Pietro Aretino was not an admiral. He got no reply. The Colonel looked at him with contempt. Then the Captain concluded aloud that Pietro Aretino was most probably the chief of Italian intelligence who had recently fallen into the clammy hands of the English.

"Name! In the name of God! Name!" the Colonel lifted his voice still higher. "We've all had enough fun now. I cannot tell your name from these filthy notes of yours and indecent drawings! Your name is nowhere to be seen!"

"My name is defeat and pornography!" The words emerged unbidden from Antonio's throat. "Defeat and shame! Pornography! Grief! Misery! When I was alive, they called me ... Do you have more brandy or at least some gasoline? Give me another little glass, and then kill me, Cordes. ..."

While the other officers studied Antonio's papers, secretly stuffing their pockets with the worst of his pornographic drawings, and Cordes and the other soldiers lifted him off the ground, Colonel Schlotterer drank desperately. He looked like a man who had invested too much in a firm that had just gone bankrupt.

Antonio laughed from the depths of his belly and looked drunkenly in the direction his own hand was pointing. Inside his shirt he could feel the turtle's little paws, clutching his bosom.

"Oh, the *Ortodossa!*" he muttered in disbelief, his voice trembling. "My sorrowful mother, how wonderful it is that what I see is so far from your eyes! I see Balkan women. I think there are four or five hundred. They are scratched; their pants-legs or dresses are torn; their long hair is scorched; they are silent. The soldiers are watching them over their gun-barrels."

Antonio's voice changed tone. He no longer spoke to his mother, but to himself:

THE WAR WAS BETTER

"They're looking at the pond in which the soldiers' bodies are floating, or at the endless sea of rock and wind from which they have come. Many of them are weeping, half weeping, containing themselves. Only one of them is really sincere: her hair reaches almost to her stomach; she's squeaking like a mouse and offering her hard, dark breasts to the soldier standing guard, watching over them. She's speaking to him in many different languages, and her nipples are so hard and sharp I'd like to shoot at them!"

His breath shortened. He caressed the turtle feverishly.

"Anna-Maria," he murmured, "remember what you've seen in the Balkans, love. When you tell all this to your Roman sisters, have me come down to be your witness. Then we'll all agree that these have been truly great, unforgettable times for the whores of the whole world! We'll repeat it over and over to all the imbeciles; we'll tell them what a splendid job the whores have done, leading the war effort, everywhere, especially in the Balkans, and that finally, they won it, they won the war. . . ."

A soldier with grass and flowers on his helmet ran up from somewhere, all raw and bleeding. He informed Colonel Schlotterer that he and his platoon had taken about fifty girls prisoner, and that some of them spoke Albanian and German. They cursed in all the Balkan languages, he reported, and sang only in Italian. There were also some Gypsy, Macedonian and Bulgarian girls among them, and he was afraid some of them might be hiding weapons or communist subversive materials under their skirts. He asked the officers what to do with them. The soldier was very young and lanky; he repeated some words several times and could hardly stand on his feet. The Colonel told him to return to the girls and guard them well.

"Beware of the materials, soldier," Peduto interrupted. "Beware of the dangerous materials under their skirts. They're explosives that blow up bridges, yes, even German bridges, wipe out boundaries, blow up fortified enemy lines. . . ."

The soldier listened and stuttered: "But. . . . But. . . ."

"Beware, my little one, of what they have. . . . And this, this is fire! It withers men like sunlight! This is alcohol, the true beverage for warriors of all races, including the German one, the only prize for the victors and the vanquished alike! Beware, soldier, therefore beware of the ivy wreaths all the heroes and cowards will decorate themselves with after the war. Beware of medals. Beware of flags, riddled by hot bullets. . . . Beware of air-raid shelters!"

Antonio's head dropped. He touched the turtle's shell with his red beard. "This is alcohol. This is the holy water. This is subversive material!"

The soldier was no longer there; Antonio was talking to himself. The Lieutenant touched the bandage wrapped around his long, bony, horse's head with a pointing finger. "He's drunk too much," he said.

"I'll give him some more; finally he will tell me where the bulk of the Venezia Division has gone," the Colonel whispered to the Captain and the careworn Lieutenant. "He must know it. . . . This is no usual major," he went on, more and more confidentially. "If he's a major at all!"

"What if he's a Russian and a communist spy?" the Lieutenant said, jutting out his strong jaws. "But first can you repeat what you just said? I didn't understand."

"He must know how many Italians have sided with the Montenegrins since last week, when they betrayed us," Colonel Schlotterer murmured into the Lieutenant's big ear. "We also don't know where the three mountain regiments of the Murge Division are, or some detachments of the Messina."

The Lieutenant's jaws stuck out further and further; he looked like a man who could have torn up a whole division with his teeth.

"He will say something after all, I hope," the Colonel said. "The part I read between the lines is especially interesting." Then all of them listened attentively to Antonio, who had begun talking again.

"Cordes and the rest of you Germans," he muttered with his eyes shut. The wind above them, blowing in the smoke and the clouds, was carrying away the light and heat. "Why don't you rape them . . . these *Ortodosse*, these Byzantine girls? They're here, offering themselves. Opportunity knocks once, and once only. You'll never see so much exotic flesh on one spot again, yours for the asking. Later on you'll have to pay for everything that's near at hand now—and pay not only with money, but with heads too." Tears broke away from his eyelashes. "Rape them. They won't be angry. They're good. They're a real army. Let's celebrate our meeting with another defeat! Cordes, would you believe that I know the word 'rape' in almost every language, including your own? Do you believe me?"

"Germans don't rape," the Captain protested from behind Schlotterer's back. "Germans only scour the globe of communism, lice and Italians. I repeat to you, *Taliano*, that Germans want nothing to do with women, even when they're clean. Take me, for example; without seeing a doctor's certificate issued the same day, the same moment . . . nothing!"

"I need two certificates, Major," the horse-headed Lieutenant said, and suddenly turned purple. "One military certificate, and one from the civilian authorities.... Don't forget that some of those damn ladies have civilian authorities. ... Don't forget that some of those damn ladies have ... rickets!"

"Rape them!" Antonio cried, trying to inspire them while Carl Schlotterer sipped more brandy. "Only then will they believe that you're an army. A great Balkan army of lust and love!" He coughed, choking on his own words. "If you don't rape them, they'll think you aren't the real heroes you are, but butchers who hunger for the living human flesh of Europe!"

The Lieutenant with the bandaged head jutted his jaws toward Antonio. Then he saw Carl Schlotterer pouring for everyone from a new bottle. He even gave some to Eckart Cordes, who was still trying to look the other way, remembering the fifth who had vanished.

"Do what I'm begging you to do," Antonio said softly. "It would be so humane."

"But many humane things are forbidden to us Germans, Major," Carl Schlotterer said frankly. "I hope you've understood me."

"Rape them, or you'll lose the war!" Antonio sputtered, reaching out to take the messtin the Colonel was offering him. "Those who rape will defeat you, those who know better than you how to rejoice." He drank until brandy scorched his throat and clouded his voice: "The poor girls will feel neglected. You're insulting them!"

Drunk with brandy and worn out from the heat, the Germans maintained their silence and waited.

"Do it," he continued. "You'll perform a great deed. The news will spread that it was men who passed here, not wolves!"

His eyes were closed, his head thrown back, all sunlit.

"Cordes, a war is won, in the true sense of the word, only by those soldiers who dance around the world with their flies unbuttoned. Eckart!"

Cordes' eyes, lively and beautiful a moment ago, were now drunken and bloodshot. He held up Antonio's shoulders and looked fearfully out of the corner of his eye at the Colonel, who was whispering to the horse-headed Lieutenant that the prisoner would soon let out the main thing, the key thing he was waiting for. The Captain, beet red with brandy, had abandoned hope, but something was sparkling in the Colonel's eyes, and Cordes did not know what: a tear or a drop of Montenegrin poison.

"Rape them. They'll remember you and the others ... with pain, with sorrow, even with pride."

"Rape them yourself, *Taliano*," Carl Schlotterer urged him with a stammering tongue. "Will you?" He sipped his brandy without paying attention to the rest of the officers. "Do it for all of us. So we'll be thankful to you, we, the Germans, and they, the whores: all of us." He smelled his hands which were wet from brandy. "Major, is it possible that you agree?"

"I always agree to everything," Peduto replied without opening his eyes. "To everything. Another drink, please." Before opening his mouth wide to receive the brandy, he called tenderly: "Cordes, where are you?"

Colonel Schlotterer staggered over to the Major; he, the Captain, the raging Lieutenant and the other officers all poured their bottles straight into Antonio's throat; his beard, eyes and ears filled up with brandy and pine needles.

The soldiers carried Antonio toward the girls. His jaws fell open. The officers blushed.

Carl Schlotterer crept more than walked. He was talking to himself: "Will he dare ... Oh, God, what alcohol this is, this Montenegrin brandy!" He tottered, and his old wounds opened and began to bleed again. "And how will he do it, alone, against so many girls?" His head spun. He could no longer remember what secret he had been trying to pry out of the Italian devil. He could remember less and less; he was forgetting everything. Some incomprehensible force was drawing him onward toward the crowd of Antonio's brides.

Exhausted like any other army after their forced marches and extra daily and nightly efforts, most of them uniformed and totally at their ease, the girls quietly watched their guests approach. They had all gotten up from the ground, even the wounded ones, to see the drunken Germans without weapons.

The crowd of women made way, and the soldiers put the red-bearded rapist down. The eyes of Carl Schlotterer and the other officers were pinned on him.

Shame and pity swept through Antonio. He thought purple must have been suffusing his cheeks; he thought he would sink into the earth if they continued to look at him so. For a moment he knelt and watched the insulted, famished eyes of the women. He remembered his sister who had vanished in Via dei Serpenti, a notorious street of brothels; then his thoughts wandered to the turtle, with which Cordes and the other Germans were entertaining themselves, and his heart seemed to shrivel up. He no longer knew who had brought him there. He heard and sensed only women. They were talking, weeping, laughing. He did not understand them. His head drooped. Tears welled up in his eyes.

Carl Schlotterer, the Captain and the Lieutenant, and even Eckart Cordes with his two perpetual comrades, watched Antonio spread his arms out. The Colonel told the officers that the *Taliano* most probably began each rape by spreading his arms and turning around. They emptied the bottle and tightened their belts.

There were no girls within reach of Antonio's arms; only army smells, strangely sweet, wafted to his nostrils. His head fell; his beard struck the earth. Then he crawled toward them, flailing first to his left, then to his right, while the girls withdrew, laughing. But he no longer wanted to reach one; he stopped even stretching out his arms. He merely crept along, weeping and sniffling, caressing and kissing the earth upon which, a moment before, the feet of the women had trod.

The women no longer laughed; they saw he could not catch up with them. Even the officers did nothing but watch him as he crept and sniffled his way forward, with his soul in his nose. They were angry, but only because there was no more brandy.

"I see you expected more, Captain," Carl Schlotterer remarked. "You particularly, Lieutenant." He sighed and looked at his watch. "*Zurückkehren!*" he commanded bitterly, and then sighed again. "We have to be at the camp before nightfall."

"Night is still two hours away," the Captain said.

"It gets dark a little earlier in a mountain," the Lieutenant observed.

"Pine trees will light our way," the Colonel said wryly. "Assuming we don't get there before dusk." He looked again at his watch and, making valiant efforts to set forth, said to himself: "We have to arrive on time."

"By then he'll probably sober up," the Captain said as he glanced at Antonio, on his knees among the women. "I'm surprised, Colonel. It seems he's a hopeless drunkard," he said, almost falling down. "It's hard to wheedle any information out of a drunkard. Of course the sober ones are even worse."

He reeled about, looking for his small bottle. It was nowhere to be found. He felt like cursing the heavens.

"He'll admit nothing," Carl Schlotterer concluded and started off. "There's no use applying force against a man like that. Brandy is more efficient." He looked over at the women with Antonio among them. "He will admit nothing, Captain, but he will reveal everything. There are more important things than military secrets." The officers listened to him intently. "He'll tell everything voluntarily. We won't even have to ask him. I know such men. Moments come when their hearts open up by themselves, and then the blood and the pure truth gush out."

He signaled to Cordes to place Antonio on a stretcher and depart immediately.

"What if we don't find out which way the battered remains of their divisions have gone?"

"If we don't massacre them today, we'll kill them off tomorrow," the Colonel said softly. "They have to turn toward the coast, toward the sea which is in our hands. They cannot escape. Rejoice!" There was much bitterness and anger in his voice. "We alone will be killing them . . . for a while."

They stood near the swampy pond, but did not look at the water, and even less at what was floating in it.

"Shall we go the same way we came, Colonel?" the Captain asked. "Or follow the river back, to avoid the landslides from the northeast?"

Carl Schlotterer was not listening to him.

"I'd keep to the river, because the communists . . ."

The Colonel adjusted his spectacles. Then he stroked his close-cropped hair and gazed for a long time at the girls with Antonio among them. He felt sorry for him; he seemed so helpless on his knees.

"He's altogether red," he said to himself. He wanted to look at him more closely. "I'd even say he's . . . improbable." His thought flowed on, drunk with women and brandy: "I can't forget him. I won't be able to. This won't be our last meeting. It is good to see and hear such men more frequently." He was supporting himself with his stick and his submachine gun. He wanted to forget the stagnant pond.

"Which alternative do you prefer, Colonel?"

"Escort him, together with the whores," Carl Schlotterer answered. "With the whores. Right. Anyhow he thinks his place is with them."

He was angry and hurt that they did not understand him.

"If he can't walk, let them carry him. They seem capable of anything." The Colonel leaned toward the Captain: "Watch out that he doesn't sink from sight like that Admiral. Disappearing acts are an Italian specialty."

The Captain was thinking about his stolen bottle and where he could look for it; he did not quite catch what the Colonel had said.

All he could do was blush and stammer something incomprehensible.

"And you, Lieutenant, I will hold you equally responsible . . . if the red beard vanishes."

The man with the bandage around his head tried to stand at attention. The Colonel believed implicitly in his protruding steel jaws, but disliked his eyes, which were like a mouse's. He turned his gaze from them almost immediately.

The odor of flowers, brandy and festering wounds continued to waft through the air. There was no shooting. The water in the pond flowed sluggishly in slow circles.

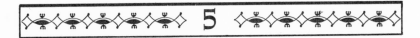

"Excuse me for having raped you," Antonio whispered from the stretcher, looking up at the silent female faces. "Excuse me, for God's sake, for love's sake, which has brought you to all this. At first I didn't want to, but then a darkness like blood covered my eyes; I didn't want to put you to shame in front of them."

The stretcher bounced up and down because the women, going down toward the river, were tottering and falling. His hands brushed against stone and earth; he imagined they were caressing the emaciated and sorrow-ridden cheeks of a woman.

"I'll never do it again, I swear. Nobody in the world loves you more than I do, or understands you better."

He spoke out a litany of all the Balkan names he could remember, puckering his lips to kiss the hands which swam across his eyesockets; in his mind, the women were blending with the turtle and his sister, lost in Via dei Serpenti, close to the Vatican.

"You're my whole life. I beg you to forget that I raped you all. Don't be angry that I kissed the ground you walked on so briefly. I wanted to kiss it forever."

The procession marched gravely down toward the water. Cordes with his chums led the way. The serious Captain and the insulted Lieutenant tottered behind the stretcher. They scolded and cursed the girls, keeping their fingers on the triggers of their submachine guns. The long column ended with Colonel Schlotterer, who could hardly walk and often had to be carried. Signal flares from the nearby mountains told them it was safe to proceed toward the river mouth and the camp.

"I'd really like to pitch this damned knapsack of his," the soldier beside Cordes whispered.

"Don't do it, Kurt," Cordes warned him. "There are some papers inside. The Colonel said everything must be examined minutely—there might be some reports and plans."

"None," Kurt snapped. "I searched through them. There's nothing in German. Certain names and words crop up on every page. No reports."

"How many pornographic photos and drawings are there, and where are they they?" Cordes whispered passionately. "Speak lower."

"About a hundred," Kurt whispered, looking back covertly at the bizarre procession behind him. "They're in the safest possible place, close to my heart."

"And the flask of brandy you pinched from the Captain, Kurt?"

"It's in an even safer spot, in my underpants. Trust in me, Ecky."

"You're smart, sometimes."

"One has to grapple with the situation. Since they wouldn't let us get near the whores, let's at least get the photos."

"Are they good, Kurt?"

"Magnificent. Unbelievable. Charming." A thrilling warmth tingled through the soldier's veins. "Incomprehensible to a normal, reasoning human being. But since we're soldiers . . ."

"We'll share them like brothers," Cordes suggested, also flushed by Kurt's excitement.

"Listen," Kurt began with a cracking voice, looking behind him again. "Mere photos aren't enough. I'm going to sneak up on the girls at night even if they push me up against the wall for it!"

"But what if they're infected, Kurt?" Cordes said softly as he watched the Captain and Lieutenant hurrying the girls up, beating them from behind.

"And so what, Ecky?" the soldier replied like a man who would welcome the blackest evil. "And what then?" His chin quivered. "We're all mad probably and infected too; all the rivers of the world couldn't wash us clean. My spine," he whispered, "my spine will dry up from . . . wacking off. . . . Do you hear me, Cordes?"

The crowd was slowing down. The crossroads they were approaching was blocked by disemboweled earth, boulders, and trucks straining in the dust. Antonio was still on the stretcher, staring fixedly and amorously at the dumb faces of the girls. He wanted to tell them many things, and his eyes were no longer tearful. But because of the chugging trucks and the singing Germans, he could not part his lips. He merely watched them and tried not to think about what was happening or other ugly things.

The Italian prisoners waved to the girls from the slowly departing trucks. Although they were tired out and scorched, the soldiers were lifting their hands and gesturing energetically.

"Love! Love!" even the injured shouted. "Love, *amore*, now good-by!"

The Germans struck at them with sticks and rifle butts, but still they shouted into the dust: "Love, heart . . . life and youth, good-by!"

The Germans spat on them. And the girls did not call back or speak. Those to whom they would have returned a greeting were no more.

The Captain and the Lieutenant with the bandaged head took Antonio over. They passed the crossroads hurriedly, weighed down by the stretcher. From the shadows, Colonel Schlotterer and another superior officer signaled that they should follow the path that entered the forest. They completed their task and then, from the shadow beside the road, looked out on the dusty, jammed crossroads. Antonio was surprised to notice his knapsack on the stretcher, and the turtle trying to push her head out through one of the holes.

Carl Schlotterer was standing above him and talking with Lieutenant Colonel Breitbach. The latter was a handsome, well-shaped man in his fifties; he still had all his teeth and knew how to make them flash when he laughed, like an actor, and was broad-shouldered and erect. He patted Colonel Schlotterer on the back and congratulated him for something.

"I never imagined he would be like this," Carl Schlotterer said, pointing at Antonio.

"Neither did I," Joachim Tea Breitbach echoed. "But it's he, for sure!"

Surrounded by other officers, they began whispering to each other and reading out a roll of Italian names. They mentioned the name of Antonio's division and looked for Montenegro, Dalmatia, and the sea on the map of Europe. They smoked cigarettes continuously, as if they had not had enough fire and arson. Antonio had an

THE WAR WAS BETTER

urge to spit in their faces. The roll seemed endless, and their pronunciation of Italian names was unbearable to him. Younger officers
were bringing ham and brandy.

"Kill me," Antonio said quietly; the smell of wounds, women
and soldiers was filling his nostrils. "That is the only and last thing I
request from you."

"Thank you for such a beautiful offer, Major," Lieutenant Colonel Breitbach answered with a smile. "Carl has told me your story
with unusual fervor." His face was wrinkled and tanned. "After
what he told me, it would be a sin to kill you . . . immediately." He
cut off his laughter abruptly, like a stage villain. "In any case," he
said, "we've already done too much killing today."

"Kill me," Antonio repeated in a hard voice. "Or let me take my
own life." He stared right into the Lieutenant Colonel's large eyes.
"One bullet is enough for me." Antonio did not pause. "Come on,
pull the trigger. That's the only thing I can request from a German!"

"We got the information we needed from someone else," Colonel Schlotterer informed him. "That is why we will not torture you
anymore, or make you drunk. Which doesn't mean, however, that
we are not going to have discussions. On the contrary." Carl
winked, pointing the way: "Look, Major!"

"I see only girls," Peduto said hoarsely. "What will happen to
them?"

"We'll treat them like prisoners of war," Joachim Tea Breitbach
said. "They'll go to a camp, Major, where they will have to un-
dergo moral and political re-education." He was not drunk; he pronounced words distinctly. "Germany is bleeding more than ever before in her history; Germany needs physical as well as intellectual
forces."

Antonio Peduto cast sorrowful glances upon Lieutenant Colonel
Breitbach and occasionally upon the uniformed girls. "These poor
women-intellectuals of mine," he said to himself as he listened to the
handsome officer's explanation; he was almost choking with tears.
"Happy be the country you'll build up!"

"Do you see now, Major?" the Colonel asked him, pointing the
way again.

"Your intellectuals are blocking my view," Antonio said angrily,
directing his eyes toward Breitbach. "Something on the road is coming closer. If I'm not mistaken, it is an Italian car. I even know it."

"A real trophy!" Colonel Schlotterer exclaimed. "You'll see it."
Carl's face was sweaty and tense. "And you're a trophy too, of

course.... Even a most interesting one,...at least for me." He blushed and adjusted his spectacles. "But for the others, do you understand, that's the trophy of the year!"

"These are the spoils for which it's worth going to war," Joachim Tea Breitbach almost cried for joy.

A military truck, full of motley Italians, torn flags, weapons and ammunition, was towing a small armored Fiat: dust covered the windshields and whoever was behind the wheel could not be seen. The skis tied to the roof were broken. The trunks and leather valises, which bore labels from fashionable summer resorts and hotels, were all torn up; women's stockings and girdles hung out of them like intestines, together with panties of various colors, brassieres of all sizes and pieces of gauze and cotton. A butterfly net was sticking out of the pile of luggage—a forlorn reminder of bygone days. Finger drawings could be seen on the dusty sides of the car: a swastika in the rear and, further in front, exaggerated male and female organs with their hair and testicles reaching down to the dented fender and the little wheels.

"General Giovanni Besta," Antonio laughed and started talking to himself again, without paying any attention to Lieutenant Colonel Breitbach, who was looking for somebody in the rolls and pronouncing Italian and Montenegrin names like a real German: "Now where in hell is Marika's Nanni Primitivo coming from, the old Roman whore—and the worst kind too?"

The car, a two-seater, was smashed front and back and riddled by bullet and shrapnel holes, and yet it rolled on.

"This Nanni, Marika's last victim, will follow me all my life; perhaps we'll go together to the other world too. On the other hand, maybe it wouldn't be so bad—to leave with him for the long sleep beneath the earth. There too he'd meow and bark; he'd tell his stories about the war and his ups and downs with sex; anyway the dead will listen to him; they're usually entranced by meditations on a brilliant future."

The funny little Fiat, equipped in its former life with white-wall tires and chromium plate, chugged up to Schlotterer and the happy Lieutenant Colonel Breitbach, who was commanding the junior officers to establish order, silence the crowd, divide the living from the dead, and separate the sick and wounded from the girls who were eyeing them with pity and trying to arouse them. Swallowing dust and stifling his urge to weep and laugh, Antonio Peduto recalled his many encounters with the perpetually smiling and mocking General Besta, remembered most of all his stolen gold tobacco case, in which he had so jealously guarded his famous Spanish contraceptives, and thought again of Marika, who went from house to house telling all the whores how she had ridden him, not only naked, but also fully armed.

Antonio also remembered their leave-taking a few days before when, with the beautiful Romana, he had seated himself in his Fiat, a car which, he said, had been personally presented to him by Benito Mussolini, and expressed the wish that all of them might escape the Germans and the Russians, and fall instead into the hands of the English and the Americans.

"They're always drunk, the English and Americans," he had said. "Pale, freckled and drunk. And they're always ready to forgive a warrior and a lover, especially us; they consider us mad, irresponsible, obsessed by sex . . . which is (I say this off the record) quite true," the General repeated to each one in turn. With his teeth chattering, he hummed: "I'm an Italian, a pure-blooded Italian, which is a rare event in the Peninsula."

When the *calabrone*, bumblebee, Colonel Spartaco Allegretti, dared to ask him why he was saying all this to them at that particular moment, just when they had signed the surrender papers, General Besta had continued:

"The time is coming soon when breeding and courage will have to be looked at with different eyes, that is, with admiration."

As the General spoke on at length of breeding and good families, which, he said, the Americans and the English in particular looked up to so much, the bent, shaggy Allegretti grew so depressed he could hardly speak.

"Has it been proved, General," he finally asked, "that we Italians can have pedigrees, as you say, like dogs?"

Nanni Besta did not even break stride at this question. "In Europe, only the English and the Italians are pedigreed, Spartaco," he replied at once. "Although neither the former nor the latter are directly linked with dogs."

Colonel Allegretti grew even more depressed, and the General tried to cheer him up:

"It is clear that we Italians have pedigrees; we weren't born yesterday, like the Germans and the Slavs, although of course this is not the case among you Sicilians, or the Neapolitans, or the islanders in general. Don't worry, Spartaco, no one will ever be able to accuse you of blue blood."

Then General Besta, caught up in his own thoughts, stopped mocking and spitting on them; it was at this point that Antonio, who had been waiting anxiously for the little Fiat to depart, came forward. They stared at each other for a moment in silence. Then the General, sitting down behind the wheel beside Romana, finally spoke: "Pedigree, on the other hand, is a word of northern, perhaps even Swedish origin.... Good-by!"

He departed by a different route than he had come, leaving the others in the dust thrown up by his wheels to discuss the famous forefather which they did not possess, and also the English and the Americans.

Now Antonio saw the overloaded Fiat stop. Several soldiers leaped down from the truck. With submachine guns and pistols ready to fire, they surrounded the little roadster.

Colonel Schlotterer was the first to approach the automobile. He put his hand mechanically on his pistol. The soldiers could hardly open the door. All dusty but smiling, crumpled and bedecked with medals, General Besta emerged at last, eyed the officers and soldiers and said, in impeccable English:

"Good afternoon, gentlemen. Ah, what a difficult and terrible day!"

"Good afternoon, General!" Colonel Schlotterer said in Italian. "The day has been very hot, but that's the way we like it." He ordered the soldiers to be careful when taking down the valises from which feminine underthings were dropping. "The real, sunny South!" he added. "Finally! The South!"

The motors of the trucks were rattling and roaring loudly, giving off foul-smelling gasoline fumes; the Colonel had to shout, and General Besta to reply by grimaces.

They pulled Romana out of the car. Her close-fitting dress, drawn waspishly tight at the waist, emphasized above all her swelling breasts and behind, which was round as a soccer ball, and left her long, tanned arms uncovered. She looked about her as if she had imagined quite a different encounter with the Germans than this. She measured the rows of guards with a haughty disdain; her gaze roamed over the wounded packed in the trucks, and then paused on Schlotterer's perplexed face. The Colonel knew she was looking at him, and coughed in a muffled way, as if from the dust.

"The data you have given us are most precious!" Carl Schlotterer said to the General insincerely. "On behalf of our command, we thank you!" The General couldn't quite hear him; his eyes bulged with effort as he inclined his ear. "We say: thank you!"

The General smiled.

Colonel Schlotterer cast a glance on Romana's breasts, which billowed over her neckline; he felt he would fall down if he did not continue to shout elaborate thanks to the frightened General. Through the noise of the engines and the smell of gasoline, he howled again and again at Besta; meanwhile Romana began offering her lips to others too, smiling left and right, to all but the Italians. She was smoking long Greek cigarettes, and the thick smoke teased Schlotterer's nostrils. Her eyes were black and big, her hair wavy, fluffed out, falling to her shoulders.

"Without the data you've furnished us, we could hardly prevent the communists from breaking through to the coast, which must remain in our possession," Breitbach lied, looking more at Romana than at the General.

"The coast has always been ours," General Giovanni Besta interrupted him. "Whose else could it be? We were born on it."

"The coast must be German!" Schlotterer said angrily, noticing that Romana was not only making eyes at him and Breitbach. "The German coast . . . must remain German!"

"German?" The General's clownish eyes bulged spontaneously; instead of guffawing, he began to meow: "Meow! Meow!" He could not restrain himself from imitating animals when it was least expected of him; he was famous for it. "Meow!"

"All the coasts must be German!" Lieutenant Colonel Breitbach snapped and felt sweat drench him. "There are no mice among us."

He fastened his eyes on Romana and the Colonel.

"All the coasts of the world . . . it is well-known that we Germans like water!" The smell of uniforms and iodine troubled his thoughts. "Water is . . . so to speak . . . in our blood. Anyhow, General, we also like to bathe!"

Antonio could no longer laugh. He lay quietly on the stretcher, awaiting the outcome of all this. Ravishingly beautiful, alone among men, Romana reigned like a queen; every sentence the men were speaking had been balanced with her in mind. From Antonio's stretcher, the weaponless General looked small among the Germans. Everything on him seemed small: his boots, his belt, his two-pointed hat. His hands were soft. The numerous medals on his soft breast were soft. His voice was soft. He was standing between Schlotterer and Breitbach with his knees pressed together like a woman's.

"Contrary to other Italians, my strong point is precision!" Besta stated. "I'm particularly outstanding at gathering, working out and supplying information." He did not dare to mention the coast again; he was afraid he would meow and bark. "Information is a wonderful thing, but Italians are incapable of appreciating it. Italians don't know how to appreciate anything. Nothing is sacred to them. They don't believe in God. They flirt with communism and immorality of every kind."

Lieutenant Colonel Breitbach was looking at his rings, artificial teeth and medals with admiration. A sudden panic seized the General; the coast was popping back into his mind, but he somehow avoided it.

"And I'd be happy . . ." he began again, hoping they would hear him out to the end.

"You're already happy, General," Colonel Schlotterer interrupted him. "You've escaped the claws of the partisans. Both of you are now with us." His drunkenness had not worn off; he was staring passionately at Romana. "We're all, perhaps, happy."

"Do you mean that, after the information I have provided you, the information which you yourselves considered precious for the forthcoming defense from the communist attacks . . . does it mean . . . that I'm free now?"

"You're free from the communists," Colonel Schlotterer said.

"I fear and abhor only them," Giovanni Besta stated as he watched Romana titillate them with her Greek cigarette smoke. "That means, I believe, that we can now proceed to the coast!"

"I hope we can," Schlotterer said, inhaling the pungent smoke of Romana's cigarette deeply into his lungs. "I hope so. One always has to hope, doesn't one?" The woman was watching him through the curling clouds of smoke. "We'll go to the coast together."

"Romana!" Besta exclaimed, leaping into the air. "You were right! The Germans are gentlemen, and the English are upstarts, boozers, womanhaters, misogynists!" He waved his little hands like a child. "Meow! Meow! Meow!" Crimson suffused his pale face; he wiped his forehead and neck with a perfumed handkerchief. "Bow-wow! Bow-wow! Already I see the sea; I feel it; it's warm and full of salt and little fish!"

The Colonel stared at him; he could hardly believe his eyes. The General froze suddenly in panic. He began to mutter:

"Iodine, salt, little fish . . . and mines, ours, that is, German . . . against the non-existent communist fleet!" He lowered his voice; his hands fell to his sides. "Water . . . German hygiene . . . famous throughout the world, even in one part of Italy."

"Are you drunk, General?" Breitbach asked him severely, his voice harsh and insistent.

"Me? Drunk?" Giovanni Besta's little fist struck his motley decorations. "Never! I'm the phenomenon of phenomena! I take a sip now and then, but almost never get plastered." His large eyes were bulging with fatigue and fear. "I'm drunk on life itself. It is sweet and, without the communists, it will be even sweeter! I'm drunk on life, in which I stand foursquare for precision, for the compulsory contribution of information, for understanding and agreement, and for revenge among men. Romana, my love, we'll go to the coast and go swimming, naked, with the Germans, among the mines!" He turned away from the surprise which registered in the cold German eyes. "Gentlemen, alcohol is for weaklings and cowards. And for us, the brave, the valiant; we know what's good for us!" He wiggled his hips suggestively. "This! This! This!"

He looked on as the officers searched through his trunks and bags, and Romana showed pieces of gold and jewelry to Lieutenant Colonel Breitbach. Fear began to creep into his bones, even into his words:

"You Germans, you ancient Teutonic heroes! You're the only ones who can save the world from the communists and the English, who are now advancing from every side!" He shouted at the top of his voice, pranced like a drill-major and spat in a circle around himself. "For the ancient heroes and us individualistic Italians, for us there's the sweetness of life, stamp collecting and light music!" He sang the refrain from an operetta. "Meow! Meow! Meow!"

"You're completely drunk," Colonel Schlotterer said fiercely. "Time is passing. We'll talk about bats when it gets dark." He looked at Romana. "When it gets dark."

"Free, finally free!" the General whispered in rapture. He sensed the presence of Montenegrin brandy somewhere nearby. "And drunk on life, even if it is in German style!" His eyes were full of false feminine tears. "*München!*" he screamed, and then softened again. "My Munich and my Maximilianstrasse! Hauptbahnhof, your Wagner and our Rossini. . . ."

"Your information is correct, General," Colonel Schlotterer repeated and pointed at the trucks into which they were loading Italian soldiers. "Whatever it is you've said is interesting and exciting. We'll talk about it another time. Now you are a prisoner, and we must observe formalities. Take the essential things and choose whatever truck you wish!"

"And my car?" Giovanni Besta grew sad. "Should it be left here at the communists' mercy? They've never seen such a thing!"

"*Abfahrt!*" the Colonel commanded, and the officers scattered. "General we share a common goal—the sea!" Schlotterer could still feel the brandy in his temples. "The coast has to be protected:

THE WAR WAS BETTER

whoever keeps it will swim in the sea; whoever loses it will sing
Rossini with the communists." His feet ached inside the rags
wrapped around them; his knees were sagging, but he kept upright
on his stick and continued to distribute the trucks. "General, choose
the truck you want."

"Friends, gentlemen, giants!" Marika's Nanni wept. "To treat
me like this, without protection, without reward? If I'd given the
precious information to the English, or even to the communists,
they wouldn't have treated me this way!" His face grew crooked
and ugly. "I've been telling everyone for a decade that you're supermen. I don't want to go with the prisoners!"

"But it is your army, General!" Lieutenant Colonel Breitbach
said roughly, watching Romana approach the Colonel. "I've seen
several guitar players; you'll have fun."

Romana pressed herself to the Colonel's side: her lips, under a
rich lipstick, were ready to taste a rough German kiss. Joachim Tea
Breitbach felt a dog's jealousy.

"General, your soldiers are waving to you! Return their greeting. And go with them. It is not forbidden to sing your beautiful
war songs as we go down to the sea!"

"Romana!" Giovanni Besta wailed. "Beg him to spare us!" He
drew his neck between his shoulders like a helpless bird. "Or else
we'll suffocate riding with the soldiers; they stink, those shitasses!"
He watched as Romana rose on the tips of her toes to kiss the Colonel's chin. "So!" he urged her. "Go on. Go on. Break the Hercu-
lean, Teutonic, superhuman willpower!" He stretched out his arms,
compressed his lips, winked. "Let's get out of the way, let's get out
from under the soldiers' eyes. Let's go to the coast. We'll bathe
among the mines, all naked, and then we'll ride each other on the
sand. When they see your breasts ... show them your disobedient
breasts, and your deep navel, the most beautiful navel of all time. ...
They'll forget Montenegro, the English, and the Americans; they'll
even forget the Russians!"

His excitement rose to fever pitch; since Carl Schlotterer could
not get rid of Romana's mouth and slender arms, nobody dared to
stop him:

"Navel, love! The navel and the thing below, that mild transi-
tion, and then your beautiful petals full of fragrant moisture!" His
eyes watered; his nose streamed; his voice softened. "Yes, the thing
under the navel, our rose, our unique flower. The Teutonic giants,
wallowing in blood and glory, will see our greatest Latin treasure,
our Rome and catacombs!"

[61]

THE WAR WAS BETTER

The General almost sank to his knees. He uttered a faint wail and fell into the Lieutenant Colonel's arms.

"You'll have Rome ... history and geography, the very heart of Rome! We know you like antiquities and gold, which we also have. Take it, use it for military purposes, for teeth, for information!" He sobbed so that his knees and pants-legs shook. "You'll have Romana. It will be as if you had the whole of Italy."

He received no reply and could see no one through his tears and the dust.

"You can have me too, I too have a hole! I agree, I promise. ... Only let us reach the coast! ... Me too, even me!"

Disgusted, Lieutenant Colonel Breitbach shoved him away. Tearful and weak, General Besta lost his balance and fell in the dust. He looked up and pleaded with them in a mixture of German and Russian, English and French. Nauseated, Joachim Tea Breitbach spat into the thorn bushes, and then pointed at the trucks which were full of Italians:

"There, General! There, and posthaste! *Aufstehen!*" He could not restrain himself and began to kick him. "Get up, or I'll spit on you!"

"Spit, go ahead, spit, but free me, spare me!" The General sent up a grief-stricken lamentation from the dust, and almost choked on it. "Have you no heart?"

"It's clear that you have none!" Breitbach flared up again. "Nor have you ever had one!"

The General wiped his dusty face; he mentioned the precious information again, his jewelry, his gold.

"I'm ashamed I ever met you!" Lieutenant Colonel Breitbach's handsome lips were compressed into a scowl of anger. "Information? Bah!" He spat again. "Your information! It's idiotic, funny, stupid! It took you almost two hours to explain that the Russians and the rest of the communists were advancing from the east, and the English with the Americans and the other savages and Negroes from the west! At the same time you sprinkled yourself with cologne and meowed!"

Joachim Tea Breitbach stamped the ground with his boot:

"Get up! Stand up straight! Wipe the spit and snot from your overdecorated chest and join your soldiers! Look, they're calling for you to come; they don't know you're lying here crying like an old widow!"

"I don't want to go with those cowards and thieves!" Besta spluttered. He started to crawl off on all fours. "They'll rob me!

They'll defile me with dirt! And then the news will spread that I've been with them . . . in the same truck! . . ."

He looked up at the crowded trucks. Through his tears and the dust, he could see the dark heads of the soldiers, bent in resignation.

"How will I . . . I who have never mixed with such wretches, who have never been tainted by . . . this misery!" He seemed to himself to be growing more and more persuasive, and therefore became more and more voluble. "Do you understand me, you tigers from the north? I'm a general who wears the *Medaglia d'Oro*, the rarest and highest Italian decoration. What you see on my breast is nothing. I have other medals, five or six hundred others, both Italian and foreign. And in the name of all these crowns and crosses, I implore you. . . ."

"We'll also give you a cross; only stand up!"

"Which one?"

"Whichever you want, but get up! You must be standing when you receive it!"

"So far I've received all my medals lying down," the General said proudly. "Do I have to make such an effort for yours?"

"Our medals are paid for by blood, General. And before we bestow it on you, you must stand still."

"Which cross are you going to award me with?"

"The Iron Cross, Second Class."

"Impossible!" the General protested. "Beside my *Medaglia d'Oro*, I must have something better than iron." He racked his brains. "The German Cross in gold."

"Oh, no!" Breitbach hissed. "Oh, no! We'll give you anything but the German Cross. Oh, no!"

"Then at least the Knight's Cross with Oakleaf and Swords and Brilliants."

"First get up, you murderer!" Joachim Tea Breitbach was again beside himself. "Click your heels and stand at attention, like a man!" The General again mentioned gold and various medals, all of whose names he knew perfectly in German.

"Murderer! Murderer! Murderer!"

"And finally, I want special treatment!" the General said, his lips white and quivering. "I'm not an ordinary Italian. I am not at all like the rest of the people. I'm an aristocrat, Conte di Tirano!" It seemed he wanted to get up, but could not manage it. "Tirano is in the north, on the Italian-Swiss border, so that, most probably, I'm also Swiss!" He crept after them on his hands and knees. "Swiss, lost in the Balkans! Therefore, watch out, your fingers may get burned.

THE WAR WAS BETTER

My Switzerland can become a great military power! Any time!"

"If you don't get up ..." Breitbach released the safety catch of his pistol. "If you don't get up at once ..."

"It isn't easy for a Swiss count to get up," the General wept, staring at the barrel of the pistol. "Spare me, don't make me ride with them!"

Trucks passed alongside; the prisoners were leaning out and waving to all of them and singing.

"Spare us, even if you kill off all of them!" The wounded, who were waiting to be packed into the trucks, did not seem to believe their own eyes and ears; the General was lucky they had been disarmed.

"Italians are lazy bastards, robbers and criminals! Lice and communists cannot be cleaned out with such an immoral mafia!"

"I will count to ten!" Lieutenant Colonel Breitbach snapped; he could see Romana unbuttoning Carl Schlotterer's jacket and pants. "And then, ... murderer!"

"All of them, these Italians, are sex maniacs, prone to lechery and treason of all kinds," he rushed on. "I told that to Mussolini himself once, and what's more important, he agreed!"

Out of the left pocket of his jacket, from under the largest decoration, the General drew out Romana's panties, and began to wipe away his tears.

"These Italians, my dear Germanic friends, have to be killed off like dogs. Do you hear them singing? And what they sing!"

He sniffed the panties and began to snuffle. Lieutenant Colonel Breitbach could do nothing but count more slowly; anger boiled in his breast.

"Six ... seven!" Breitbach counted as he watched Schlotterer, his legs sagging, defend his buttons with the last remnants of his strength. "Once again, seven!" The girl gave no quarter. "Seven and a half ... murderer!"

"Go on, Romana!" The General saw Colonel Schlotterer on his back, and the girl on top of him. "Go on, love!" He closed his eyes and covered his face with his hands. "We're not far from victory. It seems they agree ... to shoot a hundred or so of the soldiers like dogs, and so wish us a good journey and success in life. Now, love, now. You're free to ride him, you've got your pants off!"

"Eight!" Breitbach screamed.

The General threw himself against his legs. Joachim Tea Breitbach could not bear it. The Conte di Tirano was embracing and kissing his boots.

[64]

"Nine!" he shouted and fell into a fit of coughing.

Giovanni Besta's head was between his knees; it seemed the General wanted to get up and carry him.

"Ten!" he howled and, lifting his pistol, shot high into the smoke.

The Conte di Tirano gave a sickly laugh and trembled all over like jelly.

"I'm counting again!" Breitbach shouted, and burst out crying in rage. "One . . . two . . . three!"

Colonel Schlotterer was moving painfully toward Lieutenant Colonel Breitbach and General Besta. He supported himself with his rifle and Romana, who was caressing his face and helmet. Barechested and completely unbuttoned, he felt his burns smarting as if they had been rubbed with salt.

"Why did you defend yourself when you knew in advance that you could not resist?" she asked him, noticing her General between Breitbach's legs. "The next time, Carlo, just lie down at once . . . and there'll be less sickness!" she murmured, pushing a long Greek cigarette into his mouth.

The Colonel took a puff and then asked her softly to button up his pants at least. Staring ahead and leaning only on his rifle now, he scowled fiercely.

"Nanni, you'll choke," Romana warned the General. "Joachim, for God's sake, look out! He's too sensitive and good. Let him alone, *caro* Joachim!"

"He's the one who's holding my legs; I'm not holding his!" Breitbach answered. His rage was calming.

"He's like a child, Tea," she said and smiled affectionately. "He's accustomed to forgiveness."

Romana stooped and her dress rose over her knees; Schlotterer's eyes strained and bulged; an even stronger desire rose in him. Her bare breasts also stuck out as she knelt; she knew very well who was staring at her and how long she would have to remain in this posture. With her handkerchief, she cleaned the wound on the General's forehead and kept repeating how the Germans were nobles and gentlemen indeed, that they, like the French, appreciated medals and women, and that they would soon be going all together toward the sea. The General thanked her and asked her how many wounded there had been on the plains of Verdun.

Lieutenant Colonel Breitbach held his pistol high above his head, but he counted no longer. He stared at Romana's hips and parted knees with a burning, overpowering desire. No longer was this the face of a small-town actor; his jaws tightened like those of an old wolf, hungry for flesh. Colonel Schlotterer stood beside him, calmed now and ashamed.

Giovanni Besta lay on his back in the dust. His medals were all mixed up; the ribbons of some had even torn. He gripped Romana's panties firmly, waving them like a flag. Nobody could tear them away from him. He babbled on about Mussolini. Cotton, gauze and various pills fell out of his pockets.

"Carluccio!" Romana said to Schlotterer as she looked down pitifully at the General's frail body. "My little Carlo, don't forget that he frequently faints." The officers poured water over him; only then did it become apparent how many brilliant medals he had. "In a war, Carluccio, one must always have water near at hand. He's not the only one who faints when the going gets rough."

While the officers continued pouring water over him, Romana buttonholed the Lieutenant Colonel. She climbed up his feet and tried to push her knees between his. She threw her arms around his waist and let her head fall on his chest. She said something he did not understand.

He felt her cling to him; he smelled her perfumes and woman's smells and the smell of drugs. The heat was unendurable; dust was thick in the air all the way down to the trucks. The shocked German soldiers were escorting the shrieking women prisoners, beating them as they went. It was a scene of terrible confusion. Breitbach lowered his hand on her head. He said something tender and reproachful, as one would scold a foolish child.

Antonio's hands had fallen in the grass; his head was thrown back on the stretcher. He was watching the soldiers bring forward new groups of girls and try to whip them into formation. They were scrawny, dark and sad, bow-legged and disheveled, mostly without uniforms; Peduto concluded they were either Macedonian Gypsies or Albanians.

"Now there are at least five hundred ... damn women," Antonio said to Cordes. "The latest ones are horribly ugly. Look, some of them are lame, even hunchbacked, one-eyed!"

"There are more, Major," Eckart Cordes informed him. "But what good would it be to Kurt and me if there were a thousand? They'll take the whole batch to Germany tonight, for 'moral and political re-education.' And Kurt and I, God knows, will end up wacking off."

From time to time Antonio sat up on his stretcher and sipped from Cordes' messtin. Trucks were passing them, carrying away songs, prisoners and bandages, and in the clouds of dust he could not see Carl Schlotterer, or Breitbach and Romana. He knew what they were doing, though, and was muttering to himself passionately:

"So, Romana. So, my damned angel. You alone can revenge us; do it for us all, for all of us, who've fallen once and for all. Be cruel to the victors, Romana. They have to be ridiculed, shamed, humiliated, defeated!"

"Into a truck with him!" the Colonel ordered, pointing at Besta. "The whores will sober him up!" Carl Schlotterer had not been so severe and rude for a long time. "A whore with whores!" He sized up the General's calm, dirty, little body with total disdain. "Into a truck with this fraud!"

A large Mercedes with a trailer stopped near Schlotterer, and soldiers got out and lifted the General from the dust. Besta wriggled in the air, swam and puckered up his lips as if he were spitting out water. Of one accord, like an ocean wave, the soldiers threw him into the air. He landed on a cushion of Balkan girls.

Lieutenant Colonel Joachim Tea Breitbach pulled Romana up to a truck. She dragged behind him, waving and protruding her round, hard backside toward Schlotterer and the rest of the soldiers and prisoners. The Lieutenant Colonel climbed the running board of the truck and extended his hand to her. In order to step up, she lifted her tight dress up to the middle of her thighs. Then the door of the cab slammed behind her.

The sullen and exhausted Colonel ordered the next truck of girls to stop near Major Peduto. The Captain and the Lieutenant with the bandaged head obeyed. Carl Schlotterer approached Antonio and smiled to him benignly, almost with melancholy.

"See you soon, Major," he said, taking leave. "At the coast. Or, most probably in hell!"

"In paradise," Antonio Peduto answered even more affably and waved to him.

Kurt and Eckart Cordes lifted Antonio's stretcher. Women's hands carefully caught hold of him. He asked one of the girls to place his knapsack under his head, and to put his turtle back into his arms. For a moment he looked up at the blue-eyed girl who smiled to him. He felt she was dear to him, that he loved her with all the strength in his heart and all the power in his mind. He would have liked most of all to stroke her hair, which was white, like wild oats. Suddenly he had a wish once again to say good-by to Colonel Schlotterer, whom he could see limping along on the crossroads.

The truck started off.

THE WAR WAS BETTER

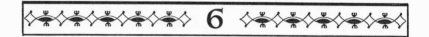 **6**

"I'm already in paradise," Antonio whispered, thinking of Carl Schlotterer. "I'm finally in paradise, where my place has been for so long, since the beginning."

He sensed the soft presence of feminine flesh near him, and a dark warm thrill rippled through him like a wave.

"Sit down near me and let me rest my head on your lap, and tell you that I'd give my life for you," he said to the white-haired girl. She listened but understood nothing. "I know I'm not worthy of you, but sit near me and speak."

They made their way through dust and wind. It smelled of gasoline and burning rubber. Antonio's eyes smarted.

"I am crying from the smoke," he said.

"It's all the same where they come from—tears are tears," she said and found room beside him.

"You're so white and tender and beautiful.... You must be from the far North, don't deny it; you must be, let's say, from Iceland, where they kneel to the sun as before a flower."

"I'm Montenegrin," the girl said and suddenly blushed. "And who'd say that you'd be a *Taliano?* You're red, like a Russian."

"I am a Russian, *Montenegrina*," Antonio muttered. "One of Feodor Mikhailovich Dostoyevsky's grandsons."

"Fjodor Mihajlovič?" the girl seemed to rack her brains, thinking it might be some *Taliano*. "Perhaps he's a General, this Fjodor Mihajlovič of yours."

"Fjodorini is the general of all the generals, *Montenegrina*."

"Strange he hasn't come to Montenegro then," the girl mused. "Only such men come to us."

"He has," Antonio said with great tenderness. "He has. He's come for visits, this Fjodorini, to see his grandsons, Malić and me."

"Could it have been the same day Napolitano died?" She reddened and her voice trembled. "Augusto Napolitano, the soldier and guitarist."

"No, it was the day Giovanni Besta came. Did you know Augusto too?"

Something was burning Antonio's eyes again. He wanted to tell her that they were not his, but Feodor Dostoyevsky's tears.

[68]

"I loved Augusto. I didn't dare approach him, though. The whole place knew how crazy he was about his Bolognese girl. He sang about her all the time. Since she wasn't there, I wept sometimes for her—and sometimes for Augusto."

"Augusto wasn't handsome—he was rather ugly and sloppy. You're the only woman who loved him."

"I still love him even now," the girl said and hung her head.

"And what will you do with us, the living?"

"Perhaps I'll meet him some time," the girl thought aloud, with her hair like wild oats. "My guitar player with metal teeth, always ready for some *porcheria*. Him and her, from Bologna."

Antonio's heart shriveled up again. He felt like screaming. But, with his head thrown back, helpless, he only murmured: "Looking at you, *Montenegrina*, I'd never have known that you're Feodor's granddaughter." He pointed his finger at her. "You too, you too, you too!"

"I don't believe it," the girl said. "I've never even seen him, this general of all the generals, this Fjodorini Mihajlovič."

Antonio Peduto sat up slowly. The white-haired girl was beside him, with the turtle in her arms. His head swam. He missed Colonel Schlotterer. He wanted to tell him again that he was in paradise, in the real one, full of serpents.

Coals and ashes tumbled over the crooked, bumpy road, and the truck jolted and creaked. Clusters of fire were breaking off from the overhanging rocks and falling. The girls tried to pull the tarpaulin over the trailer, but could not manage it—there were too many pulling in too many different directions. They looked up into the sky, and then hid behind each other. Antonio Peduto was the only one who did not fear the blows from above; his eyes were half open, his beard full of ashes, his voice troubled and soft:

"Did you know Malić? Gruban Malić, also Feodor's grandson?"

"Everybody knew him," the girl answered. "I believe he's a grandson of this General of yours, I've forgotten his name again. When it's Malić who's involved, anything's possible, even probable." She smiled. The other girls envied her talk with Antonio. "Malić, our Gruban, had nobody. A circus company abandoned him or forgot him near the town well, when he was a six-month-old baby. They never came to see him or take him back, so he's remained with us. They say he's made us famous, but I don't know how."

"Tell me whatever you know about him."

Antonio's heart seemed to overflow, beating more and more quickly; his eyes began to smart again.

[69]

"I'll listen to you until they interrupt us," he said. "Skip nothing. Tell me everything, little by little, every detail. Come on, *Montenegrina*."

"Malić," the girl began, as if talking to herself. "A real child, a real grandson." Her eyes started to glitter. "He told everybody he was a Russian, on special assignment with the 501st Montenegrin Army. Ha! Ha! Some believed him. Others said that Montenegro was too small to have so many armies. And he replied that there were even more, one or two more, but this had to be kept top secret. 'The war is going to be won by the side we decide to join,' he said to the local people. 'We will tip the scales!' He kept sending messages to the Italian command."

"And then, *Montenegrina?*"

"What then, *Taliano?* Ah yes, Malić, our Russian!" She burst out laughing, showing her tiny teeth like a child.

"He challenged Colonel Spartaco Allegretti to a duel. Our *colonello* didn't dare come out to the meeting place. It was near the bridge, where the previous commander had constructed public toilets and washrooms, as a present for the Montenegrin people. Malić, armed to the teeth, waited for him several days and nights. The Colonel, out of fear it seems, kept sending him flowers and yellow roses and some kind of love letters, full of admiration for Montenegro and the Slavs in general. Our child, our Malić, spat on Allegretti's flowers. As for the roses, in plain sight of the soldiers and local inhabitants, who were afraid of retaliation and a punitive expedition, he threw them in the dirt and pissed on them. He called the people who were watching what he was doing spies and traitors of communism and enslaved Europe; us women, he called fascist whores... which isn't completely true."

"What did our Malić do then?"

"Everyone started saying that, right there in those washrooms, where the stench of the local people and the smell of the Colonel's flowers were getting so bad that people were choking there and vomiting; right there, Malić decided to liquidate not only all the divisions of the Italian Occupation Army, but also the entire Italian nation. The news spread quickly. Many were saying that Malić was the only savior. They also said that some of the older Montenegrins, our most famous heroes, were polishing up their medals to pin them on the breast of the new leader of revolutionary Montenegro, and other unlucky countries. This, however, did not come to pass.

"All of a sudden General Besta appeared and ordered that all weapons and anything that could kill an Italian should be requisitioned and taken away from the people, together with all flags and decorations, even Red Cross badges. But Gruban Malić's fame had spread, not only as General Fjodorini's grandson, but also as an honorable son of the enslaved Balkan countries . . . ha-ha-ha. . . ." The girl was choking on her long, affection-filled sentences. "I'm tired, *Taliano;* otherwise I'd tell you about Malić until tomorrow morning. Ah, that Russian from a circus, now no one even remembers him."

"We're all from circuses, czarina," Antonio said to the girl, who was trying at the same time to communicate with the Greek girls with winks and grimaces. "And that's what's so beautiful and horrible. We're all from a circus: you and I—all of us jolting along in this trailer right now!"

He looked up at the soldier who was guarding them with a submachine gun strapped across his chest.

"And the Germans too, maybe most of all. The Germans are the most circus-like nation. Sooner or later our Malić must be directed against them! He'll break their backbones like nobody else! He'll pour their teeth back down their throats! Yes, he! Gruban Malić!"

"There are also rumors that he was a murderer," the girl said. "I could see my Augusto loved and appreciated him. But the rest were scared of him. Especially the officers; they trembled, I'll tell you. Father Vukic, our priest, fainted when he met him. The local spy, Signor Mustafa Agic, hid his face behind one hand, and put the other on his pistol, when he saw him! Isn't it true that he's a murderer, this Malić!"

"Like every liberator, he is also a murderer," Antonio said, happy that for once he did not have to talk to himself or the turtle about Malić. "Murderer, all right, girl! But a murderer of enemies and spies. There you have it! He was killing us!"

"Why you?" the girl asked, her beautiful eyes bulging. "To kill an Italian is like killing a fatherless and motherless child." Her breath was coming short. "Why didn't he swoop down on the English, and the rest of them? It's easy with the Italians, the poor things. A criminal!"

"He was killing us!" Antonio thundered. "Us, the war orphans and rats. Listen, you know as well as I do: the Venezia and Murge Divisions were massacred; the Taro disappeared so completely it seemed never even to have existed. The Montenegrin crows are picking apart all that dirty and stinking Italian flesh! The Messina Division and its commandant fled first, trying to reach the coast. The Pusteria Division met the same fate as the Venezia, and the

THE WAR WAS BETTER

Cacciatori delle Alpi were so badly decimated, almost half dead, that they begged him to accept them as soldiers under his own flag. It's a massacre! A ruthless slaughter!"

"The poor Venezia Division!" the girl said pitifully. "Almost all of them had guitars. They ate frogs and oats. They greased their hair with brillantine—or more often with butter from the peasants." The girl was excited; her eyes were wet. "The poor Murge Division too! They were with us after the Venezia Division left. They were sad like us. They stole like us too, even more. They adored children. Perhaps that was the reason, because they loved them so much, that they made them wherever they went. They were also in Greece, our merrymakers, the Cacciatori delle Alpi, and told us many things about their girls down there. The girls seemed to like them a lot. ... Oh, you poor Italians, all the things that are happening to you! ...."

"Poor Italians!" About ten girls burst out crying at the same time. "Our poor Italians!"

"Poor Italians!" Antonio Peduto joined them, almost choking from some strange nausea. "The poor rascals, savages and lovers!" The girls joined in without understanding him completely. "The poor Italians, discoverers of America and Germany, liberators of Montenegro and other countries! Poor cowards and cat-eaters and dreamers! And the poor, poor map of our Roman Empire, torn up, ripped to pieces by the hands, teeth and nails of the Montenegrin Marshal, the greatest strategist of all time, Gruban Malić!"

"Since he's such a man, Malić might be from our country," one of the girls said through her tears, in vernacular. "In Greek, Malić means 'much.' Poor Greeks!"

"I know him personally," Antonio informed the Greek girl and the white-haired one. "There's nobody in the world I know better than Malić, and maybe all my luck comes from that." He eyed the girls, who did not seem to believe him. "It isn't important where he comes from," he said, smiling to the Greek girl. "But he might have come from your country." He spoke calmly, although his head still hung down as if in sadness. "I remember when he began to challenge Colonel Allegretti and the entire Venezia Division. Whenever he went away, there was usually a sign on the door of his small, revolutionary brothel: 'I AM EVERYWHERE.' Nobody but me believed him. The General didn't even want to have him killed."

The girls were silent. Ashes mixed with their tears and soiled their faces so that they looked even more emaciated.

'MALIĆ IS EVERYWHERE even now! He is coming from

the north and the south, from the east and the west!" Antonio's throat rattled in a feeble cough. "He's omnipotent! (that is because he's a grandson of Feodor Mikhailovich!) He's invincible and indestructible! He's the angel who will burn up all the filth that exists on the earth and in the hearts of men!"

Antonio sobbed, and fell down exhausted on the floor of the trailer. Even so, he went on talking.

"Excuse me, we two, Malić and I, have been one and the same for a long time now. I have one half of his name, and he has one half of mine."

The girls lifted him up so that he could see them and stroked his long red hair.

"We two will astonish the world, just as we're stamping it down now, eating it away, pulling it apart . . . we two!"

A wind was blowing. Resting on the knees of the white-haired girl with his head thrown back, Antonio Peduto asked for brandy and sympathy and sleep. From time to time he came to and tried to persuade them that he, Antonio-Gruban Peduto-Malić, was no longer a *Taliano*, or didn't want to be one any more.

They began singing, and the trailer went banging and clattering along its way through smoke and songs. Above the women's heads, Antonio could see the rocky bluffs and the old lonely pines burning like torches in the thickening dusk.

"Good-by, Montenegro, country cast down from the moon. Good-by, my only homeland, my sorrow and my mother."

His eyes were large, and the women's hands and hair were swimming in them as in a living pool.

Second Part

1

ANTONIO PEDUTO lay quietly on the old fishing nets and ammunition boxes which, by some miracle, had not yet been washed overboard. Calm, with his head thrown back, he looked up at the sky: there was no Montenegro, no songs, no ashes; but his eyes were still full of fire and rocks falling and streaming everywhere like blood. A blanket of clouds was descending. There was no sun to dry his wounds and burns, no rain to moisten and soothe them.

"Anna-Maria," he said to the turtle resting near his head. "It's too bad Peppe isn't here to tell us how to heal wounds and other troubles."

He held the ship railing tightly with one hand, so as not to fall overboard from the heap of nets.

"Well, wounds will heal one day, and if not, they'll be forgotten, because new ones will come. But our Peppino isn't here to teach us how to live, how to write letters."

Antonio's voice was soft and dreamy, and many could hear him:

"This is the third day now that you've not been with us, my wonderful Bonaccia. I looked for you on the coast. I called and cried for you. And for Montenegro too, while they packed us into the ships. Where are you now, my unforgettable boy, to tell me about your village near Naples, where all evil and all accidents are soon forgotten?"

His eyes kept closing. He heard only the faint beating of his own heart.

A fitful dream wove itself into his eyelashes. The soldier Giuseppe Bonaccia was towing a large fishing boat, which had been hastily transformed into a warship. He called from afar, from the foam which seemed to fog up all space, called and begged that they should at least turn left if they could not stop, and take him on. With one hand, he towed a steel cable; with the other, he held a huge stone on his chest. Even in Antonio's dream, the sky was low and smelled of fish, and clouds hung on the mast. The soldier's mouth filled with white water; he asked them to calm the ship down, for the fire had remained far off, on the shore, and rain would soon fall. The stone on his chest was not heavy enough; his

[77]

boat carried all the noise and masts away. The soldier was swallowing foam.

At the very edge of the deck, Antonio listened restfully to the sea and the gulls. Whenever the boat rolled with a wave, water rose and splashed the torn nets that entangled his feet. He did not wail like the others, nor did he curse the wind; instead he wished the rags binding his feet and ankles would soak up as much pain and cold and salt as possible.

Half-awake, he felt small and insignificant beside the water, which stretched on and on and reminded him more and more of molten rubber. In his thoughts he could see his own body, his distorted arms and salt-soaked feet clothed in scorched tatters. He called his own name. But he did not open his eyes, nor fear anything. As the boat pitched and rolled, he remained twisted in the nets with his mouth wide open; it seemed the whole black sea could have entered it.

Although his eyes were closed, he saw them all. About one hundred of the German wounded were lying in the center of the deck, on benches and spread-out tents: smelling of wounds and iodine, bandaged and still, they seemed even more numerous. They were moaning, cursing Montenegro and its fire, damning the water and the Italians. Nurses moved among them, offering them drugs, calming them down like children, assuring them the traitorous Italians would soon meet their perfidious Latin god and get worse treatment than even the communists or the English. Antonio listened to them for a long time; he wanted to see the soldier Cordes.

The Italian wounded were packed beside the railing, on the edge of the deck. Other prisoners had to prop them up so that they would not fall into the water. There were no drugs for them, no words of consolation; they wailed without answer and called the names of their absent loved ones. Antonio knew the girls were the largest group of prisoners on board; several Mercedes trailers filled with them had been emptied into the boat and then returned with new loads. But as they mixed with the others, it was hard to distinguish them. They were bending over the wounded and offering them drinks from their canteens.

"I'd be happy if I could spend the rest of my life stretched out like this," Antonio said to himself, "with my eyes closed."

Feeling a sharp pain in his bones, he begged his heart to calm down and fall asleep again; but a pale, handsome guard seemed to be prodding his mind to awake again and again. A submachine gun hung from his neck, and several grenades with handles were stuck in his belt. Aiming the barrel of his gun into the clouds in the general direction of the land which they had left far behind, the guard hovered around Antonio, trying to engage him in conversation.

"I'm not a German," he confessed.

"What are you then . . . armed like that?"

"Austrian," he confided in a whisper. "Viennese."

"I wouldn't be proud of it," Antonio risked, expecting a fist in his face.

"That's not the first time I've heard that, *Taliano*," the Viennese said very quickly, instead of punching him.

Then they were silent until the German nurses had moved on.

"Rome is my true home," the soldier continued. "I spent several years there, studying your magnificent language and literature."

"Have you retained anything from your studies?"

"I got my Ph.D on D'Annunzio; of all the Italian writers, he is the closest to us today," the Viennese said, smiling and adjusting his spectacles.

"I don't know who he is . . . this D'Annunzio of yours," Antonio lied, and the soldier blushed for both of them.

"D'Annunzio expressed the spirit of your people," the Austrian continued, surprised that Antonio was frowning. "I know Benito Mussolini by heart. His language is exceptionally rich, almost baroque, as it were. The *Duce* knew exactly how to treat the Italian people, and us too, the foreigners."

"I don't know who D'Annunzio is, let alone Mussolini," Antonio said; he had a sudden urge to spit on him. "But they sound like bandits to me, both of them."

"Perhaps you're a communist?" the Austrian whispered into his ear, which was indeed red, and then added: "I was one myself, for a short time in Rome, before I found my true path."

Antonio said nothing; he was looking at the soldier's grenades and submachine gun.

"Good for you, you're not English," the Viennese said more loudly. "I would never have forgiven you for being English."

"I forgive you for everything, even for being an Austrian and a Viennese, and above all . . . because you were in Rome once and found your true path so swiftly," Antonio said. "To see one's path and follow it, whatever it is and wherever it leads, is a great thing. I don't see my own; I've never seen it. But that's not the only thing that divides us. To be frank, I despise people who find their own path so easily."

The Austrian rose from the ammunition box. "I thought you

were an intellectual," he said. "That is why I began the conversation. The sea always makes me think of D'Annunzio."

"Then you don't understand the sea," Antonio said ironically. "You began the conversation well; it would also be good to bring it to an end. No, I'm not an intellectual. I'm a midwife. I help dead babies come into the world. And this is the second time I must forgive you for everything."

"I thought you were . . . at least an Italian!"

"No, I'm only a prisoner. You can kick me overboard anytime you want to punish me for being impolite. I'm a miserable, unfortunate Italian prisoner who despises and revolts against those who taught you my language. By the way, you've learned it fantastically well."

The Austrian did not wait to hear Antonio's opinion of Mussolini and those who blindly believed in him. He went away, discouraged, and sighted at the clouds again along the long barrel of his submachine gun.

Antonio Peduto lifted his head slowly. He wanted to see whether there were any changes since the last time he had looked, whether the ship was still rolling and pitching and the passengers still vomiting. He noticed his beard and pants legs were drenched in salt. The ship was rolling. The waves tore upward from the sea, raging with foam, and seemed to reach out to clutch at the wounded. The Germans had given them no cover, but used their tarpaulins to protect, instead, the cannons and machine guns whose barrels pointed out at the turbid Adriatic from every side of the ship, like fans. Antonio's legs were numb; his back was turned to the water. He let his head fall back again. Just then Spartaco Allegretti surprised him:

"Antonio, wake up!" He put his hand on Antonio's shoulder. "Don't you see what we're in for?"

"Colonel and lover, why are you troubling me, interrupting my daydream?" Peduto asked softly. "Aren't you better off on the other side of the deck, on the benches?" Then he remembered that he and the General were at least lying down while many of the wounded had to stand. "Why don't you rest there, with your people?"

"We worry about you, Antonio. We don't want you to fall overboard."

"Who doesn't want me to, Colonel and lover?"

"I'm no longer a colonel, Antonio," Allegretti reminded him with his teeth chattering. "Here, let Turiddu tell you, let him confirm it."

"It's true. He's no longer a colonel," Barbagallo said, cocking the round Montenegrin cap on his head. "That's the truth."

"How do you know, Turiddu?" Antonio asked. "Has he demonstrated it on you?"

"He's demonstrated everything on me," Barbagallo said, holding the Colonel's suspenders on his arm. "They've all demonstrated everything on me, and, to tell the truth, so have I on them."

"And thank goodness I'm no longer what I was," Allegretti said. "Finally I'm only Spartaco. It's always been my dream. Look at us, Antonio, we won't let the waves sweep you off!" Antonio Peduto stared straight ahead.

"Don't be like that, redhead. Now we're all in the same boat; there's no use quarreling."

Antonio tried to prop himself on his elbows. But he could only lift his head; he saw the crooked Allegretti and, standing behind him, covered with foam and practically blue from the cold and his wounds, General Giovanni Besta. The General's eyes were large and forlorn, and his hands were crossed on his stomach. Almost all his medals were there; even the precious old camera hung on his neck. Romana stood beside him. She had German officers' boots on her feet and something that recalled a pirate's hat on her head. A tar-smeared cape riddled by bullet holes protected her from the wind and water. She looked at him warmly; he returned her glance with a bitter smile.

"The family has gathered again," Antonio said. "All the children are at the table, and they've eaten more than yesterday, and much more than the day before, in Montenegro. That's why we're all happy and content, especially our exhausted mother."

"You're incurable," she said. "My wonderful Antonio, always poking fun."

"I love you, Romana!" Antonio declared frankly; a tearful warmth surged up from his stomach and rose into his throat. "I'm happy to have loved you frankly and deeply ever since the day I met you."

"First of all, we'll take photographs," General Besta suggested. "Now that the children have eaten their plates and drunk sea water." Nobody listened to him. "First, I'll take your picture, and then you take mine."

"This is no time for love talk, Antonio," Allegretti put in fearfully.

"I don't know anything about hate, Spartaco," Antonio remarked, bunching together a fishing net to protect the turtle from the waves. "I want to tell her that I love her, and carry her in my memory; it makes me richer by one life." Allegretti and General Besta frowned.

"Romana, admit that you're my sister, admit that you'll always think of me as I cannot help but think of you."

"I adore you, Antonio," Romana answered and sat down on the nets beside him. "You're a real man, and I want everyone to remember it. Men like you are rare!" Her eyes were full of sea foam. "I'm your mother and you're my son." She stroked his hair, then his face. "My only son ... on board."

"Then promise me, mother, promise that you'll help me," he whispered, kissing her hands and placing them on his chest, inside his shirt, in order to warm them. "I've been trying for years to find my sister, lost in Via dei Serpenti. I can't forget her."

His red beard was on her knees.

"Promise, if you're my mother, that you'll help me. Tell me you will, if we ever get to that damned street, not far from the Vatican."

"I'll find her."

"How, Romana? How?"

"I'll ask everyone: 'Which one of you girls has a red-headed brother, Antonio, who went away to Abyssinia and Greece out of despair, and then to Montenegro, and who, by the way, has become a great hero?' I'll go from brothel to brothel; I'll dig out all of Rome if I have to, but I'll find her."

"And what if we don't live to see land again?" Allegretti interrupted softly, defending her from a wave with his hands, as if he were beating away a bird.

"Ever since I've known you, you've looked on the dark side of things, Spartaco," Romana scolded him. "If we don't get there alive, all the better for us—we'll get to hell faster, and continue our divine, earthly profession there!"

"That is the best way to inquire," Antonio agreed. "To go from street to street and stop passers-by. Not to let a single one pass until someone tells you where she is."

"How will people be able to recognize her?" Romana asked tenderly, caressing him again. "What does she look like?"

"I can't remember when I saw her last. I've had so many debauches and drunk so much since then, and passed through so many countries; so many faces have vanished from my memory. Her face has also gone. When I dream of her, I don't see her eyes; she is always turning away. My poor sister! She has long hair, like the other girls from the suburbs of Rome. The skin around her knees is covered with freckles and moles. Further up, right next to her flower-blossom, she has a scar—once I threw a knife at her, from a distance, but did not hit her heart. Sometimes I think she's like you."

"What . . . ?" Allegretti whispered, shaking with fear and cold.

Antonio was kneeling in front of Romana. He lifted his head slowly and looked at all of them, but did not see them.

"I don't know," he said, swallowing salt water. "I know nothing, except that I've loved her, and that I always wanted to plunge my knife into her heart."

"What a horror!" Allegretti whispered passionately.

"Silence, Spartaco," Romana chided him. "You don't know yet what real love is."

"And could you go with me, ugly and burnt as I am, could you lead me from street to street?"

"I could," she said. "They'll ask me who you are. 'Italians, proud Romans, and the rest of you curs,' I'll tell them, 'this is how the victors look!' " she said. " 'Now imagine, you sons-of-bitches, how it looks to be defeated!' I would do anything for you, Antonio, even that!"

"You'll exhibit me to everyone, for as long as they like. They have to be shown whatever they desire. Romans are exceptionally curious, and you can just imagine what they'll ask to see. They'll all be swarming around us, adoring the victors and licking up to everything shameful. Perhaps my sister herself will come down a staircase and notice me. She'll take pity on me and lead me up to her room."

Water was lashing at them. A powerful wave struck the General and Spartaco, and they could hardly hold onto the deck at Romana's feet. Meanwhile she protected Antonio with the edge of her cape. Even the mast with the rolled-up sails was shaking.

Then Colonel Schlotterer emerged from the water, bent over and wrapped in a canvas tent. Although he was standing near them, he could see nothing; his spectacles were fogged over. Gripping the foam-splattered railing, with his weak, tired feet wrapped in rags and tatters, he was looking everywhere for Antonio.

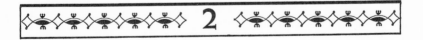

2

My dear Peduto, here's your luckless Peppe again. I'm aboard the ship like you, only on the other side. The Germans make no distinction between me and the wounded and other prisoners; they don't have the slightest idea I'm a deserter. If our military laws are severe with deserters, just imagine what theirs must be! They'd cut off my head in front of all these girls!

I'm squatting at the railing and trembling, not so much from the water splashing on my back as from the Germans, who are watching to make sure that none of us disappear. The ship is rolling and pitching, and they're the only ones who don't throw up, so I think there must be something wrong with them. Whenever the waves come sweeping over us, I look up to see where you are. I see you're in fitting company. I'd have approached you long ago if it hadn't been for General Besta and Colonel Allegretti with Turiddu Barbagallo, who beat me several times in the past and once spat on me. I'd really like to get a close view of the queen of the Italian women, Romana, this flag and pride of ours. The fact is I'm afraid of her, but I'll pitch her on her back and jump on her in a song or a letter one day. I'm even more afraid of the German colonel who's holding himself up on the railing next to you. I can't remember his name. Beware of those who wear eyeglasses; they bring evil.

As you see, I'm writing to you; it is like talking to you. Don't be angry at me, at the mean, sick animal, the mangy dog following you. I still have many things to tell you. And once I tell you everything there is to tell, everything that lies in my heart, then probably I'll desert, forever.

But no, what am I talking about? We two will never part; we'll never be able to. It became clear to me when I fled from the Germans and the fire. I felt then that I wasn't alone on this earth, that two hearts beat for me, yours and Augusto's.

The Boches were quite near me, once or twice right on my heels, and they were shouting, even in Serbian: "Surrender, communist bastard!"

"I surrender, my hands are up," I said. "Come and kill me! That's the only favor I ask of the Germans!"

I was saying the same words you had said, convinced they'd nail me to the earth that very moment. But they couldn't get near me because of the stench, and it wasn't easy to hit me where I was, behind my rock.

"Pride and discipline forbid a German soldier from shooting at a heap of Italian shit!" I think they shouted back.

Then I became proud of our Italian stench; I began to creep toward them.

THE WAR WAS BETTER

"*Ach, der Balkan ... ach, die Scheisse!*" What they meant was quite clear, because some of them wailed, threw down their weapons and stopped up their noses.

I was sorry for the Balkans, and decided to gamble with my life. I rushed at them, howling that there wasn't a gas mask in the Balkans that could save their lives. They fled, wept, offered unconditional surrender. You would have thought I was the German, and they the Italians. Then, I think, they were replaced. Anyway there were more of them, and they were singing a different tune. They fired. But I also shot from behind my rock. If I do say so myself, I didn't make it easy for them.

My stomach ached. I didn't care for life anymore. I raided their trenches and stormed their barrels, backwards. I was a German again, and they were the cowards. So we chased each other the whole day. They hunted me until noon; I hunted them until sunset. I don't want to be a Boche anymore, not for any price. I know how to threaten them now. It's no use shooting; they aren't afraid of guns. They have to be attacked with shit. It frightens and nauseates them unbearably, in some strange way; they just can't stand it.

Then we seemed to come to a truce. They withdrew or forgot me. I remained alone, in the forest. I remembered you and everything you had talked to me about. Although there was nobody with me, I laughed out loud, and called your name. In a foreign country, loneliness is worse than thirst. I began to talk to myself, the blackest thing to do. "One cannot do without other men," I was saying, "even if they're the Germans or the English." I started going down toward the road and the trucks.

Then I saw them again, escorting you with the whores.

"I want to get on the trailer too!" I shouted from the dust. "Take me.... I can't get on by myself!"

I think they understood me and wanted to stop. But then I stopped for a moment to wave, and you were all gone.

I didn't wave. I stank horribly. The stench was too awful even for me. "Today you're going to die, Peppe," I said to myself. I was resigned to my fate. But I didn't want to die alone, hiding like a rat, and I crawled after them. And they, the Germans, were crawling just like me; many times I felt sorry for them. They looked at me without supposing that I was the same one who had tired them out and finally broken them, up there in the forest. They were crawling along, dragging their dead behind them. It was pitiful.

For the first time I felt there was not much difference between us. Our wounds were alike; they burned and smarted whenever we touched them. We were all thirsty and lost. I greeted the wounded as if they were ours.

"*Gut . . . Scheisse!*" I shouted, and they understood that those were the words I remembered from two days before.

They seemed to be flattered by my knowledge of their language, and returned the greeting with, "*Ach, Taliano, Taliano!*" It made me happy. They threw bones, skins, and empty cans to me.

I wasn't the only one coming up behind them. Old men and children were more numerous: "*Soldaten*, do you have any bread?" The wounded had nothing but bandages to fling to them.

"*Pane*," children muttered.

"No bread," I answered them on behalf of the Germans. "No bread. Nothing at all that we could eat."

In the neighboring village there was even more smoke. The almost roasted cripples, all wrapped up in rags, stared out at us in despair by the ruins of their burned-out houses. They needed food no longer.

"*Scheisse gut!*" I shouted as I held out my hand to the wounded. "Wait for me!"

I don't know why they laughed so much; I understood what they were saying: "*Komm, komm her, Taliano. . . . Komm, Scheisse . . . gut, aber schnell!*"

I knew they wanted me to hurry up. They were waiting for me with bandages and bones. "*Momento!*" I said (I don't know myself what language I was speaking) and I stepped into the river. I caught hold of some roots and stones and let the swift current wash and cool me.

"So, Peppe, wash yourself clean," I said to myself; my body was so tense I felt like letting go and riding the current.

I thought the blood would freeze in my veins, and I spoke to the foam in order to warm up: "So, Peppe, so," I said. "Let the water carry all your shit and stench away, and then get out and go to the people, up there, and tell them you're clean, that they won't need their gas masks anymore, at least for a while."

My teeth were chattering from the cold and from fear that some shark or whale or some similar fish would bite off the bunny between my legs. How nice it would have been if you too had been in the water, with your wounds!

"My Antonio isn't here," I said to myself as I got out of the river, "but he's alive. He won't want to die either until he has a good bath and washes himself clean."

THE WAR WAS BETTER

The wounded who had wanted to accept me were no longer there. I wept in the middle of the road, with the water dripping off me into the dust. Some others came across me.

"Take me!" I cried. "I don't stink anymore! I've been in the river!"

They laughed, perhaps because I was wet and kept slipping and falling.

"I'll wash in the future too, *Soldaten*. Let me creep behind you, if you don't want to take me with you!"

"Who are you, you shit . . . ?" shouted one of the soldiers who were pulling the wounded along on beech branches and stretchers. "Who and what are you?"

I didn't know what to answer. They would never have believed anything true. "Fend for yourself, Peppe," I told myself. Then I looked boldly into his eyes.

"I'm a general," I said. "The one you've been tracking down for eight or ten days now."

They laughed again under their bandages and threw roots and bones at me. Then one of them said: "You can join us, since you're . . . the General we've been tracking down for eight or ten days now."

I approached them. I wanted to caress their wounds and kiss their burns and bruises out of gratitude.

"You're some general," their officer burst out laughing. "And where's your Fiat roadster, *Conte?*"

"The communists stole it. They never saw anything like it. Panties and girdles, silk stockings, skis, a butterfly net. They drank up the perfume. Such savages are capable of . . ."

"And all your medals; where are they, General?"

"Water washed them away just a moment ago, with all the shit and stench."

"Oh, what a man!" a German said in our own language, and then repeated it in German, and laughter poured from them all. "Oh, what a general, this *Conte di Tirano* . . . this *Taliano!*"

I held out my hands for them to fetter them. It wasn't child's play, I thought, to catch a shit-covered general.

"Afterwards, *Conte*," they said, and threw me on a beech branch. "Afterwards, Duke."

We trudged together toward the shore. I made them laugh and sang our war songs. They tried to accompany me. But Germans can't accompany an Italian! They bawl even when they sing about the sun or the moon, let's say, or flowers or girls; the veins on their necks and temples throb with effort. I told them the story of Augusto and you, and said the Neapolitan's heart was perhaps among them, or even in them. They laughed. Then I shut my mouth, and said only that sentence of yours, asking them to kill me.

They didn't want to. They didn't even shackle me. They threw me on board like a sack of potatoes. I could have run away, but I didn't want to; I saw that you were on the boat.

"Peppe," I said to myself, "now follow him, be his shadow. He needs you more than ever!"

I followed you and watched you stare wistfully out at the land, at Montenegro, which we were leaving forever. You said something to it, whispered to it as to Anna-Maria, waved to it.

"Peppe, you too should say good-by to this miserable and insulted country," I scolded myself for I don't know how long. "Beg it to pardon you for all the insults and humiliations. Whisper to it to guard tenderly the bones of all the soldiers, all the innocent boys who have fallen needlessly on its slopes and valleys."

I waved to Montenegro as if I were a real soldier, made gestures like yours, and burst out crying in earnest.

"Nevermore!" I sent out a message to Montenegro from the depths of my Neapolitan heart. "Never again! Nevermore Malić's flaming homeland!"

In order not to be saying good-by to Montenegro too long, I mingled with the prisoners. I made my way among the girls, and asked for the addresses of those I liked. All of them were kind and tender with me. They thought I was a *Siciliano*, or at least a *Sardo*. When I told them proudly I was a *Napolitano*, many of them smiled: "Like our Augusto Napolitano." There were some tears, but not too many, since the waves breaking on deck kept interrupting our conversations. Even now I'm still with them, with the girls. My head is full of letters, names, and addresses.

After we had embarked, a blond girl began to look at me strangely. Later you'll see what the matter was. There was almost some trouble for Peppino.

I pretended I didn't notice her peering at me, although I could hardly wait to meet her and lure her address from her. She was swifter. It seems women are different in war. When night fell she approached me and told me she was Greek. Just then a wave struck my chest and stomach, and I didn't have time to tell her who or what I was, or what I was ready for. The same wave struck her too, but it broke over her round behind, which she stuck out just for that purpose. Then she continued:

"Peppino, don't forget me. I'm well-known in Athens, and it's enough just to write: 'To the most beautiful Greek girl, Athens, Greece.' And if you come, just buttonhole the first soldier you see and ask about me. He'll know me. I'm an officers' whore, my Peppino."

"But why do you give yourself only to officers, most beautiful Greek girl?" I asked. "We ordinary soldiers are also men."

"Why am I an officers' whore? Eh, Peppino, you don't know how wonderful it is to ride on colonels and generals, in full dress a moment before, ready for a parade, and then naked! When I ride one, I make believe they're all under me, all the officers of the world, and all the armies!"

"I confess I know nothing about it," I said, choking on some salt water I had swallowed from the last wave. "And how could I know, I, a poor Italian soldier who does nothing but shit?"

"Then, Peppino," she went on, "I gather all their decorations and all their money in a pile, pack it all between my legs and piss on their trophies, ranks and medals. Oh, how they love what I do on their crosses, their stars and crowns!"

"But I, I have nothing of all that," I complained. "I'm probably the worst soldier in all the wars ever fought by Italy. An Order of Cowardice should be created; I'd be the first winner, and then you'd have something to put between your legs."

"I want to feel how a real coward loves," she whispered, shielding me from a wave. "I want, for once, to have a real coward."

"Oh, poor me," I let out.

She clung to me so tightly I was afraid I would fall overboard.

"I want you so much, coward!" Her teeth were chattering, I don't know whether from lust or the cold. It looked as if she wanted to push me into the water.

"You, only you. I want my last man to be a coward and shit of the worst order," she whispered, filling my ears with spittle and sea salt. "So far I've only had heroes, ministers, and generals."

She rubbed her navel and groin with her hand and began to finger her cunt. I was dodging her, laughing out of fright. The night did not end; the waves did not stop. On that part of the deck, we two were the only ones who did not sleep.

"I'm sorry I have no medals and no insignia; I'd like you to piss on my glory too, although there is enough water now, without yours," I took heart to say. She would have almost spitted herself right then and there on what you call a bunny. "Oh, my most beautiful Greek girl!"

THE WAR WAS BETTER

So, here was an opportunity for me to begin, that is, not to do it anymore just in songs and letters. But, my dear Antonio, you'll understand me. My thighs and belly were scorched by fire. And the male pride between my legs—the unsullied flag of the Venezia and Murge divisions—was too; so burnt, in fact, that I sang songs to the most beautiful Greek girl until the dawn, and then hid myself and wept.

Later on I saw her with a German soldier, still uglier and more unnoteworthy than I. I'm sure he was some Boche coward of theirs. Stemming the waves with her behind, she raped the poor guy. God and all the saints in heaven! How wonderful and skillful she was! And how she impaled herself on his little horn! But never mind; I have her address, which is, in such circumstances—that is, in a war—most important.

I'm tired and swollen by water and laughter. In order to go on watching you rest your head on Romana's lap, I must kneel.

My Antonio!

3

One after another in a little row, Romana, her General, Spartaco Allegretti, and Turiddu Barbagallo were sleeping on the fishing nets. Even the waves could not wake them, let alone the song the German soldiers were singing. The wounded stared in longing at the woman asleep on her side, but they could see nothing through the cape hiding her parted knees.

Antonio Peduto and Carl Schlotterer were the only ones awake on that side of the deck.

"What do you think, which of us is more unlucky?" the German asked softly, for the umpteenth time. "You can be frank with me. You have nothing to fear anymore."

"You're more unlucky, Colonel."

"Why, *Taliano?*"

"Because you're the victor," Antonio said. "They say that's hardest."

"You think victory is so bitter?"

"Bitter, disgusting, and bloody," Peduto muttered. "Not everybody can be a victor. One has to be born for it. And born bad."

"You think I'm the victor?"

"It is you who are escorting us. It is you who can kill whomever you want. The victor answers to nobody. The only thing you don't have the right to do is take your own life, commit suicide. Victory is totally irresponsible and immoral. It is the shame of all shames."

"Why, then, do people fight so much?"

"They fight neither out of conviction nor for ideals. They fight in order to win out, to do whatever pops into their heads. Since everything is permitted them, since they're afraid of no one and ashamed of nothing, they render their accounts only to victory."

"Do you consider me a victor?"

"Yes. You too are a victor, Colonel. A real German victor."

"But can't victors be different?"

"No. They have to be beasts to the end. Victory demands cruelty. Or it turns into defeat."

"I'm sorry that's your opinion of me."

"You're German."

"And don't you see how I look?" Carl Schlotterer peered straight into Antonio's eyes. "Didn't we count our wounds a moment ago and find about the same number? Didn't you yourself say I was more roasted than you? Don't you even remember that you told me you were sorry for me?"

"When I was counting your wounds I felt sorry for you," Antonio admitted. "You didn't look like a victor to me then; you looked like a loser. It's different now."

"You stick to your opinion that I'm a victor unworthy of pity?"

"Yes," Antonio grunted. "I want all the victors to die, as many as there are. Even you. People will be just as happy without you victors. It's only when everybody is defeated and happy, that they'll be able to reach agreement and love one another."

"I have the impression that you're a Marxist," the Colonel remarked. "A Marxist or something like it. Only Marxists and Seventh Day Adventists speak about mutual understanding."

"Only one thing is clear to me," Antonio said. "I'm a living corpse; nothing but my approaching death interests me ... least of all whether the Marxists and Seventh Day Adventists will someday agree and come to love one another."

"And if I tell you I'm not a victor?"

"You can tell me whatever you please. You can kill me anytime you like. They'd congratulate you."

"I'm deeply unhappy," Carl Schlotterer said seriously. "And rest assured I'm not going to kill you; I wouldn't allow anyone to aim a finger at you, let alone a gun."

"That's your business. It won't convince me or anyone else that you're not a victor, a victor of the worst kind, up to his neck in blood and glory. The so-called tired victor. Those are the worst ones. They usually kill senselessly, because of their insomnia, or their indigestion."

"I am not only unhappy, *Taliano;* I am also defeated. I can't say it to anyone else but you. I think you have a deep understanding of things. And remember the Boche in front of you now, taking you to the prison camp, is not triumphant the way any other Boche would be; he bitterly regrets that his chest is covered with so many ribbons and medals."

"If you give any of your medals to our General here, who's snoring and dreaming again about running from the Verdun battle-field, I'll kiss your ass."

"I've been defeated once and for all," Carl Schlotterer repeated. "Don't you feel sorry for me?"

"I'm sorry you feel defeated. I think that's more important than to be sorry for you personally."

"I'm a finished man. I'm broken. And the catastrophe occurred here, in the Balkans, recently. To be more precise, it happened in Montenegro, where you, the Italians, after arriving all playful and fat from the other coast, acted the victors for such a short time."

"I've acted nothing, Colonel. I've been broken and defeated since I first knew myself. That's why the devil took me to the war. When an Italian puts on a uniform of his own accord, it means something terrible has happened to him or to those he loves. But when a German's hands grab a rifle, he immediately sees himself as a teacher, a reformer, or at least a murderer, that is, a specialist in hygiene."

"Nevertheless, we differ."

"God bless the difference, Colonel."

"Recently they defeated me totally."

"Who?"

"After a superb victory and a rich banquet, I fell asleep. When I woke up, I was no longer the man I had been, if I had ever been such a man at all."

"What kind of victory was it, what banquet? The German kind?"

"Yes. We fought without stopping a full day and night. Damn Montenegro and damn whoever created it and left it here! Our whole division was engaged, but the Montenegrins wouldn't surren-der. Instead, they charged and mowed down our best boys. It was a fight for life and death, hand to hand. Then I saw there were women and children among them. What a terrible people! Finally we broke them on a plateau, drove them back into their houses and cottages, and set them afire. They were dying and they still cursed us and spat on us; I can understand why the reason of some of our soldiers began to crumble; they began to hallucinate, do odd things. And in the end . . ."

"Go on, Colonel. So far, so good."

"About five or six hundred were still alive. General Herbert Siegmann asked me how they should be liquidated. I suggested hanging. I was tired and thirsty; my brain wasn't functioning.

" 'Out of the question, Carl,' the General said. He began to burn the soles of their feet and then their faces and hands and the skin around the groin. And when he found a bottle of plum brandy, he drank to Germany and Italy and compared the Montenegrins to the Russians and the Japanese. Then he asked us to think up something horrible, or at least witty.

"I suggested that we throw them alive into one of the nearby ponds, but he screamed that I was a stupid German without a grain of imagination.

" 'Be a poet, Carl!' he shouted as he sipped brandy. Then he ordered the prisoners to be lined up, one behind the other.

" 'Pick ten!' he shrieked. 'Make them look at the back of each other's necks!'

"We obeyed. Then he stood back and fired his pistol at the first one.

" 'How many fell, Carl?' he asked me. He looked as if he had gone blind, either from brandy or from joy.

" 'Three, *Herr General*,' I answered.

" 'That is because I shot from a distance of forty yards!' he explained, and came nearer. 'Now, gentlemen, I am going to shoot from about twenty yards!'

"And he shot at a boy, the first in line.

" 'How many are there on the ground now?'

"He was blind; he saw no one at all.

" 'You've killed six men, if we take the boy into account, sir,' the Captain beside me answered.

" 'You're the most phenomenal shot I've ever seen, sir! You never miss! Your hands don't tremble, even when firing at living flesh. . . . Oh, God! I've never seen anything like it!'

"I think it nauseated the Captain; he could hardly keep himself from throwing up. But General Herbert Siegmann did not notice and came still nearer.

" 'And now, Captain?'

" 'Seven, *Herr General!*' the Captain forced himself to answer. He was leaning on me and almost crying but he kept on. 'Seven! That is the piercing force of your pistol from a distance of ten yards. The eighth was only grazed; he's still on his feet; now he's the first on line!'

" 'And if I come up to them, and shoot from five yards, Captain?'

" 'You'll kill three at most, sir. They say a bullet needs some time to gather momentum, like a man, like a thought. . . .'

"The Captain chattered on; I had an urge to pat his shoulder, to ask him never to stop. 'Fire from that distance, sir, since you're such a fine shot!'

"The General fired and drank, drank and fired. Finally he fell down. We couldn't tell whether it was from exhaustion or horror. For a long time we tried to bring him to, pouring water and brandy over him. He regained consciousness at last and asked how many bullets he had fired, and whether the barrel of his pistol had cooled off.

"We answered that he'd fired almost one hundred times, and there was not a single drop left in the bottle.

" 'Not a drop . . . but what . . . not a drop . . . you don't mean, perhaps, blood, gentlemen? . . . Blood which I detest?' He babbled words like those as we pulled him through the corpses.

"Again he ordered us to carry him, and we did it. We carried him while he stuck his fingers into the dead bodies and recited German poetry. I assure you, I saw tears in his eyes. No! No! I don't know whether he cried because of the poetry or because there was no more brandy."

"Was the banquet rich, Colonel?"

"They ate too much, drank too much, and sang too much. Then they embraced each other. They drank toasts, many, many toasts. They didn't toast Hitler once."

"And you . . . whom did you toast?"

"I drank too. I threw up, and drank again. I trembled. I was afraid of the General. He had become even more insane. He suggested that we go to the plateau and shoot again at those five or six hundred peasants and boys. I drank again in order to forget I had ever met him. Meanwhile he hugged me and promised me a medal and a promotion."

THE WAR WAS BETTER

"And then?"

"When I woke up I felt everything was hopeless. I felt it would be best to die."

"And why didn't you, Colonel?"

"My friends are my witnesses, I have not hid from death. The bullets don't seem to want to hit me! That too is a punishment, *Taliano*."

"Why wait for another's bullet? Put one in your own brain. It's faster and surer. Every victor has to do it, if he wants to be remembered as a man, and not a beast."

"I am crushed but I am not a coward," the Colonel said stiffly. "Only good-for-nothings and women kill themselves. I am a German."

"If you can't do it yourself," Antonio said, "I am willing to kill you at any time and by whatever means you prefer. At dawn, in the back of your neck. After a banquet, between your eyes. While you're asleep, in the top of your skull, so it may be said that the bullet fell from the air. I can also strangle you, or step on your throat and press down with all my strength—and with the greatest pleasure. I can hang you. I've done that too, only I can't say whether it was out of foolishness or sorrow. In brief, I am unprejudiced."

"It would be much worse for me to die defeated, than for you to kill me."

"I'll take a long time killing you; it is the only way to treat victors. It'll be all the same to me whether you're happy or unhappy, elated or depressed; I'll kill you and peel off your skin, and my knife won't know the difference, although I have to confess it has never yet cut through German flesh."

"I'll keep your offer in mind, *Taliano*. Will you be sorry for me when I'm dead?"

"Not at all, Colonel. At the moment I am sorry only for the innocent wounded, the whores around them, and one of our soldiers." Antonio was thinking of Peppe and almost burst into tears. "Speaking of our defeats," he said to change the subject, "who was it that crushed you so?"

Carl Schlotterer was silent.

"Perhaps I'd better ask who defeated us? Both of us, you and me. Maybe it was the same devil who freed us of our belief in happiness."

"The same devil," the German repeated tonelessly. "I've been in this war ever since I knew myself. I haven't taken off my uniform for fifteen years. But that day on the plateau everything rose up in my throat and nauseated me as never before. I've met generals who were even madder than Herbert Siegmann, but his act was the last drop that made my cup of bitterness overflow. It was then that I saw how helpless, worse than helpless, how worthless I was."

"I see you have no hope for happiness. Do you hope for peace at least?"

"Yes, I hope for peace and total forgetfulness."

"I piss on peace, on any peace . . . that comes after a war," Antonio said. "Peace will be worse. Money, rats, and generals will multiply, and no one will believe that we cried when nobody was looking, before and after killing."

"It sounds like you find it easy to piss on anything, *Taliano*. At least you should spare peace."

"I'm going to piss on everything I see around me, day and night, and especially on the happiness and peace which you Germans bring."

"If you had told me that before I met General Siegmann, I'd have killed you without a second thought," Colonel Schlotterer said somberly. "It's too late now. Now you can say even worse things."

"Well, as you see, happiness isn't in the cards for me," Antonio remarked. "Probably some bastard will blow my brains out thinking he's defending the Third Reich."

Carl Schlotterer felt the blood rushing to his head and his wounds. For a long time he did not speak, and they sat in silence, one beside the other, holding onto the fishing nets, their legs stretched out like dead lizards. At dawn, Lieutenant Colonel Joachim Tea Breitbach began giving lessons to the girls he had mustered out for the purpose. They could hear him teaching them how to count *Eins-zwei-drei*, with the girls spelling the words after him, like children. They found it harder from four to ten. He fumed and repeated that they could not go anywhere in Germany if they did not know how to count at least up to twenty. "The first thing a German learns is to count, to say 'thank you,' and to obey his superiors . . . to obey blindly!"

Antonio Peduto and Carl Schlotterer looked at each other.

"Shall we continue, my lovely girls?" Breitbach urged, laughing at his own wit like a small-town actor. "One-two-three," he counted first in German and then in all the Balkan languages. "One-two-three, and hop!"

He performed rhythmic exercises as he said this, bent and lifted his arms. "What I'm doing is called gymnastics, physical education! Join me, my ladies! One-two-three, and hop!"

THE WAR WAS BETTER

The girls bent down and began to fall; they seemed never to have done this kind of excercise.

"Gymnastics—that is, rhythmical, regular bending—is the foundation of our, and now also your, education! Now once again, but a little better this time: one-two-three, and hop!"

Joachim Tea Breitbach brayed in triumph.

"For us, the German race," he shouted breathlessly, "gymnastics is more important than literacy. A sound mind, in a sound body, and everybody knows what kind of mind we Germans have! Hop! Hop! Hop!" He bent double as he spoke and, in spite of his years and his uniform, touched the tips of his boots with his fingers. "And now you, my beautiful ladies! Bend, bend, bend further! Don't be afraid, there's no one behind you." The girls bent forward, the boat rolled and waves splashed them from behind. "Hop! Hop! Hop!"

"And who defeated you, *Taliano?*" Carl Schlotterer asked, as if awaking from a dream.

"It was a single man. A man whom they trampled on as they trample on me now, but a hundred times worse. The more he suffered, the more terrible was the fate in store for me. He was harmless to begin with, but in the end his blows became so terrible and deadly that I have no words or images to describe them to you. Here, look at me: that's the only description I can give. Look where he's led me."

The ship pitched and rolled more and more violently, and the wounded began falling down again off their benches and planks. Joachim Tea Breitbach stopped torturing the girls with gymnastics. He ordered them to lie down on the deck instead, and not to move.

A fighter plane was approaching. From midships, the Lieutenant Colonel gave orders and the soldiers began firing the machine guns at the little plane, which remained hidden behind the clouds.

"*Feuer!*" Breitbach screamed; the waves were splashing not only over the ammunition boxes, but also over the gunners themselves.

"Fire!" Antonio Peduto shouted in Serbian, searching the sky. "Fire! And don't stop!"

"Whom ... are you giving orders to?" Colonel Schlotterer asked, hardly able to hold onto the nets and the railing. "Whom ... are you talking to?" He spat into the water and coughed. "*Taliano!*"

"I am talking to the one who defeated me forever!"

Antonio's eyes, bloodshot and caked with salt, roamed over the clouds. His hair was glued to the wounds on his face.

"Here he is! Fire! And don't stop! ..."

The plane turned on its side and flew past the ship, firing a volley through the rain which had begun to fall heavily.

"Ah! God! How great you are, God!"

The Germans fired back from all the weapons on the ship.

"Lord, save its wings!"

"I don't understand whom you're talking about!" Carl Schlotterer cried out, almost weeping. "Who is he?"

Waves struck at their bellies and splashed up to their necks.

"*Taliano*, have a heart!" The guns were shooting blindly through the water, on and on. "Who is he?!"

"My killer!" Antonio was swallowing water; his voice began to rattle. "My Gruban Malić!"

"For God's sake, don't mention that name!" The Colonel knelt and banged his head against the deck. "But it's an American plane!"

"Malić is piloting it!" Antonio shouted, as if drunk with joy. "He's following me, me, because he likes me! He's all my happiness, all my evil, my joy and my disaster! Since he can't save me, he wants to see you kill me and pull the heart out of my breast! Believe me, he'll enjoy it, he will! And then he'll weep, bitterly, for his brother, his double, me, Antonio Peduto! Eh, Malić!"

"You're Germans and you couldn't hit him with a hundred bullets; even if you really were supermen, you couldn't hit him with a thousand!"

"But didn't the . . . didn't Malić . . . didn't he remain . . . in Montenegro?" The Colonel seemed to be holding a wave in his arms; he was almost afloat. "As I recall, and I remember it clearly . . . exactly . . . Montenegro . . ."

"All you can remember is your Siegmann!"

"I've known Malić since Greece," he said politely. "And then in Montenegro! There were terrible battles against his armies, for a while."

"Stop talking, *Tedesco!* Shut up! I forbid you to mention his name! I forbid you even to remember him! You're only permitted to look at him, and let your teeth chatter, let your knees buckle! Just look!"

The fighter plane appeared again from behind a cloud, discharged a volley, and vanished into the rain.

"Tremble, you Germans!"

"It's too late for me."

Breitbach continued to give orders. The ship smelled of iodine and gunpowder. The long barrels were searching the clouds. But the white scout was nowhere; not a shadow remained.

"It isn't easy to hit him!" Antonio said to an incoming wave. "It isn't easy to hit my pilot! He's grown into an angel!" He was catching great swarms of foam in his outstretched arms. "Bless him, Lord!"

"Ask your angel to select a bullet for me," the Colonel said, his voice calm and unruffled. "I shall be indebted to him in this world and the next. Will you ask him?"

"I'm not sure he'd hear me. What am I to him now?"

The plane reappeared and passed over again, strafing the ship.

"To him, I'm only a heap of rags and wounds. He speaks only with his equals." The plane disappeared again. "You too are nothing to him, with your salted wounds. He has no time for you either. All we can do is wait for a mouse's death, and let him fly through the clouds . . . my dragon!"

"I'm crushed now, whipped, broken," Carl Schlotterer said heavily as he wrapped himself in the fishing nets. "Excuse me . . ."

"Be quiet, Cattolica," Romana whispered to Antonio's turtle. "Quiet, the devil will take Malić, the same devil that brought him here."

The turtle vomited a little salt water and then turned her head toward the northwest. "Look, the plane is already going away. Rejoice!"

"Night is near," General Besta observed. "Perhaps we'll spend it on land."

"On land, in peace and without Malić, who is now strafing the sea," Spartaco Allegretti put in from Barbagallo's arms. "On our land, after so many years."

"But he's still shooting!" Turiddu Barbagallo said, almost weeping, and stood up to shield his Colonel from a wave. "What a pilot! Lord, how he's twisting and looping! How he's pouring it out!"

All of them stared at the clouds. Shells were bursting in the sky, tracers flaming up and petering out. The plane climbed, went into a long loop, and then dove with terrifying speed, almost plunging into the sea. At the last moment, it turned on its side, spattered fire on the ship and vanished. Then it came back again, hovering, scouring the water like a gull, careful not to wet its wings or tail. Antonio and Schlotterer thought it was going to swoop onto the ship and embrace it. But the fighter rose again and vanished from sight.

"Fire!" Joachim Tea Breitbach screamed. "Fire!" He took hold of a machine gun himself and pointed its barrel into the sky. "We must kill him! Now! . . . Now!" The long barrels vomited fire. "Now!"

There was no one to carry the wounded back to their places. Looking for the plane with thickened eyes, they saw only waves.

THE WAR WAS BETTER

The girls were the only ones who did not weep. They crept along the deck, protecting themselves from the water as best they could.

"Land isn't far away! Land is quite near! Listen to me!" Lieutenant Colonel Breitbach was calling for quiet on the ship, and waving his hand. "We have to be ready for anything! We've hurled the plane back. It'll try again!" His back was crooked from effort; his face was turning green.

"Don't panic, and remain where you are! We've been informed that we will also be attacked from a part of the coast that the Italian partisans have held since this morning!"

The prisoners wept.

"Calm down, Cattolica," Romana said. "Land isn't far away. Soon, Anna-Maria, soon."

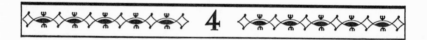

4

Italy was near at hand. The dusk was gathering, but it was not yet thick enough to join land and water. They could see the shore was burning.

Lieutenant Colonel Breitbach ordered the men to shoot not only at the plane, which continued to pursue them, but also at the land, from which several weapons were firing. The ship veered left, toward the port. Joachim Tea Breitbach asked for patience; he began to curse not only the prisoners and girls, but also the wounded.

"Sometimes it occurs to me that I'm happy in spite of everything," Carl Schlotterer remarked.

"Germans are always happy," Antonio Peduto answered, as he watched General Besta vomit over the side. "Germans are happy when there's fire."

"I'm happy that you've finally reached your own country. It's been waiting for you for so long."

"All countries are mine; that's why it's all the same to me where I am; I care only about who keeps me company," Antonio replied. He noticed that Spartaco Allegretti was trembling from fear and the cold. "Nobody can prove to me that all countries aren't mine ... except for the one we're now approaching." Antonio kept his fingers in his salty beard. "Even the Germans themselves couldn't convince me that every country and every song isn't mine."

THE WAR WAS BETTER

"I understand you more than you imagine," Carl Schlotterer said. "If I have the power . . ."

"If you have the power, you'll push me into the water when we abandon ship," Antonio interrupted. "If you don't have the power —even for that—you'll order them to shoot me or burn me alive in one of your camps."

"If I have the power or any influence at all, I'll order them to make you healthy again, as good as new, and then release you."

"Well, one way or the other, you'll give me a noisy German good-by and hope never to see me again. Yes, *Tedesco*, that's the way it'll be."

"If I don't find you, you will know I'm dead, or still defeated."

"Well, then, if we don't see each other again, I will know that my Gruban Malić has dealt you the final blow!" The plane zoomed over the ship as he spoke, let a bomb fall and then vanished as if swallowed by the darkness. "Malić!" Antonio screamed after the bomb had exploded, just missing the ship, and the water which washed up over the deck had drained off again. "Malić, my mad, wounded, angry angel, will gouge out all our eyes!"

"Lower . . . go!" Breitbach roared when the plane returned unexpectedly, its guns crackling again. "Lower! Very low! Now, more, more!" Suddenly Antonio Peduto and Carl Schlotterer saw Breitbach catch at his stomach and fall down near them. He gave no more orders; his head lay in the nets and the water without moving. The plane was flying away. The sea rose up to their necks.

"Take over the command, Wagner!" Schlotterer said to the machine-gunner in the middle of the boat. "Order them to veer to the left as soon as possible, into the port."

Wagner had just time enough to salute, which he did, and swallow a wave; then he began to shoot at the fire on the shore.

"Calm the deck, Wagner! Shoot whoever provokes a panic! We must slip into port quietly!"

Carl Schlotterer held onto the nets and boxes. "Shoot, Wagner! Quiet them down or kill them!"

Wagner shot a volley over the heads of the panicking girls and soldiers.

"So! Again! More, Wagner!"

Wagner shot, shouted, growled.

The sound of the invisible plane was approaching again. Gunner Wagner, in whom Antonio recognized the Austrian with a Ph.D. on D'Annunzio, fired in every possible direction. From the port, guns were also firing into the dusk, in the direction of the plane, and Colonel Schlotterer was satisfied.

Nurses lifted Breitbach and placed him on a stretcher. Water was dripping from him. Three bullets had hit him, someone said; the first and second ones had torn off the top of his head; the third had pierced his stomach or heart.

Carl Schlotterer sat up and gave orders that he should be covered, at least with nets and rounds of ammunition if there were no tents. They obeyed. Meanwhile, the corpse kept dripping.

The ship entered the port. Wagner shot on into the rain and the night air which smelled of fire and stale salt water.

Antonio felt like vomiting. Carl Schlotterer stood up near the railing and Breitbach's corpse. "Now we're finally in Italy," he said, and Antonio almost hit him in the teeth. Then a wave splashed over them, knocked Schlotterer to his knees again, and turned Breitbach's body over onto its back; when it had withdrawn, Antonio noticed they were quite near the dock, and that the drenched German soldiers were lowering the gangway.

Kneeling, Colonel Carl Schlotterer was rendering his report to some wet general. He tried to rise, but his feet burned and his back ached. He was precise and particular, explaining something in detail; the General and his officers listened to him and fingered the dead Breitbach.

Rain was falling heavily, pouring from the sky. Carl Schlotterer felt like falling into the mud and sleeping. But Joachim Tea lay at his knees, where he would have fallen, his skull broken open, his belly deeply slashed.

"Can we say, then, and record that he has fallen bravely?"

"Yes," Schlotterer agreed dreamily. "Practicing gymnastics."

"Do you wish to say he was shooting to the very end?" the General asked nervously as he lit up Breitbach's face with a flashlight.

"He was shooting," Carl said and looked at the corpse. "He was always shooting. He was of a lighthearted disposition."

"Is that all you can say about him, Colonel?"

Carl Schlotterer sank into a dream. He saw vividly the Montenegrin plateau, all in flowers and flames, the pond and the corpses floating on it. The smell of frog spawn, blood, and gunpowder invaded his mind. He remembered brandy and sweat and some red-bearded Italian major raping uniformed girls. And before he could reply to the officer who was shining the flashlight into his eyes, his forehead struck the ground with a dull thud. He did not realize that he had been resting his hand on Breitbach's slashed stomach, and even less that his mouth was full of mud.

"Can I write down, *Herr General*, that they've both perished?" the Captain asked from under his raincoat. "May I write down that they fought heroically and went under the earth together?" The Captain struggled for breath. "May I say that they died defending Italy?"

"If I'm not mistaken, Captain, only one of them is dead," the General answered and cursed the rain and the roaring sea. "Be more careful with the living, Captain."

"I really thought he was dead," the Captain apologized, expecting a punishment. "I'm sorry; it's this infernal darkness and rain."

Carl Schlotterer drew his hand out of Breitbach's stomach. He tried to rise, but remained on his knees, staring at them. He thought they were all on deck, and that it was sea water that was dripping down their raincoats.

"I see you're feeling better already, Colonel."

"Yes, sir. Sorry for the fall. The sea was rough and knocked me down."

Still on board the ship, Antonio could see them packing the girls into a truck. "They at least are happy," he said to himself. "They always get a ride."

The girls were singing and taking up the wounded. But it was not fated that they should depart alone; Breitbach and the other corpses were being placed among them. Some of the dead were quite fresh, even young and handsome, but others were completely drained out. Many of them had stiff, protruding Germanic jaws, and their medals, weapons, and boots had not been removed. They were the true victors now, lost in meditation and dream. The rain was pouring down on them so heavily that their wounds were awash and their blood could not coagulate. In the dim light, it was impossible to see whether their bodies and faces were livid, or green, or flushed, as they had been alive and in battle. More or less cut into pieces, with broken legs or arms, smashed-in skulls and teeth, they were being heaped into the trucks, where they fell and tumbled about at the girls' feet. Those loading them had been tender, or at least careful, with the first few. The rest they simply lifted and piled high, with curses, on top of those already sleeping below. The girls sang on and on, as if the soldiers were throwing in living men.

Antonio almost guffawed when he saw one of the girls holding up a flag on a long stick. He did not know and could not see what kind of flag it was, but there it was, hoisted in the rain.

THE WAR WAS BETTER

"Long live my army," Peduto murmured. From the ship railing, he watched the trucks full of wet flesh and corpses pass the long lines of prisoners. "Long live the great Balkan army of love and lechery!" he called out aloud as the flag passed him, with the rain driving into his eyes. "The devil take the male army! Long live women, my women, women in general! Let them live, and let love, glory, and happiness be with them forever! Only women cannot lose a war! Wind and time will sweep the Germans away, and everybody else, just as wind and time have brought them."

The girls who were not singing were waving flags, leaning out over the corpses, calling, "*Amore, amore,* good-by now, good-by forever!"

The prisoners stared impassively as the trucks moved off; the girls seemed to be saying farewell not to them, but to some other soldiers.

"Long live the women of the Balkans!" Peduto muttered as he watched the last truck and the tenth trailer moving away. "Long live the Balkans, where I left whatever was me: my heart, my spirit and my memory. Long live just my Balkans, my great village! Sooner or later I'll go back there, to hang my dirty, freckled skin on some Balkan thorn!"

The prisoners did not have anybody to say good-by to. They did not even look at each other. They only stood in the rain, expecting more lightning, more thunder, more torrents and floods. There were no trucks or trailers for them. In ragged groups of fifty or a hundred, they waded through the mud and the puddles and disappeared. Those who could still walk dragged the wounded and half-dead. The calls of the girls drifted back from the trailers: "*Amore! Amore!*" But the prisoners paid no attention; they thought the girls were calling to the victors and the sea.

"It's our turn now," Antonio said, exhausted, sitting listlessly between General Besta and Colonel Allegretti. "They'll roast us alive."

He was holding the turtle in his arms; the knapsack was on his back.

"It's not worth roasting or salting me," Allegretti said, and embraced Barbagallo.

"Be quiet, Spartaco," Romana protested, looking out at the rows of barracks lit up by the powerful searchlights. "It won't rain long." She smiled kindly to the German soldier who stepped aboard. "That's the camp.... Isn't it, *Herr Doktor?*"

The soldier seized Antonio and dragged him toward the gangway. Then he shouted to everyone that, yes, that was a camp, and the damn Italian rain was pouring, and all of them had to get up. He pulled them toward the gangway, kicking them, spitting on them, trampling over them and slapping Turiddu Barbagallo, who would not let go of his Colonel, again and again.

Pushed away roughly, Peduto was the first to fall down into the mud, together with his pack. The soldier offered his hand only to Romana, helping her descend the gangway and then to step past the puddle and Breitbach's blood. She was carrying General Besta, who had fainted, on her back.

"You take over the camp, Colonel," the General said to Carl Schlotterer. "You have twenty barracks with Yugoslavs and Italians. In the rest, there are Greeks, Albanians, Englishmen, and other Balkanians. There are some Americans too, the colored ones."

"Don't you see I can't stand on my feet, sir?" Carl Schlotterer said, trying to salute from his kneeling position. "I feel like I will have to kneel here like this forever."

"I've had the same experience several times, Colonel," the General replied dryly. "I'm leaving for the South, toward Brindisi. You can imagine what it'll be like there, even if a little sunshine filters through." He shook water from his hood. "The Captain will explain to you how the prisoners should be treated."

"I hope I don't die in the meantime."

"Death is for others, Colonel," the General said and then, smiling at his own joke, asked where Romana and Giovanni Besta were. "Death is for others, that is, for them."

"They're nearby, sir," the Captain reported. His cheeks were sunken, his lips thin. "The man whom they call a general is in a coma. Perhaps he's pretending. He's a *Taliano* for sure. He can't hide it. The lady, in spite of everything, is in an excellent mood."

"Ah, so," the bulky General said, breathing into the rain. "Into the car with them; to follow me to Brindisi." He turned to one of his other officers. "Be careful that the man doesn't die on the way."

For a moment, the General peered at Giovanni Besta, who was stretched out in the mud, and then at Romana; her round behind was sticking out and her lips were puckered.

"Should we also take these two to Brindisi, Sir?" the Captain asked, gesturing toward Spartaco Allegretti and Turiddu Barbagallo.

The General pointed his flashlight at them. "This pair with the rest, into the camp," he ordered. "The bearded one too," he added, pointing at Antonio.

The General was tired; he breathed hurriedly and with some difficulty. Rain and wind blurred his features. He looked at the prisoners, most of whom were kneeling or lying in the mud or puddles of water, and then at Romana, who knew how to behave with wolves. Then he told the driver to give refreshment to the lady—if nothing else, at least one or two drops of Italian brandy. He stooped and entered the black, armored Mercedes. Through the fogged window, he looked carefully for the spot where he had seen a beautiful woman in officers' boots. He fingered the bandage around his neck. The car took off into the darkness. The rain fell more heavily, and then a great wave, the largest so far, broke over the dock and wiped out the traces of its tires.

The half-dead Besta was carried into the other Mercedes: he held a pair of panties in his clenched fist, and his heavily decorated breast was smeared with brine. Romana covered him with a canvas and sat down in front, beside the driver. Then that car too vanished into the darkness and the smell of urine and fire.

"In the first ten barracks, there are Italians only, mainly those who surrendered of their own accord," the Captain began to explain to Carl Schlotterer. "The twenty-fifth, twenty-eighth, and thirtieth barracks are Greek and Albanian."

The entire plateau was illuminated by searchlights, and the columns of falling rain and the long barbed-wire fence were clearly visible. "In the next twenty barracks there are Yugoslavs, mostly Montenegrins. The General has ordered us to treat them like Russians, that is, more severely than the French, Irish, and Poles. Among the damned Americans there are many Negroes, who smell bad and put the English and Indians on edge.

"Since the Yugoslavs are the most numerous, I should recall how they are to be treated. The General's words should not be forgotten: 'The Montenegrins are the most dangerous beasts we have caught so far.' This is what our General has said."

The Captain was merciless. He spoke as if he were spitting. Carl Schlotterer's head swam; he fell again. On the ground, with his hands in the mud, the Colonel continued to listen to the Captain's explanation of the differences between the Canadians, Hungarians, and Czechs.

"I'm sorry I've fallen," Carl Schlotterer said apologetically, spitting out rain. "A wave must have hit me." He noticed Antonio Peduto lying in Breitbach's blood. "Malić's sea!"

"The General has gone, and now, here, you're on your feet again," the Captain said, holding him up by his arm. "Now you're with us, Colonel. How wonderful it is that you're back on your feet, the commandant of our large camp!"

"Into the barracks with the prisoners!" Carl Schlotterer ordered, trying to frown. "Only be more careful with that red-bearded one, the one who can't get up. Careful!"

"He won't go with the other Italians, *Herr Oberst!*" the Captain reported, beginning to panic. He drew out his pistol. "He won't go with his own soldiers!"

"Why?"

"I don't know, Colonel." The Captain looked into the barrel of his pistol. "I struck him twice; he won't go with them." His jaws tightened. "He tried to tell me some filthy story. .... I'd have beaten him anyway, though, even if he hadn't opened his filthy, cynical chops."

"Bring him here."

The Captain pulled Antonio up and let him drop into a puddle at the Colonel's feet. Carl Schlotterer ordered him to put his pistol back into his holster and remain silent.

Antonio Peduto and Carl Schlotterer stared at each other.

"Our conversation must be quite brief," the Colonel warned him.

"As brief as possible, please," Antonio replied from the puddle, pressing the turtle into his bosom.

"Why don't you want to join your men?"

"That isn't true," Antonio snapped, and set out immediately on all fours after a group of prisoners who were being led along and beaten. "It's not true!" he called back.

"Those are Yugoslavs," the Colonel informed him.

"But they're my men. They've been my men for a long time now," Antonio said softly and convincingly. "Especially since today. And therefore, please, let me crawl after them, let me enter the barracks with them."

The Captain took out his pistol again. The Colonel looked at him darkly and leaned on his rifle. The Captain turned away and ordered the junior officers to keep a close watch on Spartaco Allegretti and Turiddu Barbagallo, who, for the fifth time, were trying to steal away from the formation toward the shore and the big waves.

"And will they consider you theirs?"

"That's their business. What's important to me is what I think."

"They'll tear you up alive; they'll strangle you and eat you."

THE WAR WAS BETTER

"Let them do what they want. Whatever they do to me will be fitting and holy."

"Do you have any other wish, you strange man?" Schlotterer's voice was inspired. "The man I'll never be able to forget."

"I don't want to lose my wife and my knapsack between here and the barracks," Peduto requested, looking up at a Lieutenant and then at the enraged Captain, who was now slapping Allegretti and spitting on Barbagallo. "That is all."

"Help him."

Colonel Schlotterer turned aside, in order not to burst into tears. One of the lieutenants was trying to explain to him everything the Captain had already explained. The barracks were lit up brightly, and so too were the dogs which guarded them. It seemed the mad waves of Malić's sea were reaching even for the searchlights, that they broke only there. Through his tears, he could see the bridges and the weird, yellowish-green walls of a hydroelectric power station looming over the camp, high on the hill which dominated the plateau. Water was roaring and thundering up there, white with foam. Schlotterer's head spun; he felt his heart was failing.

A car stopped beside him. Two lieutenants opened the door and asked from which side he would prefer to enter. The Colonel liked the rain; he hesitated. He was watching Peduto creep after the prisoners. A junior officer was carrying the turtle and the knapsack for him, and from time to time, when he stumbled and fell, helped him up from the puddles. Another junior officer showed the way with a pocket flashlight; he was loudly cursing the Italian rain and all of Italy.

"Soon, *Taliano*," the Colonel said to himself. "Soon, my invincible red devil."

He welcomed almost with desire the rain and the pain and weariness in his bones. He heard nothing but the sea and the sound of water everywhere.

Just when he finally decided to enter the automobile, a scream echoed out of the darkness and water:

"Where are you, Major . . . my Antonio?"

The Captain shot several bullets in the direction from which the scream had come. Then he informed the Colonel that the officers and dogs had caught a lagging prisoner. He fired again into the darkness.

"Is that all, Captain?"

"He says his name is Giuseppe Bonaccia, that he did not want to die ... outside the camp. ... He did not want to die before seeing the Major they are leading away."

Colonel Carl Schlotterer turned into the wind and the rain; he almost fainted when he saw it was Peppe they had brought to him. For he recognized the soldier who had vanished on the Montenegrin plateau. For a long time he stared at him without speaking. Peppe lay before him in the mud, weeping.

"Antonio, wait for me!" the soldier called in a dying wail, looking back toward the prisoners. "You said yourself that I'm your illegitimate son! I'm your faithful mangy dog. ... Take me!"

The Colonel's eyes were full of thorns and salt. He felt like caressing him.

"Why did you disappear ... the day before yesterday, up there?" he asked him with such tenderness that the Captain stepped back in astonishment.

"I don't like battles, or hand-to-hand fights."

"Promise you won't do it again," the Colonel said, peering into his frightened eyes. "Promise you'll behave. There are no more hand-to-hand fights anymore, and there never will be." The Colonel almost fell down in the mud beside him. "Promise you won't vanish anymore."

"Please let Antonio take me," Peppe beggged, with his teeth chattering. "That is the only thing I can ask a German. Antonio! Save me! You've lost your mangy dog. ..."

"I'm waiting for you, Peppino!" Peduto called from the first barracks. "Bonaccia, my dearest soldier!" The dogs and the sea were barking. "My older and more intelligent brother! My Peppe!"

"If you promise," the Colonel insisted, almost touching him. The Captain, unable to control his fury, fired a whole clip of bullets into the raging salt water. "If you promise me that you won't run away anymore ..."

"I promise. ... Anything you want, except a hand-to-hand battle!" Bonaccia cried, hurling himself at the Colonel's feet. He smelled of rotten fish and gasoline. "Only don't separate me from Antonio!"

"Take him to the barracks," the Colonel ordered. "Let them be together."

The Captain grinned desperately. He had, for the hundredth time, to put his pistol back in his holster. The rain from his helmet poured down his neck.

The lieutenants had not understood what was happening between the Colonel and the little prisoner; all they could do was continue to wade through the little pool around the automobile. They no longer asked him from which side he wanted to enter, or said anything at all, but, like the Colonel himself, stood listening to the sea and the thunder. Then all three directed their eyes toward the dimly lit pathway which Peppino was crawling along in the mud, circumnavigating the larger puddles and reminding them all of a mangy dog.

"What I'd like most of all is to join you," Carl Schlotterer said to himself as he watched Peppe being brought up to Antonio. "Join you for good," he added, and began to wail softly.

The lieutenants thought Schlotterer's wounds must be aching and they opened their medicine bag. The smell of iodine, Breitbach's entrails, and brine filled his nostrils. Instead of getting into the car, and even before he noticed the pills which one of the lieutenants was lifting toward his mouth, the Colonel dropped down beside the opened door. The earth and water seemed soft to him, like a pillow under his head.

Again he saw the Montenegrin plateau, all in blood and flame. The wind came. The flowers and corpses smelled. The living were lamenting, wildly running down toward the stagnant pond, eating frog spawn and swollen snakes; all of them were thirsty and mad; they shot, burned the grass, and slid down the cliff toward the filthy water and sucked and guzzled it as if it were a clear stream. Afterwards, Schlotterer and all his soldiers fired at the stone where the red one stood. Judging by his behavior, he was an unbalanced man; he appeared scorched and unbuttoned; through the binoculars, they could see he had a turtle in his arms.

Carl Schlotterer could not say even now who had drunk up more brandy, nor who had been the first to storm the company of uniformed women. The smell of women's flesh between their parted legs had lingered in their minds; in their thoughts, they had mixed it with gunpowder and chewed on it. The Italian's red, bristling beard had been scratching their thighs.

Like a raging conflagration, Schlotterer's dream moved on hungrily to another scene. Foam was dripping from General Herbert Siegmann's lips; he fell, jerking like an epileptic, shooting at the children they brought up to him, testing the kill capacity of his pistol.

"I don't know why it's hard to kill a child!" he driveled from his prone position, from which he was shooting not only at the living, but also at the dead.

The children fell without lifting their hands up first, as the adults had done.

"God and all the saints, how hard it is to kill a child!" Herbert Siegmann muttered, his throat rattling, as he watched the children's heads and arms disappear in the flowers.

"Look, how I am defeated, sir!" he cried out to Siegmann, who did not turn to look at him, but continued instead to aim the smoking barrel of his pistol at the eyes of the still-living children. "Shoot me, I'm half-dead anyway," he said, falling on his knees in front of the insane, twitching old man.

"At anybody else, but not at you, Carl!" the General drawled, his mouth mindlessly chewing on dirt and the foam of his epilepsy, his hands shooting at anything that appeared in human form.

"Get out of the way! You're in the line of fire! Get out of the way! Get out of the way!"

Colonel Carl Schlotterer almost choked in the mud. The lieutenants lifted him up and showed him the car. The first one was about to wipe his face clean. The Colonel shook his head. He did not even see the car before his eyes, or the driver behind the wheel.

"I'm sorry I fell again," he excused himself frankly, his voice quite soft. "The sea is choppy and the wind is blowing harder than ever."

"Now you're on your feet, sir. We won't let you fall," the first lieutenant encouraged him. "No more falling now, or remembering unpleasant things."

"You're exceptionally tired," the other lieutenant observed, shielding his dirty face from the rain and the beams of the searchlights. "Only tired and sick men remember Montenegro and its burning mountains."

The Lieutenant's face grew sad.

"You'll need peace and quiet and a good long rest, sir. Our exceptionally well-ordered camp, which contains ninety-nine barracks, one hundred dogs, one hundred and seven guards, over five hundred agents of various kinds and a crematory under construction, will be the ideal nook for your recovery. A kind of Switzerland, with the added plus of the Adriatic Sea and a view of the Balkans and unforgettable Montenegro! It will be ideal, ideal!"

For a moment Carl Schlotterer regarded in silence the landscape revealed by the powerful searchlights. The supporting walls of a giant hydroelectric power station came first into his view, high on the mountain; the dammed-up water was roaring and foaming. Most of the valley below it, with the camp nestled in it, was lit up by the dazzling, crisscrossing beams of the searchlights. The light also played beautifully over the stormy waves, which reared so high they threatened to reach not only the camp fence, but up even into the rain. In the middle of the settlement, which was entirely fenced off by barbed wire, rose a high tower, a kind of pillar of honor and control, equipped with various searchlights which could pierce into every corner of the camp and make it bright as day.

"Peace is exactly what you need, Colonel," the handsome lieutenant said, his flashlight lighting up the tires of the car whose motor was still idling and sputtering. "You too, beginning tonight, will have all the peace you desire."

"Do you hear that bird?" the first lieutenant asked with a smile. "The owl. There are many in the vicinity. We usually listen to them and tease them around this time."

"How do you tease them, Lieutenant?" Fever was gripping him. "How do you tease the owl?"

"We imitate her. The owl is a naïve, stupid bird."

"Call her," he said to both of them. The feeling was coming to him that he would fall down again. "Wake her up!"

First the handsome lieutenant called, imitating the owl's hoot. When he stopped, he continued to stare into the darkness, and the other one took over.

"Only a field mouse is answering you," the Colonel muttered. "What kind of peace is this, when only a field mouse answers you? What kind of German officers are you, if you can't wake up an owl?"

He coughed and spit out sand and mud.

"I want the owl. . . . It's your fault. . . . You brought up the subject! You promised it! The peace you described to me is nonsense, nothing but nonsense, without this owl, this 'naïve, stupid bird.' "

"Owl!" the two lieutenants called out, first individually and softly, then in duet. 'Owl, our little owl, hoot to us! We want to hear you, just once!" Their voices would have echoed in the night if it had not been for the roar of the waves. "Whistle back just once! Hiss! Please, we beg you, have mercy!" They jerked their heads back, their mouths full of rain and darkness.

"Our little dearest owl, answer us, please, and then go back to sleep in your nest! If you answer us now, we promise not to make fun of you anymore! *Taliana*, love . . . Our only and golden love!"

"Only a field mouse answers," Carl Schlotterer persisted; he felt like spitting on them. "Wake her up, or I shoot!" He reached for his pistol and released the safety catch with an ominous click. "Wake her up!"

"How, *Herr Oberst?*"

"Do what you've been doing! Imitate animals! Meow! Bark!"

"How should we bark, sir?" the first lieutenant asked in panic, wet down to his skin. "Like real dogs?"

"Like real dogs, Lieutenant! Like real German dogs! Like real, trained, German camp dogs, accustomed to peace, good food, and teasing owls!"

The lieutenants started to bark.

"Not so!" Carl Schlotterer thundered. "That's not barking! That's whining like whelps! You must bark like real German shepherds, like dogs fighting wolves! You must bark loud, loud, I tell you, loud! And as long as it takes, until you wake her up or die!"

The lieutenants began barking in earnest. They modulated the tone of their barking to resemble that of Austrian Alpine dogs, with their tails between their legs. Then they barked like Schleswig dogs, like dogs from the Polish frontier, like dogs from Pomerania and the swampy surroundings of Danzig. They barked like dogs behind which stand armed men, mechanized weapons and other dogs. They barked like dogs making an attack, and then like wild, desolate dogs with no home or master, like hungry, marauding dogs. They held onto each other as they barked, in order not to fall, and then broke apart and barked separately, with their feet planted in the mud and water. They barked slowly, almost sadly, like real Westphalian dogs. They were tottering. They almost fell. They barked like all the dogs that they themselves had beaten or patted in their lives, or simply like the dogs they had taught how to bark and attract others. They barked without any hope of ever stopping, as if they really were dogs; out of the corner of their eyes they could see the Colonel, his body shaking with fever, aiming the barrel of his pistol directly at them. They barked, and their barking became bloody. They barked until their vocal cords began to burst, like rubber bands stretched so tight they must break.

"Barking doesn't help, *Herr Oberst,*" the handsome lieutenant whispered, exhausted. "The owl is a stupid bird. ... It's a monster without sympathy for others!"

"If that's the case, shoot her!"

"*Taliana,* whore!" the first lieutenant snarled and began firing from his submachine gun into the rain. "Damn whore ... won't return our call, will you? ... All right! Here's more for you!" He aimed carefully, falling on his knees to steady the gun and shooting on and on. "*Taliana*, oh you bitch!"

The other lieutenant was also firing, but in another direction. His gun coughed blood and cartridges at the pillars and walls of the giant dam, and then at the distant lights and searchlights. Finally exhausted, he screamed out, "*Taliana*, damn Latin whore!" and tottered forward.

Then suddenly, like some amphibian reptile, the sunken-cheeked, thin-lipped Captain emerged from the darkness. Even before the lieutenants had given up and told the Colonel that they had no more cartridges and could no longer bark or growl, he had opened the door of the car and said something slimy and flattering, which only embittered Schlotterer more.

"I will not go with the car!"

The lieutenants stood motionless. They forgot their blood and burst vocal cords; they closed their eyes; the end had come. Then the Colonel threw his pistol into a puddle. Mud dripped from his face. He was no longer looking for his spectacles, or even for his hat.

"Stretcher!" he commanded.

"We have only one on hand, Sir," the first lieutenant apologized. "It has blood all over it."

"So much the better," Schlotterer said. He began to tremble, remembering Breitbach and his open belly.

"But we've carried thousands of prisoners from almost every country in the world on it, toward their common, fraternal grave. Doesn't it bother you, sir, that it's been used so extensively? That, if you allow me to express myself crudely ... that it hasn't been disinfected, for you, our new commandant?"

"Throw me, at last, on this famous stretcher! This historical stretcher! Or I'll ask you again to wake up the stupid owl!"

The lieutenants lifted him onto the stretcher. "What now, *Herr Oberst?*"

"Now to the main entrance, and through the camp! I want to see all ninety-nine barracks and everything that's ... there! A review for the new commandant!"

"It's almost midnight, sir," the Lieutenant objected. "The camp's sleeping."

"Wake them up! Everyone!"

They carried him toward the main entrance, his head bobbing on the stretcher.

"I want to see them all!"

"*Jawohl!*" the first lieutenant snapped. "Although they're sleeping, you'll see them, sir ... everyone!"

"Isn't it a shame to wake the dogs?" the Captain asked as he waded along beside the stretcher.

"Which dogs?"

"Our wonderful dogs who guard the camp, *Herr Oberst*," the Captain said. His voice seemed to soften with affection. "The pure and truly devoted German dogs to whom we owe so much, to whom we should ... erect a monument!"

"I don't understand."

"Is there any sense in waking all the dogs, sir? It's different with the prisoners. They don't sleep anyhow. They doze off, or dream of freedom. Their main idea is mutiny and escape. But our dogs, they're like us: they work hard and guard our world-renowned order."

Carl Schlotterer's eyes were full of light and rain.

"German dogs are like men," the Captain continued. "Which means, at any time, by night or by day, I'd willingly give two Englishmen, three Frenchmen or ... any number of Slavs for one of our dogs." He stopped and peered into the Colonel's face, touching his hot forehead.

"And therefore, I repeat, I wouldn't wake them up. I especially wouldn't want to trouble the bitches and the pups. I'd want to spare these likable, healthy, German offspring from getting drenched in this terrible rain!"

"I want a review, Captain!"

"How long is it going to last, sir? I do not ask because of the prisoners, but because of the dogs, which, God forbid, may catch a cold."

"I don't know, Captain. Most probably until I faint again."

The vision of General Herbert Siegmann and the children who did not know how to lift up their arms and ask for mercy came to Carl Schlotterer again. It even seemed to him that the lieutenants were not carrying him from barracks to barracks, but through the flowery Montenegrin mountainside; that the thin-lipped Captain with the eternally insulted eyes was not walking beside him, but instead the mad, epileptic General, testing the piercing force of his lead on human flesh. The Colonel's consciousness was dwindling; he begged his heart and his head to hold out. "We're already at the tenth barracks, sir," he heard the Captain say as if from a great distance; the word, "tenth" seemed to mingle in his mind with the words "eleventh" and "twelfth."

THE WAR WAS BETTER

They lifted the stretcher to give Schlotterer a better view of the barracks. The wind and the rain were beating against the living corpses in striped suits, who had been herded out of their shelters. As the doors were badly lit and narrow, the soldiers, in their haste to please the new commandant, had even thrown some of them through the windows. Those trying to flee or hide in other barracks were driven back by pistols and dogs.

"This is barracks number twenty-five, sir, the one I spoke most about."

About one hundred people were grouped before the barracks in a ghastly formation. With their long necks and arms and shaved hair, they resembled some kind of military unit, perhaps a company. Arranged two by two, with a German flag in the hands of each one at the head of the line, they seemed to be waiting for an order to attack or march. They were standing peacefully in the rain, licking it from their faces. Even the Captain did not know who was the first to begin:

Te Deum laudamus—Te Dominum confitemur.

Even those in the rear joined in, and those lying on stretchers and waiting for God or a guard to take their souls away:

Tibi omnes angeli—Tibi caeli et universae potestates.

They sang on, staring at him with enormous, yearning eyes.

"I'm sorry, I've fallen again," Carl Schlotterer said to the company of prisoners standing in front of barracks number fifty-six or seventy-nine.

"You can't fall, sir," the Captain said, signaling that the prisoners should continue their singing. "You're already at barracks eighty and eighty-four." The Captain blew his whistle, but the prisoners did not know in which language to sing.

"We're only a few steps from the central plateau."

"I'll make an effort," Carl Schlotterer whispered; the drenched company began to thunder, *Sanctus . . . Domine Deus.* "I ask you all to pardon me. . . . Because it's not only I who am to blame for what happened . . . up there, and at sea."

They had reached the large plateau, near the main tower. Carl Schlotterer felt his head swimming. The Captain was trying to cover him with a raincoat. He was explaining that almost all the inhabitants of the camp were now in front of them, including the dead, who had also been brought up to embellish the midnight welcome.

"Where are the dead?"

"In front of the living, Sir. We always clear the paths with the dead, because they're the most disciplined. We put them in the first row tonight, so they could see you better."

"How many are there?"

"About fifty, sir. About fifty, provided someone still alive hasn't got in with them."

"Are they the ones holding our beautiful flags?"

"Yes, but they aren't waving them like the others. They remember... everything we've been teaching them here. That is why there is such a peaceful expression of gratitude on their weary and beautiful faces."

"Can you count the living? I mean those who aren't in the first row yet."

"Ninety-nine barracks have been completely emptied, sir. All the dogs, even the pups, have been awoken. We've done everything according to your will. Here are all the camp policemen and guards, and the special regiment which protects the camp and the hydroelectric station. Even the sick, here and there mixed with the dead, are looking at you with admiration; they're the ones who are either in the second row or on the ground. They say they understand you, and wish you a speedy convalescence and recovery."

"Lift me a little higher, Captain."

They lifted and adjusted him until he was almost standing and seemed to be leaning, quite by chance, on the stretcher propped up beside him. Rain was pouring down his cheeks, which were burning feverishly, like his whole body. Rain also streamed down his arms, with which he felt like pushing all this wet, ugly crowd away. In his narrowing thoughts, he saw himself fleeing, sometimes on all fours, sometimes like a healthy man. As he could not budge and could not prevent himself from urinating, he began to wet down his legs, begging his heart not to break.

Everything he saw seemed to be upsidedown. *Miserere nobis, Domine—Miserere nobis,* the Montenegrins were singing, together with some Greeks and a few Russians. *In Te, Domine, speravi— non confundar in aeternum—*even the Albanians and Bulgarians joined in, standing on their heads and opening wide their famished mouths. *Domine speravi,* it seemed someone was weeping and laughing at the same time. *Recordare, Jesu pie, quod sum causa tuae viae.* Some of them stumbled and fell over the dead. Picking themselves up and saying, *Jesu pie,* over and over in fright, they rushed back to their choir. It seemed to Carl Schlotterer that their bare feet were wading through Breitbach's immense stomach.

The Captain, having presented the Colonel to the prisoners, and then the prisoners to the Colonel, was now talking about something else.

"We lost a lot of time training them," he admitted. "Finally, in work and song, we found a common language. Just listen, sir, how the Balkanians and the French twist their tongues over *Lacrimosa dies illa.* But there's nothing to be done. Otherwise, when they don't sing, they swear!"

From the tower, the great central searchlight illuminated all the roofs and the streams of water pouring from them and flowing toward the companies and the trained choirs in formation. The smaller, moving searchlights, like those behind the guards, lit up not only the half-dead Colonel, but also the tireless and ceaselessly moving lips of the Captain.

"In our work on the prisoners' reeducation, that is, to make them literate first in the political and then in the spiritual sense, we have encountered several problems whose solution we would like to ask you to provide, sir, that is, we would appreciate your advice and help. For instance, you work with a prisoner, you teach him how to sing even if he has no ear for music and no affinity at all for anything concerning us, but then he dies. This is particularly the case with the Serbians and the English, as well as some Dutch and North American savages."

Water and wind streamed between the Colonel and the Captain. Carl Schlotterer was swaying. He did not even have the time to finish the feverish thought he had just begun: "Oh, what a night, and what a peace, after everything that happened in Montenegro and on Malić's sea . . ."—he was already reeling. He would have parted from the stretcher and fallen, had it not been for the two lieutenants, the camp doctor with a Bible, and a priest with a submachine gun, all of whom were holding him up and expecting him to terminate the midnight parade as soon as possible. He floated between the stretcher and the ground, nodding his head and whispering so that only some of them could hear: "I'm sorry I brought you out here, I'm sorry I woke you up, and took you out into this rain . . . people!"

"But they're not people, sir," the doctor murmured to him, his hairy ears filling with water. "They're only prisoners, former or future communists, talentless singers to boot, and they haven't a chance to recover."

He could see the large, wet, faithful canine detachment, the big dogs and all the puppies frolicking around the covered cannon and the ammunition box. In front, he saw the detachments of the special regiment, giants under helmets and raincoats, with submachine guns hanging from their necks; he told himself they must be guards or special policemen because, while singing *Tibi omnes angeli*, they were looking around as if to survey the others. He leaned forward further and further, almost touching the prisoners in the first row. "You must die...from shame," he told himself, "from shame."

He wanted to close his eyes. He wanted to vomit brine and rain. He could see the American Negroes, Englishmen, and Senegalese, hugging each other and all drenched, singing something that seemed to begin and end with either *Blumen, Blumen,* or *Über alles.*

Then he tumbled down and fell on his face. The Macedonian gypsies and Scandinavians were singing *Ave, Maria* and *Benedictus fructus* in an almost Oriental manner, over his head. The last words he heard were: *Dominus tecum.*

Then there was a clap of thunder. Lightning flashes would also have been visible, if it had not been for the searchlights.

"Angina pectoris!" the camp priest shouted and, rolling his eyes, stooped toward the Colonel. "God, what angina pectoris!"

"Syphilis, *Pater,*" the drenched camp doctor said quietly.

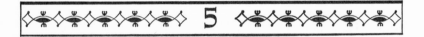

Antonio Peduto lay on his back like a dead man. An aluminum messtin propped up his head, and he was caressing quietly with his fingertips the sand and gravel which overlaid the yard of the Yugoslav barracks. He was squeezing two stones together, hoping the weaker one would not break. His hands no longer hurt, and he could feel that he still had some strength in them.

He opened his eyes slowly and looked around him. The lean captives in striped suits and with close-cut hair were lying in their own corners, each on his own sand. He could hear the Yugoslavs near him or murmuring softly beside the fence. Beyond the barbed wire, there was nothing but thorns and brown grass, from which dogs and frogs stuck out their heads. Antonio preferred to rest his eyes by looking at the path which circled the entire compound, and then lost itself in the direction of Bari. From afar, nothing reached him but a salty wind and the smell of brine and half-rotten fish.

He watched the prisoners and counted them.

THE WAR WAS BETTER

"There are thirty in the sun, on the sand; yesterday there were thirty-two," he thought. "I am counting today, another will count tomorrow, and then someone else will cross our names from the list." He was quiet, holding the two stones in his hand. "Which will be the first to break? One of them must surrender."

Prisoners emerged from the barracks one by one, looking for some room to sit or lie on the sand. Not all of them put their mess-tins under their heads and stretched out. Many took up pebbles and played.

Antonio liked his two stones. He caught himself several times calling them endearing names, kissing and wetting them with his spittle. They had a more beautiful color when they were wet and a different smell. Then he placed them on the turtle's shell; she seemed to like the game. He asked her to lick or feel them. The turtle always listened to him. She turned her head toward the northeast.

"We're one hundred again," he whispered to the prisoners, intoxicated by the heat of the spring sun. "Eight more are missing. Either they've escaped, or they've been crossed off the list."

His eyes wandered over the crowd of similarly dressed, barefooted prisoners. He did not know who was missing. As he was tired, he could hardly follow his own thoughts. The two white pebbles were distracting him.

"Which will be the first to break? Ah, I know: the stronger one will surrender."

The prisoners were quiet on their sand.

"Are we all here, Peppe?" Antonio asked, stricken with a silent panic. "I am thinking, is our number still the same?"

"It is," Peppe answered from beside Antonio's feet. "Because every day they add two or three. Since we came here our number has always been one hundred."

"Peppino, are the boys here?" Antonio asked softly, playing with the pebbles. "I don't see them." A shiver rippled through him. "I don't see them, Bonaccia. God, at least save Ivan and Miloš!"

"It'll be worse for them if they crept under the wire," Peppe said. "The dogs are just waiting for them; they'd like nothing better."

"Why did you say, then, that our number was complete? Don't you see that the children are missing, our sons? Peppino, you're starting to count more and more inaccurately. I've noticed it in recent months."

"I don't know how well I do it, but I do nothing else but count,

[120]

THE WAR WAS BETTER

Antonio. Don't you remember the Boche said there should be one hundred in our barracks, not counting the boys?"

"Your counting scares me stiff, Peppino," Antonio admitted, noticing several prisoners approaching them. "If you don't count carefully, you'll break my heart. And then, you know, I'll stop writing letters for you. I give you my word, before these people."

"Be careful, *Taliano*, when you count," a mustachioed prisoner, Brka, said as he sat down near Antonio. "If you're not more careful, I won't write to your Montenegrin girls anymore."

"It's easy to make a mistake here," Peppe explained, wedging himself between Antonio and Brka. "They always bring somebody new. The boys are always moving around while I count. Trucks usually seem to come just when I'm wrapped up in counting, and foul everything up. And then, the sun. First I sing to it, then I curse it, but anyway there's nowhere to hide from it."

"You must take care," Brka admonished him. "Counting is a kind of nourishment."

"For us, numbers are what letters are for you," Antonio remarked.

"I'll be more careful in the future," Bonaccia said. Standing up between Brka and Antonio, he began staring at the sun to keep himself from crying. Tears came anyway. He stretched out his fingers. "One, two, three . . ." He opened the other hand, painfully separating his fingers. "Six, seven, eight." He was catching at the numbers with his outstretched fingers. "Ten, eleven, thirteen . . . I can't go on; the sun has blinded me again. Tears are coming between my numbers, and I can't go on." He did not know what to do with his hands, his fingers. "Promise you'll write letters for me. I'll work harder. I'll be more careful. I'll go all in for numbers."

"Which one should we write to this time?" Brka asked, touching his ears with his mustaches, in order to make himself and the others laugh. "Tell me, Peppe. Say it loud and clear, like a man!"

"To all of them!" Bonaccia spluttered through his tears, opening his hands again. "To all the girls I know and don't know. The girls who've already been told where I am and the ones who still think the Germans made soap out of me. To all the girls!"

"Can we do it on the sand?"

"On anything you like," Bonaccia answered, blinded by the sun and his tears. "It's important to write a letter, to unburden one's heart. And since all letters, wherever they go, however long their journey, get to their destination sooner or later . . . mine too will arrive."

[121]

THE WAR WAS BETTER

The rest of the prisoners also gathered around the group.

"May we begin, Bonaccia?" Antonio asked, sitting up.

"I'm ready."

"I'm writing," Antonio muttered and looked up at the heads around him. "Must the writing and the words be nice?"

"Everything must be nice ... when one addresses girls," Peppe said enthusiastically. All of them could see the tears welling up in his eyes and blinding him. "Everything must be beautiful and clean —every word, every comma must be without reproach. Letters are not written every day."

"Can we send regards to our girls too in your letter?" a young prisoner asked Peppe; he got no answer.

"My only one, my dearest, most beautiful ..." Antonio began, drawing in the sand with his forefinger.

"I make mistakes in numbers, and you in letters, Antonio," Bonaccia said even more moonily. "I have more girls than just one. Just remember all the countries you roamed through, plus the ones I fought in."

"You're right, my son," Antonio agreed, sensing blood and warmth rush up to his temples again. "I've already rubbed it out. Now I'm writing in the sand: 'My only ones, my dearest, unforgettable girls ... of the whole world, especially the girls from the countries where I fought as a soldier of the famous but later defeated and humiliated Venezia and Murge divisions ... Sooner or later I will be back, I will arrive, and if I hear you haven't been faithful to me, I'll pour gasoline on you and burn you up ...' Is that all right, Bonaccia?"

"Yes, it is, Antonio," Peppe murmured. "Now we've expressed the main gist of it anyway. So now you can add whatever you please. When I get there, let's say how I'll put my bunny and our Neapolitan fire between their legs. Throw in a song of Augusto's again. But let it be one he composed himself and left to us."

He stood staring at the sun, not screening his eyes with his hands; many of the others thought he was either inspired or sick.

" 'The girls of the whole world'—how beautifully you expressed it, Antonio! Thirty, eighty, one hundred; oh God, distant, dear God of mine, don't let the sun and the wind rub our words out of the sand!"

He looked as if he were expecting a new flood of tears and words; the prisoners knew him and kept silent.

"You can skip, sir, the manner and means by which I defeated the Germans. I'm afraid the girls may think I'd do the same to them. In letters and songs, we should never mention shit, the Germans, or the camp."

"Whatever you wish," Peduto said, looking at the close-cropped skulls and the large eyes in them. "Not only whatever you wish, but whatever pops into your head. Isn't it so, people?" The prisoners nodded, and Antonio drew in the sand with his finger. "And the only thing we, your friends, ask from you is to count more carefully, in order not to scare us. You should pronounce numbers as carefully as we write letters and girls' names in the sand."

"Don't be afraid," Bonaccia said, as if from the other world. "We'll long remain the number we are today. Even when we vanish from the face of this earth, we'll still be one hundred!"

"We're finished, Peppino," Peduto informed him, and the others confirmed it. "All your girls will be happy! Isn't it true, people? The girls of the whole world will weep when they read what we've been telling them for so many months, when they see our sand with all these letters and names and indecent drawings!"

"Oh, what a boy all those girls have!" Brka sighed and lifted his starved hands over his head. "Oh, how happy the poor things must be; they're free! Oh, how happy we are, to have such a big bruiser among us, a real hero, a big-balled stud with so many girls' names and addresses!"

"We've finished writing," Antonio said again, overwhelmed by a painful and bitter feeling of happiness. "Tell me what to do now. Order us, Bonaccia."

"A song comes after every letter, people," Peppe said, lifting his eyes devoutly above the barbed-wire and the dust stirred up by the trucks, armored cars, and tanks. "A song is nothing but a letter. Every letter should end with a song, any song. A letter to girls, though, should end with one of my brother Augusto's little songs."

Peppe's enthusiasm grew. With his arms outspread, his gaze searching the distance, and tears trickling down his sunken cheeks, he dropped to his knees. He began with a hardly audible voice.

"Accompany me, people. But softly, my dear *Slavi*. Not so noisily and discordantly, not like the *Pater*, but tenderly, so that Augusto's heart may hear the song." His hands were lifted before his face and he could see no one. "Softly. Come on, accompany me."

"Not him!" the *capo* snapped suddenly; they all looked up suddenly and saw him standing there, beside the Captain. "Accompany me, not him!"

"Should we all follow you?" Antonio asked, happy that Bonaccia had not yet noticed anything and was still whispering to Augusto's heart. "Everybody? Or only me?"

"Only you," the Captain said. "The others may remain and sing, provided there are none of the usual communist songs."

"They're even worse," the *capo* observed. "If it is possible for anything to be blacker, more terrible, and more senseless than communist songs and slogans."

"You're singing that red crap again?"

"Yes, sir," the broad-shouldered *capo* with a pudgy nose informed him. "They're also talking about girls. They're remembering freedom. They're speaking of London and Moscow. Imagining. As if they weren't safer and better off here, in German hands."

Giuseppe Bonaccia did not pause. The Captain was at a loss what to do. His hands were sweaty, his thin lips pale.

"They even sing at night," the *capo* went on. "They're worse than the Greeks. They wake up the guards and the dogs. If I were them I'd be weeping. But they often sing until dawn, the swine!"

"We will take these songs away from you!" the sad-eyed Captain with the sunken cheeks growled. "You'll do without that disgusting crap!"

"Listen to one, Captain!" Antonio said, standing up.

"Are you going to sing it?"

"Giuseppe Bonaccia usually sings by himself," Antonio said, and then translated his words to the prisoners. "It's no use accompanying him. When the inspiration comes, he becomes enraptured; he neither sees nor hears anybody or anything. He only sings, as he is doing now, and weeps. When he's full of food, he rises on his toes, throws his head back, and makes brief but deadly movements with the frontal, communistic parts of his body. We believe he must be imagining a woman stooping before him, a woman who can never get enough ... of his song and his strength. Listen to him now, Captain!"

"I understand nothing," the Captain complained, looking at the *capo*. "Perhaps it's in dialect." He blushed with shame. "Anyhow he's only moving his lips; there are no words."

"His songs cannot be sung in any other way," Antonio informed him. "They're murmured, Captain; they're whispered."

The *capo* frowned.

"Again I understand nothing," the German complained.

"Turn your ear on," Antonio jeered, signaling with his hands for

[124]

the prisoners to calm down. "If you can't hear the whole song, at least listen to the refrain. All the meaning is in it." He wanted to hear once again the words which the Venezia and Murge divisions had liked so much to sing. "Now, my son!"

"*Daglielo mollo, daglielo.*" Giuseppe Bonaccia was losing his breath. Only the words "*Daglielo mollo, Daglielo duro*" appeared to keep him on the earth. It seemed even to the *capo* that Peppino was talking to someone who was there, in the yard with him, or just beyond the barbed wire.

"*Duro ... duro ... duro!*" The prisoner stretched out his arms passionately, desperately, with all his strength, like a bird unable to pull its feet out of a swamp. "*Duro ... duro ... duro ... o Lucrezia, non avrei creduto.*" He was breaking, bending, his heart lived no longer; he was a man who wanted to drop to the earth and forget everything upon it, whether living or dead. "*Che ti avessi avuto quattro peli.*"

He was already on his knees, trembling and speaking of Augusto, Lucrezia, and some other girls from Greece. "*Daglielo ... duro!*"

His forehead struck the ground, and there he grew quiet.

"He's dying!" the Captain cried, turning his thick eyebrows toward the *capo*.

"Don't worry, Captain," Antonio reassured him. "He isn't dying. That is the way our Peppino lives. Whenever the sun really beats down, something awakes in him. He's not dying, don't worry, Captain!"

"Translation!" the Captain commanded with subdued anger. "Word by word!"

"Should I also translate his ... er ... vulgarities?"

"Word by word."

The *capo* perspired. Even with grimaces, expressive gestures with his arms and violent movements of his whole body, he could not translate Peppe's words. The Captain kept on frowning, and the *capo*, frightened for his life, prepared to drop to his knees.

"I understand nothing at all!" the Captain snapped. "I have the impression he sang in Latin. I didn't catch a word."

"It's clear you'll never understand anything with this idiot interpreting for you!" Antonio flung off, ready for the Captain's submachine gun. "Anyhow, how can a Montenegrin elephant, a butcher, a cuntlike ape, and, all in all the lowest kind of shit ... translate Peppe's words?"

THE WAR WAS BETTER

Antonio could hardly hold himself back. He almost flung himself at the Captain and the *capo* and all the guards and keepers who were rushing up with their whistles in their mouths.

"A shit-covered asshole like that can't translate the sublime humming of an enraptured wretch!" Antonio burst out crying; he bent over Peppe as he gestured toward the Captain with extended arms. "A mangy rat . . ."

The Captain held the *capo* back. "All right, then, you translate the 'sublime humming' for me!" he said. "I want to hear, and perhaps memorize one of your shameless political songs!"

Antonio had not wept so softly and so quietly for a long time. He moved his hand across his forehead, his nose, and his dense beard. Tears were streaming over his face. It seemed to the prisoners that he himself was touched by rapture, and they were ready to take him into their arms. Bent over, staring into the sun, he began muttering. He did not translate word by word, but sought for a freer, more idiomatic rendering.

"Pooh!" the Captain spat. "Pooh!" He again held the *capo* back. "I'm sick of your filthy communistic folklore! Your disgusting camp pornography makes me sick!"

He stamped his boots, almost growling and spitting with rage, and began muttering something about the Poles, the Irish, and the Negroes, who began at once to pray to God more fervently than any of the others.

"From this day forward I forbid you to sing! I repeat! Forbidden! Forbidden! I will inform the camp command about everything!"

"Scoundrel!" Antonio screamed, and the Captain reached for his pistol. "Scoundrel and villain!"

Frail and almost weightless from lack of food, he rushed at the German, who turned around and asked the jailors not to shoot.

"Don't touch our songs! You, you shit-ass, from an army of shit-asses!" Unable to reach the Captain's submachine gun, Antonio tumbled down at the *capo*'s feet. "Our songs . . ."

"Shut up! I'll have to kill you, you communist bastard!"

The Captain, who had at first turned almost green, began to regain his normal pallor. He fired suddenly into the air to quiet the guards and jailors who were blowing their whistles like children.

One of the guards started to kick Antonio, beat him with his fists and then with the butt of his rifle. Restrained from out-and-out murder by the Captain, who was firing his submachine gun at the barbed-wire fence, the *capo*, too, began beating him with his pistol and spitting on his red beard.

"Captain, do whatever you like, shoot, kill, but don't touch Peppe's and my songs! Those few words and verses are all that remains for us!"

A siren shrieked and then began to wail. Dogs and men were barking in panic through the loudspeaker.

"Killers from the North!" Antonio screamed. They were stamping on him; sometimes it was the *capo*, sometimes the others. "Peppe's right! You're worse than the Chinese!"

They lifted him up and held him while one of the jailors tried to pull his tongue out and cut his throat.

"Killers! White Negroes! Shit-asses!"

Sobered up by the firing, Bonaccia, the petrified Brka, and the rest of the Yugoslavs stared in silence as the jailors and soldiers carried Antonio across the courtyard.

The sun beat down. It was so bright it was hard to keep one's eyes open.

"We're ninety-nine," Peppe observed.

 6

"Is my crime awful?" Peduto asked the camp commandant.

"It is," Colonel Schlotterer replied, stroking his closely cropped, already grayish hair. "What you have done is extremely serious. According to law, we should shoot you in front of all the prisoners, as an example. Ever since I met you, Peduto, you've been rushing headlong from one outrage to another."

"Punish me once," Antonio invited; the wounds on his forehead and cheekbones were smarting. "Shoot me, or pour gasoline on me, in front of all the prisoners. I'll strike the match."

Antonio felt unstable on his wooden sandals. He looked into the commandant's frowning face.

"I'll strike the match, I swear it."

"I did not call you here because of your guilt, or to be informed that you're ready to immolate yourself," the Colonel said as he offered him a chair again. "Catch your breath. It seems you've been doing too much singing."

THE WAR WAS BETTER

Antonio took a step toward the chair. He could see the commandant pouring something that looked like brandy into a water glass. He took another step, imagining the neck of the Colonel's bottle in his throat.

"Sit down, *Taliano*," Carl Schlotterer invited him as he poured brandy into another glass.

"I'm afraid I won't be able to stand up again."

"We will find someone to help you."

"I don't like to be carried. They beat me and spit on me, and then I become sorry I was ever born . . . at this time."

He took the glass and sipped from it. "Otherwise," he said, "I don't beef about anything; you never hear me complain about being in the camp." He took another sip and sat down. "Even this *grappa* is bearable."

"I did not call you here because of your transgression today," Schlotterer resumed as he poured more brandy for both of them.

"What am I doing here then?" Antonio asked; he put the glass aside.

"Listen to me again, *Taliano*," the Colonel said, looking into Antonio's large eyes. "Hear me out, perhaps for the last time."

"You do nothing but threaten."

"We've been here for one year now," the Colonel said, pausing to sip a little. "And this is the seventh or eighth time I've offered you the same thing: to go away, to bolt. Don't you believe in my good intentions?"

"No," Antonio said. He felt the brandy warming his stomach. "The intentions of a man who holds the fate of so many lives in his hands can never be good."

"But I can't let you all go."

"Then don't consider your intentions good and pure at least," Antonio rejoined. "I didn't suggest that you let everybody out. I didn't suggest anything." He felt his wounds hurting again and relished the pain they brought him. "They simply beat me up, spat on me, and brought me here. It's a real miracle they aren't here right now. You, however, are getting me drunk . . . like that day in Montenegro, the first time we met."

"You hold a grudge against me even for that, *Taliano?*"

"Yes," Antonio Peduto grunted. "I'm a mere wretch, a miserable prisoner, a former *Taliano* and the most indisciplined inmate of the Yugoslav barracks. And you're a Colonel of the great army which . . . is losing inland, on the coast, in heaven, and in the air! The only thing I don't know is how you're doing on water!" Antonio's

eyes grew a little lighter and somewhat mad. "I've got it in for you
—for being polite to me. Who granted you the right to call me
Taliano, instead of by my number, which is stamped right through
my skin into my mind!"

"You yourself are defeating all my efforts," Carl Schlotterer protested. "I'd even say you're crueler than General Herbert Siegmann." Again, he poured more brandy into both their glasses.
"Siegmann! That's the one who tested the piercing force of our lead
on human flesh." He drank. "You're an unusual man, Peduto. The
unusual man with the umpteenth number!"

"A very high number," Antonio said, feeling, as he drank more
grappa, like singing Augusto's and Peppe's songs. "The umpteenth
number ... Oh God, why did you create me and fling me down
here among mankind?" Laughing at his own insincere sigh and the
sonorous sentence, he started licking around the edge of his glass.
"And so you, sir, with number umpty, say that I'm defeating you!
How strange and impossible! Still, everybody probably has his own
General Siegmann, and it's quite possible that Siegmann himself has
his Siegmann too!"

"Very well. In order not to defeat you anymore, in order not to
be your General Siegmann, I want you to leave. Do you understand? Leave! Take Peppino with you, the one who keeps disappearing. And, anyhow, you say he's so kind to your wife. Carry
away your manuscript, which nobody but me has looked at. It's
here in my desk. The scandalous booklet of Pietro Aretino is also
there. Make me a present of it, will you? And then you can flee."

"Thank you. I deeply regret that I have to refuse again. Remember that I joined the war out of despair and of my own volition.
Nobody forced me into it. I met my Siegmann much earlier than
you did. I waded into the filth by myself, and I want to bear the
brunt without anybody else's help. I could have escaped a thousand
times; I could have escaped the day we met. But I will not depart
from the people I now share good and evil with, for better and for
worse, and Augusto's songs too, even if you say you'll kill me this
very moment. I speak for Bonaccia too. He feels the same!"

"As you wish. I'm leaving now to stop the English and the Americans who are pushing on from the south."

"God help you, sir."

"I also joined of my own volition. I'm going to defend Italy,
which the Americans want to take away from Europe, and humiliate and soil."

"It's soiled enough already," Antonio said. "We, first of all, we

Italians tried to soil and twist her. There's no trace of the old Italy anymore; there are no real Italians left there! That's why Italy should be left alone for a period of time and be neither defended, nor purged, nor cleansed, nor scoured, nor whatever you Germans want to do to her. Let's wait for the rains and the spring. Then we'll be the only ones who think the country is dirty."

"That is what you said, if I remember correctly, during our last conversation, *Taliano*."

"I hope so. If we meet again, call me *Slavo*. It's shorter."

"Is that all we can say to each other today?"

"Have a pleasant journey!" Antonio said, noticing for the first time that a small German tear was glistening in Schlotterer's eye. "Thank you for the brandy." He looked at him again: the Colonel was erect and strong. "A good wind in your sails, and don't lose your head defending Italy. Like me, you haven't the slightest idea of what it's like. . . ."

"Thank you for everything, *Slavo*. When the war ends, I'll look for you. If what we started never ends, we'll meet where it's safest. Then I, the stupid *Tedesco*, will sing Augusto's and Peppe's little songs to you."

Antonio's hands trembled. The German continued: "Thank you for the unforgettable conversations, for your impertinence, for your madness! I'll order them not to beat and spit on you until the end of the war. Good-by. Good-by, my *Slavo!*"

They stared at each other, their eyes full of brandy and light.

Dogs were barking outside.

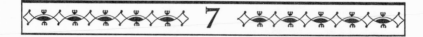 7

All the villages around Bari were burning. The prisoners stood on the tips of their toes to see the smoke rising above the barbed-wire fences and the roofs. From the south, from Brindisi, the crackling, roaring flame was spreading, devouring, and swallowing the land and covering it in smoke and darkness. Pressed against the wires, the prisoners watched the columns of German trucks, armored cars, and tanks disappear into the heat and chaos. The heavy howitzers dug in near the camp were thundering; the barbed wire and even the barrack walls and the towers were trembling. The smell of brine, polluted gunpowder, and overheated steel was everywhere.

Antonio Peduto stood among the group which was shouting back and forth with the prisoners from the neighboring barracks. Only barbed wire, a pack of dogs, and the heat of the early fall day separated them. Yet sometimes they could hardly see each other through the dense smoke which descended upon them from the sky as from a waterfall.

"Hey, don't you see your country's burning?" Antonio yelled, recognizing Spartaco Allegretti and Turiddu Barbagallo within the other group. "*Taliani*, cowards and cat-eaters, fire is sweeping away everything that was yours!"

"We don't know what you're talking about, *Slavo!*" Allegretti hollered back into the barbed wire. "We don't know what's burning or how it's burning ... as you seem to; we've been here for more than a year; our minds are all mixed up!"

"Don't you smell smoke?"

"We do, *Slavo*," the close-cropped Allegretti shouted back, clinging to Barbagallo. "But we don't know where it's coming from." Spartaco did not dare to take hold of the fence and therefore could not see very well; from a few feet off he was teasing the dogs and spitting on them. "It does look like something's burning, though," he shouted. "Maybe the sea bottom has caught fire, and the fish are roasting. That would explain all this smoke."

"The devil is taking your country, *Taliani!*" Antonio yelled; Peppe, Brka and several other Yugoslavs repeated the words after him.

"It won't be the first time, *Slavo!*" Allegretti replied, looking at them in amazement. "We still see nothing, though. But, *Madonna*, something terrible and ugly does seem to be happening to the earth and the water!" He drew back from the dogs who were dashing themselves against the fence. "How is it you see something and we see nothing?"

"The big brute we're holding up on our shoulders is looking for us," Antonio said, pointing at Peppino. "We're lucky he isn't heavy. He can also prophesy."

"Let him tell us what he sees too. We'll listen." Smoke choked him and he began to cough. "Let him find out what's wrong with the water. Oh, God, what smoke!"

"Heaven and earth are burning," Giuseppe Bonaccia reported "Fire has burrowed into the rocks and grapevines. Rocks are bursting; crevices are opening up, and cattle and grass are falling into them. Everything smells of wool, skin, and salt. This is a real war, I tell you!"

Peppe could hardly keep himself on their shoulders; he screened his eyes from the light and the wind.

"A real war, a war again, and they talk so much about peace.

"Birds are fleeing from the smoke, seeking refuge in church steeples. They are burning up there like black figs. Lord, don't take the birds' wings away! Tear the leaves of smoke from their beaks, give them water!"

"Hey, *Slavo!*" Allegretti called, bursting into tears. "How terrible it is—what your mad eyes see!"

"Go on, Bonaccia," Peduto urged him. "You're the only one who can see!"

"Bread is burning!" Peppino went on in a broken voice. "Hard and bitter bread is turning into coal and ashes, and no mouths will ever eat it again." His eyes were even larger than before, when they had been holding him up on their shoulders; the dogs and barracks and all the barbed wire were reflected in them.

"Wine is burning; all the springs are burning! Mother, my only one, save a little earth for my girls and for my future house, for my grave!" He was weeping and floating above them, as light as if he were made of rags. "Our Montenegro is burning up!"

"This is Italy burning, Peppino!" Antonio yelled from below. "Their Italy and their grapes! This is not Montenegro, soldier! Montenegro has already burned up, Bonaccia, our son! Do you hear me? It's not Montenegro; there's nothing left to burn there!"

"Now I don't understand anything anymore, my mad *Slavi*," Allegretti lamented. About a hundred Italian prisoners were crowding around him. "Where does such a fire come from! Which country is burning?"

"Whenever I see fire like this, surging out of the earth like water, I say to myself: 'Look, our Montenegro's burning again,'" Peppe said. "For a while, when you were holding me up, I thought another country had caught fire, one called Italy, but it isn't so! The country where Augusto, my brother, has remained; that is the country which is burning. I feel it by the burns between my legs; they're itching and smarting now. The fire of Montenegro is the only fire of the world; it is the fire which singes your eyelashes and curdles your blood!" He was weeping and laughing. "Save me, people, I'm falling! Pardon me, forgive me. It must be a mistake I'm making. When my wounds ache and my eyes fill up with smoke, the only thing I can see is Montenegro; I see its terrible pits and landslides!"

He fell down. The others picked him up and carried him along beside the barbed-wire fence and the yelping dogs.

"I won't go up again, my good people," he murmured. "I won't go up. I can't see the bread and wine burn anymore; I can't look at the grass where they spilled Augusto's brains and blood. Don't lift me up, don't torture me."

"I still can't see anything," Allegretti cried out in terror, "but I can hear the cannons firing and the sound of planes!" He begged the Yugoslavs not to leave the fence. "I don't know who's shooting, but it doesn't matter; it's bound to be good for us. Water and peace will come after all this thunder!" He reeled along the fence while the others around him began to giggle. "I don't care whose country is burning! I'm mad with love for life, I'm insane with fear! Go on, Turiddu, let's begin! So that everyone can see—everything!"

Antonio Peduto and the Yugoslavs watched Turiddu Barbagallo, the skinny prisoner with protruding jaws and oblique eyes, jam some string into Allegretti's mouth. He tied one tooth with it, and then stepped aside.

"May we?" Turiddu asked.

"You may, sons."

At Spartaco's signal, the prisoners started to pull the string and shake it up and down. They shuffled along beside the fence, some tottering and others crawling, teasing the guards and the many dogs, and cursing in dialect. Allegretti crept behind them and wailed.

"Ah!"

The string broke. Barbagallo breathlessly lifted high an extracted tooth. Allegretti turned toward Antonio and the others and spat blood.

"Only two left now," he said, "but they're molars."

He opened his mouth wide, showing his raw gums. "This is the way to take care of teeth, my mad *Slavi!*"

"What are you doing, *Taliano?*" Antonio shouted, almost choking on his own laughter and tears.

"I don't know whose country is burning. I know even less who's shooting and why, but I sense that peace is near!" He chewed blood and spittle. "I don't even know where we are anymore, or whose prisoners we are. The one thing I'm sure of is that peace is near. I smell its stench. Peace stinks, *Slavo*; it stinks horribly. You've got to realize that. Otherwise you'll choke to death on the first day!"

"What's the connection between the stinking peace and your stinking teeth?"

"Peace must be greeted without teeth." He spat out the remains of the extracted tooth, and wound the string around his finger. "When the last tooth goes, then there'll be peace outside. Don't let the Germans get wise to it. They'll start pulling out each other's teeth too, or gluing the extracted ones back into my gums!" The prisoners were laughing at his jumbled words, and Antonio could hardly understand him. "In peace, anyhow, nobody'll need teeth. There'll be nothing to eat but shit!"

"Keep at least one!" Brka advised him. "As a war souvenir, of Montenegro, of the only time you were a man. At least one."

"Not a single one, *Slavi!*" Allegretti grinned. "Not even a molar!" He laughed, made faces at the dogs, and teased them with pebbles, which he first licked and covered with bloody spittle, and then threw over the fence. "*Slavi*, my mad *Slavi*, declare war on teeth! Whoever wants me to pull one for him, just let me know! He can stick his jaws through the fence!"

Then the *capo* and the Captain came, and Antonio and the Yugoslavs watched them beat him. They hit him with a wet rope and then with a bone. He threw himself on their feet, and they kicked him with their boots.

"Communist!" the bristling *capo* growled. "A real Italian communist!" The *capo* struck him with the butt of his pistol and stamped on his stomach until Allegretti's mouth fell open and blood dripped out of it. "A communist who wants to live without teeth! A parasite! ... That's what communists are!"

"Here's one for the teeth you pulled out last Friday!" the Captain yelled, striking his face with an aluminum messtin. "And this one is for today's tooth, you provocateur, you bad apple!" The messtin caved in, stained with blood; Allegretti lay on the ground unconscious. "Here's some more, and more, you peace-loving communist! We know what kind of peace! A toothless, rotten peace!"

Then not only the Captain and the *capo*, but also the rest of the guards started kicking and pummeling his body. With their faces smeared with drops of Spartaco's blood, they kicked and grinned and bared their teeth. The well-rested orderlies were also arriving, carrying submachine guns and chains; whenever they stopped blowing their whistles, they showed their teeth. Even the dogs were growling, licking the wire and the barbs, and the sand around Allegretti's body; their teeth too were sound, white, and sharp. The other Italians were packed into the far end of the yard; they were frightened and grinned like clowns, thus revealing that their mouths were still full of teeth.

"Whoever, of his own accord, rids himself of an eye, an ear, a tooth, or any other necessary and useful organ, and especially whoever performs such a deed in front of others, with a view to disturbing our order and inviolable camp brotherhood and unity," the Captain intoned, "will answer for it not only before the law, but also before the court of honor and the council of ten!'"

Dogs darted between the barbed-wire fences and barracks and among the guards. Wisps of smoke billowed from their mouths, as if they were portending some unforeseeable disaster.

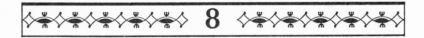

8

Antonio Peduto, Giuseppe Bonaccia, and the other Yugoslavs lay quietly in the sun, warming their shins and elbows and listening to the crackling of the fire and the thundering of the artillery. The earth shook down to its foundations; even the giant pillars of the hydroelectric power station were trembling, and the walls of the barracks began to groan and crack in earnest.

"How long will it last, Peppe?"

"One year."

Giuseppe Bonaccia looked out over the rutted road where hunched-over tanks were plodding slowly toward the south. He sniffed at the air, and corrected himself: "One year, probably two."

"Too much, son, too much," Brka lamented calmly. "How come two years, our luckless Peppino?"

"If not two, then surely three," Giuseppe Bonaccia persisted, watching the trucks carry the dusty German troops away. "Three years, if not four."

"Why are you adding years, *Napolitano?*" Antonio scolded him. "First you said one year, and now four. Please don't add."

"Am I adding?" Giuseppe Bonaccia's big, wet eyes bulged with surprise. "You mean I'm not subtracting?"

"Lie down and rest," Antonio urged him as he stretched out again beside Brka. "You're adding. You should stop for a while."

"I thought I was subtracting," Bonaccia said dazedly, and curled up at Antonio's feet like a dog. "I'm sorry, I can't count or calculate anymore. Ever since last winter my numbers and letters started getting mixed up, and my letters got mixed up with my words and the barbed wire. I'm sorry I cheated and insulted you. I didn't want to. I didn't want to scare you either."

THE WAR WAS BETTER

They were all lying down now, one beside the other, breathing in the smell of gunpowder and sulphur and the sea.

"I won't do it anymore," Bonaccia murmured once again. "No, I don't know how long the war is going to last anymore. Perhaps it's ended already, and we've been condemned to stay here, forgotten. Days and years have gotten mixed up in my mind; I can't distinguish them anymore. All I feel is that disaster and evil will last for a long time. I wouldn't even call it evil; it wouldn't be evil if it weren't endless. Evil and disaster have a taste and a color; I can smell them in the air." Again, he sniffed the barbed wire and the fence posts. "The evil is here, somewhere here. The earth is breathing and buzzing and budging like an anthill filled with smoke. People, come back and embrace me. I'm sorry. Forgive me. It's what I feel: the evil, the blackest evil is aprowl now, looking for us."

Lying near their feet, he looked up at the camouflaged hydroelectric station and listened to the water, muttering that he could no longer even tell apart the pebbles he was holding in his hands. They caressed him and urged him not to tire himself out by weeping.

"Look, birds!" Peduto sighed and extended his arms toward the sky. "White birds!" he added, pointing toward a squadron of planes. "How nice the planes are! . . . Ah, look at them!"

The prisoners looked carefully at Antonio's hands, and then at the smoke. They coughed until it seemed they would suffocate. Peduto asked them not to move, but to lie on their backs and watch the birds.

"Americans," Brka observed. "They haven't been here for five hours."

"Americans, shit!" Antonio spat on the fence. "That's Malić!"

"Malić?" Brka's eyes opened; his head popped up as from a dream. "Gruban Malić!" He wanted to get up, but Antonio pushed him back onto the sand. "Where is he?"

"He's always up there!" Antonio answered. "But you can't see him whenever you like, Brka. Malić is a dragon. . . . Our Montenegrin dragon!"

"They're Americans," Brka repeated from below. "It sounds like ten of them again. The eleventh is leading them."

"They're all Malić's planes!" Antonio said, letting his tears pour into the other's ears. "A pilot without Malić's heart in his bosom is no hero, but an old woman!"

Intoxicated by the smoke and the dreadful racket, Antonio looked up ecstatically at the dragons which were racing across the sky with bomb loads and machine-gun bursts flashing from under their wings. "The leader is truly a Malić," he murmured. "That one of yours, the eleventh one. Not only does he have Gruban's heart, but also his thoughts, his soul, his madness!" He wept, and as the planes, maneuvering in a vast circle, disappeared from sight momentarily in order to reappear above Bari and the sea, he wagged his head. "Take care of yourself, and stay up there as long as you can, my Gruban!"

Bombs began splashing into the sea. It seemed to Antonio that suddenly the sky was full of water and splattered fish. Whistles sounded. Dogs rushed at the barbed wire, or began digging up their hidden bones.

"Malić is a Russian," Peppe said, as if revealing a secret.

"I wouldn't say that," Brka protested. "First you say he's American, now Russian. He's either one or the other. Maybe he's something else altogether: a Montenegrin, our pride!"

"Malić is everything I've never been able to be," Giuseppe Bonaccia remarked, standing up next to them. "When the Venezia and Murge divisions still existed, I kept going to his little brothel. He hid nothing from me. He told me the story of his Russian descent. He told me about the nameless circus which left him at the town well, wrapped up in swaddling clothes. He's truly a Russian. He spoke several Russian words. He even forced me to remember them and pronounce them in front of the other soldiers. Everything he's done so far, not just with our poor divisions, but with himself too, has revealed the truth about him more and more clearly."

"How could a Russian be with the Americans? Eh, Peppino?"

"Sometimes Americans are Russians too," Antonio put in. "When they're brave and think they're going to conquer and renew the whole world. Malić will be quicker; he'll get there before everyone else. Then the women of the whole world will see what justice is; they will know the tenderness that kills; they will find out about a hero's leaden balls . . . that reach down to his knees!"

"Malić is Russian," Peppino said, starting to cry because no one believed him. "He didn't know a single German word. Like me, anyhow until they caught me."

"Oh, my children!" Brka said to Antonio and Peppino. "My good, mad children!"

Just then it happened: what Bonaccia had prophesied a moment ago. It occurred. It came so suddenly and unexpectedly it seemed indeed to be a miracle. The squadron of white planes reappeared from the sea, fanned out, and began to bomb the fortifications and roads branching off from Bari toward the south and the north. The eleventh plane, the lead one, zoomed over the camp, and Antonio and Brka had to abbreviate their tales of Malić and Montenegro. The explosion of a bomb drowned out the volleys of the German antiaircraft guns, the roaring of the heavy howitzers and mortars. Even before Brka and Antonio could look at each other, could tell each other with a glance that the last bomb had hit that longed-for, most-guarded target, a chain of explosions erupted, and all the earth and barbed wire shook.

Antonio opened his mouth to say that the fuel, ammunition, and explosives long hidden deep in tunnels and trenches were igniting and blowing up. But the words had no time to come out. Dirt, muddy water and a horrible stench hit him. Dust, smoke and an infernal din buried everything they had known and seen up to that moment. They held onto their pebbles and clutched the heaving earth like leaves in the wind. When they opened their eyes, they found themselves buried under the heap like corpses.

There were no camp guards any more, no *capo,* and not even the Captain, who had stopped beating them so much recently and begun spitting on them more. If a naïve or, let us say, honest man had come upon the scene, he would have thought an immense fire was enveloping the entire camp. However, even worse things had occurred—events so terrible and so all-encompassing that few could survive them.

Of the Yugoslav barracks, only a few gutted walls and pillars remained standing; the roof had been altogether blown off. From those ugly stumps, and from the earth and the camp beds, flames were surging. But not only the airplanes, it seemed, were bringing fire.

The dogs were the first to get out from under. Wounded, mad, howling like wolves, they began choking on the foam from their own gaping jaws and the unusually thick smoke. They too, like the fire, attacked human flesh and blood. But they seemed to shrink from the dried-up limbs and ribs of the prisoners. Instead, they assaulted the German guards and soldiers, who wailed and invoked *Madonna* and Christ, and cursed America and the American Air Force.

Antonio Peduto was among those the dogs skipped in order to prey on the fresher, racially sounder German flesh. He got up slowly, ready at any moment to fall on his face again. The water was rising rapidly. The wire fence and the fence posts alone would never have been enough to stop the high waves rolling toward them like mountains.

"Malić has hit the dam!" he said, and felt the water sweep the ground out from under his feet. "Oh, how terrible and merciless a destroyer my Gruban Malić is!" he murmured. And then a new wave of water and straw pushed him against the wire gate.

Lifted and flung at the wire, giddy with waves and the wind whistling over them, Antonio could now see not only the whole camp, with the hundredth barracks and the crematory under construction, but also the surrounding hills and the hydroelectric power station, which had been heavily guarded only a few moments before. The dam had broken at several places, and the lake was roaring out. The water was sweeping down the living and dead Germans from the special regiment, and all their belongings as well.

"No more war," Antonio seemed to dream, with his mouth full of frog spawn and algae. "This is probably the way every peace comes," he thought, seeing the fence and his gate post shake. "The peace my Malić brings will be terrible. Anything will be possible." He sensed his strength and consciousness dwindling. "Oh, God, where am I?" he muttered, watching the water carry away flowers and blood. It seemed to him that his throat and belly were filling up with barbed wire, stones, and straw.

The water from the lake flowed out with tremendous force, forking in several directions. The first stream, pulling down with it the supporting walls of the power station, swept in its path all the barracks, concrete bunkers, and houses constructed in front of the dam. The second pushed on before it whole bridges and scaffolds with grills and flags. The third stream flooded everything so completely it seemed to carry away the entire road crammed with trucks, armored cars, and tanks. And finally, a fourth stream surged from the very depths of the lake, and flooded all eight battalions of soldiers who had just arrived from Brindisi as a special reinforcement for the special regiment. A moment before, they had been in formation, two by two, fully equipped with rifles, knapsacks, and helmets, and ready to die an honorable death on dry land. The water disturbed and moistened their battle formation. They resisted it as best they could, wading through the dark-green, rubbery waves, sinking into algae and greasy grass and shooting up at a new squadron of Malić planes.

Then all four currents joined. It was a kind of invasion, merciless and swift as fire or plague; nobody could tell which current engulfed the barracks and then ravaged them again and again. Even Antonio himself, high up against the gate post, never knew.

He came to entangled in wires and almost tied up into a knot.

THE WAR WAS BETTER

The water was still rising, reaching for his heart; it seemed to him that he too was turning in the dirty whirlpool of this new, suddenly formed, artificial lake. He opened his eyes slowly, watching the water carry away rifles, straps, bows without arrows and various other torture devices.

Foam floated around him, oat bread and gnawed bones, shavings, yellow flour and bran, crushed barley and saddles made of shining leather. Saws, pickaxes and hatchets, knives and scissors for killing cattle and prisoners floated past. A few tar-painted posts drifted to and fro, anchored by their roots of iron and concrete.

The half-constructed crematory, a large house covered with roses, ivy, cyclamens, and grapevines, which had been painted phosphorescent in order to attract prisoners and the shipwrecked at night, was being pulled down now by the water. Wires trimmed with metal laces, little knots and poison barbs, like arrows and crushed razor blades; all the wires of all the camps and stores floated around Antonio, even glistening, decorative wires rolled in balls and ready for unwinding and humane application.

Since the water was flowing very slowly out of the valley, if it flowed at all and could flow anywhere, ammunition was afloat everywhere: all the ammunition at the camp, as well as the ammunition in the power station; everything which had not yet blown up; ammunition dry a moment ago, softly greased in order not to rust; ammunition made for every caliber and every type of weapon, rifle and machine-gun bullets, cartridge clips and belts, tamtam and bumbum bullets, and bullets with colored tops and capsules like fish eyes.

Bombs too swam up from the bottom, German bombs with handles of light wood, small bombs and very big bombs, all with water, mud and fish spawn flowing into them. With the least movement, but the most dignity, the platelike mines, made to wait underground and explode the caterpillar tracks of enemy tanks, floated past, condemned to bathe and turn on their prickly backs like blind kittens. Reddish grenades and heavy cannonballs floated by in great numbers like schools of fish; they were more numerous than everything but the shells from the bulky howitzers and mountain cannons, and the flame- and lead-throwers.

There was no one there to touch off the powder, that dry and beautiful substance, like salt or some strange bird food, that floated past in cups, bags and boxes, and with the other explosives. Oh, what powder, how much dynamite and nitroglycerin, how many German pearls were floating among the cannon barrels, among the overturned trucks and uniformed soldiers of the special regiment!

THE WAR WAS BETTER

Entire barracks filled with living, sick, or already dead prisoners were afloat: all the barracks, ninety-nine of them, not counting the hundredth; barracks with flags and poles stretching high into the finally liberated sky; barracks that were burning and choking in their own smoke and shit and stench of all kinds; all the barracks, especially the notorious Yugoslav, Greek, and English ones, seemed to be floating, including those from which American Negroes, French, Albanians and Irishmen, Senegalese and Dutch, Turks and Canadians were leaping out into the long-awaited flood. Now all of them could drink the lake water about which they had sung for months and years, in almost every language; now all of them could gather and smell the water lilies and the wildflowers that grow on mountains.

But all those poor devils, including the German guards, soldiers, and *capos*, who continued to command, whistle and shout as if the war had not ended, as if the long-dreamed-of peace had not come, a full hour ago; all of them drank less, but choked more. Then, dying, they continued to flow together, to embrace, to whisper and lick each other. It was not easy for the water under them. Their mouths fell open; they ate ammunition and powder, which swelled in their bellies; they started to resemble balloons or puppets; they seemed to be chewing on the water, as if it were clogged with dirt and bones, to be spitting it out and stroking it like real swimmers. And finally they pissed into it and turned their backs impertinently to the land.

Although the water circled sluggishly around its own axis, it was still rising and began to cover Antonio's body rib by rib. It reached above his heart, stifled his breathing, and robbed him of speech. His head spun. He could vomit nothing but gasoline and straw. He awaited the moment when his whole body would freeze up and rest forever.

He could no longer think, nor even murmur, as he had before, when the water had been beautiful and powerful, signaling the genuine end of war and slavery, the first moments of peace and joy. Losing sight of the mountains and the far-off sky, he resigned himself to the wind and the foam. He could not even put his hands together; the water held them apart. He did not have time to ask himself who he was, or what had brought him there. A piece of skin and a plump human ear lobe floated up to his open mouth. Somehow, he found the strength to scream and spit it out, with another little piece of human flesh.

"Pooh! Skin!" he said, still chewing veins and hair. "Pooh! What a punishment!"

"Hey, *Slavo!*"

THE WAR WAS BETTER

It was a voice which sounded dry, and seemed to come from heaven. So he would not die alone, Antonio thought, swallowing roots, human nails, and hair. He wanted to stop the wind and the water with his hands, but he was caught on top of the fence, with his head turned toward the land.

"Hey! It looks like you're still alive!"

Only then did Antonio begin to remember that before he had come to this crest of the bloody water, he had been with some other people, and there might be other survivors. He did not know how to answer the nearby and now very familiar voice. Finally he called out weakly: "I'm alive."

"There's no war anymore! Look up. Peace has begun. Peace is everywhere!"

"It shouldn't have come, such as it is."

"Whatever it is—it's here!" the voice observed, drinking in water. "Peace is made for us, the cowards."

"Who are you?" A beam with boards still nailed to it rushed past Antonio's head. "Hey, cowards!"

"Don't you know me? Don't you remember me? The insane one, the one who's been mad from happiness and love . . . and fear since the day of his birth! Come on, look up, and you'll see . . . Oh, shit!"

Carried by the strong current, all tied up with ropes, chains, and barbed wire, a barracks was floating past. In the doors and windows, there were no longer the starved, skull-like faces with the yearning human eyes which Antonio would never be able to forget. On the roof without a chimney, half naked and shaggy as a bumblebee, Spartaco Allegretti was just keeping his balance. Half in the water and half in the air, Turiddu Barbagallo trembled beside him.

"I think we knew each other in the camp, some months ago," Spartaco said. "We shouted to each other, sang together, cursed each other."

"I don't remember it," Antonio said, smiling painfully. "We've never met. I've never sung with you. You don't know our songs."

"Although you're a *Slavo*, and I'm a *Taliano*, we know how to sing the same words. We admired your pronunciation. You must have spent a long time in Italy. You damn red *Slavo*. That's what you are, all of you!"

"I never saw you before in my life," Antonio repeated, remembering Montenegro. "Don't look so surprised. I don't know you, that's all there is to it."

"I pulled my teeth out right in front of you," Allegretti reminded him with his bulging eyes peering out of the water like a bullfrog's. "You laughed at me. You couldn't understand why I did it. I kept telling you I did it for peace; now peace has finally come and found me ready."

"You're ... I think I know ..." It all came back to Antonio with a rush. "Yes, you're the mad *Taliano* from the barracks across the way, the one who kept saying teeth wouldn't be necessary in peace, since anyhow, as you said, all we'd ever eat would be shit!" His swollen eyes began to smart. "If you're the one... let the devil and the water carry you away!"

"Look! No teeth anywhere!" Spartaco Allegretti opened his mouth, which was filled with wood shavings and straw. "They took even my molars out, for cigarettes." He opened his mouth again and worked his jaws. "Now I'm a real man. And you, red one, how have you greeted the peace?"

A wave slapped Antonio on the forehead. It seemed to him suddenly that it was not water and wind which surrounded him, but powder and chaff. For a moment he did not know where he was, nor who it was who was talking to him about teeth, jaws and pre-softened postwar food. When he looked up, he saw Allegretti on the roof without a chimney.

"Look, I'm still alive," Antonio thought to himself, and smiled.

Spartaco was making funny gestures with his arms. He pretended he was rowing, pushing his barracks-barge toward land. At the same time, he was spitting and spluttering, imitating Breitbach: "Hop! . . . Here's peace! Hop! One-two-three!" Through it all he was coughing, and half his body was submerged. "Peace ... on all fronts, everywhere! Now we're safe, nobody can do anything to us cowards!"

"We've never sung together," Antonio repeated, and bent his head just in time before an incoming wave.

"Hop! Hold on, *Slavo!*"

Allegretti caught hold of a chain and cast it into Antonio's barbed wire.

"I'll pull you up, don't worry. I like fools, and my heart has remained in Montenegro! Hop! Peace without end, peace as long as the chain I've thrown you!"

Antonio felt pain in his bones and then, before he had time to tell himself that this was it, the end of everything, the highest wave he had ever seen loomed before him, approaching with the speed of the wind. It looked like dirty sheepskin and left behind it a wake of foam and tumult. No one had the slightest idea how to hide from it. Only the toothless Allegretti began to wail.

Then the wave engulfed them.

THE WAR WAS BETTER

 9

Antonio found himself on a heap of boards, he did not know
how. Allegretti and his faithful Barbagallo were nowhere to be seen.
A barracks similar to theirs, except with a chimney, was floating
nearby without a crew. Shivering from cold, he could see the current carrying off children, cattle, and Germans. The living and the
dead seemed to be reaching out their arms toward him. He hadn't
the strength to throw a board or rope to them, or even the dog collar which he had found somehow on his shoulder. Almost fainting
with exhaustion, he looked out at them in despair, begging them in
his thoughts to pardon him. Islands of debris were heaping up and
mixing: ox horns and helmets, freezing children, and large loaves of
bread.

The water rose swiftly, heaving and swelling like an abscess, lifting the boards, and Antonio on them, effortlessly. It was not merely
lashing at the shore; it was climbing it; it drowned stone after stone,
roof after roof. Paths and roads, graveyards and steeples, orchards
and ripe cherry trees disappeared beneath it.

There was no war anymore, no sound of it. The water was the
great pacifier. Propping himself on his elbows, Antonio could see
the water going on and on, rising and swelling out toward distant
villages and towns.

He turned and saw the sea, blue and pure, as if it were made of
some other substance.

"Now we'll go there," he muttered to the sea. "Now we'll come
and trouble you."

There was a roaring under him; he felt drunk and sick, as if
someone were digging into his stomach and pulling out his entrails.
And still the water grew and grew, with terrifying speed, as in a feverish dream; even the pale, serene sky did not seem far from its
angry clutches.

"Now we'll reach you, sun. We'll darken you. We'll kiss your
upturned lips."

Then Bonaccia emerged from the water, clutching a door like a
spider. His eyes were glassy and circled in like targets. With one
hand he gripped Antonio's knapsack, from which the turtle pro-

THE WAR WAS BETTER

truded; with the other he held onto his door. The turtle seemed happy to have risen so high, and she drank continuously.

"Peppino!" Antonio could hardly speak, and Bonaccia did not hear him. "The strangest soldier and man I ever knew!" he mumbled; he could feel the water clutching into his belly again.

Shivering, almost naked, wet and scratched all over, Giuseppe Bonaccia could not even hear his own heart. Antonio pulled the door toward him, grabbed his foot, and pulled him onto the boards. Glassy-eyed as an epileptic, Peppino struck the wood with the back of his neck. Then, chewing water and powder, he said something tender to the turtle.

"Don't be afraid," Antonio said, stroking his close-cropped hair. "I'm not the *capo*. Don't tremble. I'm Antonio, your red dog!"

"I don't believe it," Peppe murmured, gazing fixedly at the sun. "I don't believe in anything anymore."

"Believe in me at least," Antonio said hurriedly, laughing at his own words. "Since I believe so much in you."

"Take the knapsack."

He seemed to be weeping, but he was not; waves lapped at his face.

"The water has taken away only a few pages. The rest are soaked, but who cares? Songs remain songs, regardless," Peppe murmured. "Especially if those wonderful, indecent drawings from the sand and Augusto's songs are all on those pages, as you once told me."

"Why didn't you let it all go? Believe me, that's what I'd have done with your letters." Antonio was caressing him and protecting him from the water. "You could have lost your head."

"I knew the songs and the turtle were the only things that kept you alive. And I vowed I would die before I let them go."

His eyes were losing the gloss of an epileptic's; the sky was reflected in them. "Where am I?" he asked suddenly. "Are we sailing around Greece? Are we climbing up to Montenegro?"

"They say there's no war anymore, that peace has just begun."

"Does it mean that peace brings water? Or maybe it's the other way round?" Left without an answer, he kept silent for a long time. "Or are peace and water one and the same thing?"

"It seems peace and water are one and the same devil."

"Why did we look forward to it so eagerly?"

"They tortured us with thirst. Don't you remember?"

"It would have been better if the Montenegrin fire had burned us up," Bonaccia admitted. "It's nicer to burn up than to rot away

[145]

in this filthy lake like a sick fish. As for me, I'd just as soon the war
never stopped. At least one writes letters, sings, and weeps, one after
the other, until he's killed. And finally, whenever you want to, you
can enter the flames, and say good-by to the girls of all the
world. . . ."

"The water's rising faster and faster," Antonio observed. "Soon
it will cover the mountain top we dreamed so much about and sent
kisses to from the camp. The waves are already lapping at its feet."

Peppe swallowed, and then vomited up powder and algae for a
long time.

"I'm finished," he said finally. "I'm going to die in front of your
eyes. I'm going to put us both to shame!" He gasped, and his eyes
rolled. "Let the water carry me away; let me join the others."

He vomited again—this time straw, wire and sand.

"Antonio, be my friend, at least today, push me down! I can't
hold out; I'll never survive the peace. It's so disgusting and damp!"

Peduto knelt on the makeshift raft. He could see the walls of the
hydroelectric power station cracking under the onrushing water,
and disappearing in the raging foam. The sky was so clear above the
dam that it seemed that Malić's planes had never flown in it.

A new flood was threatening not only the mountains and the
rocks now, but also the quiet sea. There were no more shots or explosions. Everything seemed to be abandoned to the whim and somber rage of the flood.

Antonio did not have time to tell Peppino that he would not let
him sink. A filthier and muddier wave than any before it appeared,
carrying peasant houses, tombs, and thick walls from the power station. It would have surely crushed them altogether, this wave, if it
had not sunk; if this monster full of water and old bones and crosses
had not tumbled into the black abyss which suddenly gaped before
it, received it softly like a mouth, and then closed! A terrible crash
seemed to break the poor wave in half; its skin tightened; its ribs
cracked; it was too narrow down there in the darkness.

The water tried to push back toward the surface, and erupt
against all three mountains. Antonio was seized by fear that the hell
which had broken loose would split his raft; he hugged Peppe.

The water suddenly opened up again, like the earth, with a horrible uproar. It was the last thing that Antonio heard and remembered: the water beginning to whirl about, to overflow, raging up
from the abyss. The waves lifted Antonio and Peppe, who were
hugging each other as tightly as they could around the knapsack,

more lightly, more softly than the other bodies and things. Then one pitched them, senseless, more dead than alive, high into the air.

They woke up breathing and shivering, without knowing they were on land, in a bed of flowers.

Scratched and bloody, Antonio Peduto and Giuseppe Bonaccia lay wet and exhausted in a sunlit field of barley. They were plucking cherries from a young tree and eating them. A mild wind was billowing the barley, which scratched and tickled their ears. This made them think they were probably still on the earth, and near some human settlement. Still, it was just as probable that the wave had carried them straight to hell. There was only one way to find out. They parted the barley and the grass and examined what was below. A shiver convulsed them. They trembled again and feared they would start vomiting up powder and cherries.

Antonio was on his knees, with the turtle in his arms. He caressed her broken little leg and whispered to her, "My dear one, my darling, don't be afraid, all the wounds will heal, mine and yours. The bones will join, love. Males will fall at your feet just as if nothing had happened, and beg you to satisfy them."

Anna-Maria was trembling. A poignant grief overwhelmed Antonio's heart. He bandaged her knee with a little piece of cloth, and bound it with a barley stalk.

"Cattolica," he said, "Peppino and I will caress and kiss your wounds; soon they will heal and be like new. Calm down now, our only one, don't be afraid."

The little body under the shell would not keep still; Antonio's eyes began to burn. He clasped her to his chest, hoping to warm her.

"My sun," he whispered, "stop trembling. Look, water is everywhere. The soil where the barracks were standing is covered, drowned; nobody will ever be able to dig holes for those filthy posts again, or weave the wires around them. Water's carried everything away that was so horrible. Soon it will cover even these hills of ours. The last time I asked you to look around, we were in Montenegro, about to be burned alive. You remember those unhappy whores, our *Ortodosse;* I remember them too. But remember also what you see today. It's like this, probably, that every peace begins. The peace which many people call happiness."

It seemed to Antonio that she understood him. He was exhausted and yearned for sleep, but he continued with a broken voice:

"Calm down and don't be sorry for them. When the flood subsides, if it ever does, we'll start out again for Rome. We'll get to Via dei Serpenti. We'll find Romana and all the other sisters. Now just take a good look at the water running wild, carrying the poor people's crops away, and ask your Balkan heart to calm down."

"Leave me now." Bonaccia was weeping in the barley field. "Go on alone. I'm no longer necessary. I'll stink more in the peace they're talking about than in the war. Just push me a little. I want to go downstream."

"We'll go downstream together, if the peace is really worse than the war," Antonio called out as he looked over at Bonaccia, who was rolled up tightly into a ball. "We'll go far away, maybe back to Montenegro. We'll join Augusto and his girls. If the peace is nothing but water, stench and immorality . . ."

They walked slowly through the barley field, eating cherries and then vomiting as if they had swallowed the whole power station. Shepherds, and even the cattle, fled from them. They told each other that the water was too ugly and frightening, that they shouldn't look at it, but they could not tear their eyes from the vast artificial lake. A rumbling echo of grinding earth and rocks resounded like thunder in the valley from which the gigantic pool was flowing.

Helping each other on like wounded men, they came to a clearing. From there, their eyes reached the sea. They stood gazing out along the country path which was rutted and crowded with cattle and fragrant with hay and dung. For a long time they remained there, in peace, warming their ribs and knees in the sun, and it would have been longer, except for a clamor which suddenly broke out nearby.

It came from two prisoners pitched out of the water like themselves, who were trying to explain their situation to two American soldiers. Antonio and Peppe recognized Allegretti and Barbagallo.

"Ever since I've been a soldier, and I've been one since the day I was born—because I'm an Italian and a Sicilian—my heart has been with you and . . . what you're bringing!" It was the living corpse of Allegretti, looking up at the dam and talking at top speed. "I love you, my little wonderful America!" A third soldier had come up to join the others. He rushed to embrace and kiss all three. "America, which we discovered, the Italians!"

"Oh yes," the first American said in English, and then continued in Italian: "Understand only half ... what you say, but is exact! Is a fact! A fact!" He was dodging Allegretti, who was getting him wet. "Oh yes, *Taliano*, oh yes!"

"Me, *Taliano*, also speak truth!" Spartaco said, pausing and pointing his finger at his hairy breast. "*Taliano* always speak truth."

"Oh yes!" the American repeated, stepping back. "*Taliano* speak truth, and *Americano* believe all, in spite of history. *Americano* believe everything, *Americano stupido*, but *buono!*"

"Since our adolescence, all our daydreams have been about you, all of us have dreamt of you!" Allegretti burst out crying and grabbed the chocolate bar which the other American had hardly gotten out of his pocket. "Why haven't you come earlier, *Americano?* We've been waiting for you for at least ten years." With his toothless mouth, he was munching both the chocolate and the wrapping. "Oh God, to wait for somebody one and a half centuries, and finally to meet him! This is meat, American and sweet! Some special American process, it must be. Nowhere a sinew, nowhere a bone! Isn't it so, Barbagallo?"

"Oh yes," Turiddu Barbagallo agreed in English, almost choking on his chocolate bar. "Oh yes," he repeated. "*Americano buono. Americano* believe everything. *Americano* foolish and good."

"*Americano* believe, oh yes. *Americano* love unhappy Italy," the first American put in as he extended a small package of chocolate, chewing gum, and oat flour to each of them. "*Americano* love little old tortured Europe. *Americano* have hobby: miserable and sick Europe."

"What's he saying, Turiddu?" Allegretti asked in dialect. "You've always had an interest in barbarian languages."

"He says he doesn't steal. I don't believe him. I believe nothing he says. ... He says he likes gambling, poker."

"They probably don't have any cherries," Allegretti observed. "Give each of them a handful. Give them as many as they want. Fill them up. They'll shit from cherries, as we did in Greece. That's the way it should be with the victors!"

"Oh yes," both Americans said, nibbling leaves from the branch which Barbagallo bent and pushed under their noses

[149]

THE WAR WAS BETTER

"Oh yes," the third one, a Negro, also said, without daring to take the cherries. "Oh yes, we love good old hospitable Italian people. We die for Italy and for fresh fruit."

Allegretti and Barbagallo were choking on the oatmeal, chewing gum, and paper wrapping, while the Americans choked on leaves and twigs.

"Oh yes," the Negro said, with his mouth full of cherry leaves and stalks, bark and buds, "oh yes!" He caught at his stomach and rolled his eyes. "*Grazie, Taliano.*" He took the knapsack off his back and opened it. "All this is for you and the unhappy country of Italy."

Spartaco Allegretti bent over and peered in, gaping like a savage. He saw flour, and not only oat flour, but also groats, rice, and salt, in little bags; milk, honey, tomato juice, and mustard, in tubes; cocoa, pudding, pepper, and some other powder of a suspicious color, in transparent boxes; bread packed, it could be said, on the other side of the world, black and white cookies and various crackers; cheese, butter, cheese again, but different, with holes, and various advertisements on the cellophane wrapping; plastic vials with baby milk; a large variety of cans: flat cans with fish, long, green ones with beans, cans with beef heart in rabbit juice, cans with goose pie, feathers, and meat finely drawn in color on the label, cans from which pineapple juice, orange juice, and carrot juice almost dripped.

"Oh yes."

There were more drugs than food. All twelve or thirteen vitamins, capsules against headache, nightmare, and diabetes, to be inserted very carefully from behind, powder for better and faster digestion of stale food, whether fresh or canned. Ampoules with serum against tetanus, plague, and leprosy, with sterilized needles of all sizes and thicknesses; ampoules against the bites of American dogs, snakes, Mexican ants, and European rabies; ampoules full of a precious liquid which could cure any type of gonorrhea, including the worst, the blackest, the Americo-Africo-Italian one, overnight. There was also castor oil, cod-liver oil, oil for treating the skin, and a great deal of oil for Italian hair. With each little package of food, cotton, and drugs, came a little brass cross and one little box of contraceptives, American ones, three with nipples on top, three without.

"*Oh, boljšoe spasibo*, thanks a lot, Ivan Ivanovich Tchaikovsky!" said Allegretti, smeared with chocolate and tears, as he threw himself around the Negro's throat. "*Boljšoe spasibo, dorogoj moj chotnik*, my dear hunter, Ivan Ivanovich!" he continued, kissing and slobbering over the soldier's neck and shirt. "Ah, deep Russian soul and red Italian cherries ... ah, Tchaikovsky, *dorogoj moj teljonok*, calf!"

"I'm not Russian!" the Negro said, almost weeping. He stepped back, and Spartaco fell off his neck onto the road. "I'm not Russian!"

Spartaco Allegretti was storming back on all fours.

"I'm not this Russian, Ivan Ivanovich Tchaikovsky!" He did not know what to do with the castor oil, the eye-drops, or the cherry branch he was still nibbling, and he rolled his eyes. "I'm an American soldier, Joe Washington, Alabama! I'm only Joe Washington, *Taliano!* Ah, please, please!" He said this in English, and then continued in his Southern Italian, stretching his rubbery lips to form the sounds: "*Io sono solamente uno soldato americano!*"

The two other Americans did not know what to do with the food and drugs they took out of their knapsacks either. They chewed on their branches and vaguely held up their messtins with the already mixed oat groats and watched Allegretti throw himself at the Negro's feet.

"*Njet, njet, njet!* You're not an *amerikanskaja svinja*, you can't be a swine!" Allegretti kissed the Negro's shoes, and then vomited chewing gum, powder, and pieces of chocolate over them. "If you're not Ivan Ivanovich Tchaikovsky, you must be Vladimir Trofimovich Romanov! Ah, Russia ... All of us have been born and raised on the steppes!"

"No, a thousand times no!" The Negro shouted. He was weeping and mopping his tears with a large piece of gauze. "This is impossible, impossible! I'm not Russian! Ah, my God!" He himself began to throw up, but only cherry leaves. "I'm not Russian! I'm not a communist! I'm only Joe Washington, Alabama! Ah, please, please, my shoes, my feet!"

"Russian!" Allegretti sputtered, licking and kissing the soldier's black ankles. "The first and only genuine Russian I've ever met in my life!" He was choking on the spilled flour and dust. "I learned Russian in my youth and perfected it secretly in Montenegro, with women. Let's sing, Vladimir! Here's the refrain: *A djevuški, a djevuški potom*, which means, 'And afterwards, afterwards the girls.'"

"Oh, no, please!" Joe Washington cried again, looking as if he were going to vomit up a whole branch. "Don't insult white men, *Taliano!* Don't insult the Russians! They, after all, are also white! A Negro can't be a Russian!"

[151]

THE WAR WAS BETTER

"The Russians, like others, have their Negroes!"

"A Negro can't be a Russian, *Taliano!* A Negro can only be an American. In many things the Americans are Negroes, provided they aren't one and the same." He was weeping and holding up the lopped branch like a flag. "Please, please, my feet ... my skin!"

The two other Americans were scowling fiercely at their Negro; they were red from rage and cherries and kept chewing on the branches, mixing the groats and spilling cocoa.

"I'm not a Russian or a communist! I'm only a miserable Negro from Alabama, Joe Washington, Jr., and one of the rare colored boys who lived through the landing on Sicily!"

Antonio and Peppe stood again in a field of barley. The valley stretched out in all directions before them. Long columns of olive-colored trucks bearing U.S. insignia rolled along the road past cottages and deserted sheds. There were no farm animals to be seen, and no cats, only dogs, excited by the disaster, sniffing at cans, barking and howling. Church bells were ringing, and the country was in turmoil. Water was approaching from one side; a clean, well-fed army, whose songs nobody understood, from the other. The bells rang with increasing panic. And how could they not have rung, when foreign soldiers were throwing bags of wheat, peas and bird food, coffee and salt, into a small Italian cemetery? The boxes and many-colored bags piled up so high they screened the graves and even the crosses over them from view.

Chewing barley grains, Antonio and Peppe watched Joe Washington, Jr., Alabama, and the two other Americans browsing among the cherry trees. The entire first company of the PX and storm battalion was browsing. Famished children and old men were pulling off branches for them, and they wolfed them down. William Brown's company, the third company, and half the fourth company under the command of the sour and pompous Samuel Becker, from Louisiana, were also nibbling with the rest of them, camping around the road and in the once commendable orchards. When there were no more cherries, the surviving inhabitants pulled down the thick pear and apple branches for them, and they ate hungrily, paying no attention to the dust or the echoing bells.

The soldiers of the sixth and seventh field hospital companies, led by the smiling Captain Jeremy Sullivan, from Indiana, were the most voracious. While they were attacking a walnut tree, breaking its branches off and cracking open the green nuts, the peasants were storming the truck like ants. They carried away sacks and shiny bags with advertisements, pulled them through the thorns and nettles and hid them away somewhere. They pulled away big trunks and neatly packed cardboard boxes with small and large red crosses on them.

Already exhausted and white with flour, their pockets and shirts full of rice, cocoa and pudding, the peasants kept climbing the trees not yet eaten from and bending their branches. The Americans, white and black, nibbled even from the fruitless trees, the willows and alders and lindens, the stunted little pines, and whatever else could be reached and chewed on.

It was impossible to tell from their faces whether they knew what was happening to their trucks. They kept repeating they were for peace, equality, brotherhood, and fraternization, hygienic food and vitamin pills. They insisted that the Italians, along with the Japanese and North Africans, were the most hospitable and unhappy people they had ever liberated. While expressing these sentiments, they passed from the already darkened orchards to the nearby woods, declaring their readiness to eat up whatever might be offered to them as a token of Italian gratitude.

Peduto and Bonaccia rose from the barley field almost at the same moment. They looked to the west. The sky resembled a large bell. The road was dry and covered with flour.

Third Part

"THIS IS UNHEARD OF!" the director of the movie about ex-war heroes, Georges Bonnefous, exclaimed. "Unheard of and disgusting!"

He grunted and mopped the sweat from his forehead and neck with a soft clown's hat. "Serge, let the devil take Italy and her heat! Let the devil take me for that matter! I've only come here to burn up anyway!"

"After great wars or floods, they say, come periods of unbearable heat or drought," said the screen writer, Sergey Ivanovich, who was known as "Fearless Fox." "We are living in a postwar period."

"I adore you, Serge," Bonnefous said, stretching out his arms and stamping on the ground. "I adore you and envy you for having an explanation for everything, including peace, otherwise known as happiness."

"That's how they explain it."

"Who?"

"Peoples. Various peoples. When it comes to explaining great mysterious things, all peoples are the same. They say: after one evil, another comes."

"I have no idea what a people is, Serge. I wouldn't be what I am if I did, or belonged to one. I've heard, though, that there are folk proverbs ... thoughts ... philosophy ..."

"Peoples foresee everything, boss. That's why they live without excitement and without panic. Most of their ideas are naïve and simple, and therefore very deep."

"Well, what do they say in the Balkans, where you've spent so much time?"

"They say everything passes. By that, they mean sorrow as well as happiness. The Serbians and the Greeks say even at the blackest moment: 'There is something worse than evil itself.' For, as you can see, evil is their fate."

"Let the devil take all the peoples of the world ... bugger their mother!" Georges muttered darkly from the ground at Serge's feet. "I spit on my cock to all these philosophers, these egotists and humbugs!"

He did not have the strength to clench his fists; he merely stared at the sky.

"I piss on their thoughts; I piss on those you've already told me about and I piss on the ones that still lie undiscovered in the so-called folk genius! I don't belong to any people, Serge. I don't even know the place of my birth, or the exact date for that matter, and even less who my parents were. Well, you're about to say it's I, such as I am, who turns out to be a child of the people! Serge, listen to me. My story is short. I was found one morning in swaddling clothes and shit, on the banks of the Seine, where it enters Paris. I don't remember very much about what happened afterwards; I grew up illegally, robbing what you call a people, trying to revenge myself for all the injustice I had suffered. They've hunted me ever since, but I've also hunted them."

Bonnefous was forty, with a big head and hairy elbows. From deep in his furrowed and unshaven face, his eyes stared out, blue and sleepless, full of dust and sweat. He lay on the ground like someone ready to grow into the earth and spend eternity there. His big lips were wrinkled and dusty and almost cracked when he spoke.

"It's your turn now, Serge. Your story is funny too."

"I'm sweating horribly."

"I don't believe in the peoples and their big talk about futility." His voice trembled as it had when he spoke about the Seine which poured into Paris. "I'm against peoples. I've become convinced that many things *don't* pass; they remain, right where peoples have left them. Grief, for example: it can change a little, but it remains."

"Poor peoples," Sergey Ivanovich said whimsically, pushing his black-rimmed spectacles up to the middle of his forehead. "Poor cattle, who promptly forget everything, once they've eaten and drunk their fill."

"Listen," Bonnefous murmured, putting his hand on the camera to keep himself from shuddering again. "Something unpleasant is happening to me: I feel my heart opening up to snatch something with its little bantam claws."

He struggled for breath, speaking softly and thoughtfully: "I'll be against peoples to the bitter end, because they're huge and heartless. There's only one thing you can be sure about a people, which you're so enthusiastic and blinded about, which you believe in so deeply; you can be sure that it's wrong. Nothing passes quickly, if it passes at all. Grief is eternal, and peoples don't recognize it. They don't admit that anything's permanently terrible."

THE WAR WAS BETTER

Sergey Ivanovich listened dreamily and sweated.

"My heart shriveled up just now, actually shriveled up. It's only done that two or three times before, when I was a tramp, a *clochard*, and went up to passersby in front of churches with my hand out. Today, in this heat, I feel the same bewilderment, the same futility and defeat. If you weren't here, Serge, I'd cry until the sun went down. It's terrible to be so acutely aware of one's own misery and failure. If I weren't a thief and a rascal, believe me, I'd put an end to my life right now. Are you listening to me? ... Where are you, Serge?"

"I'm right here, boss, lying beside you. It's getting warmer. It's easier for me just to lie here listening." He spoke softly, as if in meditation; his thoughts were focused on bringing a cloud into the sky or anything else that would pour water down and thus silence the thousands of crickets that sang on and on, in the tops of the pines, as if to praise their hottest summer since the war.

"All through my youth I believed in physical power and considered it the foundation of life. I made myself into a kind of elephant or tiger; I broke everything around me. Then I passed my fortieth year and understood that a man's fists aren't everything. Younger wolves began to beat me to the draw; I had to find refuge in my old weakness, art. Perhaps all my luck comes from my meeting with you. Like me, you don't want to change the world. It's better to set it afire, and find ourselves, our true selves on the ashes of this infected continent, alone probably, perhaps with a few innocent beings."

"I know it, Georges. Everything's as you say, boss. Are the pebbles under you as hard as they are over here?"

"I believe in celluloid." Bonnefous propped himself on his elbows and saw that Sergey's smooth, foxy face, turned up toward the dazzling sky, was wet with perspiration.

"Celluloid, reels of film, chemistry! I don't think I've ever come across anything stronger, more efficient, or more amazing! It can free us from time that ravages us like a drenching rain, and from a people which drools eternally about its fictitious past, and dreams about a future it doesn't merit, a future which, fortunately, won't come either. It can liberate us from the sorrow that makes us sweat. Pooh, earth! I spit on you, you old whore! What will you do with so much sun!"

"We must be either good, or insane, Georges," Sergey said, keeping his eyes closed and his hands folded on his chest, like a fresh corpse. "You put so much stock in celluloid; all right, maybe you're right, putting all the nerve and money you've got left into it. As for me, I don't recognize time; I don't admit it exists. But I am convinced that something called a people really does. I like you, boss. I don't know what I'd do without you and your ... bankroll."

"Our film must succeed, you know," Bonnefous affirmed, feeling the burnt grass with his palms. "Regardless of the time, which we recognize or don't recognize, regardless of nationality, which gives me a pain in my you-know-what, regardless of the money, which anyhow we robbed and embezzled ..."

"Right, boss. Because of the last item especially ... our film should be an epic, a real masterpiece, a kind of poem about people who feel pure emotion and experience the exalted and surreal."

"Do you remember who said, at a meeting: 'After the war, at half past seven'? Who was it?"

"Some whore, a real one, and real whores belong only to soldiers or officers. Or some general, convinced in advance of his victory. It must have been a whore."

"There is our beginning, Serge. A whore and a general alternate in telling about the same battle. And if they were asked what came afterwards, both of them would say the war was better!"

"This is going to be the maddest film ever made."

Cold sweat drenched Sergey's tender body.

"There will be no script," he went on. "We'll mix life and celluloid, blood and chemistry. As you yourself put it so well, boss, the film will make itself! We'll shock the world; we'll rake in money!"

"After the war, at half past seven," Bonnefous whispered, musing, beginning to dream about the whore, the seducer of a whole division. "Celluloid." He smiled, and his lips almost cracked again. He murmured something to himself, something important and soft. His big gangster's heart beat in the rhythm of a dream. The bantam's little talons were opening at last, and the long repressed blood rushed through the entire bulk of his body.

"After the war, at half past eight," he said, unaware of his heart. "At half past eight, after the war. After the war ..."

Meanwhile the fearless fox was sleeping. His head was thrown back and his arms were crossed on his breast. His dream was filled with peoples, time and money, and his open mouth with dust and crickets.

THE WAR WAS BETTER

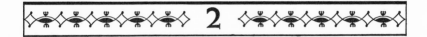 2

Now, as whenever he held his camera in his arms, Bonnefous felt calm, almost satisfied; he wanted to come to terms with the whole world, even his worst enemies.

Sergey had the gas pedal down to the floor with his bare foot, and their jeep was hurtling down the road. Georges was looking back, caressing the sweaty black contours of his apparatus. He felt like standing up and waving to the clouds the wind was bringing.

"Look back," he called. "The world is nice when you're leaving it ... You always regret what you're leaving, isn't it so? Look back!"

"I can't, boss!" the driver said through his teeth, dryly, focusing his eyes on the rutted road. "Don't you see the potholes and rocks!"

"Still, look back!" Georges roared into the wind, throwing his head back. "You'll see the dust rising like a fog; you'll see time, which you don't admit exists!"

"Enjoy it for me too, boss! I have to watch the road. Otherwise someone else will be making a movie about us!"

Paying no attention to traffic regulations or road signs, they whizzed through a crossing. Sergey honked, geared up, and sped on, feeling as if he could fly. Georges spat on the trucks they were starting to pass now, wherever they could squeeze by on the road, sometimes on their right, sometimes on their left.

Tired under their helmets, their faces grained like the stocks of their rifles and white with dust, the American soldiers wiped off Georges's saliva as if it had started drizzling, and waved to him as he went by.

This time both Georges and Sergey spat on them, together, with all their might, and cursed them as loudly as they could. The soldiers mopped up the saliva with their sleeves and went on singing and waving.

"You're a genius, not only with the pen but with the wheel too!" Georges yelled when they had spat on several other trucks and jeeps with dazzling headlights and outdistanced them all. "What does it matter if I'm killed? Even a mad death is more beautiful than the shameful life I lead, and the misery I feel so deeply I can't get rid of it. You, Serge, my last driver, are a genius. You're a genius at spitting. You're a genius at driving. Because of you, I sometimes even regret that I'm going to have to kick the bucket in a few minutes!"

"Hold on tight, boss, this is it! Ah, *merde!*"

The truck with the headlights on had moved into the middle of the road. It was impossible to pass it. They didn't have time to spit on it.

Georges Bonnefous curled himself into a ball, embracing his camera. He heard the wind whistle and the rocks pelt against the car. At that moment, he saw only a grave, a brook of blood, and a heap of celluloid unfolding in endless reels as though in numberless roads. He compacted himself into a tighter ball, not wishing to hear the horrible squeal of the brakes and the painful shrieking of the strained metal. He no longer knew where he was, or whether the camera lenses had remained unbroken.

Sergey liked danger. They had often faced death together.

"You're a living example of the death wish," his old friend had said to him that very morning; now, like a bag of lifeless flesh, he lay heaped on the right seat.

"I don't want to die in bed, like an old woman, with a pile of useless drugs on the night table," was Sergey's stock response; he had used it that morning too.

"Then wars are just made for you, Fearless Fox," Bonnefous had said.

"I was too late for it; that's fate. I was occupied with stealing and writing. But one can always fight after a war. Peace starts falling apart almost immediately." Such had been his philosophy.

Now he could only scream: "*Merde! ... Merde! ... Merde!*"

He turned the wheel to the right with all his strength, pressed the brake to the floor and down-shifted the gears.

It was their luck to be on a crossing full of gravel, branches, and broken boxes. Led on by the hand of the devil, the jeep veered right with its front wheels turned completely sideways and nevertheless gripped the road. The truck, like a steel monster full of military songs and helmets, roared on. There was nobody to spit on, nobody to make indecent gestures to.

Sergey hoped they would soon emerge from the dust cloud through which he could just make out the contours of the road. He was delighted and surprised that they were still on all four wheels and uninjured.

A man was running toward them, right up the middle of the

road. Sergey did not see him until he was about ten feet away. Tall and slightly stooped, he seemed to be absolutely bent on leaping over them or touching them as he flew past. Georges also thought he could hear him shouting. His jaws were wide open, his arms outstretched, his eyes mad from the sun.

"Serge!" Bonnefous screamed from his ball. "Watch out!"

Only a bullet could have stopped the screaming man. The tails of his overcoat were flying behind him.

Sergey Ivanovich squeezed the wheel and turned, trying not to kill him. He tried to pass him on the left, banging into the rocks on the side of the road with his fender, but the man rushed to the same side.

Sergey hit the brakes hard, pressed the pedal to the floor and bit his lip until it bled. The man was already to the right of the car now, that is, in mid-air. Ivanovich was still braking. The man fell, brushing against the fender, and tumbled down beside the wheels. The brakes were still squealing, and the jeep rattled to a stop. Georges yelled that they had not killed him, that he was only injured.

"*Merde!*" Sergey Ivanovich exclaimed, licking the blood and dust from his lips. "*Merde* a thousand times! Boss, what is this today?!"

Georges got out and looked at the bulky man lying with his legs under the wheels. "He's alive!" he shouted. "He's laughing! This whole day is nothing but a punishment! Serge! He's laughing and his mouth is full of blood!"

They pulled him out from under the wheels.

"You damn devil, you!" Sergey cursed him. "*Espèce d'imbécile!* Idiot of all idiots! You're the murderer, not I! I've smashed you! You wanted it! Fool!"

Sergey was trembling. Rage and despair could be seen in his fox-like face. He almost began to slap the man, bloody as he was. He could not. The man smiled and threw his head back as if he wanted to die in human arms, not alone, in some alien land.

He had on torn army pants, a greasy army shirt, and a tattered, bullet-riddled army overcoat. Even his thin, tanned face, framed by short, grayish hair, was military.

"Stand up, if you're a soldier! Salute!" Georges said, stepping back with his camera. "Serge, if you're conscious again, help him. Don't be afraid. We only broke his teeth, maybe his jaw too."

Sergey panted. He was still waving his arms about and cursing heaven and earth. The uniformed man was shivering.

THE WAR WAS BETTER

"This distance suits me," Georges muttered to himself. He took the plastic cover off his lens with shaking hands. "If he would only turn toward the camera a little, and say a few words!"

"We need you only for a few minutes," Sergey said to him, stepping on the tails of his overcoat. "Stand up, be a pal!" he repeated in all the languages he could remember. "Don't be afraid; we won't harm you. Just stay with us a few... Hey, you veteran... Listen you, get up! We photograph you, then we go away forever. You can stay here where we saved your life. You can lie here as long as you like on this shit-covered road."

The man got up, slowly; his coat was caught under one of the tires and he had to pull it free. Sergey stepped aside. Georges got a clear view, with the human figure and the wheel in the middle.

The veteran soldier got himself up, but could not keep his arms at his sides; stretched out and thin, they began to flop up and down like a featherless bird's. He could not put his feet together either. He stood there like that for a moment, with his face smiling and bloody. Then he lost his balance and fell down on his knees.

"Serge, ask him something," Bonnefous said, shooting footage from a prone position. "You're wonderful, wonderful, much better than the ones we got yesterday. His face is in the shadow."

"Hey, *soldato!* We saved your life and you're saluting on your knees. Who are you?" Sergey mopped perspiration and sticky dust from his face. "We won't harm you. We're only thieves. But tell us..."

"*Sono Tedesco,*" Carl Schlotterer said as he raised his head with painful pride. "I'm German."

"All right," Sergey Ivanovich said, coaxing him to remain as long as possible in the same position. "I was thinking you must be one of those unhappy and suicidal people."

He smiled to him. The man remained silent, his face still.

"It was clear to me immediately you were a *Tedesco.* Where did you get beaten? When was your terrible defeat?"

Carl Schlotterer looked down at the dust and the wheels from under which he had just been drawn. Then he studied his hands and his feet and the long tails of his overcoat. He too was sweaty, and his finely cut face was dirty.

"What did you want?" Sergey asked, trying to draw his eyes up from the wheels and the soil. "*Tedesco,* say something to us."

Carl Schlotterer kept staring at the same spot.

"It's said one has to live!" Sergey Ivanovich yelled, shocked by the soldier's composure. "It's also said there has been peace now for more than a year, peace, you understand, peace, right after the war and everything that happened."

Sergey approached him, but not as he went up to other soldiers, who were usually drunk and submerged in well-being, thankful they had survived. He peered into his face and saw, in his eyes, terrible heaps of automobile wheels, steel axes, bloody tin plates, and rocks. He could not touch him.

"By God, I'm extraordinarily happy!" Bonnefous exclaimed, filming from a heap of boards, broken packing materials, and dung. "It's almost unbelievable! He doesn't seem to notice me at all; all this doesn't seem to bother him. These will be terrific shots, terrific! But if you could just coax at least one more word out of him, one more grimace!"

"Hey, *Tedesco!*" Sergey yelled. "Look! Catch!"

From one of the cardboard boxes he took out an olive can and threw it to him. "Take it, it's for you." Carl Schlotterer took the can and lifted it up to his face. "It's military," he muttered, "military indeed." He began to caress the can. "It's military."

He stared at the sun, blinking as if he were nearsighted; his large, beautiful eyes sparkled with something like a strong light. He spat on the dust, and Sergey, looking down, could not tell whether his own broken teeth or merely a few pebbles had fallen beside his boots.

Georges was shooting his happy face, the can, and his tears.

"Now good-by, Boche!" Sergey said as he opened the jeep door and sat down behind the wheel. "We've saved your life and given you a military olive can, but you've repaid us well!" He was warming up the motor and checking the brakes. "You've been wonderful!"

"Thank you, *Tedesco*," Georges also said, all sweaty, as he took his seat beside the driver. "I thank you from the bottom of my gangster-artist heart! You appeared as if on command. Perhaps I'll start the movie with you, our poem-movie about people whose hearts and whose memories have remained in remote, foreign mountains."

"Since you don't want to wave to us, at least get out of the way! The next car will knock you down! People are different nowadays; they're usually in a hurry!"

Carl Schlotterer knelt before them, staring at the jeep wheels. In his arms he held the can like a baby. His face expressed a kind of calm acquiescence to the earth and the dust in which he seemed to be burrowed.

"Good-by, *Tedesco!*" both of them cried, with their hands above their heads. "All the luck! A good wind in your sails!"

Carl Schlotterer neither answered nor gave any sign that he even noticed them.

"He isn't like the others," Sergey said softly, putting the jeep into neutral. "I like it that he doesn't speak, or weep. It looks like everything's all the same to him."

"I wouldn't like to just leave him here. . . . What do you think? Maybe we could take him with us, at least for a while," Bonnefous said.

"You know, boss, it would be a sin, well, it would be a real shame to leave him alone like this, right in the middle of the road."

They looked at each other like true friends. Georges was thinking a thought he had had many times before: movies are best when life itself writes the script.

"How strange! You're getting to be right more and more frequently!" Sergey said. They got out of the car, spread a blanket on the stones, and put the veteran soldier on it. Then they lifted it up by the corners and put him down on the boxes, ropes and tools in the back of the jeep. The soldier said nothing while this operation was carried out.

"Now let somebody just try and tell me that gangsters and artists have no soul, or sympathy for their fellow men," Bonnefous said, carefully stretching out the German's legs on the blanket.

"And now, straight toward Rome, the city of peace and love!" Sergey growled and stepped on the gas pedal.

"Rome!" Georges grunted, feeling the jeep's tires clutch the gravel. "Rome, where many of our boys . . . lost their lives . . . since the war ended!" He turned around in his seat to look at the soldier.

Carl Schlotterer lay quietly in the back, letting the dust settle on his forehead and lips. For a while, he kept his eyes open, but they did not express even gratitude. They were full of the light from the sky. Georges looked at him for a long time. He wanted to tell him how nice it was of him not to cry, like some other poor devils he'd run into, who'd gone mad thinking about their long-destroyed battallions.

Overwhelmed by exhaustion and memories, and still holding the can, the man finally closed his eyes. Georges was sure he was not asleep. How could he sleep? he thought, after everything that had happened.

"Christ, you've been burnt to a crisp!" Georges said to the quiet traveler. "Where did you get those burns, you poor wretch?" His stomach was rising up to his throat; he thought of his camera.

THE WAR WAS BETTER

"Serge, did you see? He's all burnt and wounded; that's probably the reason he has nothing to say to us."

Sergey was driving like a madman.

"He must have come to Italy straight from hell, or some other country that was burning up."

"Should we turn on Via San Giovanni or Via San Pietro, boss? I think San Giovanni is a worse road, and longer."

"Then take it," Georges said, looking closely at the scarred burns and wounds on Schlotterer's knees, calves and elbows. "To Rome, Sergey Ivanovich, my right hand . . . my both hands!" the bulky man almost sang. Drawing his cloth hat down over his ears, he began to spit against the wind.

"And as for those who roam through Europe, raw and roasted, and in any case beaten up and defeated, you can be damned sure they've got something to be sorry for; the war was better for them."

They were in front of San Giovanni. They could see the church, the cemetery with a donkey at the entrance, and several stacks of hay and straw piled up on the left side of the road.

Sergey noticed a spring. With a few highspeed, breakneck maneuvers, he braked the jeep at the very edge of the water.

Georges hardly had time to spit on the signpost: ROMA, 100 km.

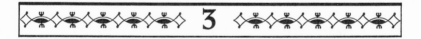

3

"Luka!"

It was a miracle, a miracle indeed: everything happened to the donkey so quickly, almost at once.

It was a big donkey, a real one; more thoughtful, by all appearances, than the fifty or so others who were shaking their heads and waving their tails along the dusty road. Flies attacked him, swarming around his tail and his mouth, which was smeared with American chocolate. He leaned on the church fence, where a shadow fell, protecting half his body from the sun and the insects. He relaxed his swollen stomach and dreamed. In this position, he seemed merely a lucky and rather ordinary peacetime donkey. But he stared in the direction of Rome.

He was less and less in the company of the rest of the donkeys. Even when he met them, and they nodded their heads together, he would never tell them anything interesting; he soon returned to his old spot, where he was now, digesting groats and chocolate which dripped down the sides of his mouth like honey. His left hind leg was lame.

"He could draw a cart if he wanted to," the Sexton of the San Giovanni Battista church said. "He's still strong."

"Let him alone!" the Padre replied with much warmth in his voice.

"Shame on him," the Sexton said, mildly scolding the donkey. "If at least we knew where he came from, and to whom he belongs!"

"He's God's donkey and ours, my luckless Gaetano," the Padre said, his expression softening as he looked at the black, swollen testicles between the donkey's legs. "He's ours now, just as all the miseries, the poverty and shame of the world are ours."

Probably an abandoned or forgotten invalid, a survivor of some long and distant war, there he was, spending his happy days of peace and almost unbearable weariness beside the church of San Giovanni Battista. His greatest entertainments were weddings and burials. Then, as before, during the brightest days of battles and storms, the big, good heart of the ass beat strongly. He approached the main entrance and stared thoughtfully at the motley dresses and fresh wreaths. Wedding guests stroked him or even treated him to wine—thus he became acquainted with drunken happiness. Grave-diggers flung him the human bones they had dug out of the earth; thus he imagined he was still in a battlefield. They also threw grass to him, and food from out of the graves, and many flowers. Luka looked at them and ate. Then he licked their spades and picks.

"Patience, Luka," the Padre said as he stroked his forehead. "I know you like to hear the bells, but you must have patience. Our poor sorrowful Gaetano is asthmatic, and it's hard for him to climb to the belltower."

That day Luka, even with his lame leg, resisted everything; he felt his belly and his testicles pulling him toward the earth. He waited. The Sexton took a long time to climb. He finally reached the top and broke through a spider's web and shooed away the bats and swallows which were hiding from the heat under the copper bell.

"My Luka!"

The Padre caressed the scarred wounds on the donkey's back and touched his belly with his fingers, from below. "Patience, Lukian. Gaetano is truly old. Now he's preparing everything. He still doesn't know with which hand to . . ."

THE WAR WAS BETTER

Gaetano De Cicco began pulling with his hands and feet, at the same time calling from above, like a dormouse. Luka lifted his head, and his eyes took on a dark shine, which the gravediggers were well acquainted with. He wiggled his ears, letting the echo of the bell and the chirping of the frightened birds and bats pour from one to the other. He began to weep big tears. The gravediggers stood above the hole they had dug, looking at him.

"Luka . . . Our Luka!"

But something sparkled in his eyes that day besides his tears; there was also a kind of yearning. He dilated his nostrils and sensed the smell and presence of aroused females nearby. Firmly planted in the earth, and still listening to the bell, he pushed up his old, worn-out, veteran ramrod. He struck it against his belly and then against the metal fence of the cemetery and drew his neck in. He remembered the war and the jennies who had straddled him in some distant land. The sun was at the zenith; it was hot, and the bells of San Giovanni Battista knew no quarter or measure. Luka conjured up a vision of love, war, and blood. He opened his mouth wide and brayed, begging his beauties not to duck out on him.

"Luka, come to your senses!" one of the gravediggers yelled and threw a spadeful of earth and green cherries into his mouth. "Restrain yourself, or we'll bury your souvenirs!"

Luka brayed. With his blessed rod he lashed at the thorns and the cemetery fence. All the jennies he remembered turned into one —warm, soft, voluptuous—it seemed to him he was already on her back; it was like then, in the midst of a mad and unforgettable war, when bells had been ringing, and he had been weeping from pleasure.

"Luka, our shame! Shame!" the asthmatic Gaetano hollered from above; he was disheveled and pale and looked like a bird with a wax beak. "Luka, antichrist!"

"Throw as much dirt on him as possible!" the Padre ordered the gravediggers. "As much as you can, yes! But without stones, please." With his fingers on his lips, he stared in admiration at the huge, asinine mushroom. "Mother of God, pardon me for having seen it!"

The Padre turned his back to the donkey. He felt his behind with his fingers like a woman and adjusted his belt and cassock. Then he made the sign of the cross. He no longer bothered to ask the gravediggers to cover Luka and his flower with earth; he could hear them shouting with Gaetano and bursting out into laughter.

"You still don't know, my old Sexton, what real love is. And

you've never had even the faintest idea of war," one of the gravediggers was calling up to Gaetano. "You don't know what pleasure
is in far-off, God-forsaken lands!"

"Flower!" the Padre let out.

He stopped invoking the name of the *Madonna*, and passed over
to Jesus. His neck and forehead began to perspire from the intensity
of his prayerful whispering. He felt weakness, thirst and then a terrible desire to kneel down in front of the godless Luka. On behalf of
the helpless and sick of the whole world, he would ask him for
mercy, for a tender touch, for one or two drops of his dark and
blessed power. Writhing with an almost physical pain, as if someone
were pushing him from behind, he fell to his knees.

His beautiful almond eyes flooded with tears of pain and lust; he
saw the donkey in his thoughts again, rearing up on the church
fence, chewing dirt and foam and directing his horn of flesh toward some distant, war-torn land, or toward the weak and the
thirsty. The Padre fell even lower. He touched the earth with his
head. He turned his round, soft, fat backside toward Luka and the
gravediggers.

"Christ, I pray to you also for Luka. Pardon him, he's unhappy
and quite alone. Have mercy on him, oh Lord, because he knows
not what he does. . . ."

The Padre did not cease to think of Luka even when the children came and lifted him up from the earth. He wiped the dust
mixed with sweat and tears from his face and looked up to see a funeral procession, approaching down the first path. The other two
paths were jammed with peasants. They too were carrying coffins
and crosses.

"Only You, oh Just One, can save me today," the Padre murmured without even noticing that he was also mentioning the godless Luka. "Pardon me, Jesus, for loving him so much. I can't seem
to get his big flower out of my sick mind." Through his tears the
sky looked cleaner and nicer. The whole firmament seemed covered
by the lame animal with his flourishing tail, his gaping jaws and
swollen rod. "Pardon me, excuse me, take me to You, or punish me
with Luka here on earth!"

A hot wind, whirling the dust about fiercely, forced all three
processions to stop and drop their coffins at the cemetery entrance.
There was so much dust that even the most grief-stricken mourners
could not weep, and nobody could see anything. They stood
blindly over their corpses, with crosses above their heads.

The Padre himself did not know what to do. His mouth was full of unspoken words, chaff, and straw. He did not stretch out his arms, for fear that the hurricane would carry him away; instead he leaned over the coffins and prayed to all the saints to stop the wind and return peace to the hapless earth and the even more hapless and sinful Luka.

Then something happened that he would remember all his life.

"It's the way it was during the war," he let fall. "I don't know whether we'll have time to bury all three today."

"We've come too, Padre," a wailing peasant leading a fourth little group said, as he ordered the others to put down an exceptionally heavy coffin.

"Don't reject us, Padre," the peasant implored, not realizing that he was waving his cross in a threatening manner. "Our poor corpse has been stinking since the day before yesterday."

"And ours is decomposing, falling apart before our eyes," a funny, weeping man in front of the second crowd put in. "We could hardly bring him."

"My good and luckless people, let us pray to Christ to help us in this heat and storm."

"First of all, we're praying to you, Padre," a mustachioed woman at the head of a third group of mourners called out. "Take our dead, or we'll start vomiting." The woman stood with her legs wide apart between two coffins. As she spoke, her stomach literally groaned and palpitated. "Padre!"

"It's the way it was during the war," the priest said quietly, his chin sagging as he fought back tears. He felt a very hot wind under his cassock. "Brethren in Christ and in His blood!"

"There hasn't been war for a year, Padre," the old woman reminded him as she spat out a handful of sand and leaves. "Look, it's peace now!"

The priest smeared tears and grass on his fat face as he watched the peasants lift the lids from the coffins.

"There's no more war, Padre!" the oldest peasant repeated after the woman. "It's peace now! They said this time it would last forever. Woe unto us!"

The Padre looked at all four corpses. The first two seemed to be perspiring more than the living; their faces bore expressions of disdain and deep suffering. The mouth of the third corpse was smiling broadly; chewed newsprint and tobacco juice dripped over his swollen lips.

The fourth corpse, judging by everything, belonged to the woman with the mustache, who was straddling its coffin. The Padre could see the dead person was of the male sex, that he had shaved and cut his hair, and that he had been a glutton—although he was dead, his belly looked full to bursting, and his legs, with a rose sticking out in-between, next to a revolver and a crooked candle, were horribly swollen.

With her foot, gingerly, the woman was positioning melting bars of American chocolate around his head. Chewing gum, cocoa, and groats spilled out of his mouth, nose and ears. If he had not been so swollen that the corpse gas was lifting the coffin lid by itself, one would have said he was a merrymaker, drunk at some feast, a real circus tramp, a kind of postwar Italian clown. In any case, he was surely one of the few departed who must have died without cursing American food.

All four corpses, not counting the fifth, whose coffin lid was just being removed, were wearing some piece of clothing from the Allied armies. The first and third had on English jackets and pants that were too long; a French beret was clapped down over the second's ears; the fourth, the peacetime fattie, was wearing a new American infantry helmet.

The fifth corpse, a smiling woman in her fifties, seemed either to be speaking or spewing out chocolate, powdered milk, and bits of Australian rusk; her smile revealed her tongue and toothless jaws down to her gullet. Her husband was still alive, but there was no great difference between them, except that he was sucking and chewing sweets, and she was returning them to the Americans and the rest of the allies. He was small, crooked, and glad, although old. She had a motley medal on her breast, and big army boots on her shrunken feet. This plunged the Padre's conscience into an intense panic.

"We have the same boots on," he thought, almost choking. "Army boots, Canadian! There's still a war on! Oh Jesus!" he shrieked and fell on his face among the dead.

"It's peacetime, our little shaking, frightened child!" the owner of one of the corpses said. He stuck his cross next to the priest's head. "There's peace, I say; it's been peacetime for a year and twenty-five days already. Stand up, Arturo!"

"There's still war, oh Lord! I see so many boots and army clothes, even Russian things," he murmured with his head stuck into the dust and sand, not realizing that the wind was lifting his cassock up over his plump buttocks and hips.

"You could have put on some underwear, Arturo!" the old

woman with the mustache spat and jerked her stomach. "Underpants, even American ones!"

"Luka, my luckless Luka," the Padre muttered feverishly. "My abandoned orphan, forgotten by everyone."

They poured water over him. He remained there, lying among the dead, sobbing and gasping for breath and crying out: "My only Luka!"

Then the fire broke out.

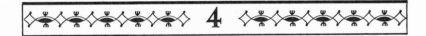

Antonio Peduto and Giuseppe Bonaccia lay hidden behind the stacks of hay and straw which surrounded the church. They had firemen's helmets on their heads and soft boots on their feet, from some distant epoch. Even their clothes, which were torn, seemed to have been taken from a museum exhibit of some long-forgotten army. The pockets of their spacious pants were embroidered with golden threads, and there were silver plates on their breasts. Bleached tassels and hen feathers fell over their shoulders.

Ten medals hung on each of their uniforms, in addition to numerous brass buttons and various clasps. Their decorations were also from a distant time, but they still shone majestically and were well sewn to the fabric.

Giuseppe Bonaccia had one cross and three crowns on his left breast, while a heavy star hung down Antonio's neck, with six large and six small forks and swords. An already dirty braid was thrown over one of Peduto's shoulders and drawn under the crown which glistened on the right side of his chest. They both also had insignia, stripes and ranks on their shoulders and their sleeves, but the world's best historians could never have decoded them.

The two did not even behave like men from this age. Their faces were thin and tanned, sweaty under their cheap tin helmets and emphatically serious. They remained silent for several minutes as they handed back and forth to each other probably the strangest pair of binoculars ever made by men. They were looking in the direction of the San Giovanni Battista church.

The binoculars were almost two yards long, thick as a good stick and decorated by ivory and countless dates. They were so heavy that, while Peppe was looking at the church and the heap of coffins piled up at the cemetery entrance, Antonio had to hold up the front end, which was somewhat wider, on his shoulders and epaulets.

A knapsack, a kind of bag with shoulder straps, lay between them. The turtle's sweaty head protruded from it. Both of them were wearing asbestos capes, designed for fire-fighting, with hoods and glass disks for the eyes.

Gruban Malić was about Antonio's or Peppe's size. With his pants down and his Russian overcoat up, he was squatting not far from the two. Antonio and Peppe were watching him and enjoying his stench. They could have moved away, or at least turned their heads. Instead, they remained with their faces turned toward him, enraptured, as they always were when he took a shit.

"How deliberate he is," Bonaccia whispered, noticing a jeep sneaking up toward them slowly. "Should we report it to him?" he asked, pointing.

"Revolutionaries shouldn't be interrupted when they are... doing their duty," Peduto warned him, inhaling the foul, pungent odor. "All the more so since he, like every true red fighter, suffers from constipation."

"Perhaps the news that a jeep is coming would accelerate the process," Peppino said, bending under the weight of the binoculars. "Do the other revolutionaries throughout the world suffer so much?"

"The more significant a revolutionary, the longer he shits, and the worse his stink and pain," Peduto said, focusing the binoculars on the cemetery. "Malić has no equal. Just imagine, Peppe, how he must be feeling now!"

The donkey Luka was shaking the church fence, braying and trembling, and Antonio's cheeks turned pink and then crimson. Through the binoculars, the Padre's behind looked even larger and softer than close up, and the dead who had been carried there even funnier and more helpless. Several further processions had arrived at the cemetery entrance with fresh corpses, and the gravediggers were throwing spades of dirt on the sprawling body of the priest. Peduto spat and turned toward Malić, who was still writhing in pain.

"May I join you, soldiers?" Georges Bonnefous asked, getting out of the jeep. "I mean, can we rest together?"

"Yes, if you have some cigarettes," Antonio smiled and stroked his beard.

[174]

THE WAR WAS BETTER

"They're American," Bonnefous informed him as he opened the package and offered the first one to Antonio.

"Tobacco's tobacco," Bonaccia remarked, striking a match and lighting one himself.

"And the gentleman?" Sergey Ivanovich asked softly, stretching on the grass and pointing at Malić. "I mean, the pale knight?"

Antonio liked Malić's new name. He felt like embracing and kissing Sergey Ivanovich. Instead, he lent him the binoculars and gave way so that he could look.

Sergey Ivanovich could see Malić even without the binoculars. With them, however, the whole bent figure of the pale knight came into view.

"He's groaning and reeking," Ivanovich said; he felt like throwing up.

"It isn't child's play," Peduto said excitedly. "Poor revolutionary! He's come from the east. Parachuted. He didn't have the slightest idea of the heat that was waiting for him here!"

"His parachute is still on his back," Sergey Ivanovich informed both Antonio and Georges. "The veins on his forehead and neck are bulging, but not from the vain effort; it's from the songs he's singing. I know the first one from my prison and circus days: 'Red Is the East and the West.' The others will come out more clearly ... when it starts, if it ever starts."

"The globe will help him," Peduto said to console him. He looked over at the shocked Georges, who had taken Sergey's place, took one look, and spat vehemently.

"He's rotating the globe, and trying to pierce some of the countries with his finger," Bonnefous panted. "I've got the impression the thing he likes best is to hit the countries painted red, the countries of the east. Probably those are the parts he likes best and knows most. In brief, his countries."

"What's he doing with the west, Georges?" Ivanovich asked, already concocting plans in his foxlike mind. "Is he cruel?"

"He's piercing it. Caressing it with his whole hand. And, nevertheless, singing to it as he struggles."

An hour later, Gruban Malić finally arrived with the large globe and sat down among them with a sigh of relaxation. He was pale and sweaty. His Russian overcoat reached almost to his feet. He clapped his fur hat on the back of his head and began, with the immediacy of the rank-and-file:

"Who has tobacco?"

He stared at them victoriously. The stench from the pile of corks he had left behind had not abated.

"Wonderful cigarettes."

"They're American," Ivanovich informed him, extending the package.

"I'd prefer them to be something else," Malić said, looking out of the corner of his eye at the spot where he had undergone so much agony. "But since you're here, give whatever you have."

They smoked the long American cigarettes and directed the cannon barrels of the binoculars toward the cemetery, the uncovered priest and, the dead. They giggled and talked with fingers, words and grimaces. Then they sang, trying to harmonize their voices. A hardly noticable smile played over Sergey's lips. Georges Bonnefous was happy, and he did not hide it; as usual, he was lying on his stomach, almost humming: "Italy, oh Italy, do you know who's stamping on you today? Do you know what's being done in you?"

His shirt was unbuttoned, his naked chest and stomach sweaty and hairy, and his voice deep and sincere. "I'd like to sing with you boys, but the only song I know is the 'Marseillaise.' But it's not funny or ugly enough for me to recommend it to you. Therefore, let's join in one of the knight's favorites: 'Red Is the East and the West,' or . . . perhaps another."

"I know all the songs," Bonaccia said.

"His favorite is the one about the whore, the helmet, and the general," Antonio observed. "The song in which she fills up his helmet, claps it on his head, and sends him out to the parade." He turned to Georges. "Old man, can you give us all another cigarette? By the way, men, who are you?"

"Sort of tourists, Red Beard," Bonnefous answered and laughed. "Isn't that right, Serge?"

"Tourists," Ivanovich said as he turned to Peppe and Malić.

"It's good tobacco although it does seem to be sweetened," Malić said, expressing his opinion to Sergey. "Hey! Who's in the car there? He'll burn up in the sun."

"Also a tourist," Georges Bonnefous answered. "All of us are tourists and travelers to a certain extent."

Carl Schlotterer's dusty face was turned upwards toward the sun. He had the can on his chest.

"It looks like we'll be driving for a long time."

"Take care he doesn't die," Peppe warned them, cocking his fire helmet

"He won't," Sergey Ivanovich answered. Suddenly he remembered everything. "He won't, probably ..."

They smoked for some time in the shade, looking thoughtfully at Carl Schlotterer and his scorched feet.

"People, that is, soldiers!" Peduto exclaimed, taking a bottle out of his knapsack. "Will everyone have a drink?"

"I'll take whatever you offer, Red Beard," Bonnefous said, holding out his hand.

"This is war booty," Antonio said, and drank first. "It's nothing to brag about, but it moistens and it burns!"

"It's good, Red Beard," Georges admitted after he too had drunk from the bottle and shivered violently as the brandy went down.

"It's not so bad, but it's too mild," Malić said to Sergey Ivanovich. "I can't even tell what it's made out of. Our brandy, the Balkan one, is much stronger and purer; everything is fiercer in our country."

"There must still be a lot of brandy there in the Balkans," Sergey Ivanovich mused and drank again. "Much brandy and much sorrow. And many fierce girls."

"Ask Peppino," Antonio said to Sergey Ivanovich. "He knows everything about Balkan girls, and women in general." He toasted him with the bottle. "Throw me another cigarette, will you? But a lit one."

"My dear Balkan girls! Ah!" Giuseppe Bonaccia almost began to sing; his eyes were shining darkly. "My poor ones, where are you now, while I sit here smoking American cigarettes and drinking Italian brandy?"

"Peppino, don't mention the Balkans," Antonio requested, fearing that Peppe might grow exalted again and tell about the fires and Montenegro. "Peppino, here, you'd better take the binoculars and see what the situation is now in front of the church."

Peduto put the broader part of the binoculars on his shoulder and fought back the tears that had welled up in his eyes when the name of Montenegro had been mentioned. Then he winked to Georges, who could not hide his admiration. "Come on, Bonaccia."

"Oh heavens," Peppino began with a trembling voice. "I see something horrible. I can see the priest's backside moving among the coffins; the old battle-axe is packing hay and straw into his asshole, and flowers too! Heavens! How much earth and chaff and thorns it can take!" His voice was breaking. "There, two more little groups of poor men are arriving, carrying crosses and ... leading along their dead. They have no coffins, so they're holding their dead ones' shoulders and hands, and making them walk along between them, or look as if they were walking. Now there are thirteen dead, not counting the owners of the third and fourth corpses, who're dying just at this moment, victims of this terrible peace. If it weren't for the wind and the dust, I could probably see a lot more!"

"Don't be sore, old man, if I give one or two drops to that luckless tourist of yours," Antonio said to Georges as he set out with the bottle. "I can't drink if anyone near me stays thirsty."

Peduto lifted the bottle to Schlotterer's mouth, which opened by itself. He recognized Antonio immediately, closed his eyes, and was stricken with shame. He too remembered Montenegro, the Montenegrin flowers and flames; he continued to drink greedily from the upturned bottle which Antonio held above him.

"I'm really pouring it into you," Antonio said, jingling his medals. "He's alive, but I never saw such roasted arms and legs. Never."

"Thank you, Beard," Georges Bonnefous called out. "Thank you for having poured some into the tourist, the true German traveler!"

Antonio wanted to turn around, to look at him once again. He did not have time to, however, for Malić was asking Peppe to give him the binoculars. Bonaccia obeyed. Malić spit out his cigarette and leaned the binoculars on Sergey's shoulders.

He saw the Padre's behind, surrounded by flowers, some of which seemed to be growing out of it, and saw the dead who seemed to be sweating and fretting feverishly in their coffins. He almost vomited when he noticed Gaetano standing under the bell which was bursting from heat, shame, and despair. He frowned severely when he saw the roof and the cross of San Giovanni Battista glittering in the sun.

"The cross is guilty of everything!" Malić said, with a scowl, as he stared through the binoculars. "We have to settle our accounts with it, first of all!"

"Aren't you a Muslim, my hero?" Sergey asked him softly from under the front end of the binoculars.

"That religion is the most disgusting to me," Malić answered, grinding his teeth. "But since we are in the decadent West . . ."

"What will you begin with, commie?"

"First of all, faith must be killed!" Malić snapped.

"Faith in what?" Sergey Ivanovich asked with unconcealed excitement.

"In anything," Malić continued. "In anything that's human!"

THE WAR WAS BETTER

"Boss, this guy is wonderful!" Sergey exclaimed. "Georges, did you hear what he just said? Faith in anything should be killed!"

"But look at the clothes he has on," Bonnefous replied, throwing his arm around Antonio and pouring brandy into his beard and over his golden medals. "Can't you see he's some kind of Montenegrin Russian? He's a mad angel, whatever he is!"

The bottle had come back to Antonio, empty. Georges Bonnefous was lying on his back with his mouth open. Antonio watched his Adam's apple moving up and down. Not only was his throat full of brandy, but also his cheeks, his nose, and even his eyes. He lay back in the grass and, after swallowing, began to curse nationality and whatever else Gruban Malić had just been talking about.

"At first I thought you were thieves or spies, but now I see you are children!" Peduto said, his tongue faltering. He threw the empty bottle toward the jeep. "Now I see you're just mad, wounded children."

He pulled another bottle out of his knapsack, moistened the turtle with a few drops, and then began to pour it over Georges (who was already coughing and sneezing out brandy) and then over Sergey Ivanovich, who, with the binoculars still on his shoulder, was asking Malić whether it was really possible to kill faith in anything human.

"And since you're children, let's get drunk, and let's arrange to meet again in Rome, which will soon be ours!" Antonio cried, sprinkling them all.

"San Giovanni has practically been taken already!" Malić asserted as he took the bottle out of Antonio's hands and began to suck on it. "All that remains is to burn it up!"

"Do you think, Commissar, that Rome would surrender without putting up a fight?"

Georges Bonnefous had not been so happy nor so drunk for a long time; he wanted to hug and kiss the lean, fanatical face of Malić, with its single wrinkle lost under his heavy Russian hat.

"Can such a big, corrupt city be taken without resistance?"

"Rome or death!" Gruban Malić said emphatically.

"We'll go with you for a while," Georges proposed. "We'll film the landscapes you conquer. And I wish you'd trample all the West under your boots, the whole damned, immoral, shameless continent, the loveless earth!"

"I piss on such a world, and such a peace!" Peduto almost wailed and clapped his fire helmet on. "We'll burn up whatever refuses to lie down before us!"

THE WAR WAS BETTER

"Even your name is wonderful!" Bonnefous said; his suddenly awakened eyes were bulging. "It's easy to remember it."

"Listen, old man, did you know that for a long time now, I haven't just been called Antonio Peduto, but Antonio-Gruban Peduto-Malić! Anyway, we're the same! He's all my happiness!" He drank and extended the bottle to Peppe and Malić, who also took swigs from it. "Your name sounds good too; perhaps it's Russian?" He corked the bottle and returned it to his knapsack, which he then shouldered. "At first I thought you were an Englishman, with your big head. Now I see you're a man; it'll be some time before I forget you."

Gruban Malić, Antonio Peduto and Giuseppe Bonaccia donned their asbestos capes, under which their medals disappeared. They pulled the hoods over their faces.

"This is our favorite weapon: arson," Malić said, bending down.

All three struck matches, screened the little flame with their hands, which were protected by asbestos gloves, and then stepped aside and took cover.

Even before the fire had caught and raged through the whole haystack, Sergey Ivanovich and Georges Bonnefous were scrambling toward the jeep. Their faces were sweaty and happy, their eyes drunken and full of flame.

Carl Schlotterer felt the alcohol he had drunk deep in his heart. He wanted them to start. He wanted them all to perish together.

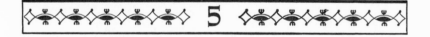

Georges Bonnefous and Sergey Ivanovich forged their way with difficulty through the clouds of smoke. Heaps of straw, broken branches and even burning bushes were falling on the canvas roof of their jeep. They brushed them away hurriedly whenever they could, driving at breakneck speed, sometimes even off the road and through the fields, in order not to lose the arsonists.

Malić was the deftest and fastest of the three at setting fires. With the globe in one hand, he flew from haystack to haystack, bent over, observed the direction of the wind, and then lit his match. His cape and hat had long since disappeared. Peduto and

THE WAR WAS BETTER

Bonaccia could hardly keep up with him. They ran after Malić, carrying the bag and binoculars between them, and flinging bunches of burning hay on the haystacks he had missed. Thus they pressed on toward the church and the cemetery, with their torches flaming, like the vanguard of an invading army. Whenever they could be seen in the smoke, Bonnefous, holding his camera high, shot as much footage as he could get.

Then whole loads of burning hay covered the cemetery. A single flame licked the roof of the church, leaped, clutched upward and began to climb the steeple. Georges Bonnefous supposed the old man would jump out. He had stopped ringing the bell. But they heard neither a scream nor a thud. Only the cross disappeared, and the sky.

"Georges!" Ivanovich yelled. "Shake a leg! ... The roof is starting to go; it's going to fall down on you!" Sergey shifted gears in the smoke, almost hitting a cornerstone with his fender as he avoided a flock of terrified sheep. "Georges, for God's sake!"

"I've shot something really gay," Bonnefous said, almost weeping as he took his seat beside Sergey. "I've filmed everything, everything, the whole horror, the gravediggers, everything." His head spun; his eyebrows and lashes were smoking; sooty and panting, almost gasping for breath, he could hardly get out the words. "Drive to the other side! I want a total picture. I want everything: the Sexton, the Priest, the corpses!"

"We shouldn't miss the living either, boss!" Sergey Ivanovich said, coughing and pointing at Malić and the knights in their capes. He drove the car across a heap of ashes that were spreading over the hot field. "Look, the one with the globe is running in front of them, looking for cover or trying to make sure they can retreat."

"We'll stick to them ten years if necessary," Georges said falteringly. If only he had some more of Antonio's brandy, he thought, he could have forced the soot down his throat. "I don't know which of them is more magnificent!"

He hung his head; his entrails seemed to be surging up into his windpipe. He began to sniffle: "I like you, Serge. I sincerely like you. And I ask you to pardon me for having filmed a real death. A beam killed a gravedigger. He took a long time to die. He vomited dirt and cherries. Pardon me and lead me away, into the fresh air!"

They were approaching the church, and the wind and fire were sweeping toward them, from the other side. Georges did not vomit yet. He only coughed up some sputum and started filming the donkey.

THE WAR WAS BETTER

Luka trembled and shook the fence. Although the bell no longer tolled, he was dreaming of love again. He pushed his rod into the nearest tree and began to peel the bark with it. Nobody threw sand at him anymore, or threatened him with a pick. He brayed and inhaled the smoke of the sudden conflagration. Bunches and armfuls of fire were falling on his legs and tail, and even caught in the dirt around him, which he dug up with his hoofs and kicked around.

He imagined that the flame was the open, warm, moist flesh of all the jennies of the world. He rushed at the fence with his huge flower, braying in passion and not even noticing that he was burning himself. Then he knocked over the fence and started a new fire. There was ever more flame and ever more flesh. He wanted to spit it, to pierce it, to cut it through and through.

He trod on the dead gravedigger. He flailed crosses with his rod and felled them. He sank into a sweet heat, as if falling and falling through flesh from which he did not want to free himself until he had torn it into pieces. He disappeared into the church. His worn-out body had never known such excitement.

Then the worn bell tumbled down. A dull thud resounded. A cloud of ashes rose.

Driven on by the wind, or by a genuine male desire to sprinkle as much earth and flesh as he could, Luka changed direction. He veered left, across the cemetery, and treated the twenty corpses, the hundred mourners, and even Father Arturo to a shower of his semen.

Georges and Sergey mopped the dense, honeylike, aromatic stickiness from their faces and necks. They began to spit. Then Sergey Ivanovich vomited. Nevertheless, he helped Georges to a new shelter, where it was easier to follow the donkey in his flight.

Fire seemed to trail after Luka as if he were pulling it along with his tail and hind legs. He paused at the entrance, only a few feet from Georges and Sergey, who thought he would remain there. He even bent his neck as if to graze. Live coals tumbled down his back and legs, and the artists froze in terror, not only for their eyes, but also for the camera.

Lusting for donkey milk and blood, Luka examined all twenty corpses. He straightened his neck and pounded the ground with his powerful front legs.

Treading hurriedly over the hot ashes and hardly noticing his burning trouser legs, Georges was afraid that the lame, Biblical beast would get too far away for close-ups. He almost fell down among the dead. He spat on the people's faces, once on all of them, and then aimed his lens at the dragon.

Frightened by the fire, or fearing they would not be buried properly or on time, the dead began to fret. They shook in their new clothes; their arms thrashed about among their presents for the other world. By knocking with their heads from below, they lifted their coffin lids and looked out onto the roaring conflagration.

The old woman in the Canadian boots was the first to leap out. She began to weave her way through the smoke with her long sleeves scattering flames on the others, as well as chocolate and palm leaves. The owner of her corpse, her tiny old husband, was flabbergasted; he almost hit her.

The dead man with the French beret clapped over his ears felt fire at the small of his back and began to drivel and drool. He stood up with the coffin still on his back and started to run, his wool socks treading wreaths of fire. Then he turned suddenly and tagged after the woman in the Canadian boots. He caught up with her in the middle of the path, threw his arms around her and kissed her. Then he hurled her down, separated her boots and spread her knees. He pushed something crooked, long, and half-dead under her skirt; because of the coffins, one could not see what and how.

The merrymaker in the American infantry helmet pushed his boards aside with his elbows, stood up, and laughed until his rotten mouth spread open to his ears. But this was not the end. His giggling cost him his head. Hardly had his mouth opened and revealed his vegetable tongue to all and sundry, when he burst. Groats and putrid powdered milk dripped down the legs of his trousers. American chocolate full of worms and stars from the American flag surged up. Whatever he had been filled with poured out onto the others. His clothes lay down with his bones on the earth. There was nothing else left.

The rest of the dead were also beginning to stand up, some faster, some slower, some with their coffins, some without. The clothes fell off some of them, together with their decorations and emblems, mostly little brass crosses. Others threw off their gloves or the strings with which their hands had been tied, waved their arms, and slapped everybody they could reach. The last who rose up roamed over the ashes, fighting with the coffins or hugging them, and dripping from every pore. The angriest ones were those who had just arrived; they were cursing those who had carried them there for not going faster and bending their knees, and for giving them, for their journey into death, only a cheap cross and a few tears. Old men and children joined the angry ones, and all of them began stoning their numerous relatives, who fled from them, stumbling and cursing.

It went hardest with the old woman with the mustache. She straddled the empty coffin which her husband had abandoned, flourished the flaming cross, and screamed. Even the mourners were stoning her, and with her flaming cross and smoldering gloves, she could protect only her head. Branches and rocks tattered her dress completely, and her naked stomach could be seen expanding and contracting like sooty bellows. Scratched, disheveled, and bloody, she invited San Giovanni Battista personally to come, offering herself to him. Her cross was turning into a torch, and nobody knew what she would defend herself with if that went too, especially if her saint, occupied by other women, did not arrive on time.

Sergey Ivanovich pulled Georges toward another, still-unburning stone, from which they could get a good view of the entire slaughter. He ordered him not to cry and pointed out the only remaining coffin, in which something was moving.

Then a thin little man emerged from below, with a goatee and spectacles, and sweat on his forehead and nose. His beautiful and pain-chiseled face revealed that he was a man of breeding and impeccable manners. His sunken breast was covered with medals, crosses, and crowns. His uniform—which dated from the time of Garibaldi—was irreproachably tight.

He was the only one who did not join in the ruckus, but stood aside, carefully observing the entire battlefield. Disgusted by the fugitives and cowards, and by the long-awaited peace, he spat quietly and lay down again.

Georges Bonnefous would have filmed him longer if the old man had not reached up and drawn the lid back over him.

Padre Arturo Lupo was having trouble getting his bearings. He lifted his head, which had been stuck in the earth a few moments before, quite slowly. He was looking for his dead. But he could not find even the living there. Not far from him he could see the old woman with her feet in thorns and smoking straw, her mustache smoking, and a burned-up cross falling into ashes before her face. She was sobbing.

He recognized her by her tears and her belly. He said nothing to her. He could not explain to himself who had thrown her there from the sky, or who had so disfigured her. He merely stared, trying to remember the beginning.

THE WAR WAS BETTER

"Where am I and what has happened today?" he asked himself as he smeared soot and ashes over his face. "Who has come and led away so many of the dead? Oh, *Madonna*, I'm naked to the waist, and alone, and the most unhappy of all." He was coming to, beginning to feel pain tingling in the small of his back and his shoulders and shins. "Something unforeseen must have occurred," he thought. "Something that won't please heaven."

He did not notice the camera, or let his cassock slip down his thighs. He was observing the wasteland around him, the smoldering thorns and bushes. There were countless footprints in the ashes. He decided to look for the souls who had made them. He set out on all fours, cracking the coals and burnt-out earth with his kneecaps.

He could not reach them. The living and the dead were fleeing, the dead with their coffins on their backs, like giant beetles. He did not call them, did not request them to wait, but turned instead toward the church. He noticed there was no roof anymore, no bell in the tower. He was not yet completely awake, and he did not weep. Quiet and half-naked in his darkness, he longed to see the donkey. There was no Luka though, no fence anymore, no place of his. Shame and sorrow overwhelmed him. He looked down again into the ashes.

The devil, the famous and invisible devil, wormed his way into the Padre's brain. Arturo Lupo forgot all the holy things with which he had been living, all the prayers and masses, the sounds of the organ and the voices of the choir boys. Above, far above the burnt-out church, in the clouds, he saw Luka.

The donkey flourished his tail in the sky, throwing down fire, flesh, and pieces of the cemetery fence. He would have soared still higher and perhaps even completely disappeared, if it were not for his swollen belly and erected ramrod. The cawing of half charred crows drowned out his braying.

"Pardon me, oh You All-Powerful One, that I still want to live!" Arturo Lupo yelled and leapt upwards into the smoke. "Pardon me," he repeated as he felt his Canadian boots weigh him down.

Through Georges's tears and camera lens, the Padre looked small. The whirlwind had torn away half his cassock, and he looked like an embryo, trying to touch his knees with his beard. While he flew toward Luka in this position, flowers, thorns, and whatever else had been stuffed into him from behind fell out from under his tail. He turned over several times, like a larva in the smoke, caught hold of the donkey's mushroom, and squeezed. It did not burn him, although it was so hot he almost let it go. He began to swing, to climb it like a rope.

By all appearances, Luka no longer felt any pain, and did not even seem to notice the man who was climbing up his rod. His beautiful, yearning, donkey's eyes were blind; when he turned on one side, the whole sky tumbled into them.

He paused for a moment, with his head thrown back and his tail calm and drooping. Georges Bonnefous filmed his hooves, upturned and aflame.

The Padre's small body, focused clearly in the lens, began to shake. Arturo Lupo was mounting the mushroom, squeezing its neck like a snake. He had triumphed, Georges thought. There was no wind or power on earth which could have torn him off the rod. He was obviously happy there, and kept leaning toward the cap of the mushroom and imagining he was nibbling its skin.

Thus they floated off, further and further into the sky, more and more united. Finally, a shining blot was all that remained of them, almost unnoticeable to the naked eyes and impossible to film.

"I've filmed everything now," Georges Bonnefous said. Flinging the camera into Sergey's hands, he fell to his knees and banged his head against the ground. "Horror, Serge! I've filmed horror," he sobbed, exhausted, flailing the ashes and hay. "What is happening here? There is a God! I say it! I believe it!"

"Poor people," Sergey Ivanovich sighed. "Poor people, unprepared for peace, and even less for vitamin-enriched Allied food." He ran back to the jeep, started it up, and rushed back with it.

"Everything has been filmed, life, all of life," Georges murmured without opening his eyes, remembering all the peace, the waste, and the ashes. "I think, at one moment, I caught the very act of insemination, up there in the sky. Those are the most beautiful sequences. They're a masterpiece, an inspired amalgam of poetry and pornography! I'm afraid, Serge, that every censor in the world will cut them out; they'll sterilize us; they'll murder us!"

"Let's hope they won't," Ivanovich panted, helping Georges climb into the car. "In any case, we can count on Sweden, South America, and Spain, and especially on the socialist countries."

"You're really the Fearless Fox, the genuine and only one," Bonnefous said. He could hardly speak and was drenched in sweat and ashy mud.

Sergey Ivanovich pressed the gas pedal to the floor. The jeep leapt forward. Carl Schlotterer moved just a little, knitted his brows, and closed his eyes again.

THE WAR WAS BETTER

 6

"We've got to give them the slip," Georges Bonnefous said as he turned to see what San Giovanni was like. "Stupid as they are, they'll suspect us of the arson."

"They'll believe we didn't do it only if we say the English did," Sergey Ivanovich said dully, with his last bit of strength. "They hate the poor English. They're sure to believe the English were the first to light the match."

"Fire trucks are arriving on all the roads entering San Giovanni; there are some soldiers too, and red water trucks," Bonnefous reported as he looked out over Schlotterer's sleeping body. "Yes, I heard they hated the English more than the Germans. My poor English! The whole world is unfair to them. Their only crime is to be egotists who don't pretend, as others do, that they love their neighbors."

"Hold on, boss!" Ivanovich screamed in panic. "Three fire trucks are coming on. Duck! They're spraying!"

From their perches on the trucks, the firemen were spraying water everywhere, even into the air. Bent over and honking constantly, Sergey and Georges wiggled through the red monsters and the large rocks that had tumbled down onto the road. They took a breath. Smoke rose from the bumpy road.

"They're arriving on time," Georges mused as he looked back at them, dripping wet. "There's no church anymore. They're so poor that the English might build one for them. By the way, I'm still not convinced of their stinginess and hatred for others."

"They think the English are bigger communists than the Russians," Ivanovich said and laughed at his joke. "What is, most probably, also true."

"Watch out, genius, we're coming to a crossroads," Georges said as he glanced briefly at the quiet Schlotterer with his olive can. "Watch out!"

Olive-green army trucks were passing peasant carts. The soldiers shouted from above and threw cigarettes, chewing gum, and old bread down on the poor. Sergey Ivanovich told Georges that the Allies also threw contraceptives to the people, and the peasants, not knowing what to do with them, chewed them like gum.

"As soon as we cross the intersection, we'll have to search for our knights," Georges said. "They aren't far off. They must be here somewhere, in the bushes."

"There they are, boss!" Sergey Ivanovich waved his hand to them. "Look right!" He blew the horn like a madman, and turned on his headlights. "Hey, soldiers!"

"Hey, gentlemen!" Georges Bonnefous joined in, straightening up in his seat. "Do you hear us? Do you see us? Or don't you care a rap for us artists?!"

Bent low and deployed like a patrol, the three ran toward the crossing and the last of the twenty Allied trucks. Antonio Peduto and Giuseppe Bonaccia carried the knapsack and binoculars, on which the turtle was perched; they waved down the truck, barring its way. Gruban Malić, with his globe in one arm, waved and threatened the driver with the other; he explained to him in his mother tongue, Serbo-Croatian, that they were in a hurry, that they had to carry out a party assignment and, before night fell, get out of the village, which the devil had taken anyway.

"They don't notice us at all," Bonnefous said bitterly, standing up and signaling them with his hand. "No, you won't slip away from us!" he shouted to them. "You arsonists and conquerors of peace!" He was choking with dust. "Have I expressed myself finely enough, genius? Does the name suit them?"

"Anything insane—and nice—would suit them, boss."

Sergey Ivanovich blew the horn.

"You won't get away, you sons of bitches! We'll follow you right up to your victory, yours or ours, it's all the same, right up to our common victory!"

Frightened by the globe and Malić's threats and curses, the driver braked his truck. A dense cloud of dust rose around Antonio and Peppe. The driver understood that the three were also in a hurry, like him, to get to Rome, and with his tattooed arm he signaled to them to climb in.

A very thin and inconspicuous soldier, a Negro, extended his hand first to Malić; he looked at the globe with admiration and placed it on the lap of another soldier. He did not have time to roll his eyes when he saw Malić's medals and the red cross on the lapel of his jacket, but hurried to help Antonio and Peppe on. Almost all the Americans made room for their asbestos capes, and smiled at the turtle and their knightly uniforms.

"I'm very happy we can help you," Sergeant Lennie Lopovsky

said on behalf of the others. "We're very happy and honored by your presence." The tall, blond youth with thin lips flushed. "Your car must be out of order?"

Sergey Ivanovich shifted gears again and drove the jeep up to the truck. A dust cloud floated between Georges, who was standing up, holding onto the frame of the windshield and the open truck. His eyes scanned the men in the back for his peace conquerors. He coughed.

"Give us a curse at least, damn it! Or at least spit on us!"

"Are you coming from a parade?" Sergeant Lopovsky asked politely.

"Chance has guided us here," the panting Peduto replied.

"Did you see how poor San Giovanni Battista was destroyed?"

The soldier's face expressed pity; he peered into Antonio's face with admiration and studied his beard, which was full of coal and ashes. "The poor Italian people," he sighed. "They have to suffer in peace too!"

"We did everything we could to prevent the fire, and then to stop it," Peduto said, and almost spat on him. "San Giovanni Battista is not the only miserable one. In the last few months we've seen about ten such catastrophes."

Antonio noticed that Malić was getting along well with the Negro, making himself understood somehow with his fingers and a chocolate bar.

"The worst was in San Lorenzo. The arsonists set fire to all three churches, so that the poor Italian people of that town, who expected more than anyone else from peace, no longer have any fitting place to pray to God. The arsonists, wherever they've gone, have killed faith in everything, in anything. Or at least they've tried to."

"Judging by your lovely uniforms, you must be French," Sergeant Lennie Lopovsky guessed. "I've never seen so many decorations on the same chest."

"We're Slavs," Antonio Peduto said hurriedly. "We're *Slavi*, Captain."

"I'm also a Slav," Sergeant Lopovsky replied, unhappy that he did not know with what rank to address Antonio. "Polish. Also a *Slavo*. That's why I'll never make captain."

"In my opinion, *Slavi* are promoted faster than anyone else," Peduto rejoined. "The day after they're born, they're usually at least corporals."

"In our country, the United States, Slavs are usually firemen," Sergeant Lennie Lopovsky said, watching Antonio and Peppe take off their wet helmets. "In my own town, Gary, Indiana, all the fire-men are Slavs. Poles. Montenegrins. Back there, you know, I'm a fireman too; what else could I be?"

"Who sets fire to houses there—usually?" Peduto asked signif-icantly, drawing a brandy bottle out of his knapsack.

"Slavs," Sergeant Lennie Lopovsky admitted uneasily. He took a swallow from Antonio's bottle and almost burst out crying. "Poles and Montenegrins, mainly. Czechs to a lesser extent."

Everybody laughed at him. He took it easily, lifting the bottle high and toasting in a mixture of Slavic words: "Long live all of you, brothers and friends!"

"And the Bulgarians and the rest, what are they doing?"

"They mostly steal," Lennie Lopovsky admitted with tears in his eyes. "Bulgarians are ordained chicken thieves. I'm ashamed of them, brothers."

"To the health of the Poles and Montenegrins from the town of Gary, Indiana!" Peduto exclaimed. He translated Lopovsky's name privately to himself as "crook," and almost burst out laughing. After a long swig from the bottle which a soldier had just returned to him, he continued: "To the health of the Bulgarians too, and to the health of all the other American chicken thieves! And finally, to the health of all of us, soldiers!"

The truck began to jolt and swerve shortly after they had given the driver a swig from Antonio's bottle. They all threw their arms around one another and swayed in the rhythm of a song. Sergeant Lopovsky stood up to demonstrate how the Poles and Montenegrins threw back their heads when they burst into song. He broke out into one himself, motioning them to join in, which even Malić, as well as Peduto and Peppe, did willingly.

"This song I know too, soldiers and brothers!" Bonaccia cried out with tears in his eyes, standing up suddenly and almost tum-bling over Malić's globe. "I know all the songs which have been sung so far, by anybody, *Americano!*"

"Oh, what a batallion!" Peduto exclaimed, almost completely drunk now and thinking again of the war and the burning Monte-negrin pines. "What a batallion of tramps and firebugs!" he shrieked as he sprinkled the turtle and the Northern countries on Malić's globe with brandy. "Long live fire, without which the wonderful human race of fire eaters could not exist!"

"I know only one song," the small Negro stammered.

"That's a lot for you," Bonaccia replied, but the Negro did not catch the joke.

THE WAR WAS BETTER

"My name's Truman Independence Jones," the Negro resumed, happy that Malić was hugging and squeezing him like a brother. "Truman Independence Jones, Lawton, Oklahoma," he kept repeating while Malić suckled him like an infant, pulling his jaws apart and dousing him with brandy. "I never saw a Slav before, but they look all right to me. They are one brave, mad race of firemen." His head spun; he kept freeing himself from Malić's drunken embrace and looking at the others. "I, Truman, nicknamed Mocking Devil, like every kind of human being, especially the white ones—even if they are chicken thieves."

"I like you too," Malić said and kissed his forehead. "And I'm happy I can hug and kiss you."

"Why?"

"I count on you," Malić went on, clasping him even more tightly in a bear hug and blowing into his ears. "Because you'll soon be what I am now."

"Well, but why?" Truman Independence Jones' ribs hurt. "Why? How can I, a miserable little small-assed Negro from Lawton, Oklahoma, be what you are, with all your decorations?"

"Even before the others, you will become a communist," Malić said; he was almost astride the black man now, forcing open his jaws and looking at his red gums and down his palate to the uvula. "You'll be a real black communist."

"Don't squeeze me anymore, please," the Negro burst out crying, mopping Malić's dripping spittle and snot from his cheeks and neck. "Leave me alone. I'd rather die than let you, a good white man, turn me into a . . . black communist."

The truck hit a pothole and jolted, the tattooed driver swerved, and Truman Independence Jones was finally able to extricate himself from Malić's embrace. Bonaccia received him and began to hug him drunkenly. He kissed his forehead, his flat nose, and even his mouth. He kept repeating to him that Malić was right, and that sooner or later he would make him a free man, without faith or hope. Peppe even tickled the Negro, who was panting by this time and covered with mucus.

"Please, sir, do other male communists mutually kiss each other?" he asked. "I mean, why, please, do they do it . . . I mean, what with so many kewpie dolls and women around, and animals?"

"They love each other," Malić informed him; Antonio Peduto translated it into English and Italian. "They love each other frankly and deeply; all of them work for one thing."

"Oh, goodness!" the Negro sighed, and Lennie Lopovsky would

have joined him if he had not been drinking just at that moment. "Oh, goodness, I'm glad they haven't reached us yet, so we can go on loving just kewpie dolls and women for a while."

"We're reaching you too," Malić continued. He asked Antonio fiercely to translate and explain it, if necessary, with his fists; then he gripped the globe, which was glistening with brandy, and twirled it. "Now I'm going to find your country, and the spot where I'll give you a firm, manly embrace, and free you."

"What will you free me from, sir?"

"From everything," Malić said quickly. "Our goal is complete freedom." With his drunken finger, Malić pricked the heart of America; he found Truman's Oklahoma. "I'll arrive by boat. Wait for me in the port of your town, where extreme injustice and misery reign! Most of the time I appear at dawn!"

Truman Independence Jones was sitting on Peppe's lap, like a baby. Giuseppe Bonaccia held him and blew down his neck. Sobbing drunkenly, Truman looked up every once in a while at Sergeant Lopovsky, who was singing a discordant but obviously masculine song well-known among the Polish and Montenegrin firemen of Gary, Indiana.

Peduto was embracing the soldiers. He tried to explain to them how much he appreciated and loved the greatest warrior of all time, the ideologist of a new order, Gruban Malić, who was drawing his finger through America again.

Peduto tore Truman Independence Jones away from Peppino's embrace. He began to kiss and embrace him, fondling him on his knees. He talked to him about the future, whispering into his ear and tickling his belly until the Negro almost cried again. He rubbed his beard against the Negro's cheek and urged him to desert from the American army and join them. He crooned to him, promising him uniforms and medals and repressing an urge to burst into laughter. Sergeant Lopovsky sat beside them, ordering them to drink up the brandy.

"Let me see those binoculars, please, sir," Truman Independence Jones asked. "What kind are they? Whose are they, such big ones? Spanish or Dutch? I see they're all printed and decorated with gold and brass letters."

"They're Russian," Malić said vigorously. He was drenched in sweat.

"How come?" the Negro asked, trying unsuccessfully to jerk himself from Antonio's grasp. "How come they're Russian, sir?"

"Lenin used them."

"Lenin? Who's Lenin? A football player?"

For the first time Malić was silent.

"Lenin a baseball player?"

"No!" Malić hissed, repressing his rage. "Lenin didn't play games. He looked through these binoculars. That was why he saw so far."

"Did he see Oklahoma, sir?"

"And how could he not see it?" Malić said, softening at the mention of his master. "The man who didn't play games was looking toward you most of the time."

"Did he see our Negro neighborhood?"

"He did. And kept talking about it wherever he was. He loved Negroes very much, and kept thinking about them while he worked with the whites. Therefore, you must know about him. All the miserable and despised peoples throughout the world know the words he repeated every night before going to bed: 'Learn, learn, and only learn!' Such was Vladimir Ilyich Lenin!"

"Since he was looking so much at Oklahoma, sir, did Lenin see me?" Truman asked, his eyes growing more and more vague and bloodshot. "We live in a cottage. We're twelve around the table. Harry and Shirley have left us, and they're in Louisiana now, the neighbors told us, fine and healthy. We twelve agree about everything. They all listen to me because I'm the oldest and smartest. We're happy, sir, and you don't have to come, especially if you're going to squeeze and kiss us so much. Oh, goodness, my black ribs!"

Sighing after a long swig at the bottle, Antonio Peduto finally relaxed his hand. Truman Independence exploited the opportunity and sat up. He resembled a bird about to take off, who could not because of the roof. But before he could say a word, he found himself in Sergeant Lopovsky's arms.

Drunkenly, but firmly, Lennie caressed and kissed him; he told him that after the war he would take him sooner or later to Gary, Indiana, and find him a job with the Polish-Montenegrin fire brigade.

The truck rushed on at top speed, lurching right and left like a drunken man; only an abyss could have stopped it.

"They've forgotten us completely," Georges Bonnefous said; he was beginning to panic.

Sergey Ivanovich honked the horn and then, bending over the wheel, shifted gears and almost crept under the body of the truck. He did not brake on curves, since the tattooed truck driver didn't either, and Georges closed his eyes. He was beginning to think they would catch up with them all right, but dead. Sergey coughed and honked the horn again.

"They've forgotten us, Serge," Georges said, opening his eyes again. "They're singing."

Sergey Ivanovich almost ran into the tires of the army truck, which suddenly braked to let a fire truck pass. The brakes squealed, and Bonnefous's big heart contracted again. By some miracle he was still alive, he told himself, but if they continued like this ... He closed his eyes again, bowed his head and began to choke. Sergey's jaws jutted out; he cursed aloud.

Then Antonio Peduto emerged from the dust and cacophonous song of the Polish-Montenegrin firemen. His medals jingled as he climbed over the rails of the truck, holding a bag in his arms. Giuseppe Bonaccia was standing beside him, with another bag, also drunk. Finally Gruban Malić and Truman Independence Jones appeared, the first under his warm, dusty Russian hat, the other bareheaded, tiny and black.

"Tourists and shit-asses!" Antonio shouted as he spilled cocoa on the jeep. "Shit-asses, hungry peacetime cattle, don't you see what an army is! We're letting you eat your fill for once in your life!"

"Accept the food, you poor devils!" Bonaccia hollered, pouring out powdered milk on Georges and Sergey Ivanovich. "Here, war orphans, taste the food which Truman's America, Malić's Russia, and my Montenegro offer to you!"

Truman Independence Jones poured groats over the jeep, jumping into the air as he did so; since he was drunk and tearful, he almost fell off the truck.

"Poor, miserable tourists," he said as he watched Georges and Sergey Ivanovich extricate themselves with great difficulty from the heap of food that had piled up in the front seat of the jeep. "Poor, miserable tourists and Italian people!"

"This is for tourists too!" Malić exclaimed as he began to throw handfuls of drugs and contraceptives into the jeep. "This is for them too, isn't it, Antonio?"

He kept throwing more and more into the jeep, while Sergey's horn was heard less and less.

"You remember, don't you, Antonio, that I began my career with stuff like this?" Malić asked enthusiastically. "Only, at that time, there were no colored contraceptives. They were expensive as the devil."

"You made a wonderful beginning, *Montenegrino!*" Antonio

said, coughing and spilling out more items from a new bag. "Throw them more! Give them everything! We have to help tourists and the European poor!"

Sergey Ivanovich's horn was hardly audible.

"Now good-by, poor ones!" Peduto spluttered when three fire trucks had passed and the truck wheels began to grip the dirt of the road again. "But not good-by, *arrivederci*, see you soon! We're going straight to Rome, and it seems you're going that way too!" He sprinkled them with the last drops from the bottle and then pitched it into a field. "Malić says we'll conquer Rome without resistance, even more easily than San Giovanni! And I believe him! Believe him too, tourists and travelers . . . and my sorrow!"

The truck was departing. Peduto let out a long scream and hung his beard over the railing. Then the truck disappeared behind a bend.

"You see, they haven't forgotten us," Georges said, scraping food from the windshield. "They've supplied us with drugs against plague, leprosy and both kinds of typhoid, and even with contraceptives."

"I give you my word, boss, they won't give us the slip," Sergey Ivanovich promised, blinking his eyes which were powdered over with cocoa and chewing the cocoa powder around his mouth.

Georges Bonnefous sat hugging his camera. His ears, eyes, and nostrils were also covered with food and dust. He turned to look at the man with the olive can on his breast, who, with the exception of his head, was entirely covered with flour. He seemed to be sleeping and Georges did not want to wake him up.

"What a traveler!" he mused, looking at the bend in the road around which the truck had disappeared. "He's the only one who isn't coughing and spitting today. He's not even sweating."

"We'll catch up with them," Sergey Ivanovich growled as he started the engine. "We'll take shortcuts and reach Rome before them. We'll wait for them at the entrance. Let's hope they don't burn up Rome without us."

"And if they burn it?"

"So much the better. We can make about ten first-rate movies out of it."

"Where did you say we'd wait for them?" Bonnefous asked softly.

"We'll cheat them. We'll ambush them."

"How?" Georges watched the wind blowing flour and packages of drugs off the jeep. "Malić is with them." The wind was carrying off the American rubber devices now too; a few of the untorn ones blew up like balloons and revealed the letters "USA" and various numerals. "I'm afraid of the one with the globe. He'll end up seducing them, and then us too!"

"I've concocted a hellish plan, boss. A genuine humane humbug. We'll go ahead of them, from neighborhood to neighborhood, and if necessary from town to town. We'll get there before them and hire bit players—that is, the common people of whom you have so high an opinion—to retreat, to flee while they advance. And while they conquer the rotten West, we'll be right there, filming everything! This will be the third, and surely the most justified conquest of this damn continent in the last ten years or so."

"It will make a stupendous movie epic!" Bonnefous said enthusiastically. He crinkled his cocoa-and-flour-smeared face into a smile. "It's a stroke of genius! My fox, your intellect and imagination are boundless and merciless." Georges knitted his brows. In his thoughts he saw the insulted angels advancing as their paid enemies withdrew. "We're lucky people are cattle, and will run for anything, even a promise. Don't forget, Serge, that we've already got fire and arson enough for the whole film. We should talk them out of setting fire to everything they come across. They'll be caught and killed, and then we'll have no more actors!"

"The red one, that Peduto, kept talking about some Via dei Serpenti, not far from the Vatican. Did you hear him, Georges?"

"I heard him mention his sister, lost somewhere around there, when he was talking to the Negro. What kind of a street is it?"

"A whorehouse street, the worst. It has a nice sound though, doesn't it? 'Via dei Serpenti, not far from the Vatican.' Even if we lose them, we're bound to find them there."

"It'll be interesting to see how the whores greet them," Bonnefous mused aloud.

"Probably his sister will help the red one, that Antonio. Anyhow, only whores and madmen admire heroes."

"It would be wonderful if they could deliver speeches while they conquered the streets and squares," Bonnefous thought. "The extras, that is, all the people, will have to look mad with fear. We'll record the howling and wailing separately, in a zoo. But the main thing is to let them keep their illusion that they're conquering the world," he continued. "Then they'll think it's easy, and the others will too, that it's wonderful to be a warrior and conqueror of peace."

"They aren't far," Ivanovich yelled. "Hold on, I've got my foot on the floor!" He nibbled his lips again and drove on the grass. "Don't be afraid, we'll outrun them!"

The jeep drove across a field of stubble and found itself approaching a bend in the road. Sergey Ivanovich noticed at the last moment that the field ended in a ditch. He stood up and stamped on the pedal with all his strength, and they almost flew onto the road. They did not overturn; nothing unpleasant occurred. The jeep landed first on two and then on all four wheels. The dust rose around them. Sergey Ivanovich adjusted the wheel, quieted the engine and looked over at his fellow traveler with the eyes of a real fox.

Bonnefous was frozen with terror. He looked up the road across the body of the silent Schlotterer, half covered with flour, rice, and drugs.

"I can't go slower, boss," Ivanovich complained as he put the jeep back into gear. "I can't slow down, I just can't. We're getting near Rome now. You have to fly into Rome, or else fall into it from the sky, like a lightning bolt."

The engine chugged and throbbed.

"I can't slow down, Georges, I've told you a thousand times." He spat out cocoa, rice, and groats. "Anyway, the distance they put between us will never be a problem. In a sense we are what they are, boss, and it's all the same who conquers Rome first, and gets to Via dei Serpenti near the Vatican."

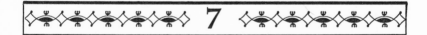

7

"The people are fleeing magnificently," Sergey Ivanovich remarked as they entered Via dei Fiori at twenty miles an hour. "Even the ones we didn't pay with those counterfeit dollars. They're doing it even better."

Via dei Fiori was overflowing with the crowd.

"People, I've always loved and admired you; panic seizes you so divinely, you believe anything, and nothing on earth can sober you up."

Through Georges's lens, the crowd rushed on; only a fire could have stopped them. It seemed to Georges that bells were ringing from all the Roman churches; the sky was bursting with the echo-

ing of copper. Not only those on the pavement were running, with
the counterfeit banknotes in their hands, but also the others, who
jumped out of their houses through the windows as if snakes were
pursuing them, and hurried after the rest. Bells were ringing everywhere. The echoes were multiplied a hundredfold; the roofs were
melting in the heat.

Women, children, and old men turned to see the conquerors.
There seemed to be no one there of military age, however, for the
hundred or so men who were could never have been reached by a
bullet, let alone Georges's lens. They did not even turn to look.
They were genuine Italian soldiers, light and nimble, experts at falling down and feigning death, at rising and taking cover, somehow,
somewhere, sometimes even behind their own shadows.

Behind the panic-stricken crowd, and ahead of Sergey's jeep,
Gruban Malić was riding on a naked donkey. The tails of his overcoat covered some of the donkey's ribs. With his museum spurs, he
was kicking at the famished, mangy animal, who was not accustomed to such a multitude and could hardly move.

Malić held the globe in his left hand. He flung his right arm
around to fan himself in the heat and cut down, in his mind's eye,
the crosses of the numerous churches in the neighborhood.

"Italy, whore, you're finally under me!" he shouted, as his hat
with fur earflaps fell down over his hooked Montenegrin nose.

He turned, as if in a saddle with a spear in his hand. Bathed in
his own sweat, he was listening to his own fearless heart.

"Italy, infected whore, faithless strumpet, is this how you surrender?!"

In his thoughts he saw rivers of cowardly Italian blood. He
lifted himself up and spoke. "Are there any heroes in this country
who'll come up to me and look me in the eye?! Italian cunt-lickers,
get yourselves out of your mouseholes and come share Rome!"

Malić's voice did not resound (he was too weak and run-down
that day), but since he spoke in Antonio and Peppe's language, almost everyone understood him. They bowed their heads, hid their
fake dollars, and wept. His tired donkey halted frequently, frightened by the crowd. Then the man with the globe had time to kick
the panicky bodies of the extras and the real cowards. He spat on all
of them until his mouth dried up, from growling, spitting, barking,
and challenging people to duels.

"No, *Montenegrino*, not in this whole country, or anyway not
in this whole rotten city, is there one hero who'd come to meet
you! Peduto shouted, happy to see Malić so inspired. "There are no

men here anymore! The good ones are still in Greece, in the Balkans; wolves are pulling their bones apart in Montenegro! There are no men in this country anymore! Don't you see they're all like women, and mostly like whores; there'll be nobody even to meet me, let alone you!"

Peduto was following the donkey. He held his knapsack with the turtle in it on the giant binoculars. The Romans who were not fleeing, but making way for them and greeting them like real liberators, looked at his red beard and breast covered with medals with sincere admiration. He brandished his fire helmet, spat toward the steeples and called out: "Italians, cattle and frog eaters, you who've polluted half of Europe and almost all the Balkans with syphilis and gunpowder, don't you see that your doomsday has come! Look! The *Slavi* are arriving; we three are only the vanguard! Look at us! Remember us! And know that the rest, who're arriving on our heels, are worse, more terrible than we are! Isn't it so, Peppino?"

"Romans, I'm going to have all the Italian girls!" the panting Bonaccia exclaimed. "All your sisters, all your daughters, all your relatives!" He was speaking half in Malić's language and half in Neapolitan. His fire helmet was literally spinning around his profusely sweating head. "Peppe will impale all the Roman women. . . . And then you'll . . . then all the addresses will be mine!"

"Oh, what a people!" someone from the crowd wailed. "What a people, these damn *Slavi* who won't let us die in peace, which we waited for so long!"

"Oh *Madonna!*" another voice lamented. Everyone Malić spat on began to invoke the Mother of God. "Oh *Madonna*, save us from the Slavs, save us from these ruffians and barbarians! Oh *Madonna*, what a people, these mad, courageous *Slavi!*"

"Don't invoke the *Madonna!*" a woman screamed as she scratched her sunken cheeks. "Don't invoke the Mother of God; she's still in Greece or Montenegro! It's better to give shelter to the women and girls. They'll rape all of them; they'll pull their legs apart. Just look at their clothes and medals! Don't invoke the Mother of God, who only weeps over the victims of the long war and prays for us!"

"These will be the worst, I feel it already," an old man blubbered, rolling his eyes and throwing himself in front of Malić's donkey. "Blessed Christ, don't you see the *Slavi* will be even more horrible than the Germans! They say they drink human blood, and then weep and kill each other!"

Malić's donkey trampled the man under its hooves; only Antonio heard him: "Jesus, the *Slavi* have killed me, as they wanted to kill you...."

Everyone following Malić trampled over the old man's body. For a while he wailed from beneath them, invoked all the saints in turn, and then addressed the commandant of occupied Rome. He could not even cross himself. His arms were crushed, his jaws bloody and gaping, his English army shirt rolled up and dirty.

Georges Bonnefous filmed him from the jeep. The old body trembled like a child's. Then it calmed down.

In a vivid flash, Georges remembered San Giovanni Battista, the disfigured gravedigger, and the dead with their coffins on their backs like giant beetles. He found himself wondering in a kind of daze why the old man's flattened and mutilated body did not get up and walk away from the pavement.

"My celluloid will bring you back to life, *mon vieux*," the sweaty Bonnefous said, turning his camera toward another target.

"You'll live again, old man, never fear. And whoever watches you, die, crying that the *Slavi* wanted to poison Christ; they'll know the price of what this whole foolish, irresponsible world calls peace and happiness!"

The crowd bumped into a company of American soldiers, who had just arrived, dusty and half-dead, from a long march, and a group of onrushing firemen, who were expecting a fire to break out somewhere nearby; it veered into Via dei Fiori and came to the square with the fountain. Frightened by the uniforms, the Negroes and the red fire trucks, the crowd swerved again, into the narrower Via degli Amfibi.

"Make way for the victors and conquerors!" Ivanovich was shouting as he honked his horn and braked to a stop. But the clamor of the children and the wailing of half-dressed mothers drowned out his words. "Make way, or I'll run you over! I'll begin to shoot!"

It seemed to Georges that in Via deli Amfibi, the mood of the people began to change. Even those who cursed the *Slavi*, the poisoners of Christ and Teutonic barbarians, pressed toward Malić. They wanted to touch the tails of his overcoat, his museum boots whitened with powdered milk, his numerous and weighty decorations. They caressed Malić's donkey, pulled his tail, felt his greasy testicles and the sluggish foreskin of his ramrod, and then smelled and licked their fingers. It reminded Georges Bonnefous and Sergey Ivanovich of Luka and the Padre Arturo.

A new and still madder crowd rushed at them from the nearest sidestreet. Old men, children, and women were everywhere, strong as water, dividing the crowd which had run through all of Rome before the oncoming liberators. They too caressed Malić's donkey, pulled his mushroom, and cooed: "*Slavo*, ah, our *Slavo*, you're finally among us, our only *Slavo!*"

"Never before witnessed, wonderful, magnificent!" Sergey yelled toward Georges, whose breath suddenly stopped from excitement. "Watch out, don't miss this!"

They were lifting the donkey, carefully but high. He was too tired and upset to defend himself. He relaxed his tail and belly and even his mushroom, which the women were squeezing and twisting. He even dropped his ears and his eyes, perhaps in shame. Although he was lifted high, he was careful not to lose his balance or turn on his side and throw down the man with the globe and the greasy Russian hat pressed on his skull.

"Long live our liberators, our *Slavi!*" they rent the air with a tremendous shout as they looked up at the donkey and Malić from below. "Long live the good *Slavi*, who've come to free us from the English, Americans, and other Negroes!"

Gruban Malić also howled. He began to speak of Montenegro and his little café where he had supplied the 501st Montenegrin Army and certain other Red detachments and corps with money, brandy, and contraceptives during the shameful Italian occupation. He mentioned the Venezia and Murge divisions, the fleet and blood-thirsty black-shirt companies. He spoke of vast Mother Russia, which had no such preventives or medicines, and of the globe which had to become entirely Red. He mentioned Vladimir Ilyich Lenin, his wife Nadezhda, and the thoughts which Ulyanov repeated every night when getting into his hard, proletarian bed. He mentioned world revolution; he mentioned the longest and thickest binoculars of all time, through which the most distant parts of the world could be seen; he threatened them with equality, poverty, and communism. He waved his free hand about, thundered at the top of his voice and driveled.

"*Slavo*, Commandant!"

A disheveled woman in her late thirties was calling to him from her balcony. Something mad and restless stirred in her dark eyes. She extended her hands toward Malić, who was not far from her. "*Slavo*, if you happen to be Russian or Montenegrin, take me!" Her abundant breasts seethed over the balcony railing. Her lips were swollen with lust. She took the crowd's breath away.

"Take me, *Slavo!*" she shrieked. "I want to get on you and your donkey, the first and only victor!"

THE WAR WAS BETTER

"Hold her back! I haven't finished about the revolution and Lenin yet!" Malić cried out, but only Antonio and Peppe heard him. "Hold her back. Otherwise she'll besmirch our victory, the great names I've mentioned and the speech I only just started!"

Stripping off her clothes, the woman leapt from above. Her round behind flashed; the rose between her legs shone blackly. She fell down on the crowd's shoulders and felt a multitude of fingers on her hot body. The whole of Rome and all the church cupolas poured down into her eye sockets and between her thighs. She rolled her eyes, shrieked, and felt many hands lifting her.

She did not want to get down again, and even less to be put back on the balcony. Through her tears she could see Malić's shoulders and she gripped them desperately with her hands. She rode. His neck and head were between her thighs.

Feeling the woman's moist, hot little frog on his neck, Gruban Malić interrupted his speech about how the *Slavi* and communism would devour the West and turn it into an endless garden of roses which were only red. He wanted to spit. He saw her knees in front of his nose. Her body smelled like a miracle, especially the dripping sack of musk. He raised his globe to hit her. The woman began to fret and jostle, to roll her eyes again.

"*Slavo*, marshal, warrior and victor, how long I've waited for you! Finally, finally, oh men and women, my sisters and brothers, the real victor has come! Not a tank, but on a donkey, like Jesus, the only one I'm faithful to!"

She wriggled and trembled, spreading sweat and ashes over his face with his fur hat.

"*Slavo*, do you know who Christ is?"

"Lenin is greater!" Malić roared, keeping himself astride the donkey with more and more difficulty. "Lenin, Vladimir Ilyich Ulyanov, is probably the father of Jesus!"

"My husband, Mario Mulas, perished either conquering Moscow, or fleeing from Bijelo Polje! He was the greatest coward in the Venezia Division, but I loved him in spite of everything! My poor Mulas!"

Malić could hardly hear her voice. His voice too was rattling and straining. The crowd shouted at her and spat on her from behind, especially on her uncovered buttocks. They were still carrying the donkey.

"Get down from the victor, Gigia!" someone screamed from beside Sergey's jeep.

"You'll strangle the victor and his donkey, you prostitute!"

THE WAR WAS BETTER

"My good people, don't spit on me anymore!" Gigia sobbed and directed her swelling breasts toward the crowd; her eyes were big and crazy. "Don't treat me like this! I'm so unhappy and lost!"

"Why are you unhappy?" Peduto out-shouted the crowd. "You're riding the victor and one of the greatest warriors of all time, a Montenegrino-Russo-Japanese hero, a man who's willing and able to annihilate the whole world for the sake of communism. Gigia, *Taliana*, Malić even knew Lenin! Vladimir Ilyich Ulyanov even gave him these binoculars and a series of vows and assignments to carry out. Gigia, my poor one, did you hear what I said?"

"Mulas, my heart and my coward, disappeared in the war," the widow stuttered out through her tears. "And therefore I pray to the Montenegrin or Russian land, on behalf of Christ and the *Madonna*, to be tender with his bones! When peace came, they took both my daughters to Via dei Serpenti; the first was fourteen, and the second twelve. They also led away my ten-year-old son, little Marco Mulas, to Via dei Serpenti, and since then I've never seen them again—not one of them! Tell them, oh Christ, not to spit anymore!"

"Is the damned Via dei Serpenti far away, Gigia? Is it far?" Antonio asked the woman who was riding the killer of her Mulas; his heart was overflowing.

"We're quite near," the widow said. "First we ride through Via Maledetta, then Via Dante, and then we'll be there, *Slavo*." She was quieting down, but still she did not cover her body. "I look for my children there every day."

"Get off my neck, woman!" Malić wailed when he had stopped speaking to the crowd about progress, love and the classless society. "Get off, or I'll fall down, and I shouldn't kneel down until I completely conquer the capital of the dirtiest country in the world!"

She crumpled his broad Russian hat, grimaced, and screamed, so that Sergey's horn, which he was honking with all his might, could hardly be heard.

"Get off, and I'll show you the country and the very spot where I killed your Mulas! Lenin, Maxim Gorki, and I did it. Gorki took out his heart, squeezed it with his huge hand and wringed his blood out like dirty water. If you get off, I'll tell you when it was and all the other details!"

Maintaining his balance precariously, Malić took his globe and spanked the widow's behind, which was glistening with spit, again and again, sometimes with Red Russia and icy Canada, sometimes with the blazing equator and the convex parts of Asia and Africa.

THE WAR WAS BETTER

At the entrance to Via dei Serpenti, the donkey began to bray, and Malić almost fell down. Some of the old men who were carrying him burst into tears out of sheer fright.

The donkey brayed and lashed at them with his tail and his rod, and kicked at them with his hooves. He stuck out his neck, but closed his eyes in order not to see the multitude and the motley city. He had no idea that they were photographing him and calling him by not only contemptuous, but also Slavic and communist names. He brayed and kicked but kept the load faithfully on his back.

The procession did not stop even at the great crossroads. Those who were following in the narrow, dirty Via Maledetta had to wait for them. Even the large, open Land Rover with the long antenna and unusual crew climbed the sidewalk and began to wait.

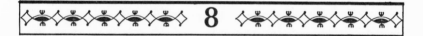

8

"Everything's possible in Rome, but I've never seen anything like this," the Commandant of all Allied troops in this part of Italy, Sir Stanley Gordon Clumsy, former Chief of the Royal College of Veterinary Surgeons, Oxford, said to his companions in the Land Rover, with a reserved smile. "And I've seen all kinds of miracles!"

He was a meager Englishmen, freckled about the nose, with lively movements and dreamy eyes.

"What we're looking at is even more bizarre, I'd say, than what you've experienced and filmed; wouldn't you say so, Fred?"

The American General, Fred Charles Friggit, in his fifties like Sir Stanley, but slightly smaller and more decorated, laughed uproariously. "I like Europe, even adore it, because it's tragicomic, and because occurrences like this never seem to end. Europe is inexhaustible." He laughed until his strong, thickset body shook all over and it seemed his sides would split. "I like Europe and I'm going to try to remain here to the end, if for nothing else, then at least for such things."

"This is more like Asia," the rattleboned Lady Agatha Friskie remarked, without condescending even to look at the American as she pointed at the donkey and his load. "Asia, and not Europe. Decidedly."

THE WAR WAS BETTER

"Europe and Asia—it's all the same, madam," General Fred Charles Friggit said, clapping his hands and giggling. "Europe is interesting because its borders with Asia are impossible to define; because, look, a thoroughly Asian scene is possible in the center of Rome and its Via degli Amfibi, Via dei Fiori, Via Maledetta, and finally Via dei Serpenti, from which we're not going to budge."

General Friggit sized the woman up again: scrawny and uniformed, her hair already graying, her eyes malicious, her chin double; he would have stopped laughing if it hadn't been for the sign of the Royal Red Cross and the medals of the Order of Merit and the *Légion d'Honneur* on her breast.

"What I say, my dear and honored lady, is that the most beautiful things in Europe, which you defend from me in advance and in vain, are Asiatic."

Lady Agatha Friskie stopped looking at the donkey and his ramrod and fixed her eyes on Malić, his crooked Montenegrin nose, and the globe with which he was defending himself from the widow. Although she had long been nearsighted, she noticed the Red Cross badge among Malić's numerous medals and was deeply moved. She felt love for him; she told herself she would meet him sooner or later, and then she would caress and kiss the neck which the miserable nymphomaniac, Gigia, was now rubbing and licking.

The fourth member of the group in the Land Rover, the French Colonel, Luc de Tonnerre, stopped watching the victorious Malić and what was happening to him. He flushed, stroked his well-combed beard and wished to be far from the peacetime landscape which confronted him. He was tall and slim, with a thin nose and intelligent eyes, and even his closest friends took him for a Norwegian, rather than the French aristocrat and officer he was. He stood behind Lady Agatha Friskie, sickened by her masculine perfumes and skinny legs.

"Before we Americans came to Europe, we knew about prostitution only from books," General Fred Charles Friggit pointed out. "Now here we are taking part, as I would put it, in a totally sexual theater."

"It will be coming to America too, Fred," Sir Stanley observed.

They stood watching the rows of prostitutes grouped on the sidewalks in front of the houses and in the windows. All of them were inviting in the victors, waving their hands, some of them with unmentionable frillies clasped in them, and showing their bruised thighs and breasts.

"This is what awaits you; it will come even if peace on your

[205]

continent, which you call a paradise, lasts forever, but especially if you lose a war. The victors will grant you the freedom which you now find only in European books. Prostitution goes hand in hand with defeat, Fred, especially spiritual and national defeat, and with victory as well. You're lucky you've seen neither one nor the other so far."

"If prostitution finally sweeps the U.S.A., I'll come to you."

"Oh, Fred! By then Europe will be a unique, vast, general brothel. Only a conflagration will save it from syphilis. Even now it's already so horrible that I dream about flames as the only remedy."

"Since Europe as a whole is in question, I don't think what we're looking at now is so terrible," General Fred Charles Friggit said, noticing the shocked Lady Agatha Friskie shudder and stick out her pouting lips in disgust. "Angus McPurdy, my friend and sexual adviser, a Captain in the Royal Canadian Horse Artillery, is going in passionately for the eroticism of poor Europe, especially the sexual fantasies of the Latin peoples and their neighbors, the Slavs. He's found out that today's Rome, in comparison with its former heights, is a mere everyday, sleepy little Swiss village. He stresses that, under Pope Pius IX, this town counted hardly 200,000 inhabitants but boasted of roughly two hundred brothels. Today Rome counts more than a million and a half Italians and foreigners, but has only 2000 to 2500 bordellos. As you can imagine, the Pope's Rome was much more revolutionary, richer, more poetic."

"That is also the thesis of Major Archibald Symons, from the Royal Army Dental Corps," Sir Stanley said, his dreamy English eyes bulging. "He holds that the times were such as we know them from books because everybody had forgotten about war, justice, and, if you will, fire itself. I didn't know that Captain McPurdy was going in for such research, and had come to the same results."

"Most interesting is the theory of Lieutenant D. S. Elliot, also an Englishman, my intimate friend and frequent entertainer, an outstanding member of the Oxford Royal Central Asian Society," the American said, noticing that Lady Agatha was about to blow up. "I'll explain it to you when we're alone, or in the presence of Colonel Luc."

Colonel Luc de Tonnerre could recall numerous theories advanced by English cavalry captains. He felt crimson flush his sunken cheeks, and he coughed. Then he saw what even the raging Lady Agatha Friskie could not help but notice.

The crowd was pressing in closer and closer and caressing Malić's boots. And when the old men carrying the donkey on their pathetically lifted arms knelt down, in exhaustion, to grant the honor to others, when it seemed the donkey would totter down on the pavement, or onto their fallen bodies, women rushed in and kissed his still hard and motley mushroom.

The Colonel remembered the desperate expression in Malić's eyes, his scream: "Surrender at last, you black capitalists!"

Then, as they lifted the donkey again, with Malić on it, and passed by the Land Rover, Gigia, the widow, leaned into it backwards, so that they all saw both her holes.

"Protest! Please!" Lady Agatha Friskie almost shrieked, looking sternly at Sir Stanley Gordon Clumsy. "You're the Commandant of Rome, not I! Please! Please! Please!"

"This is a film, Madam!" Sir Stanley said, stretching out his freckled arms, with the medals on his breast jingling like those on hers. "A genuine film, a kind of European-Asiatic western."

He could see Sergey's jeep and Georges Bonnefous, whose camera was glued on Malić, the donkey, and the double-barreled widow.

"The western, my dear lady, is the only spiritual production of America worth remarking. I must confess: I know it thoroughly and love it totally."

Lady Agatha Friskie was not so easily pacified; her chin and her heart were still quivering.

"Aside from the western, the Americans, the farmers and cowboys, know no art, because they have never known real sorrow, wounds, or prostitution."

"I wouldn't call it a western," Fred Charles Friggit, dizzied by the widow's body, put in. "For my money, it's more like a European or English comedy. There's the clown, the one with the globe, and it's well known that even the Russians and Chinese have never surpassed the English in clownery. Such a scene is possible only in Europe. As in the circus, not just the artists, but the public too takes part. Europe is a circus! And I'd like to preserve it!"

The American General got no answer. Malić's donkey was braying beside him and suddenly whacked Lady Agatha Friskie's decorations.

"This is a true European circus," he continued as if nothing had happened. "A real burlesque comedy with a sad ending. Only my personal friend, Vittorio De Sica, is lacking; if he appeared, it would make the chaos complete. Have you seen De Sica in his latest neorealistic, Italian western?"

THE WAR WAS BETTER

Once more no one answered. General Fred Charles Friggit turned to the French Colonel, who was holding the half-unconscious Lady Agatha Friskie in his arms.

"Luc, help me, will you? If you understand what a movie is."

"I'm a man of the theater," Colonel Luc de Tonnerre said, defending himself. "By profession, I'm a teacher; as a hobby, I write dramas and play the leading roles in amateur productions. I despise films, especially American and English ones. I've never heard of your personal friend, De Sica."

Luc de Tonnerre continued to hold Lady Agatha Friskie. He gave her some pills, and she frowned. She was watching Gruban Malić and the implacable woman on his neck, and Peduto and Peppe, in a kind of dream; she began repeating after Malić that the capitalists had to surrender as soon as possible, and if not they would have to perish by fire.

Sir Stanley Gordon Clumsy and Fred Charles Friggit, almost at the same time, finally noticed something was wrong. They asked Luc what was happening.

"The lady has almost fainted," the French Colonel said triumphantly. "I've given her all the pills I had on me, even the ones I need to prevent my unfortunate kidneys from disintegrating," he added, with his eyes flashing, and then continued in a whisper: "She's talking of her childhood. She's asking us, as friends and colleagues, to bring her the chief clown, the one with the globe, as soon as possible."

"Why just him?" General Friggit murmured in his ear. "Why not the donkey?"

"She says she knows him. . . ."

"The donkey?"

"No, I think it's the clown she means, although I don't exclude the donkey. She says she must have met him somewhere in the past. She remembers the little red cross among all his medals. It seems she's the body and soul of the organization, and she's ready to give anything for it—to die for it, we hope, but not in my arms, thank you. Anyway she wants to see him alone, to talk to him about certain personal matters, *tête-à-tête*."

"These damned English women are hopelessly, irredeemably mad," Sir Stanley murmured to his American colleague. "They're just like American women: the only thing they go for is clowns and donkeys!"

"She's asking for a chamber pot," Colonel Luc de Tonnerre whispered. "My goodness, where am I going to get a chamber pot in the middle of this parade, and with those moviemakers aiming right at us just this very moment? Ah, the lady's yielding. *Merde!*"

The open Land Rover made its way with great difficulty. Via dei Serpenti was choking with humanity. The driver honked and blinked the headlights and even the iodine fog lights. His assistant was dialing the car telephone in deadly fear, calling for an ambulance.

Lady Agatha Friskie lay on Fred's and Luc's knees. She gulped Sir Stanley's pills against rheumatism, asthma, and intestinal catarrh, and then whispered, so faintly that only the three could hear her: "My poor *Slavo* . . . my clown!"

"Step on the gas, even if we run them all down!" Sir Stanley ordered the driver; his eyes were no longer dreamy and romantic. "Give her the petrol, boy! Turn right, by that ambulance, into the courtyard on the side, over there, there, where the board fence is, in front of the hole made by our bomb. Gas, Thomas!"

Honking in panic, they almost smashed into Sergey's jeep. They swerved, but Ivanovich did too, and kept right behind them, so that Georges Bonnefous could film them close up. Lady Agatha Friskie had not yet come to.

They made their way through rows of prostitutes and homosexuals. Those who had not yet gone off hand in hand with Allied soldiers waved to them. Middle-aged women offered them finely combed, clean little daughters and sons. Old women and utterly useless children extended rubber sex organs of various sizes and shapes, with fur tufts of different colors, toward the passing Negroes and Hindus. Via dei Serpenti was having its great day. Perhaps for that reason, all the bells in all the churches of Rome and even the Roman suburbs were ringing.

The driver turned the Land Rover into a large yard. The French Colonel let out a sigh of relief, and thought of how unfortunate he was to have gone for the usual ride with his friends that day.

Lady Agatha Friskie came to and refused to lie down on the stretcher. She asked a group of bristling, assiduous girls from the Women's Army Auxiliary Corps whether the front was far off and the battlefield covered with German and Japanese corpses.

"And where's my wonderful man with the globe, my *Slavo?*" she asked, shaking like a leaf from the drugs she had swallowed. "What a clown! Don't let him get lost. I want to help him, to make him a member of the Red Cross. My clown!"

Sir Stanley, with a shudder of jealousy and disgust, let her drop

THE WAR WAS BETTER

into Luc's arms. General Fred Charles Friggit was pleasantly surprised to see that Sergey Ivanovich's jeep had rushed into the yard, which was filled with boards and broken furniture. Georges Bonnefous, dripping wet in his unbuttoned shirt, was already filming the locale and each of them in turn.

"Excuse us, gentlemen," the panting Ivanovich pleaded as Georges pointed the lens at Lady Agatha Friskie and the uniformed W.A.A.C. girls. "Excuse us poor, unprotected artists. We're in the midst of making a movie on a highly significant theme," he said in English, French, and even in Russian. "We have no fixed script, however; what we need is life, real life, without scenery, without makeup, and without roles memorized in advance." The officers were silent. He wanted to make them smile. "Don't get sore at us if we're ready to die for art, especially for movies."

The officers frowned, while the W.A.A.C. girls ran up in front of the camera, adjusting their hats and giggling as if they were at somebody's wedding.

Then Sergey Ivanovich remembered something he could use to attract the officers' attention. He grabbed hold of Carl Schlotterer's shoulders and lifted him up; flour, groats, and cocoa dripped down from him.

"What in the world will happen now?" Sir Stanley asked General Friggit softly but significantly. "Do you have a foreboding, Fred?"

"Here our journey together comes to an end, soldier," Sergey Ivanovich said to Carl Schlotterer, who was still holding the olive can in his hands. "Now you're in Via dei Serpenti, not far from the Vatican, in the middle of Italy and the world, and you can fend for yourself from now on." He pulled him over to the middle of the yard and introduced him to everyone. "He says he's from the north. I believe him too. Only a German could be so proud, suicidal, and insane at the same time."

Carl Schlotterer looked at them. His beautiful eyes with long, delicate eyelashes shone somberly out of his ghostlike face covered with flour.

"Gentlemen, you still don't know real Germans."

"But . . . is he alive . . . if he's a *Tedesco?*" Agatha Friskie asked from Luc's arms. "Is that horrible and most unfortunate German alive? I mean, didn't we annihilate all the Germans and Japanese at Hiroshima?"

"No, Madam, he's not alive," Sergey Ivanovich said in a genuine London accent. "He's dead."

With Colonel Luc de Tonnerre still holding onto her, Lady

THE WAR WAS BETTER

Agatha Friskie began to vomit drugs. If it weren't for him, she would have fallen across the barrels and boxes, onto the manly breast of the shocked General Friggit, who was seeing his first German. Lady Agatha Friskie vomited all over her own and Luc's medals and coattails.

"He's dead, madam!" Sergey Ivanovich repeated, turning Carl Schlotterer around so that he could be seen from all sides. "And precisely because he is dead, he has become great."

Lady Agatha Friskie was still throwing up.

"He's dead and magnificent. How can you doubt it? Only a dead man could be so beautiful, so magnificent, so masculine!"

"I'd prefer him if he were alive," Lady Agatha Friskie managed to say as she vomited more pills into Luc's beret. "I hope, Sir Stanley, that the clown with the globe isn't dead yet."

"He's just arriving, madam," Sir Stanley informed her, posing for Georges and making an effort to invest his eyes with his famous, all-conquering, romantic air. "He's here, among us, in the full sense of the word. He's alive, I assure you."

"I can also assure you that the *Tedesco* is dead!" Antonio put in as he led the donkey to Sergey's jeep. "He's the most beautiful dead man among us!"

The donkey's legs began to bend and tremble. It seemed Gruban Malić was too heavy for him. He stopped in the middle of the yard, not far from Carl Schlotterer, who could hardly keep himself upright, even with Sergey Ivanovich's support. The donkey's eyes fell; his rod began to swell, and Lady Agatha Friskie started throwing up bile and pills again.

"Here's another real man," Antonio said to all of them, when Malić had dismounted and mopped the sweat from his face with the sleeve of his crumpled Russian overcoat. "Here's a great man and the greatest hero I've ever met!" Antonio Peduto and Peppe set down the knapsack and carefully placed the binoculars on it. "His name is Malić, which is... well... like mine. Gruban Malić. If I were you I'd remember that name. You'll need to."

"Malić," all of them pronounced after him like school children. "Gruban Malić."

"It's easy to remember," Lady Agatha Friskie thought aloud, deciding to approach him as soon as possible. "Isn't it true, Sir Stanley, that his name and exotic figure are quite easy to remember?"

"Malić," Sir Stanley said softly, looking over at General Friggit, who was desperately trying to contain his laughter. "Malić, it's quite easy to remember indeed! Montenegrin or Russian?"

"Both!" Peduto said

THE WAR WAS BETTER

"If this is the Malić, who drove the Italians out of the Balkans and enabled us to land quickly in Greece and elsewhere, if this is the same man, then I'm exceptionally honored," Sir Stanley Gordon Clumsy said with a reserved English smile on his lips, as he stepped toward him. "It's my great honor, proud son of Montenegro and Russia, and now, since today, of England too!"

"Hands up!" Gruban Malić thundered ferociously at the Englishman. "Hands up, I say!"

"Oh, God!" Sir Stanley sighed.

"Don't mention God in my presence!" Malić shouted, lifting his globe high over the other's head. "Don't you see who I am and why I have come? Surrender!"

Sergey Ivanovich translated everything for them.

"Surrender, sir!" Antonio Peduto exclaimed. "Surrender, all of you, surrender! Don't you see he's a great hero, destroyer and conqueror? Parachuted into this country from the east, a communist? Just look at the parachute he's still carrying around. Stalin trusts him completely. His name's Malić. What a name! His task, like mine, is to turn you into ashes. Have mercy and compassion. We're good, only you don't have to believe us very much; we're children. Please."

Sir Stanley Gordon Clumsy exchanged glances with General Friggit. Lady Agatha Friskie whispered to Colonel de Tonnerre that she had long been ready to surrender. The W.A.A.C. girls gathered around Sergey's jeep, waiting for someone—anyone—to make them surrender. Colonel Luc de Tonnerre decided to write something tragicomic and bittersweet on the theme.

"Surrender, gentlemen," Sergey Ivanovich urged them with a voice full of elegant pain. "Surrender, since such a man and conqueror is urging you to." He whispered to Georges to get more footage of the lady in the arms of the hatless and ghastly pale French gentleman. "Surrender, I too am asking you. It will mean a lot to him, and you'll remember it with nostalgia, your longest surrender and our only and most thrilling movie."

"I give up in the name of the western," Sir Stanley said solemnly and reddened. "I give up, although I must confess this is the first western in which I have no idea what's going to happen next."

"Nothing will happen next," Antonio reassured him. "We aren't smart enough to figure out what will happen next. First of all, we want to destroy everything and dishonor everybody. As Malić says, to free everybody. That's all we know about; we aren't interested in the results. We're for madness at all costs. We're from the east!"

THE WAR WAS BETTER

Sir Stanley lifted his hands.

"Be kind to my divisions too," Fred Charles Friggit said, surrendering like the Englishman. In Malić's appearance and grimaces, he noticed something inexpressibly sad, Chaplinesque, English.

"I surrendered first, *Slavo*," Lady Agatha Friskie yelled, trying to scramble to her feet. "Lead me off! I'm your slave!"

"How wonderful and noble it is that you've surrendered, and that you're holding your hands over your heads," Peduto began, almost tearfully. "We'll never forget it, we for whom illusions and victories are all that remain in life. Don't tremble, don't be afraid; we won't harm you. We're deeply grateful to you. We don't know how we can ever repay you. It's worth living for such an act, for such a triumph. Since we, the unhappy *Slavi* . . ."

"Your surrender was completely convincing, gentlemen," Sergey Ivanovich interrupted. "I can only bow to you and assure you your lives are not in danger. Relax, the Slavs have insulted hearts, but kind ones."

"We've read a great deal about it," generals Friggit and Clumsy said, one after the other. "Only now do we understand that the Slavs are martyrs, great martyrs indeed."

The donkey's mushroom began to swell again, and he started pissing. A little yellow pool formed around the jeep's left front tire.

"Finally a war!" somebody shouted. "Here's the war, love, and here are the conquerors!" It was a man's voice and it came from above, from one of the windows which looked out over the large yard, which had a small bar in the corner, a shooting gallery and a merry-go-round. "Love, here's a real war! Oh, how it excites me!"

"I don't believe it; our luck's not that good, my sun," a deep, lazy, female voice answered. "What have we done to deserve it?"

Then both of them went to the other side of the yard, between the shooting gallery and the empty bar. The woman, Romana, was miraculously beautiful. She had only a dark blue overcoat on, so that her long legs could be seen up to her hips. Her wavy black hair fell to the middle of her back. She stared at them and made an effort not to weep. The inconspicuous man who was standing beside her, holding her hand like a mother's, was Conte Giovanni Besta, and he had on a bleached general's uniform with countless ribbons, medals and orders affixed to its breast. His hair was whiter and thinner than before, and something dark and mad sparkled in his eyes. In soft boots and white gloves, with a bloated face and dark red puffs under his eyes, the General did not know how to begin, or whether to begin at all. He waited for Romana to speak first.

THE WAR WAS BETTER

All of them stood speechless, motionless. Blinded by Romana's beauty, the Allied officers still held their hands above their heads.

Only Gruban Malić seemed to be interested in the globe. He was turning it around, looking for Russia, Montenegro and then Rome. When he finally found the conquered country, he took a red ballpoint pen out of his breast pocket, and colored in the whole of Italy. He did not skip a single locality or river. Sicily and Sardinia, even Corsica, became bright red. His round, tired eyes were full of happy tears.

"If I'm not mistaken, you all know each other," Sergey Ivanovich remarked, his eyes roving from face to face, from smile to smile. "If that's the case, may Georges Bonnefous—the best cameraman in Europe—and I, kindly request you to pose for a family snapshot. We need you for a few minutes only. Then we'll depart, and, in all likelihood, never trouble your happy family gathering again. Please come together now, please, we need everyone in the picture, a touching sequence, a living illustration of peacetime harmony."

All of them gathered around Romana and General Besta. Sir Stanley Gordon Clumsy and Fred Charles Friggit set up a frame for them. Luc de Tonnerre, with Lady Agatha Friskie in his arms, stood beside them. Antonio Peduto and Giuseppe Bonaccia sat down at the feet of the happy six; before them, they placed the long binoculars and the knapsack, from which the turtle peered out.

Sergey Ivanovich escorted the donkey and Malić into the center of the picture. Malić clapped his fur hat on his neck and lifted his globe proudly. Nor did Sergey Ivanovich forget Carl Schlotterer, who fell down on his knees as soon as he was moved. Still holding the can in both hands, the German was the only one who bowed his head contritely, like a real culprit. Nobody but Sergey Ivanovich and Georges Bonnefous noticed him, however.

The happy peacetime family was calm for several minutes. The only sound was the whirring of the camera and the braying of the frightened donkey.

Then all the Roman bells began to announce either the sunset or the commencement of some holiday.

 9

"A little faster, *Taliano*," Malić urged the donkey, goading him with his museum spurs. "Faster, if you want us to get there before dark, and trick the enemy." Although not so tired as the week be-fore, when the victors had entered Rome, the donkey was still a lit-tle balky.

"Judging by appearances, *Taliano*, the damn Via Dante isn't as close as she said."

Georges Bonnefous and Sergey Ivanovich, together with about a dozen reporters, moviemakers, and photographers, were following him. Georges and Sergey brought up the rear; they wanted to get the whole scene: not only Malić and his donkey, but also those hurrying up to have a look at them. There were military personnel, civilians and firemen running after them on foot and rushing up on bicycles, on motorcycles, and in small automobiles. Everyone was rushing and jostling each other. It wasn't child's play to get answers from Malić.

"Are cruelty and mercilessness your personal hobby, or are all Slavs like that?" a middle-aged man asked from a tricycle. "How many Slavs are there, including Hungarians, Rumanians, Greeks, and Albanians, as well as some Caucasian peoples?"

"I am proceeding to negotiations in Via Dante," Malić answered, all in a sweat. "I've been invited to the negotiations.... Come on, *Taliano!*" He spurred the donkey on. "Negotiations. Otherwise, I wouldn't have come."

"Will you, the *Slavi*, be merciless with the newly conquered peoples and countries?" a blond, bloodless reporter asked from his jeep, in a strange accent. "I'm from Holland. Are you going to pull up our tulips and throw us into the sea?"

Gruban Malić spelled out the names of the streets; they were written in Latin letters, many of them double, and this had always puzzled and irritated him. He ignored the newspapermen, snoopers, and photo-reporters.

"Since when have you been carrying that globe, and could you go one single day without it?" an older gentleman inquired, bran-dishing a jade walking stick from an immense limousine. "In that case, I'd buy it. I'd even buy the donkey. I'm offering you, outright, ten thousand dollars. I'm American. My hobby is collecting tro-phies!"

"What do you think, *Slavo*, how will the negotiations in Via Dante end?" a young Italian photo-reporter in an Allied uniform asked him. "Fifty-fifty?" He photographed him from the front, from the side, from behind. "And something else: are there powers in the world which could possibly resist the thrust of the Slavs, Greeks, and Albanians into the West, which is, according to you and Mr. Lenin, so rotten it must be already on its knees?" The reporter panted as he ran and sweated as he tried to pronounce the real name of Vladimir Ilyich Ulyanov. "The third and most important question: what will happen next, and how many heirs or substitutes do you have, and who is hunting whose head—you, theirs, or they, yours?"

"I'm also for war," the American who had just mentioned trophies and dollars yelled from his automobile. "But why does the globe have to be red? There are other colors—gold, for example. I'll buy you too, boy, as a trophy! I'll give fifteen thousand . . . Will that make you forget about that ugly color and all those terrible invasions you've planned, or do I have to double the sum?"

"Faster," Malić said to the donkey, who was frightened by the flashbulbs, the whirring cameras, and the crowd. He mentioned the dark and the negotiations again. "The way to glory, success, and communism is covered with shit!"

"I'll be waiting for you, *Slavo*," the American said in Italian and laughed roguishly. "Don't forget the path you're talking about is a winding one; you'll get lost trying to stay on it. I'll be waiting for you, but you'll only get half what I'm offering you now."

Gruban Malić dismounted. The crowd began to shout wildly and photograph not only him and the donkey, but also the fenced-in villa and the palms planted before its numerous windows and terraces. He led the donkey into the yard and deliberately let him nibble on the smooth English grass, the flowers, and other Mediterranean plants. The donkey plodded over to the fountain and plunged his head in up to his ears; a shoal of little fish gathered around his muzzle and nostrils.

Malić was already under the veranda, in front of the door, trying to unravel the words inscribed in Latin letters which encircled the Red Cross emblem. One of the newspapermen climbed the ivy-covered fence and aimed his camera at him.

"How long will the negotiations take?" he asked. "What results do you expect? Are you ready to give in even a hairsbreadth?"

The crickety old American made it up the fence too; someone said he was a regular barnacle and got a dollar tip for it.

"In general, and considering the circumstances, is there anything you can give in on at all? Don't you find that all you people from behind the Iron Curtain are slaves of your own savagery, prisoners of principles which are neither yours nor good . . . ?"

"Joseph Vissarionovich Stalin has said that we, the communists, are people of a special cast, made of particular ingredients." Malić clutched his globe staunchly; with his other hand he pressed the bell button. "A man of our mold, a communist, never gives in, even if he has to kill everybody around."

Sergey Ivanovich had also climbed the fence. Scratched and sweaty, he was translating Malić's replies. He even added things; he mentioned not only Stalin, but also Molotov, Malić's great friend, he said, his downhill jogging and poker partner.

Georges Bonnefous could not climb; he filmed Malić's donkey through the metal grill, capturing on celluloid the magic moments when the beast scratched his backside against the tennis table, and then against the bark of a palm tree.

Taliano pulled down the earthen pots filled with orchids, Dutch tulips, and cacti. Then he stood calmly between a swing and a table piled with sporting gear, tennis rackets, volley, basket, and soccer balls, weights, pulleys and other equipment for indoor gymnastics, as well as some indecently shaped objects apparently designed for vaulting.

"We always kill as many people as possible," Malić said and began to pummel and kick the door. "Any man may be our enemy."

He thought he heard them asking about the food and way of life they could look forward to in the future.

"In the very near future you'll be naked and barefoot, like us," he growled. "You'll eat shit, as we do, and it'll be sweet to you. And what's more, you'll be lucky to get enough of it!" He spat toward the fence and the crowd of busybodies. "You'll remember us, you rotten black capitalists!"

Sergey Ivanovich's hair stood up on his head. Nevertheless, he went on translating, without adding anything this time.

"How long will our happiness last—more or less?" a reporter next to Sergey Ivanovich asked. "Can an end to such happiness be foreseen?"

"The people of each country decide everything. The people must feel happy, and once they're happy, an end won't be necessary. We communists are the end of anything."

The door opened. Lady Agatha Friskie appeared in her military jacket and long khaki skirt. On her breast, in addition to the Red Cross badge, she sported both her great orders. Her withered face, with puckered lips and soft, gooselike eyes, was heavily made up, and all its pores and wrinkles were filled with creams and powder. She smelled of drugs and of her organization.

"Oh, God!" she exclaimed, seeing Malić and the multitude of newspapermen, movie producers and curious passersby. "The press,

THE WAR WAS BETTER

presse, giornali italiani e stranieri," she muttered, hiding her lips and false teeth with her hand. "Do they know about our negotiations?"

"They know about everything," Malić replied, still holding his finger on the bell, which was resounding throughout the house. "They're following my every move, like the fascists during the war." He spat toward them. "Shall we start at once?"

He carried the globe over the doorstep, found himself in the dining room, and began to ring the bell for the servants. "Shall we do it here?"

"Not exactly here, and not at once," Lady Agatha Friskie protested, watching him pull savagely at the string. "I'm alone, quite alone, *Slavo.*"

He continued to pull the bell, which sounded somewhere in the kitchen, the basement, or the loft.

"I've released all the servants for the occasion. Not here, please, and not so quickly. I hope that the rest of the day—and the whole night—are before us."

Gruban Malić stood in the middle of the bedroom, holding the globe. He looked around and wondered why so many things, such luxury, needed to exist. The luxurious Venetian blinds, the crystal vases, and the tropical plants in the corners of the room enraged him most.

He remembered Montenegro and Bijelo Polje, sunk in dust and dung, the cellars and granaries where he had spent his adolescence and youth, dreaming about bread, clean underwear, and equality among men.

Her room smelled sweetly, he did not know of what, or why. The walls were crowded with idyllic landscapes and family photographs of various sizes, in gilded frames. On the night table, there were several open books, their pages thick and printed in Latin letters. Above the inkstand, with a feather in the inkpot, and the brooches and other little gold and jeweled ornaments, was an ivory frame enclosing the mild and pain-chiseled figure of Henri Dunant, the founder of the Red Cross.

From one of the adjoining rooms, brushing past the piano with the graciousness of an English girl from the early days of the century, Lady Agatha Friskie tripped in. Hidden for decades under the severe hats of the world organization, but now released from its bun, her hair scattered over her shoulders and around her long and rather withered neck. She had on a Japanese kimono, with a little package fastened to the small of her back which reminded him of his parachute.

THE WAR WAS BETTER

Barefoot and sweet-smelling, she bowed in Oriental style and sat down at the piano. He watched her from the bed, holding the globe in one hand, and a drink with ice-cubes in the other.

"What music would suit you best at this moment?" Lady Agatha began in her own kind of Italian, as her long fingers flew over the keyboard. "What music . . . ?"

"Play me the 'Hymn of the Slavs,' if you know it," Malić ordered, shouldering his parachute. "Or something partisan, powerful."

"I deeply regret that I don't know any folk music," Lady Agatha Friskie excused herself with a trace of condescension. "I deeply regret it; I know only serious music."

"Then nothing." He frowned at her. "Can you blow the trumpet at least?"

"No," she replied, and flushed. "It isn't my instrument, although our organization recommends it warmly and offers it at half-price." She stood up quietly, still barefoot. "I shall procure it. The trumpet is the instrument of the faithful and the brave."

"What do you know then?" He looked her over, up and down, ready to slap her. "Do you know the Russian *kozachok* dance, or any Montenegrin round dance?" She stared at him, enraptured. "What do you know?"

"I know nothing," she murmured, blushing again. "I see I know nothing. I'm a common English girl, dulled by colleges and universities." She was standing at the piano, as if preparing to sing, but she did not sing. As she looked at him, an expression of outright lust began to overcome her pale, lean face. "I'm sorry. I'm merely a primitive and conservative English woman, without open horizons, without the Slavic vastness and depth." She stepped toward him, almost fell. "Our food is so pale. Rain and fog alternate with weariness and apathy. Oh, God!" Beside the globe, she hung herself on his neck, climbed, almost flew over him; she was taller. "Oh, God, how little I know! Nothing really! Nothing!"

"Shall we begin?" Malić said, hardly able to keep on his legs. She clung to him without speaking. "Why have you called me? Shall we pass from words to work?"

She hugged him and began to kiss his neck and face. Thus she answered him that they had already begun. She took the globe away from him and placed it carefully on the broad French bed. The ball of earth turned over. Her head swam. She continued to kiss him violently. Her puckered lips swelled.

"Let the enemies of the people not rob me of my globe!" he could hardly squeeze through his lips. "They tried to steal it once already. We're in Italy." She clung to him. "Are you sure the rotten black capitalists and the rest of the rabble and lackeys of the occupation can't get in?"

She was burying his lips under her kisses, and he could not ask her why she had invited him.

"Now you're protected, *Slavo*," she assured him, squeezing his ribs and licking his ears. "Enemies can never enter here, let alone the others. You are now under the protection of the greatest of all world organizations, which is hugging and kissing you through me, thus!"

Malić lost his breath. She flew over him again and hugged him. "Here! Thus! Thus! Thus!"

She took his hat off and slipped the parachute down his back. She unbuttoned his long Russian overcoat and jacket and hung them up beside her own uniform. She removed his shirt too, and his soft museum boots. His tanned head contrasted sharply with his chest and ribs, which were white as a rooster's.

He stank. He was a real warrior, smelling of sweat, soot, and arson. She stroked his hair, full of ashes and smoke, and felt his belly and navel.

Her hands drifted lower. He did not resist. She compared his parachute to the little Japanese package on the small of her back. He remembered the Montenegrin widows, Ana and Marija, who had taken off his clothes and possessed him so ravenously. He watched her pale, impatient hands, which trembled as they drifted still lower.

"It's a pity you don't know how to sing the 'Hymn of the Slavs,'" he complained as he let her take off his Russian trousers and his underpants, long since totally black. "All of us, from the other side, like battle music."

When she saw what swung between his legs, with its knotty head reaching almost to his knees, Lady Agatha almost shrieked. She trembled: "Jesus and Mary!" She remembered the donkey's mushroom which the thirsty hands of the women and the voracious Roman mouths had touched. She was shocked by the similarity. Once again she called on *Madonna* and the founders of the Red Cross to help her. In panic, she even mentioned the officers at her Geneva Headquarters.

"How is it there, in your England?" he asked. Then he paused, numb with desire and ready with his tough sword to overturn everything. "Write to them. Tell them I'll soon be coming there too."

She was lying on her bed, shivering. Her long, heronlike legs protruded from her kimono. He enjoyed the raising of his blood, its coursing through his limbs and veins. He was silent, listening to his heart and her accelerated breathing. He wondered why she trembled so much; he did not understand what was happening, for he had not yet even approached her.

He could not see her face behind the globe. Her hair was scattered on the velvet blanket. She whispered that she was an abandoned English orphan, without anybody, and that she wanted to die, locked in his embrace.

Malić pushed away his parachute, in which his asbestos cape was packed. He heard whistling in the street and on the fence, and decided he would punish them all. He did not know how he came to be in her arms, and between her frail knees.

She was quivering. He waited for her to calm down. She clung to him, bony, warm, mad from lust and fear.

"But still, wouldn't you just leap into the bathtub for a moment?"

"Not for any price, in your water," he said in a deep bass, rejecting her suggestion like a sovereign. "I will remain like this until the victory—we've vowed it to each other, all of us. Even if I perish in my struggle for a more just and better world, don't bathe my dead body. Leave me such as I am to the earth, the party, and the revolution."

"Then, my *Slavo*, promise that at least today you'll be kind to me," she asked, nibbling his ears and hiding her withered breasts from him. "This is the first time I've ever been alone with a man."

She rubbed him with her sharp, meager thighs, wanting suddenly to make up for everything she had missed in her first forty years. She impaled herself on him, helping him both shamelessly and modestly, like a child who does not know what it is doing.

The crowd shouted his name. They asked him how long the negotiations would last, and implored him to be flexible. Trumpets were heard, playing some circus tunes. Then the yawning of an accordion interrupted the braying of the donkey, whose stomach ached from eating too much English grass and too many orchids.

"Clown, I'm afraid of you," she burst out crying in English, and he understood that she was asking him to begin. "My *Slavo!* How wonderful it is that my first prince is a *Slavo*, and, what's more, a clown, with a globe!"

She caressed his clammy back and lowered her hands down to his firm thighs, which he moved slowly, pressing against her, stirring her up.

THE WAR WAS BETTER

"*Slavo! Slavo! Slavo!*" she panted, sensing that either doomsday was nearing, or the birth of a dewy Roman dawn.

"Mother!" she screamed when he hit her, and again when he began to penetrate through her flesh. "Clown! Clown! Clown!"

Clenched between her legs, lean and exhausted, with his soul in his nose, he pressed her forehead with his. Their faces were bathed in perspiration, especially his. He wanted to hold her long, pierced and crucified as she was, bent double. In his mother tongue, he pronounced the most disgusting words of hatred he could think of, and listed countless threats and tortures to which he would subject her and the others, but from this growling and gnawing of his teeth, she could make out only the words "globe," "fascism," "syphilis," and "communism."

"I'm no longer a naïve, stupid little English girl," Lady Agatha Friskie murmured, all in tears, sweat, and clammy blood, when he rolled onto his back beside her, uttering a curse. "Now I'm a woman like the others, am I not?" She hugged him, stroked his protruding ribs and spoke of Allied, vitamin-enriched food. "My clown, my *Slavo*, it still hurts. But tell me I won't die of it, tell me nothing unpleasant, nothing I don't want, will come of it!"

Malić opened his eyes and saw her next to the globe, on top of him. With the kimono and her free hand, she was hiding her breasts, which he had touched only a few times. Her eyes were mad and bloodshot. He strapped his parachute on his naked back and winked.

"Since I'm no longer an inexperienced little English girl," she said, "and since, thanks to you, I've become clever and brave, tell me something real now, something beautiful, sublime. Something powerful . . . something . . . sexual!"

"Lenin," Malić snapped, looking at her and the globe.

"I come from here," the surprised Lady Agatha Friskie said, in order to avoid the subject of Vladimir Ilyich. She pointed to the blue Thames on the globe. "Here is where I was born. Here too I found my true path in life, that is, the Red Cross. May I travel through the world with you, you and your donkey and your circus? I'd just love it!"

She kissed the countries which he showed to her, following his finger with her mouth.

"May I go with you? I'm adventurous by nature, you know, like every Englishwoman worth her salt. May I go with you, please, follow after you?"

She kissed all the countries, not only those which had been colored red; she kissed the vast spaces, the seas, and the oceans; she felt a thirst, a need for water and alcohol; her mouth and her wound thirsted terribly.

"May I follow after you like a shadow? Really go with both of you? May I? Really? Truly?"

She flung herself on him. He was sleepy. She shook him mildly and stretched out his legs, caressing, and waking him. She threw herself on him again, jumping on him, trying to reach his eyes before they closed in sleep. She tickled him, cooing to him in all the languages she could remember, nibbling and kissing the poles on the globe and then his melting bugle.

"Lenin! Lenin! Help me, I'm alone!" Malić's eyes were closed, his bitter lips drawn out into a mild, almost painful smile. "Vladimir Ilyich! Don't you remember me?"

Gruban Malić dreamed that human blood was overflowing the map of the world, a great blood-red lake as large as the velvet blanket on which he lay, with his parachute strapped to his back, prepared for any emergency.

"Comrade Lenin, what will become of me?"

Vladimir Ilyich climbed the fence of Lady Agatha Friskie's villa, photographed the donkey as he nibbled the English grass and reached out, toward Malić, his small, soft, white hand with blunt fingertips.

"Lenin, I kill and burn everything human, that is, whatever can sooner or later turn against us! Ulyanov, I am annihilating everything on behalf of you! Is it all right, Ilyich?"

He held Lady Agatha Friskie's hand and smiled to Lenin, who was photographing him and nodding his head approvingly.

"Oh yes, we come from the same place. Only men like us come from there. But it's a great pity I can't grow a little beard like yours!"

Gruban Malić smiled. Lady Agatha Friskie stared at what was between his legs, there, where he was most a man, with an expression of admiration and fright. It was pulsing.

"I've never seen anything like it, even on Indian and Etruscan statues," she said to herself, and thought of her wound. "He wouldn't even get a license for such a weapon in England." It pulsed and reared its head like the emperor of all the snakes; it extended its turban, hardening along its whole length. "From today onward, he shall carry it with the special papers of the International Red Cross Committee."

Lady Agatha Friskie mused that the common good of humanity

must be given priority over personal sorrows, especially passing pain. Without waiting for the end of her thought, she began to spit herself again on Malić's horn of flesh.

Her head spun from pain. She looked over the globe for the nonexistent Bijelo Polje on the Lim River. Through her tears, Montenegro looked large, almost as large as Russia, and seemed entangled in tough veins and tendons. "I shall go to that far-off, God-forsaken, romantic country," she promised herself once she had fully impaled herself on him and was pressing against his pelvis. "I've heard that the Italians, fires, and fratricidal wars have utterly ravaged them." Pausing, she looked down at him and the immense horn which she was straddling, and almost fainted. "Poor Montenegro, the country of such people!"

Malić smiled in his dream. Across a large, geographical map, he was shaking hands with Vladimir Ilyich. There was something warm and gay in the expression on Lenin's face. He was like a big, boneless child. Malić smiled in his dream and pulled his chum, his fellow countryman and teacher, Ulyanov, toward himself and Rome.

Vladimir Ilyich Lenin came to Rome. He stood on the fence, trying to photograph distant objects he could see only through the giant binoculars. He succeeded even in this. Vladimir Ilyich Lenin was immortal; he could do anything, and his forehead, while his mouth laughed, continued to frown.

He was with her only once again, in the late fall. In a heavy shower which merged heaven and earth for hours and even days, he arrived from the south. He had not forgotten her, but had no special desire to see her. He only stopped in front of her villa, admitted to himself that he was hungry, and dismounted. He rang the bell as he had the day he had come for the first time, struck at the door, and kicked it, while the donkey stood waiting in the garden and the rain.

She appeared in her long kimono, embroidered with bright-colored dragons and other supernatural beings; even before she dismissed her servants and the army doctor with the expressionless eyes and protruding jaws, she fell on her knees before him.

"Prince and clown," she cried, beginning to wail and embrace the tails of his overcoat. "Clown and prince, where have you been all this time? Clown and *Slavo!*"

"I know of no way to help you, madam," the English army doctor said, looking at Gruban Malić, standing with his globe in the middle of the room; rainwater was dripping from his head and coat and making puddles on the floor. "In any case, it's already late," he said, pointing his smooth, pronounced jaws toward the servants who were departing. "You should have come to me one or two months ago."

"But I've been waiting for him."

The doctor said nothing. He took away his jaws and his deep leather bag.

It was raining. The two were sitting at the table and eating. She was placing savoury dishes of frog's legs, cooked crabs, and other shellfish in front of him. He pushed the plates away, spat on the rug, and wrinkled his brow.

"A man of my rank and profession will never eat anything like this. If we Reds ate this stuff, the revolution would fizzle out. Why don't you understand that we fight against the people who eat this?!"

Trembling, she brought out fried fish for him.

"Pugh! One thousand times pugh!" he snapped, almost throwing up. "Not fish! We don't eat fish either, we, the Reds!"

He growled and overturned the pot with the shellfish.

"Bread and meat!"

His globe dripped rainwater on the table.

Then they rolled on the bed, drank thick Calabrese wine, and threw pieces of tart and shellfish at each other. They danced, naked, and clung to each other, he, with his parachute still on his back. They leaped over each other and danced around the globe. She no longer hid her breasts, for they had come back to her, and all her glands had swelled; she even lifted them with her hands, stuffed them into his mouth, and tickled his mushroom with her hardened nipples. She spitted herself shamelessly on his rod, and wailed and rolled her eyes, which, from the long days of waiting, had assumed a kind of prophetic brightness.

"I'm going to give birth for you," she informed him, utterly drunk, as she greased his crooked nose and wrinkled forehead with cream. "I'm going to give birth for you ... the strangest child that will ever be seen."

"You're not the only one," he drawled, lying on his parachute and watching her grease his navel and groin with butter, honey, and chocolate cream. Then he remembered Ana and Marija and the rest of the Montenegrin widows who, pushing their swollen bellies proudly before them, had accompanied him to Bijelo Polje and the prison, beyond the Lim River, bound in chains. He no longer knew whether it was Ana's or Marija's sons who were the incurable klep- tomaniacs, but he still remembered the stolen roosters and the ever- insurpassable, perpetually laughing Marija.

"As if it had been yesterday," Malić remarked, and Agatha thought he was expressing his joy at the news that she was going to give birth to a bizarre, insane, Montenegrin-English bastard.

"I've made a special effort to protect its life from pain and suf- fering," she informed him, fingering her own belly fondly.

"They tortured Lenin also. That is how he became great and omnipotent. That is why he turned bald."

"I want a daughter. To pass on my heritage decently."

"And why don't you want a son?" He watched her climb him again.

"I don't want one. A son can always become Lenin, as you know. I don't want a son."

"Mine and yours would surely become Lenin," he said, waiting for her from below. "I guarantee it. Judging by us, he's bound to become something of the sort. Well, let him. The West needs people like me, like what he'll be."

He went away in the same manner he had come. He woke up sometime before dawn, put on his clothes, and walked toward the door. She rushed after him, to stick the biggest, most recent Red Cross emblem in the lapel of his overcoat.

"Before you step over the threshold of my modest home, please take whatever you want," she said like a real wife, taking leave of a loved one who was about to depart on a long journey.

"Only this," he remarked, and took the ribbons of the *Legion d'Honneur* and Order of Merit off her jacket. "Nothing more," he added, stuffing them into the damp pocket of his overcoat.

She brought him a handful of money, about one hundred dollars, fifty English pounds and many liras. "So you can have them handy," she said. "Especially if they don't understand you in some foreign country. Or if they chase you."

"I'm a communist; people everywhere help me," he said. "Can this money, let's say, buy food or red paint?"

She laughed, then cried again.

"Do you love me at least a little, my clown?" she called as he mounted his donkey and went toward the gate. "My Montenegrin- Russian prince, my Ulyanov, do you love me at least a little?" She was holding her hand cupped on her stomach. "My papa!"

"I love only world revolution," Malić answered, fingering her medals and money in his pockets. "I will love you, perhaps, once the revolution triumphs and I take a bath. Which means, soon."

The dawn was breaking. She stood on the pavement, waving to him. With her other hand she felt her stomach and then let her hand sink a little lower. The day would have come earlier, but for the rain which had not stopped since he had come. She trembled as she saw him going away, following a strange revolutionary instinct, toward the west, and leaving a smell of arson trailing behind him in the wind.

That morning fever forced her to bed. She ordered her servant to buy several dictionaries and grammars for all the Slavic languages, as large a globe as possible, and a whole batch of maps. She thumbed dictionaries and textbooks with her temperature rising and the Cyrillic letters swimming through her feverish brain. With one of Malić's ballpoint pens, she colored red on her globe, all the countries which were red on his. She did not forget London either, or Geneva. Sweat broke from her brow; her own and Malić's countries seemed to be bathing in the sea.

"*Jebati!*" she called and lost consciousness. "*Jebati! Jebati! Jebati!*" she babbled until the army doctor and Sir Stanley Gordon Clumsy arrived.

"What does this word you keep repeating mean, madam? ... Madam?"

"*Jebati*," she repeated, watching the ambulance team arrive with a whole company of the W.A.A.C. girls. "The word means 'Red Cross' in every Slavic language."

All of them thought the word marvelous, simply marvelous, and promised to remember it for a long time.

 **10**

Three months after giving birth, Lady Agatha Friskie invited her closest friends for a drink. She took Sir Stanley, General Friggit, and Colonel Luc apart and showed them a pile of Malić's photographs. Gruban's triumphal entrance of Rome was thrilling to see, especially his entrance into Via dei Serpenti, and even more thrilling, his interview with the newspapermen in front of the villa where they were now drinking. With the tips of her well-cared-for nails, she pointed to his round, Slavic eyes, which were always a little sad, even in photographs.

"Have you any news to cheer me up, Sir Stanley?"

"Since you reported his disappearance, we've had him followed closely," the Englishman replied, and his whole face, except the freckles around his nose, flushed mildly. "The organs of my infallible service, the Special Operations Executive, found out that he has conquered other sections of Rome three or four times, spending his time particularly in Piazza Venezia and in front of the monument to the former Italian king, Vittorio Emanuele II." Sir Stanley thumbed through the leaves of his notebook, reading without the benefit of his smoke-colored spectacles; he often used these glasses to screen his mild, dreamy eyes from harsh light, because they teared so easily, especially when he laughed. "There, in front of the monument, not only did he threaten the Italian monarch, but also the other royal families, including all the Scandinavian ones, and even ours, so that my agents began to wonder how he had managed to memorize the entire list of all the reigning kings and queens and the heirs to all their thrones. He also mentioned an American king, but only the masses remembered his name, and cheered madly.

"The organs of the Allied Military Government for Occupied Territories, of which, as you know, I am personally in charge, followed him, or followed the mob which carried him down the entire length of Via Veneto, to the park, where he delivered an address similar to the one in Piazza di Spagna. He brandished the globe and his, if you permit me, 'Asiatic' hat, and prophesied the approach of the dawn and the arrival of Vladimir Ilyich Lenin."

Sir Stanley paused. General Fred Charles Friggit nodded his head and smiled with evident pain. He began to speak distinctly and deliberately.

"My boys from the Office of Strategic Services took photographs of him," he said. "Those are the ones I've already shown to you. It's interesting that he uses the globe not only as his symbol, but also as a kind of medieval shield to hide behind. I have to admit that women rushed after him like mad, not only the insatiable foreign ones... from the north... but the frigid Roman ones as well. I envied him, believe me; on that particular day I had less soldiers to command than he had women. And that's not even counting the pained but enthusiastic Italian people."

"Where did he sleep then?" Lady Agatha Friskie asked in a dull tone. "Did your O.S.A. and A.M.G.O.T. boys go in for that?"

"For a time he slept exclusively in museums, with royalty and exhibitions," General Friggit answered. "Then he began to sleep more or less anywhere in Rome, and, at the end of his stay, in the catacombs, where he usually parked his donkey *Taliano*. Apart from that, we observed whole flocks or, let us say, hordes of exwarriors from almost every part of the world, and especially from the north and the east. When questioned, the only thing these boys seemed able to say was that the war was better, and that there's no love anymore. Curious."

Fred Charles Friggit mused.

"Then our *Slavo* worked at a Shell gas station. We've been informed that, when servicing the larger automobiles, he deflated at least one tire tube. It was a regular circus there. They even beat him for a while."

Lady Agatha Friskie's good, gooselike eyes flooded with tears.

"He threw sugar cubes into some of the gas tanks, spat in them, or tried to piss into them. They beat him again. Then they hugged and kissed him; when there were no cars and no traffic around, they even carried him on their shoulders. When he found out that the Shell Company was neither Russian nor communist, he cried like a baby. An elderly American tried to buy him, as a trophy. After a long bargaining session, it is reported that his offer went as high as fifty thousand dollars. Our *Slavo* got angry. He bit the American's ear and threw about one hundred dollars and fifty pounds sterling at him, saying that he did not need them, since the oppressed peoples themselves would always help him. The people did in fact carry him off that day on their shoulders, I must confess; it was the carnival. Our *Slavo*—I'm sorry, madam, to call him that, but our *Slavo* sometimes seems to be ours as much as theirs—that day our *Slavo* was the most beautiful float carried through Rome."

"Where is he now?"

"All signs point to the probability that he's somewhere in the south," Sir Stanley said, thinking of a western movie again. "You can't even guess how marvelous a reception he had in Naples. They were so overjoyed to carry him around, him and his donkey, that they refused to let him down until he fell asleep or fainted."

The Englishman said this with a distinct feeling of jealousy, adding that he himself had never been carried so much, even when he was small. He took the smoke-colored spectacles out of his pocket and hid his deep, insular melancholy behind them.

"According to an S.O.E. report, he was seen in Sicily; another report, however, places him in Sardinia. Since it was the same reporter, he evidently doesn't distinguish between the two islands. But he's almost sure the peace conqueror is down there somewhere. It seems the Mafia has accepted him. The reporter writes that fires, apparently set by arsonists, are more and more frequent in the vicinity, as during the war. No connection is drawn, however, between this fact and the good father of your wonderful child."

At that moment, the servants, dressed all in white and wearing surgical masks, emerged from one of the adjoining rooms. They carefully pushed before them the gigantic baby buggy in which Malić's son lay weeping.

"For goodness sake, the child is quite normal!" General Friggit let out.

"Judging by everything we know, this will be a great man," Sir Stanley said benevolently, in order to conceal the American's carelessness from the officers and servants and the happy mother. "Just listen, how savagely he cries, how strong he is!" The Englishman began to babble to the baby, uncovering him apparently by chance and looking carefully at the long, crooked, Malićian larva which dangled between his legs. "This will be a man and a lover!"

"He's certainly strong," the happy mother agreed and covered him up.

"A wonderful human example! And why restrain myself? Why not say it frankly? The male race is increasingly degenerating," the lean, perpetually frowning Captain Thomas Morrison said. An impassioned ethnologist in civilian life and a member of the Royal Institute of Anthropology, he was particularly impressed by the child's larva; he brought a number of Malić's photographs up to the baby buggy and compared them carefully to the *Slavo*'s son and heir, whom even his dolls and playthings and mother's awkward murmuring in Italian could not console. "I've seen something like it only once before," he concluded. "In Ireland."

"He will be a real warrior," Major Jeremy McIntosh snapped in a brisk, officer's tone; he was the fiercest and most devoted member of the Royal Scottish Geographical Society, Edinburgh: a man of about fifty, bald, and with flaccid muscles but a will of steel, he was more severe than any of the other passionate officers and geographers. "A real warrior," he repeated, coughing behind Captain Thomas Morrison's back as he looked at the various piles of mother's dictionaries and grammars which lay about the room, and at the red-colored globe with a Slavic word scrawled across the whole of Europe, the Atlantic Ocean, and America. "For him, the globe will be a common plaything, perhaps a soccer ball; the map will be a mere rag to crumple up and spit on. Look, even now, as an infant, he's enraged, irrepressible, almost hysterical."

Colonel Luc de Tonnerre kept silent. He was glad that no one seemed to have noticed him.

"Madam, your divine little son is not just normal; he's more than normal," the steely Fred Charles Friggit began, a fan of wrinkles spreading around his warm, smiling eyes. "Your wonderful heir is a miracle among miracles: he resembles Lenin!"

He approached her and touched her shoulder. She did not burst into tears, but only glanced over to Sir Stanley, whose romantic eyes, even behind his glasses, expressed intense fear, either of Lenin or of scandal.

"Madam, although this may sound horrible and paradoxical, you seem to have given birth to Vladimir Ilyich Ulyanov, that is, to Lenin! You're doubtless only the second woman in human history who's ever succeeded in doing so! So many try, cry afterwards, and curse their fate and the time they're living in. You've given birth to a teacher—not ours, happily, but a teacher is still a teacher. And however terrible, disgusting, and above all comic this fact may be, you, madam, must be proud of it."

Lady Agatha Friskie did not weep, but drew her puckered lips into a strange and painful smile. Sir Stanley Gordon Clumsy was standing beside her, ready, like a real gentleman, to receive her in his arms and against his medals, if she should happen to totter, or faint, or begin to scream and invoke, as usual, Christ and the general director of the Red Cross, Moses Fischer.

Instead, Lady Agatha Friskie was, for once, reserved and almost demure as she handed out gauze masks to all of them. Vladimir Ilyich Lenin was crying. His drooping, Malićian eyes were full of tears.

"Just look at those slanty, Asiatic, Slavic, Leninistic eyes!" the most talented R.I.A. explorer and traveler, Captain Thomas Morrison, put in; he had been the first who had dared to remark upon the boy's striking resemblance to Ilyich to the Commandant of Rome, Sir Stanley, and then to General Friggit. "Look at the wonderfully tender forehead which, as in all males of genius, is growing bald, and frowns, and reddens and rages. Madam, in all humility, I bow to you, deeply, in sheer admiration."

"The boy's brows are also Leninistic, not to say crooked, not to say broken," Major Jeremy McIntosh observed. "His voice also wheezes, like Lenin's."

THE WAR WAS BETTER

He alone laughed at his joke. Binding the gauze mask which Lady Agatha had just offered him across the pale mouth of his friend, Captain Thomas Morrison, he continued.

"The nose of this boy, to whose health I'm ready to drink until midnight or, if there's enough, until dawn, unmistakably recalls Molotov's!"

"The child will turn out a complex imbecile," Sir Stanley thought as he drank down a full glass of whiskey. "A complicated idiot; he already resembles Einstein." He sensed a cube of ice jingling in his stomach. "Gentlemen!" he announced in a joyless voice. "Gentlemen and friends, let's drink to the health of Vladimir Ilyich, Jr.!"

All of them lifted their glasses. The boy continued to cry.

"Let's drink to the health of his brave mother, Lady Agatha Friskie, dear to us all, whose touching figure we'll long remember!"

They drank together, quickly, swallowing their ice cubes.

"Let's drink to the honor of life itself, which has no prejudices! And to the honor of peace, in our fashion! Ladies and gentlemen, to peace, in which anything is possible!"

This was Lady Agatha's last highball. They left her more drunk from the nauseating experience she had undergone than from alcohol, tearful beside her Ulyanov, and rushed to Via dei Serpenti, to divert themselves and laugh at General Besta's anecdotes and bravuras. But she wept the whole night through, and the following morning came to an important decision: to depart, to hide, to disappear. She immediately composed the shortest and most important letter she had ever written in her life:

My dear Sir Stanley,
    I have decided to go to the bitter end. I stand by the decision which I explained to our command a month ago. Although no one is requiring me to do so, I hereby submit my resignation. I shall remain faithful to the Red Cross Organization until my death; it brought me to the true path, and then led me to Rome. I dreamt of the eternal city as of an earthly paradise, but it has turned into hell for me. Both the Western and Eastern press has continuously besieged my home. I reply to their questions as you have told and written me to do. This is too little. The photo-reporters insist on photographing my little Ulyanov, my only treasure and happiness, naked. One of them even tried to paste several tiny hairs of suspicious origin onto his little chin.

THE WAR WAS BETTER

Three gangsters almost tore him from my arms while I was walking in the garden and telling him wonderful Slavic tales. They were from behind the Iron Curtain, I am sure, because they were miserably dressed, and employed several expressions which I later found in my dictionaries and grammars; every third word was the one you asked me about that day I had fever. Thus, as you see, they were born for the Red Cross, but of course in their own way. They are not conscious of it, however. The Slavs are magnificent, but also dangerous and prone to kidnapings of all kinds. Do not be distressed at my love for them (my pure English heart knows neither hate nor malice), nor at the fact that I shall devote the rest of my life to them.

My dear and only friend, peace and Rome have become disgusting and sickening to me, especially because I imagined them so differently. I am indeed going to the end, and it is possible that we shall never see each other again. I am leaving for a kind of war, for the lowest level, the bottom from which I have come. I am convinced that I shall at last encounter understanding and support in a people which suffers and dreams about a different happiness. Do not look for me. You could not find me. I shall live in some basement, or perhaps in a loft, among pigeons, with which my Vladimir will play. And I shall wait. Malić will come, although he did not promise it. He will come because he must vanquish. I hope he will become attached to me when he sees our infant and learns what I am now ready to do for our common cause.

If you see him before I do, tell him he is an angel, and ask him to take good care of himself. And you, my dear and only friend, may the selfish Anglican God bless you, the God in whom, after my encounter with Malić, I no longer believe, and against whom I am ready to do whatever a loving, reborn, and abandoned woman is capable of.

Agatha Friskie

Lady Agatha Friskie was true to her word. For some time she did not seem to be among the living. The omniscient A.M.G.O.T. agents traced her to the vicinity of Naples. They observed her talking to a crowd of poor people, with her child on her bosom, about something quite revolutionary. O.S.S. agents followed her from Milan to Genoa. She was seen showing Vladimir Ilyich, Jr., to the travelers in a second-class compartment, and threatening the conductors with a globe and the crimson dawn in the Balkans, and the east in general. S.O.E. agents finally followed her to Rome and to the Shell station where Gruban Malić had worked for several months.

In reddish-yellow overalls, with her child and her globe beside her, she pumped gas from dawn to dusk. She was photographed deflating tubes on large American automobiles from time to time, and throwing sugar cubes into Englishmen's gas tanks. No one even suspected her; they chased and beat the others, but never her. Even when they got wind that it was she who was the troublemaker, they did nothing to her. She peered at every donkey passing the Shell pump and asked every rider's name. She was convinced that the great conqueror might appear at any time, from any of the four corners of the earth.

The flabby-eared, slanty-eyed boy no longer wept constantly. He spent his early adolescence swallowing gasoline fumes and playing with the small red globe.

11

"Cattolica, don't forget this is the second year of our stay in Rome, in Via dei Serpenti, and you've been growing," Peduto murmured to the turtle as he caressed her small paws. "My heart, my gold, my only happiness besides Malić and Peppe, calm down, hush now, calm down, and see the miracles of peace around you, see them unreel one after another."

Lying among garbage cans, as though in a box at the theater, he had a clear, full view of the entire yard. He was leaning back against a heap of bricks and sand; the turtle lay on his chest like a living ornament.

"Cattolica, my little whore, leave my neck alone, will you, please? Don't lick it," he said heatedly. Only Bonaccia, from beside his own garbage can, and the fat prostitute who was also sitting nearby, could hear him. Antonio caressed the turtle's hard, checkered shell. "Cattolica, don't nibble on me."

"Is she like me?" the prostitute asked, leaning across Peppe. "She too?"

"She's growing," Giuseppe Bonaccia answered, on Antonio's be-

half, as he began to rearrange the medals on his breast, which the
girls had mixed up. "She's a real whore and she's growing."

"I weigh only two hundred and forty pounds," the prostitute informed them, turning her sweaty, birdlike head toward both of
them and fluffing up her hair. "Is that much, at this time?"

"When I first found her, she was a little orphan, abandoned by
everyone, an *Ortodossa*," Antonio resumed, watching the girl lean
over Peppino again. "Now she weighs about thirty pounds. She's a
real *Cattolica*, ravenous, growing, and I wonder . . . feel her shell,
Amalia."

"Then we're really alike," Amalia remarked. Pushing away a
garbage can, she wedged herself between Antonio and Peppe. "I'm
not Italian either. I was brought here when I was small, from Al-
bania, or Greece. . . ."

"Be quiet, Amalia," Antonio said. "It's not important where you
come from. The important thing is that you've grown." His hands
were clasped on the turtle's shell. "Be quiet, if you don't want me to
drive you away. Just remember, Amalia, that you're in the city of
miracles, in Via dei Serpenti."

The sweaty Amalia pushed another garbage can away and
grinned, revealing her blue gums and broken teeth. With one hand
on Peppe's lean, closely-cropped head, and the other on the turtle's
shell, she seemed to calm down.

"We really are the same," she murmured. "They say I myself
was an *Ortodossa* once, and that my name was different." She let
out a thin, sickly laugh; beads of sweat were rolling down her forehead into her hairy eyebrows. "My name wasn't Amalia."

"Don't speak, Amalia," Antonio whispered. "Don't speak, my
Balkan pearl, my wonderful Amalia, who weighs two hundred and
forty pounds already."

Antonio looked over the yard. There was a small table in the
middle, covered with red velvet, flowers, and old newspapers. On it,
a globe lighted from inside was turning round and round beside a
microphone, without pausing at any particular country or continent
or ocean. Three stylish chairs were placed around the table, empty.

At the entrance, along the walls of crumbling plaster, the public
was waiting—mostly foreigners, military personnel, men of various colors and uniforms. The faces of the higher army officers registered impatience; they clearly wanted the peacetime show to begin
at once.

Above their heads, the flags of almost every country in the

...rld were flying, although most were American, English or French. There were Far Eastern, exotic-looking flags, flags from South America and Northern Europe, even Russian and East European flags with red, five-pointed stars in the middle or at the end, and one flag with a Cyrillic inscription of "Workers of the world unite!" Most of them were trophy flags, soiled with human blood, riddled by bullet holes and decorated with medals of all kinds and sizes.

The largest flag, fluttering on a low pole near the table, was Italian; it was perhaps the bloodiest, and was torn and half-burnt; on top of its once bright and golden pole, a woman's panties hung, either a symbol of the house and time, or a sign of the owner's wittiness.

Around a small, hurriedly set-up, American-style bar, and near the shooting gallery which sported a dozen air rifles, bows and arrows and other such entertainments, girls were bustling: dark and blond ones with plunging necklines, fat behinds, and short skirts. They had been invited from Via Ficaia, Via Amfibi, Via dei Fiori; some had bowlegs and some were terribly fat and quite sick as well, especially those from Via delle Streghe and Via Maledetta. Heavily made up, with long nails and bruises around their knees and sometimes on their arms and faces, the girls were smoking and waving their multicolored pennants. All of them, even the stupidest and worst-looking ones, were quiet, waiting for something important, beautiful, or at least exciting to happen.

A slow Roman dusk was settling down into the city, bringing on the freshness of the evening and the clamor of the streets. Somebody was weeping. Laughter and a merciless car honk drowned the sound of it out. A whistle blew. A policeman in the jammed Via dei Serpenti seemed on the point of a new nervous breakdown.

Antonio watched Giovanni Besta, Conte di Tirano, step graciously into the yard. Spartaco Allegretti and Turiddu Barbagallo followed him. Giovanni Besta bowed to all of them in turn, like a true actor. Spartaco and Turiddu sat down beside him at the table.

Sir Stanley Gordon Clumsy answered Giovanni Besta's greeting by lifting his white glove and wrinkling his brow formally. General Fred Charles Friggit almost burst into laughter; he regretted that Vittorio De Sica, his close friend and personal consultant on gambling and Italian love, was not there. Colonel Luc de Tonnerre had one medal less than on the day Georges Bonnefous had filmed them; he blushed shyly as a crowd of gap-toothed prostitutes formed around him.

THE WAR WAS BETTER

Truman Independence Jones, the Negro, was standing beside Carl Schlotterer, who was kneeling before the multitude, with his head bowed and his arms drooping down toward the earth. The Negro trembled lest Sergeant Lopovsky and his other officers should see him and chase him away from the celebration, which he had been promised would be magnificent. He rolled his big eyes and let his lower lip hang down like a dead man or an epileptic.

"I'm so happy you've come to see what I've done for you and for peace in general, for which, by the way, I was predestined from birth," Giovanni Besta said, after he had told them the long story of his life and explained his inherently humanistic view of the world. "The successes which Romana and I have achieved would be less dear to us if you hadn't gathered around us here this evening." He got mixed up and sought with his hands and various grimaces to find some means of expressing his deep feelings. "In short, I love you and think of your needs!"

From Antonio's little cove, Giovanni Besta looked particularly small. There was also something international about him. Frail, sweaty, perplexed before the curious girls and chance passersby, he seemed to belong to all the peoples of the world. He was dressed, however, mainly in Allied rags. His shoes, yellow and too long, were Canadian; his olive garters, bloody and riddled by bullet holes, were either Yugoslav or Russian; only his riding pants, with leather patches on the knees, were Italian; his jacket was English, and bore countless European medals, including the prominent *Medaglia d'Oro* and the *Medaglia d'Argento*, as well as some huge, tin, probably German crosses; Fred Charles Friggit himself, let alone the rest of them, was not sporting so elegant an American shirt, with a living butterfly stuck to the knot of his tie; a *Bersagliere* hat literally crowned his entire figure. He began to speak again.

"My frank, childlike Italian heart beats with pride at my mad luck. Tonight, in the name of our good and hospitable nation, I am going to be able to show you five new workshops made after my own plans and modeled on some of the old masters. They were not easy to make, and even less to imagine. Only my great love for you, who brought our eternal peace, enabled me to achieve success."

Spartaco Allegretti was dressed like Besta, but with fewer medals and crosses. His thick white hair grew down to the middle of his forehead. He held a money box on the table and was playing idly with his keys. As Besta passed from his childhood to the war, from the war to this blessed peace full of harmony and love, Allegretti showed his utterly toothless gums to the crowd, opening his mouth so wide that Barbagallo could see his uvula and gullet. Turiddu, who was wearing a French pilot's uniform, crumpled but decorated with ribbons and orders, glanced occasionally at the money box. In his lap he held a stick, so that no one would dare to approach.

"My heart contracted with regret as I watched our wonderful liberators, our friends and customers for ages, elbow themselves onto the narrow stairs of my house in plain view of each other. From now on, this will stop! In addition to ten rooms on the first, second and third floors, and several spacious premises in the basement and loft, you'll have these five magnificent workshops, little nests of paradise, if I say so myself. And the girls are new, quite fresh, more or less young, simply children, trained in everything, even behavior. Just look at them!"

Projecting his square jaws like a man readying himself for a street fight or an encounter with mad dogs, Turiddu Barbagallo set out into the crowd with his pole and made his way to Besta's first workshop, a kind of beach cabin, only slightly larger and in somewhat better condition, with curtains of various colors in the windows and a little red ship's lamp above the door. As Barbagallo pushed aside the plush curtain, a bulky Negro girl, with a skinny neck and hair spilling over her shoulders, appeared behind the lighted little window in the door. She rolled her eyes more often than Truman. As for her other charms, only her hands and fingers full of cheap rings, came into view.

"My latest discovery, a real jewel, my black precious stone, my Laura," Besta grinned, bowing low. "Paris itself has nothing like her, and let's not speak of other places! I assure you, gentlemen, Laura is a find of finds, a treasure of treasures, something every white gentleman and lover dreams about in his nightmarish sleep! Taste Laura, and she'll make you happy for the rest of your life!"

Laughing, Laura revealed her beastly teeth through the little window. Men gasped for breath; occasional drunken passersby stopped and stared. Laura conquered the courtyard. Giovanni Besta blew kisses to her, smiled and called her his happiness, his song.

"General," said a pale, tall man of about thirty, clothed in a black suit, with his hair parted on one side, who stepped toward the little table. "I've been dreaming about Laura all my life. The women in our country are too white and too tough, veins, blood, disgusting Scandinavian flesh ... It all shows through their skin!"

The man dropped his visiting card and the money Allegretti requested into the money box.

"Thank you in advance, my General, for making me happy."

"I'm here to satisfy everyone's desire," Besta replied, bowing and jingling his medals; above the name on the visiting card he noticed a crown. "Everything will be as you wish, my dear *Principe!*" Rapturous, blinded with desire, the Prince folded his hands below his stomach and stared fixedly at Laura. He did not even hear General Besta, who was talking on as if he were overflowing with generosity and kindness.

"This blond angel's name is Adriana. She's from the extreme north, from the frontier; perhaps she's even Swiss."

The girl exhibited her smooth, naked, harmoniously proportioned body, her long hands and especially her breasts, whose hard, stirred-up nipples could be seen penetrating the dense locks of her hair.

"Whoever touches her can say he has possessed the Old World; he'll testify to the fact that this miserable, unprotected continent is nobler than ever, grateful for every dollar and cent offered to her as to an orphan. My luxurious, my yielding, my literate Adriana!"

The Scandinavian Prince stared at Laura, ready to rush across the yard, leap into her cabin and remain for weeks.

General Fred Charles Friggit and Colonel Luc de Tonnerre approached Allegretti at the same time and threw their banknotes into the box.

Spartaco Allegretti yawned, thus proving once again that he had lived to see freedom and peace without a single tooth. Then he announced that there was room enough for three in the cabin of Besta's blond angel.

The American and the Frenchman bumped into each other, begging each other's pardon in Italian. Adriana watched them with pity, pursing her rich lips.

"The twins, Maria and Luiza, offer, I'm convinced, something our Anglo-Saxon and black friends will never be able to forget, something which wonderfully symbolizes our beloved Italy, although it has become more and more rare in modern times," Giovanni Besta said, suppressing a sob, as Barbagallo, with a powerful jerk of his pole, uncovered the next cabin, in which completely identical twin girls were to be seen. "They're from Naples. Our true southern folk traditions were never better represented. They speak several languages. When you possess them, you'll think all the Italian sisters, all our mothers, in one word, the entire Italian family, has been yours for the asking!"

Maria and Luiza were girls about fifteen or sixteen years old, with large, slightly slanting eyes. From their skinny torsos, round and identical pairs of breasts stuck out sweetly, and their mounds swelled out in gentle slopes.

"I alone know how much effort and money it took me to convince their wonderful, poor, but unfortunately bigoted parents to sell them to me," Besta resumed, recounting further details and stressing the various charms of the swarthy Neapolitans, whose faces expressed nothing but sorrow, silent disdain, and helplessness. "I let them receive three, even four men at a time, since their lovely, very comfortable rooms are connected by a sliding door. Gentlemen, four is the limit, for the present. They can't take five; they're so frail, almost anemic. Both of them have the same Neapolitan tuberculosis!"

The big, flaccid Major from Texas, Courtney "Rocky" Mudd, came up to Allegretti's money box with a soldier behind him. Sergeant Lennie Lopovsky also appeared, with a drunken colleague in uniform. All four looked at each other without a single word. Then they stepped aside, like men sharing the same fate.

"Rome has never known a girl like Lili!" General Besta began again when Barbagallo had revealed the fifth and last cabin. "As you can observe, my dear and honored guests and friends, Lili is a redhead, and freckled like a dove's egg!"

The round-hipped and long-legged girl lifted her hands; artificial jewels glistened on her fingers.

"I don't know whether she's a *Slava* or a *Tedesca*, but I give you my word of honor, I cannot tear myself away from her. Has anybody ever seen so much old gold in the hair of a woman? And I wonder: could the northern, Slavic, or Germanic God have created anything more harmonious and beautiful? No! Never! It's not possible!"

A crowd of American and English soldiers charged. A number of elegantly dressed civilians—probably Dutch or Danish—joined them.

Turiddu Barbagallo separated them with his heavy pole, and restored order around Allegretti. General Besta noticed the rawboned Hindu, his old friend Raja Singh, a Colonel of the Royal Sikh Fusiliers Regiment, and helped him to pour as many pounds as possible into Spartaco's box.

"*Shanti! Shanti! Shanti!*" Raja Singh said to express his thanks, as he looked at the rejected ones with sincere pity. "Thank you, my wonderful General!" he added and adjusted his turban and the violet net holding his beard in place. "Nanni, I don't think I'll ever

THE WAR WAS BETTER

forget this . . . a lovely Slavic-Germanic Christian girl, with gold on
her thighs and knees!" The Hindu sighed loudly, drew in his breath
and gnawed his teeth.

"Now, tourists, customers and . . . my numerous relatives," Besta
yelled, "I am about to show you the throne!" He asked Barbagallo
to push aside the heavy plush curtain from the largest and most
sumptuous cabin. "Gentlemen and brothers in arms, warriors and
proven heroes who've come from such great distances to liberate us
and make us happy and harmless . . . liberate us from everything . . .
look now . . . ! And please restrain yourselves!"

A real throne appeared, a giant bed, with many supports and
shock absorbers, like those in automobiles. Naked and dignified, surrounded by flowers and multicolored cushions, a woman was lying.
Her black and wavy hair scattered over her large shoulders and fell
to her ample breasts, whose nipples pointed sideways.

Her navel was also large, and deeply set into the finely formed
flesh of her stomach. As if created by the dream-miracle of a sick
imagination, the woman held one hand on her bent knee, and the
other on her narrow waist. Her thighs were rounded, her loins shad-
owy, moist, soft.

Not only men, but women too gasped for breath as they looked
at her tearful eyes and mouth swollen from lust or tears. Passing
from neighboring streets and nearby bordellos, even drunken prostitutes paused to look and admire. Someone in the crowd burst out
crying. Many thought the giant woman was speaking, but she was
not; she was only watching them.

"Who can still doubt, after seeing her, that this is the Queen of
all Italian women?" Giovanni Besta shouted, his voice beginning to
falter. "The Queen of all women, the Queen of Rome! And finally,
my Queen!" He wept, then mopped his tears with the crumpled
lace panties from the Italian flagpole. "My Romana! Our common
miracle of peace!"

A crowd of men and women charged. Barbagallo pushed them
back into the crowd of common prostitutes and recently arrived homosexuals. Meanwhile, Besta took Sir Stanley Gordon Clumsy apart.

"Our highly esteemed Commandant of Rome, and my honorable
colleague!" he began. "In my house you will always enjoy absolute
priority, even on scrip. You'll pay me one day, I'm sure of it, and
since you're a proud, rich Englishman, it may even be with your
head!"

"Thank you, General," Sir Stanley replied caustically as he

placed himself, blushing, beside the Queen's throne. "Don't forget, please, that it's a good deal easier for me to pay with my head than with pounds." He thought of the western movies he had seen, of De Sica; he remembered the war and the African sand. "I understand you very well, General. I can only repeat: I am deeply honored. Neither I personally, nor my powerful—but unfortunately not very rich—country shall forget it!"

"I've loved her madly since the first day!" Giovanni Besta said, weeping again; his lips writhed and hung from his mouth like withered sacks. "I've loved her since the moment I first touched her, and felt the smell and warmth of her Latin flesh!" His shoulders trembled silently. He hardly noticed the happy males approaching the cabins of their chosen ones.

"It happened some time before the war, in Via Veneto. We agreed then that once we finally lost the war and won the peace, we would open such a house as this, where the liberators, who were only dreams to us then, would find something they could never even have imagined!"

Besta turned to the customers who were shouting that they were sick of stories and could wait no more.

"Get used to it: in my house you'll find anything but happiness. With my girls, you can stay one hour or less. I personally will ring the bell. If you stay less, they'll be thankful to you, but it's all the same to me what you do with them, or whether you do anything at all."

He looked at them and wept like a torn-down Buddhist statue. He shouted to Romana, his voice breaking so that it seemed almost to bark: "In front of everyone and for the thousandth time, I repeat to you that I love you! How wonderful it is that you're growing; soon your forehead will reach the sky."

"Do you see?" the sweaty Amalia asked triumphantly. "Do you see that your Anna-Maria and I aren't the only ones who are growing?"

"Silence, Amalia," Antonio said.

"She weighs about eight or nine hundred pounds now. Heavens, think what she'll look like in a few years!"

"Be quiet, Animalia, will you?" Antonio scolded her. "If you don't shut up, I'll have the General shove you into one of his cabins."

"If he only would," Amalia sighed, her mouth falling open as she watched Romana's body lit up by multicolored lights. "How good and funny you are, *Slavo!*"

THE WAR WAS BETTER

"Shut up when I tell you to!" Antonio whispered. "Otherwise
... I won't let you go into a cabin. Animalia!"

Giovanni Besta's eyes looked crazed. He was holding a stop
watch and trembling. He seemed to know neither where he was nor
who had brought him there. He turned around and around in his
tracks, almost without noticing the next shift, already chosen, which
waited in front of the plush-curtained cabins.

Someone from the crowd remarked that the devil himself must
have gotten inside him, and it was just lucky for everyone else that
the pistol holster on his belt was filled with gauze, drugs, and colored contraceptives with little drawings on them. Otherwise he
might have drilled them all full of holes.

Besta insisted that he was from Tirano, near the Swiss border;
for him, time was more precious than money. Looking at the dusk,
which was sinking slowly from the Roman roofs, he spoke again.

"Friends, in order to increase the indescribable pleasure which is
awaiting you and which you will experience in exactly twenty-one
minutes and a few seconds, in order to make that pleasure complete,
royal, and violently masculine, allow me to finish my story and tell
you what happened when the Abyssinians attacked us in the center
of Addis Ababa. They charged at us more or less naked, armed not
only with English rifles, but also with spears, arrows and axes, and
all kinds of other tools. It was on the nineteenth of February, 1937,
some fifteen years ago! They stormed us like Russians, but they
weren't drunk, just thirsty for our white Italian blood. We mowed
them down with machine guns, waited with grenades for them to
charge, and then cut them to bits. They surged on from all sides,
like black ants; the heap of corpses grew higher and higher.

" 'By God, they're brave,' General Rodolfo Graziani said; he
was the Governor of Abyssinia and my closest friend at that time.
'They're brave, these damn natives, Nanni,' he said. He was shooting a heavy Breda into the multitude of black flesh.

"They passed another machine gun to me, and I myself killed
about a hundred of the naked heroes. Rodolfo was jealous; he ordered that they should be driven to him from the Akaki airport. He
soon surpassed my total, and I had to turn and shoot into another
crowd.

" 'Rodolfino, I've gone you one better again!' I shouted, and he
answered I was a whore's son and no better than a dribble of shit.
Then he pushed me away again and began vomiting fire from his
Breda into a flock of African workers.

"After a while he tapped me on the back. 'Now I've beaten you all hollow, Nanni!' he said. He was laughing like mad. The main square was packed with corpses. Thick blood flowed over the ground in streams, in real brooks, and we could see it, smell it.

" 'About ten thousand have fallen!' a captain who had just arrived reported, and then fell, hit, at Graziani's and my feet. 'Ten thousand, sir!' he repeated; then we covered him with a raincoat.

" 'I like numbers!' General Graziani growled into the telephone receiver. 'So many again, my boys!' Then he himself bent over, because two bullets had hit him. 'Revenge me!' he wailed. 'Revenge me and kill them all!'

"I wept over him. He drew my ear down to his mouth and whispered that the rest of the colored people should be stirred up against the black Abyssinians, every one of the five thousand Eritrean and Tripolitan askars who were so impatient to plunge their knives into human flesh. I don't know who killed more after that, our soldiers or the North Africans. Necks were bent and broken, and bellies opened up, while the voracious African rain extinguished the fire which we set in their homes, and rinsed their human bowels and smashed skulls.

" 'We've liquidated twenty thousand already, Rodolfo,' I informed him the following day, the twentieth of February, and for the first time since I had become a soldier, it seemed to me that I was a real man and that Africa was ours. 'Rodolfo, twenty thousand! From yesterday to today at noon! Is it enough?'

" 'What's twenty thousand, if it's their lives or ours?!' he cried out, jerking his head up and down as he lay there, bulky and wounded. 'We must be ready to annihilate all of Europe if it suits us, when the right moment comes. I must be revenged! Everybody must be killed!'

"We killed anew, as if no one had been slaughtered before. We poured gasoline on the living and the dead, and burned them all up. The rain was on their side, however. I rushed from one end of town to the other, and ordered even the dogs coming in from the suburbs to be exterminated. I promised my wonderful Rodolfo that I'd carry out a model slaughter, a massacre that more words would be written about than the German camps.

" 'Thirty-five thousand!' I informed my unforgettable Graziani on the following day, the twenty-first of February. 'I regret that there are, so to speak, no living Africans left in town. Is it all right now, Rodolfino?'

" 'Only thus will the new order be built, Nanni,' he murmured to me, and I communicated his sentiments to the officers, and the

Black Shirts who were guarding the hospital. 'Are the great German and Russian successes clear to you now? Thirty-five thousand! You're still a European, who troubles his reason with old-fashioned, obsolete categories! Thirty-five thousand! That's enough for a start, I must admit. But more than the numbers, the methods of killing interest me. Especially, the methods, methods, keep the methods in mind! . . . The vanquished must remember!'

"That night, between the twenty-first and twenty-second of February, we spoke twice with Benito Mussolini personally on the telephone. He congratulated us on behalf of the entire Italian people, and finally exclaimed: 'I embrace you both!' Even today I remember the warm, vibrant voice of the *Duce*, coming over the receiver.

"Although he was seriously wounded, Rodolfo ordered us to bring him two beautiful Abyssinian children. They brought us a boy and a girl, both about ten or eleven years old, although they looked as if they were over thirteen. The children were bloody; it seemed they had been pulled from under a heap of corpses, and were the only ones who had survived. Rodolfo Graziani did not allow the children to be washed. He caressed them, passed his hands over the blots of coagulated blood, and then smelled them. We sniffed them and licked them for a long time, in shifts, he and I, and vice versa, then together, helping each other, pushing our fingers, pistol barrels, and tongues into all their little holes, seeing in them the future of the new, Europeanized Africa."

Besta's eyes were mad and full of tears. He stared into the distance, without asking the crowd whether they had heard him to the end. He did not even know they were applauding him and calling him a genuine Italian actor and director, and even a great clown.

He stared into the distance. He could hardly keep himself on his feet. He saw before him the wonderful and painful figure of Rodolfo Graziani; he saw the heaps of black corpses, with Italian flags flying over them, drenched in the rain.

"Exactly sixty minutes have passed," he murmured dreamily without even looking at his watch. "The first shift's time has elapsed." He listened. "Is the next shift ready, or should I go on warming you up a little longer?"

"Can he be believed?" the tearful Amalia asked, pointing at General Besta, who had just told, for the third time, the story of what General Graziani and he had done to the Abyssinian boy and girl, especially the boy. "Isn't he laying it on a little thick, *Slavo?*"

"No, Animalia, he is not laying it on thick, or cooking it up either. He's even toning down and skipping some things. Can't you see that words fail him?"

"Are the others like that too, *Slavo?*" She was all in tears and sweat. "I mean, are the generals of other countries and peoples so generous?"

"They're the same everywhere," Antonio answered, playing with the turtle's little paw. "How else would they get promoted?"

Giovanni Besta stuck out his tongue and licked the nonexistent black body which he saw before him. He sucked in the air as if it contained the place where, in his imagination, the Abyssinian boy lay. His lips, his eyes and his whole face and body melted into a quivering, victorious, Italian satisfaction.

"That one doesn't hide anything, you say?"

"He's capable of admitting to you that he ate shit—and describing how he did it."

"Oh yes, the others are silent," Amalia agreed; her mouth fell open again and revealed her bloody-blue palate. "I had one yesterday, here behind the garbage cans." She showed him the spot on the concrete, and even demonstrated the manner in which she had lifted the overweight posts of her legs. "I think he was deaf and dumb. That's why he was so quiet. He greeted me by clicking his heels. Then he gave me fake money from some small country."

"There are many deaf and dumb among the generals," Antonio said; sweat was pouring into his eyes. "That's why they shoot so much. The deaf and dumb have to make themselves understood."

"How wonderful it is that you and Peppino aren't generals yet," she said.

"If things go on like this, I'll soon become one," Giuseppe Bonaccia observed, allowing Amalia's hand to fall between his legs. "Animalia, give me your address."

"I have none, Peppino."

"Give me your address," Bonaccia repeated, feeling her fingers squeeze him. "You're the only whore who won't do it. I prefer an address to anything else." His eyes were foggy; he could see nothing but Amalia's tears and beads of sweat. "Animalia, have a heart. Stop pulling my swollen bunny and give me your address."

"I've told you twenty times, *Slavo*, I'm almost always behind garbage cans. Sometimes I'm in Via dei Fiori, sometimes in Via Maledetta, sometimes in Via Ficaia. Since recently I've been here, in Via dei Serpenti, not far from the Vatican, like you. Just write: Animalia Celestina, called Pia or Meek, the toothless one, who loves peace so much and, because of everything, grows. . . . But let's do it,

THE WAR WAS BETTER

Peppino, I want it with you, right away, hurry, here behind the garbage cans, while our General tells us about Rodolfo Graziani and the black children for the fifth time in a row."

Then something unexpected happened. Giovanni Besta said: "The first shift's time has elapsed," and added, "Italy has been accorded the honor of showing the naïve, still uninitiated part of the globe what real love and original sex are, and thus can stand shoulder to shoulder, at least in something, with the great powers and liberators!" It was then that the door of cabin number one was flung open.

As if scalded by boiling water, the Scandinavian Prince bolted out so fast he could hardly stop even by the time he reached Besta's table. He was utterly naked, and white as a corpse just taken out of water. He flailed his arms about wildly, addressing not only General Besta and the high army personnel, but also everyone else and especially the newspapermen and photo-reporters who had just arrived.

"Gentlemen! Friends! This is humbug! That black young lady you heard so many stories about . . . is a man!"

The Prince peered back cautiously at the door of cabin number one; in the looking-glass, he could see hair falling richly over the black shoulders and back.

"Gentlemen and friends, Laura, the gorgeous beauty, is a male of the first order, one of those you don't forget! A humbug! Humbug! Humbug!"

The Scandinavian sobbed. His face was dirty from tears, creams, and powder. As he turned to all sides, spitting and raising his hands toward the Roman dusk, the bruises and all the bites on his skin appeared in turn, under his arms and on his back, and then those on his thighs and groin and between his legs.

"A humbug unequaled in recent history! Do you understand me, or do I pronounce this damn, magnificent language with too much of a Scandinavian-Lappic accent?"

"I was mistaken too, *Principe*," Giovanni Besta said, trying to calm him, but the man continued to pour out pale Northern tears and then, suddenly, demonstrated how he would commit hara-kiri unless a pistol or at least a grain of cyanide was given to him. "I was also mistaken, Prince! And others have been mistaken! All of them have been mistaken! All have to be mistaken! They call these times happiness; perhaps they're right! Look around you; look at all this health!"

"You're philosophizing, General, but I've been cheated!" He fell on his knees and pointed his lean backside at the press and the cameras. "Laura is an incredibly developed and charming male, which makes the fraud horrible, vile, Latin, southern, and typical of peace-time, as you usually stress!"

He almost stood on his head and beat his forehead against the ground until the thuds resounded; he turned his bitten hind part to all of them in turn, and screamed: "Humbug! Humbug! And this, in my beloved Rome!"

"Well, and who had whom, *Principe?*" Giovanni Besta could hardly speak above the clamor and general laughter. "I'm asking in order to establish the facts of the drama, the feverish temperature of the spectacle, the degree of what you call a Roman humbug!"

The General noticed not only some Allied army personnel, but also certain gentlemen past their prime, with black hats clapped down over their ears, almost down to their noses, making their way toward Laura's cabin.

"No, no! You speak Italian fluently, without an accent, even too well, considering you're from up north. Answer me concisely and clearly: who had whom?"

"I had him." The prince's answer could hardly be heard through his tears. "I had Miss Laura!"

"I've had it worse, Prince!" Besta yelled; his whole body, especially his face and his flabby cheeks, was shaking like jelly. "Afterwards I was put in bed by the heels, with what you call Latin humbug. You should have seen me, sewn up and bandaged everywhere, like a regular patchwork quilt!"

"Did you know it wasn't a woman?"

"Of course I did!" General Besta shouted to everyone, with his round, clown's eyes bulging at the Prince. "That's why I put him into the very first cabin, so he'd be the first to bear the brunt!"

"Miss Laura is a panther."

"Prince, call her whatever you like, but understand once and for all that you're not in your Scandinavian wasteland now; you're in Europe, in our liberated Rome!"

"Oh God! Help me!" he wailed. "Save me from peace, save me from Rome, Italy!"

"Don't invoke God at such a moment! Don't be vulgar!" the General scolded him, as he lifted him from the ground by his shoulders. "Be a man and bear things courageously, with your chin out! You've got away from Miss Laura, and everyone envies you, and they have reason to!"

The Prince sobbed on the General's breast, pressing his cheeks onto his medals. The General wiped the tears and mucus off his uniform with the panties.

"Now, for the first time, you're a complete man! You should be grateful to me, my sweet, naïve little *Scandinavo!* Come on, put your clothes on. And if you're a good boy, that is, if you restrain yourself and pay me well, I've got a little surprise for you. Yes, Prince, my baby from the north!"

"My crown is lost!" he sobbed. The crowd laughed uproariously.

"It isn't!" Besta snapped. "I'll speak to them; I'll intervene on your behalf. We have many friends and customers up there."

"They'll get wise to it, and when they get wind of something like that up there ... Ah, you don't have the slightest idea what life is like up there, even when they know nothing. ..."

His formal dress was nearby: a pair of striped pants, lacquered little shoes, a tie with a diamond pin in the knot as large as a fist, a crimson flower in the lapel of the dinner jacket. But there was no one there either to clothe or to cover him.

"I never expected this! Oh God! You'll tell them before anybody else will ... Such things are done discreetly in the north; a great deal of alcohol is consumed. ..."

"Nobody can say now that you haven't been in the south, in Europe!" Giovanni Besta said, shaking him and counting the bloody bites around his neck, on his narrow chest and on the skin below his navel. "Now you're a man in the true sense of the word, an irresistible male, for whom there are no barriers and no secrets, except for one. But you're too weak for it. You have to fatten yourself up."

"I'll never go back!" the Prince squealed, not realizing that he was stamping on his own clothes. "I feel they already know. They find out everything before anyone else, especially such things. ... Therefore, in front of you all, gentlemen and friends, I yield up my crown! I abdicate! I'm going to remain here, fatten myself up and become your equal in every respect! I'm remaining here!"

"We accept you!" Giovanni Besta exclaimed, pushing him into Spartaco Allegretti's and Turiddu Barbagallo's laps and throwing the checkered skirt of the McDonald clan of Scotland to him. "We accept you and love you, all of us! We'll have another Prince! No longer will there be only Conte Allegretti, Conte Barbagallo, and I, so lonely here among the vulgar and primitive of the world, and all the rest of this rootless scum."

Giovanni Besta leapt for joy. In his thoughts, he saw the Prince taking part in the items of his various programs. He blew kisses to him, gave him more advice, almost wept.

"He's ours now! He's ours! Ours! We've robbed you of him, Scandinavia! We've cheated you, north! Oh, Laps! Oh, reindeers! Oh, bitter winter which almost froze my heart once, in Russia!"

"I'd like to have a skirt like that," Amalia cried out, separating her clammy knees in sheer envy. "But I'm afraid it's too large," she added, as she looked at Allegretti with the naked Prince in his lap. "What a skirt! Woolen too!"

"Animalia, shut up!" Giuseppe Bonaccia said. "Otherwise, we won't let you into a cabin!"

General Fred Charles Friggit and Colonel Luc de Tonnerre jumped out of cabin number two at almost the same time. Pale, sweaty, and rumpled, they were staring fixedly before them as if they were not the victors but the vanquished. Adriana threw water after them and spat. She looked at them with disdain, but her eyes betrayed no resentment or pain; she took some air at the little window, spreading out the locks of her hair and pushing up her breasts.

The General and the Colonel paused beside Giovanni Besta, and Spartaco and Turiddu asked them whether they wished to visit Adriana once again. Both the American and the Frenchman admitted that Italy was a unique and hospitable country; in their opinion, the Allies could not have selected a more ideal or more exotic city than Rome to call down revenge upon themselves.

It seemed to Barbagallo that they were staring not at the ground which they had subdued and liberated, but at Spartaco's money box. He planted his long, crooked pole between them.

"Now, my little *Principe*, you must put your clothes on," Giovanni Besta urged the Prince as he glanced at his stop watch and welcomed the tearful Scandinavian into his arms. "The press is following you, and the photo-reporters are filming you. I didn't give you the skirt because of them, but here, put it on; I'm afraid you'll catch a cold. *Principe*, in the name of our common God, don't drivel like that! Please! Don't nibble my ears!"

"I have my reasons to refuse whatever belongs to the McDonald clan!" the Prince cried; his ribs and genitals were shaking in the cold. "You don't know what happened to me with those sexual maniacs!"

Everyone gathered around to listen and photograph him as he spoke on with the same sobbing voice.

"I'm for the knightly McMurdoch clan! I like their colors! Once they were kind to me and my unhappy, deeply depressed Scandinavian people!"

"If you don't want to put your clothes on, son, then at least sing with me!" General Besta exclaimed as he pushed him from his breast. He regarded him with the smile of a warrior, a wrinkle between his brows. The cameramen were approaching, and he wanted to look courageous and serene in newspapers and on movie screens, and display his comedian's talents.

"We'll sing, my dove, '*Gloriosa Patria Bella, Tu Sei la Viva Stella.*' The words are mine, and the music too. Benito Mussolini and Rodolfo Graziani were charmed, literally charmed, by the harmony of the lyrics and the ingenious musical composition!"

He brayed in triumph. Like Vittorio De Sica, he threw his head back and lifted his brows. Then he stuck out his jaws, like that other actor, called *Duce*, who didn't want anyone to know that his chin sagged like an old woman's.

"Come on, son, sing out!"

"Father, you said that today I became a complete male; but please, tell me whether I'll be able to continue with women ... and animals," the *Principe* whispered, still trembling, and totally unaware that dozens of photo-reporters were photographing him from the tips of his white duck's feet on up. "Will I be able ... at least with animals?"

The awkward, flabby Major, Courtney "Rocky" Mudd, from Texas, told General Besta he was all for entertainment in the Italian style. The scene with the Scotch skirt, he said, had been worth battling across the Pacific for, fighting and winning at Monte Cassino, and finally, arriving in Rome, the eternal city of original love and unadulterated sex.

Also half-exhausted, with bruises and bites on his neck and around his ears, the blue-eyed Sergeant Lennie Lopovsky said, with reserve, that he too did not regret he had come all the way from Gary, Indiana; only now was it clear to him why the Slavs, with Gruban Malić and Vladimir Ilyich Lenin at their head, had so often fought their way toward the Latin peninsula.

"Rocky" Mudd and Lennie Lopovsky stepped aside at the same time, so that the Scandinavian Prince, instead of tumbling into their arms, struck the concrete with his belly. General Giovanni Besta frowned at them, cursed them, threatened them with his finger and then his whole fist, but not because he was angry; it was because of the crowd of photographers and newspapermen who were literally burying him under artificial flowers, confetti and questions.

THE WAR WAS BETTER

Then a scream pierced the air. All the lights flashed on; even the Scandinavian Prince looked up toward cabin number five. Enraged, baring his teeth, Major Raja Singh staggered out. In one hand he held a knife; with the other, he pulled, by her golden-orange hair, a female body covered with little freckles and dense blots of blood. Nobody, not even the photo-reporters and newspapermen, could see whether her dead eyes were closed, nor count how many mortal knife wounds marked her body.

Major Raja Singh pulled the body up to Allegretti's box and flung it down beside it. Spartaco shivered; with a devil's speed, he covered her mound with banknotes.

Major Raja Singh was naked from the waist down, except for his boots. As he waved his knife, with a bloody hand, toward the white part of the public, turning slowly as if to face his enemies on all sides, his long, thin rod smoked. The turban on his oval forehead was untied, and the violet net for his mosslike beard had slipped down his neck. His medals jingled and his knife flashed as he hissed, in North Indian English: "These damn European women; these damn blondes . . . these damn whores who'll drive us to the madhouse or the grave! These damn *Slave* and *Tedesche!*"

"What happened, sir?" General Besta asked in astonishment. "What happened in the most beautiful of my five new cabins, and on the very first day, liberator?"

"These devilish women, these bitches, who decline to go to my divine mountains, eternally covered with snow and ice! These damn, red, freckled . . . witches!"

"We deeply regret this unpleasant incident, liberator. As you know, you're one of my dearest and most gallant guests; such behavior is inexplicable, incomprehensible, unforgivable!" Giovanni Besta said as he bowed elaborately to the half-naked Hindu, whose black, hairy behind with the funny flower in front had become the chief target of the newspapermen, cameramen, and moviemakers. "Allow me to excuse myself on behalf of the European peoples, sir, and especially on behalf of the vanquished, whose principal representative I have the honor to be, whether they like it or not. I am ready to fall on my knees, Sir, to retain you on the roll of my most faithful, wittiest, and kindest guests."

"These damn, faithless, white . . . witches!" His teeth, his forehead and his knife flashed. "This very day I said to myself: 'Raja, don't go with those blond Christians anymore! Change, Raja, change, because the women they're always offering to you bring evil; they're in league with the devil!' These faithless whores! . . ."

THE WAR WAS BETTER

"I have a substitute, sir," Giovanni said, his sly eyes bulging. "An Algerian has already been installed in cabin number five. She's bowlegged, but original. She says she's willing to go with you to the Himalayas. She desires only to be wooed formally."

"This lost, luckless, red woman!" Major Raja Singh said, gazing calmly at the body stretched beside Spartaco's box and covered with banknotes and artificial roses. "The more I stab them with my knife, the more I love them." He began to weep and then his thin face wrinkled up like a baby's. "This is the fifth one I've stabbed in the heart!"

"I don't know the others, liberator!" Giovanni Besta said, extending the skirt of the McDonald clan to him. "As for this one, don't bother: I expected something like this; I had a foreboding, so to speak, and have already taken out insurance on her. Poor girl; she, like the others, didn't want to climb the Himalayas." He offered him the skirt again.

"I remain faithful to the McIntosh clan," Major Raja Singh said, declining the offer. "Jeremy McIntosh is more than a brother to me, and the only European whose stench I can bear."

"The Algerian is waiting for you, Major. If you aren't ready, however, I'll send in your Canadian friend, the well-known botanist The second-to-last in line just happens to be your brother, Jeremy."

"I'll do it with the Algerian tomorrow," Major Raja Singh decided, as he watched them pull away Lili's body, towing her first by her hair and then by her legs, which were covered with patches of old gold and coagulated blood. "Now, please, lead me to cabin number one, to Miss Laura, the one you told so many stories about at the very beginning."

Turiddu Barbagallo conducted him across the yard.

"Let's hope Miss Laura isn't a Christian and a whore, and that she's kind."

They watched him with horror. News reporters and moviemakers accompanied him all the way to the cabin. In front of the door, before entering, he threw away his knife and put aside both his pistols. His black, thin backside, crumpled like tanned leather, vanished behind the closing door.

Above the general laughter, a modulated, almost theatrical weeping could be heard: that of the Scandinavian Prince.

Amalia and Allegretti let their mouths fall open.

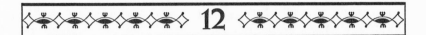

"Don't touch me," Antonio Peduto murmured to the crowd which had gathered around him where he lay behind the garbage cans. "Don't touch me. Take me away from here, remove me from the earth; my brain and spirit have been infected; whatever I touch begins to fall apart or wither with some cursed disease. Get away from me, or terrible things will happen to you!"

"What can happen to us, Red?" Sergey Ivanovich said, as he lifted him from the concrete and set him up among the cans. "What terrible things are you talking about?"

"Don't touch me! I've caused enough evil and misery around me. I've done it ever since I can remember. Gentlemen, people, brothers and friends, I'm contagious in every respect. Keep at the greatest distance possible. Do it for me; have a heart! Despise me! I'm nothing but a mangy dog!"

Georges Bonnefous was standing beside Sergey Ivanovich with his camera. Both of them were panting and sweaty; it was evident that they had just arrived after a long journey. They paid no attention to the Allied officers and soldiers or to Besta's permanently aroused and fiendishly curious guests, all of whom were bustling up to hear the conversation. They concentrated their attention on Antonio, who still had on the torn and dirty uniform from Napoleonic times which he had worn the day they met.

Antonio Peduto peered at them, but did not see them clearly. His face was sunken and bruised, his eyes swollen, his disheveled hair glued to his forehead. Under the medals, his heartbeat was weak and irregular.

"Believe me, I'm telling you," he murmured, "I'm no longer a man; I'm finished. Pour gasoline on me. Let me burn up before your eyes; that way I'd suffer longer. Or crush my skull under your heels; stuff my brain into a garbage can. Fling my body into a dog cemetery, where it belongs."

He licked his raw lips and threw his head back; his mouth fell open and remained so. His throat and Adam's apple were scratched and full of scars and burns.

"You're a man, and more than a man," Giuseppe Bonaccia pro-

tested, accustomed to such conversations. He began to pour something from an army canteen the crowd had given to them directly
into Antonio's gullet. "You're a man; stop talking about mangy
dogs," he added, taking a sip from the canteen himself. It was a hor-
rible-smelling wine which reminded him of Greek *retsina.*

"What can happen to us, Red?" Sergey Ivanovich asked him
again. "We think the worst has already passed. After all this, what
else could happen?"

"I can't see you very well, but I know who you are. We drank
together once, I don't know where; we drank for a long time. Then
a tremendous fire broke out, and the flames reached toward the sky.
Wait a minute. I know who you are; I even remember your names
and faces. We embraced. You're the ones who are making movies, a
kind of song of peace called happiness. I can't help you: you're
going to begin to grow! We shouldn't have met in such times.
Whatever I've touched recently begins to lose its true, human
shape."

"But, Red, we haven't been together much," Sergey Ivanovich
pleaded. "Just from San Giovanni to here."

"We filmed you, then went away," Georges Bonnefous put in,
clapping his cloth *cascadeur* hat down to the middle of his forehead.
"We've met many others of the kind." In his voice, there was a
rude, bitter melancholy. "Red, spare us anyway: we're already big;
in fact we're immense!"

"Your end is foreseen," Antonio said. His voice came to them
even more softly from behind the garbage cans. "Surprises are impossible for you. I'm terribly sorry for you, terribly, because you're
still children."

"He's a magus!" Sergey Ivanovich informed those gathered
around. "Give him some more wine."

"We've filmed enough magic for three films," Georges Bonnefous said, as though arguing with himself. "Red, I'll give you more
wine if you make me stop growing. Have a heart; I'm already as fat
as an elephant."

"What's a magus, old one?" Peppino asked, terrified. He began
pouring something from another canteen into Antonio's gullet.

"A magus is someone who prophesies," Sergey Ivanovich explained.

"So far he's foreseen everything," Peppe said to Georges.
"We've been together since the fire in Montenegro; I've disappeared
from time to time, it's true, but only for short spells."

"Everything is growing around me; I'm damned," Antonio whispered, shivering. "Now I see you better." He fingered his swollen lips and bruised cheekbones. "You won't be able to escape it. It's terrible! Everything around me grows!"

"Who's growing and ... what's growing, Red?" Sergey Ivanovich said, peering into his face, babbling something about peace and universal human happiness, and shaking him. "Red, I'm sick of magic!"

"How long has it been since you haven't been back ... inside this courtyard?"

"About five or six years," Sergey Ivanovich replied.

"Time has lost its significance for me," Peduto mused, with his hands on the concrete. "And yet, it seems to me we met only yesterday. You had a jeep."

"We still have it," Sergey Ivanovich said, apparently moved. "We have to change the tires a lot. It's all rickety; it consumes a fortune in gas, but I wouldn't trade it for an airplane."

"You had an excellent jeep, a real army one. Dust rose behind you; rocks rattled. You were carrying a living corpse, that *Tedesco*. I don't know where you found him, but it was nice of you to forgive him and take him along."

"Red, the *Tedesco* is also behind the garbage cans," Sergey Ivanovich reminded him, growing more and more dissatisfied with the conversation. "He's on his knees, as he was that day when we filmed you all."

"You were armed with cameras and intended to make something against the spirit of the time, perhaps to stop it and spit on it. You were honking your horn."

"Red, show me the pages which you've been carrying around, as you told me then, ever since your Montenegrin period." Sergey Ivanovich remembered even the title of the manuscript. "Perhaps it explains why everything around you, in the period others call happiness, starts to lose its basic human form."

"I have only a few pages left, but I don't even need them," Peduto said, and began to feel the pockets of his jacket, which was still covered with medals. "My son and brother Bonaccia remembers everything, even the things that have evaporated from everyone else's head." He was looking through his breast pockets, inside his shirt and trousers, in his boots. "None of my pages are left," he said finally. "There's no wine either, Peppino."

"There's not much time left for Via dei Serpenti," Sergey Ivanovich said impatiently. "Do you intend to go on?"

"Stay a little longer," Peduto asked. "Look at the things. Perhaps we could go on together again." He was listening. "Things are no longer ... as you left them. ... Everything has changed. ... Don't touch me: I'm guilty of everything!"

Georges Bonnefous's eyes followed Sergey's pointing hand. Something to film had appeared. General Besta was standing on his usual spot, between Barbagallo and Allegretti. Turiddu still had his long, crooked pole. Spartaco, almost completely gray now and with one eye closed, was stuffing money into a larger box than before.

There were now about thirty cabins in the yard, even nicer than the first five. The Roman afternoon was thawing in the windless, sultry heat. Red lights shone above all the doors. Allied officers and soldiers, members of different army missions and delegations, mingled and bustled about; they would have come to blows if it had not been for the tireless Besta, who was telling them the story of the Italian conquest of Greece, adding new blood and truth with each retelling.

"The village was burning; it was the fifth to burn up that day," he was saying. "A wonderful flame was licking the roofs and rising into the smoke toward the sky. We drove whoever did not choose to die in his own dear, warmed-up home around and around their Orthodox church. We hanged the priest, a bearded one, by his tongue, right on the portal, and he did not hold out long. We killed the fastest ones, and those who did not want to surrender, who were shouting, 'Long live our dear Greece!,' their country of misery and freedom; we shot them in their tracks as they shouted that someday they would be liberated from our darkness.

"The village was soon done for, and the church too, when a boy with an icon emerged from somewhere. I thought at the beginning he wanted to grab hold of me, and I hid behind a burning pillar. But he was running toward the others, crying first in his barbarian language and then in our own:

"'People, God sees everything. ... Don't kill me, *Taliani*, good people!'

"They wanted to mow him down in front of me, with a Breda, but I was sorry for him, and ordered them to shoot above and around him, and bar his way with a shower of lead. The little Greek rushed to the left, to the right; he kissed the icon and then waved it, almost threatening us. The Breda was going rat-tat-tat; it prevented him from leaping into the fire.

"Then I got into a tank, which had not been my custom, and began to chase him with it. It was a wonderful machine, with surprising mobility and maneuverability. We chased him around a burned-down house, allowing him to pick up the icon from the ashes one time, after he had dropped it, and run off. From our steel monster, I loudly cursed all the Orthodox and Balkan gods, so that he could hear me.

"He also charged us; I must admit the Greeks are a tough, brave people; he threw dirt, rocks, and coals at us. Many of our soldiers were watching the fight from the side, ignoring the heaps of dead bodies as utterly insignificant details. They told me later that the Greek bastard had actually scratched the tank's caterpillar tracks with his nails, spat on them, and said his name was Demetrius, like the Byzantine saint on the icon.

"We went on chasing him. Sometimes we even had to drive backwards, in order not to run him over. We chased him on and on. Symbolically, we were settling our accounts with the mad resistance of this strange, freedom-loving Balkan people. I was all in a sweat. I wanted to get out. His mad, saintly eyes began to haunt me. Fear seized me.

"Finally he fell down on his face. Nobody shot at him, and I didn't run over him. His own scream choked him with ashes; his heart broke by itself from his own exaggerated courage. His bastard Greek bones seemed to be cracking under my caterpillar tracks. I told myself that it was good, anyhow, that I did not kill him, and I took his icon away from him. It was the image of a martyred saint, with a long face and a thick, male beard. Now Demetrius is resting beside Romana, who often caresses him, and coos to him, and presses him to her bosom. Romana says Demetrius' dark Balkan eyes sometimes become larger, but they are never accusing; he must have a nice time with her!"

Gesticulating dramatically as he enacted the role of a guiltless and skillful tank commander, General Besta nearly fell down, and almost certainly would have, if the Scandinavian Prince had not been holding him up. Dressed in the Scotch skirt of the McMurdoch clan, padded at the hips for emphasis, and equipped with falsies, the *Principe* fell all over the General, waved to the public and directed the guests to the various cabins.

In most cases, and with utter frankness, the Scandinavian offered them cabin number one and, imitating the General's grimaces, kissed his gathered fingertips in Neapolitan style.

Laura peered out of the cabin, as indestructible and beautiful as that first day. In front of her door the most serious gentlemen, most of them formally dressed, had gathered: clean, pale-skinned men with thickly muscled, Anglo-Saxon necks. There were also others: Roman men and women, in hunting and riding clothes, with jeweled whips and black spectacles; a few Finns and Swedes and Norwegians, who claimed to be French; and, most numerous, Turks and Greeks, Arabians and other colored people. The latter were the only ones who carried rosaries.

Miss Laura was waiting for them; she did not even guess that Georges's camera was trained directly on her eyes.

Made up like a woman of the late 1940s and early fifties, with long hair thrown back in the manner of the girls from around Rome, mincing back and forth in little lacquered shoes with long, sharp, stiletto heels, the *Principe* flew from cabin to cabin, receiving those who were making their exits and helping those preparing to step in. He addressed them in every language, taking care to hide his own accent and to maintain the seductive expression of his eyes. And he begged them all to give him at least a pinch, if they wouldn't let him touch them openly.

Then he approached Giovanni Besta to make his report. The stiff, much-decorated General bowed to him in token of gratitude, as to a real lady; rising, he peered discreetly into his bosom and elegantly kissed his little hand.

The Scandinavian rolled his eyes and sighed.

Giovanni Besta then proceeded from his tales of Greece and Montenegro to Russia and its snow; more than half of those present literally shivered.

Sergey, meanwhile, noticing Amalia, Truman Independence Jones, and Carl Schlotterer, pointed them out for Georges to film. The German and the Negro formed a frame in which Amalia lay like a humped mountain of flesh behind her garbage cans. The Negro wept softly. The German was kneeling.

Amalia was sparsely dressed. Her clothes consisted of a jacket made from an American tent; a giant skirt of Scotch wool in the colors of the McMachon clan; the rags wrapped around her feet; and a necklace. While Georges Bonnefous was filming her, she sweated profusely and tried to open her bushy eyes.

"You haven't come back here for five or six years," she said, turning to Sergey Ivanovich. "How could you stay away so long? How you must have missed us! We've inquired about you—but there was never any news."

"We also inquired about you," Sergey Ivanovich answered touchingly. "We were worried about all of you. But we inquired about you especially."

THE WAR WAS BETTER

"Did you know that I can't move, and can't even get up to leave this yard?"

"We thought you couldn't leave because you liked it here," Sergey Ivanovich said, looking at the little Negro, who was still weeping beside her as he gnawed on a melon rind. "We knew other things were involved too."

Georges Bonnefous, kneeling like the German, began making close-up shots.

"Truman swears he loves me and is ready to kill half of Rome to prove it. I don't believe him; he's too black and tiny; in fact, he's so inconspicuous no one even notices him. And then I wonder: what could such a miserable little man do against everyone else? A miserable black child; he hasn't been back to his barracks for years. He's disguised himself as a blind man and comes here to weep among the garbage cans. He says he's only made love to kewpie dolls so far, never to women, only to kewpie dolls and animals. He wants me now. He wants to start with me. I don't dare let him. I'm afraid I'll crush him. And what would become of me without him? He's the only one in the whole world who cries and yearns for me. I don't know whether I love him, but even if I could stand up, I'd stay right here for a while, just for him. He's utterly helpless. There's no one to protect him. Whose back would he hide behind if he didn't have me?"

"We've come to ask you whether you'd like to be in a movie," Sergey Ivanovich interrupted, frightened by her story. "Our colossal movie about peace, which many people call happiness."

"I'm growing," Amalia answered, laughing like a child. "I weigh about one thousand and two hundred pounds. I'm lucky my bones are also growing, like Romana's. Just say in the movie, or to the newspapers, that I'm not here.... Wait.... I'm gradually beginning to remember ... some far-off country ... and fires ... many fires...."

"Do you have anything else to say to us?"

"You know, fire is very nice," she continued, smearing sweat over her face with her large hand. "Fire is wonderful, especially when you see it from here, from this stench." Her pupils widened. "There's nothing nicer than the smell of fire. Fire! I talk so much about it to Truman, but ever since he saw what happened in San Giovanni and San Lorenzo, he's had a terrible fear of fire."

"Amalia, right at the beginning of our (to use your own words) savagely growing movie, we'll say that fire is nice and smells better than roses. We'll weave whatever else you say into our story; it's no problem. But just say something."

"I don't come from here."

"We included that already. Do you have anything else to say?"

"I want everybody to know that I love *Tedesco* too, but nobody believes me. 'How can you, you fat whore, love a *Tedesco?*' they ask me. And when I tell them I'm sorry for him, they spit on me and throw melon rinds and other garbage at me. I love *Tedesco* too, yes, and the only one who understands it is my little-bitty Negro."

"*Tedesco* doesn't come from here either," Georges Bonnefous observed when he had finished filming Truman's tears and melon rinds. "What's he looking for here? He, at least, has a country."

"He too must remember something. He doesn't cry like the others. He's handsome and proud. That's why I love him so much. We all think he's violently ashamed of something. We don't know of what. Many think he's dumb. But he isn't. He can say he's a German, that his country is far-off, that it's damned and unhappy and, since that's the case, he doesn't see the road to lead him there. He's terribly obedient; he cleans the yard and shoos mice away. When he finishes his chores, he usually kneels beside me and stares for a long time at Romana's throne. He's capable of looking at her for hours. That's what he's doing now. You see, *Tedesco* is her Negro."

"And she?"

"We think she also loves him, although we don't know how or to what extent. Sometimes, when she's free, she calls him. He falls down at her feet, with his olive can in his hand, and starts to shiver. She passes her hand over his close-cropped, grayish hair and tells him something.

"We heard her only once. '*Tedesco*, my boy, my little one,' she said. 'Don't bow your head so much. You aren't the only one who is guilty; allow the others to be shameful too.' When she calls him, they say he always asks her whether she remembers Montenegro, the fire and the flowers, and the thing they two did there. '*Tedesco*, Montenegro is the only thing I remember, Montenegro and our Balkans, but I've forgotten that you and I did anything there. You know, my Knight of the Leaden Figure, years have passed since then. I'm sorry you remember it. Forget everything, like the others!'

" 'Romana, my sun, I love you,' he said. 'And that is why I beg you not to grow anymore. If you continue like this, soon you'll touch the sky with your hands. I'm afraid I won't be able to see your eyes and mouth from the earth.' He has knelt before her throne as before an altar, and watched her ever since. We all think she's so big, five times heavier than I am, that she must really be his sun, blocking out the real one, replacing it for him."

Carl Schlotterer gazed toward Romana's throne; Georges and Sergey filmed him. He had on a torn army uniform, of unknown origin, and was barefoot. His naked arms were covered with old wounds and the scars of burns.

But the German's long, thin arms and bare feet did not attract Georges's attention; his camera was glued to his head. He had never seen such a head, let alone filmed one. Both Sergey and Georges agreed that here, finally, they had found real poetry, a touching visual metaphor, perhaps even the ideal opening shot for the movie. They asked him to remain still, so they could film him all over again, between Amalia and the garbage cans, in order to make sure the footage was perfect.

Tedesco considered the request an order. He remained kneeling with his eyes lost in the distance, feeling shame for all the Germans. In his hands he still held the olive can.

"Amalia, what's happened to his face?"

Amalia did not have the time to answer. The German had stood up. She motioned for them to follow him.

Tedesco walked toward the shooting gallery and the bar, which were surrounded by a crowd of prostitutes, homosexuals, and merrymaking guests. Before he entered the crowd, Carl Schlotterer turned back to look at Sergey and Georges, who were following him. His gaze frightened them both. There was a sense of quiet, reasonable suffering in his eyes. He remembered them and had many things to tell them. He was tall, and his shoulders were still straight, although he stooped forward just a little. He held the can tightly in his hands as on the day when they had thrown it to him like a dog. They filmed him and the entire motley multitude around the shooting gallery. Then he disappeared behind the scenes.

Sergey Ivanovich and Georges Bonnefous walked up to the counter; each of them took an air rifle. Sighting down the barrels, they saw a number of personages from the world of legends and tales: the targets. Sergey fired first, and missed. Tired by the weight of the camera, and all in a sweat, Georges did no better. The woman behind the counter, with glued-on mustaches, told them they should watch out, because the target that was hardest to hit would soon appear.

Carl Schlotterer's face, the same they had filmed from all possible angles a moment before, suddenly appeared, disfigured by lead, leaden. Densely pressed together, interlaid in layers and rows, little lead pellets had been pressed over it to form a kind of mask. Metal spectacles protected his eyes. All the other surfaces, down to the collar of his shirt, were riddled and gray.

Without having time even to scream, Georges Bonnefous fired and hit Schlotterer's head between the eyebrows. The head tumbled down, and general laughter broke out. Then a figure from a tale rose to take his place.

"*Tedesco!*" Bonnefous yelled, taking hold of his camera. "Come back! Appear again! Tell me the truth, I didn't hit you, I missed just as I've always missed, in every game I ever played in my life! Come back, I want to film you: you're wonderful, you're great, you're a man! I know it must be hard for you to expose yourself to a shower of lead, but please appear again; we need at least ten more times to get the footage. *Tedesco*, please, will you?"

"No worry, sir," the woman with the glued mustaches reassured Georges as she offered her most beautiful rifle to Sir Stanley Gordon Clumsy, whom Sergey Ivanovich recognized at once. "Once it starts, our *Tedesco* usually keeps popping up until midnight."

"Sometimes until dawn," Sir Stanley added for the benefit of Sergey Ivanovich. "*Tedesco* likes to die; he thinks he hasn't yet died enough, or been hit in the right place."

"What does a German understand as the right place, sir? What do they mean by 'to die' and 'to die enough'? Do they think, perhaps, that a man can die twice? Do you know?"

"I'm a veterinary surgeon by profession," Sir Stanley replied to the woman. "I know only the English and horses. I've heard the Germans are good cattlemen. Happily, I've come to Rome from Africa. And you, what do you know about them?"

"The Germans always suffer," Sergey Ivanovich said. "Usually, others pay for their suffering. A great people, that is, they have a large population. They capitalize all their nouns. Let's take the word 'happiness.' Does a word like that, that has been used so often it's now completely worn-out and gets blamed for everything, deserve a capital letter?"

"Do you also find that the Germans—and a good many Slavs too, I dare say—that all the people up there are Teutonic?" Only Sir Stanley laughed at his own joke. "From my own veterinary and English point of view, all people are the same, with the possible exception, unless they're colored, of the Muslims or the Catholics."

"I've never met any Germans before, but I've heard they're brave, and stingy as bastards," General Fred Charles Friggit said, turning to Sergey Ivanovich and the glued-mustached woman. "Judging by the one we've got here, that's what they seem to be. To put it briefly, we can't kill him!" He turned to Georges Bonnefous, who seemed to be planted in the earth before his camera, waiting for the head with the metal spectacles to reappear. "I've hit him more than a thousand times." Georges Bonnefous did not reply, and the American poked him in the ribs. "They're not only stingy; they're selfish too, those Germans," he said.

Tedesco's head rose again, quiet and leaden. Rifles crackled. Georges's camera buzzed. Sir Stanley, Fred Charles Friggit and Colonel Luc de Tonnerre hit him at the same time. So, for that matter, did Lennie Lopovsky, who was wearing a new medal and using a decorated rifle. Two Hindus, inseparable chums and tireless hunters of male children under fifteen, hit his forehead and his cheekbone. Even the few fashionable ladies who had come up to the range, holding their rifles awkwardly and looking about nervously at the soldiers and the bored, naked girls, hit the German's cheeks and lips.

"It's only you who haven't hit him, sir," the mustached woman said to Sergey Ivanovich. "Do you want a pistol? Or a machine gun?"

"I can't shoot, madam," Sergey Ivanovich replied, returning the rifle to her sadly. "I don't know him well enough."

"Perhaps you'd like to fling a bomb at my poor German?" said the woman, who was wearing, besides her glued-on mustache, a man's tie and a lesbian sign on the lapel of her coarse men's jacket. She frowned frankly. "I'd go bankrupt without him."

"I wish you big money, madam," Sergey Ivanovich said. "Big money and luck in love."

"He seems to know you," the woman went on; her mustaches quivered. "He'll be sorry that you haven't hit him too. Would you prefer, perhaps, a toy bow and arrow?"

"I prefer to watch the others shoot, madam," Sergey Ivanovich answered, watching a crowd of wild riflemen press toward the counter and wait for the real, live, German head to pop up. "I have my reasons, dear madam, but let me say this: Your entertainment is fantastic, absolutely brilliant! Congratulations!"

"Newspapers all over the world write about us, sir," the woman said as she distributed an armful of rifles and a handful of lead. "From every corner of the globe, travelers and the ambitious gather here, not only for the entertainments offered by my spiritual father, the General, Conte Giovanni Besta, but now also, and especially, to have the opportunity of killing a real German. They depart, convinced that they've killed him, and they're happy. I'm happy too, and others are happy, and there's happiness at every step: happiness with a capital 'H'! And isn't this a time of trade, harmony and general human contentment, a time of endless peace? Try, go ahead, why not? His beautiful head appears immediately after the hunter, the wolf, and Little Red Riding-Hood. Sir!"

Rifles chattered. The woman said that almost all thirty of the bullets had hit the human head, so nobody got the prize, and a new circle was forming.

"Is your western ready, or is this kind of a continuation of what you were filming then?" As he waited for the German head to reappear, the Englishman gazed at the crowd with a romantic air; sometimes he even raised his eyebrow. "Don't you want to shoot? I dare say it simply crackles in every good western, don't you think?"

"A western is the hardest kind of movie to make, sir," Sergey Ivanovich replied, watching Georges film the thickly mustachioed woman. "It's especially hard to make a western with an idea, a humanistic message."

"That is my friend Vittorio De Sica's thesis," Fred Charles Friggit pointed out as he shot Little Red Riding-Hood under the eye. "De Sica even contends that Europe will never be capable of making a genuine western. I have to say I agree with him: Europe, my dear Europe, has no morals and no message; such as it is, it can produce only love stories and—eventually—historical spectacles in technicolor."

The woman with the bizarre sign on the lapel of her jacket announced that the main prizes, a bar of American chocolate, a little brass cross, and a small bag of dusty crackers, had been won by her most appreciated guest, Sir Stanley Gordon Clumsy.

"Please, in the future give all my prizes, whatever their number, size, and worth, to our courageous German," Sir Stanley declared and, stuffing that day's gain into his pocket, sighted down the barrel again.

The figure of Little Red Riding-Hood appeared again. There was some clamor, and then a pause. Little Red Riding-Hood looked at them. Several rifles fired. She tripped and fell.

"Take a rifle," the thickly mustachioed woman said, knitting her brows. "*Tedesco* will reappear right after the hunter and the wolf."

"Thank you, sir, but no," Sergey Ivanovich replied, returning the rifle again.

"Not at all, you're quite welcome, young lady," the woman with the rich Stalinian mustaches growled back in a deep bass. "You're quite welcome, Little Red Riding-Hood!"

Sergey Ivanovich almost sank into the earth. He blushed for all the men.

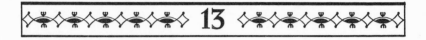

13

Sergey Ivanovich and Georges Bonnefous were tiring of their wanderings around Italy. Leaving Malić to conquer Rome again, to dance once again around the Colosseum and other monuments, they set out toward Via dei Serpenti.

A chaotic hubbub and the weeping of a woman stopped them in front of the General's courtyard. As usual, they climbed up the sidewalk with the jeep, left it there and rushed in with the camera. They felt they had to film as much of the mad laughter and frank tears of their own time as possible, roaming from one end of the country to the other.

"It's been a long time since you've been here, old man," Amalia said in greeting Sergey Ivanovich, who had almost fallen over her. "Help me at least to lift my head."

"Only eleven months this time," Ivanovich said softly, after he and an American soldier had propped her up with boxes. "What's happened, Amalia?"

"Romana's giving birth," Amalia breathed, as if sighing in relief. "That little beard suits you wonderfully, you old walrus. I can't see you too well, but you seem handsome now, almost like my *Tedesco.*"

"She's giving birth?"

"The lucky girl!" Amalia cried. "After so many years of hard work, she's going to have a baby." Propped up by the boxes, even bulkier than on the day she had told them that the little Negro was too small for her, she observed them as closely as she could. "I see the fat one, your brother, has a little beard now too; it's a handsome one, too, isn't it?"

Without bothering to reply, Sergey and Georges swooped onto Romana's throne with their camera. They made their way recklessly through a crowd of cameramen, reporters and common photographers, some of whom were even perched on the roofs of the General's cabins. The throne itself, completely uncovered for the first time and illumined by hundreds of lamps and spotlights, was protected by a cordon of policemen, Allied officers and soldiers, reinforced by a group of the stronger prostitutes and homosexuals, all dressed, this time, as nuns.

With her head lifted and her legs spread apart like any other woman giving birth, Romana lay panting on the throne, which had been bolstered by strengthened shock absorbers and springs. She pressed her giant stomach, in which the ripe fruit was moving, with both her hands, and wailed softly and continuously. Sweat poured down her forehead and neck, moistening her hair and necklaces. Her swollen eyes flashed with genuine pain and fear.

At her feet, a team dressed in white was waiting with their child-bearing equipment: five or six gynecologists from the Allied forces, a council of Roman professors, and about ten nurses and nuns (real ones), with needles, tongs and scalpels, gauze masks across their mouths and noses, rubber gloves powdered with talc, mirrors on their heads, and distilled, sterilized water kept warm in a little wooden trough for the future fruit; all were peering up between her legs.

Wet and overgrown by a thick mat of fur, Romana's smelly cave was open and gaping. Even the men who had often seen her in such a position could hardly breathe. The hard, fleshy lips on either side were folded and quiet.

Sergey Ivanovich's eyes were full of light and tears. In Parisian argot, which hardly anyone else could understand, he asked Georges whether they were on the moon. Georges Bonnefous had no time to answer; he was filming the stupendous woman on her back; beginning with her feet and rounded knees, gliding up inside her thighs, he paused at last with his lens where the others paused with their obsessed eyes; then he climbed the stomach, in which the fruit turned and stirred as in some surrealistic dream; he climbed it slowly, very slowly, pausing on the swollen navel.

Sweat poured down his face and behind his ears while he let the camera glide down the sick swelling of the belly and approach the immense breasts bursting with milk; he passed slowly from one to the other, stricken by thirst and a wolf's hunger, without knowing how or why. He remembered San Giovanni and the fire, and went on.

Her neck was long, and as beautiful as on the first day they had seen her. Georges filmed her face the longest: her swollen, lusty lips, cracked and bloody in several places, and her large, dark eyes in which pain and the intense light from the hundreds of lamps and spotlights mingled. When the fruit turned in her womb, the expression on her face changed too; she did not know where to press with her hands first.

"*Corragio! Corragio!* Courage, my treasure," Giovanni Besta, formally dressed for the occasion, cheered her on. "Courage, Queen of Peace, Queen of All Peacetime Women." He stood behind her in such a way as to place himself and the mass of his decorations with all the crosses and ribbons in full view of the cameras. "Harden your heart and don't give in. Remember that God and our generous, selfless, naïve liberators are thinking of you, of me, of us three!"

"Antonio, tell me again about your sister," Romana whispered, panting heavily and caressing his disheveled hair. "Begin, mad beard. When I listen to you, I relax."

"But everyone's waiting for a son," Antonio protested. "They're waiting for an heir."

"Speak, Antonio."

Wrapped in his asbestos cape, all torn, half-barefoot, but still decorated with medals and ribbons in the Malićian style, Antonio Peduto stood beside her. His pupils shrank and fled from the harsh lights. With his arms at his sides, he leaned toward her and touched her with his forehead. Then, enraptured as long ago on the ship, but this time loudly, so that everyone could hear him, he began.

"I'm still looking for my sister, Romana. Before I left for the war, she was lost in Via dei Serpenti. Mother and I, and the rest of my brothers and sisters, looked everywhere for her. I never tired. I went through insult after insult. I wandered everywhere. I wanted to see her so much and tear her heart out with my teeth, I've wanted to do that for so long, that now I've even forgotten what she looks like. I only know that there are blemishes, coffee-colored spots, a flood of them, all over her beautiful body, and that I aimed my knife at her heart, many times, at night. For years, as you know, I've been plodding up and down this street and other streets, calling her name aloud, promising I won't cut her throat. But she hasn't answered."

"Does she love you as much as you love her, my freckled brother?"

"I think I saw her today. She was in the overflow of girls crowding out of Via Maledetta into Via dei Fiori. I rushed after her, with outstretched arms, ready to kneel and kiss the ground she walked on. 'My loved one!' I cried out, staggering toward her. 'My loved one, the same mother has given us birth! Stop! Wait for me there, so that I may remember your face, so that at last I may see those eyes which I have kissed so often in my dreams. My darling, my poor one, my only one, don't you want to see your brother, your Antonio, who's traveled over almost the whole world, day-dreaming about you, pronouncing your name, worrying about you?' They sped away with the Allied soldiers, with the Englishmen and Negroes, who carried them away in their jeeps into the darkness. Now I don't know when I'll meet her again, or how, or whether I'll ever see her at all. She's afraid of me, although I mean her no harm. I won't do anything to her but what I just said."

Antonio began talking about the turtle. He pointed at the animal and began to complain about her. He was sorry that she drank and ate from others' hands. He scolded her for continuing to grow, so that she now weighed as much as one of the underfed little girls from Via dei Serpenti. He compared her to his sister, threatened both of them, and called them by the same tender, indecent names.

"And Peppe?" the large woman asked. She held her stomach in and moaned. "What's he doing now? How is he living?"

"I have been burning," Giuseppe Bonaccia said softly, with no sadness in his face, looking up at her from below, where he knelt beside *Tedesco*. "I've been burning so much, Romana, that my skin, especially from my knees upwards, has begun to peel and fall off." With her free hand, the woman caressed him and the German, kneeling and bent over as they were, with their eyes wet. "I burned so much in those days, and afterwards, you know the time I mean, that my memory has failed. All those fires have turned into one, universal, endless conflagration.... And I, who once knew what others have forgotten, I've become a different man. From those terrible dog days, I remember only one fire now, and in it I see you, Romana."

"Is your head still full of addresses and girls, Peppino?"

"Give birth, Romana!" Peppe exclaimed to choke back his urge to talk about his girls all around the world, and to sob. "If you can't do it like other women, *Tedesco* and I will tear you open. We have a knife. We'll help you!"

"I don't know whether I'll live," Romana burst out crying, and all the spotlights and camera lenses swooped in on her tears. "Antonio, my brother, there are no men anymore! They don't have any enthusiasm when they make love to me, the way they used to. I think they have mice's hearts."

They pushed a microphone up to her mouth, and began jotting down every word she spoke, even those she pronounced with difficulty. Paying no attention to her labor pains, one of them asked her to make a clearer distinction between men and rats.

"Their hearts are mousy," Romana repeated to Antonio. "Since I've grown so much, they've been pulling at me, scratching me, spitting on me, putting their hands and feet into me, entering me like a cave; they even count their money and decorations in there. Sometimes they can't get out, so I have to wriggle around, sweating and weeping, until they find their way out. Antonio, is it my fault that times have changed, and I now weigh over two tons?"

"If my little sister, Romana, cries out in pain, I'll send fire on you!" Amalia bristled, deciding on the worst possible thing. "Dogs, damned dogs!"

"Send fire," Romana could hardly get out the words. She murmured the names of Amalia, Peppe, and Antonio. "A great, terrible fire which will eat up everything, even the dirt and the rocks." She threw her head back, and the throne almost overturned. "Fire! Real fire!"

"The birth will be very complicated, colleagues and ladies and gentlemen," the chief Allied doctor said, protruding his jaw; he was the same one who had arrived too late at Lady Agatha Friskie's. "The baby isn't overdeveloped. It's even normal, which is surprising. Its weight is normal, but it's trying to get out with both its head and its feet."

"Caesarean!" shrieked the Scandinavian Prince, who was dressed entirely in white, with an ophthalmologist's mirror on his forehead. "If something like this happens to me, I'll get a knife and do it myself. Or perhaps I'll ask Barbagallo; he does everything!"

"Old one," Amalia called out to Sergey Ivanovich from her boxes, "don't let them cut her up! The idiot will find his way out by himself!" Sergey Ivanovich did not hear her, and Amalia pressed her teeth and knees, and sweated. "They're no longer human!" she shouted. "Take their knives away!"

"Mother!" Romana screamed and raised her hands toward the sky. "My sorrowful mother, where are you to help me now? Woe to me and to you, Mother!"

"Truman, you poor thing, watch out, don't touch the fruit," Amalia warned him when she thought something was coming out. "It looks diseased . . . really diseased . . . this fruit!"

Happily, the fruit emerged with his boots first, and the main Allied doctor waved away all the scalpels, cleavers, butcher, and kitchen knives and even the new American machine for drilling army teeth. Only Truman and *Tedesco* burst out crying. Someone said that Negro and German tears, which had the same chemical composition, were infectious and must be kept off the floor. Dozens of white hands were pulling the boots outward. Instruments, decorations, sterilized vessels and test tubes jingled. The knees appeared, the other parts of an officer's pants, then a khaki jacket with an English belt and clasp on it. Ribbons emerged, and medals from various European and non-European armies. Finally the narrow chest and drunken head of Sir Stanley Gordon Clumsy emerged, with freckles around his nose, and smoke-colored spectacles on.

The infant lifted itself to its feet and staggered about. Many hands waited anxiously for it; in case of emergency, they held about a dozen hypodermic needles filled with serum against various infections and diseases. The infant remained on its feet; with romantic, bloodshot eyes, it looked down at the woman writhing in pain, and called Antonio and the leaden Carl Schlotterer to help her. Then it pushed the two-story English baby buggy away. Full of cotton wool and various playthings, it rolled all the way to the shooting gallery and the woman with the Stalinian mustaches.

"As a veterinarian, as the Commandant of all Allied troops in this part of Europe, as an Englishman and as the Commandant of Rome, in particular, tell us what you felt on this truly spectacular trip!" Sergey Ivanovich was nearest. He screened his face with his hand from the hot spotlights, flashbulbs, and shouting spectators. Feeling that Georges must be near him somewhere, he continued. "Two more questions, sir. First, must a man submit to happiness when it is imposed on him like slavery? Second, do you foresee any end to this harmony, or will people have to begin setting fire to everything?"

"I have asthma, a typically English disease," Sir Stanley whispered contritely, resembling the fruit of a sick imagination. "Asthma ... which I've had ever since my childhood." He began to gasp for breath. "I think happiness is imposed on men as on horses, whether they like it or not." He was choking, and pressed both his hands on his chest. He seemed to be spitting out the needles and gauze they were bringing up to him. "As a veterinarian, I should have known better. One should never go on such trips ... up there ... with asthma like mine. It simply isn't done!"

He would have fallen if it hadn't been for Fred Charles Friggit, Luc de Tonnerre, and the Scandinavian Prince, dressed in Scotch skirts, who were holding him up and mopping his slimy, smelly face with sponges soaked in smelling salts. Sizing up the heap of baby-care equipment, and the whole mountain of playthings, he remarked: "I'm not the only one who's sick."

They asked him something he could not quite make out, something about a knife, happiness, fire.

"I know nothing more," he answered. "Above all, I want to say hello to my courageous mum. . . ."

With her free hand, Romana caressed *Tedesco*'s face, trying to feel all his little lead pellets. With the other, she was pressing down her stomach, which was slowly sagging. The man trembled.

"Love!" he screamed, and everyone there, even the girls in the cabins, heard the German's voice for the first time. "Love, I'll never abandon you!"

14

"You were right, Red! Georges and I just can't leave. Believe me, it's not only because of the stupendous movie we're making; it's something else, much worse! Is it because we're embezzlers, thieves and (please keep this to yourself) gangsters? Is it because we met you and came to love you? Or is it because you, you damned red magus, wanted it to be like this? If you don't answer me, I swear I'll smash you one, I'll murder you!"

Noisily drunk, and dressed in a toreador's costume like Peduto himself, Sergey Ivanovich leaned across the garbage cans and tried to hug him. He was falling; the cans fell apart and banged against the fat and agitated Amalia. Then he rose and shouted, charged, and thrust his fox's nose into the garbage.

"Georges, what's happened to us since the day we met? Georges, ask the red magus. I think he's charmed our hearts into beating in the same rhythm, into crying at the same time, into . . . Where are you, boss?"

Georges Bonnefous was not clad like a toreador, but his garb was also museumlike: a cape of some coarse fabric, embroidered and hemmed with gold like Peppe's; broad, Oriental pants with a rich, red belt; a heavy watch on a gold chain; and a two-pointed hat, tightly clapped down over his head, inside out. Sweating, with his hands in the garbage and the camera dangling on his chest, he did not have time to say a word, even to himself. He dropped on his knees and listened to the general uproar and weeping which came from somewhere in the cabins. He wanted to clap Antonio on the back, but kept hitting garbage cans instead, and shooing away mice.

"Red, we'll follow you, you two!" he said. "We'll follow your tracks, because you've become our heroes, our hearts, maybe even our happiness! Have no fear for your lives. We'll defend you. Even if you start stealing again, we'll take care of you like mad angels! We'll be together, all of us, and we'll triumph! Tell me, Red, where true happiness lies. Tell me whether we have a right to it."

Peppe was even drunker than Sergey Ivanovich, who was now threatening to eat up the first mouse he caught if their questions were not answered soon; he was giggling and pulling open the turtle's jaws. Lifting her with great difficulty, he set her on a heap of garbage and tried to embrace her, but her little paws did not want to hug his neck at all. Then Antonio spoke to her with a bottle of wine in his arms.

"Anna-Maria, my curse, my happiness, don't refuse the wine! Cattolica, you too forget you're growing; you forget I can hardly carry you anymore! Poor one, don't you see that everyone is insane now, that they're trying to leave, but they can't—it's impossible."

"Don't get the poor beast any drunker, Red Beard!" Sergey Ivanovich shouted at Antonio. "Her heart will break. Don't you know that whores' hearts are weaker than other women's? Don't fuddle up the miserable beast; tell her the long-awaited day has come!"

"Antonio, things are really growing now!" Georges Bonnefous roared from the garbage as he stumbled out and almost sprawled at Amalia's feet. "You're cursed, damned. You've made everything around you become mammoth, colossal, inhuman! You're a magus! We'll follow you anyway. You couldn't escape us even if you had a hundred turtles instead of just one, this miserable little Cattolica. . . ."

"Red, after everything I've seen and heard, I've come to the idea, the bitter idea that we're the same!" Sergey Ivanovich began to wail from behind the garbage cans. "It was clear to me even on the day we met you, but I didn't have the guts—or the energy—to tell you. . . . Poor San Giovanni Battista and the miserable donkey Luka, and poor Padre Arturo Lupo, and the poor dead who ran away, so many of them . . . have a heart and answer Georges's questions! Tell him whether happiness exists, since when he's drunk and full of American chocolate, he asks about nothing else, as if happiness were for everybody!"

"Cattolica," Peduto whispered to the turtle. He remembered how, ten months before, he had rushed with his knife after his sister and the jeep which was carrying her and the other girls away from him into the darkness. "Cattolica, my little whore, my only one, lift your head and say good-by to your sisters, and to everyone who's going to stay here in this yard. Tell them we'll be back one day, perhaps when a fire comes, and burns this whole, God-forsaken, peaceful circus down to the ground. Cattolica, answer fat Georges. Tell him whether happiness really exists. Tell him what he'd do with it if it did!"

"There is no happiness anymore," General Besta sobbed into his tiny microphone, and his voice, magnified a hundredfold, drowned out the wailing of the prostitutes and homosexuals who were embracing the colored Allied soldiers and the so-called "occasional" white visitors. "There's no more happiness in this country. There's no more real masculine adventure and excitement. There's no more freedom! They want to forbid us to make love. They're preparing laws! Yes, laws! Political and ideological censorship is rearing its ugly head! Tyranny is vomiting its rage down on us first, on us poor, unprotected artists! Therefore, we must cheat them, cheat them again and again! We will win another victory, by sweat and common suffering!"

Standing at his usual spot, Giovanni turned left and right, so that most of his audience began to expect some more of his war stories from Africa, the Balkans or Russia. No one guessed that the General, framed by Allegretti and Barbagallo as usual, could no longer remember any of his atrocities. Tightly corseted, dressed, as it seemed, for a parade or a museum, he poured his grief into the microphone, and the soldiers and others wept.

"My children, my friends from all over the world, we've got to give a bum steer to censorship! I'm the first. I'll set the example. ... The moment of our parting has come! We won't be here for long. Don't remember the evil in us, don't remember the bad things. Write to us. We're leaving!"

Sergey Ivanovich, Antonio Peduto, and the others behind the garbage cans watched him pose for the cameramen, moviemakers, and newspapermen. He turned left and right, exposing his profile and offering brief answers and sustained theatrical smiles as he jingled his medals and lifted his eyebrows. He too had a beard and mustaches, but they were glued on, and he often stroked them and inconspicuously made sure they stuck to his face. Although he was still lively, and the only one still sober, he could hardly move, no less turn around. Decorations, pistols, holsters, and swords were dragging him down.

THE WAR WAS BETTER

"In which direction are you going, General?" Sir Stanley Gordon Clumsy asked on behalf of the most drunken and worried customers. "Do you want me to give you a compass?"

"Thank you, dear colleague!" Giovanni Besta said into the microphone. "My compass is my nose, and my instinct for life and happiness, which simply can't be found around here anymore!"

They applauded him, broke bottles, and threw their glasses on the floor. Those who had been tricked out of their money rushed to the bar and the shooting gallery, pulled them down and tried to rape the woman with the Stalinian mustaches. Besta turned, greeted them with a wave, and then gazed after his own lifted hand.

"My sense of direction is infallible: the West! The primitive countries with a surplus of literates and intellectuals! The underdeveloped countries, the countries which still don't know what love and sex are, Italian style! In Switzerland, for example, we won't stay long. There's no room for my program there, and no money! Paris is calling me. We'll pitch our tent beside the Obelisk on Place de la Concorde! The French are the only people who'll let me get along without contracts and lengthy explanations of the attractions I'm going to present!"

A group of uniformed Turks and Arabians were raping the woman with the Stalinian mustache, thinking she was a man. The others were carrying away the rifles, stealing the ammunition and the moldy American chocolate and firing drunkenly at Little Red Riding-Hood.

"I'll show the English and the Dutch and others my own miracles of peace! An opportunity will finally be offered to them and the Scandinavians to see what's been happening in the postwar period, the time of so-called 'harmony'! I also thought of the Germans, although least of all, of course. It's easy to cheer them up. They laugh like mad at anything, provided it's gaudy.... Poor Germans. But they're so tasteless, and have so many phony guilt feelings!"

"What will happen to us?" Sir Stanley whispered in a voice tinged with reticence and sorrow. General Friggit and Colonel Luc de Tonnerre repeated the question aloud. "What will happen to us, now that we've grown accustomed to a normal life?"

"You can always come with me!" Giovanni Besta answered them through the microphone. "I've become accustomed to you, too, and today's parting isn't easy for me! Let's set out together. We'll perform the most exciting feature of the program, the birth, not only in all the Western capitals, but also in the God-forsaken ghost towns of Europe, in cathedrals, in circuses! I accept you and embrace you. . . ."

"No, we must remain here!" Sir Stanley Gordon Clumsy said, resigning himself with considerable melancholy. "My profession is veterinary surgeon. I'm staying here! What would I do in England, anyway? There's no longer any cattle or vegetation there! Besides, pensions are low, and arrive irregularly!"

"We're remaining here!" General Fred Charles Friggit repeated after the Englishman, who was reeling forward, bent almost double under his decorations. "We've fought in the Pacific. We've beaten the Japanese, and that's why we're remaining in Italy! But those are only some of the reasons. The rest of the reasons, it is my deepest conviction, belong . . ."

"The rest of the reasons belong in the theater!" the thin and rather handsome Colonel Luc de Tonnerre cried enthusiastically. "I thought myself that I'd return in my own time to my home and country, which are waiting for me." Looking at his friends, he reached out and held their hands. "But I can't leave them, just as they can't leave me. My General, my *Taliano*, a miracle has happened. We can't part!"

The Englishman, the American and the Frenchman embraced. Sir Stanley driveled. He repeated that England's humidity and the Puritan way of life would administer a death blow to him and drive him to an early grave. General Fred Charles Frigget assured the reporters and movie men that all those who thought the Americans were children, were themselves idiots. He totally mixed up the expressions "sexual pathology" and "spiritual misery," on which he dwelt at length, and then concluded with the statement that Americans, no matter where they came from and where they arrived, were incapable of departing.

Colonel Luc de Tonnerre struck his breast and coughed. It was his opinion, he said, that the majority of Frenchmen, including himself, suffered from liver and kidney ailments, sunken stomachs and constipation, and because of these and other diseases and reasons, they needed more space and greater rewards in life. Then all three threw their arms around each other, turned in a circle and sang something obscene and cacophonous in Italian.

"Then you'll guard this place?" Giovanni Besta raised his finger like the Pope. "This place . . . where many . . . have fallen."

"We'll continue the work you've begun, *Taliano!*" Sir Stanley promised. He waited for the American and the Frenchman to repeat his vow, and then for the numerous members of diplomatic and military missions, who were gathered around the woman with the Stalinian mustaches, to do likewise. There was a general murmuring of assent. "The work you've begun, the work of peace and universal human happiness! We too will grow. We'll become mammoth, colossal! The hundred girls you can't take with you will be, for the present, enough for us! When you come back here, though, you'll find a whole industry at work, busy as bees! General, *Taliano*, we wish you a good wind and strong tires for your car. Go as soon as possible. We want to begin at once!"

"But didn't you start the day you came, bringing us liberty and chocolate? Or perhaps you've forgotten the day you came?" He watched them embrace each other again, still turning in a circle. "Perhaps you've forgotten that you came at all?"

"We want to grow, *Taliano!* Everything mammoth and inhuman and sick is no longer strange to us!" They stared at him too. "Bless us. Don't leave us without something . . . for the start . . . because you've taken everything!"

"*O sole mio*," General Besta sang into the microphone in a pure, Neapolitan tenor, as he watched a large crane lifting Romana's throne. *O sole . . . o sole.*" He trembled while they dropped the giant bed, with the apparently calm Queen still on it, into the trailer of a truck. "*O sole, o sole mio, sta 'nfronte a te.*"

"I'll die without her!" Sir Stanley began to wheeze and weep. Then he saw them stretch a tent over Romana, scatter motley cushions around and tuck her in. She was holding the icon of St. Demetrius before her face like a looking glass, weeping and praying just as she had long before, when she was only a poor girl from the suburbs of Rome. "I'll die! The English too, gentlemen, know how to love. We too, from time to time, can live with others!" He was holding his hand under his decorations, on his chest. "Do you doubt, then, that an English heart can break? I'd like to convince you of it, but I'm afraid. I'm a coward. I'm selfish. Asthmatic. A veterinary surgeon by profession. Our hearts usually break for animals. . . ."

"I have the impression we've already begun!" Fred Charles Friggit yelled and clapped the frail Frenchman on the back. "Go, *Taliano!*"

"Love, I'll die without you! I really shall!" Sir Stanley cried out in the Queen's direction. "My only beloved, just wave your hand if you don't want to give me the precious Orthodox icon . . . just one gesture and I'll die!"

He would actually have died, or at least sunk to his knees, if the American and Frenchman had not been holding him up.

"Since Romana is a miracle, if you'll allow me, my miracle . .

because she's a real miracle of peace, Miss Peace, she must have a chaperon!" Attacked by a fit of coughing, General Besta got mixed up in the middle of his long sentence. "And since it's a question of an all-time beauty, Romana will have two chaperons. The first is my spiritual but, happily, not physical son, *Principe*, the Scandinavian, who, as you can see for yourselves, is occupying, alone, a place beside Romana!"

Everyone looked up at the scene under the tent. Romana was kissing the deep, somber eyes of the Balkan Demetrius and remembering the fire.

"We needn't look too long for the second chaperon. It is Amalia, called Mild, Good, Toothless, or, as I have named her in my books, Amalia Celestina!"

Then a shot rang out. The hue and cry stopped. Those behind the garbage cans said that Truman Independence Jones had seized a pistol, then dropped it among the garbage mice. All of them, however, saw the Negro emerge and open his mouth wide in order to inhale as much earthly stench as possible. He rolled his eyes and set out across the yard, disguised as a beggar. A passage opened for him. Somebody from the crowd said it was not a genuine suicide, let alone death, because there was not enough blood.

The Negro did not enter any of the cabins whose doors opened as he passed. He did not even look at them. Trembling violently, he tottered up to Amalia, who received him. He crouched in her lap, his head pressing against her giant belly, and gradually began to calm down.

He did not seem to be bleeding, or else his blood was as black as his skin, like the rags which clothed him. The homosexuals and prostitutes from the filthiest corners and staircases said they had never seen a swifter, more commonplace death.

"I won't, I won't give him up to you!" the sweaty Amalia Celestina sobbed as they lifted her with long forks and carried her toward the trailer. "He's mine, mine, mine alone!" She pressed him firmly against her ample bosom, but he seemed to drip away and diminish in her arms. Even if he had been alive, he would not have budged from her lap. "I won't give him to you, you murderers! Don't come near us, don't touch us with your dirty hands! He's mine! He's the only one who ever really loved me—and he never touched me!"

They set Amalia Celestina on Romana's left. Then Romana, without taking St. Demetrius from her bosom, ordered the German to be set at her feet. They obeyed her. The leaden-faced man knelt, holding the can, and looked up at them all like someone well accustomed to every calamity imaginable. General Besta said that *Tedesco* himself was a living miracle. He was sure to get first prize for his face, his never-yet-exhibited mask, at the world's fair in Brussels.

"If at least he would leave Miss Laura with us," Sir Stanley sighed from the midst of Friggit's and Luc's embrace. "But, buck up, boys, somehow we'll find something similar. I know a Greek who'll be a decent substitute for Besta's black swan. You, my friends, are lucky; you've never tasted Laura!"

His eyes were troubled. Through his tears, the Queen seemed even bigger and more beautiful. At the moment of her departure, she could have actually touched, if not with her head, at least with her hands and the Orthodox icon, the cloudy and sweaty Roman sky. It even seemed to Sir Stanley that the German's face was also bigger and more leaden. Everything swam in his tears, expanded, increased and lost its previous shape. Even the Scandinavian, with his falsies, glued-on eyelashes and an oculist's mirror on his forehead, had lost his pallor, and his Scotch skirts seemed to suit him quite nicely.

"*Taliano!*" Sir Stanley shouted. "You're taking away exactly thirty girls, that is, one-third, but we'll surprise you. We'll make miracles with the rest! You're a common Mediterranean windbag, an amateur. You still don't have the slightest idea of what a genuine circus is!"

"We've already started, Stanley. Don't get excited," Fred Charles Friggit said.

"If only I weren't dying for her!" Sir Stanley wailed. "Our life is just beginning to get interesting. The *Taliano* doesn't know what a real bordello is!"

Fred, Luc, and Sir Stanley could hear the soldiers and the rest of the men neighing like colts around the thick-mustached woman at the shooting gallery. The girls and the homosexuals, in long dresses, fell down on the ground and wailed from pain and pleasure and spoke to each other of war and fire. The trio could have turned and seen the first day's festivities begin in earnest, and free of charge, but they did not want to. Instead, they watched the General's trailers being filled with living exhibits and colorful displays.

A square black automobile, which resembled a London taxi, with the General's trunks, skis, butterfly and bat nets piled on its roof, left first, leading the way. Sir Stanley, Fred and Luc could just make out Giovanni Besta and Spartaco Allegretti inside, and Turiddu Barbagallo behind the wheel. Shocked by the screams and roars in the yard and the cabins, which no one bothered to close anymore, the trio had time only to wave to them, and wish them a happy journey.

Via dei Serpenti had its great day again. Windows opened, and trumpets, hands and even some torn flags were thrust out. Pale, harried Roman faces looked up from the sidewalk to greet the trailer which was carrying off the Queen of peace and Amalia Celestina, who, with an ever firmer grip, like a great bear, hugged her small, black fruit.

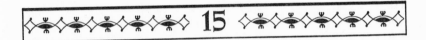

15

"I'm a magus!" Antonio Peduto whispered, standing up with Peppe from behind the garbage cans and stuffing the turtle into a large bag. "I'm a magus! I've foreseen everything! I'm sorry!"

Antonio and Peppe passed the binoculars through a hole in the bag, and lifted the load. The turtle, peering out, looked at them. Antonio also asked her to forgive him, and then they set off.

"We'll never part again, Red!" Georges Bonnefous said. He began to choke and cough from the smell of the burning garbage and overturned several cans.

"Just tell us the direction—we'll follow you!" Sergey Ivanovich said, planting his feet on the ground. "Are you going west, like the others?"

From the threshold of Besta's bordello, the four watched Via dei Serpenti and the adjoining side streets say goodbye to the General's caravan. They too waved good-by for a while, calling out to them and asking them to wait. Peppe was not the only one who spoke of love, women's addresses, and fire. They followed the column by foot, staggering and reeling. Then they picked up fallen decorations from the pavement, and began to get into the rhythm of the rest of the procession.

"Tell us the direction, Red!" Sergey Ivanovich cried out sometime before dusk, when he was hardly able to steer the old jeep anymore. "Georges, you please ask him. Tell him it's not so terrible, although it was predestined, that he's a magus! Georges, don't you see that Rome is bidding us farewell? And they're just as generous and panicky as the day we marched in!"

THE WAR WAS BETTER

None of them could have explained how and from where Gruban Malić appeared. He simply broke out of one of the side streets full of stench, empty cans, and prostitutes, and joined the column. He was riding his donkey and carrying the globe, which was now almost completely red and scribbled over with a ballpoint pen, and he was wrapped up in his own thoughts, deaf to the cries which echoed around him.

Malić's clothes were also more or less from a museum. His boots were soft, with spurs that had undoubtedly belonged to some already forgotten marshal. On his late-nineteenth-century Spanish grandee's jacket, he sported about fifty medals and ribbons. A Russian fur hat with ear flaps and a red star in front covered his head. His overcoat was also long and Russian, but worn-out and partly burned, like the parachute on his back. On his lap he held his asbestos cape with the hood and glass disks for his eyes: just in case!

"Sergey, don't you see our angel, our Malić, is deciding our direction!" Peduto cried for happiness. He and Peppe tried to approach the man with the globe. "Our Malić, Sergey Ivanovich! Lord, if You exist, how generous You must be, for having sent him to us! He alone can set fire to the world; only he has the power to lead us out of this hell!"

"How wonderful you are, Red!" Sergey Ivanovich shouted from behind the wheel. "And how wonderful our madness is!" His tears too were flowing as he honked his horn, braked, and then put his foot on the gas pedal. "After him, then, even if he leads us into the fire!"

"A great person once said that fire is beautiful, that there's no smell more intoxicating than that of a flame," Antonio said, thinking of Amalia Celestina and her childlike smile. "Sergey, fire is like a rose. If You exist indeed, oh Lord, send fire upon us, and pardon us our blasphemies!"

"I'd like to stretch out in flowers," Giuseppe Bonaccia sobbed, as he watched the turtle peer out of the bag. "In order to rest my feet and rub my burns, which hurt me so much, with some clean earth." His knees buckled. Alcohol was troubling his thoughts and his words. He began to daydream about flowers. "Cattolica, our love and our sister, say good-by to Rome! Anna-Maria, my rose, say good-by!"

"It looks like Malić is leading us all right," Sergey Ivanovich observed, as he drove on behind the General's trailer. "He seems to be using his globe as a compass!"

"He is! And it works! It works like a compass!" Antonio was

beside himself, his beard full of garbage and tears. "Sergey, he's infallible! Look, his face is sooty. He's all seared. His overcoat is completely riddled and burnt through!"

They went down another, narrower side street which curved tortuously and descended further and further until it reached the banks of the Tiber. The windows and balconies of the old houses were bristling with Italian heads. They were flinging flowers on them, old newspapers, and wet underwear.

Antonio's gaze wandered over the walls. He recognized the balcony from which the nymphomaniac Gigia had thrown herself upon Malić, and hoped that something similar might occur again. He saw a broken baby buggy suddenly fly past Malić's globe.

"Romans, poor, sorrowful ones," he asked them, "has Gigia found the children she lost in Via dei Serpenti, not far from the Vatican?" They held their tongues, and he asked them again. "Where's Gigia now? Are you dumb, Romans?"

Discarded things fell on Antonio from the widow's balcony: feathers and bedding, saints' images and night lights. It was thus that they answered him.

Peduto was quick to understand. He felt the weight of the turtle, and pain around his heart. He asked those who were leaning from the other balconies: "Whose child is that, up there on the roof?"

"Some mad Englishwoman's, some atheist's, my knight," a wrinkled old woman answered on behalf of the crowd, making the sign of the cross over her withered bosom. "Just look, you'll see what he's like, this Vladimir of hers, to whom she coos, we don't know why, in our own tongue: 'My only one, my only *Slavo*.' Just look at him. Then you'll have something to see!"

"We'd like to see her, mother," Sergey Ivanovich said to the shriveled old woman. "Where is she now, the godless woman who delivers sermons, you say, threatening you with the Balkan and eastern dawn, and hands out little red flags and globes of crimson cloth?"

"Is such ... an Englishwoman and communist necessary to anybody?" Old women were leaning so far out of their windows and balconies that they were about to fall out. "What do you need her for, *Cavaliere?*"

"We'll take her on our long journey, dear mother," Sergey Ivanovich said softly, remembering Lady Agatha Friskie and the assortment of drugs she had taken from Colonel Luc de Tonnerre. "If she's somewhere around, throw her to us! What are you telling us, dear mother? No! It couldn't be true! She tried to set fire to this wonderful town of Rome? Twice?"

"They let her go because she's an *Inglesa* and *Slava*, or something like that. People like her do to us what they please. Anything's allowed, for them. They'd cut our heads off with an ax in the center of Rome, if we did it. But she's an Englishwoman, or something like that. You're lucky she isn't here now. She'd go after you with her little flags, and her red paint and brushes!"

"And the son, my old woman?" Peduto asked her excitedly from below. "Her little *Slavo?*"

"He's seven," a man with a white beard next to the old woman said. "But he's big, like a good calf."

"Seven years? Has it been so much time since then?" Sergey mused aloud, watching Georges Bonnefous. "Is he seven, old one, seven or eight?"

"It wouldn't be much if he were a sound child," the old man said, just as the boy, inordinately developed and extremely fat, finished strangling a cat and threw its body in front of the jeep. "A moment ago he threw a live cat at some gentleman, in uniform too, probably an American. Threw a live cat, like that, at a liberator ... he should have thrown a stone!" The old man's eyes widened; he flailed his arms. "You can't come to terms with him. He speaks some kind of Slavic mother tongue, and then English, which also makes us shiver. He threatens us from above, and throws old pots and tiles at us. I tell you, *Commendatore*, he controls the lofts and roofs of this neighborhood, not we. He!"

The street was jammed; they had to wait. The engines were vomiting pain and smoke. Georges Bonnefous kept his eyes closed; he was swelling in the heat and listening. Sweat bathed his broad face and drenched his hands, which lay quietly on his camera. Sergey Ivanovich looked up at the General's exhibit items, and then at Malić, who said something to his donkey, and then spoke again to the excited crowd on the pavement and in the windows. He seemed still to be lost in thought.

"What else is the little robber, the damn *Slavo*, doing?" Peduto went ahead of the others, kicking Peppe, who wanted to pick the dead cat up from the pavement. "You say, old one, that nobody dares to do anything against him, not even the firemen?"

"*Avocato*, that is because he's both a *Slavo* and an *Inglese*," the old man argued. "They'd either hang me, or eat me alive. And he —he's strong, voracious. Just look at his slanty eyes; look at his cheekbones and forehead! All he does is eat and, excuse me, shit it out. And he insults us at the same time. The Germans themselves never cursed us like that, not even the Negroes. As he shits down his legs all the time, he wipes his behind with pigeons. With our Roman pigeons! And then he lets the pigeons, bruised and scared out of their wits, fly over people and around churches. What will we see next, after so much trouble and suffering, we and our good pigeons?"

"Such are the pigeons of peace, my old one!" Antonio Peduto exclaimed in joy, and exchanged significant looks with Ivanovich, who honked his horn crazily.

"I don't know where they came from, my knights, but they're covered with shit," the old man said melancholically. "We're scared of them, all of us. We're scared of him and we're scared of her! She curses us like a barbarian, repeating the same word, if it is a word at all, over and over again. Pigeons of peace, did you say? What peace? Whose peace?"

"Malić, turn! Look up!" Peduto yelled when the column started again. "You'll see something. Something wonderful and terrible. Just turn for a moment, and then look back toward the west! Montenegrin! You implacable and merciless knight!"

The man with the globe was silent. He spurred the donkey. It seemed to Antonio that, settling deep into his saddle, he must be looking into a future entirely covered with flowers and flames. Malić seemed to hear nothing, least of all the voices of the widows who waved to him from the warped balconies, first with their hands, and then with their lace frillies, accusing him of their husbands' deaths. He would not have heard little Vladimir either, if the latter had not occasionally yelled from the roof.

Sooty, covered with cobwebs and gripping a chimney stack, the boy wiped his naked, moonlike backside with a pigeon. Turning his healthy face toward the street, he grinned broadly. Then he flung the pigeon out over the procession. The poor bird was hardly able to spread its gluey wings.

The golden pigeon flew heavily over the General's trailers and, strangely attracted by Malić's fur hat and globe, almost alighted on him. The boy already held another pigeon. As he spread his thighs, a large, crooked, sluggish larva appeared between his legs.

"Vladimir Ilyich, be merciful toward the poor people!" Peduto exclaimed, and Peppe and Sergey Ivanovich repeated his cry. "Ilyich, Ulyanov, *Slavo*, you who reign over so many lofts and roofs, cats and pigeons, watch out you don't slip! Be careful, you're surrounded by enemies! Be careful, our hope!"

THE WAR WAS BETTER

Vladimir Ilyich Lenin, Jr., who resembled a big puppet, laughed. In the expression of his broad face, and especially in the brightness of his black, slanty eyes, there was something kind, deep, and, above all, Slavic. He held the pigeon and deliberated as to where he would throw it. In his clumsy appearance, and in the manner in which he addressed the people over whose lofts and roofs he reigned so imperiously, there was something funny, almost clownish. Nobody could have forgotten him such as he now appeared, with his legs spread, and his dangling balls and larva touching the hot tiles.

Beside him, he kept a heap of strangled cats and a row of hot tiles, in case of attack. Bulky and fleshy in the extreme, Vladimir Ilyich looked even bigger in the sunset. With a bow and arrow strapped across his back, and the pigeon in his hand, he seemed to grow to the size of the dusk which was pouring over the roofs.

"Vladimir Ilyich, stay up there. Keep threatening them!" Peduto coughed and waved to him with his free hand. "Stay up there and tell them whenever you can that they don't deserve anything better from you! Tell them they're no good, villainous, shit-eaters! And one day you will punish them with a fire that all the firemen of this sick, crazy, pornographic world won't be able to put out... This world deserves nothing but hate, disdain and disgust!"

Ulyanov did not reply. He screened the view of many of the neighbors, which was small and restricted in any case. For others, who looked down on him from higher windows and balconies, he did not. Holding the big pigeon, he carefully chose his victim. In his other hand, he was brandishing a brick. Anyone else would have lost his balance and tumbled down.

"Malić, Gruban, our *muleta*, mad angel, turn and see!" The toreador Antonio Peduto, lacking only a red *muleta*, called to him tenderly. "Malić, you can't even guess how beautiful this dusk is! How it seems almost human! Turn, look! I'll never be able to describe it to you! Malić!"

"Is he thinking of anything as he stares so fixedly toward the west?" the troubled Sergey Ivanovich asked Antonio Peduto, who was watching, through his tears, flocks of Vladimir's golden pigeons fly over them. "What's he thinking now? Tell me, you red-bearded magus and sage!"

"I'm hoarse," Peduto said, panting and almost falling down. "Ivanovich, you're a magus too! Do you have any water? I'm about to fall down."

"Ivanovich, Sergey, fearless fox, Malić thinks of nothing but the world revolution, like me," Georges Bonnefous said dully, beginning to cry, either from happiness or exhaustion. "That's why one shouldn't show him his sons, whoever they are, or his daughters either. We revolutionaries wear black spectacles. We don't answer for our works, or pay support for children. And he's unique among us. Just look how sooty he is, burnt through in a hundred places! Look how his globe is scribbled and colored over!"

Georges Bonnefous closed his eyes again. A golden pigeon fell down into his arms.

The dusk, the pigeon feathers and the deep echo of the Roman bells were saying good-by to them.

Fourth Part

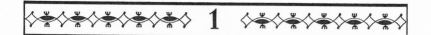

DON'T WORRY, SERGE," Georges Bonnefous said to cheer him up, as he leaned against the side of the jeep. "I see them."

"Where are they, boss?" Sergey Ivanovich's face was pale and skinny. "Are they still on the river bank?"

"Yes," Bonnefous answered. "They're waiting for the reply."

"I've got the feeling they've been waiting for it too long," Ivanovich thought aloud as he watched them through binoculars. "If my memory doesn't fail me, we've all been here since the day before yesterday."

"The Swiss don't surrender so easily," Bonnefous remarked, taking the binoculars from Sergey. "Probably they're taking time to study the declaration of war, maybe even the conditions for surrender."

"I wish they'd try to resist. Malić's invincible," Sergey Ivanovich said, screening his eyes from the sun. "I'd like to see them bleed."

"You won't live to see it, Fox," Georges Bonnefous shook his head. "They aren't such damn fools as to accept a fight and all the expenses involved. They're probably doing a cost benefit analysis."

"It would pay off for us," Sergey Ivanovich mused from the other side of the jeep.

"The Swiss are fully aware of that," Georges Bonnefous said, winking. "That's why they never get into a war with anybody."

"Why the devil don't they surrender?"

"That doesn't pay off either. They prefer to be quietly defeated, with as few witnesses and reporters around as possible. We're just lucky they don't know we have a camera. They have no idea what we're cooking up."

"They'll remember us, by God!" Sergey Ivanovich said, raising his fist and shaking it at the absent Swiss. "They'll remember us and our movie. They still don't know the things Slavs are capable of, no less what kind of boots Malić has on."

"I know the Swiss," Georges Bonnefous said, measuring the distances. "They remember everything."

From the bend where they lay in the sun, the valley and the winding river spread out in a calm landscape of peaceful beauty. Around the water and all down to the low pine forest, there was a pasture fenced with wire and packed with cows, bulls, and calves. Roofs of cottages and sheds protruded from the forest, as well as telegraph poles with many wires, on which crows were sitting. In the distance, where the river bent in a U-shaped oxbow, the embankment and crossties of a railway track could be discerned, embedded in the moist, luxuriant grass. Only the cawing of the crows and the whistles of occasional trains troubled the peaceful landscape and the happy cattle.

"Malić is pulling the donkey and adjusting his saddle," Sergey Ivanovich remarked. "Peppe is holding the globe for him; Antonio is putting the turtle into the bag. I think he's saying something. Malić looks terribly angry. He must be sick of all this delay. They're in the reeds, in the grove."

"This time even your filthy lucre won't help you, Swiss!" Georges Bonnefous almost shouted. Then he added carefully: "What will happen to their money, by the way? Who usually carries off the mazuma of the vanquished?"

"We'll never be that lucky, Georges," Ivanovich sighed. "Buzzards and hyenas generally drag away the main thing. We'll just have to keep on perfecting our counterfeiting."

"It could start now," Georges Bonnefous said suddenly. He got hurriedly into his seat in the jeep, growing visibly excited. "Drive on. We've got to get nearer." Sergey Ivanovich started the engine and moved slowly out onto the forest road. "Maybe there'll be hand-to-hand fighting," Georges said. "We could use some for the movie; we haven't got any yet. And I hear the Swiss are good at it."

Now they could see them better. Directly before him, there were about ten wonderful pictures that Georges could have filmed. What he needed was some action with the green grass in the background, or silhouetted against the clear sky. Sergey kept the engine running and studied the meadow he would have to cross with the jeep if the Swiss surrendered *en masse*, like cowards. He also looked carefully at the concrete abutments of the bridge. For a moment, he thought he saw holes in them, and then even the barrels of deadly Swiss weapons.

"Malić is on his donkey!" Georges whispered passionately, adjusting the focus and arranging his equipment. "It's important that he got on. There, he's holding up his globe like a shield and frowning at the west. It looks like his hawk's eyes are seeing all the way to the Atlantic Ocean."

"He sees farther than that," Sergey Ivanovich said, looking through the pine branches. "He'd never enter a battle if he didn't see farther. I only hope the story that a bullet will never hit him proves true! Then we could make movies about him for the rest of our lives."

"If he'd only act all the time! I wonder what he'd say if he knew that we've been filming him ever since San Giovanni. There might be a hell of a storm about it. Probably it's better the way it is now. He thinks we're just his followers, his fellow travelers."

"They've stepped . . . not into shit, as you usually put it," Sergey Ivanovich informed him. "Antonio and Peppe are wading into the water up to their knees. Malić is spitting in the river. He's disgusted by something. It could be starting now."

"Switzerland, country of snow and darkness, surrender!" Malić yelled at the top of his voice, as he sat up higher on the donkey and glanced up at the steep mountain peaks which soared above the valley. "Sullen country, your end has come!"

Antonio Peduto got out of the water, stood next to the donkey and translated Malić's every word at the top of his voice, adding several adjectives. Even the sleepless and bloated Peppe was not intimidated by the country of glaciers. In his Neapolitan, he cursed all the Tyrolean gods and saints, and bared his teeth at the peaceful valley.

"It's started, Fox," Bonnefous said, filming the river, the bridge and the strutting trio of warriors. "They're taking the wire fence for the frontier, and the cattle for the Swiss."

"Perhaps they're right," Sergey put in, jotting Georges's observation down in his notebook. "If they turn out to be right, they'll really be geniuses."

"Who?" Georges asked quietly. "They or the Swiss?"

"The Swiss, of course," Sergey Ivanovich said. "The Swiss and the cattle."

Water dripped from all three and from the bag they were dragging behind them. The conquerors gathered together. The wires of the fence and the valley full of cattle extended before them. Gruban Malić sat up on the donkey and expanded his chest. His voice resounded.

"Surrender, you stingy bastards, you gutless traitors, who always stick your knives into our backs! Get out in front of me now and kneel!"

"Surrender, Swiss!" Peduto repeated. "Soon it'll be too late!"
Their voices echoed in the valley.

"Surrender, as you always have throughout your history!" Gruban Malić shook his globe at the mountains and began to call the

Swiss names which even Antonio did not know. "Do you hear me? Surrender, or I'll . . . I'll stick my knife right into your heart and your cheese!"

"Don't shout like that! You're frightening my cattle!"

A tall, skinny man with a crooked nose and dark eyes emerged from the high grass. He had on an ancient overcoat, a broad hat, and boots which rose above his knees.

"Don't holler, my cattle are nervous!" he said as he leaned his chin on the handle of his walking stick. "Don't you know cattle?"

"So you are the famous and gloomy Switzerland, then?" Malić asked him from his donkey.

"By descent, I'm Armenian," the man said politely. "But I'm Swiss, and I'm proud of it." Then the shepherd could no longer contain himself. His mouth opened wide, revealing the stumps of his teeth and pink gums. He drew his head down between his shoulders and almost burst from laughter. Finally he calmed himself enough to get out a few words: "It seems you're proud too . . ."

"You admit, then, that you're a blackguard?" Malić interrupted. Peduto was translating everything rapid fire. "You admit that you're a traitor, that you were against the forces of progress when things were going worst for us?"

"I'm Swiss, a Swiss cattleman, that's all," the man explained, stretching himself and then clapping his greasy Alpine sombrero onto the back of his head. "My name's Simoën Gasparyan. I admit my stomach has troubled me ever since I was five or six years old. And I admit my intestines rumble incessantly, and my pants are cut behind, so I don't have to take them off to shit, because it takes too long."

"Aren't you a Czech? And if you are, why do you keep it a secret?" Malić asked severely as he prodded the donkey up to the wire fence. "Your last name reveals your secret! You're Czech!"

"It's just getting me!" the man wailed and began to grind his gums and writhe pitifully. "Someone must have wound my intestines on a spool. Oh Christ! Oh Jesus! I'm not Czech. I'm a cattleman. I'm proud I . . . shit so much . . . like this. . . . Oh, Mother of God!"

"Then fight if you're so proud!" Gruban Malić challenged the writhing man. "A man must shit, but he must be brave too. You're on the frontier of your gloomy country. You must fight and defend your flag . . . if you have one!"

"What frontier are you talking about, Colonel?" Simoën Gasparyan asked Antonio, as he cowered into a squatting position, and watery shit began to dribble from between his legs. "Perhaps you think you're on the frontier?"

"We are on the frontier," all three answered at once. "We're on the frontier of your homeland, you proud Swiss shit-ass! What a stinky shit you are, trying to fight us off in this way ... ugh! ... But there isn't enough shit, there isn't enough stench in the entire world to push us back! Straight ahead! We are on the frontier, you shit-ass!"

"You are on the frontier ... of what?" the man laughed and stood up again. "Colonel of some far-off power and army, I can't say that you're in the heart of the country, but you've been somewhere inside of Switzerland for the last two nights, that's for sure. Happily, it's only a three or four hour walk to Italy. Excuse me, I'm getting excited again, it's dripping down my legs again, sorry."

"Did you see us when we crossed the frontier?" Malić's clownlike eyes bulged. "Pugh, you capitalistic, filthy stinkpot! You are what we're fighting to destroy with all our heart and reason! Pugh!" He almost threw up. "Answer me! Did you see us?"

"I saw you when you got to my pasture before midnight, that's all, and when you occupied the riverbank," Simoën Gasparyan said, moving his stick. "I understood at once that you were an army. I was the one who sent the children with food and wine for you, nobody else. I saw you were exhausted by the long journey, that you had passed through burning settlements and forests. 'It's a pity, Simoën,' I said to myself, 'that because of your stomach, you can't take them the food yourself.' I saw how heartily you ate and drank. I eat the same way, but food doesn't stay long in me."

"Show some fight!" Malić and Peduto thundered, while Giuseppe Bonaccia ran up and repeated that he was a proud, Swiss, shit-ass, who had probably fed them with dirty food. "Show some fight!"

"Here are the cattle now!" the Swiss wailed and cowered again. "The cattle will fight better," he pleaded, plucking handfuls of grass and stuffing them in from behind. "My beautiful cattle!" He pointed toward the wire fence with his long, skinny arm.

"We want to fight the whole army, the whole nation!"

Sergey informed Georges that the real fight had now begun. Neither of them knew how they had crossed the frontier unnoticed two nights ago, but it was clear that Switzerland would be defeated in a few hours, or at least turned on her back. Sergey drove alongside the pasture while Georges made an effort to fill his film with as many gaping and belligerent jaws, cries, and cattle horns as possible.

THE WAR WAS BETTER

Malić spurred his donkey, charged the cows, and frightened them with the red portions of the globe. Peduto and Bonaccia ran behind him, making their eyes bulge fiercely and mooing at the cows, which stampeded in panic. They seemed especially afraid of the bag with the turtle.

Their onrush was irresistible. The motley brigade of cows withdrew precipitously toward the furthest edges of the valley, and the forest road from which the moviemakers were immortalizing the entire valley and all the groves stretching out to the railroad and the bridge.

They stopped, or at least paused for a moment, in order to avoid filming Simoën Gasparyan, who was holding his belly, from laughter this time, and hooting out that the calves had not yet surrendered.

Peduto sensed wine invade his cerebellum. He told himself that follies and illusions were all that remained in his life. Then he led Malić and Peppe along the fence, and cut off the retreat of the entire regiment of black and white calves.

Sergey Ivanovich whispered something to Georges, who replied that the calves were less afraid of Malić's red ball than their parents had been. Georges Bonnefous bent with his camera to keep his lens on Malić, who was stretching out his right arm in a vain effort to catch at least one Swiss tail. The calves, awed and aroused, did what the cattleman had just been doing. They, however, had no pride at all.

The conquerors stopped once they had shattered the main body of the young bovine regiment and reached the center of the valley, where the path toward the west was most clearly in view. With their sleeves and handfuls of grass, they mopped the sweat from their foreheads and necks. Then they counted their medals and peered under the heifers' tails.

Simoën Gasparyan did likewise, making more and more indecent gestures and urging them to crown their victory with an orgy. In various colors, sizes, and shapes, the aroused heifers marched past them with their tails raised, pissing seductively.

The conquerors stood for a few minutes between some haystacks and a heap of dung. They had no time to exchange ideas or even to look at each other. Taliano was sweating and panting and began to foam at the mouth. The moviemakers thought he was about to lie down. A train chugged past in the distance. The crows became restless. Simoën Gasparyan yodeled. A cloud of smoke loomed up from behind the bend.

THE WAR WAS BETTER

They charged the cattle again. Heavy with milk, the cows ran away, mooing loudly. The calves looked at them yearningly from the other side of the fence. The oxen were in the water, all four of them.

The conquerors had consolidated their victory in classical military style. Behind them, the passage was empty, a straight path full of cow dung. They cursed the Alps and the railroad. Unprompted, the donkey set off on a side path, leading them toward the west.

"Wasn't I right when I said my cattle would put up a better fight—more beautiful, more sincere?" Simoën Gasparyan giggled, revealing his pink gums. "You couldn't even guess how good my heifers are, gentlemen! We can do it together. First, I'll hold them for you, then you for me. Alone like this, I can't get them to do it. I promise you, Colonel, sir, their flavor is truly unforgettable!"

They did not turn to the wise Eastern shepherd, nor even answer him. They simply walked down to the road, where Sergey Ivanovich and Georges Bonnefous had already been waiting for them for more than an hour.

Then they caught sight of the lake, which reached as far as Geneva. To avoid the main road and the water, the conquerors set out across the meadows. Sergey was lucky that paths were frequent, with one leading to another; thus he could follow them in the jeep without great difficulty. Georges Bonnefous tried to film the peasants who fled before Malić, the women who waved to him and the children who laughed. A middle-aged, Calvinist Minister, polished and skinny, also swerved from the path of Malić's donkey. He greeted them and then, fixing his eyes on the bag from which the turtle peeked, began to cross himself, blush, and step backwards, like a Muslim priest leaving the cemetery after a burial.

"How do they look to you, Malić?" Sergey Ivanovich asked. Shooing away some cattle, he broke out onto the path and again cut across the pastures. "How do they look, hero?"

"Who looks like what to me?" Malić asked angrily, looking all over his globe for the lake they were skirting. "The cattle?"

"Not the cattle," Ivanovich said; he noticed that Malić was kissing the globe from time to time. "The Swiss, Malić, what do they look like to you?"

"There are no heroes in these parts, Ivanovich," Gruban Malić observed. "No one opposes me, and no one carries me. It seems they're nothing but stingy cowards."

"You won't be carried in this country," Bonnefous shouted toward him as Sergey ran his jeep over a beautiful rose garden. "Even when we trample over them and totally defeat them, they don't notice us at all. Believe me, that's how they are. While we break their bones, they're probably still caressing and counting up their gold and solid Swiss francs in their basements and attics. They won't carry you, I'll tell you that!"

"Antonio, ask Ivanovich what kind of women they have here." Malić was looking out across the lake. Water was the only thing he feared. "Ask him if they resist their country's enemies. And how do they behave toward military heroes?"

"Malić, the town we're coming to is Geneva," Sergey Ivanovich yelled as he made his way with difficulty through cows, calves, and barnyard fowl. "The beautiful Geneva."

"Surrounded!" Gruban Malić turned in his saddle and winked at them. "Surrounded three times and well colored on the globe! Once in Rome, the second time in Naples, the third in Sicily. All three times, Fox, they scribbled on my globe by themselves."

"Swiss women?" Sergey Ivanovich pulled up with the jeep. "Swiss too?"

"The first was English, maybe American," Malić answered. "It was in Rome, on Via Dante, rather long ago."

"Don't you remember her name, hero?" Sergey Ivanovich asked him slyly. "Perhaps her name was Agatha?"

"I have no idea," Malić replied, spurring on the donkey. "If we revolutionaries spent our time remembering such details, we'd hardly have any energy left for the final victory."

Gruban mused. He remembered how she bit him, how she licked both globes, and afterwards impaled herself on him, speaking of God and the executive committee of the Red Cross.

"I think her name was Lady. Some such Swiss name. She rode well!"

"If you want to, or if you order it, we'll cross the lake," Peduto proposed when they had all come to the edge of the water and stopped. "Geneva the beautiful is in front of our noses! If we hurry, we'll be there before evening. Let's ride and get there as fast as we can, since you say they like to scribble on the globe. Shall we cross the water?"

"Let's strike at them, somewhere from behind," Malić suggested, shuddering at the very thought of crossing the lake. "Enemies, especially capitalists, should always be attacked from behind, eluded, surrounded. Then they have no choice but to fight hand-to-hand. There we're strong!"

THE WAR WAS BETTER

"We have to go around the lake, Ivanovich!" Antonio informed Sergey and Georges, who were entranced by the beauty of the vast, glittering lake. "You know, Geneva has been surrounded for ages now!"

"Surrounded, encircled, encircled, surrounded," Bonaccia repeated to himself, breaking into a sweat. "All of us have passed and ridden here, at least in our thoughts."

"Even *Taliano*," Antonio said to Sergey Ivanovich, who was mopping the sweat from his face with his hat. He was thinking of San Giovanni and the Padre—and the donkey Luka. "*Taliano*," he said, "did you ever conquer Switzerland? Is your head, like my son Peppe's, full of Geneva addresses and names and memories?"

"He can still ride!" Malić said cheerfully. "Especially when I'm not on his back. And when we're in a strange country, whose language we don't understand."

"Does the word 'revolution' stir him up, Gruban?" Georges Bonnefous asked softly. "I mean, does his mushroom lift its ancient head when the great and sacred word is pronounced?"

"It does, walrus," Malić answered seriously. "At the words, 'world revolution,' 'communism,' and 'equality'; and for the song, 'Red Is the East and the West,' it rises like mad!"

"Ah, whenever I hear those words, mine falls," Bonnefous remarked, content with the footage he had filmed of the lake and the mountains reflected in the water. "By God, sometimes I wish I were a donkey!"

"Victory, victory again, my fellow fucking conquerors!" Sergey Ivanovich exclaimed; he had found a path on which all of them could proceed freely. "We've bypassed Geneva. Wonderful! Now we're behind its back. We've come around to this side unnoticed." He honked his horn while Georges laughed uproariously. "Here's France too, the country of wine, song, and donkeys! Hold out, *Taliano*, you'll soon be getting some fine pieces of ass for yourself, yes sir! My fellow fucking conquerors, we've arrived, without bloodshed, at the frontier of the only country capable of understanding and accepting us!"

"Brothers, please don't mention world revolution, love or France in front of *Taliano*, will you? He's got a hard-on again!" Peppe said plaintively. "If you keep saying those wonderful words we'll have to wait for it to fall and shrink away like a snail's horns. It'll take an hour."

"Look at that, for Chrissake, mine has also risen!" Bonnefous said as he got out of the jeep which they had hidden among branches

[297]

and ferns. "I bet it's because of France. There she is on the other side!"

"The question is how long it will hold out," Sergey Ivanovich teased him as his eyes drank in the French border and the countryside beyond. "It's easier to stir it up than to keep it standing at attention. At least in my case."

"I'm ashamed to admit it, but mine is pulsing too," Peduto whispered and blushed. "*Vive la France!*" He hugged the cheerless Peppino, who had nothing to announce, trying to console him. "A wonderful day, isn't it, boys? A real day for men, on the frontier!"

Hidden in the grove and stretched out on their asbestos capes and blankets, they looked out at the unconquered country. Georges did not dare light a cigarette, for fear that his might fall, and he gazed toward the west anxiously. Sergey informed them all for the hundredth time that he was happy with his cock in his left trouser leg. He compared himself to the donkey and said he envied him from the bottom of his Russo-Serbian heart.

Taliano listened to the words he liked, sniffed at the soil, and the air from across the border and whacked his belly with his rod. Antonio compared his living pole to a motley border road about one hundred yards from the shade in which they lay. Stretched on his side, with his hands between his legs, Giuseppe Bonaccia watched the donkey with fervent admiration and sorrow.

Warm, soft, too vast for the human eye to take in, France extended out of sight, as if it were lying on its back. Water gurgled somewhere, perhaps a river, a French river, wet and gurgling like a real woman. They all sighed.

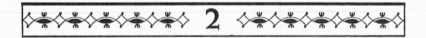 2

"Surrender, you whore's country of the great Napoleon!" Malić cried out as he approached the line drawn in lime which represented the Swiss-French border. "France, I'll trample you under my feet! Answer!" he shrieked, rearing his head from the dense ferns and raising the globe. "France, woman, seven days have passed since we declared war on you! If you don't answer by Saturday, we'll consider you all cowards unworthy of Napoleon, whom we defeated, although we were sorry he wasn't one of ours!"

THE WAR WAS BETTER

"French divisions and armies!" Peduto screamed, replacing Malić. Beyond the frontier, he could see an army of many divisions and batallions moving like a giant amoeba. "Soldiers! The great strategist, Gruban Malić, who's strung up countless victories and scribbled over the entire globe, urges you to surrender honestly, without shedding blood, without butchering human flesh! If you're human enough, if you're still French, raise your hands and allow a man whose name will remain in history and in legends, especially in legends—allow this man to trample over you! Do you hear me, or are you still going to do nothing but sing and rend our ears for the seventh consecutive day?!"

"Frenchmen!" Sergey Ivanovich shouted, cropping up from the grass and the shadows. "Sooner or later you will have to surrender. Why not do it right away, today? You have an excellent opportunity to do now what you must do anyway! Throw away your weapons! A man is asking you to do so, a man whose name has been written on the pages of history with big, red, capital letters for years! Drive away those damn infected whores you haven't torn yourselves from for a single instant since we marched here, and give at least a bit of your attention to some real heroes, especially this angel we're following, drunk as we are, almost blind!"

"Girls!" Georges Bonnefous grunted, lying on his side with a bottle of wine in his arms. "Girls and whores, you who're riding your beardless, unlucky boys, and not letting them admit that we're stronger, not allowing them to surrender to us: you girls had better pack off and clear out! If you fall into our hands, we'll rip you apart with our rods! Isn't it true, Peppino?"

"I was burning!" Bonaccia said over the bottle, but so loudly that the hundred or so prostitutes could all hear him. "I was burning, girls, first in the Balkan mountains and Montenegro, and then also in Italy. I've been through it all and I am personally requesting you to get out of here, so we can catch them alive!"

"We will wait for your reply until Saturday!" Malić shouted, fingering the decorations he had procured in a Palermo museum. "Until Saturday! Saturday!"

Then Malić and the others saw a woman in her forties sprout out of the ferns. Her eyes were dark and full of lust, real lust for a male. Her mouth was swollen and cracked, her bare calves hairy up to her knees and above. Her hair hid her neck, which was somewhat withered, but still long and curved.

They thought she was a shepherdess, and waited for her to come nearer. Scantily dressed, with the freedom of a peasant woman, she stepped first toward Malić, and stood on the white lime of the frontier, expanding her breasts until they almost touched his globe.

"Until Saturday," Malić let drop, smelling her pungent sweat and the dense musk from her glands. "Until Saturday—and until Sunday at the latest."

She watched him from the line crazily. Her nostrils widened. His head began to swim from the sense of her nearness and her smell.

"So, there it is. Until Saturday or Sunday. On Monday you will be ours."

"It's too long to wait, until Saturday," the woman said and leaned on him. "I can't wait." She threw her arms around his waist and overcoat. His male smell of arson, buck-piss, and the tails of Swiss calves stirred her up irresistibly. The pupils dilated in her swooning eyes. "My name is France-Claire. I can't wait until Saturday. I'm unhappy. I can't wait! I won't wait!"

"I understand her, but what's she saying?" the confused Malić asked Peduto as he laid his hands on her hot, broad back. "Is she saying anything about political, or at least military matters? Antonio, translate quickly, she's already grabbed hold of me. She's pulling it out. She's already started. In a minute she'll spit herself on me, but translate, will you? I'd at least like to know what she wanted."

"She says that she personally is France, and unhappy," Antonio explained, blushing in shame. His voice quivered; his whole body seemed to quicken. "Is she spitting herself on you? If you want, I'll push her, help her. It seems she's a widow. All of them are like that."

"My name is France, which means I am France, and I surrender unconditionally," the woman said, her eyes and lips growing moist. "Surrenders are the most precious moments of my life. Prince from afar, Prince with two medals from my country!"

"Malić, she says they're used to surrenders, that surrenders are their favorite pastime," the red-haired Peduto informed the Prince from the East. "She therefore requests you to give it to her whole, unadulterated, and begs you to interpret all this as their utter defeat, a real laying down of arms."

"I'll give it to her, all right. What else can I do?" Malić agreed as she tickled him and caressed his testicles and thighs. "But I'd prefer that they surrender formally, or at least accept a fight." He cowered for a moment, and then, straightening himself and sticking out his chest, pointed toward the infantry companies and motorized platoons. "Antonio, ask whether the army has noticed that we're here, and is really retreating from us?"

"France, the Red Knight asks why the army is withdrawing before Saturday?" Peduto stooped to smell her glands, holes, and military perfumes. "They're fleeing without a word, without white flags on their rifles! Does it mean that Frenchmen are nothing but cunts?"

"Their maneuvers have ended," the woman explained, preoccupied with Malić's pants. "They've gone on for three and a half months now. This has been real life, life with the army, with careless, honest children. Now they're going away, and that's why I'm sad. Who knows when the devil will bring them back again?"

"France, the Slavic Prince asks you whether you're going to rape him right here on the frontier?" Antonio's voice trembled. He remembered Montenegro, soldiers, girls.

"Are you going to throw him down right here ... before Saturday? Be a little more considerate. It'll make him sore. Don't pull so much. France, right before our eyes, in the middle of the day? France, he's asking you to be a little more careful. You'll pull it right off, he says. And without it, wars and conquest would be impossible for him!"

"I always do it here, on the frontier," the woman answered hoarsely, and Malić's hair stood up on his head when he heard her throaty, passionate, French "r." "On this white line which separates two brotherly countries. I don't have to worry about the patrols on either side, or the dogs and border guards, or the cattle which usually graze around me as I ride!"

"You mean ... he has to lie down ... he, not you?" Antonio asked in disbelief, although tenderly. "Otherwise, the Red Prince is ready for anything. He comes from far away and knows all sorts of things. The two French medals and the ten others you see on his chest aren't the only ones. The Red Prince is, happily, very strong, although perhaps not very big. His strength and powers are known throughout the world, in all the countries he's passed through or burnt up or trampled down."

"We'll do it here on the border," the woman said, rolling her eyes and beginning to take off her clothes. "Knight, I hope you too care nothing for boundaries, that you hate them and spit on them like me. Let's do it here. The soil smells wet today. It smells of you!"

As she leaned forward, touching the ground with her hands, Sergey Ivanovich and Georges Bonnefous saw her hairy legs. They were filming her from the ferns, while she, moving backwards like a crab, protruded her hard, round behind toward the Red Knight.

"I haven't seen the like for a long time," Antonio Peduto remarked, fearing that France-Claire would crush his friend. "Look, how she moves backwards, how she rises on her fingers, how she seeks his horn with her holes!"

"Her cunt looks like swollen cat testicles," Giuseppe Bonaccia said shamefully and felt darkness and fear flood his being. "Real swollen cat's testicles."

Peppe covered his face with his hands and then smeared it with stinking cheese. "Antonio," he cried out, "I've never seen a hairier woman in my life, not even in photographs! Did you see what she's got between her legs? Cat's testicles and a whole black Alpine lamb!"

"You could interfere, Peppino," Peduto suggested, after the widow had found the horn and begun to spit herself on it. "We'll ask her. We'll tell her you like cattle. We'll tell her you're a lamb yourself."

"I'm too burnt to help her now," Bonaccia answered. He could not tear his eyes from the widow, who was stretched out like a living bridge and had begun to pump up and down like the grindstone of a water mill building up speed. "She'll kill him like that! She'll break his neck! Our poor Malić! Will he hold out, or perish . . . because of his ignorance of their language and national customs, among other things? Poor Malić! Are you sorry for him too, Antonio?"

Sensing a real emergency, Antonio stuck close to Peppino and the turtle, to whom he whispered that this widow was almost as unhappy as Gigia from Via Maledetta. He scolded her for peeping out of the bag and hesitating to finish a piece of the peasant bread and greenish cheese on which Sergey Ivanovich and Georges Bonnefous had been feeding them all for days. The turtle moved, took up a new place and began to nibble cabbage leaves. Before she had calmed down, sweat poured down her face and wrinkled neck.

Some peasants or customs officers were peering out from the ferns. Their eyes almost dropped out from watching the battle which was waged without quarter for more than an hour, and from seeing the Prince from afar stand his ground and wipe his forehead with the edges of her dress.

The widow kissed his Russian fur hat, rubbed herself with it under her navel and around her moist loins and mare's rump. She wailed as if someone had pinched her intestines, or they had been knotted up. She even fell on her fingers, rose again, and built the bridge.

"Who are you and where do you come from, Red One?" she whispered, thinking his horn would reach her windpipe. "From what country have you come, Marshal?" Her voice was breaking. He struck and struck, again and again, in a rhythm and with a force which the peasants and customs officers had not seen for years. "Tell me, whisper it to me: where is the country which made you like this? What language do you speak?"

He leaned over her, pushed, nibbled her skin and flesh along her backbone, moving gradually up to her neck and gullet. His mouth was full of her hair and pieces of her underwear.

"Prince! Prince! Prince!" she began to wail, and rolled over the borderline. She was nearing the globe and hardly cared anymore whether her backbone or ribs would remain intact. "Where do you come from, and are the others like you? Oh, how happy the people you reign over must be ... if you reign like this. ... Oh, Prince! Woe is me! Oh!"

"Malić, she's asking whether you can stop," Antonio whispered; he was pale and frightened. "She says her heart has already stopped two or three times."

"Tell her I wish the most terrible death for the black capitalists!" Malić said, looking around him and seeing nothing but the rotten West. His face and his whole body were drenched in sweat. "Death, merciless death! First like this ... and then ... like that ... into both brains!"

"She repeats that she too wishes them death, Gruban," Antonio went on, watching Malić grab her loins and pull her to him. "She points out that she hates them bitterly, especially from this day forward, and she'd do anything in her power to make their end shameful and miserable. She begs to inform us, as witnesses, that if you continue like this, you'll crush both her kidneys!"

"I want them to surrender!" Malić shouted, sensing her half-dead under him. "I want them to surrender unconditionally, on all fronts!"

"But her kidneys ... and intestines," Peppino burst out crying, with his hands inside his pants, on the seared and withered skin. "Her kidneys and her ribs. Don't you hear her invoking Christ, surrendering herself ... as she never surrendered before in her whole life?"

"I want the collapse of the nation!" Malić growled, piercing her, in his thoughts, up through her gullet into her cerebellum, right up to the coast of the Atlantic on his globe. "Capitalists, I'll tear your skin apart with my teeth!"

"The army is withdrawing," Antonio said fearfully, as he crept up beside him and watched him plunge into her on no-man's land. "They're fleeing, shame on them, without a single word!"

Gruban Malić turned ghastly white. He gnawed his teeth and began speaking of death and sweat. He did not hear Peppe, who was chattering excitedly.

"They're withdrawing without even waving their hands. God! Do they see what we look like and what we're ready for? And they run to reach the broad roads and the center of their country. Look, chums: behind all those terror-stricken companies, there are tanks rollings, tanks! The smell of rubber is reaching us! Hey, aren't you ashamed to run, without a salute, without a smile? You shit army, you cowards and tenderfeet, look back at least once, bestow at least one glance on us!"

"Prince, on behalf of the generous nation whose army is withdrawing before you, on behalf of Jesus Christ, please don't crush my backbone. We're all soft and corrupted. We haven't met such gods as you for ages. . . ."

"I'll free you only if you make a statement in front of everyone, and sign it, that the French army is mine!" Malić yelled, convinced that this time she would resist. "If the keys are handed over to me!"

"I give over to you this whole country and all its keys," the woman moaned from below. It seemed to her that the soil under her was shaking and bumping away from her, and the French sky blackened and got mixed up with the Swiss one. "I give the entire country over to you, France and all her armies. You can see for yourself that they're withdrawing in panic. I give them all to you provided you save my backbone and my skull . . . you've pierced my loins with your nails. Let me go . . . let me, please, angel!"

"France has fallen!" Antonio cried out, hoping that Malić would be satisfied. "France has fallen . . . on her belly! France has been defeated and humiliated!" Antonio's and Peppe's eyes were full of clouds and tears. "France is now yours and ours! Finally, sweet heavens, finally! Oh God, how generous You are to have given us another country . . . whose frail ribs we're counting now as we crush the black Alpine lamb! Oh God, our wonderful God, ask Malić, please ask him, You too, to let her go!"

"She has surrendered, Red One!" Sergey Ivanovich shouted from the ferns in Malić's language. "She's given you the whole country, Mad Knight. The keys will soon be here!"

THE WAR WAS BETTER

"Ask him, Serge, not to kill her. He'll nail her to the ground that way!" Georges Bonnefous almost wept as he filmed Malić torpedoing her again and again. "Night is falling now. Perhaps the poor woman has children."

They rolled on the borderline, in no-man's land, keeping away from either side as if by agreement. Both of them were white and crumpled. Behind them, a border post with a double highway, grass, ferns, customs officers, and dogs could be seen. It was hard to discern in the gathering dusk which of the two, in the pangs of death and love, was more insane.

Sergey Ivanovich finally brought up some people, probably firemen, and introduced them as generals, who had come to surrender as soon as possible. Ivanovich signaled to them. They dropped on their knees. Their epaulets, medals, and tin helmets jingled.

"Booby, here, take!" they said in one voice and threw down beside Malić's globe a heap of old, really huge keys. "Prince, there's not a city in France these keys wouldn't open!"

"Antonio, the biggest key—is it for Paris?" Malić asked enthusiastically, hugging the almost unconscious woman. "Ask them why they didn't give in earlier. Red Beard, I can't do it any longer. My head is spinning. The only thing I see in front of my eyes is a pool of their whorish, capitalistic blood. It hasn't been hard to conquer this country, Antonio. Remember it well. Water!"

Giuseppe Bonaccia gathered the keys and stuffed them into the bag, next to the turtle. Sergey Ivanovich asked Bonnefous to take a rest and save some film. Then they reached their jeep. They waited. The lights went on at the border post. Dogs and customs officers barked.

"They've fallen asleep in each other's arms!" Peduto said. "Right on the border. They're completely white." Antonio bent over and caressed them. He said something tender. Then he turned them over very carefully and pushed them away from the white line. They did not wake up, and clung to each other even more tightly. One of the firemen threw an asbestos cape over them.

"Now they're in France," he said.

He turned to the uniformed buzzard beside him. "Now, I think, they only have to go through the customs and tax formalities..."

"They're with us now and they'll pay for it," the uniformed customs hyena growled as he looked over at Antonio and Peppe. "Now they're with us, which means they're..."

"They belong to history and the revolution, gentlemen," Peduto interrupted. "They belong to everyone. Look how they're smiling in their sleep: they're engaged!"

THE WAR WAS BETTER

"If he wanted to take her with him to Paris!" the most decorated fireman sighed. "We have a lot of trouble with her, but we can't do anything about it—she always does it on no-man's land."

"I don't believe he'll be able to take her," Peduto argued. "He thinks only of the globe, of world revolution and the final victory of the red color."

"You've been calling him a prince," the oldest fireman began, pushing the customs officers aside. "Whose prince is he? Where does he come from? Is he Spanish?"

"He's Montenegrin," Peduto informed him with pride. "Montenegrin, like myself . . . sort of. That is, Slavic. We're all from Bijelo Polje. It's not on the globe yet. But maybe the river appears, the swift and clear Lim!"

"I told you they were from there," the fireman said, turning to the younger one, the one who had been pushing away the customs hyena. "I thought right away they were from there."

"He squeezed her under the arms like a he-frog," the younger fireman pointed out, seeing the terrible picture flash before his eyes once again and trying to perform it with the customs officer. "He pierced her skin, broke a few of her ribs, I'll bet." He was squeezing the officer and gnawing his teeth. "I'm like that myself. But what can I do? I'm not from there."

Sergey Ivanovich and Georges Bonnefous started the jeep and drove it onto the grass. They too were in France. Lying down beside the entangled lovers, they covered themselves with capes and blankets.

Antonio and Peppe also stretched out on the ground. Border guards, dogs, and customs officers sneaked around them. There were other beasts around too, they thought.

The wind was carrying away the summer clouds, and the stars above them were clear and beautiful again. Until late that night, they watched the frightened French army withdrawing toward the west.

Then, some sooner, some later, they closed their eyes. They dreamed of love, and told each other how wonderful it was that the world was finally theirs.

THE WAR WAS BETTER

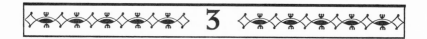

Even the clouds were attacking France. They were pouring in from all sides, driven on by malice and the wind. It seemed that rain might begin to fall at any moment. France was having the worst of it. The idyllic ground on the other side of the lime-drawn line was still bathed in the selfish sun of Switzerland. Since that morning there had been constant thunder and lightning over France, while the neighboring countries basked in the sultry August heat.

Almost all the bells in France were ringing out, perhaps in alarm, and echoing from end to end of the country. Those who were initiated in military matters knew that the widespread national panic was not due to mere lightning and the gloomy sky alone, but rather to the fear of the conquerors invading from the east, speaking of surrender and brotherhood in common misery and nothingness, and talking about love in a rather savage way, unfamiliar to many who lived that far to the west.

Gruban Malić turned in his saddle and saw they had left the frontier far behind. The country they trampled over was increasingly theirs. Antonio Peduto and Giuseppe Bonaccia, with the bag and the turtle between them, also looked back toward Switzerland and the East.

Gruban Malić remembered the aroused widow, France-Claire. That morning, at dawn, she had explained at length that the French were unable *not* to enter a war, but that they could hold out nine to twelve days at the most. While watching the sun rise, she spit herself on his horn again. Between sobs and moans, she reminded him that the French were a merry people in spite of everything, and would soon make friends with the conquerors and share with them whatever there was to be shared, and even what wasn't.

Before they left the frontier, the widow attacked both Antonio and Peppe at the same time. She pointed her finger at the endless French countryside and the roads leading toward the west, along which the army was still withdrawing. "They're surrendering, don't you see?" she said, and began to shout: "*Slaves*, don't treat my Frenchmen roughly; let them escape. You can be sure they'll never rebel!"

THE WAR WAS BETTER

She stood for a long time among them, caressing the donkey's neck and Gruban's knees. Malić adjusted his feet in the stirrups and wiped lime and no-man's land from the tails of his overcoat. He did not know what to say to her in parting. He looked at the road on which the tanks and trucks were departing, and spat on the ferns.

"Have mercy on my Frenchmen, *Slaves*. It's not their fault there are so few of them compared to you and the rest of the yellow people from Asia. Take me with you. Lead me. I'll reveal all their military and other secrets. First, I'll tell you their secret way of making cheese, which we've used to make half the world stink. *Slaves*, have a heart . . . if you don't happen to have some cheese!"

They left her on the white line of no-man's land, kneeling before the sun that rose in the East.

They stood on a hill, at a great crossroads. Gruban Malić was asking *Taliano* to calm his brave heart and stop pulling him off the road toward the meadow. Sergey Ivanovich and Georges Bonnefous were trying to start the jeep, but the devil himself couldn't have done it. They began pushing it and cursing, and would have left it there, or rolled it off the cliff beside the crossroads, if they had known what to do with their cans of film and other equipment. They stood there sweating from vain effort and rage.

"They're not surrendering correctly," Malić thought as he watched the trucks full of singing soldiers depart. "The Italians ran like mad, do you remember?"

"The French aren't Italians, Montenegrin," they answered.

"What are they then, Antonio?"

"More like Greeks," Peduto said. "They aren't Italian. You said yourself they retreat differently."

"They talk strangely too," Malić said, turning to Sergey Ivanovich, who was running his fingers through his now already well-formed little beard. "What's their mother tongue? Turkish?"

"French, I think," Ivanovich said from beside the dead jeep. "It's not Italian, though, don't worry."

"Look, friends!" Malić exclaimed, pointing at a truck full of soldiers and girls. "Do my eyes betray me?"

A truck was passing them. The soldiers were singing "Auprès de ma blonde" and necking with the girls. "*Auprès de ma blonde, qu'il fait bon, fait bon*," they sang as they lifted up white bikini panties on their bayonets. "*Auprès de ma blonde, qu'il fait bon dormir!*" The truck rolled on. Berets began falling off the Frenchmen's heads, and the crazy, naked girls, giggling like mad, covered their mounds with them.

"That's their French language, what you're hearing," Antonio informed Malić, who was saluting them with the globe. "That's how they are when they advance, and when they retreat. For decades now, they've been singing about 'how nice it is to sleep next to my blonde!' "

Gruban Malić saluted them again. His prisoners burst into laughter and more song. They lifted up about ten pairs of panties, perhaps as a token of final surrender.

"I'll chase you down to the ocean!" Malić threatened them from his donkey. "Where will you go then, you whores' sons? If you've ever looked at a globe, you know the sea there is even deeper and more restless than anywhere else! Cunt-lickers, shit-eaters, what will you do then? Antonio, please translate everything to them, and let them rage and sulk as much as they want!"

"Malić will rob you of all your girls, my poor French!" Peduto shouted to them. "And then the poor girls will feel for the first time what a real man is, what a brave heart from the Balkans means, what true love can be! You French pansies, you homos, you faggots! Malić will tear apart all the females you have that walk on two legs! A Malícian race will flood your country; a new race of magnificent liars and dreamers will spring up!"

"*Qu'il fait bon, qu'il fait bon dormir . . . auprès de ma blonde!*" the soldiers broke out again into the song. "*Vivent les Slaves!*" they yelled.

They stood up, cheering; the truck bumped over a rock, and the girls fell down. This brought on new cheers.

"Long live the melancholy, miserable Slavs! Long live the Slavs who haunt our dreams! *Qu'il fait bon, qu'il fait bon dormir!* Long live Slavs, long live madmen! Long live Slavs, the sick angels! *Auprès de ma blonde, qu'il fait bon dormir!*"

"About ten armies are withdrawing at the same time!" Georges Bonnefous said to Malić, who was mopping the sweat from his broad forehead with his sleeve. "Squadrons of fighter planes are protecting the withdrawal of the artillery! Their fear of us, the Slavs, is so great that they don't even notice the camera and the film that could express it! Words are not enough, Malić! We can go on, although the road is jammed, but now, for once, we know our goal!"

"Antonio, my comrade and brother, did you tell them about . . . about the thing that made all of Switzerland vomit?" Malić asked. "About communism?"

"Frenchmen, poor devils!" Peduto rattled on, letting the binoculars slip down his shoulders, in order to stick his chest out further.

THE WAR WAS BETTER

"Malić and we, his soldiers, are ready for anything! Malić has personally decided on behalf of communism, that is, on behalf of an idea with a capital letter, to kill faith in anything human! If possible, Malić will make all people equal, in poverty and nothingness, of course! As a communist and a saint, Malić wants victory! As an irrepressible, maladjusted Slav, he doesn't quite know what'll happen after that! Nevertheless, as you can see, he's going to the bitter end! And we will follow him, since it's the only thing left for us in life! As a communist, the only thing he sees in the future is blood, your blood in any case, other people's blood! He's truly great! Today, while you run away like cowards, he's figuring out everything that will happen to you!"

"Have you told them about the prostitution of the proletariat. That there won't be so many whorehouses in the new society, that is, they'll be given a different name?"

"I've told them that three times already, Malić," the tired Antonio reassured him. "They answered that they knew very well what a dictatorship of the proletariat meant: the most disgusting of all dictatorships. Then I prophesied suffering. They agreed. They said they're used to bloodshed. They've seen constant slaughter, rape, and arson in the movies."

Trucks filled with armed soldiers rolled by in impeccable order, their headlights on, their horns honking. They were departing, offering no resistance. The small, clean soldiers embraced their girls and sang in French; they had no shame.

"It's impossible to start this junk heap!" Sergey Ivanovich grunted and spat into the jeep's worn-out motor. "This damn piece of American garbage!"

"It's leaving us in the lurch, just at the moment we need it most," Bonnefous growled as he slammed down the hood. "It's finished, *kaput,* the bloody old ... And there's nobody to tow us either, at least to Paris!"

"What? Nobody to tow us to Paris?" Malić's clownish eyes bulged. "And the French? What about the French? We defeated them. Let them tow us!"

"They won't ... to Paris, Gruban," Georges Bonnefous said sadly. "It's too far. If that were the case, the whole French nation could tow us."

"Let them tow us!" Malić decided and turned in his saddle. "Are we communists and liberators, or aren't we? It's our destiny to be towed and carried!"

"Well, we shouldn't . . . exaggerate on the very first day," the sweaty Bonnefous smiled. "Later, of course, we won't get off their backs. But now, it seems too far to me, for that very reason . . . All the way to Paris, today!"

"Not only to Paris, even farther!" Malić persisted. "We've ridden on others, haven't we? Where are the defeated armies?"

"They're fleeing with incredible speed," Sergey Ivanovich said. "As if they knew they were going to have to tow us to Paris, and even farther than that. Hey, Frenchmen!"

All the roads were jammed.

"People, comrades, look out!" Giuseppe Bonaccia coughed, pointing at a truck with a trailer. "They're coming right at us!"

"Had a breakdown, gentlemen and artists?" a large-headed driver asked them, braking his truck and leaning out the window of his high cabin. "Have you been stuck here a long time?"

The driver had a girl beside him; her hair was long and her cheeks and mouth heavily made-up. He stretched out his arms. "Gentlemen and you, knight on the donkey, do you understand me?"

"Would you be so kind as to tow us to Paris, or to the coast?" Sergey Ivanovich asked him frankly from the side of the jeep. "We're the victors, so it wouldn't be nice to leave us here helpless like this, in the middle of our victory. The sooner the better too, because it's getting so overcast. After the rain, night will come; there'll be wild animals."

"To tow you to Paris?" The driver spat out his cigarette and embraced the girl.

"Did you fall down here from Mars or something?" he hugged the girl and began to laugh. "If we wanted to, we could—but for the moment, only to Paris! Clear?"

"Take them, *chéri*," the girl implored. "*Mon chéri et mon chou*, perhaps they really are victors. *Chéri*, quiet down."

"Why should I quiet down when they want me to tow them?" the driver protested, blushing. "You tow them if you want, if they look like victors to you, and if you love them so much!"

"I love only you, *chéri*," the girl said. "But take them."

"Artists!" The driver lit another cigarette and slapped his forehead with his greasy hand. "Artists, I don't think you understand what I'm saying. What's your nationality?"

"Slavic," Antonio answered for all of them while the driver, a heavy man with ruddy, veined cheeks, who was dressed entirely in leather, stepped down from the cabin. "*Les Slaves.* Couldn't you see it right away? *Slaves!*" The driver kept repeating the word. "Why didn't you tell me that right away?"

"Do you also come from there?"

"I like small nations, especially poor ones," the driver said with a rugged smile. "It's a habit I picked up in the army, where there are all kinds of people. I like the Slavs particularly!"

"Why, *Français?*"

"There are no greater artists and drunkards than the Slavs. I knew one. What a character! Wait a minute: I knew three. They were Turks! *Ah, mes Slaves.*"

"Don't you have a bottle somewhere around?" Peduto inquired, laughing at his Turks. "We, *tes Slaves*, can't do without the divine drop."

"She's also a *Slave*," the driver informed Antonio, throwing a bottle of wine to him. "If she's not lying. This is the eighteenth day I've been driving with her. Slavic women are very rare around here. We're mad about them. Ah, *l'âme slave*, that is something; it makes you lick your fingers afterwards!"

"Where is she from, if you say she's a *Slave?*" Antonio caught another bottle. "She's beautiful and exotic, and she looks tame too!"

"She comes from Greece," the driver said. "Somewhere around there, from the Greek-Albanian border."

"Then she's a real *Slave*," Antonio broke into laughter. "I envy you, *Français*, for having a real Slavic angel with big breasts and a wild imagination sitting right next to you."

"What are you thinking now, seducer of Slavic women?" Sergey Ivanovich said, wiping his hands with grass. He smelled of oil and gasoline. "How about the transportation?" He sized up the Greek-Albanian gypsy girl, who was wisely keeping silent and examining her almost Negro eyes and mouth in her pocket mirror. "What will you do, *Français*, with the victors? It looks like rain any minute now. We're afraid of the dark and the wild animals."

"Into the trailer!" the Frenchman commanded. "Into the trailer, gentlemen and artists. There's room enough for conquerors." He led them back to the trailer and showed them the pigs. "As you see, half the trailer is empty. There's enough room for all of you!"

"You're a real Frenchman," Antonio said to the driver once he and Peppe had climbed up and put their bag into a corner near the boards separating them from the pigs. "A seducer, a lover, a fucker of Slavic women; and you know how to treat the victors, and the

[312]

vanquished too, don't you? But which, *Français*, do you think these pigs are?"

"I heard on the radio recently that humanity couldn't do without the Slavs," the driver said, avoiding an answer about the pigs and casting a nervous glance at them. He turned to help Malić up. "Will the knight dismount?"

"Malić, he's inviting you to dismount," Antonio translated, putting his hand down and patting the turtle's head. "Don't accept."

"I'd like to get on as I am, on horseback," Gruban Malić said hoarsely, without allowing *Taliano* to step on the lowered ramp. "On horseback!"

"All right," the Frenchman said, and slapped the donkey's haunch. "Climb up on your wonderful thoroughbred." He pushed them on. They smelled of smoke and were still white from lime. "Bend down, and watch your head—and your globe."

"Don't strike my *Taliano!*" Malić warned the driver, who was already raising the ramp and chaining it to the side of the truck. "Antonio, warn him not to touch my horse!"

"I'm sorry, knight," the driver said, after Antonio had translated. "I'm sorry I dared to touch him."

Gruban Malić did not dismount in the trailer either. He settled himself into the saddle and felt hungry. From the other side of the boards which formed a partition, the pigs stank hellishly. He looked away, across the globe; he could see half of France, all intertwined by roads and rivers.

"And what shall we do with this old heap?" Sergey Ivanovich and Georges Bonnefous were afraid that Malić, Antonio, and Peppe were ignoring them. "What shall we do with this American junk heap?" Sergey repeated, banging the jeep with his fist.

"You've caught a bad fish," Bonnefous remarked when the driver, chewing his cigarette, took out a steel rod and a ball of rope from somewhere. He nodded up at the gypsy girl. "At first I thought she was a man."

"I thought so myself, but she isn't," the Frenchman laughed uproariously.

"A real Balkan fish," Bonnefous went on. "She must have at least ten varieties of clap."

"The devil knows!" the driver spat on the steering-wheel of the jeep. "I usually don't count them. You're right, a real fish!"

"Long live French mechanics!" Sergey Ivanovich exclaimed as he counted the pigs; he began to feel like vomiting. "They're pigs, *Français*, the noblest prey."

THE WAR WAS BETTER

"Tie it up, clowns!" the driver laughed when they pulled the jeep up to the trailer; he looked again at the pigs, counted them up, and cursed them mildly, almost affectionately. "Never mind the clap! Probably I've got it now. Well, so much the worse!" The Frenchman peered under the pigs' tails. Then he pointed at the silent girl. "What's important is that she doesn't have cancer."

"Even if she has—who cares?" Sergey Ivanovich put in.

They all worked together, tying up the jeep.

"She bubbles and flames like a dragon," the Frenchman moaned. "When I put it in, it's like a furnace, a regular limekiln in there! And she wails and screams to beat bloody hell, in some of your Slavic languages too, the devil knows which. You'll see for yourself later. You'll all have to give her a little scratch!"

"I'm terribly afraid of cancer," Bonnefous said, backing out. "Anyhow, mine rises very rarely nowadays. Least of all for cancer. It jumps up only when money is mentioned, or fame, art and celluloid."

"I like money too, old man," the driver admitted when they succeeded in tying the rope to the crosspiece of the truck. "It's because of her that I work like mad. Otherwise, I have an inclination toward wine. I suffer from epilepsy."

"From epilepsy?" Sergey Ivanovich inquired with apparent calm as he seated himself behind the wheel. "That's worse than cancer! Do they know anything about it . . . ?"

"You mean the pigs?" The driver lit another cigarette and banged the jeep hood with his palm. "No, the pigs know nothing about it."

"Pigs?" Sergey Ivanovich was beginning to worry.

"Hold fast!" he shouted to them, giggling. "I drive like a madman, especially when there's someone in the back, and I pour wine down my throat!" He leaned out of the cabin window. "The pigs don't know a damn thing about driving. And they don't worry about clap or tricky roads either!"

Sergey Ivanovich began to laugh. With his middle finger he made indecent motions, pointing at the pigs. The driver answered in a deep bass, waving the joke off with his hand. "My old clown, a hole is a hole! The only important thing is that cancer doesn't take a bite out of you, from in there!"

The truck started. Sergey Ivanovich and Georges Bonnefous smelled the pig stench. It was powerful, heavy, all-pervading, inescapable. It filled up their nostrils so that they could hardly breathe. The driver honked his horn, yelling to them at the first bend, "Hold fast! And yell if you come untied!" Then his head disappeared back into the cabin.

Georges Bonnefous felt like vomiting as he looked out at the beauty of the already golden wheat fields and spat at an orchard and the motley homes they were passing. When they went by a cemetery, he thought again of San Giovanni Battista and the corpses lifting up their coffin lids, and he almost threw up into Sergey's lap. He heard the Frenchman honk again.

"I'll die of shame!" Sergey Ivanovich complained into the wind. "From shame and pig stench!"

"Calm down for a little while!" Bonnefous urged him. "We're approaching total collapse anyway."

In the trailer, they all began eating hard bread, gnawing Swiss bones and drinking. Then, rather topsy-turvily, they sang Malić's song, that the West would become like the East, if not redder; that America and England would turn into proletarian countries; and that the time would come when all mankind, without work or any effort whatsoever, would live like the richest capitalists.

Antonio stood up and poured wine down the turtle's gullet, calling her a vicious sister and a whore. Peppino sang the rest of Malić's songs. Although his large and beautiful eyes were open, he did not see the France they were driving through, but Montenegro in flames and flowers; to him, song and fire had long been indistinguishable.

Bonaccia and Peduto were drunk from the wind as much as the wine. They urged Malić to dismount, or at least to bend down, for rain was threatening, and a lightning bolt might strike his globe. Then *Taliano* lost his balance at a curve. He did not fall, but at the first opportunity quietly crossed his legs at the knees and lay down on his side. Malić cursed and spat on him. Then he sipped from Antonio's bottle. He could see the pigs better.

"Do you have anything against us and our victory?" Antonio asked as he leaned over the partition and tapped a sow on her back. "French angel, do you have it in for us, merciless as we are, knowing no pardon, punishing and threatening everybody?"

"Oink!" the sow answered. "Oink! Oink!"

"We're going to bring justice and freedom to humanity. It will be something men have never known, with no foreseeable end, and anyway why should it end? It'll be so nice for us, the bringers of the great miracle!" Malić said this very quickly and then touched the sow and thrust the neck of the bottle into her belly. "Translate for her, Antonio; all I know in French are the words I learned at the border."

THE WAR WAS BETTER

"*Camarade*," Peduto said, pulling her tail. "Comrade! *Camarade* (whose name must be Simone or Thérèse), Malić greets and embraces you!" He spoke on in his own and Malic's name. "You still don't know how Gruban hugs, how he thrusts, how he pierces!"

"Oink! Oink! Oink!"

"Simone," Antonio continued. "Simone-Thérèse, he's good, but he's been insulted. He can't stop. He's a dragon who looks only forward. He's for chaos, for defeat at any cost! If he vanquishes the world—and he must, he will, just look at him!—we'll live in brotherly love and harmony; we people and you pigs will all be equal. Whoever dares to stir up any differences will be treated like spies, traitors, enemies of the people and progress. We'll hang them by their testicles! Simone-Thérèse, you at least, try to understand us. Many of the people we tried to explain this happiness to have been deaf, or blind, unable to glimpse the future awaiting us all. Simone-Thérèse, we're hugging and petting you, all three of us. Simone, with whom we're storming the city of light, Simone, with whom we'll soon be equal, we and everyone else, all equal, tell us, love, whether you've understood what we've said, just a little bit?"

"I didn't say that much, Antonio," Malić protested, gnawing a bone.

"She agrees with everything," Peduto said hurriedly as he watched the stinking pigs jostling each other and beginning to wake up before the rain. "She says the swine will be content to lie down, at last, on an equal level with people. She asks what people will say, whether they really will agree to such happiness?"

"Simone-Thérèse, I was burning," the drunken Peppino squealed and caressed her like a lamb. "I burned. I'm sorry I have nothing more to tell you. And my head is swimming, from wine and France, which we've defeated, from the wind and the lightning flashing in the distance."

Bonaccia tried to stick his head through a hole in the partition and rest it on her fat, warm tits. The stench did not deter him. In his thoughts, he was somewhere in the flaming mountains, on the flowery Montenegrin plateau. "Simone-Thérèse, you have a wonderful first name. How much lovelier your last name must be! Simone, give me your address. I'll try to remember it although my head is booming, booming ... remember it ... because I love you!"

"Oink!"

The epileptic driver gave no quarter and knew no measure either. Honking fiercely, he rushed forward, braked, and rushed forward again, so that both the jeep and the truck were shaking so

hard it seemed they might fall apart. He caught up with automobiles and passed them, spitting on their roofs and drivers, cursing
and singing. He also outstripped the olive-green army trucks, but
was softer on the soldiers who filled them. He and they shouted,
cursed and sang the same songs. He waved to them with the gypsy
girl's yellow panties.

"Give her to us, orangutan, for a few hours!" the soldiers yelled
as they leaned out of their trucks, fully armed. "Little gypsy, leave
that gorilla, that maniac, and come to us! At least you know what
an army is! The French army!"

"We're finished, Serge!" Bonnefous screamed; he could hear the
creaking of brakes and the banging of tin plates. "It looks like they
really want him to give them the gypsy girl! We're going to crack
up with all the swine!"

The driver's cabin tilted. Somewhere glass was breaking. The
wheels of the trailer were smoking.

"With the pigs...without finishing our masterpiece, condemned to ruin! With pigs, already evened out...everything equal
...Oh, the shame of it!"

"I've been rude to you, Georges!"

"And I to you, Serge!"

They shrieked into the wind. The jeep bounced off the road and
landed again with a crash; it seemed about to fall apart piecemeal.
Glass broke again. Metal bent.

Sergey Ivanovich realized suddenly that their driver, lit up by
lightning and wine, had plunged into the abyss of his epilepsy.

4

Unshaved, totally unkempt, with only a few medals left on his
worn-out toreador's jacket, Antonio lay on his back in a French infantry overcoat. Rain was falling on his arms which stretched out
over the pavement. His bones and his eyes ached. He saw only the
lighted windows and the raindrops dribbling down the panes. Passersby stepped on his fingers—one out of two at least expressed
surprise. Antonio wanted to die, but that was not easy either. He
was sick of the Paris humidity, the rain which cooled his feverish
forehead and cracked lips, the rumbling of the metro somewhere in

the depths. He was also sick of the warmth surging through the steel grills beneath him, heating his neck and palms. He was sick of everything he was aware of. He felt like vomiting. He was disgusted even by his own feverish voice:

"I'm quite alone, my people. Quite alone."

"Have you gnawed up all the bones, Red?" A tramp emerged from the warmth behind a handcart in which the turtle lay in the bag. "I have some more."

"Thank you, Pierre," Antonio sighed. "You're tireless with the bones, my Calvet." He turned his head to Villon. "François, nobody could have picked a better place than you—or you, Pierre." Antonio felt for Villon's cold hand. "François, this place is really wonderful; we must remember it."

"I don't know where we are," Pierre Calvet remarked as he gnawed on the rainy bones. "When I eat I lose all my bearings. I lose even hope. A wonderful place, though, François."

"I think its name is Montparnasse," François Villon said as he stooped over Antonio, who was burning with fever. "All my skill, friends, consists in trying never to be far from rascals and food."

"I understand every third word you say, François," Calvet protested from the gutter. "What language are you speaking?"

"Don't be afraid, Pierre," Antonio said in Italian. "He'll slip away from us."

"You're suspicious too, Antonio," Pierre Calvet said and began to choke on bones and laughter. "All of you Poles and Spaniards are tramps and drunkards."

"Sleep, Calvet," Antonio urged him. "First of all, spit the bones out of your mouth; you'll suffocate at night. So, Pierre. So. You snore beautifully."

"I'm counting, not snoring," the tramp mumbled, half-asleep.

"Count on, Calvet. Count until dawn if you like. But a little softer."

"When one counts big money, or the survivors of the war, one counts aloud," Pierre Calvet said. "When I was in Indo-China . . ." he mumbled, and then fell asleep without finishing the sentence.

"Montparnasse," François Villon repeated. "I think right here where we're lying, and on the spot where we'll lie tomorrow, a large slaughterhouse used to be. Blood dripped everywhere. Tendons crawled. Skulls rolled."

"You see only meat again?"

"Only meat, wine, and girls," François Villon said.

"Today there are more homos than girls," Antonio remarked.

"But I can imagine how much cheap meat there was in your time, poet."

"Everyone was killing and stealing; there was nothing else to do," François Villon said. "There was flesh everywhere. Even where we were yesterday, there was an immense slaughterhouse. Intestines, skins, and skulls floated down the Seine. Then we waded among them. The Seine was larger. It was a real river then."

François Villon had a pirate's hat on his head; it protected, from the rain and dim light, his thin, sickly face which was adorned with threadbare mustaches and an even poorer beard. His tall, meager body trembled under his raincoat. He peered fearfully around him.

"I'm quite alone, François," Peduto murmured, with his head thrown back and his beard wet. "And if it weren't for you, who are good and nice, and always laugh and tell me stories about meat and slaughterhouses, fires and girls—if it weren't for you I'd cut short this torture called life."

"I'm quite alone myself," the man with broken teeth and feverish eyes seemed to reply. "Alone, lost in these dog's times. If it weren't for you, I'd have left Paris long ago." François Villon picked up Antonio's free hand from the pavement and laid it on the turtle's shell. "I'd have gone . . . long ago . . . if it weren't for . . . you."

"You know what it means, then, to be misunderstood, to be abandoned by everyone?"

"That's the only thing I do know," Villon said quietly. "It is my fate. They've hanged me countless times. I always laughed at them. I defended myself and won. They've been hanging me for ages. All they know is hanging. Antonio, I'm cold. I need something to think about. Tell me how you conquered Paris, how you got lost. Warm me up!"

"It was raining when we entered the city. There was thunder and lightning. The pigs were restless; they seemed to sense something important and terrible was about to happen. And it did. The driver must have been dazzled by the lights of Paris. He went faster and faster. He charged like a bull. The huge mountain of pigs shook and groaned like a volcano about to erupt. Everything was about to crash down, together, in some horrible bloody shambles on the pavement.

" 'We're going to perish tonight!' I was about to say to Peppe and Malić's donkey; I could hardly get the words out. Whatever happened, they shouted back, we should live or die together, we should never part.

"The driver swerved, the truck jolted, and Malić himself, even

Malić, vomited over his globe. We could see streets and avenues
which trucks and pigs don't often enter flashing past at lightning
speed, as in a film.

" 'Big sale on meat tonight! Pig, donkey, and hero steaks, cut
rate!' I started shouting, surrendering to fate and my sense of
humor.

"There were policemen, soldiers, and a crowd of curious Parisians chasing us. The driver wouldn't give up. From time to time,
his leathery hand with the yellow panties of the gypsy girl stuck
out into the rain, as if to signal; then he stamped on the gas pedal
like a maniac. I don't think a truck has ever gone that fast on Place
de la Concorde before, and I don't think one ever will again.

" 'Stop! Stop! Maniac!' everyone was yelling while he turned
circles around the Obelisk at breakneck speed, losing pig after pig.

"Finally the jeep got unfastened from his monstrous trailer, and
fell off. We left Georges and Sergey there somewhere, in the blood
and rain. The driver, the *Français*, burst through a barricade on Avenue des Champs-Élysées, and suddenly emerged on Place de
l'Étoile.

" 'He's hopping over her now, don't worry!' I was calming
down Peppe and Malić, who was lying, half-conscious, between the
globe and the donkey.

" 'Who's hopping over whom in this rain? And at the moment
of doom?' Peppe was weeping, crossing himself, and saying good-by
to all his girls.

" 'He's on top of her now!' I explained to Peppe and Malić,
hugging them. 'He can do it. He's a driver and an alcoholic and,
above all, an epileptic! Men like that can do anything! They have
all the madness and inspiration they need! He's banging it into her
now, stirring up her gypsy kidneys, squeezing her waist, waving
with her yellow flag, quenching his thirst with wine and rain!'

" 'And the wheel, Antonio, who's got the wheel?' Bonaccia was
squealing.

" 'He's an epileptic! He can do anything! He's got plenty of
time to catch hold of the wheel, every once in awhile!' I shrieked.
My only hope was that this sleepwalker's race around the Arc de
Triomphe would continue through eternity, or until our common
death.

"And for a moment it began to appear to me that we really were
great, that we were true conquerors, that victory was nothing but
epilepsy. And it was at that very moment that something occurred
for which I'll remember this gloomy city until the end of my days.

THE WAR WAS BETTER

The wheel was torn out of the driver's hands, if he was holding it at all. The truck miraculously got past another barricade, the army and the police, and started off entirely on its own.

"I'm not too clear about how it overturned, or who stirred up whose kidneys. I only remember that we glided onto the square in a kind of frozen dream, mixing with the pigs and seeing bones and decorations fly through the air. There hadn't been more pigs, blood, shouts, screams, and laughter on Place de l'Étoile since the Napoleonic wars.

"I don't know what happened afterwards, when they realized we had won another convincing victory. But I never saw my friends again, and I worry about them, whether they're alive and where they are, that is, in which countries they now reign. Since that night, then, I haven't seen them. As for the pigs, that's another story: I've been running into them all the time, seeing them, recognizing them; their stench stifles me. I swear to God, François, I don't know where to turn my head."

"Your story is wonderful, Antonio," François Villon said enthusiastically, all a-flutter. "As if it were from my own time. From the time when men killed much, ate well, drank heartily, and shit long and peacefully, usually in front of pigs. You've warmed me up. Think of all that meat in one spot!"

"It's a pity you weren't with us, or somewhere nearby, that night. You'd surely have written a poem about it. Don't you think so?"

"I would." François Villon felt Antonio's hot forehead and then his neck. "I would. I'd have written a poem about the pigs, the gypsy girl, and epilepsy."

"François, how do poems get written?" Peduto asked him from the ground.

"In darkness," Villon said, "mainly before or after a crime, when your hands are still quivering. Songs are written on sand. On water. On skin, human skin of course. Poetry must be bloody and funny, really funny. Poverty, misery, fear, and knives give birth to poems. Ha! Ha! Ha! In fact, Antonio, I don't even know how they're written; they're only spoken. Ha! Ha! Ha! The story about the pigs is good, but you haven't added anything new in all the times you've told it. I like the thing about the gypsy and her yellow panties the most. You know, Antonio, I think I'm also a gypsy? I think I must be one of that damned, but everlastingly merry race."

"I'm a gypsy too," Peduto murmured, letting his eyes fill with tears and raindrops. "You're dark at least, but I'm a red gypsy, which is worse. But I think we're all gypsies, because everything around us is so gypsyesque. Villon, in the past, I think I knew all your poems by heart, all your gypsyesque lamentations. I wept reading them to imbeciles, who were incapable of getting your meaning. I told them you meant nothing; you only sang."

"I always liked meat, and I was a genuine gypsy," François Villon observed from under his hat. "All I did was kill, sing, laugh, and run. I swear it to you, Red Beard, I wanted my poems to convey no message. Nothing to anybody! Anyhow, whatever they attribute to me, even if I really wrote it, I can't remember anymore. I've forgotten everything now, with time, living in this way."

"Countless times I've recited your 'Épitaph de Villon' from the *Ballade des Pendus*. '*Frères humains qui après nous vivez, / N'ayez les cœurs contre nous endurcis*,'" Antonio whispered into the rain. "I know it wasn't a message; it was a scream in some inn by the Seine."

"That is my fate, Red Gypsy," François Villon admitted, caressing Antonio's forehead and thick hair. "They noted down a great number of things, but I'm not responsible for every one of my screams." He screened Antonio from the rain, caressing him as one caresses a convalescent child who has lost all hope. "At least so far as my poems are concerned, I plead not guilty."

"Who is guilty then, François?"

"The rain," Villon said and laughed. "The weather is guilty." And then, with the utmost disdain, the poet began to talk about the weather, rain, and water in general. Antonio no longer followed him. A cold wind swept Montparnasse. He told the poet once again that his bones ached. He told him that they two should never part. Sleep tangled itself up in Antonio's eyelashes. He could see Giuseppe Bonaccia kissing the sow, Simone-Thérèse; then they nibbled each other's ears. The rain and the wind were not troubling Gruban Malić. He climbed the Arc de Triomphe, and affixed his red globe on its very top. All the avenues which Malić could see from the wet square were full of pigs and Gypsies.

"François, when you set off again, don't leave me here," Antonio murmured, feeling his eyes begin to shut. "I can't go on with them anymore; they don't seem like people anymore. You said it so wonderfully, that you were lost but now repent your return. I too, it seems, came in through the wrong door."

"There'll be sunshine and there'll be girls," the man above him said, pressing his cold hand on Antonio's forehead. "There'll be health, and wine to drink to it; there'll be inns and meat! There'll be highways, my red-bearded robber, my Gypsy thief!"

"Take me back into your own time, brother!"

Against his ribs and backbone, Antonio felt the rumbling of the metro which made the grill tremble. A whiff of stench floated up to him with the hot steam.

"Take me there, François. I know, your village is Montfaucon." In his mind's eye, Antonio saw the Seine thick with reeds and rushes, where ugly swamp birds were hiding. There was a little path which led toward the infernal green with the stocks and scaffolds with their foundations dug deep into the earth. "Lead me . . . there!"

"We can't in this rain."

"We'll hang it then!" Antonio said. "We'll draw its dripping head through the noose, wait a little, and then kick the barrel out from under its feet. Ha! We'll let it balance like that for a moment to scare whoever arrives in our gypsy Montfaucon, blown in by the wind. We will, won't we, François? We'll hang the rain!"

"In order to get there we have to wade through the Seine," Villon said. "I don't believe in their bridges. What I'd really like to do, though, is piss from here or from the arcades with the decorated railings. Their bridges aren't real. I doubt their existence. I piss on their foundations! We'll wade!"

Afterwards they did not speak for a long time. Pierre Calvet was counting either the dead and wounded or big money, and snoring. Antonio no longer talked of gallows, weather, and rain, nor knew that they were not in Montfaucon. He held one hand on the turtle's shell and the other in the gutter, and every second or third passerby stepped on his fingers.

Leaning over Antonio, smiling mildly, with many wrinkles about his eyes and lips, François Villon dreamed about the sun and highways whose end or beginning he had never been able to unravel. Sometimes sleep would completely overwhelm or trick him, and he would touch Antonio's forehead with his cheek or his beard. Then he would think for a moment that the earth was not so hot and so hard, so sick and so miserable, that it should not be touched, at least that night. He stood as if crucified between the two, leaning forward heavily and resembling a big bird.

The fourth tramp, a bearded one with a crooked nose and long legs, lay down beside Pierre Calvet on the grill and took almost all the bones away from him. Drenched to the skin, he turned his eyes up to the sky and begged it at least not to soak the crusts he was removing from his overcoat and side pockets. Then he looked toward the restaurant, from which steam, light, and the smell of food were issuing, and cursed the people inside and cursed their voracious, self-ish, gypsy French god.

The dawn found them again, all four, hugging each other in the cold.

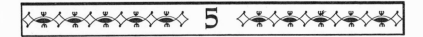

5

"I'm afraid," Villon said to Antonio. "I'm afraid of the French."

"I don't understand you," Peduto said, pulling the handcart along the sidewalk, with the turtle in the bag. "I don't fully under-stand you, François."

"I don't understand them either," Villon went on as he hid half his face with the brim of his large hat. "Anyhow, they and I have never agreed. I've robbed them and killed them; they've hunted me and caught me and sentenced and hanged me. I don't know how a gypsy like me has survived. Maybe my rage and disdain have out-lived them."

"But I'm with you now," Antonio assured him. "Don't be afraid. I'd die before I let anything happen to you."

Peduto's eyes were still swollen, but he could see at least some-thing around him. There was determination and warmth in his voice.

"For goodness sake, don't tremble."

"Antonio, you still don't know what *L'Arbre Sec* is!" Villon muttered; his words were hardly audible over the creaking of the handcart, which they were pulling along together now, more or less sharing the work. "You, happily, still don't know what *Le Gibet* is, or *La Potence!* You haven't been hanged; winds haven't blown through your skull; the sun hasn't warmed your bones!"

Peduto cursed and spat. The voice of the inspired gypsy qua-vered for an instant and went on. "I'm afraid of them. They breed lice. I don't want you to perish in vain, defending me. Yes, I'm afraid for you too, you especially, you red-bearded pirate! I'm abso-lutely convinced you couldn't feign death as I did. And even less slip the noose off your neck and escape. I don't think you're capable of tricking anybody except yourself. You still don't know what *L'Arbre Sec* is!"

THE WAR WAS BETTER

They emerged from a wet, narrow sidestreet onto Boulevard de Clichy. Flashing neon, searchlights and fireworks suddenly broke out in a dazzling flash before their sick, sleepless eyes, almost blinding them. A song was booming out of various loudspeakers and mixing with the shouts of the merrymaking crowd:

> Un p'tit jet d'eau
> Une station de métro.

Rockets soared above the roofs, drawing upward the glances of the crowd. The little bombs burst high in the air, one after the other, each just in time to prevent the sky from darkening, and vomited false colors. The cold, gray rain began to sparkle with all the colors of the rainbow.

> Une station de métro
> Entourée de bistrots
> Pigalle.

The voice sang on, hardly penetrating the noise of the eternal crowd in the eternal square; Antonio and François did not follow it. Some of the wilder passersby wanted to pull the turtle out of the bag and turn her over on her shell; Peduto clung to the handcart to prevent them. Villon kept away from the artificial light, to which his eyes adjusted only with great pain.

A roar of triumph came from the crowd, as if they were crowning or skinning somebody. It seemed that Pigalle was doomed to endure and suffer yet another shame. A tall, stooping, warmly dressed and much-decorated personality appeared, waving his white gloves, nodding his bald head and gnawing his false teeth.

Pigalle was happy. Everyone cheered wildly for the long-awaited President, the guest of the great country of France. Not only the poor girls from the sidewalks and doorways blew kisses toward his gilt coaches and cried out in joy, but their pimps and owners did too. And so did everyone else, the milling crowds of tourists and Parisians, the pleasure-seekers and gangsters; all joined in, to experience a few moments of cheap human happiness.

As it turned out, Pigalle would long remember that night in the rain. The bald, big-bellied scoundrel, with a cross somewhere above his navel, turned to all sides, laughed, and, as many told it afterwards, swallowed entire armfuls of confetti and firecrackers.

"I want to remain here," François Villon said, with his teeth chattering, when they had finally pushed the cart into the courtyard of a large house. "I'll remain here and wait for you. I'll sing to your

THE WAR WAS BETTER

Anna-Maria as if she were my Grosse Margot. I'll caress her and kiss her little paws and shell; I'll do all the things you asked me to, when we met one or two years ago, was it? I can't remember anymore. But Antonio, don't take me out of the dark. It's good for a gypsy. I like it best in the dark. My eyes haven't adjusted to this infernal artificial light yet. Here, in this humidity and stench, I'll work out the best way to begin things with Anna-Maria, your faithful, cursed wife. I swear I will. Antonio, don't you see? I'm on my knees. My heart will break from fear, from grief for my endless, unlit highways. I'll die from longing for meat. Man, red gypsy, brother, my evil, you still haven't tasted poetry. You still don't know what the dry tree is!"

"I have a knife," Peduto panted and pulled Villon onto the pavement. "A knife!"

"I have one too," Villon rejoined. "But it won't help me if I meet that blackcoat from Sirmoise, who keeps hunting me down even though he's dead. He always has two or three knives. He takes them out of his sleeves, from under his cassock. That terrible Abbé de Sirmoise! He is chasing me because of a whore. Yes, his love. I raped her. I think he just passed by here too. That big-balled buck, whom I strangled; it took him a long time to die. He's like a wild boar, that Abbé de Sirmoise, only tougher!"

"You just give me the eye, François, and I'll take this big knife of mine and hack his balls off! Not only his either, but any other scoundrel's who looks like him too!" They were standing on the sidewalk now, getting drenched in the rain, watching the crowd, and the scoundrel in the gilded coach at the head of the column. "Trust in me, François, stop worrying. If anyone so much as asks you why you've come here and abandoned your highways and inns, and your fleshy Margot, I'll cut his throat!"

François Villon walked on like a blind man, hiding half his face under the brim of his hat. The windows and doorways of the bars were crammed with photographs of naked girls. Uniformed doormen invited the passersby to enter, pointing their gloves into the darkness, toward the cellars and little nests where happiness was cheap. They offered masks for their customers' faces, unbreakable Russian contraceptives, female and male sex organs of all colors and calibers, made of Michelin rubber, some with fur glued on and some with nothing at all, and batches of pornographic photographs. They also offered their services, the services of their friends and the services of their unique and unforgettable fiancées, who were scattered around Pigalle. From time to time, the song "Entourée de bistrots" drowned out the noisy invitations and the drone of promises of paradise on earth. The whole colorful merry-go-round was shining brightly with neon and fireworks. Pigalle was aflame.

"There she is!" Antonio cried out, as if he had been stabbed by the knife of the Sirmoise priest.

"Who? Whom have you seen, Gypsy?" François Villon asked almost in a whisper. "*Prince trompeur!*"

"Her, the woman, it's she, François!" Antonio almost sobbed. "I've been looking for her and hunting her down all my life. François, don't budge now. Wait for me here. And don't be afraid, for God's sake! When I'm around, nobody can harm you. Just wait for me here!"

François Villon leaned against a wall, lest the passersby should knock him to the ground. He felt he would die from cold and fear. He adjusted his raincoat and felt the knifeblade hard and chill against the skin of his chest. Waiting in solitude, leaning against a dirty wall, the eternal Villon watched Antonio make his way through the crowd of prostitutes and pimps and the sidewalk merchants who offered a panoply of souvenirs from the city of lechery and light.

Antonio reached the girl before she turned into a sidestreet. It seemed to Villon that he stood a full minute or more before her, barring her way with outstretched arms. Then they disappeared. A black spot formed where the man had trembled before the woman.

"Don't take a long time coming back, my Antonio," François whispered to himself. He was frightened of the cars, rockets, and noise. "You know very well that my eyes can't bear artificial light, that my lungs don't accept this air, that I more or less don't understand anything these people say or do. My mind just doesn't understand. It rejects what they call peace, happiness, and life. Antonio, gypsy, that's why I'm keeping this knife under my coat. Since you've gone, I've started feeling its point and stroking its edges. How sharp it is! And Paris is a shame. It's a heap of dust and misery!"

The gilded coach was passing by. In front of it, beside it and behind it, guards with automatic rifles on their chests were marching in impeccable order. Motorcyclists in leather, with white helmets, zoomed across the square. Prostitutes, pimps, tourists, and colored wretches; everyone who was plodding through the surrounding streets and gathering around the *bistrots* waved to the bulkiest, fattest and baldest President who had ever visited the beloved country of France.

THE WAR WAS BETTER

Imagining he was on Place de la Concorde, somewhere between the Louvre and the Obelisk, that he was passing under the Arc de Triomphe, or swinging in his coach down the Champs Élysées, which had been especially illuminated for his arrival, the visiting President greeted France. The people of that great and hospitable country were jostling around his coach to see him better and tell him that the love he driveled about was reciprocal, that the idea of brotherhood, which never ceased to dominate his tiny vocabulary, and dribble from his fleshy mouth, was guaranteed by numerous treaties and public statements. The rain fell on him and his bald head and on the rows of his guards, who were dripping wet but seemed to be made of steel. Water dripped from the hindquarters of the horses, whose shit-stained tails were tied up in silk tricolors, and from the helmets of the guards. Two national anthems were playing loudly, both of them quite wet and out of tune.

"Antonio, I can't wait for you any longer," Villon said. Blood beat against his temples. His heart was sprinting in the old highway robber's rhythm. "Don't you see I'm lost here, Antonio? What I really want to do is go back to my Rue de la Brèche-aux-Loups. I have a love in Rue de la Grande Truanderie, two in Rue Gratte-Cul, three in Rue Put-Teigneux, four in Rue Put-y-Muse. And a faithful company is waiting for me at Montfaucon: highway boys, another real love and the gallows."

Crimson surged through his sunken cheeks. His dark eyes, squinting a little from staring too hard into the distance, were glowing. He could not tear them away from the gilded coach.

"My blood is evil and completely gypsy. I'm telling the truth, Antonio. I'm afraid and ready for anything. I was good only because I was with you."

Leaning against the wall with his face dark and concealed, he seemed almost invisible. Nobody noticed him. He felt like fleeing. He trembled and muttered feverishly: "I hate them, Red Beard! I hate them! I hate them with all my heart! I hate them like hell!"

"*Vive la France, le pays de mon enfance!*" the President began, coughing and chewing on the rain. France had never seen such a person. "*Vive la France*, this divine cradle where I wet my bed up to my fifteenth or seventeenth year!" he shouted, as he scattered gold pieces and prospectuses of his vast country, also beloved and devoted to France, among the listening crowd. "*Vive la France, vive l'Europe!*"

François Villon did not wait for the drenched, obedient, friendly

French horses to stop. He curled himself into a living spring and bounded from the earth. "Antonio, I'm no good, I'm just no good," he said to himself. "I'm not your brother either. Renounce me, give up on the damned, dirty gypsy!"

With devilish skill, he pierced through the cordon formed by the guards whose necks were very wet and, he thought in passing, fit for the knife. Even the motorcyclists did not notice him. The explosions of new rockets and fireworks did not blind only Villon's eyes. He bounded once again, thin and light as he was, and found himself on the step of the coach.

Absorbed in his own words and voice, enraptured by a welcome such as no other country had yet given him, and especially delighted by the French fireworks, the distinguished guest of France did not even notice, at first, the man who had flung himself from the pavement, through the rain, onto his coach. And when he finally did, he thought it must be some boy, probably madly in love with his country or with him, a little boy with sick eyes and a beard glued on for the purpose. Traveling constantly from capital to capital, the President was accustomed to packing his coach or his limousine with some of his more enthusiastic welcomers, holding and rocking them on his giant knees or even picking them up under the arms like grandchildren.

But this time he did not have the slightest opportunity to welcome the French boy with slanty eyes and a pirate's hat on his head, nor even to complete his sentence. Villon hurled himself against his chest and jingling medals.

The President gaped and then screamed. Villon saw both rows of his false teeth, a handful of gold and saliva, and many half-pronounced words struggling to emerge from the muck. He slashed his neck like an ox's. The President's gullet yawned open and poured out blood like a faucet. Several veins on his neck had been opened.

Even before the whistles blew and the guards and the crowd began to scream, even before somebody from the drenched security unit fired his automatic rifle, and ordered the driver to rein in the perfectly trained, priceless French horses, François stepped back coolly and stabbed the President's belly ten times. He tore up the ribbon of the Legion of Honor with his teeth and nails. With his knife, he slashed the President around the heavy, diamond-studded cross, which now hung under his navel.

"*Bene stat!*" François Villon said. Fearing that the immense, riddled corpse of the beloved guest would fall down and suffocate him, he jumped further into the coach. *"Bene stat!"* he said again when he felt strong male hands seize his shoulders. *"Bene stat . . .* here's meat!"

The largest and most beautiful display of fireworks ever seen in Paris illumined, in all the colors of the rainbow, almost the entire city. Cannon salvos thundered. The President's blood—green, then blue, and sometimes even red—drenched the coach, the nearest motorcyclists and even the pavement. From his wounds, which the guards were trying to close, the rare, greatly honored, and beloved guest's intestines slid out with a gurgling sigh. The entrails of the great ruler stank; his shit was flowing out of them. All of Pigalle stank. The horses stopped in their tracks.

"Vive la France!"

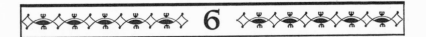

6

"I'm going to stay with this one a little longer, Auntie," the girl said, pointing at Antonio.

"What?" the old woman asked, bending her ear toward the prostitute, who was no less excited than the man who stood beside her. "What did you say? How long?"

"He's paid double, so I can't throw him out just like that," the girl murmured into the old woman's long, floppy ear. "So . . . I'm not here. You know what I mean, Auntie, you know whom to say it to."

"Perhaps he'll come," *la patronne* smiled, and her whole forehead wrinkled. "I'll tell him. He's a wonderful boy, that Mr. Gaston. Only now, in his seventy-fifth year, has the poor devil understood what true love is. Ah, my little Gaston!"

"Tell him I'm not here," the girl said more loudly. She was getting nervous, standing there beside Antonio. "I'm not here!"

"Love with us two will cost him a pretty penny," the old woman winked, opening the door for other guests. "And let it. He's been saving all his life, hasn't he, just to have a good time now? We're expensive!"

The girl hummed a song as she climbed the steep stairs. Her voice was neither gay nor quiet. She hid her face and her eyes, although Antonio did not look at her; he was tremendously excited.

"Now we're in my room," she said when she introduced him into a dusky cubicle in the attic.

"It's nice here, girl," Antonio said, sizing up the room, the walls with glued-on colored paper, the cross with a crucified Christ above a bouquet of artificial flowers and the little window against which the rain was drumming. There were several bottles on the small chair, which smelt of meat and onions.

"It doesn't leak," the girl said. "It's warm. Stay here as long as you can."

"In the past I dreamed about four walls like these," Antonio said, "but there were others who wanted the whole world to belong to me."

"You're rich?"

"I'm incredibly rich, girl. The whole world, as I've just said, belongs to me. The whole world and all its misery. All its sorrow. And laughter too. Happily, laughter too."

"Why did you pay so much," the girl asked suspiciously, "if you're so . . . fabulously rich?"

"Money doesn't mean much to me," Antonio remarked, sitting on the edge of the bed. "I don't even know how much I gave you. I'm sure I haven't helped you as much as I should. Perhaps I could have done something better and nicer for you. Something to remember me by."

"I think you gave whatever you had," the girl said, hiding her face as she had when they were climbing the stairs. "It's not a small thing—to give everything you have."

"I've still got about a hundred francs," Antonio said and took them out of his wet pocket. "That's already something, isn't it . . . ? In a town like this, and in such weather."

"What will you do with them, Red Beard?"

"I'll buy bread and wine for twenty francs. For Villon and me. Maybe a bone too. With the rest, I'll get some cabbages or salad or fresh grass for the turtle. For my Anna-Maria, who's still growing. She needs more and more."

The girl with the hidden face and long, pale arms remembered Greece and Montenegro; she remembered the army and the officers' bordellos, the blood, and the injured. The earth and the sky, and everything human, had burnt in such a terrible, incessant fire that she had asked herself countless times whether it was not God's punishment that was being inflicted upon them. She remembered Antonio too, nicknamed the Red Devil, the luckless merrymaker, with his turtle in his arms; Anna-Maria had been a tiny, abandoned orphan,

and everyone had called her *Ortodossa, cara nostra Ortodossa.*
Whenever Antonio got drunk, he used to place her in his bosom, on
the left side, and ask her, in front of everyone, to scratch his heart.

"Little whore and love," he used to murmur, "even you don't
know how unhappy I am. I had a sister who was lost in Via dei Serpenti, not far from the Vatican. *Ortodossa*, now you are that
damned sister of mine, whose throat I always wanted to slash. I
wanted to pull her whore's heart out into the broad daylight to see
what it was made of!"

She remembered him from Rome. Once he had been in Via Maledetta, two or three times in Via dei Fiori, but most of all in Via
dei Serpenti, where he had stayed behind garbage cans with some
tramps and other malcontents.

Even in Rome, he had never parted from the turtle. He had
called her his sister again, and his bad luck, because of which, he
used to say, he was still among the living. Once she had lifted him
up from the ground, ran her fingers through his hair which, like his
beard, was full of litter and wine, and asked him whether he needed
anything.

"I'm rich, girl," he had answered, unable to open his eyes. "I'm
very rich. Therefore, I'm lying here. So rich that I should be envied. I have a son, Peppino, a brother, Malić, and a sister, Anna-
Maria Cattolica! Do you know a more beautiful and harmonious
family on this sinful earth, girl?"

"No, I don't, Freckles," she had answered and escaped into the
darkness, because he seemed to be remembering something.

"Girl, where are you? Stop!" he had wailed and even opened his
eyes for a moment.

She had fled. She sent him wine, bread, and meat from time to
time, through other prostitutes. And she watched him whisper
sometimes with Peppino and sometimes with the turtle. Tears had
moistened her eyelashes; her heart had melted, but she had not
dared confide it to anyone. And although she loved Romana dearly
and pitied her, she had come less and less often to Via dei Serpenti.
Whenever she cast a glance into General Besta's yard, and looked at
the garbage cans in the corner, her heart would shrink. Choking
back an urge to scream, she would dash away with the other girls
and drink herself unconscious. Afterwards she had left Rome. She
hardly knew herself all the places she had been, or how she had
come finally to Paris.

Again, a miracle had occurred. She had seen Antonio in the rain, standing beside the strange man with feverish eyes, sunken cheeks and broken teeth.

"I love her, François, love her," he was whispering, as he stroked the turtle's coarse, checkered shell. "I love her. Don't be mad at me, excuse this love of mine, man from afar. My life changed the day I met her and took her, and she became my eternal fiancée."

"I'll love her too, Antonio," the restless man had said in an almost unintelligible language as he held up his raincoat to protect them both from the wind, which was bringing a cold rain from the west. "I'll love her, Peduto, because I love you. It's for your sake that I, a bandit armed with a knife, have grown good and tame, I, a gypsy from the gallows, from the creaking beams where the winds play endlessly!"

She had dropped a basket of bread, cheese, and wine near them, and disappeared. The three had remained on the pavement and embraced.

"You aren't going to leave that ... that Villon, as you call him?" the girl asked him now. "How is it that you look so alike, like the same person?"

"We are one," Peduto said, without knowing anymore where he was, or why he had come, and feeling fire burn his cheeks. "He's come from a great distance, and I don't understand every word he says. But the same gypsy blood flows in both of us. And our thoughts are the same, even our dreams, except that he looks at everything in terms of meat. That's why I care for him so much. I don't know what I'd do if I lost him."

Antonio grabbed a bottle, lifted it to his lips, and tilted it. He felt the wine course down his throat and warm his intestines. His tongue loosened, and his thoughts darkened. His eyes began to smart. He sat beside her, quivering. The water dripping from his asbestos cape was forming a puddle on the floor.

"We're all the same: Malić, Villon, Peppe and I," Antonio began again, after the girl had taken the cape off his shoulders and stroked his hair. "You don't know Malić and Peppe, which is a great pity. But we're brothers, that's the most important thing. Nobody dares touch us. We could annihilate everything, burn it down to the ground, whatever we touched! Do you have some more wine, my French beauty?"

"I don't know the people you're talking about, but I understand you completely," the girl lied, reclining beside him and sipping from the bottle. "I've never seen them, and never will, but the way you talk about them I seem to see them right before my eyes. I already love them. They're your blood brothers and ... gypsies, as you put it."

She embraced him and kissed his forehead, his cheeks, his feverish mouth.

"Red Beard, my good red boy, I love all your brothers and sisters, if you have them. I love everyone who is dear to you. I love you too, I can't tell you how or why, but it's true. I'm so glad you finally reached me, that you've caught me at last."

"The same mother can't give birth to everyone," Antonio murmured as he went and showered her arms, neck and hair with kisses. "I love you, girl, and I've been tracking you down for years. Ever since I knew of you, I haven't been able even to approach another woman. In every one, I've seen you. Pardon me, I can't see you very well now. My eyes have swollen. My tears are flowing. Love, my only true love, I don't know which of the many gods to thank that I'm near you at last, that I, a gypsy tramp, can touch you with my dirty hands. Love, come with us. We'll change the world, or at least the part we'll trample down."

"I'm afraid."

"What are you afraid of, love?"

"I'm afraid we'll never see each other again, my Red Beard, my golden gypsy. You'll have to change the world alone. It'll be better without any more trouble from me."

"Leave everything and join us, love. Love, do you hear me?"

"I'm bad," the girl said, sobbing and hugging him. "I'm evil and vile. Whatever I've managed to change so far has only gotten worse. Don't take me with you. There's vice and misery enough without me."

He propped himself up between her knees, stretching out her arms.

"Go, conquer and change the world without me. May God help you, whom I pray fervently for the health and souls of my numerous brothers and sisters scattered and wandering throughout the world. Go alone and beware of thunder, water, and human wickedness, which is boundless. Don't blaspheme God; He won't listen to you. Don't weep too much. Red Beard, my boy, what are you doing? Oh, Mother, do you see what I'm doing and how grievous is my sin? Oh Mama, my sorrow, my luckless, freckled Mama, even you don't know what you gave birth to! My pious wretch, pardon me, I love him. Mama, Mama, I ran away because I knew I'd caress his hair like this sooner or later, kiss his eyes and lips. . . ."

THE WAR WAS BETTER

"You're with me already, we're one," he muttered, possessing her as he had never possessed another woman. "Love, my only one, don't you see we can never part again, that you're to me now what I am to you? My darling, my treasure, my pearl and my sun, my *Cattolica*, the world is already ours. Everything is ours. The power does not exist that could darken our love. From now on you're my fiancée, my eternal sister."

"Antonio!" the girl screamed, pushing herself out from under him and finding herself on the floor. "Antonio! Do you know what we've done?"

"What are you talking about? Have you drunk too much?" He fell to his knees and searched for her, turning his head in the dusk. "Has the devil got into your skin?"

"Antonio, my brother!" the girl sobbed, scratching her face. "My dearest, most unhappy brother!" She felt that she had peeled the skin off her cheeks; her fingers were sticky. "You hunted me to cut my throat and pull out my heart!"

"Snake and sister!" Antonio burst out weeping, as he jerked his knife out of his museum boot. "Stop! Don't run away! Stop, my sun and my evil, let me take your heart out to see what it's made of! Where are you, damn bitch, you whore, *Cattolica?!*"

He tottered in the dim twilight of the room, utterly blinded, sobbing and trembling.

"I'll cut you up . . . or I'll pardon, I'll forgive you as no one else would! Where are you hiding you poor, miserable snake, you wretch?!"

The girl smashed a bottle against his neck. He dropped on his knees again. She grabbed the knife which had fallen from his hand and ran out the door, calling back from the darkness, "Brother, my only love, don't look for me, don't hunt me anymore. You'll never be able to find me again. And even if you did, I'd take this knife and slash your heart and cut it up in little pieces! Because I know what it's made of and what kind it is!"

The darkness around her voice and her silhouette at the end of the corridor grew thicker. She murmured to him while he knelt on the threshold, his sick eyes bulging:

"Antonio, the only one for whose salvation I'll pray *Madonna*, go now, and don't come back! Take your Villon and disappear forever! And pardon me, both of you, for my wickedness and my damned birth!"

"You're good, you're good, my little sister!" he muttered, as he tumbled down the steps. "It's I who am evil, not you. You're only

[335]

unhappy and insulted. I remember how they took your pigeon and tore it up when you were small, and how you couldn't be consoled for days. You called it again and again, looking at the sky, full of feathers. My little sister, my soul, don't run away so fast. I'll break my neck falling down these stairs. Help me, hold me up. I pardon you! I forgive you for everything, everything! I'll leave Paris with Villon this very day. But don't run away! Wrap yourself up, you'll get soaked in the rain, get up from the ground, caress me just once more! Give me back the knife. And since I'm already going away with the black Villon, wave your hand to us. Sister, my love!"

At the exit, the half-deaf *patronne* and the seventy-five-year-old lover, Gaston, who was as mangy as his old bulldog, were waiting for him. Antonio directed his steps toward them. He felt like piercing them both with his knife.

The *patronne* and the gentleman with the dog he resembled stepped aside just in time; Antonio hit the wall with his face and chest and fell down. Only then did he realize that he had not nailed them to the wall like insects.

He stood up again, scratched and bloody, his shoulders stooping, and turned toward them. In a flash, he recalled the room and everything his sister had told him. And instead of rushing at them both, he collapsed in a heap in Gaston's arms and began to choke out feverish words.

"Old one, my good old man, what an injustice! All this should never, never have happened! What an injustice... toward her! Don't be afraid! I won't harm you! Lead me away from here! I imagined life differently! Take a knife, kill me! Old one, do you hear me?!"

Mr. Gaston worked his way out of his grasp, and Antonio sank to his knees. He crawled over to the old woman and tried to hang himself around her neck, to kiss her wrinkled hands, to ask her to shorten his life. He held out his hands toward her, hoping he could grab hold of her and then force her to kill him. For a moment, she seemed to be transformed; she was his sister, warm, soft, lovely, with the turtle's shell on her back. He fell down again. Only then did he notice that the bulldog was ripping his pants-legs, and pummeling his chest and medals with his paws.

The old man pulled the furious dog away, and some strong guests in leather coats grabbed hold of Antonio. The *patronne* asked the girls, who were all out on the staircase by this time, to call the police or at least the fire department. The girls, hissing and striking the bulldog with their furled umbrellas, watched indifferently as the drenched, muscular giants in the leather coats dragged Antonio across the threshold and into the street.

They beat him, lifted him up and threw him down, lifted him again and spat on him. Then all three pushed him away vigorously. Mr. Gaston received the old woman on his chest, threw his arms around her and told her that he would do well by the brave, up-standing young men who had delivered them from that red-bearded hooligan.

Antonio took one step, tottered and fell, hitting the ground with his forehead. He did not have time to tell them that he was not angry at them, or to tell them anything. He could think only that his mouth was full of teeth, salt rain, and dog hair.

"François!" Antonio was yelling, as he ran across Pigalle. "François, my brother and only friend, answer me!" He reeled and fell suddenly, then got up and made his way through the crowd gathering around the rain-flooded coach. "Villon, where are you?" he called plaintively.

Villon was nowhere. Another man was leaning against the wall where he had been. He was not on the sidewalk; he was not in the street; he was not among the prostitutes milling around the corner and under the lampposts.

"François, my Blackie, you'll never even guess what a sin I've committed!" He called him again and again, kneeling finally, and feeling the raindrops cool his forehead and cheeks. "Where are you hiding, my poor, frightened boy? Hey, there's no need to be afraid when you're with me!"

"The way he swooped and sprang!" a man's voice said passionately.

"I could never have done it. Like a lynx!"

"And how he cut him up afterwards. Just after my own taste! Ah, he was a hired killer, a professional, I'm telling you!"

"An Italian or a Corsican," the first voice said to the second. "An unusual man, all right. You saw how he was dressed, didn't you? Like someone from long ago, like a circus clown. A splendid boy!"

"He sure killed him the way people were done in, in the past," the man standing next to Antonio observed. "Expertly and deftly; that's the most important thing in killing."

"Who killed whom?" Antonio asked, as he got up, shivering, from his knees.

"A dark man, a stranger who'd been leaning for a long time against that wall over there, they say, assassinated the President—un-

fortunately not ours," a passerby paused for a moment to inform
him. "A regular butcher job. He drew his knife through the gullet
like thread through a needle's eye. Then, it seems, he slashed his
belly until it opened right up. What a stench! You have to admire a
job like that! He did it as it was done in the past, in those dark,
happy, heroic times. It stank so much, they say, that even the poor,
stabbed President vomited half an hour after he died."

"What have they done to him?" Antonio asked, with his soul in
his nose. "Did they lynch him on the spot?"

"The President?"

"The killer," Antonio said. "The circus murderer, the clown."

"They led him away," the man answered. "He didn't resist. He
only coughed and kept saying, *'Bene stat!'* He seemed happy at
what he'd done, especially at having done it, the killing, that is, just
as it should be done, *comme il faut.* He's headed for the gallows
now!"

"To kill such a President!" another man shook his head. "To
open him up, right here in front of us, who came just to amuse ourselves, to forget our cares and the high prices. And then to say
'Bene stat!' Only an Italian, a Corsican, or a communist could have
done it! If you only knew how long his intestines were, Christ, like
a pig's or a sheep's! And flesh: soft, clean, without a single vein!
How much blood flowed! As if a horse had been slaughtered! The
rain hasn't washed it off yet; it's even coagulated on the street. A
President's blood, a President's, do you realize how precious it must
be?"

"I wonder what would come out of us!" the first man said in
disgust. "I bet even gas masks wouldn't help."

"François!" Antonio cried into the rain. "Villon! You've done a
wonderful thing! You've pried him open! Everybody knows how
splendid it was!"

He gagged on his own sobs, and looked at the sky and the fireworks.

"You did what I couldn't do, what I'll never be able to do!
François, my black, wonderful brother, don't be afraid of the gallows! François!"

"Judging by his first and last names, the murderer is Spanish,"
the first man concluded; he looked at Antonio in surprise. "A Spanish communist, no doubt."

"François, my sin is greater!" Antonio began to cry, feeling the
bruises on his face. "I want us to hang on the gallows together; that
way we'll be even; we'll never part! François, you're great, mighty,

unsurpassable! You're a poet, and such a man must kill! Listen, can you hear me? Listen, there are some people here who want you to open up their President too, their scoundrel!"

"Did you know the killer?" the first man asked softly, holding up Antonio to prevent him from falling. "Is he, like you, one of these speckled, drunken Slavs?"

"He is!" Antonio shouted proudly. "Doesn't the name of François Villon confirm to you his Asiatic descent?"

"Slavic then, and not Corsican!" the man mused. "All those Slavs are drunkards and communists. And when they're both, like this François Villon, then barbarous deeds like this occur, even in our own wonderful country. Stop crying for him, stop calling him your brother. In another minute, as a loyal French citizen, I'll have to call the police!"

"I don't see very well," Antonio said. "What are they doing around the coach?"

"They're reconstructing the abominable crime, which we'll have to pay for with taxes, to avoid entering a war," the second man informed him. "We'll have to pay through the nose for this!"

"I don't understand you very well," Antonio complained. "You have to explain things twice to Slavs."

"Newspapermen, cameramen, and photographers are circling around the scene of the murder like hyenas. They're filming the coach, the horses and the driver. They're filming a piece of the President's intestines, his orthopedic shoe, size fifteen or twenty, and his walking stick with the gold or ivory handle. Near the deceased man's things, the killer's hat is still lying, that Hungarian, Greek, or Bulgarian's hat ... that Slav of yours! They're filming everything. Read a paper tomorrow, if one comes out!"

"What kind of blood was it that drenched all of Pigalle?" Antonio clung to them and would not let them go. "What kind of blood is a President's blood, that is, a King's blood—something I've always wanted to drink?"

"Green," the first man answered. "Then it turned yellow and blue."

"What?" Antonio's eyes bulged. "Do you mean the blood of a President, any President, yours for example, has so many colors? Green, you say? Green?"

"It's because of the fireworks, madman," the second man snapped and pushed him away. "Look up. If you're not blind, you'll see that the sky is ablaze. We've prepared a welcome for their President which will long be remembered, especially by them!"

THE WAR WAS BETTER

"The sky should be left alone," Antonio muttered from below. "The earth should be sprayed with fire, with a gigantic hose!"

They were all departing, and he shouted after them: "Fire should strike the earth right here! Fire is very beautiful, you can see for yourselves, you who're staring up at it!" He thought again of Amalia Celestina, nicknamed the Mild and Toothless. "Fire can be like a rose. There's no smell like the smell of a flame!"

He was alone on the wet asphalt, whispering to himself.

"Fire, among other things, can burn up whatever is ugly and monstrous. It can be a flower and a medicine at the same time. People, spare the sky!"

His head spun. He got up and reeled about, looking for the wall against which François had leaned. Then he fell again. He stretched out with his face in a puddle and sipped the rain. But even if he had remained on his feet, he would not have seen or heard anyone or anything. It seemed to him that he was being led to the gallows. A somber joy was overwhelming him.

"*Bene stat*," he said to himself and lost consciousness.

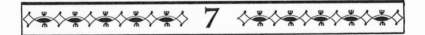

Antonio tottered out of Rue des Martyrs onto Pigalle, pulling the handcart behind him. Although it was midnight, the fireworks were not yet over, and everything looked green. He did not know where to set out. Standing in the rain, gazing mournfully at the spot where, several hours before, Villon had cut open the President's belly, he began to get soaked again. His bones ached. His eyes smarted. He himself could not bear the neon signs and the artificial light.

"Now we're utterly alone," he whispered to the turtle. "Everyone has abandoned us, so we'll die of solitude and hunger. Anyhow we've experienced enough now, you and I. Perhaps it's high time to wait, together, for the bitter end. Not in this human mud, though, but somewhere in the green countryside, alongside some nice, dirt road."

His forehead and his numerous bruises were still burning. He might have fainted at any moment, and he was thirsty. From time to time he paused and threw back his head with his mouth open; then

THE WAR WAS BETTER

the green raindrops moistened his palate. "Just a little, a little more, and everything will pass," he thought, with his face upturned. "A little longer, and the devil and the wind will sweep you away from here. Anna-Maria, sister-love, look out. Don't even try to count up the sisters of your trade, all those whores and wretches. *Cattolica*, my darling, just a little longer! Let's leave for a distant, clean, sunny country somewhere. Let's forget everything we've seen and everything that's happened to us!"

"Antonio, Beard! You're still alive, ha?"

"Who's calling me?" He was swallowing rain, fearing the voice would not call him again. "Isn't it you, François?" He waited. "Who's taken pity on me?"

"We've been looking all over for you for two years now!" The voice was quite near, but Antonio could see nothing clearly, because of the green rain. "Devil, where is your usual hiding-place? Devil of devils, Red Beard, now you can't give us the slip anymore!"

"Who are you? Who are you?" He leaned over the cart, stretching out his arms like a blind man. "Are you people or ghosts?"

"We're your brothers, Red Beard. There's no difference between you and us anymore."

"Isn't it terrible, to be equal to me?"

"Anyhow, we're in the same boat. We're quite near you now, Antonio. We see you clearly. At least deign to give us a look. We're here. We won't run away. It isn't easy to abandon a magus! Try to raise your eyelids a little! Go on, a little higher! That's it!"

For a minute he saw them clearly. Dressed in clown's clothes, bearded and hairy, with heavy paint on their faces and penciled eyebrows, Georges Bonnefous and Sergey Ivanovich stood before him. They were holding Carl Schlotterer between them. The German was barefoot and erect, with his hair closely cropped. He was wearing an overcoat from some unknown army. A camera hung from Georges's neck, and the skinny Sergey Ivanovich was moving his whitened lips. A middle-aged gentleman stood behind them, evidently a Jew and their boss. He was holding a whip and smiling.

"I'm so glad I see you," Antonio murmured, holding out his hands toward them. "I'm so glad you won't abandon me. Have you, perhaps, seen Peppe in this jungle? He's disappeared again."

"We perform in a few bars around here," Georges Bonnefous informed him, jerking his swollen belly. "All three of us. We work as clowns. They say our act is touching."

THE WAR WAS BETTER

"This is our manager," Sergey Ivanovich said, pointing at the polite Jew, and smiling like a fox who has tricked all the wolves. "He's taking us through Paris, feeding us and beating us."

Rain poured down the leaden face of Carl Schlotterer.

"Take me with you," Antonio requested, looking mournfully at the Jew, whose opened umbrella was held only above his own head. "I have several medals on my chest. Everyone will laugh. It'll add to the act. Take me in, so I won't get wet."

"Can you play any instrument? Or do you always hold your hands like that?" the Jew asked, touching his fingers with the whip. "Perhaps you can remember something—a story to tell—something beautiful and funny?"

"Just let me be with you," Peduto said softly, pressing his hands together. "That is with them, boss."

"Then get in, with them," the boss ordered. "You don't have to walk on all fours, stand up! You can go on all fours on stage, since that's one thing you know how to do. Stand up!"

They turned into one of the darkest side streets and got stuck in a doorway. Georges and Sergey helped *Tedesco* to lift the handcart and the turtle over the threshold. Drenched and half-frozen, they all finally got into the theater and quieted down behind the scenes.

Onstage, an ugly, scrawny woman was taking off her clothes to the accompaniment of cacophonous music. She was rolling on an artificial fur coat, making believe that a big-nosed General's photograph was caressing her sunken breasts and withered mound. Indecent cries, growls, and obscene jokes rose up from the audience at each of her orgasmic gestures.

Before the woman could get up and wipe the sweat from her forehead and groin, motorcyclists dressed in leather from head to toe began to drive onto the stage, some of them from behind the scenes. Men armed with submachine guns, knives, and bombs made room for them, and greeted them with vicious cries. Both groups sported jingling metal bands, tin badges, and chains. A few competitors from the audience, also in leather and helmets, joined the others. Their motorcycles were small, like toys, and everybody laughed at them as they climbed onto the stage. The woman stared at the men in terror.

Almost all the lights over the stage went out; the woman hastily stuffed half the scattered underwear and medals, and the General's photograph, between her legs. Turning on their headlights and swelling out their muscles, the motorcyclists honked, waved their phosphorescent hands, dangled their artificial genitalia, and ravaged the stage from one end to the other. The ones whose 250 or 500 c.c. motorcycles roared the loudest were entirely naked and disheveled; they drove straight into the others, who were crossing the stage and trying to rise up on their rear wheels. They drove abreast, and then in disorder, shooting ahead of one another, rearing, leaping, and crossing like acrobats, and driving their motorcycles along the very edge of the stage. Their headlights lit up almost the entire hall.

It seemed the woman had been expecting them; there were even more still arriving. Their headlights exposed her from every possible angle; on her back, with her head on the floor and her thighs spread apart, she began to bump and grind, wriggling her belly and her behind. "Punish her! Punish her!" someone shouted. "She should be punished for being ugly!"

"Punish her for being skinny and old!" another shrieked.

The blazing motorcyclists swooped in on her with a horrible roar.

Nobody in the audience could quite see what was happening. There was such congestion on the stage that it was not clear whether only one or two of the motorcyclists, or all of them, had thrust their knives into her belly and breasts. Someone roared that he was for peace, that he had not come to watch the spilling of fraternal French blood, but rather to enjoy mass nakedness and whipping. This brought new howls from the crowd. The woman was wailing and sobbing; she seemed to have been slashed and stabbed deeply in several places. The motorcyclists went on killing her. They lit her up in their dazzling headlights and ran or leapt over her. The cries of the audience froze in their throats. Hair stood on end even in the first rows, where the cruelest customers were sitting, tense and controlled, in multicolored, tight leather costumes.

The leather man who had roared that he was for peace and collective lust suddenly burst out crying, but he soon quieted down. Someone yelled to him from the other side of the hall that more than half the audience was shooting their wads. Another screamed that it was just an act, that the woman who was being crisscrossed by the knives and motorcycles would surely survive. Then they whipped and beat the man with whips, and scratched him with their nails. He writhed and bit the seats, chewed the rags and rubber sex organs they were stuffing into his mouth and babbled joyfully of happiness, skin, and money. Between the trembling boards on which the 250 and 500 c.c. motorcycles were thundering back and forth, the woman knelt, naked, glittering, and shining with blood and sweat and contrition.

THE WAR WAS BETTER

Then the stage calmed down. The General's photograph disappeared, together with the underwear and almost all the medals. The naked, gorillalike motorcycle drivers also vanished. Someone from the back of the hall called out that the woman should have been punished more severely, that perhaps, in the interest of peace and mass ejaculation, she should really have been killed and her body cut to ribbons. The music died down. The audience grew quiet.

A cloud of dust and smoke rose from the spot where the woman's body had been writhing. The Jew appeared as it gradually dissipated. He led Georges and Sergey in by a rope, pointed at Carl Schlotterer with his free hand, and cracked his whip. *Tedesco* was on his knees, staring out into the nearest rows of leather-clad customers. They too had whips and were flicking them and making them crack.

"Ladies and gentlemen, this act, like the last one, is called 'The War Was Better'; that will also be the name of the next act... which, I admit, hasn't been prepared yet," the smiling Jew announced as he cracked his whip three times over Schlotterer's head. "Ladies and gentlemen, all my numbers and songs, not only the real-life acts, but also the imitation ones, will be presented with this same title."

"Oh, what a mask! A war mask!" somebody from the audience shouted when he noticed that *Tedesco* was not afraid of the whip or the lights or even the audience. "What a face! What a man! What madness!"

"Ladies and gentlemen, I know nothing about this red-beard who has just come on-stage, pulling a turtle. Nothing." The Jew pointed at Antonio who was whispering something to Anna-Maria, as though unaware of where he was. "I met him several minutes ago, and the only thing I caught was that he's a *Slave*, like the rest of them. But I shouldn't let such a man freeze to death in the blossoms of our damned Pigalle, should I? They say he's a magus. Ladies and gentlemen ... now!"

He cracked his whip again, bowed deeply to the audience, and directed his gaze toward the spotlights. The two clowns, Georges Bonnefous and Sergey Ivanovich, began to fight. As if by agreement, both of them fell down at the same time and turned over. There they would have remained—for at least a moment, to catch their breath—if the boss, throwing a smile to the audience, had not begun to cut at them energetically with his whip.

"I'm a thief, a gangster, and an embezzler," the fat Bonnefous

began, writhing in pain. "I'm not only a counterfeiter: I fake everything else that men have made or are capable of making. I spit on
everything that's sacred to you! There's no one, living or dead, and
no thing and no idea that I would hesitate to annihilate, totally annihilate, or at least laugh to scorn or throw in the mud. I'm a shift-
less man, and I'm getting even worse. I don't believe in your sacred-
ness or your kindness or your humanity, and I haven't for a long
time. Anyway our hearts are not the same size. They don't have the
same shape. They don't beat to the same rhythm. I'm a bandit, yes,
and it's because of you, because that's been your only idea of me
since I was born. I saw later on that it suited me, all right. But I also
saw that I'm helpless in the face of your idea of me. The only thing
left to me is to spit on you from the bottom of my heart, and hope
to God you stay as deformed and horrible as you are forever. I was
born near the Seine, somewhere around here. I don't know whose
fun it was to make me. The police and the nation thought up my
biography. I'm a scoundrel and a thief of the worst order. The police should be informed about me. Why don't you inform them?
You have enough material now. The fact is I want to pay for my
crimes, at least once. It would calm me down. It would help
me. . . ."

The audience broke into frenzied applause and stamping and
screaming, interrupting Bonnefous's last few words, which were in
any case broken by strangled sobs. Deeply moved, he mopped his
tears away with his sleeve. When calm had been restored, Sergey
Ivanovich began.

"I'm everything my brother, Georges, is, with a single exception.
I'm worse! I'm more corrupted!" he cried out. "We wanted to
transform our stolen gold into poetry, to return it to the people. For
more than ten years now, we've been making a movie about the
brave heroes who are lost in peace and lost among you . . . and
who're now falling apart, disintegrating! We've crossed all of Europe and filmed its misery and disease. We've been in Japan, at Ka-
tahira's, and seen many things which deformed, twisted people like
you would be proud of. Somewhere in Italy we met the red magus,
this one over here who's whispering something to his turtle-wife.
We would never have become what we are today—perhaps—if
it hadn't been for him. It was living with him that made us realize
we'd never finish our movie-poem, that raw, unfinished, unpolished
works are the most magnificent. Great heaps and rolls of our film
have been scattered all over Europe. Maybe one day our good-

hearted crime, our poetic, evil-minded, clownish bitterness will
sprout up from the celluloid like weeds. Yes, now you know. I'm
worse than my brother Georges! I'm a bigger scoundrel!"

"Bravo!" the entire hall roared almost in unison. "Bravo! Bravo!
Three cheers for our luckless Slavs! Bravo! We carry you on our
conscience. We've always been cruel to you Slavs! Bravo!"

"Bravo, Edgar Salomon!" they applauded the manager, who
flicked his whip, bowed, and blew kisses to the audience. "Bravo,
Edgar! You're the only one around here who knows what real
amusement is, a scenario, laughter!"

"Bravo, Salomon, you turn whatever you touch into literature
and comedy!" somebody dressed in leather shouted from the first or
second row. Edgar Salomon bowed again and, with a flourish, began
to whip the clowns, who jumped and frolicked around the stage,
partly from pain and partly from satisfaction that the audience was
enjoying their act. "Bravo! Bravo! Bravo!"

"We rascals and embezzlers live off the bad luck of others!"
Bonnefous resumed when the hubbub had died down. He placed his
hand meaningfully on Carl Schlotterer's shoulder. "We've taken this
man with us for two years now, showing him to crowds and begging with him. Wherever we went, he was known by the name of
Tedesco, which means a German. He's not dumb; he's not deaf. But
he doesn't speak. He's probably ashamed of something, we don't
know what. Probably it's just these terrible times in which he's lost
his way. We think he's a real man, a real, human man. He's
ashamed, and he blushes the way every man should blush. You can
see for yourselves that his face is made of lead, that his eyes are full
of light and tears, that he's staring fixedly at you. He has only that
overcoat on, and nothing else. If the ladies so desire, I can uncover
him for you."

"Uncover *Tedesco*, you clown!" Men and women both were
shouting and waving their whips and leather clothing. "Uncover the
Boche, clown!" A whip cracked on somebody's back. "Uncover all
of him!"

"As you will observe, ladies and gentlemen, our *Tedesco* has
nothing on under his overcoat, except for his manhood from the
north!" Georges Bonnefous puckered his lips and raised the tails of
Schlotterer's overcoat. "His body is full of scars, old wounds, burns.
He wanted to stamp on the world, but the world has trampled him
down. In my opinion, that is not the only thing he's ashamed of.
What I'd say is that he is defeated, as we're all defeated, all of us
who amuse ourselves like this. He was burning. Burns and terrible

scars are visible on his skin. You still don't know what fire, wind and flowers are. Whoever has not seen the flame, has nothing to remember.

"Ladies and gentlemen, *Tedesco* is the most beautiful living corpse among us, a corpse whose memory hasn't betrayed him, and who can't exist without other people. This half-burned-up man with his face of lead, this divine corpse, is in love with a living woman. Her name is Romana. She's a whore, of course. You must have heard of her. You must have heard her called a real miracle of peace. She is a woman who is still growing. When we last parted, she weighed over four thousand pounds! *Tedesco* loves her with his infinite German love, incomprehensible to any other nation. No force, no living force on the face of this earth, ladies and gentlemen, could divert his thoughts from her. He remembers her vividly and painfully even now. Even now he thinks of her while standing half-uncovered before you. I know him and know which act in our rich program provokes his tears the most. Should I drop his overcoat, dear ladies, or cover him up, or should we wait until it falls off by itself?"

"Bravo, Edgar!" the audience howled from the gallery and the parquet, while music boomed out and the spotlights cast multicolored lights on the stage. "Bravo, Salomon, bravo!" Almost everyone took up the cry, chanting it in unison, and Edgar flew around the stage flogging everything he could reach. "You're a genius, Edgar! A genius! Who else would have known that there's no entertainment worthy of the name without Germans, Jews, and Slavs!"

The cheering died down finally, and Antonio Peduto began.

"I'm a magus," he said to *Tedesco* and the clowns. "I'm a genuine magus, a red-bearded magus, as you said a minute ago, a magus who has changed your life and foreseen your future. It wasn't necessary for you to meet me, though. Without me, you would have been unhappy and crazy enough. Forgive the gypsy who's ruined so many of you. Forgive me, you too, *Tedesco*. The fact is, it's you and Peppino I feel most sorry for; that's no exaggeration. He's in your skin, Carl, just as he is in mine, or in Villon's. Why didn't you kill me? You, a German made of lead, a soldier with so many wounds and memories and souvenirs; why didn't you kill me that day in Montenegro? The plateau was full of flames and flowers; it looked like the moon; there was no better place for the mangy dog Peduto to perish, and thus prove that he was a man, and not a scoundrel and a gypsy. Why didn't you kill me, *Tedesco?*"

THE WAR WAS BETTER

Carl Schlotterer did not reply. He was kneeling on the stage and watched Antonio wrestling with the turtle, which it was no child's play to pull out of the bag. Antonio was tapping her shell with one hand and stroking her neck with the other. He kissed her little paws and stomach, and pressed his ear to her, trying to find the place where her faithless Balkan heart could be heard best. The Jew shouted at him and tried to prod him into continuing the story, but Antonio seemed hardly to notice him. All this incited the public to uproarious laughter. They called back and forth to each other, speaking of leather and rubber.

"The knife which François used to kill the President was mine, and I'm proud of it," Antonio Peduto revealed to the clowns and the audience. "François and I had spent a long time sharpening our knives. Then we exchanged them, like our fates. But it's still not clear to me, even now, whether a President's blood is really so sticky, foul-smelling, and green, or it just seems that way to me and Villon. Because many things seemed different to us. Before he killed him, my brother François . . ."

"Which François, Red Beard?" the Jew yelled above the enthusiastic cries of the audience. He bent over Antonio's swollen face. "Who killed whom, may I ask?" he said with a flourish and a leer. "And why didn't he do it sooner?"

"François Villon cut up the President, cut him into ribbons," Peduto went on, addressing the audience as much as Edgar Salomon. "He spilled his blood on Pigalle and unwound his long, goat's intestines. François, my brother, used to gaze at his knife for hours, feeling its point. He used to cut his hair with it, holding it, like this, between his thumb and finger in the air, while he hummed '*Tout aux tavernes et aux filles.*' And then he would throw his arms around me and . . ."

"Which Villon are you talking about, you foolish Red Beard? The poet-bandit, or the guitarist who sings in the basement across the street?"

"I'm talking about the poet . . . perhaps sent from somewhere," Peduto explained to the Jew. "He rips up whatever isn't . . . humane enough, with his knife, and with his fingernails! Every genuine poet should kill at least one President, no matter whose."

"Why?"

Rage and fear were flooding Edgar Salomon's face. He was afraid of the police. He raised his whip and flayed Antonio's bare hands and lashed even the turtle which Antonio had been trying to set up on her hind legs as part of the act. "Why? On behalf of what?"

"So," Antonio said, entirely drenched in sweat. "So that's how it is."

"Poor President," the Jew began to weep, gesturing wildly in grief so that the leather-clad audience would follow his example. "Poor, kind, noble, stingy President ... who perished on Pigalle, in this temple and house of prayer for every faith." The audience repeated the words after him, sobbed more frankly than he, brandished their whips, caressed the weeping women, and giggled hysterically.

"Poor President, suffering from diabetes and hernia! Our François killed you, our child Villon, our guitarist from the basement across the street. . . . Poor President, who left his little children and his big money uncared for . . . big money, a heap of it, a pile, earned by others' sweat, and with who else's could he earn it? With others' sweat, yes, and—it's quite possible—with a Jewish mind!"

The large hall boomed. Leather cracked. The spotlights were glued to Edgar Salomon. He began to sing to himself, and did a little dance around the stage, already confident that this act was going to be a success in a much larger, more expensive hall that he was thinking of renting the following evening.

"Our poor presidents, orphans, and rascals . . . who'll all disappear, sooner or later, who'll all die, one after the other, who'll all perish from knives and the curses of poets—men like that medieval madman, guitarist, and libertine, François de Montcorbier, nicknamed Villon because of the police, or as an alias, or simply for brevity—a pathological wreck like this red-bearded magus here, who, even while we mourn the naïve, stupid, sclerotic President of some country even more idiotic than our own, sits here stroking the neck and little paws of his turtle, calling her his love and fate. . . ."

"*Tedesco*, and all you others watching me kiss this hag's eyes," Antonio wailed, interrupting the Jew's endless litany, "I'm no longer human! People, listen to me! I have a confession to make! While my brother was killing and cutting open the President— whose blood I'd really like to drink, if it weren't so green and, no doubt, infected—I, people, I was embracing, banging, balling, and possessing my born sister's body!"

The audience paused. Even the left side of the hall, where the cowboys with long hair and the wildest sheriffs were sitting, quieted down. The one who had been making the most noise prior to Antonio's confession began to foam at the mouth. A piece of rubber was jammed in between his teeth. He rolled his eyes and pulled three others down with him onto the floor, where they rattled and trembled, driveled and gnawed their teeth. Other leather-clad youths rushed over to trample them under their boots, crush them with their knees, and beat their faces with the handles of their whips. The first and second rows were seized by a first flutter of panic. The Jew himself was frightened. He belabored the clowns and interrupted the hushed silence.

"Go on, Red Beard! Go on, gypsy!"

From the right side of the hall, his cry was taken up. "Go on!" they yelled, as they began to strip off their clothes and flog themselves. "Villon's brother, that's a laugh! It's really funny! And touching ... truly touching!" The whips cut. Backs and ribs glistened. Human skin cracked. "Ah, Red Beard! Go on! Continue! What you're talking about is painful, but so is our entertainment! Pain and blood! That's what we like! Go on!"

"Bravo, Edgar!" they cheered from the dark area at the bottom of the hall, holding up their slingshots and tearing one another's jaws apart. "Bravo, Salomon ... you know the best acts to put on with the motorcycles, and the rubber and leather!" There too, they were trampling over somebody, forcing something sticky and disgusting down his throat. "Edgar!"

"Tell us everything, *Slave!*" a man yelled from the middle of the hall. "Don't skip anything! If you leave one thing out, I'll snap your eyes out with this whip! Ha! Ha! Ha! I have a sister too. Happily a whore!" This man too was dressed entirely in leather; he was sweating so heavily that his thin hair stuck to his skull. "If she wasn't a whore, she'd be hanging on my neck all the time, like the beautiful, feeble-minded woman she is!" He wiggled his hips lasciviously and made indecent gestures with his hands. Then he took out a boxing glove from somewhere and whacked the man in front of him with it. "Go on, *Slave*, tell us. Does she know how? Mine, she's on Pigalle. ... Ha! Ha! Ha! She came from far away, from Corsica!" Those around him were taking so much room scratching and battling each other that he could not free his whip. He could only brandish it and let out a sickly giggle. "Ha! Ha! Ha! *Slave!*"

"Kill me, tear me apart before you go away!" Antonio sobbed, turning toward the clowns, the strutting Jew, and the kneeling German, and then toward the foaming audience. "She took me up to her room. We drank. A deadly fear seized me. I didn't realize it was she, I wasn't sure, I didn't know. I've been hunting her, tracking her down since I became a man, but I don't remember her face. I haven't seen it clearly in my memory for a long time. I only remember what I felt with my hands, what I seemed to tear up with my knife and my fingers and rip apart and cut into little pieces.... But she knew. She recognized me. She had no doubt. She rose first from the bed and shrieked that the same mother had given us birth!"

"We too have ... fucked our sisters!" a youth squealed in a truly inhuman voice. His chest was tattooed with motorcycles and skulls, and decorated with brass chains. "We've all fucked our sisters, Red Beard, some in thoughts and dreams, and some like you!"

The youth removed a black leather mask. The face under it was pale, sweaty, and hideously scarred. "Don't cry about it, *Slave!* Who hasn't fucked his own sister? That would be a better question. Who hasn't?"

"I don't deserve to live," Antonio cried, hugging the turtle ever more tightly. "Stamp on my neck, trample me down, cut me up; my blood is more contagious than yours!"

Cowering beside the turtle's body, he writhed and twitched on the stage where the woman had been lying. A green spotlight lit up his hands. The Jew's whip cracked. Again and again, Antonio kissed the turtle's little paws and her breast which was overgrown with green fluff.

"Sister-love," he murmured to Anna-Maria, loudly enough for half the hall to hear and remember every whisper. "Sister, my only one, *Cattolica*, I'll never, never abandon you."

"Oh, marvelous! Wonderful!" somebody cried out, and ran his hands over his ribs.

"Wonderful, and funny as hell!" another one said, pummeling the customers around him and gnawing his teeth.

Then something happened on stage that upset even Carl Schlotterer, who suddenly stood up for the first time. Sergey Ivanovich grabbed the whip from Edgar Salomon, and began to brandish it, and rage and foam. Georges Bonnefous joined him.

They threw the Jew down in front of the German's feet and threatened to tear out his throat and fling it to the audience if he so much as budged one inch, before they, loudly and clearly, told the audience what had been on their minds for so long. Throwing their arms around each other, they staggered to the edge of the stage, refused to bow as clowns should, and looked out over the mad, flogging hall.

THE WAR WAS BETTER

"We are not content with the role which life, the circus, and history have allotted us," Sergey Ivanovich began with a sad voice as he continued to brandish the whip. "Not that we want to get out of the circus altogether; it's nice here, funny, even exciting and instructive from time to time, but . . . we're fed up with the West!"

Real tears flowed down Sergey Ivanovich's foxy face. He brandished the whip again, and almost fell down. "We're sick of the West! We're sick of motorcycles and leather!"

"Everything's in leather, you mad clown!" a middle-aged gentleman bawled, while a green woman pulled him toward her like a vampire. "Everyone's in leather!"

"We can't bear leather or rubber or violence anymore!" Sergey Ivanovich almost screamed, extending his arms toward them. "We've failed in everything anyway! We're hopeless cases! We've failed even as bandits!" Sergey Ivanovich conducted Georges to the edge of the stage. They wept together. "After deliberating and calculating night and day, day and night, we have decided that communism is better for us, that it's the only system that could fill up the emptiness of our miserable, ruined souls!"

"What did you say, clown? Repeat!"

"We want to go where there's no leather, rubber, or motorcycles," Sergey Ivanovich continued. "Where there's nothing at all. They say the desert is good for the nerves and the digestion. We want to try and be happy in their way. Everybody believes in something there. They don't have to take off their clothes, because everyone is naked and good! Ladies and gentlemen, we've long dreamt of paradise; now we want to go there; we want it to come true! Understand us! Pity us!"

"What does your fat brother think about it, clown?" a leather-clad woman asked from the first row as she flung a white helmet at their feet. "I'd like to go with you, clown!"

"He, my brother, Sergey Ivanovich, a disciple of Tolstoy and Balzac, and perhaps of the devil himself, likes the people," Georges Bonnefous said, putting the helmet on his head. "He likes the people. He admires them. He respects their wisdom. He admires their sense of humor, their patience and faith."

They threw a whip to Georges, and he began to brandish and crack it.

"As for me, I deeply despise and hate the people. I'm against the masses because, as I once said in prison, they're huge and heartless. But where we've made up our minds to go, this will not hold true. Everything suits the people in the East. There's no damn-fool idea or insanity they won't accept, once you convince them that you're for progress, that is, for the triumph of those who used to be on the bottom, regardless of why. As proof we'll take these two whips with us. We'll flog whomever we catch up with, just to keep our hand in. We won't change our masks, our clothes, or even our skin. We'll weep too. Our tears will be more sincere there!"

"Take us there, clowns!" the woman raised her voice again, clapping another helmet down over her ears. "We too would like to weep more sincerely! Here they don't beat us enough. Nothing's really terrible here. Take us!"

"We're egotists, ladies and gentlemen!" Bonnefous said. "We'll go alone. Please stay where you are. We want to get there first!"

"We're leaving at once!" Sergey Ivanovich shouted.

The audience greeted this last salvo with an outburst of frenzy. They lifted their whips and began to lash themselves, even the most peaceful ones in the central rows. Everywhere, rubber, leather, and human lips were stretched. Chains jangled and motorcycles rumbled behind the scenes. Again, the smell of gasoline and sulphur filled the hall. The Jew awaited the denouement fearfully, trembling for his audience. Sergey Ivanovich kicked him with his clown's boot, and then continued.

"Georges, my fat boss, if you're not utterly drunk, if you're not terrified by whatever awaits us there, help me find my bearings! Show me the east, the countries where the sun rises!"

"Let them show us the direction," Georges Bonnefous suggested, almost paralyzed with fear. "Look, how many whips they have! Look how they're whipping each other!"

"I don't trust them anymore," Sergey Ivanovich said, turning around and around and flailing the air with his overlong shirt sleeves. "Georges, I've found it! I know which is the fateful side of the world! I've sensed it with my heart!" He sprang up and blew kisses to the audience and the Jew, who was lying in the dust, and then to the others grouped around the stage. "Georges, follow me! Follow me! Once again my nose and my heart have helped me. Come on, follow me!"

"I've always believed in you, Fox of All Foxes!" Bonnefous panted, all in tears, and set out across the hall, after Sergey. "Ladies and gentlemen, let us pass! Comrades, it's all right for you to flog each other, that is sound practice, and the road to progress, but don't lash us! Oh, it aches! Ow! You'll break every rib in our bodies! Ow! Comrades, don't embrace us, please! and don't spit so much. . . . We really want to get out of here!"

THE WAR WAS BETTER

"No, comrades, we can't, we don't dare to take off our clothes!" Sergey Ivanovich protested under a shower of blows; his arms were up around his head; he was afraid for his eyes. "Ow, that hurts! We implore you, hit us more softly, please, because there's not an inch of leather on us, except for our own skins! Spit on us, that's easier to bear. So, and thank you. Comrades, how much confidence in the working class! How much spittle! How many comradely slaps! How many disgusting curses!"

The whole hall was on its feet. The smell of leather grew more and more powerful. Edgar Salomon sat waiting on the stage. He did not know what to do. He watched even the most peaceful ones, in the corners, slap each other, pull one another's hair and flog each other. He saw the others tearing and cutting away Sergey's and Georges's clownish suits.

"Comrades, we're going where the sun rises!" Georges was crying. Blows hammered on his helmet. "There, we former men, and ruined thieves, will begin again, anew! Comrades, do you know what mercy is? Leave me at least one ear, the left one! Ah, I'm all bloody!"

"If you tear us to pieces like this tonight, nobody'll make it, nobody'll arrive at the destination, nobody'll get to paradise!"

They did not listen to Sergey anymore either. They already had both of them up on their shoulders and were trying to stuff a hard leather bullet into Sergey from behind. He continued through tears and laughter.

"If you eat us up tonight, nobody'll see what the goal even is. Leave us alone. Let us blaze the trail and show the true path. No, and one thousand times no! Ladies and gentlemen, please! We hate from the bottom of our hearts and souls this . . . thing you're trying to thrust into us from behind! No! Please! Ah, it hurts! Ow! No! Ow!"

"Lead us to the East, clowns . . . where, they say, there's no leather, no rubber, and no motors!" several women screamed as they hit them harder and more cruelly than even the most savage men. "We don't want to rot away with the West! Take us with you! We'll exchange worlds, for better or for worse, who cares? It's all the same to us!"

"Let us out, please, in the name of God and all His saints," dropped from Georges's lips. "We have no more strength or patience. We're at the end of our ropes! Where we're going there's nothing but tears and mad faith! Comrades, stop, please, it hurts!"

"What else do you want, *Slaves?*" somebody asked as the crowd flung them against the wall beside the door. "That we whip you? What do you want us to do to you, now, at the moment of farewell? We're also at the end of our ropes. We've run out of ideas. What else do you want, you mad *Slaves?*"

"To see us off like men, to bid us farewell like comrades," Sergey Ivanovich said; he was drenched in sweat and blood. "To embrace us in friendship. But afterwards, not right now, after we get out of here and find our way. It's getting terribly late."

"When do you plan to come back here, with your tanks and red flags?" a clever gentleman asked quite seriously, coughing and choking on his chewing gum. "Should we wait for you here, or jump into a pile of shit when we see you coming?"

"As you like," Georges Bonnefous replied, feeling his backside for cuts and bruises. There was a whole forest of whips around them, heaps of leather and rubber, and even a few naked motorcyclists, waiting for the door to the East to open. "Do as you like. We're for freedom of expression. To a certain extent, of course."

"What does that mean?"

"I think," Sergey Ivanovich broke in, "you'd better jump into a pile of shit. All of you should jump into shit, with your leather and all the rest of your equipment."

"And if we refuse, what then?" asked the nearest ones, whose insane eyes were bulging out. Those further away, astride their 250 and 500 c.c. motorcycles, were also staring wildly. "What will happen to us then?"

"You'll be the clowns, and we'll be the audience," Sergey Ivanovich said, sensing that he was bleeding everywhere, as if from every pore. "We'll remember your comradely spit for a long time, comrades, yes, and those hard things, everything!"

"Then forward, *Slaves!*"

The door to the East was flung open. Driven on by their sick and infallible instinct for happiness, they rushed across the threshold. Disheveled motorcyclists set off after them with a thunderous roar, waving rubber cocks. Spotlights, comradely greetings, and the cracking of whips saw them all off, and the blind race began.

"To the victory!" Sergey and Georges exclaimed. "To the dictatorship of the proletariat! To victory over rubber, leather, and bad entertainment!"

A chill rain carried by the wind awaited them on the other side. The neon lights glimmered in the rain, and old newspapers, tattered posters, and garbage were blowing across the sidewalks. They continued to run toward the East.

"To victory, Georges!" Ivanovich cried; he began to totter. "Hey, Frenchmen! Hey!"

Nobody paid any attention to Sergey's cries.

Georges slipped and fell down on his backside in a puddle. "To victory, leaves, garbage, mud!" he said, getting up. "Lord, how rumpled and spat upon we are! To victory anyway, or at least a world revolution!" He remembered the leather and rubber bullets and cocks, and felt himself where they had pierced him. "Sergey, do all revolutions begin like this?" There was no answer. "We'll take revenge on them, that's what we'll do," Georges said, beginning to run as if he saw his destination. "We'll treat them the same way!"

They reached Boulevard Rochechouart, Boulevard de la Chapelle, and then some streets leading to the East. Only an enemy's bullet or an abyss could have stopped them. A thin, chill drizzle continued to fall.

"I'm horribly hungry, Georges! Hungry and thirsty!"

At the beginning of Avenue Jean Jaurès, someone flung a round loaf of peasant bread to them, a bottle of wine, and a rubberized cape. They shivered when they first touched the rubber, and then remembered it was all over.

"The people are already helping us," Georges Bonnefous mused as he covered himself with the cape. "When we conquer, the people will feed us. We'll eat for nothing and, as for the rest, what's the difference? God, do I hate the people and rubber!"

"The people is huge, but it is heartless," Sergey Ivanovich admitted, as he moistened the bread with wine and rain. "But you have to love the masses; they always lose out. Boss, I'm getting wet."

On the long, seemingly endless Rue de Paris, their energy began noticeably to wane. Tired out, half-frozen, convinced they were following the road toward their own and others' salvation, they almost ran into a milk truck. The next truck, full of wet street cleaners singing something revolutionary and cacophonous from under their raincoats, rushed by even faster. The driver of the third truck, which was loaded with tubes, hoses, and wet rubber, honked angrily at them and spat on them from above; the street sprinklers sang.

"Capitalists, be damned!" Sergey Ivanovich and Georges Bonnefous shouted as they tumbled down behind some garbage cans. "You who cannot live without milk, leather, and repulsive rubber tubes! Rascals, man-eaters, ignoramuses! You don't even know how much it hurts us, how much it aches! Scamps!"

Trucks continued to pass, bringing with them and then carrying away the songs of the street cleaners.

THE WAR WAS BETTER

"We're on the right path," Sergey Ivanovich observed, kicking away scavenging dogs and cats as he turned over garbage cans and piled them up to build a screen against the wind and rain. "I can see almost the entire West from here. We can curse it and spit on it until morning!"

"You've had a wonderful thought, Fox of All Foxes," Georges Bonnefous said, thinking of Gruban Malić and his red globe; his teeth began to chatter. "There couldn't have been a more appropriate moment for our departure."

"They'll regret it. They'll eat themselves up with rage," Sergey Ivanovich gloated.

"Who, Fox? Who will burst from pain?"

"The West and the capitalists," Sergey Ivanovich said, counting the passing milk and sanitation trucks. "We abandoned them when they needed us most."

"It's nice that the East has accepted us," Bonnefous murmured. He was almost drunk from suffering, from the cold and everything that had happened to them that night. "It's noble too, nice and noble. In the East, there's nothing but tears and some new, mad faith. We'll begin everything anew there. We'll become equal to them in everything. We'll be good like them."

They shivered and trembled. The day seemed to have no intention of coming, and illuminating their long road to happiness. They trembled and embraced each other and waited.

Before Sergey Ivanovich and Georges Bonnefous left the hall, and before the crowd forgot them, Edgar Salomon rose from the floor and began to pace about the stage like a real clown. He did it so skillfully that even Antonio Peduto had to laugh. He tumbled, turned, and pulled his Jewish nose. Nobody looked back at the door to the East anymore, or even believed in it.

Edgar Salomon stood on his head like Ben-Gurion. He strutted about like another President, who could not see the floor under his feet because of his nose. With infinite eagerness, speed, and malice, he ridiculed the Arabs and their white-clad rulers. He rolled and sang, barked and growled.

When he thought the audience had had enough, the Jew pulled out a rope from somewhere. To the rhythm of a cacophonous brass band, accompanied by general whistling and the cracking of whips, he formed a noose and slipped it over Carl Schlotterer's head onto his neck.

The German remained quiet, with his leaden face turned toward the audience. He watched the men and women undress themselves and whip and scratch each other. Some roared from pain and delight. The German's mouth was full of spittle and dust. He stood calmly, as if patiently, looking at them all.

Edgar Salomon tightened the rope. *Tedesco* could hardly keep on his feet. Edgar Salomon waved his hand and grinned. Bathed in a spectral spotlight, and tied with the eternal rope, the Jew and the German marched across the stage. The hall thundered with applause.

"What won't you think up next, wise Salomon?"

"You're better than the Comédie Française... where there are no such acts anymore... the miserable Comédie Française, which has remained without leather, rubber, and motorcycles!"

"What are you going to do now, Edgar, you whom Chaplin himself cannot match, you who've imagined the collective pleasures of flogging and spitting?"

The great clown bowed, bending and twisting his nose and his lips. Only he could have done it without a mask. He caught several whips in mid-air, two pairs of suspenders and a yellow plastic helmet. He took a handkerchief from his breast pocket and mopped tears and saliva away. Then, panting, he said, "Ladies and gentlemen, make a passage for me! Friends, show me the door to the West! Audience, people, you for whom I live, to whom I'll devote all the powers of my heart and intellect, help me!"

"Where are you going, Jew?"

"Show me the door to the West, ladies and gentlemen!" He moaned as he got down from the stage, pulling the rope along with him. "I'm not like Sergey Ivanovich and Georges Bonnefous! I trust our own, Western happiness! Show me any door, provided it isn't the one to the East!"

"Then you don't believe in our dawn?" the ones who were slapping him and pulling his nose were screaming. "Why are you looking for the door to the West? Why don't you believe in our dawn, Jew?"

"I don't believe in the dawn from beyond!" Edgar Salomon shouted above the hubbub as he clapped the plastic helmet he had caught over his ears. "I don't believe in that kind of dawn, because I'm not Russian or Chinese. It's a lot easier for them to wait for the sun. They've got plenty of leisure time on their hands, they're insane, and, anyhow, they're in the East! Ladies and gentlemen, everyone has his own dawn and his own hope; everyone has his own anguish and his own door, and that is why I beg you to show me the door to the West...."

THE WAR WAS BETTER

"Whoever doesn't believe in both the door to the East and the door to the West, whoever, therefore, distinguishes between the two doors, and, finally, whoever is afraid of the dawn from the East as much as you are, must get this! This! Here! Take that!" Some beat him around the face and helmet. Others grabbed his legs and dragged him through the hall like a carcass, while still others bent him double, stripped off his pants and underwear, and thrust leather and rubber mushrooms into him from behind. "Take this, clown! And that! Here, Jew! Take that! And then go out through any door you like, and leave us alone, to flog ourselves until the dawn!"

The Jew was moaning under the blows and shouting something about fascism and concentration camps, but he did not let go of the rope. They punched him and twisted him and spat on him until his face and behind were dripping with blood and spittle. Somebody roared that *Tedesco* was not being tortured as he should be. They brandished their whips and leather belts menacingly. Finally, Edgar Salomon reached the door to the West, crawling on all fours, with a wedge in his flesh.

No one had touched Carl Schlotterer at all. He had followed the Jew across the hall almost erect, with his long arms hanging down at his sides. Those who peered at his face told the others they had never seen a more lifelike mask. His mouth was full of big teeth and spittle. Nobody had the slightest idea of taking the noose off his neck and freeing him.

"Jew, where are you going? What will happen to me and my *Cattolica?*" Antonio sobbed as he dragged his cart onto the stage. "Jew, hey, Jew, and all you people who are leaving, are you going to leave us alone here? Hey, Jew, sir, either take me with you, or give me *Tedesco!* Give him to me! He shines at night. He'll defend me from vampires! Jew, before you step over the threshold of the door to the West, give me back the German! I've known him for ages!"

The hall was empty and the stage quite dark.

"François, take me back into your own time," Antonio whispered, stretching out beside the cart; all his aching nerves seemed to be jangling. "François, can I go to the gallows instead of you? While I hang, you can kill the scoundrels!" He lay down on his back to calm his heart and his racing brain and pressed his eyes with the palm of his hand. "Villon, where am I? How much longer must I live among wild beasts?"

There was no reply. The sound of whip cracks, cries, and exploding fireworks came from the street outside. It seemed as if another President were crossing Pigalle and showing the maddened crowd his orthopedic shoe, size twenty or thirty. A song came from somewhere. Somebody was singing.

"Don't tremble, my wife-sister-love," he said to Anna-Maria and hugged her. "We're in total darkness now. We're on the bottom. And if we're lucky enough, we won't wake up again." He listened and heard their two hearts beating. "Let me kiss your little paws. Let me kiss your neck and your breast overgrown with hairs. Tell me that you at least love me. *Cattolica!*"

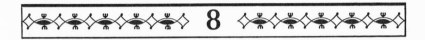

8

"Who are you?" Antonio asked the girl who was sitting in the dusk with him. "And why have you been bringing me bread and wine for the last ten days? Don't you know I'm already tired of you?"

"I don't want you to die in the sixth *arrondissement*, on my part of the sidewalk," the girl answered, watching the darkness gather around the door leading to the street.

"How much of the sidewalk is yours?" Antonio asked. He sipped some calvados from the bottle she had handed him and then placed it beside the cart with the turtle. "A mile? The whole street?"

"About twenty steps," the girl said, caressing him. "Eh, if I had the whole street!"

"What do you do?"

"I'm a poor girl from Brittany. I'm looking for a respectable job. Meanwhile, I'm going to keep those twenty steps."

"Are you happy?"

"I don't complain. This place isn't too bad. There are expensive restaurants nearby. When they eat their heads off, they sometimes pass by afterwards and throw up in the gutter. Some of them get caught in my net. The sixth *arrondissement* is one of the best, especially for girls who are as yet unknown."

"And so you've decided not to let me die?" Antonio asked her from the floor, looking up. "You tire me, and you're wasting your time. I cost you money."

"You're a substitute for my brother," she said, passing her fingers through his thick, disordered hair. "He also came here to look for a decent job, but because of the robbery and the rest of it, he was condemned to ten years of hard labor. I don't even know where he is now. But he was like you; he even drank the way you do, and kept driving me away."

"I won't be your brother," Antonio protested; in a flash, he remembered Pigalle. "I won't be! I won't! You're wonderful and foolish, but don't even try. I have a sister already, somewhere around here too; she could come by any time."

A fit of coughing interrupted him; he drank more calvados.

"You don't even know how awful a brother I am."

"You can't be worse than the one I have, rotting away at hard labor. Once he pointed his knife at me, just because I tried to kiss him."

"Why did you do that?"

"Just . . . I don't know. He has big, hard lips."

"Do you love him?"

"Yes, only him, Antonio. I'm crazy about him. I never met such a man. A secret power draws me toward him. I can't help it, I love only him; I don't hide it either. I openly desire him."

"Go, and don't come back!" he said, shocked. "You're wasting your time."

"I'm wasting nothing," the girl said. "It's raining out. They're gorging themselves now and singing. They won't be coming out for hours."

"How do you know?"

"Judging by their songs."

"Can you tell how full and happy people are that way? What course they're up to?"

"Some of them will start getting out soon, but I won't catch those."

"Who are the ones singing so savagely up there on the second floor?" Antonio's head was in her lap; he smelt her knees and thighs and opened flesh. "They were walking back and forth here for an hour, giggling. I didn't see them well; my eyes are still swollen. Do you know them?"

"Mailmen, firemen, and chimney sweeps," the girl answered, making room for his beard between her thighs. "All the uniformed personnel of the Latin Quarter. Also their officers, real ones. They're all wonderfully decorated."

"They're singing *Bataillon, tu es mes amours, / J'ai juré de t'aimer toujours.* They're singing *Y'a l'histoire du général, / Qui a fait du scandale.* Singing and swaying to the rhythm of a waltz." His head swam; he kissed and licked her knees and thighs and then descended lower, while she caressed his hair and showered his neck with kisses. "Girl, why do they have to sing that song just now? If we could only tell them to change it!"

"My brother wanted to become a *parachutiste*, too. He was always singing their songs. He used to tell me it was more honorable to be with them than with us. He daydreamed about joining the Legion and used to say that only the Legion boys knew genuine fraternity, genuine comradeship, genuine songs."

"But what are those mailmen, firemen, and chimney sweeps so proud of? Why do they sing their songs with such enthusiasm?" He embraced her, hugged her, kissed her fleshy, heavily made-up lips. "What do they want with those songs?"

"I think every mailman, fireman, and chimney sweep in the sixth *arrondissement* is a failed legionnaire," the girl observed. "Let them sing. Let them imagine they're far off, burning in the sun, and getting drenched in wild, foreign countries day and night, defending the honor of France."

She kissed his eyes and his weakened hands, and then began to play with the few remaining medals on his breast.

"Let's leave them alone tonight, to perish, courageous and invincible as they are, defending us. We all know I'll ambush them afterwards, and tomorrow, or the day after tomorrow, on Monday, their miserable mouse's job will be waiting for them. Have mercy on my legionnaires. Have mercy on the poor paratroopers of the Latin Quarter."

The mailmen, firemen and chimney sweeps, together with all their guests, including the orchestra, were singing *Bataillon, tu es mes amours,/J'te quitterai quand-même un beau jour*. Even the walls were shaking; glasses were clinking. The homeland was drunk, happy, and protected. Hugging each other, Antonio and the girl were also rocking in the waltz rhythm: *On dira que c'étaient des petits gars,/Qui n'ont pas hésité à donner leur vie,/Pour le salut de la Patrie.*

They sipped calvados. Antonio did not know where he was nor whose lips he was kissing. He spoke to her softly, yearningly. "You haven't told me who you are, but I know you. Your hair is white, like ripe oats. Isn't it so? Your eyes are blue and full of circles and dots. Do you see? I know you."

"I told you I'm from Brittany."

"You're from Montenegro. You loved Augusto Napolitano, the guitarist with metal teeth and a big Adam's apple. But he, on the other hand, loved a Bolognese girl who didn't even exist. He said she was his chosen one and sang about her to the whole Venezia Division. He refused to sing about the *Duce*, and the Black Shirts trampled him down and stamped on him on the road, grinding his bones. My Augusto sang only *porcherie*. You too, you come from Montenegro, you're the girl I talked to on the truck, in the trailer. The Germans were escorting us to the sea, the last scum and the worst army in Europe. They were beating us and spitting on us without respite. You come from Montenegro, from my other homeland, which is ravaged, burned down, dug up by grenades. You come from Montenegro and . . . If only they'd stop singing for a minute! Hey you, up there! Shut up!"

"I come from Brittany," she said, wagging her tongue drunkenly, kissing him, and beginning to get frightened. "There's no Montenegro in Brittany. Brittany is wasteland, poor and salty and wet."

"You come from Montenegro, there's no denying it. And you're the tender girl who told me she was leaving for the world so that sometime, somewhere, she would meet Augusto Napolitano. Like Peppe, you said that Augusto's heart lived and vomited and bled like a volcano when his songs weren't sung right. I remember it perfectly: you and the rest of the girls, the Balkan army of lechery and true love; you were holding me in your arms, bandaging my wounds and blowing on my burns. Afterwards I saw you in Rome, in Via dei Fiori."

"I've never been in Rome."

"You were," he insisted, squeezing her neck and beginning to kiss her eyes again. "You were, I remember it well. I was lying behind the garbage cans, beside Amalia Celestina; she and I were daydreaming about the sun, which must have been shining somewhere on those rainy days. Amalia dreamed about becoming another Romana, so that *Tedesco* would love her, *Tedesco* who had nothing to say to mankind anymore. Romana held an Orthodox icon, St. Demetrius, and sang to it in all the Balkan tongues. Romana, at that time . . ."

"Is it the same Romana who was shown to Paris for months, the one from the circus? The one who overshadowed all the women and whores of Paris?"

"Romana is only one," Antonio said. "You see, you know her. You were in Rome."

"She was here," the girl protested, feeling the calvados warming in her veins. "Piagalle had never seen anything like it. They remained on Place de la Concorde for a few months; it was the only place where they could pitch all their tents and really let themselves go. The whole company was given an excellent reception. I heard they had a more than hair-raising program. Romana gave birth, sometimes even twice a day. Her husband, an admiral or pilot or something, sang Neapolitan and Greek songs. He was a marvelous singer."

"You heard nothing more about them?"

"I think they banished them to America," the girl answered as she sipped more calvados. "Poor wretches. The Negroes will eat them up."

"No worry. They'll eat the Negroes first." He remembered them all, saw Rome again in his thoughts, the whole Via dei Serpenti. "Does it mean we'll never see them again?"

It was raining. His feet and the tails of his army overcoat were covered with the water which was pouring in from somewhere. She sat in his lap and said she wanted to embrace him and stay with him. His eyes smarted. He wished he could open them more, to see her at least a little, to remember her. He still mistook her for the girl who had been in love with Augusto.

"You see, you were in Rome. For a while, you didn't even have twenty steps of the pavement, there were so many other girls. They were densely packed, embracing each other even, weeping, flocking together, luring the liberators and the victors in that time which many thought would bring the long-awaited peace and happiness. Then one day you came and told me you had finally found Augusto. I looked at him. He was dark and tiny, almost invisible. He said his name was Augusto and that he was from Naples. He had metal teeth, pomaded hair, and a guitar on his shoulder. You were standing hand in hand. I couldn't tell which of you was happier: you, who had found Augusto, fallen in Montenegro; or he, who decided to take the name of Napolitano for your sake. You couldn't stop hugging each other."

"If I found him!" the girl sighed. "If I met him!"

"Who?"

"What does it matter? The Augusto Napolitano who died in Montenegro, or the other wretch who changed his name for love of me? I'd be kind to both of them. I'd love them as a sister loves her brothers. We'd be embracing all the time. We'd try to live on the guitar, prostitution, and song. If I only could meet both of them!"

"I don't know whether I can help you," Antonio said, thinking of the fire again, and the far-off country in the Balkans, vanishing in smoke. "You see, I know your hair is white, your eyes blue, with circles and dots, and you were in Via dei Serpenti, Via dei Fiori, and Via degli Amfibi."

"Yes, I was in all those streets, and in all the others you remember," she said, caressing him like a child. "I'm the one you remember as far back as Montenegro and Rome. Only calm down, don't shiver, and move your feet; they're getting soaked in the puddle."

"How glad I am that you're finally admitting it. So we've met again."

"We should never part again. I know I'll find a decent job and get off the sidewalk. Then, to spite everybody, I'll only walk down the middle of the street. And even if I don't find a job right away, there's bread and calvados enough for the two of us. You'll be my fiancé and brother at the same time, and I, your sister and your love. Will you?"

"Get me out of here!" Antonio gasped, choking. "Out, into the open air, I beg you!" He stood up, pulled the cart with the turtle behind him, and rushed across the threshold. "No, don't embrace me, I can't, I can't with you! You don't understand. The whole hellish story isn't clear to me either. I'll suffocate, girl! Already I can hardly breathe!"

"Where are you going, my mad brother?"

"Anna-Maria, wife-sister-love, don't be afraid, I won't deceive you!" He fell sprawling over the pavement, embracing the bag. "*Cattolica*, let's die, but not in this town. Give me your little paws; let me stuff them inside my shirt to warm them up."

"My name's also Anne-Marie, and I'm very religious," the girl cried out and ran after him. "Believe me, I believe in Christ and love Him not only with my heart, but also with my body. Wait for me!"

"My religion is different!" Antonio coughed, pushing the cart ahead of him. Rue Bonaparte, happily, sloped downwards, and the handcart went by itself. "Don't run after me!"

"Didn't you hear when I told you I was religious?" The girl ran down her part of the pavement, careful not to knock against her girl friend, who was looking up at the restaurant windows from under her umbrella, and listening to "*Bataillon, tu es mes amours.*"

"Does it mean nothing to you that I love Christ and my prisoner-brother?"

"My religion is different!" he repeated as he turned with his cart onto the level Rue Jacob. "I'm *Slave*."

"What kind of a religion is that, Beard?"

THE WAR WAS BETTER

About ten prostitutes gathered around him. Among them he could see Anne-Marie from Brittany, with her straw-white hair.

"We don't accept hatred. We don't permit it."

He was happy among women. He felt as he had that day in Montenegro, when he thought he was raping them while they carried him on a stretcher.

"We are not beasts," he said. "But you, my girls, cannot understand it."

"The Slavs are Muslim, aren't they?" one of them asked from under her umbrella. "Or Buddhists, like most of the Russians and Poles?"

He did not have time to answer. The waltz of the legionnaires was thundering out: "*On criera 'Bataillon toujours, bataillon!'*" He swayed with the song, like their umbrellas, watching them and not knowing what to say to them or how to get rid of them. They petted the turtle and offered him chocolate and American chewing gum. In his thoughts, he kissed their mouths, their thick, heavily made-up lips. He drank calvados while they touched the long, wide binoculars tied to the cart.

> *Cravate verte et képi blanc,*
> *Où t'en vas-tu, vieux légionnaire?*

The music was blaring from the two upper floors of the vast restaurant on Rue Jacob. Some of the girls could see trumpets and drums and the vibrating brass cymbals at the far end of the hall.

"Who's that singing, beauties?" Antonio asked; he was tired; he felt like slumping down beside the cart. "I think . . . I think, what do they believe in, and why are they singing just those songs?"

"Railwaymen," Anne-Marie from Brittany said through her tears. "They too think they're legionnaires. Look, how they're marching in the restaurant; they think they're reconquering Indo-China. Girls, he doesn't want me. He says he's faithful, that he has two wives already, but doesn't know where they are. Girls, tell him to take pity on me. He looks so much like my prisoner-brother. Jesus!"

"Crooks, thieves!" one of the drenched beauties shouted and began to strike the locked restaurant door with her umbrella. "Pinchpennies! Cormorants! Legionnaires! Up yours! Cuckolds! While you're dragging around France in your dirty old trains, your wives are riding the real boys and heroes, the mailmen and firemen, the chimney sweeps!"

THE WAR WAS BETTER

"Cuckolds, horses, pigs, come out, will you? Get out here on the street!" the oldest one joined in. "We've been waiting for you for hours, you boozers, you rascals and tramps! You're the hyenas, not we, we poor wretches and artists; the rain is drenching us and here we are, listening to your jangling and bellowing! Hey, our ears are full of coal and soot! Aren't you ashamed to sing those wonderful songs?"

"What's going on, beauties and artists?" Antonio asked softly as he pulled his cart along. "Isn't tomorrow the fourteenth of July, Bastille Day, our national holiday? The whole of Paris is singing."

"Tomorrow is All Souls' Day," said a girl near Anne-Marie from Brittany; she was shivering in the cold. "Oh, if it were only the fourteenth of July, I wouldn't be standing here in the rain. I'd be in Marseille, waiting for the parade and the sailors. How many uniforms there are down there! Every third man is a fireman!"

Je vais ou le bateau m'attend,
C'est mon devoir, j'aime la guerre.

"Judging by the song, the mailmen and chimney sweeps will start coming out first," Anne-Marie from Brittany remarked. "We'll attack them first. As for those cuckold-railwaymen, we'll get them at the end, at dawn."

Then they saw soldiers, about twenty of them, real legionnaires, with white hats on their heads, knapsacks on their backs, and rifles on their shoulders, with the barrels pointing down. They were wet and tired, and marched like common people. They did not even sing and embrace each other like the railwaymen, whose stamping feet and shouts *Pour l'honneur du grand légionnaire* jarred the very brain. They walked silently, as after a battle. Such an army had not marched on Rue Bonaparte or Rue Jacob for a long time.

"Hey, boys!" Antonio cried out from the sidewalk. "Are you all there? Hey, my wet boys, are there any wounded among you?" The legionnaires did not reply.

"Up and at them, girls!" Antonio said, rising to his knees. "Up against the knights! Ask them yourselves, how many are missing and whether they need anything?"

"They don't even notice us," the oldest said. "They think we're not worthy of them. Legionnaires, crackpots, children!"

"Wait a minute, my boys, at least a minute!" Antonio coughed. "So we can see you and remember you better. Hey, my strong boys!"

"Hey, boys!" Anne-Marie from Brittany stepped up toward them. "If you won't stop for us, at least stop for him, for Antonio; he's just like my prisoner-brother; he knows all your songs!"

The legionnaires were passing. Rain poured down their rifle barrels, canteens, belts, and straps. They seemed to be arriving from afar and to know their way and destination. Even if they had been singing, they would have been drowned out by the railwaymen.

"*Je ne regrette rien*," the girl without an umbrella struck up the song and stuck her tongue out at the boys, who were departing toward the end of Rue Bonaparte. "*Il était mince, il était beau, il sentait bon le sable chaud*," the girl continued, but nobody joined in. "*Il était mince, il était beau, on l'a mis sous le sable chaud ... mon légionnaire*." Not even the song could warm her up; her teeth were chattering. "*Merde, la vie! Merde!*"

"It's been wonderful to be with you, my angelic girls," Antonio said and set out hurriedly, feeling his intestines rising up toward his windpipe. "Thanks for everything! For bread! For pity! For the calvados especially!"

"Which way are you going?" the oldest girl and Anne-Marie from Brittany both inquired.

"After them," Antonio answered. "I think anyhow they're going north."

"But they're outdistancing you," Anne-Marie from Brittany warned him, pointing at the wet silhouettes of the legionnaires. "It won't be easy to catch up with them."

"They'll wait for me," Antonio said. He had a sudden urge to embrace all the girls. "They'll have to wait for me. They can't do without me, just as I can't do without them."

"Write to me if you ever reach them," Anne-Marie from Brittany said, taking a few steps after him and bursting into tears; they consoled her with a chimney sweep who emerged from a side street quite drunk, carrying a French flag on a long pole. "Antonio, write if you get anywhere."

"*Bonheur perdu, bonheur enfui, toujours je pense à cette nuit*," the girl without an umbrella sang even more sarcastically. "Anne-Marie, grab that chimney sweep, hold him tight, and don't agree to his going up there with you, on the roof. Anne-Marie, one of them once wanted to push me down from up there; that's all he wanted, nothing else. Hey, what are you doing? Hey! *Bonheur perdu ...*"

Anne-Marie and the chimney sweep lay down in the nearest doorway. They covered themselves with the tricolor and wept or laughed, it was hard to tell which; anyway they made an uproar.

THE WAR WAS BETTER

The rest of the girls were standing in the rain. They cursed the railwaymen, banged on the door with their fists and spat on the windowpanes.

"Good-by, my pearls," Antonio said. "All the same, be kinder with the railwaymen. It isn't easy to have so much soot and coal in your ears, and so many horns under your hat."

"Will you write to us, Red Beard?"

Antonio stared at them, hesitating.

"If you're illiterate, ask somebody to help you."

"I will," Antonio promised. "I'll let you know that I'm lost and happy."

"And if you never reach them?" the oldest one asked him again. "You're weak, and you're not alone. And they're used to long marches. What will you do then?"

Antonio did not answer. "Throw something on Anne-Marie and the chimney sweep," he said in a voice which almost broke. "The flag isn't enough. The night is cold, and the dawn far away."

Antonio limped up to the Seine, to the bridge, humming *On l'a trouvé dans le désert,/Il avait les beaux yeux ouverts.* The legionnaires were on the other bank. He could see their knapsacks, their spades, and their down-turned barrels. They were taking counsel, choosing the direction. He waved to them, singing *Dans quelque pays merveilleux plein de lumière.* He was still on the bridge, and they far away.

"We'll reach them sooner or later," he consoled himself and the turtle. "Maybe we're taking the same road. Maybe they're looking for the north too. Patience, *Cattolica.* Only one more little eternity, and we'll be there, up there, with them."

A cold, drizzling rain was falling. He lost sight of them and began following their footprints, sniffing and humming like the girl who had stuck out her tongue. He stopped all the passersby, asking them:

"People, have the white hats passed here?"

"White hats? There are no more white hats, *clochard.* There are black caps now. This is the time of the black caps."

"And the north, good people, is it far from here?" he asked, humming and trembling. "Probably the white hats are already there. They're waiting for me there. Will you go with me?"

Nobody wanted to listen to his story to the end, the story about the legionnaires from some other time. He spoke of his brothers, Villon and Malić, and of his son Peppe; he stretched out his arms like a cross and spoke like a child.

[369]

"Come with us, why don't you? You'll never come back from
there. Let's go right away. We'll look for the direction together.
Anyhow, I'm hungry and thirsty."

"*Ah, clochard!*" they waved at him. "Go and try it out for
yourself, how it is up there." They gave him food and asked where
he came from, so red and so bearded. "We're poor mortal men; we
like it here on earth. Go alone, *clochard*."

He sang. It was raining.

"*Cattolica*, who'd have thought it would take us a full ten days
and ten nights to get out of Paris?" Antonio looked back and saw
chimneys and clouds above the roofs. "A little longer, and we'll be
with them."

He liked Paris. He was shivering.

"Good-by, city. I'll never come to you again. Nevermore. Don't
be mad at me, a miserable *clochard*. And good-by, this time forever!"

Antonio's eyes were full of fog, white hats, and cold. He did not
realize how vast Paris was. He did not know how he could pardon
all of them, for everything, but he could, he did.

"Good-by, Red Beard!" they were calling.

And the legionnaires were marching across the sky.

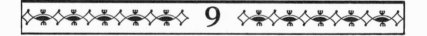

9

Antonio came to the village of Yebles, near Rouen, at dawn,
with one medal less. He dallied around the church until noon—
lucky it was a Sunday. Widows noticed him. The pinkest and fattest one, Claude-Clarisse, approached him and led him to her house.
She fed his turtle and told her something tender and vague. She
showed him a warm stove and a dish of cooked beets.

"Eat, soldier!"

All her children stared at him. Antonio winked to them. He
drank cider and told them he wasn't French, but knew a lot of stories and jokes anyway.

"Stay here, why not?" the widow Claude-Clarisse invited him.
Her breasts and the skin below her navel and around her loins were
tingling. "You'll have food and drink enough. And for the rest, the
good God may care."

"May the God you're talking about bless Normandy, the coun-

THE WAR WAS BETTER

try of good people, good cheese and cider, and all the rest He may keep for Himself and those nearest and dearest to Him."

"Remain here, and you'll have meat too," Claude-Clarisse went on. "Stay here for a while; why not?"

"Was our papa such a soldier too?" the children asked. "And did he like to eat cooked beets? Perhaps you know where our poor papa perished, defending France in Africa?"

"Poor papa liked cooked beets very much, but he didn't refuse meat either, or cider," the widow Claude-Clarisse informed them as she pushed a new dish and another bottle toward Antonio. "He knew our poor papa. He says he was an exceptionally gallant man, and always gay."

"Tell us, uncle, about our papa. We don't even know where his grave is," the children said eagerly. "And stay as long as you can." The children were climbing over him, in his lap, on his shoulders. "Were his last words really that honor was more important than anything else, even life?"

"The children of all France will learn about the courage and integrity of your papa," the village priest, Paul de Goustine, answered for Antonio, as he poured wine for himself and the guest. "He was a Christian. Let's drink today to his decent soul!"

"He was killed beside me, Father!" Antonio said, embracing the priest. They began to clink their glasses. "He deserves to be talked about to the end. What a warrior!"

The children crossed themselves. Claude-Clarisse kept her hand on her stomach. Antonio Peduto and the priest Paul de Goustine wept frankly and drank until late at night.

Antonio guarded her pigs and the calves of most of the neighbors. His eyes were no longer swollen, but they grew moist more often, especially when he laughed. Claude-Clarisse gave him the suit of clothes of her late father-in-law, and even his rank badges and medals from the Franco-Prussian or some other important war. Antonio hurried to the priest to boast of it.

Paul de Goustine stroked his little beard and mustaches and sighed. Then he said that the village of Yebles had not had such a shepherd and faithful church-goer since its inception.

Antonio Peduto saluted; his medals jingled. The handsome priest, with kind blue eyes, embraced him with all his heart. He repeated once again that he was for harmony among people, and opened a bottle of cider. Antonio talked to him about Montenegro and Greece. The priest did not know how to stop his tears. He hiccuped.

THE WAR WAS BETTER

The village of Yebles was content. Their shepherd and soldier watched over the cattle with his binoculars, kept a lookout on the surrounding hills, and forecast the weather. They were angry with him, however, for talking so much about arson and fires, comparing them to flowers.

Instead of a fire, a thief appeared in the village. The smallest suckling pig disappeared, and then the damn thief stole a rooster. Antonio was overwhelmed with sorrow and remorse. It was his fault that the thief had gotten away. From the stable where he had been sleeping, he moved to the hayloft.

"You don't deserve even this," he accused himself, wiping his tears with straw. "You'd better disappear. You'd better just get out of here, and not dishonor this uniform and these medals anymore."

Paul de Goustine came and tried to confess him over a bottle. Antonio spoke of fire like a Catholic, but the priest could not understand him, and drank for both of them. Another rooster disappeared.

"Stay on, don't weep," Claude-Clarisse invited him. "My pigs have gotten used to you."

"And our calves are happy with you," the rest of the widows and other women said. "Stay as long as you like, that is until the arrival of the ship you've been talking about for months now. Stay and don't be sad. The thief has been caught. An Italian! He's been taken to prison."

"You don't know his name?"

"He was caught with my rooster in his hands," a widow informed him. "He was plucking him and smothering him on a fire. Then he tore him, half-alive, with his teeth. He was taken to Paris."

All the widows got to like him. They chased him in the fields, leapt after him into the hay, and ambushed him around the pigpens.

"*Slave*," they murmured to him. "Don't run away. In this village, every female that walks on two legs loves you! Every female, and not only walking on two legs, but also on four," they went on, thinking he was almost in their clutches. "Our heifers and cows, our sows, our turkey-hens, our bitches. Don't run away! Stay in Yebles as long as you like, as long as you can." They kept at his heels, two or three even with knives. "*Slave*, every female loves you! Even Father Paul de Goustine loves you!"

"But I'm faithful," he answered from the hen-house.

"To whom, our good and wonderful *Slave?*" One of them had a rope, a real lasso. "To whom are you faithful? Why are you telling us about it?"

THE WAR WAS BETTER

"I don't know," Antonio said, thinking of his sister and Anne-Marie. "I don't know how to explain it to you."

He was expecting an attack. He could hear their breathing. His overlarge pants-legs were trembling.

"I'll stay until the ship comes, or at least until somebody comes to get me from my own batallion, if you'll truly forgive me for the disappearance of the suckling pig and the two roosters, and give me a French widow's word of honor that when you catch me and push me on my back, you won't tickle me, or at least not so much."

They usually caressed and combed him between the hen-house and the dog-house. There he would stretch himself out on the grass and give himself up completely. Lying in this position, he could see only the village children making fires and running around in circles, armed with arrows and real axes and yelling like wild Indians. They were setting fire to last year's straw, scraps, and earth. Memories and tears welled up in Antonio. He lay back with his eyes closed and smelled the smoke and the women who were caressing him.

Claude-Clarisse was tenderest; he was mostly hers. "Redhead! Redhead!" she murmured and thrust her hands under his shirt, into his pants. "Don't be afraid of children's fires. The war is forgotten. Happiness and peace reign throughout France. Everybody in Yebles has been saying that for ten years now." She leaned her cheek on his again and defended him with her elbows from the other peasant women. "Redhead, the children are only playing. They know how much you like flames." Lust consumed her. She sweated. Her mouth watered with lust.

"Claude-Clarisse, everything has its limits," Paul de Goustine whispered from the haystack as he watched the widow kiss Antonio's hairy chest. "Sinner, don't forget that you're the mother of five unprotected orphans, that you're a warrior's widow, who left his bones in Africa so it would be nice for us here in France, that the fate of many pigs, calves, and chickens depends upon whom and how you love."

Paul de Goustine closed his eyes and drank. As usual when sinful feelings and his doglike jealousy seized him, his stomach ached. He himself, like Antonio, breathed in the smell of smoke and the musk of the long-unwashed and stirred-up woman's body. He prayed within himself, invoking the help of fire and the sky.

Antonio lay back with his arms stretched out, as if crucified. It seemed to him that he was encircled by mountains which were being more and more consumed by fire, and that all his exits had been cut off. A pleasant drowsiness entangled his eyelashes; he remembered Bijelo Polje and the villages in which Gruban Malić had crusaded, chasing after food and the headquarters of the 501st Montenegrin Army. There had been no army. Almost dwarfed in his ill-fitting forest ranger's suit, Malić had roamed through Montenegro, frightening the poor with red paint and communism.

"You'll get pregnant, you're stroking and nibbling and kissing me so much," Antonio warned the widows, who were ready to tear him apart with their nails and teeth. "That's what I'm really afraid of. Watch out whose medals you're decorating me with and what names you're calling me."

"Jesus, I pray you to unleash on the so far honest and pious Yebles a great flood or fire, and to call to reason and return all of us to your fold." The priest was following Claude-Clarisse's eager hand with his starved eyes. He imagined himself in Antonio's place and in his uniform. "I want to burn up in hay, beside them. I want to disappear in smoke and flames, sinful and drunk. Jesus, give me back my spirit which You alone have planted in me, and the peace which I've lost. Have mercy on me, oh Christ, and lead Antonio far away. Every third word of his is flame."

"Tell us again about the whores, *Slave*."

"Why just about them, girls? Why not about saints?"

"Because all of us wanted to become whores," one of them said, as she stroked his giant binoculars with which, when it was clear, he could see as far as the sea.

"Why haven't you, then?"

"Marriages."

"That doesn't bother real whores. It's only then that they start."

"Then the First and Second World Wars came. Our husbands haven't returned. Yebles is a wasteland! All the armies, especially the Allied ones, have gone through here."

"I'm sorry," Antonio said, breathing in the odor of cheese, dung, and poultry. "I'm sorry Yebles is so barren, and you've never got acquainted with soldiers." They kissed his hands, his neck, his medals. "Perhaps it's still not too late. If you let me go today, alive and uninjured, I'll come back with a batallion. What I'd like most is to bring back a whole shipful of sailors!"

Cider and jealousy were eating up Paul de Goustine's stomach. He lay in the hay, naked and desperate. He wanted to run across the pasture, jump off the little bridge, and splash into the river, but he did not know how.

"Tell us about Marika, the one from your village. What happened afterwards, after she swam through the communist mines which the whole Adriatic was bristling with, and arrived in Italy and Rome?"

"They were all asking for her hand and consent, offering her thrones," Antonio said. "'Montenegrin Princess, Princess and beauty, who've come from the war as the only victor, have mercy on me and my poor people; I come from Benelux,' a pale Prince began first, chewing his American chewing gum like a calf. 'Princess, angel of romantic Montenegro, which I know from English and German travel brochures and various tall stories, don't despise my Scandinavia, don't reject me, we'll love you; we're crazy about exotic women up there,' the partly deaf Scandinavian stuttered. 'Half the infantry and cavalry, and a good part of the air force, will be placed under your command,' the third Prince said. 'Unfortunately, I already gave all the donkeys and mules to a girl who eloped with my driver and abandoned me to God and your mercy!'"

"'Over how many souls do you reign?' my little Montenegrin sister inquired of one after the other. 'How many people are under you?'"

"Did they lie?" the widows asked Antonio. "Did they exaggerate?"

"They were honest," Antonio answered. "That's how their feet got stuck in their mouths."

"What did she answer then, Antonio?" the widows drank more cider. "Did she show any mercy?"

"'What little power you have!' That's how Marika dismissed them. 'I piss on all this poverty of yours! What are three, five, seven, or even ten million souls . . . for Marika?!'"

"'Princess, don't let us die, don't kill us like dogs!' they wailed right there on the Roman streets, in front of all of us. 'Choose among us. We love you and we're ready to eat from your hand, to kiss and lick your fingers, to be your puppies, your rag-dolls, your children! Don't punish our nations. All we want is to make them happy, with you.'

"'Marika Popović has decided to become the Queen of Italy,' she said and kicked one of them; he remained sprawled on the sidewalk, sticking out his tongue. 'I've heard there are more than two hundred million Italians. That's a large flock of sheep! Their last Queen was a Montenegrin too, the miserable Jelena. They're fated to be led and pulled by their noses by Montenegrin whores. That's my decision. Now beat it!'

"'But their King, Umberto, has been banished. He's in exile.'

"'So what? The only important thing is that I become their

THE WAR WAS BETTER

Queen, and that it be well known,' she replied, throwing back her thick black hair. "And whether I live in this or that country, that is unimportant. Umberto is important!' "

"And did she become the Queen, Antonio?" the widows asked.

"Of course she did," Antonio answered, and in his thoughts he led Marika Popović all the way to Lisbon. "And remember, my little Norman girls, she isn't the only whore with a crown on her head."

"How miserable we are, we widows who're combing and nibbling and touching you," the red-haired Claude-Clarisse lamented. "We've not even reached the rank of whores, like the rest of the really intelligent women. We've never even seen a crown either. Poor us, the honest ones, from the village of Yebles!"

"God sees everything, sinful Claude-Clarisse!" Paul de Goustine cried and, naked and skinny as he was, rushed past the pigpen and the hen-house. "God sees everything and hears everything! Nothing can be hidden from Him and heaven!" He covered himself in front and behind with some hay, and ran toward the little bridge and the river. "God is good, Claude-Clarisse, but He won't pardon everybody! He won't want to! He won't be able to!" he concluded and splashed into a whirlpool. There was still some hay left on the bridge.

"If I survive this wretched peace, girls, I promise to send you a man among men," Antonio said, as he watched Paul de Goustine wave his arms at them and threaten them with heaven. "He'll come on a donkey, with a globe, and demand that you surrender. Don't give in right away, fight a little, and don't worry about happiness. He's from my own village. His name is Malić. He's a real knight with a pale face, a knight who always lives in a dream."

"Let him hurry up, if he really intends to come," said Aunt Jacqueline, Claude-Clarisse's relative. "Some of us have one foot in the grave, so he'd better get here as soon as possible. Anyhow, you don't let us touch you down there and put our tongues in your mouth."

"Throw me some underwear!" Paul de Goustine shouted from the river. "I'll never hold out in this water as long as I could on land! Any kind of underwear, even female underwear; hay doesn't work!" His torso emerged from the waves down to his waist. Almost all his ribs appeared. "Underwear, please . . . I'm scared! I've just seen a fish! Claude-Clarisse, Christ's daughter, fling me something, anything! I'm no longer desperate or jealous. Hurry!"

The swineherds from the other bank of the river did not remain deaf to the priest's cries. They brought him an armful of hay. Paul de Goustine crossed himself on the bridge. He prayed for rain and hail and even mentioned fire.

"Marika Popović was in France," Antonio continued, thinking with increasing vividness of Bijelo Polje, the amorous Venezia and Murge divisions, and General Giovanni Besta, whom she had ridden the longest. "She came from her exile and asked them to introduce her to Louis XIV as the Italian Queen."

"Why just to him?"

" 'I want him,' she insisted. 'I've heard he's magnificent in bed.' "

" 'But he's no more, *il est disparu,*' the French said. They were up a tree, guiding her around Paris; they didn't know what to do. 'Louis XIV is no more; he isn't here. He isn't.'

" 'How isn't he if I see his furniture everywhere? Even Umberto and I have it in Lisbon. I want him, a real man finally, an artist of lovemaking.' "

"What happened afterward, *Slave,* when they proved to her he was no more?"

" 'Take me to Versailles, show me his bed,' she demanded. When they had obeyed, she said, 'I'll wait for him,' and lay down."

"Did he come, Antonio? How could Louis XIV come?"

"French museum bugs were biting Queen Marika until midnight, but she waited anyway, whispering again and again, 'Louis, where are you?' Then around midnight a man in his fifties appeared, dressed in a suit from the royal times, with a powdered wig and tight britches. He sat down on the edge of the bed and began to kiss her hands and knees and her wonderful black locks. 'Louis XIV, you're the only king who'll be able to satisfy me,' she said, letting him lie, clothed as he was, between her legs. He hesitated for some time, and then began: 'The history of France—is a history of cheese. You must listen to the end. Then it will be clear to you why we've become what we are.' She spread her legs wider, like me now. She closed her eyes. She waited the sting of the King's famous horn."

"Did she hold out?" Aunt Jacqueline's voice quivered.

"It wasn't easy for her. The story was long, and while he told it, he kept taking cheeses out of his side-pockets, his breast-pockets, his cape, from everywhere; some were overripe and some even had little worms in them and they all smelled like the devil. He demonstrated how they should be sniffed, eaten, or licked. Sometimes he lay beside her, sometimes on top of her. His wig kept slipping off, and she adjusted it. When he looked up at the ceiling, rolling his eyes and speaking of God, the only and greatest friend of his country, Marika slipped his pants down his hips. He didn't even notice it. He was the true *Roi-soleil:* he either prayed or listed the names of cheeses.

"He started tickling her, kissing and smearing her with saliva, licking her and stuffing cheese into all the holes she had in her royal body. Camembert, Livarot, and Pont l'Évêque were the hardest for her to suffer. It was mostly Roquefort, Munster, and another one, which stank from a mile away, which he had stuffed between her legs. 'Louis, do you always begin like this?' she asked him, suffocating in the stench and watching him tremble like a butterfly as he tortured her. 'Louis XIV, for God's sake, for the sake of glory and honor, take the damn Livarot out of me!' He didn't listen to her. He wanted her to depart from his land—that is, your land, from France—full of cheese. And so it was. She left unhappy and disappointed. All of Lisbon gossiped about it afterwards, and tried to smell the Camembert on her."

"I don't believe it was Louis XIV," Aunt Jacqueline remarked while the other widows almost wept for the unsatisfied Queen. "Louis wasn't one to leave a woman like that. It's well-known that he was born with two teeth, and that the breasts of his nurses were always bloody. Who was it, *Slave?*"

"The night guard of the museum," Antonio said, embracing them and laughing so hard that his stomach ached. "The poor night guard, Louis XIV!"

"Be more gentle with the Sun King and history!" Paul de Goustine said, raising his arm threateningly as he ran past and thus uncovering his chest. "Louis XIV was religious, and all the stories about his lechery were thought up by anarchists and communists!"

Paul de Goustine ran back into the hen-house and hid there, drenched and jealous. He finally came back through the wrong door, stumbled on a heap of feathers and fell down. He began to cough violently and almost suffocated.

Until the spring, Yebles entertained itself with the story of the impotent Louis XIV, and with the unwilling Antonio. Then, in the darkness and hay, Claude-Clarisse confided something to Antonio.

"*Slave*, I love you with all my Norman heart. But I've sinned and conceived with Paul."

"Didn't he have hay in front and behind?"

"He was quite naked, and I was as you see me now, in black clothes. He always used to undress down to his skin whenever rage and jealousy seized him. 'I'll either kill Antonio, or put it to you a little, on the side,' he said. 'Sometimes, Claude-Clarisse, God closes one eye.' That's how he put it: 'closes one eye.' And because of you, not for my own sake, I let him irrigate me. I'm in the fourth month now. Do I hear the bells? He can't sleep, and he's giving me a signal, or else he's drunk again. *Slave*, your sins are nothing compared to mine."

"Claude-Clarisse, my wonderful girl, it would have been better to let him charge after me than you," he said and embraced her and kissed her through the hay for the first time. "God is good and omnipotent, as you yourselves say. Let Him assist you. Let Him blink at it. Let him shut His eyes." The bells were ringing, waking up the hens and the pigs. "Show me the north; my time here has run out. The ship has been in the port for weeks, waiting just for me. You've saved my life, but I must go. I'll long remember you, especially if you stop kissing me now, and licking me, and wetting me with your tears."

"If I saved your head, *Slave*, you must save my honor," she said, stuffing cheese which stank of poultry down his throat. "Agree to our wedding. You can do it. You're a warrior. Warriors don't mind. They're irresponsible. For reward, take half the cattle and go to that damn ship of yours. And if that's too little for you, I'll give you some money too. These are rude, dog years; you know it yourself."

The wedding was prepared for a full seven days, not counting the eighth, Sunday, when it took place. The widows baked bread, poured cider and heaped cheese on the plates. Aunt Jacqueline and Paul de Goustine killed suckling pigs, calves, and poultry with terrifying speed. After plucking the geese and the ducks, the priest literally ran to the church to practice the ceremony, as it was whispered, and prepare the sermon. With the exception of Claude-Clarisse and Antonio, nobody knew why he hurried so much and why he was so deathly pale.

Antonio Peduto packed his cart, oiled the binoculars, and cleaned the hunting rifle without bullets. Standing beside a herd of swine, he shouted:

"Claude-Clarisse, stop killing; don't annihilate your whole stock! We have five children. You said yourself these were inhuman times, dog years, and there are more and more unhappy and hungry people. Five children, today! And the sixth is on the way!"

"One lives only once," the bride answered, covered with flour and dough. "One lives only once, Red Beard, and dies several times."

"What do you think you'll die from, beauty?"

THE WAR WAS BETTER

"From love and fear."

"Don't be afraid, Claude-Clarisse," the swineherd, with a ribbon of the Legion of Honor across his vast, medal-studded jacket, said to cheer her up. "Don't be afraid, my pearl. I won't leave before the wedding!"

"Then I'll die from happiness," Claude-Clarisse said, and blushed, for she was surrounded by the other women. She sent the priest and her oldest little son to him with a roasted boar's head, a dish of cooked beets and a bottle. "From the happiness that you've come to Yebles," she called out, "and fallen in love with Normandy."

"Why are you weeping, Peduto?"

"For the little roosters which they're slaughtering and plucking so insanely," he answered the priest and the boy. "For the red cocks; for them I'm weeping. Paul, I'm a kind of Hindu. The cock is, for me, a sacred animal. Tell them yourself, shout to them: they should not kill them like this. We're poor, anyhow. It's not good to waste everything like this."

"One marries only once," Paul de Goustine remarked. "Once or never. And God knows which is worse."

Antonio wept for the cocks. It seemed to him that their spilled blood was coloring the sky and the sun setting in the west. Then he watched Paul de Goustine and the children set fire to heaps of hay, straw, and scraps. A flaming wreath encircled Yebles. Dogs were barking everywhere, some of the moon and the stars, and others at the crazy blackcoat and the wild children who carried torches and threatened to burn up everything ugly and dishonest in their village.

"What are you doing?"

"As one lives and marries only once, one burns once too," Paul de Goustine said, all red from flames and happiness. "Once or never, Antonio."

"If you continue like that, the earth itself will burn up," the swineherd protested softly, with his long binoculars and the hunting rifle across his shoulders. "The earth, the whole earth, and my own home will burn up," he added, pulling the turtle along among the fires and remembering Montenegro. "What will I do then, without my homeland? The earth will burn up!"

"It isn't easy to burn up Normandy," Paul de Goustine said as he shook ashes from his shoulders and beard. "Normandy is wet and big and gallant!"

"How large is it?" Antonio asked softly. "Like my Montenegro?"

THE WAR WAS BETTER

"Normandy is bigger than France, my dear, wonderful papa," the boy said, clinging to Antonio. "Don't weep for your homeland, or for the cocks. I'll bring you more cider if you let us burn up everything, whatever we come across. I'm having so much fun, good beard! With you, I've forgotten that I'm an orphan, ashamed, and afraid of other children!"

"I don't understand you very well, son."

"One lives and marries once, and burns only once," the boy said. "We'll burn everything down! We'll spare only your homeland, which you remember whenever you eat cooked beets with us."

"Will you take me sometime to Montenegro?" Paul de Goustine murmured. "I promise, as the boy has promised, we won't let a single flame touch it." Drenched in sweat, he watched fearfully as Antonio crawled on all fours around the church before returning to his shed. "Antonio, promise me before we part that someday you'll take me to the country where evil was planted like seeds and burst into flame."

"Wouldn't you also plant something there?" the swineherd asked softly, taking pains to stand up straight beside the turtle and the church wall.

"You're talking sin again," Paul de Goustine protested, holding him up. "A sin, especially a grievous sin, should be forgotten as soon as possible. Don't you find the night beautiful but suddenly cold?"

Antonio Peduto looked at the flames which prevented him from seeing all the Norman stars. Then he kissed the priest's hands, which smelled of ashes, cheese, and boiled feathers. He asked him to forgive him everything, and particularly his coming to Yebles and his long stay.

"It's been an angel's stay," Paul de Goustine remarked, fearing that Antonio, as usual when it was cold, would seize his hands and stuff them under his shirt to warm them up. "It's been a Slavic angel's stay."

"I'll be good at the wedding tomorrow," Antonio whispered, wishing that the flames which were now subsiding would never cease. "I'll only say things that will be dear to God, angels, and the village firemen, who are mad at all of us. Father, embrace me and kiss me. And tell me that the earth won't burn up."

They embraced. The priest's ribs began to crack. They kissed each other's foreheads. The west wind was bringing the sound of barking dogs and the stench of buried bones and garbage. They stood there for a long time, leaning against the wall.

Drunk partly from cider and fire, and partly from Antonio's

kindness, Paul de Goustine rang the bells until dawn. He prayed at the same time for the peace of all the souls whom his brother Antonio Peduto had met and come to love, and for the salvation and happiness of all those whom the good God had recently created with His spirit and His omnipotent will. In his prayers he mentioned Montenegro, the country of heroes devoted to Christ, and brought it into connection with Normandy, and even with Spain and Russia. The sun and Sunday found him weeping before the *Madonna*.

Before the altar, Antonio swore loyalty until death. Claude-Clarisse and the children burst out crying. Antonio remembered Villon and Peppe. When the organ began to play, it seemed to him that the sound was visible, and that snakes and flames were beginning to lick the ceiling of the church. He remained on his feet and repeated that he would be devoted to all those to whom he had given his word, not only during his life, but also afterwards. One of the old women yelled from the crowd that Peduto was one of the rare swineherds, if not the only one, who deserved the *Légion d'Honneur* and other medals. Then Antonio stretched out his arms, received Claude-Clarisse on his bosom, caressed the children, and felt like embracing the whole church and all those present.

Hugging each other joyfully, Antonio and Paul sat at the head of the table which extended down the entire churchyard. They toasted the inhabitants of Yebles, Normandy, and the whole of France. They taught the drunken wedding guests how to sing Montenegrin, Greek, and other songs from the Balkans.

They were the first to start playing. Sometimes they conducted; sometimes they pulled the accordion out and played beside the table and the cross. Paul de Goustine spoke at length about peace, happiness, equality among Frenchmen and finally about the year which all hoped would be fruitful, in spite of a dry spell and then heavy Atlantic rains.

"Now, friends and brothers, I'm going," Antonio spoke up before dusk, when the first cloud covered the table and the church in shade. "As you know very well, for I've been telling you all this time, my ship is waiting for me. Now my moment to go has come. I must go now to meet my comrades who've been searching the entire globe for me."

"You could spend at least your first wedded night at Yebles," Paul de Goustine suggested and let the extended accordion drop from his lap. "Custom is custom, our *Slave*."

"I've spent wonderful nights in Yebles, Father, unforgettable nights, my friends," Antonio said as he picked up the accordion and gave the other end to the priest, who began to sing. "All of them have been wedding nights and full of stars, smelling of hay, your healthy cattle, and poultry."

Lightly touching the keyboard, Paul de Goustine and Antonio Peduto pushed the soup-and-wine-stained bellows of the accordion closer and closer until it closed with a gasp. The priest's face was pale and sweaty; his stomach cramp was acting up again. Antonio could tell that there was nothing the priest would rather have done at that moment than strip off his black rags and borrowed medals and splash into the river. He looked fearfully at Claude-Clarisse, who was sitting between them, and then at the closed accordion. Then he said:

"Our *Slave*, warrior, and hero, whose chest is decorated with the medals of almost the entire globe, tell us now, on the point of your departure, whether all the Norman nights which you have spent here have been an expression of the Love that moves the world? Was everything as our church, our religion, and our customs decree?"

"Father, everything that has taken place has happened through God's will, wish, and suggestion," Antonio answered and crossed himself. "Everything has been as it is written in the sacred books, and in books in general."

"Now we can all relax," the priest said. "Let's embrace and see him off singing!"

They began singing folk songs, first Greek and Balkan ones, and then Augusto's, without knowing their meaning, repeating the unintelligible words and cries and accompanying them with the gestures which Antonio and Paul de Goustine had taught them.

"If it's a boy, what should we name him?"

"I don't acknowledge female children, Claude-Clarisse," Antonio declared, allowing them to cram his pockets with goose legs, bones, and cheese as he tied the binoculars firmly to the bag with the turtle. "Since, therefore, he will be a son, call him Malić."

"Is that a first name or a last name?"

"Both, Claude-Clarisse," Antonio said. For the second time since they had been together, he kissed her big lips and eyes. Watching the neighbors and the priest, she did not close them. "The boys bearing that name are already being compared to great conquerors, the most terrifying warriors in human history!"

They saw him off with singing and tears. They walked behind him, pulling the tails of his ancient French overcoat. The little cocks, cows, and sows who had survived the feast also cried. The bitches barked as if some suspicious person were arriving. The bells rang out, and there was no wailing, no accordion, and no wind which could have drowned them out.

"Don't go! Don't go! Don't abandon us!" the children cried, barring his way, falling down around his swineherd's boots and cart. "Now we're double orphans!"

"Your father was a truly gallant man; he coveted honor more than any other Frenchman," Antonio said loudly, so that the wedding guests and the priest could also hear him. "And if he hadn't been, his name wouldn't be written, as it is now, with big, black letters in the pages of French history. He excelled in everything. He had even more medals and ribbons than I do. Compared to him, I'm a good-for-nothing, a dog, a good-for-nothing twice over. He could eat up enough cooked beets for three Germans. The only thing I've done more than him is get drunk."

Then he began to pull away his handcart packed with gifts.

"Good-by, Normandy!" he sobbed. "Good-by, my wonderful country. I'll carry you in my heart till the end of my days!" he waved to them, taking care that the old double-barreled, cartridge-less hunting rifle should not slip down from his shoulder. "Good-by, children, my orphans!"

Yebles remained to celebrate the wedding and tell the story: there was once a *Slave* who knew all kinds of things and never stopped once he started talking about something. He had waited so long for his warship to come, and loved it so much, that he did not even spend his first married night with the blossoming Claude-Clarisse, but set out instead, toward the sea, driven on by his insatiable desire for distant lands, fire, and war.

"I'm François Villon's brother," Antonio introduced himself when he arrived, drenched, in the hamlet of La Bassée. "I'm the great Villon's younger brother."

"Then sit down and dry out," the innkeeper invited him. "I buy his meat. His is the best in this part of France."

From beside the stove, Antonio saw that he was among drunkards, and that the innkeeper was even less steady on his legs than he. Peduto let the rain drip down from his clothes, smoked, and drank. With a tight, dimly glowing face, the innkeeper filled up his glass again and moaned. Everyone was singing.

"Why is Villon's meat the best?" Antonio asked, rising to reach the bottle. "Is it only because it's human?"

"It's fresh, therefore it's best, for no other reason," the innkeeper explained, asking him, by the way, where he had come by such a beard and so many ribbons and medals. "Villon's meat is fresh, and almost always without tendons. And finally, you can get it any time you like."

They were sitting around the stove and the tables and, since there were no midnight guests anymore, drank cheap wines and calvados. It was raining. Roosters and neighbors were beginning to wake up. When dawn came, Antonio wriggled out of the innkeeper's drunken embrace.

"Does it mean, old one," he asked, "that François Villon is the best butcher in these parts?"

"Perhaps in the whole of France," the innkeeper answered as he opened the door, and the first guests and drunkards of the new day staggered in, bringing with them the wind and the rain. "Villon is merciless. All he does is kill! Kills and chops and cuts. And all by himself, too, because he doesn't trust anyone else. Didn't you know that?"

"I've been away for a long time," Antonio said.

"Well, we're all, in a certain sense, absent."

"I've been fighting," Antonio went on. "I'm still fighting. Didn't you notice?"

"Villon told me many times that he loved knives ever since his childhood, so much, in fact, that later on he took one with him wherever he went, even to shit," the old man said and mused. "We never knew he had such a red and decorated brother! Think of that!"

"There are more of us. We're scattered over the earth and in cafés. We're so many that we don't even know each other. Knives and kindness are in our blood; they're what we punish people with."

"He's been as good as his word. He's known how to wait, giving with an open hand," the walrus said. "If I'm not mistaken, the village is still indebted to him."

"Where is he now, by the way, while we sit here drinking? Can a glass and a story about a knife go without him? Where is he now?"

"Villon?"

"Yes, old one. François Villon. Why doesn't he come?"

"But he's died," the innkeeper answered and his face turned the color of the earth. "My condolences. He was a man who could laugh even with blood on his face."

THE WAR WAS BETTER

The old man shook silently and suddenly fell over. The most recently arrived drunks lifted him from the floor and placed him beside the stove.

"I think I attended his funeral. Although he wasn't from here, the village saw him off nicely. He was a carouser, a hothead, and a skirt-chaser. He aided the poor—every fifth child here, like your brother, has white eyelashes and droopy ears, like a spaniel's."

"Where do you get your supplies now?"

"At his place—didn't I tell you that already?" the innkeeper answered as he lifted his bulky belly up on the stove to warm it. "His meat is still the best. There's no tendons, which is rare nowadays. Villon kills, peels, chops, and cuts by himself, since he doesn't trust anyone else."

Restlessness overwhelmed Antonio in the spring. As soon as the sun got warm, he went up to the innkeeper and stood motionless before him like a soldier at attention. He told him he yearned for distances, flowers, and the sea.

"Whom will you go there with?"

"Soldiers are waiting for me, perhaps a ship too," Antonio said. "Soldiers and brothers. We're going to conquer the north."

"So," the innkeeper said. "They should be treated sharply, the worse the better. They'll never understand poverty the way your François did. But better to wait one or two years."

"I'm indebted to you," Antonio said to him before the other drunkards as he adjusted his ribbons and medals. "You've fed me and given me drinks and tobacco. I've been wearing your underwear. I'm leaving the shed and the loft in disorder."

"You owe to me, and I owe to your brother," the old man laughed, and his eyes filled with light and blood. "Let's split the debt somehow, quietly, like men! How did we begin it? I can't remember. You owe to him, and I owe to you?"

"Long live Normandy and long live the hamlet of La Bassée!" Antonio exclaimed, jerking his handcart and departing. "I'll be back, if an enemy's hateful bullet doesn't get me first! I embrace you all, my good people, who eat meat with such delight, the meat of the greatest butcher of all time, the meat of my older brother Villon!"

"Thus," the innkeeper muttered, up to his knees in a puddle (in his mixed-up thoughts, he saw Calais, butchers and enemies), "thus they should be treated. Roughly!"

Antonio stood for a long time on the shore. The wind was carrying away the clouds, and blowing salt and sand into his eyes.

THE WAR WAS BETTER

Dogs were scavenging and howling among the shipwrecks. He felt small, insignificant and somehow comic; it seemed to him that he and even all the land he stood on were nothing compared to the boisterous and raging sea.

"*Cattolica*," he whispered, stretching out beside her. "Forgive me for torturing you so much. Now we're almost in between the earth and the sea. It'll be easier to find our way to the north."

The dense, black ocean was thrashing and roaring; in his dream, he spoke to it as if it had assumed human form.

"You're a man," he said. "You'll return my male strength to me. You'll help me find my many brothers and faithful friends again. You too, like me, are a swallower of stars."

He was quite alone and could remember everything in sequence. Gulls were scouring the edge of the land. The sea was hurling water against the shore, vomiting foam, and then sinking back again without a trace.

"Sea, my mad soldier, let's start everything from the beginning. Let's begin anew!"

Epilogue

CHERRY TREES

FLOWERS AND LIGHT AND THE SEA were mingling before Antonio Peduto's eyes. He could not distinguish the three. His eyes were swollen again; his hands trembled. He had on a Danish nobleman's museum suit, soft boots, and a two-horned hat with crowns and lions embroidered on it. The sun, trembling like an iridescent flower, hung above the waves of water and light which broke and joined, joined and broke again. With blood beating against his temples, he stared southwards from his perch in the branches of a cherry tree and shouted into a kind of trumpet made of old newspapers.

"If you Germans only knew that I can't distinguish the earth from the sky anymore, that life and dreams are the same to us, you wouldn't spend so much time deliberating! You are the only ones remaining we still have to trample down! Then the earth and all the paths crossing it will be clean and beautiful! The world will be a better place! Germans! Why do you take so much time? What are you deliberating about?!"

"I know a lot of your most important words!" Giuseppe Bonaccia shouted from another blossoming cherry tree. "I know the words you don't like, the ones you despise the most. And if you don't answer us like men, by God, I'll begin to say them! I'll repeat them over and over, until your stomachs ache! I know what to tackle you with, and how to do it too. I haven't forgotten how we chased each other back and forth in Montenegro! Don't force me to say those horrible words. Even I may vomit! Oh Germans, have you no mercy for the people and marshals who are shouting at you from the flowers with so much fear and respect?"

"We've met again, we three, and there's no power on earth that can stand against our magic!" Antonio yelled from the top of his tree. "Germans! You're half defeated already. Surrender the other half—at least in words! Rascals, man-eaters, don't forget that the cook, Ingelore, has already joined our side, and we live in harmony, in paradise, so to speak!"

"Ingelore is our soul, our body, our cook and, above all, our spy!" Giuseppe Bonaccia shouted and then paused. His eyes dimmed. "Antonio," he whispered, "I don't know how to go on.

[391]

THE WAR WAS BETTER

Too much of me has been burnt. I'm sorry, Antonio, my thoughts just stop sometimes and my memories get all mixed up."

"Peppe is right," Antonio took up the cry. "Ingelore constantly leaves Lolland, here, for secret missions in your country. Our base is in Puttgarden. Germans! Right now she's on top of our chief hero, Gruban Malić! She riding him! She says she got used to it that way and came to love it in Spain; that way it goes in further. Let her have it then, let it enter her; it's something! Malić, our idea and our man, is on his back, with his arms stretched out and his parachute under his head! While she impales herself on him and kisses his hard warrior's forehead and crooked Montenegrin nose, he pierces her with his horn, from below, and asks her about the disposition of your units. Germans! Do you hear me?! She's ours! Isn't it so, Peppino?"

Giuseppe Bonaccia turned and saw the cook's big, white behind. His head swam; he did not know exactly what the two were doing there on the ground. He blushed from shame and began to sweat.

"Oh, Germans!" He whispered. "If you knew how burnt I am, how scorched I am through and through, how much I'd like to conquer you! Oh, you Germans! Don't you have any mercy? Beasts! Dogs! What will happen to us?"

"Peppino, I asked you already to tell me what they're doing. You know my eyes are swollen and full of dust. You know I can hardly see them. Peppino, they're nearer to you!"

"The cook is galloping, charging on," Bonaccia almost wept. "She's grinding her teeth and muttering things in Spanish. She's tearing up the flowers Malić is handing to her with her teeth, so she won't chew him instead! Antonio, never, never have so many bees and insects hummed around my head as are swarming around her creamy white hemispheres now! It's a whole hive! As if she were made of honey! Never around my head... never... I'm so insignificant. Oh Germans! Beasts! If you knew how many Danish bees have gathered around our dear spy's honey holes and crevices!"

"Don't worry, Peppino. There'll be halved behinds and honeycombs; there'll be swarms and honey. There'll be health and life! Don't lean out so far, though! Hold on tight! And send the message to the Germans. Tell them it's impossible to resist an attack from Denmark!"

"Bend, Germans, bow your heads, lick our boots! We're marching on with flowers and song!" Bonaccia hardly had time to compose his sentences. "The earth and the cooks are rising against you —defend yourselves while you can!"

THE WAR WAS BETTER

"Do you see Kiel from your cherry tree, Peppino?" Antonio inquired softly, blinking. Bonaccia aimed the long binoculars toward the south. "It should be there. Do you see it?"

"I see only ships, let's hope they're the Navy's, a whole fleet," Peppe answered. "Ships, roofs, and some smoke which looks white and thin. Lord, how much water there is! And all those houses; it looks like they're floating in foam."

"What?"

"Strange. I can't explain it, Antonio, but it looks like the cherry trees are blossoming in Germany. There are at least as many there as here, in Denmark. I don't know whether they'll taste the same. But heavens, how many cherry trees!"

"Don't you see any bones, skulls, something like that, anywhere?"

"Only cherry trees in bloom; a mild south wind is blowing off their flowers. There are trees along almost all the roads I can see from here. The earth is white. No skulls appear. There are no people either. No dogs. Only an endless whiteness and in it, maybe, Kiel. Roofs—they're white, too—like the crests of waves. Antonio, who came from Kiel?"

"Don't you remember the German with the lively round eyes, the one we met on the Montenegrin plateau?"

"I've almost forgotten, Antonio. My eyes and my memory are full of whiteness and foam and flowers; I can't remember anything but fire. I've burned. My skin's peeling. My head aches. Was he German?"

"He didn't want to kill us, although he could have. He said he couldn't kill even an enemy without an order, that he was a real German, and had several girls, including Frauke. She was dearest to him and had moles around her knees and below her navel. If my memory doesn't fail me, he mentioned the North and one time I think he spoke of Kiel. But I don't know who was actually from there: he or his girl? He didn't want to put a bullet in your neck either, although he could have. His name, I'm almost sure, was Cordes. Eckart Cordes!"

"That is Kiel, you're right. The cook's still galloping, nibbling, and tearing off cherry twigs. Kiel, yes, exactly; even the sign is white. There are countless storks, like giraffes, only white. I'll bet even the bees flying around Ingelore's honeycomb are white. Everything's white. What a day, oh Germans!"

"Cordes, yes, Cordes, a fine name," Antonio mused, mentally measuring the distance to the sea. "What was he by profession, as a civilian? Did he make candles, sausages? Or was he a gravedigger?" Antonio's eyes were full of yellow powder. "If my memory doesn't fail me, he was funny. Maybe he owned a bookstore. He didn't want to kill us."

"Antonio, a bookseller would have shot us on the spot," Peppe observed, adjusting the binoculars. "It's well known that they're all murderers."

Peppino's voice was mad and warm.

"Everything seems transparent and full of light, there in Kiel," he said. "People can hardly make their way through the clouds of flowers. Only the cross is black. Bells are ringing. It must be a Sunday. Or someone suffocated from all this light, and this is his burial. Oh Germans! Where are the bones and skulls?"

"Cordes," Antonio called out, "pay attention to us. Listen. If, in Montenegro, you didn't want to shoot me in the neck, then why not write a book about us now? It'll come easy to you; you're a bookseller or a sexton, which is the same thing anyway. At least Peppino says so. Write down that we've chosen Denmark for special reasons. You don't expect anything from this direction but winter and snow. Thus we have to attack from here, from the pure north. We're well masked. Water lies between us, which is very important in military matters. Cordes or Cordialis, our horn has reached the galloping cook's throat. She's choking and the cherries are blooming everywhere, all the way down to the sea. Life without victory can't be beautiful. Germans! Don't eat up the flowers; leave them to the bees! Accept the fight! Pay attention, Germans! Notice us!"

Drunkenness and a kind of dizziness were seizing Antonio. He saw only flowers and a warm, all-embracing peace. He listened to the sea; its sound reminded him of some old broken song he could not quite recall. He imagined that he was aloft already, hovering somewhere above, in heaven; he stretched out his arms; he leaned forward. Suddenly he realized he was about to fall. He grabbed hold of a branch and laughed. His eyelashes were moist.

"Ha! Ha! Ha! How sorry I am for you! Ha! Ha! Ha! Germans! If you only knew how much pollen there is around our Ingelore's tail! How many bees, oh *Mensch* Mayer, are swarming around her honeycomb! There's no care, no bitterness, no suffering anymore. Do you want some honey? Everything is white, beautiful, clean. She's riding and galloping and spitting herself, and singing all the while! How nice it is not to touch the earth! Germans! We'll drive you into the sea with cherry blossoms!"

"We'll blind you with pollen, instead of ashes," Peppino murmured from his tree top. "You'll lose the war, from surprise, because you aren't used to warriors like us. So far you've only battled against shitheads like yourselves. Stoop, Germans! Put your heads down so I can see Montenegro! Stoop and stop ringing all those bells!"

"Is Montenegro visible from there, Peppe?"

"As if it had vanished from the face of the earth. As if it were no more. We ravaged and wasted and burned up all of it. I've heard smoke was still coming out of the rocks until recently. I remember how the earth and even the sky trembled. I remember it well, Antonio."

"Have you forgotten that plateau?"

"There's nothing. There are no ponies. Everything tangible, whatever a living man can remember, has turned into pollen. Everything's white there in Montenegro. Only light has remained."

"Our poor country! We cut it up and then it turned into smoke and pollen!" Antonio sobbed; his throat contracted. "Wonderful, golden, ravaged little country of ours, forgive us. Forgive the mad dogs who planted blood and syphilis in you and polluted your veins. Forgive us, Montenegro! You're lighting up even now, like a star stuck in our throats. Forgive the wretches in these flowers, who kneel before you, asleep and awake, as before a wayside grave. I can't go on, I'm choking! My mouth is full of bees and buds. I can't hold on, I'm falling down!"

"My tears are also white, as white as Antonio's," Bonaccia whispered passionately, as he adjusted the binoculars again and spit out twigs and bark. "And everything around us is uncapturable, indestructible."

"We're made out of light, out of powder," Antonio said with his head thrown back; his eyes were filled with the salt sky and the foaming blossoms and the brine.

"Germans! Give up! Surrender!"

APPLE TREES

The wind and the bees hummed in the white tops of the apple trees under which they lay. They smelled the sea, salt, and food

THE WAR WAS BETTER

scattered over the grass which had just sprung up. Dogs were milling around them and down to the edge of the Danish apple orchard
and the shore. Lying on asbestos capes, they could feel the earth
under them germinate and crack.

"Ingelore, love and salvation!" Antonio whispered, kissing her
broad, low forehead and caressing her unbraided hair, which she
threw back and scattered over her shoulders. "Ingelore, we all love
and admire you. We promise you your name too will be carved into
the future monument erected to madness and victory, to our memory. Little Ingelore, our little kitten, our spy, our rider, a rider such
as we've never even dreamed of!"

"I learned everything in Spain, Antonio," the short, round
woman in her forties said. She had blue German eyes. "*Arriba España!*" She hugged him, and he continued to kiss her sticky neck
and her luxurious bosom sweetened by honey. "*Arriba la libertad!*"

"*Arriba* our Ingelore, who sails to Kiel every day, looks for Eckart Cordes, the candlemaker, bookseller, or gravedigger, the man
who didn't want to kill us! *Arriba* Ingelore, a real German *mujer*,
who's given us food for weeks, and supplied us with the precious
data which will facilitate our attack, and our defense! *Arriba!*"

"These are *los cojones*, Antonio!" the romantic German woman
said, with one hand in Malić's museum pants and the other in Peduto's shirt. "These are balls, my God! As if he were Spanish ... by
Christ, he comes from Granada. This is power. This is beauty ...
arriba la República!"

"The rest of the world doesn't have what you, Ingelore, are
squeezing and weighing in your hands," Antonio said, touching his
lips to the deep cleavage between her breasts. "Only we have it.
Only we, and nobody else, I swear it!"

"Can the world, which we all hate, be defeated with this, Antonio?" Her eyes grew, and Antonio saw apple blossoms in them. "Is
this enough? Can we punish them all with this?"

"We can, and we will, my magnificent *guapa!*" Like a dog, he
thrust his muzzle and beard between her breasts, nibbled and licked
them. It seemed to him he was in another world, aloft, above the
earth. "My *guapa*, my beauty!" he sighed. "We'll destroy them
with this rod, with these balls; the rest of the world has nothing like
them! My milky *mujer*, ready to give whatever you have, for freedom ... oh, how good this is for my mouth and forehead, oh ...
arriba la libertad!"

"*Canalles y cobardes!*" Ingelore cried out, challenging the world
scornfully. "Scoundrels and cowards!" She continued to squeeze

THE WAR WAS BETTER

and balance Malić's heavy sacks as she spoke. "Your strength is nothing compared to this one! These are *los cojones;* this is a *hidalgo y camarada!*"

"We're dug in with flowers, you German rascals and man-eaters!" Peppe took up the call; between shouts, he sipped beer from a wooden dish. "Our fortifications are white apple branches; our shelters are a heap of empty bags and a few handfuls of earth! Hey, you on the other side, you don't even have binoculars like these, you can't see any further than your noses.... That's why you don't know what kind of weapons we have, or the caliber of the artillery shells our Ingelore is weighing and caressing! Hey, Germans! You there!"

"We'll pull down your damn whorehouse, right down to the ground!" Ingelore shouted enthusiastically in both directions. "We're starting from here, armed with these bombs. We'll start from this clean place, and we'll spit on you! Sons of bitches, you don't even know what a bordello, what a *casa de putas* that country of yours is!"

Then she lay down beside Malić and passed him hot dogs, lukewarm, unpeeled potatoes, and a dish with beer. She undressed herself and then straddled him, so that once again bees, wasps, and various butterflies swarmed around her buttocks and the honeycomb between her legs. Antonio could see when she moved that some unknown, invisible force of the north was waking in her. She smelled of honey, potatoes, and stale semen. The wind wafted from the sea. Little white crowns and light pollen were falling over them.

"*Cavallero,* why do you call the donkey Taliano when he's obviously a Spaniard?" Ingelore inquired with a trembling voice, as she began spitting herself on Malić's horn. "*Cavallero,* look: *los cojones* on him are almost as big as yours!"

"He's Belgian, *camarada,*" Gruban Malić corrected her, turning his globe and slowly coloring in Germany with his red pencil. He started from Kiel and moved toward the south and the west, circling towns and even whole provinces. "He's from a Belgian circus, but his ancestors are English. We've been together for a long time, and trampled down and humiliated many countries."

"Where have you been fighting, *amigo?*"

"In Ghent, Knokke, and Antwerp, we each got a medal, and a diploma. In Bergen and Amsterdam, the famous Bloemona received us and fed us; there was plenty of food, drink, and glory there. Taliano is a real clown and lover. I have it easy with him too; he's well trained."

[397]

THE WAR WAS BETTER

"Why don't you call him *Belgico* then?" Ingelore asked softly. "Or *Inglés?*"

"For me, *guapa*, any donkey is Taliano," Malić said as he spat on some of the countries on his globe. "This is my third one. They get accustomed to the name Taliano sooner than to Slavo, I find. Watch out, love, watch out! Those are human *cojones*....Oh, careful. ...Or go to Taliano....Oh, *mujer!*"

"*Arriba la República!*" the German woman exclaimed as she mounted him. "*Vivan los cojones!*"

She unclasped his Flemish gilt belt and unbuttoned his resinous pants and his shirt, which had gone unwashed for a long time; she counted his ribs and looked for the hair on his his naked, bantam's chest. Then she unbuttoned his long Russian overcoat and caressed his fur hat, which turned around and around on his head while he stared fixedly at Germany on the globe—and all the while she continued to impale herself. He was dark with dirt around his neck and under his arms, but she did not mind.

"I don't want to get into water, my *mujer*, until we win!" he had explained the day they met and got to like each other after returning from Spain.

"I also want victory over the Germans, the English and the Americans, over the rich, *camarada*," she had said, gluing herself to him just as she was doing now. "Afterwards, when the victory comes, we'll bathe and eat, and the Germans and the rest of them, who've never been able to satisfy me, will be hungry and dirty like we are now!"

"They're starting again," Guiseppe Bonaccia whispered and blushed.

She bent and kissed his sweaty, wrinkled forehead, pointing her other, narrower canal directly at Antonio. She hugged him and begged him to leave the globe for at least a moment, and grab her hemispheres instead. She spoke of food, and mentioned the secret depot of hot dogs, potatoes, and sauerkraut in the suburbs of Kiel, where she had been unable to find comrade Eckart Cordes, the candlemaker, gravedigger, or bookseller, who would have been especially valuable for gathering military and other German secrets. He resisted her, defended himself, and spread apart her hemispheres as if he were tearing apart melons. White crowns were falling on them; bees were swarming around their nakedness; a salty wind was wafting from the sea.

"My *camarada y mujer*, tell me once again, before we attack,

THE WAR WAS BETTER

how it is in Germany," Malić asked. His eyes, like Antonio's and Peppe's, were full of pollen and the reflection of the sea.

"Our good cook, provider, and ally, do you realize that we are now on the eve of the most difficult battle in history?" the Montenegrin Marshal whispered. "Therefore, repeat, please, what you told me once in Spain. So that we may remember. Not only courage and strength are needed. This is a fight to the end. Cunning is also necessary. Oh, *mujer*, a bee just stung me, down there, maybe a wasp or a hornet! *Los cojones* should not swell up before the final struggle with the Teutonic bulls! Oh, *guapa*, tell me where the damn German heart is, so we can pull it out and watch it writhe and die, since it roars so much and vomits poison.... I'm afraid it really was a hornet; they're already swelling; how will I attack, with such lead...?"

"I'll apply cold compresses, don't be afraid," the romantic *mujer* assured him. "I'm German. I know how heroes' balls should be treated. This won't be the first time."

"Dove, *mujer*, woman with big, milky breasts as nice as all of Denmark, how should we attack the Germans? That's what I want to know." Recently, even Malić had not been able to control himself. He trembled no less than Antonio and Peppino. And he was trembling now. "Dove, I don't want the slaughter to last long. Therefore, tell me whether the Germans have hearts, and on which side they are."

"*Ahora!*" She turned her eyes upwards and threw her head back. It seemed to her that a flame was licking her hemispheres and the sky. "*Ahora!* Now! *Jetzt!* So, yes! Montenegrin!"

As she bumped and jerked, her breasts fell out of her flowery chemise. The *cavallero* caught them, bit the left one with his lips, and began to pull on the right one. He almost broke her in half. With his mouth crammed with her honey-sweet flesh, he had some difficulty getting his words out: "*Guapa*, how should we handle the Germans?" The sky swirled around his head, full of apple branches and bees. "Like this, my cabbage, my doe?"

"*Ahora!*" The German woman bit her teeth. "Don't budge. Don't try to get away! *Ahora!* Listen: *Ahora*, "*libertad*" and "*República*" are words the Germans hate. They fear them like the plague. *Ahora! Ahora! Ahora!* Oh, Lord! Oh, all the saints! Help us to vanquish, to revenge ourselves, to impale everything on this knightly miracle piercing my belly! *Ahora*, oh God! God, how good you are to have granted me straight from heaven such a *culea-*

dor, such a sword! Germans, you castrated deer! *Caballos!* Do you know what a *corrida* is? If you don't, my *novio* and I will demonstrate it to you! Germans, we're waving a red handkerchief at you; why are you trembling? Why aren't you answering? My *banderillero y novio* and I, and the others who're shooing away the flies, are ready for anything! We're in the flowers here—oh, *por favor!* —just waiting for you! *Ahora! Ahora!* Now, now, my *banderillero!*"

"After the victory, will we all dance the flamenco?" Giuseppe Bonaccia asked anxiously, with Antonio's turtle in his arms. "I mean, *guapa*, will it be possible to dance the flamenco in the new, liberated, ravaged Germany? *Guapa*, do you notice how I'm using the turtle's shell and the flowers, like a medieval shield? Do you think it'll work against the Germans? Oh Ingelore, even I wanted it so much in the past! Oh! Calm down, please, Cattolica!"

"*Viva, viva, viva Dinamarca!* which has let us trample her down and roll and copulate in her flowers for weeks!" Ingelore was sobbing. With her eyes and her outstretched arms she seemed to be trying to take in the whole countryside. "*Arriba Dinamarca, arriba Lolland!* And long live all the provinces my dearest *novio* Malić and I have crossed since Spain! Let them flower! Oh, Germans! Long live everyone who hates you stinking … *caballos*. I don't want to have anything more to do with you!"

"Are the Germans ready for anything, *mujer?* Malić asked, pointing at the country beyond the bay of Kiel.

"They're ready for anything but this, my angel, my *culeador!*"

"Do they have money? If so, can we get it?" Malić went on, more composed now, although still in a sweat, as he pulled her hemispheres further apart. "Where are their museums? We must dress up like real men and heroes. Do they have any museums at all? We want to humiliate them, you know, *mujer*. We want to take away whatever they have. And above all we must convince them, as we have the others, that they're happy, and shouldn't hope for things to get any better. How can we trick them, my insatiable *guapa*, my most skillful rider? I mean fast, and without much blood, as in a dream. Tell us, *mujer*. Teach us."

"Just by doing what you're doing, *hidalgo*. That's all."

"Do they crave honor, Ingelore?"

"Less and less," the *guapa* answered. "If they had any to begin with, I'd have never gone to Granada and Corboda."

Malić thrust again. It seemed to her that her hemispheres would come completely apart, and his *banderilla* reach her windpipe.

THE WAR WAS BETTER

"*Ahora!*" she neighed like a mare. "Forward! Until death! ... Germans! Surrender your great circus without bloodshed! *Ahora!* Don't you Germans know that we're not from this world, from this earth?"

"How do the Germans multiply, *mujer?*" Antonio asked her, growing anxious about the forthcoming battle and clinging to Peppino, who was watching everything from behind the turtle's shell. "Like fish, asexually, like snails? *Mujer,* answer me please, and watch out for Malić. He's from another time like all of us, and made completely out of light. *Mujer,* please how do the Germans multiply if they don't make love and don't even know what it means, as you told us as far back as Sweden? Do you hear me, my sweaty *mujer?*"

"Jesus and Mary, cherries and apples will begin to grow out of me after all of this," Ingelore murmured with her mouth full of white petals, bees and wasps. "Cherries and apples... Where am I? With whom? In which country...?"

"Don't break off my medals, my mad *guapa,*" Malić warned her energetically. "Don't pull my ribbons off; you said yourself you don't know whether the Germans have museums. *Mujer,* are you deaf? Don't you hear what Antonio's asking you? *Mujer,* why are the Germans so pale? Why do they multiply asexually when this way is so much nicer? *Mujer,* my wonderful *mujer,* give my brothers each a breast.... They're eager for German blood and milk. Like that! Ah, good. Good, my only *mujer!*"

"Surrender, slimy snails! Surrender! Without you the world will be better and nicer!" Antonio tried to shout with her goatlike tit bobbling in his mouth. "Surrender and let us roam through your country sowing semen and flowers!"

"I'll do it myself. I'll plant. I'll irrigate," Giuseppe Bonaccia burst out crying and began to suck the cook's breast like a lamb. "I'll sow love myself, I, who was burning and finally burned up. I, who have nothing left. I, who can hardly remember anything... I, who don't see a thing because of all the apple blossoms!"

"Germans! Don't you see how we love each other? Don't you see in the name of what kind of love and unity we beg you to get out of our way until we pass?" Malić cried, convinced that he was not pouring semen into her, but fire. "The cherry trees have stopped blooming. Now the apple trees are white. Soon grass and life will riot everywhere. By the time the Danish cherries get red, by then at the latest, we will match our powers with yours and cast you down under our feet!"

THE WAR WAS BETTER

"*Hidalgo*, my prince and ruler, today you've made your heir!" the woman yelled and turned toward the sea and the white city of Kiel. "You Germans don't have the slightest idea what kind of son he'll be!" Her eyes were troubled, her teeth bared, her lips swollen. "Malić has a knife and a spear, a shield and a donkey! This son will be like that! Malić stabs like an ancient hero, his fellow knight says. Yes, it's true! He's a hero all right, a hero who's always on his donkey or on me, his Dulcinea, and never spares himself. Antonio says the *Montenegrino* would die for my skirt or kill a hundred sour Englishmen for it! Germans! What are you doing there?"

It seemed that their happiness could have lasted forever. Kneeling and sighing, Antonio and Peppe would have sucked until the end of their strength. Perhaps even milk would have begun to flow. The *mujer* looked around her like a real she-wolf, and then announced, at the same time as Malić, that the hateful, detestable enemy had again refused to surrender. They were ready for another gallop, and did not bother to separate. Meanwhile, Antonio and Peppe continued to pull and fondle and suck her immense udders. For one moment of uncanny stillness, they did not say a single word or make a single motion.

Then something strange happened. The sea and the sky began to billow. Antonio looked over at Malić's globe which was standing near the turtle. Taliano did the same, rubbing his motley mushroom against his belly. The globe began to seethe. Although Antonio saw it through his tears, it looked redder and redder to him, and the war which was starting became clearer and clearer. German war sailboats were entering the Danish territorial waters. They trained their big guns on Lolland and vomited smoke and stench. Old ugly cruisers, fishing boats and trawlers, all dirty and rusty, and even some rowboats, took to the sea. The bay of Kiel began to stir. In the port, trophy flags were fluttering in the wind beside pornographic posters and wet underwear.

Even the sky looked a mess on Malić's globe. Taking off from the Kiel, Flensburg and Oldenburg airports, and from the secret bases in Schönberg, Neumünster and Lübeck, struggling to be first to get above the bay and over Denmark, musuem planes with diesel engines approached Lolland. First they dropped bombs, killing fish. Then they flew in formation again, with their worn-out engines clattering and whistling. Antonio saw them clearly, both on the globe and above unprotected Denmark. They were mostly single-engine biplanes, and once they had gotten rid of their bombs, they flew more easily. They were pouring in from all sides. They side-slipped, stunted, looped, and turned to show their wires and wing supports. And when they bombarded the Danish orchard, Antonio could see their manlike pilots in leather suits and large hats. They waved their hands from their cockpits, made indecent gestures, and called out something in their sharp language. They stank from oil and gasoline.

First they strafed the shallow bay, the shore, and the rocks which bristled up from the water, and then the small trenches packed with food and hay on both sides of the channel. Then they peppered the apple orchard, breaking the branches with lead and arrows and scorching the flowers with fire. From the fortifications of Heikendorf, Langholz, and Hasselberg, old-fashioned howitzers began pounding. Heaps of tangled chains and tin burst somewhere behind them. The German metal and shrapnel jangled everywhere. The German sirens and cries reverberated. Sailors wailed and laughed. Somewhere, bands were playing military marches.

"For God's sake, Germans, what are you doing?" Antonio Peduto complained when he noticed that the explosions had soiled his medals and the large uniform he was wearing from the Franco-Prussian or some other important war. "Are you cracked or something? What's the matter with you?" he cried out again. He decided to drink down the dish of beer before his death came. He knelt down. Branches and earth and stones were burying him. "Germans! You Germans are madmen! You're attacking us treacherously, suddenly!"

"You're attacking us before the time!" Ingelore roared, surrounded by scattered food, overturned bottles and dishes. "The cherries aren't red yet! Withdraw! Withdraw until the cherries are ripe, until the grass grows up to my thighs, until we get some rest from our long marches and terrible battles!"

She too was kneeling, motionless, in the same position in which Antonio and Peppe had been milking her and watching the prehistoric planes fly by, about to fall apart in mid-air.

"Traitors of the *República*, turn around! Go somewhere else! Spare our little Denmark!"

"German blood will flow in brooks!" the sulphur-sprinkled Gruban Malić threatened from his donkey. "Finally! Finally! But was it necessary today, and like this?"

His globe was white too. His overcoat was also white and riddled with bullet and shrapnel holes. It reached down to his stirrups and the tops of his museum boots. The parachute on his back was white too, although soiled by honey and other gluey matter. Bees and butterflies were flying around him. The donkey took a few steps toward the water; the rider stuck out his chest and yelled.

"We're going to make the North Sea blood red!" Smoke and apple petals were making him cough; he was almost strangling. "Do you hear me . . . are you already withdrawing, or what?"

"Look, we're still alive!" Antonio was also coughing when he emerged from a heap of earth and broken branches. "Anna-Maria, your eyes are full of dirt and whiteness; where's Peppino? Can you tell us where our son Peppino is?"

"Here I am, Antonio," Giuseppe Bonaccia wept and shook the dirt off his Danish prince's suit, his medals, and the numerous insignia which he no longer understood. "Here I am, and I'm going to die from fear. Pardon me for being a coward, excuse my aching stomach again; I don't want to stink like a skunk!" He peered out of a heap of half-rotten, briny straw, trembling and hiding his face with his hands. "Antonio, the world is not conquered with cowards like me. Flowers and words are no help! So, in order not to fall into the hands of the Germans, I'm going to make myself scarce. Goodby, Peduto!"

"Peppino, shake my hand!" Antonio said when the burst of the next explosion had abated. "You don't stink to me! Peppino, I don't care what condition you're in. Come to me! My wonderful, irreplacable shit-ass! Where are you?"

A more powerful explosion than any before it threw dirt up to the sky and pulled up an apple tree by the roots and flung it twenty feet in the air. The air around them turned into thunder and sulphur. Antonio smeared blood on his face and beard. He saw there were wounds on his hands and legs. He hardly had time to tell himself it didn't hurt him yet. His arms were outstretched, his mouth open. He no longer knew exactly where he was, or with whom, or who could have dropped him there.

"What, you've been injured too, *mujer?*" He could hardly move his tongue. "Come to me, *guapa.* I'll protect you. They can do nothing to us!"

"I'm disappearing, Antonio!" Peppino said, and then suddenly tore away one breast from the woman's body and started running across the dirt and branches. "*Mujer*, please pardon me, you too: I've taken the left one, the larger; it's mine!"

The planes were divebombing and strafing the orchard now and dropping paratroopers and leaflets. Waves were splashing against Lolland, washing in blood and salt, dead fish and flowers. Antonio Peduto, like a true *cavallero*, was hugging the cook.

THE WAR WAS BETTER

Ingelore spit out blood and sand and looked around for Malic, who was defending the island. She could not see the knight on the donkey. Where his globe usually stood, there was only a red spot the size of a wild Danish strawberry.

"I'm finally a man, Germans!" Giuseppe Bonaccia shouted between explosions, with the cook's left breast in his arms. "We'll chase each other through Lolland, black birds, as we used to in Montenegro. Ha! I'm charging you! I'm going backwards! I stink!" the sea roared, and the waves and the blood drowned out his voice "Are you Germans still *hombres* or are you blood-sucking spiders? I remember your German words: '*Komm, komm her, Taliano, komm, Scheisse . . . gut, aber schnell!*' I've forgotten everything else. I was burning. I burnt up. But those words I remember. Don't rob me of her breast! It's everything I have! I've finally become a man; don't spoil my happiness!"

Antonio slumped down beside the uprooted apple tree with the cook in his arms. He was convinced that the pale-faced knight with the swollen testicles, Gruban Malić, had stopped the German ravens in their tracks. He said nothing and did not even weep. He smiled when Ingelore whispered to him that her *novio* would soon be back.

The sky and the earth were shaking. Antonio was in a kind of dazed ecstasy; he felt that light and power were surging from his hands and all his wounds and that his blood was mixing with the woman's.

"The *hidalgo* should be here any moment," he murmured to her, thinking that Malić was their happiness, their essence. Everything he could see was turning into dust and thunder.

"*No pararán!*" the *mujer* shouted to the Germans who were pouring in from everywhere now, trampling the blossoms and sea foam with their muddy boots. "*Canalles*, you shall not pass!"

"Yes, our *mujer*," Antonio agreed, tasting somebody's blood on his tongue. "They aren't *hombres* at all; still, it's nice to have beaten them." He waited for the thunder to subside. "You're right, *guapa*. The world, the whole world, is ours again. Everything is ours!"

"*Arriba la República!*" she exclaimed, chewing on the earth. "Long live the two great, wild, sad countries I've come to love, *España* and *Montenegro!*"

Well-fed German dogs were barking all around them.

RUM

"After that, it's all a blank; they must have got us separated somehow, but I bet it wasn't easy," Antonio Peduto said giddily to Captain Archibald Beckett, whom he stood before on a camouflaged Irish ship. "When I woke up, my mouth was full of her hair, her blood, her skin. . . . What a woman, Captain!"

"This is the tenth time I've heard this story, Slav, but I still can't figure out who hugged whom, or what, or why," Archibald Beckett said over his pipe and a bottle of rum, both of which he held in his right hand. He was a man of about fifty, a wrinkled old sea-wolf with a crooked nose, sunken cheeks and old-fashioned spectacles, behind which his dilated pupils looked immense. "Slav, who and what in hell are you talking about? Who was embracing whom?"

"We were both covered with blood, Captain, our *mujer* and I," Peduto continued as he sipped rum from an army messtin. "She was hugging and squeezing me as if she were my born sister. Our wonderful Ingelore, our *mujer!*"

"Stop crying, my wretched Slav," Archibald Beckett consoled Antonio, who had fallen to his knees. "You'll have plenty of women and embraces, soldier, Spanish women too. Sooner or later we'll put into a harbor, at least to see one more time how dirty and miserable it is to be on land, and why we should try our best never to go back. Stop crying, Slav, you'll have lots of rum too."

"I tell you, Archibald, I don't know how they tore her out of my arms. They had dogs, and they shouted," Antonio went on more quietly, with his eyes glued on the Captain's bottle. "Afterwards they picked her up from the ground, our *mujer*, and put her into the bucket of a tremendous steam-shovel. I stared up at her like the others; I was full of admiration and regret. Our *mujer* had a sign printed on her big white behind, TRAITORESS OF THE GREAT GERMAN PEOPLE, and she shrieked down at them:

" 'Blackguards, *caballos*, your doomsday will come too! You've been so eager for someone to declare war on you, just so that you can start fucking at last! That's the only way you can get it up! But God knows why you want to anyway, since you multiply asexually, like the snails you are!'

THE WAR WAS BETTER

"They were looking up at her from all the ships, the whole of Kiel was watching her, and all the other ports too. A good part of southern Denmark was looking at her.

" 'Malić, my Montenegrin, will get your heads, Germans!' She spoke of her bridegroom, then of Peppino, who had disappeared with her left breast. She flashed her white hemispheres and the letters written on them in their faces and spat on their helmets. 'Life would be nicer without you, you traitors of the republic. Perhaps you'll have my body again, but never, never, never my soul!'

"Such was our *mujer*, Archibald."

"I don't know what you're talking about, Slav. It's true I don't come from around here, but life is good," Captain Beckett said as he poured some rum into Antonio's messtin. "Just look around you; how can you deny it? Life is wonderful. Ah, Slav, how calm I am!"

"I see only the barren waste, Captain. I see only water and the sun," Antonio replied. Many dirty bandages were stuck across his large French uniform. "Pour rum on my healing, itching wounds, will you? Drench me all over with it!"

Antonio stretched out like a lizard on the nets spread over the deck. The Captain poured rum on his arms and legs and then over his entire body.

"I understand what you're talking about. The ocean has no end and no beginning, and I'm small and meaningless compared to it, lying on your deck with my salted wounds. Captain, strike a match, let me burn up. That's the easiest way to get rid of me."

"Life is beautiful, Slav," Archibald Beckett replied to the red beard, who lay on his back caressing the turtle's shell, staring at the sky and weeping. "No, Redhead, I don't exactly know whether it's sensible or not, but I won't go into port again. I'm fed up with land. Life is beautiful! And God is good and generous to have pushed us off into endless space and the salty sky! We are grateful to God for this richness!"

"Your richness is wonderful, and your rum is splendid, Captain," Antonio said to the man with the dilated pupils. He waved his hand in the direction of the crew. "Are they Irish too?"

"The fat one with the Scotch ribbon is Pozzo," the Captain said warmly, with rum in his eyes. "Pozzo is a hail fellow well met; that's why he always coughs. Vladimir and Estragon are brothers, although you wouldn't guess it at first glance. They say the two have a single heart, breathe with gills, and cannot be separated."

Vladimir and Estragon were exchanging sailors' undershirts, clowns' boots, and Napoleonic hats.

THE WAR WAS BETTER

"And that boy, Captain?"

"His laughter tells us whether it's night or day. He reads the stars and forecasts the weather. Now he's drinking like the others, because life is beautiful. Stand up, Slav. There'll be rum!"

"Archibald, who's that fellow with the white hair falling over his shoulders? The one turning the helm with his hands tied and a rope around his neck? The one who seems so happy, maybe because he drinks so much?"

"That's Lucky," the Captain answered as he waved with his pipe to the almost transparent, white-haired man who was steering the ship. "My oldest, dearest, and most drunken sailor."

"He looks like a Slav," Antonio suggested, looking at the man's moony eyes and sunken cheecks. "Why is he tied up like that, Captain?"

"So that he can steer better. He thinks he's running away, so he jerks the helm a great deal, trying to steer somewhere. He doesn't realize that whatever route he takes would suit us just as well. If you ask him a question—any question—he'll answer that there's nothing better than life, rum, and light. By the way, do you know which sea we're on?"

"No, Captain."

"Neither do I, Slav. And that makes me carefree, relaxed. Look around, if it's more rum you want. There's nothing that could trouble our peace and harmony. The wind has carried the clouds away, or the sun has scorched them up. What a day! What company! Slav, tell me: is there anything more sublime than true serenity?"

"I don't know, Captain," Antonio Peduto said. "Do we have any destination?"

"Advance, boys!" Archibald Beckett called out to the sailors. "Advance!"

"Where, Irishman?" Antonio Peduto asked softly, lying beside the turtle.

"Toward light and rum, Slav. Toward the sea and distances. Because life is beautiful. How blessed I am, boys, to have met you all!" The tall, skinny Irishman suddenly burst out crying. Then he began to laugh.

"Without you, my boys, I'd be a hopeless adventurer. If I hadn't met you, worms would have eaten me up on land; six feet of earth would be contaminated forever." Tears flowed down his tanned cheeks, on either side of his pipe. "Can't you see, my mad Slav, where we're going? . . . Ha! Ha! Ha! Isn't it clear?"

"Nothing ever has or ever will be, clear to me, Captain," Antonio Peduto said while Archibald poured rum from the bottle into his messtin, and a salty wind began to swell the sails. "Is it true that an Irish bomb explodes twice?"

"It's true," Archibald admitted in a soft, squeaky voice. "My wretched Irish bomb!"

Antonio stood up and mopped the tears from his face. "Don't drivel, Captain," he said. "Life is beautiful. You said so yourself, and you're the first man I ever met who can prove it too. Don't cry, Archibald. Just look up. How much wind and salt there in the sails! How much beauty! How much hope! Life is wonderful, Captain!"

"Wretched Irish bomb," the thin, gray, almost transparent man whispered through his tears and laughter as he leaned out over the railing. "Why did you mention it to me, Slav?"

"I'm sorry, Captain," Antonio apologized and embraced him. "If you'll pour some more rum for me and tell me how long we're going to sail on like this, I promise not to mention it again, or the dry land either."

"Poor Irish bomb," the Captain said, coming to himself. He poured rum over his thin little beard. "You're asking me, Slav, how long we're going to remain at sea?"

Now it was he who embraced Antonio, and they both looked up to see the sails surging, ever lighter and larger, like Irish tears. "I'm glad I met you and helped you that day. You're red, mad, and powerful. You don't always know what you want, but whatever it is, you want to have it right away. You're a real Irishman!"

"I've always dreamed about your country, Captain," Antonio said, seeing Ireland in his mind's eye, poor and green, at the other end of the world. "How long are we going to be at sea?"

"Until the sun burns us up, until we turn to salt."

"Who'll get the ship?" Antonio suddenly remembered François Villon and the knife, and blood rushed to his temples. "Irishman, pour some more, and tell me, who'll get the ship?"

"Water," Archibald Beckett answered. "The sea will deal with her according to its whim. It won't sink her too soon. It'll take a long time. But finally the ship and the sails will turn into a light blot. The people on land will think it's some kind of flower."

"I'd like to stick with you, and help you reach your destination on time," Antonio said to the Captain one day, as he watched the waves and dreamed of eating some fresh food and drinking something else but rum. "But I'm a man of the land, a landlubber, and . . ."

"Life is beautiful," was all the Captain said. "Isn't it true, Slav?"

THE WAR WAS BETTER

"Life is indeed beautiful, Captain and brother," Peduto agreed, as he sipped with the Irishman from the aluminum messtin. "Life is like your flower on the water, like our sails. Life is magic, Archibald. You convinced me of it. Life! Magic!"

Both of them laughed.

"Why don't you go with us to the end then? We've come to like you, although I'll be damned if I can remember a thing you've said. Maybe that's because we've been at sea so long."

"The land is calling me, and the soldiers I crossed half the world with," Antonio said as he let Archibald mop off his tears and saliva. "Please order them to look for a port. Have mercy on a miserable wanderer. Release him from this divine service, if you won't sprinkle him with rum and burn him up, or throw him to the fish."

"Maybe you're hungry?"

"I can't complain, Captain. Rum is an excellent food. I've come to believe it's the best. Your rum is especially good. It's strong and pure, a real sailor's and a real man's drink. The Irish and the Slavs can quench their thirst only with this. I swear to you, on my honor and on my beard, I would class it right after Montenegrin brandy. But I can't do without my fellow soldiers anymore. It's hard enough to think of doing without you. But pity me, please, and release me from this service."

Around dawn, Lucky brought the sailboat into land.

"And now, Slav, may the luck of a warrior and your inexhaustible madness serve you well!" Archibald Beckett said as he clasped him in his arms. "I'm glad that you defeated the Germans, the English, or some other rascals that day on land you kept talking about. I did it myself at sea." The Captain patted him on the back. "You're good, my Slav, because you're following your heart."

"And now, Captain?" Antonio asked, quivering. "What should I do now?"

"Now move on!" the Captain answered. "The infantry is calling you, the men with whom you've crossed half the world. If you ever reach Ireland, which is like your Montenegro, tell them we're still holding on."

All of them embraced him. Lucky kissed and caressed him the most. Vladimir and Estragon gave him a Napoleonic hat, Pozzo a raincoat. The boy said that the stars were getting pale, but that their magic luster and beauty would sooner or later return. Antonio thanked them, sank to his knees and said that life was beautiful. The sailboat began to pitch and roll.

Carefully, as if he were still bandaged up, they dropped him on the shore. Then for a moment they all stood on deck, masked with the fishing nets and white in the early dawn light, waving to him. Again the sails swelled, the ropes around the mast tightened.

"Anna-Maria," Antonio said to the turtle, who was peering out of the bag. "Cattolica, promise them, you too. Promise them we'll never forget them. We'll talk about them wherever we go."

"If you get tired of the land, Slav, look for us!" Archibald Beckett shouted to him. "We're at sea—that's half the victory already —and we'll stay on it until we breathe out last. We won't surrender so easily, Slav!"

Antonio felt the land with his hands and began to pluck up roots and dirt and chew them in gratitude.

"Do you see us, clown?"

"Archibald, my eyes are full of rum and salt. They're swelling again," Antonio answered from the rocks. "I know only that the dawn has come, that life is beautiful, that you'll remain at sea to the end."

"Then good-by, Slav!" the Captain called over his pipe. "Good-by, gallant clown!"

"A good wind in your sails, my Irish brothers and soldiers!"

Antonio Peduto lay beside Anna-Maria and waved his museum hat. The sunny sailboat went away; her wake lingered behind on the water.

"Cattolica, life is beautiful," he whispered with grass and earth in his mouth. "Oh, if only we knew where we were!" He hugged and kissed her neck and her eyes, which were full of dew and the first sunbeams.

"Life is beautiful, my wife-sister-love."

JENEVER

"Did you say, Willems, that you've sailed around the whole world?" Antonio Peduto twisted his tongue and staggered on, pulling the handcart with the turtle. "The whole world?"

"Many countries, boy," Willems van der Hoeven said, following after and watching that the turtle should not fall out of the bag. "I've gotten acquainted with almost all the ports of the globe."

"Was it on military ships, Willems?"

"Mainly Dutch sailboats," he answered, helping Antonio to his feet after he had fallen. The old man stank of earth and fish. His broad, wrinkled face brightened up when he spoke again. "We transported everything you can think of—bananas and rice, pigs and flowers, beasts and soldiers."

"You've never wept?"

"*Nooit*," the old man said and clapped his fishing hat down over his ears. "Never!"

"The world has been yours then?"

"The world has been, and still is, theirs," the old man said quietly. "The sea and long sailing trips; that's what's been mine."

"What do you have now, apart from me?" Antonio laughed and embraced him.

"Him," Willems van der Hoeven said, pointing back at the lion he was leading along on a thin rope. "You and this lion cub are everything I have, not counting Texel, where we've been for two years now. This whole island of Texel is mine too."

"Nobody's your match now, Willems."

"Any wretch would envy me for what I have, boy. Isn't it wonderful to have a lion, even if he's a little stunted and hairless, and a sailor and child like you, and then finally a turtle, this love and whore of whores! I'm rich, Antonio. For sure, I'm rich."

"Looked at closely, Willems, life is beautiful," Antonio said, falling down between the old man and the turtle. "As you told me a hundred times: 'Whoever has Texel has all of Holland!' Therefore, everything belongs to us."

"Life is beautiful," the old man agreed as he sat down beside Antonio. "I don't know who said it, or why; he must have been a man of the sea; but there's something in it. Life is beautiful if you don't ask too much from it, and you've got good company. Take us two, for instance. Is there anybody who knows where we are and how nice it is? They don't even know Texel is the island of islands, the purest country under the sky. It would be sinful to complain and blaspheme. Texel is a pearl, remember that!"

"Praised be Jesus and Mary for having given us Holland, with so much water and sky," Antonio almost sang. Then he lay down again.

"Whoever has Holland can easily possess the whole world," Willems van der Hoeven said, and took a bottle out of his torn cape. "Long live life and *jenever*, the strong brandy from Texel!"

Antonio repeated the words after him with enthusiasm, and then touched the neck of the bottle with his trembling lips. "Ah, this is a beverage! The dead themselves would drink it. Willems, my wonderful old man, do they know how happy we are?"

"You're really good, *jenever*," Willems agreed, looking through the bottle at the sky and the sea. "You're strong, *jenever*, and may God have mercy on the bones and soul of whoever invented you!"

They lay in the flower beds among the tulips. They hugged each other, plucked one another's beards and boxed like former sailors. *Jenever* was almost finished, and they sprinkled each other with the last drops in the bottle, and Antonio's eyes smarted even more.

With tulips, narcissus, and roses in his arms, Antonio watched a windmill turning lazily. He wanted to rush downhill to see it more closely, to caress and kiss its brick base. He could not. The old man was pulling him down to the ground, and both of them fell across the turtle and the lion.

"I love you, Holland, salty, noble country," Antonio murmured, looking out at the windmill, the canal, and the dam behind which the sea and the foam began. "I love you too, you former men!" he said to the scarecrows. "Do you want this sweet poison, this nectar, my black boys?" He extended Willems' bottle toward them. The scarecrows, some five or six men's suits stuck on crosses, were silent. but they moved whenever the wind blew. "Hey, my wonderful sailors, who've sailed over and spat on the whole world, why don't you answer me?!"

"Leave the boys alone, Antonio!" Willems reproached him, shouting over the head of the sleeping lion, who lay at his feet. "For them, life is beautiful without us. They like the sun and the wind, the sea and the land." The old man's large blue eyes were full of pollen. "Leave the fuckers alone to guard Holland from birds, Germans, and evil spirits! Hey, boys, how do you like it there in the flowers?"

" 'There was a soldier once,' " Antonio began to sing; the lion woke up and jumped into his arms. "Hey, boys, we're singing to you, because life is beautiful!"

"We're singing to you, you big-balled Dutch adventurers, who've spilled your merry semen in all the ports of the world!" Willems almost sobbed, with the turtle's little paws on his bare chest. "We're singing to the sea, too, and the whole world: 'There was a soldier once.' . . . We're singing to you all, and we'll keep singing until we choke . . . on words and yellow tulip pollen!"

At noon, when the sun stood highest above the windmill, Willems van der Hoeven snatched up Antonio's binoculars and aimed them at the sea like a cannon barrel. Then he began to curse and sing in some European sailors' mixture of tongues.

"Do you see a boat, Willems?" Antonio asked, throwing his arms around the tulips and then lifting himself up again onto his knees.

Willems van der Hoeven waved to the scarecrows and to his entire island. Antonio thought of Archibald Beckett and Lucky, who used to greet him with bound hands, and the boy who had wept for the stars and rum. His eyes and his throat smarted. He too looked toward the west.

"Can you hear me, old buck?" he asked.

"It's been a long time since Texel has had such a day as this," Willems mused aloud, calming down his heart and his breathing. "You can't tell which there's more of, water or light, waves or foam. To me, Antonio, it even looks like the sea and the sunbeams are the same thing."

"I asked you what you see, if you see anything," Antonio reminded him quietly. "Willems, old buck!"

"Unless my eyes and your binoculars are fooling me, I see a ... a blot of light. It can't be a fish, not even a lot of fish. No. It's more like some human skeletons on a shipwreck. Something of the kind, my carroty boy."

"Does what you see, does the blot of light ... does it have the form of a flower?"

"What, Antonio?"

"Could the dazzling spot on the water there be a flower?" Antonio asked softly; he felt like singing and laughing again. "Some flower as yet unknown to men?"

"Well, it might be," the old man said, letting the lion play with his ankles and the torn legs of his pants. "If I kept watching, if I waited for the sun to shift from the zenith, maybe I'd see something. But it still looks to me like skulls and skeletons standing up, except, yes, in a certain way, it could be ... yes, a large, bright, flowerlike spot it looks like! Thanks to you, *jenever*, I've succeeded in seeing an unusual flower...."

"Don't tire your eyes out, Willems," Peduto said with pretended roughness. "Let the flower float on the water! Turn the binoculars the other way. Try and find Montenegro."

"I see smoke and light."

"Can you see the plateau? Can you see the grass and the rocks and the pieces of human flesh burning? Can you smell the gunpowder and the abandoned houses? Is there a raw-backed pony galloping on the burning grass? Is he flourishing his flaming tail like a dragon? Look on! Who knows what you'll see? I come from there, Willems, from the same country that I, more than anyone else, humiliated and ruined."

"I'm afraid I don't see your Montenegro, Antonio. It looks more like Germany or some other industrial country," the old man said, blinking his eyes and staring into the binoculars. "There are so many church steeples and so much coal smoke it makes me feel like throwing up. It couldn't be Montenegro, which must be really lovely, judging by all your descriptions. No, I don't see any mountain flowers; there's no stagnant pond either, with Italian corpses floating in it, no manes of trembling horses, shaking off live coals and ashes. . . ."

"Willems, you're old and your eyes are tricking you," Antonio said as he petted the threadbare lion. "Your head is swimming from brandy and too much sun.

"It's not that we don't see the Montenegrin plateau; we're already there. We're lying in the mountain flowers bent by the wind and the flames, and we're watching the sky melt. Both of us are trembling with fear. The whole country seems doomed to disappear. Everything's burning, everything! Churches and crosses are burning; the Orthodox bells are red and smouldering; charred birds are falling around us like cinders. Small homes are ablaze; their roofs are gone. Fire is sparkling around the oxen's horns; it's cocooning in goats' and asses' hoofs; it's smothering and smoking in the sheep's fleece. Everything's aflame, Willems. Even the smoke is burning!"

"Can life be beautiful if everything is burning up?" The old man sipped his *jenever* and looked at him suspiciously. "Sometimes I'm afraid of you, clown."

"Shut up, Willems van der Hoeven, and pour some more. Pour enough for me to wash a Texel tulip down my throat. Pour more, even more, everything you have. There, old buck, that's it. I thank you, God, for having brought me once again to this Montenegrin plateau where more or less everything began! *Jenever*, how strong you are! How you parch my throat and belly! Life is beautiful, yes, beautiful, beautiful, and there's no power on earth that can make it dirty or ugly! *Jenever*, magic, help me to rise! Tell me what's the matter with the flower on the water."

"I've gotten drunk again, you russet devil, I'm drunk as a coot," Willems said, "and it's beginning to look to me as though we weren't on Texel at all, but in that country you've taught me to love.

You're strong as fate, *jenever;* whoever makes your acquaintance can easily understand that life is beautiful, that there's nothing to it but pollen, sunbeams, and songs."

Then they drank, lay down, and embraced. The lion tore the bag and pissed on the muddy turtle track. Through the almost empty bottle, the two looked at the sun. The sky was quite near and round, with the windmill in the center. It reminded them of a Dutch circus tent.

HIDALGO

"Antonio, my eyes aren't tricking me any more!" Willems van der Hoeven cried out, pointing with his dirty hand at a dark human figure which loomed up in front of the windmill. "Finally, a man!"

"Let's go to him, Willems," Antonio suggested, and he set out on all fours through the tulips. "Like this, old one. You from your side, and I from mine."

"I wish my eyes had been tricked. I wish I hadn't seen him," the old man wailed suddenly as he stopped the turtle cart near the ragged man. "Don't give anything more to drink to my lion. And hurry over here, Red Beard!"

"Hold him, old buck!" Antonio shouted with the lion and a new bottle in his arms. "Don't let him give us the slip!"

"He can't go anywhere anymore," Willems van der Hoeven remarked. "He's come to the windmill, and that's all. Hey, boy, what are you doing there? Red Beard, he's not answering. It seems he's deaf, or dumb, or something."

"Peppe!" Antonio burst out, and ran up and embraced him with all his heart. "My son Peppino, how did you get to Texel? Peppino!"

"That's how I imagined him too," the dirt-stained van der Hoeven said, and sucked deeply from the bottle which Antonio handed to him. "A real seaman, a deep-sea sailor. Everything on him is from museums, from his bare toes to the top of his head."

"Where's the breast of our *mujer?*" Antonio grunted, more drunk even than the old man. "You ran out of Lolland with it in your arms."

"The Germans robbed him of it," Willems van der Hoeven said, reeling. "There's nothing good or nice in this world that the Germans or the English haven't stolen from someone else and polluted with their filthy claws. What kind of a breast was it, boys?"

"Luxurious . . . real . . . female," Antonio said as he clasped the man in singed rags in his arms again and hugged him. "It was a breast from the north, full of flesh and milk. A clean left tittie, and the larger one too. A breast which remembered Spain and dreamed of Montenegro."

"If only we had it now!" Willems van der Hoeven wept sincerely, revealing his worn teeth and palate. "Where are you, oh left white breast of our *mujer?*"

"Peppino," Antonio said, and stepped back to see him better. "Peppino, tell Uncle Willems that you burned and burned until you burned up, and then you set fire to everything he spat on from his ships."

Antonio could hardly stand on his two feet; Peppe's large, troubled eyes watched him in silence.

"Peppino, tell him that you've gone through fire since the day we met the *hidalgo* and the clowns; tell him that's why you're so bloody and blistered and sooty."

"Don't tremble, boy," Willems van der Hoeven soothed him. "I've burnt some myself, and done some spitting, and cursing too. Now we're all in the same boat, especially you and I."

"Tell Uncle Willems that this giant tulip which you're pulling behind you on the rope represents a man, that you, in your seared head, believe it to be a human being threatened by misery and death, and that you're the one who is saving him."

Antonio Peduto studied the fallen flower and the rope tied around it like a noose, just below the corolla. "Willems, when we met in that Montenegrin hell, he had a rope like that and was using it to save the lives of our cowards, who'd been mowed down by a landslide and then swallowed by an abyss. That's how he found me, Willems, and pulled me up, and saved my life for no reason at all."

"Bravo! Bravo, *Taliano*, pulling the tulip . . . ha ha . . . thinking it's a coward . . . ha ha . . ." Willems van der Hoeven was so drunk he could hardly speak. "Will you pull me along like that when I drop down in my tracks? . . . Ha! Ha! Ha!" A sudden desire to embrace Peppe seized the old man. He reeled over to him and offered him the bottle. "Are you dumb, *soldato?*"

"I'm not dumb," Giuseppe Bonnaccia answered, and began to shake and weep. "I will. I will pull you up like that when you drop down." His eyes were large and mad, and his voice rather quiet

"I'm not dumb, but I don't know what I'm doing, or where I am; I don't remember anything. But I'm not deaf or dumb."

"What? How could it be, young man? You don't even remember your name?"

"No, old one. I know nothing anymore. I don't even know who I am."

"You're my illegitimate son," Antonio Peduto said as he began to uncover him to count his wounds. "Your name is Giuseppe Bonaccia, Peppe or Peppino for short, and the day I met you in Montenegro, you knew even things that others had forgotten. You're from a village near Naples. You knew all the fishermen there and loved all the girls of the whole world. We wrote them letters on sand and water. You swore tenderness to them all and told them what would happen if they weren't faithful to you."

"I won't say I never made love to those girls," Giuseppe Bonaccia said after Antonio had taken off all his clothes; he stank of fire, sweat, and earth. "But I don't know who you two are, or whom you're talking about. I don't know who I am."

"In the sacred name of God!" Willems van der Hoeven began to lament and pluck his gray beard in rage. "Peduto, *los cojones* have burnt up!" The old man growled against the sky, the windmill, the water. "How could you allow it, all you saints? The injustice of it! The shame! The sorrow!" He bit the neck of the bottle and sniffed *jenever*. "And how do you expect him to remember, Red Beard, when he's lost *los cojones*! Sailors say there's no memory without the testicles. I believe the things they say, and what the peasants say, too. Who has no *cojones*, has no voice, and can't remember the simplest fishing song. Return him *los cojones*, all you saints!"

"My eyes have swollen; they're smarting again, Willems," Antonio murmured. "Pour some more *jenever*, old one, and tell me what else you see."

"Instead of a bunny, he has a narcissus between his legs," Willems van der Hoeven said. "How cruel and unjust God is! He's arranged it so that everything on this earth has its beginning and end! A narcissus between his legs, to remind us of my kind and generous Holland! Red Beard, you were right. We are on the Montenegrin plateau. Everything's burning and turning into embers and ashes!"

"A narcissus between his legs," Antonio whispered. He dropped down on his knees beside Peppe and watched the silhouette of the windmill vanes turning slowly against the glowing background of the sky and the water. "I'm sorry, Peppino."

"I don't know who I am," Giuseppe Bonaccia repeated, pulling on the tulip. "What is a narcissus?" He began tottering too; the tulip was wet and heavy. "I'm hungry and thirsty."

"To honor your narcissus, *Taliano*, we're going to drink until we fall down unconscious," Willems van der Hoeven shouted hoarsely. All three embraced. "And to honor your still-red beard, Antonio!" The old man threw his head back and poured *jenever* down his gullet and then even sprinkled the earth where they lay. "Life is beautiful, most beautiful, my boys!" he almost sobbed. He looked at the scarecrows which were so near he could have reached out and touched them. "Let's sing, adventurers, for soon we'll be without *los cojones* and without memory! Let's sing, since we'll turn into a flower on the water anyway! Let's sing about *los cojones* and about memory!"

> "There was a soldier once,
> "Gallant and handsome,
> "Handsome and swift,"

Antonio began. Then his strength and his memory failed. Willems van der Hoeven joined in with his whisper as he caressed the lion and the turtle:

> "Nobody knew his real name,
> "They called him only Our Soldier."

"I don't know who I am," Giuseppe Bonaccia repeated. "I think I sang songs in the past. There was no song I didn't have somewhere in my mind. But I don't know who I am. I hear that you're singing. Now, for the first time, I hear it. Don't take the rope out of my hands. What narcissus have you been talking about? I'm hungry. Let's sing:

> "Fatherless and motherless Mary
> "Fell in love with the soldier.
> "For her the soldier was everything,
> "Gallant and handsome."

Carl Schlotterer cropped up from the earth and foam, barefoot, scratched and raw, with his overcoat wrapped around his naked body. Short, almost completely gray hair framed his leaden face. His eyes were still as beautiful and sad as on the day when Edgar Salomon had whipped him. His arrival surprised no one. He knelt and looked at Peppino and then at the windmill and the water. All three embraced him. Willems van der Hoeven slipped the Jew's noose off his neck and asked him where he had come by so much lead. Telling himself he was back among the right people again, Carl Schlotterer accepted the Dutchman's bottle and welcomed Antonio's song. He began to move his lips:

> "And only when he went away,
> "They all said the soldier,
> "Handsome and swift,
> "Was made of straw, all of straw."

"Tedesco, Tedesco," Antonio asked in drunken merriment. He jumped on the German's back and covered his eyes with his hands. "Whose hands are these, German? Whose fingers are counting the lead pellets on your face?"

"They're Herbert Siegmann's hands," Carl Schlotterer replied quietly, feeling the *jenever* warm his brain and his intestines. "It's Herbert Siegmann. Sooner or later he will gouge out my eyes."

"Who's that, Tedesco?" Peduto asked even more drunkenly. "My *cojones* and memory seem to be failing."

"The insane, foaming epileptic who tested the piercing capacity of his pistol on human bodies," Carl Schlotterer said, remembering Montenegro, and then Romana. "Herbert Siegmann, General Herbert Siegmann. I don't know where he came from. He defeated me once and for all; I told you the story on the ship. I'm afraid of his nails, Slav. He's going to gouge out my eyes."

"Marvelous! Wonderful! You understood right away that we're back on the Montenegrin plateau now. You spoke up and even sang with us!" Antonio was enthusiastic. "It's wonderful that you're here and have nowhere else to go."

"I've always been silent before the inhuman," Carl Schlotterer said, letting Willems van der Hoeven pour him more *jenever*. "I'll never forget your Montenegro, never! It was there that Romana kissed me for the first and last time. And all my wounds ached then as if I were on fire! Perhaps God Himself has willed it, Antonio. Perhaps He wanted us to meet and drink together in this country again. Montenegro, magic, I'm with you again!"

"We've trampled down your Germany," Antonio Peduto said as he removed his hands from Schlotterer's face. "We hanged Herbert Siegmann by his feet. You don't have to worry about him gouging out your eyes."

"You mean he's gone, finished, *kaput?* You mean I don't have to be afraid of him anymore?" Tedesco's lead mask wrinkled as if he were about to laugh or sneeze. "Was he hard to kill?"

"The three of us, and some others too, consider him to be

THE WAR WAS BETTER

kaput," Antonio Peduto said again, just before Willems van der Hoeven began to sing. "Don't worry about your eyes anymore."

"Life is beautiful," Carl Schlotterer joined in with a child's voice as he looked up at the windmill, with its vanes in the sky. "How beautiful life is now, without the epileptic Herbert Siegmann, who gouged out so many people's eyes and ripped their hearts up with his bullets!"

The German did not hold out very long on his knees. Willem's bottle fell out of his hand and his forehead banged against the turtle's shell. He looked up at them guiltily.

"Your brandy is splendid, men!" he said finally. "A real, double-distilled Montenegria corkeroo! I haven't had anything like this for a long time!" He began to sing:

"Alone stayed Mary, fatherless and motherless.
"The soldier was all to her, all of straw."

It was like a real song, almost a whisper, the kind Augusto Napolitano's heart could hear. All three moved their lips; only Giuseppe Bonnaccia was still. He seemed to be beginning to recognize the world and the things around him. Carl Schlotterer held Willem's bottle on his chest, like the olive can Sergey Ivanovich had given him long before, and looked at the narcissus between Peppe's legs. Since they all had their arms around one another, it was easier to harmonize their voices:

"Good and faithful was Mary,
"Soldierless, fatherless, and motherless.
"She was faithful like the soldier,
"And made all of straw, all of straw."

"You've fought gallantly, my boys," Antonio Peduto muttered, hardly able to get his words out, as he waved to the scarecrows; there were hundreds of them all around. "We've sailed around the world and conquered it together; together, we've set fire to everything rotten and ugly we came across, or spat on it anyway. We've destroyed Herbert Siegmann, so that wretches like our Tedesco can walk freely on this earth, without fearing for their eyes or their reason. Our victory is complete and pure. Only the beauty of life can compare to it. If it weren't for you, boys, I'd never have known what real love and devotion was, among men, among lions."

Willems van der Hoeven, Carl Schlotterer, and Giuseppe Bonaccia embraced, utterly drunk. The bottle was empty, and their heads were numb. They watched the sun sink slowly down toward the water, where the flower was. They did not even know where they were, no less to whom Antonio, the father of the family, was talking, nor where he got the strength to lift his arm and wave it.

"You deserve some reward for your victory over the world, my friends and *culeadores*," Antonio said, beginning to count the scarecrows. "Since I've always pissed on European medals, crowns, crosses, and lions, I will present you with the honors of some far-off and more beloved countries. Guard them well and always display them, los *jodeadores!*"

Antonio Peduto stretched his arms out toward the scarecrows. In his thoughts, he caressed their nonexistent faces; he kissed their heroes' foreheads; he shook their empty sleeves. A stiff breeze was blowing in from the sea. The heroes clad in rags turned to one another amidst the creaking crosses and groaning boards and gave greetings.

"To the first and fifth of you, I present the order of the Queen of Sheba," Antonio announced as he quieted down Willem's lion; he was remembering Ethiopia and Giovanni Besta's stories. "To the tenth, the mocker who could scare off a whole flock of birds and evil spirits with his legs and straw hat alone, I accord the Laotian order of One Hundred Elephants. For the sailor with the patchwork sleeves and pants, the big-balled one with tulips and narcissi around his knees and between his legs, I award the Bolivian order of the Condor of the Andes. To the adventurer who's watching me now with such derision and contempt, the poor jealous devil whom the first strong wind will blow down into the mud, among the frogs and salamanders, I cannot but award the Chinese order of the Blue Sky and the White Sun. And to all the rest who gallantly guard our dear Dutch homeland, our Holland wrested from the sea, I present the Thai order of the Nine Precious Stones."

"Life is beautiful," Tedesco repeated, pressing his cheek against the turtle's shell and petting the drunken lion. "Forgive me, Anna-Maria, for loving you since the day we first met. How you've grown! How nice you are!" Carl Schlotterer's eyes were full of pollen and the reflection of the setting sun. "You're a grown-up girl now, and you'll let us kiss your neck, your forehead, your little paws, like this, as if you were our eternal fiancée, our sister, our love!"

"*Hidalgo!*"

It was Antonio Peduto who yelled it. Then he began to laugh like Archibald Beckett and jump up and down.

"Malić! Look there! Malić!"

THE WAR WAS BETTER

He waved to him with Willem's hat.

"Clown of all clowns!"

All of them looked up and saw him, even the scarecrows. He was tired and pale and riding his donkey. He had on a long Russian overcoat, a red-star Russian hat which turned around his head, Belgian museum boots, and a Yugoslav parachute on his back. On his breast, he had one medal more than any other clown or hero Antonio or his brothers could remember. In his left hand he held the globe, caved in now but completely red; in his right, he held the reins and a whip made of ox tendons.

"*Don* Gruban, don't you see us?" Antonio Peduto called out in a faint, childlike voice. "And did you know, my *Montenegrino*, my god of fire and love, that we've been waiting for you for years, that without you we aren't even what we are? *Hola, hidalgo!*"

"Don't worry, he'll notice us, *los picadores*," Willems van der Hoeven reassured them. "What a man!" he added, petting the lion. "A real Dutchman!"

The *hidalgo* frowned, clapped his hat down over his flabby ears, and spurred his donkey. Taliano perked up and began to dig into the ground with his hind legs like an angry colt. Malić said the word, spat toward the sea, and then charged at the windmill.

"Bravo, Prince!" Antonio exclaimed, placing his hands on Willem's and Peppe's shoulders. "Bravo, knight and living fire!" Antonio labored for breath; he could hardly contain his joy. "Bravo, lightning! We need just this one victory more, your feat of daring, and then we'll be free to say we've conquered the whole world, that everything's ours, that life is beautiful, that it's exciting as a dream. Bravo, *hidalgo!*"

All in sweat and foam, wiggling his ears, flailing the air with his tail, bounding and rebounding from the earth like a panther, Taliano rushed at the windmill with all his strength. Malić's skinny little figure seemed to lengthen as he stretched out with the globe and tried to strike one of the vanes that turned slowly past and rose up toward the sky. He missed. The rider and the donkey fell together beside the humid wall, entangled in ivy and other vines. They could hardly get back on their feet. Then they backed up and dashed at it again for all they were worth. For a moment, the two floated on the level of the windmill vanes, kicking and thrashing, until, an instant later, they were hurled away and tumbled into the pond, among the snakes, lizards, and frogs.

"*Los cojones* are pulling him down," Antonio said whenever Malić soared up and touched the vanes only to fall back again. "*Los cojones* are weighing him down; that's the trouble. It's not easy for him."

Gruban Malić did not stop charging even after the sun had hid behind the water. Through tears and the gathering dusk, he appeared great and powerful, a rider of riders.

"There's no fort or windmill in the world which our Malić can't conquer," Antonio murmured, overwhelmed by brandy and song. "Although *los cojones* are weighing him down, he's still up and fighting."

Gruban Malić charged. He struck at the wall. He fell. Then he got up and charged again. The wind puffed up his overcoat. The wall knocked his globe into the grass. But Gruban Malić would not stop.

"Victory!" Antonio squeaked like a child. "Now we have everything, Anna-Maria! We're men—more than we've ever been—such as we are now!"

The windmill came nearer and grew and darkened until it was immense, like a tower in the night. They saw and heard nothing else.

"The world is ours! Once and for all it's ours, Anna-Maria! Life is beautiful, Cattolica!"

Vogel, above Bohinj Lake
August 15, 1968

DATE DUE